THE COIL
COLLECTION

3 NOVELS IN 1 VOLUME

~ DISTANT CONTACT ~

~ DISTANT FRONT ~

~ DISTANT HARM ~

D.I. Telbat

In Season Publications
U.S.A.

Printed in the United States of America

The COIL Legacy Collection / D.I. Telbat -- 1st ed.
Christian Suspense, Collection

D.I. Telbat / In Season Publications
https://ditelbat.com
https://books2read.com/ap/8NV7l8/DI-Telbat

ISBN 978-0-9864103-7-6

Book Layout © 2016 BookDesignTemplates.com
Cover Design by Streetlight Graphics

Acknowledgements

Every book requires a team,
and every series requires commitment.
Thank you to the blessed souls who strive with me,
correcting, advising, editing—Dee, Jamie, Sharon, and Ed.
Thanks to Uguku Usdi, for his patient instruction in astronomy, and
Scott Fitzhugh, who developed the Caspertein characters with me.
Most of all, I acknowledge the saving work of God in us
and the finished work of Jesus Christ for us.
May the work of our hands bring Him honor and glory.

CONTENTS

DISTANT CONTACT

BOOK ONE

The COIL Legacy

D.I. Telbat

Note from the author

Dear Reader,

In the *Distant Contact* pages that follow, I have created a Muslim extremist organization from Iran called the *Soldiers of Mahdi*. Although it is a fictional entity, its practices inside Iran and intentions abroad are factually based on existing modern groups and ideals. Knowing that this darkness exists better enables us to love and care for these people who are in such bondage.

But since love never fails, the Cross of Christ will always hold the answer for humanity's darkness. Continue to pray.

David Telbat

Dedication

To those who are far away,
yet very near to our hearts.

Russia

Through his drunkenness, Oleg Saratov realized he was being followed. For two weeks, he'd been thrown out of one Moscow club after another. Every establishment inside the city's Garden Ring knew the ex-Interpol officer had been fired. Returning to the land of his birth, he had ranted against the authorities he'd failed, and who had failed him.

Near Tver Square, Oleg fell against a wall and tried to focus his blurring eyes. Yes, three men were closing on him, men who murdered and robbed at night. He thought he'd lost them at Boulevard Ring, but these thugs stalked him with purpose. The money he'd flashed around for weeks had apparently attracted a few predators.

"Come on!" Oleg waved them closer. Three men in their thirties swaggered nearer, spreading out. "I'll tear you apart!"

But Oleg couldn't stand without leaning against the wall. He cursed through his stupor and held up a weathered fist.

When the three were a few feet away, they rushed him together. Oleg fell toward the first, swinging a fist that seemed remarkably slow even to himself. He was on the cobblestone in an instant, feeling their boots against his ribs, then their fingers in his pockets, scratching for his wallet.

Suddenly, three dull thumps registered in Oleg's hearing. The robbers leaped up, then fell over dead. Oleg's senses flooded back to him, thanks to the blows, and now the silenced gunshots. He sat up and saw a tall man in a jean jacket walking toward him. From the glow of the street lamps, the figure seemed almost like a guardian angel. Until he realized who it was.

"*Titus Caspertein!*" Oleg spit blood past his swollen lip. "You coward! So, you've finally come to kill me?"

"Kill you? Nah." Titus, with his Arkansas drawl tainting his otherwise perfect Russian, knelt next to Oleg. "Seems you're doing that well enough on your own. Corban Dowler sent me to fetch you."

"Fetch me? Haven't you heard?" Oleg burped. "I've finally been put out to pasture. And I blame you. If not for you, I'd still have a job. All you had to do was let me arrest you, and my life would've been different."

"I'm sorry, old friend. Maybe I can make it up to you."

"How? By putting me out of my misery?"

"No, I work for the Commission of International Laborers now. They brought me on." Titus holstered his weapon under his left arm. "I helped them design some new tech that'll put us ahead of the real bad guys. State of the art satellite and spy stuff. Because of Corban's guidance, I'm not the man you used to know."

"So, it's true? You're a Christian with COIL? For real?"

"Gone are my past ways, old friend. The women, the stealing, the smuggling— Well, I still smuggle, but just Bibles now."

"Unbelievable. Apparently, you're still killing, though." Oleg spat toward the three muggers. "Old habits die hard with us, huh?"

"No, these boys are just tranquilized. With newly-designed non-lethal weaponry. Custom handguns and rifles, even bullets. It's all about saving lives with me now."

Oleg sighed. Titus had always lived a charmed life. That's why Oleg had begun to hate him so much. But if he'd truly left his criminal ways behind . . .

"Why are you here, Titus?"

"Corban asked who I would trust with my life to do what needs to be done around the world. All the people I know are crooks. Except you. Even when we were on opposite sides of the law, I still trusted you."

"Last I checked, we're not even friends, Titus."

"We've worked together, though."

"I was trying to arrest you. And I failed."

"Sure, but you got closer than anyone else." Titus sat down next to Oleg and handed him a handkerchief. "It seems you could use a job."

"No kidding! But no one will hire a disgraced Interpol agent. Nobody with any honor, anyway." Oleg pointed his finger at the thieves. "Wait a minute. If they're not with you, why didn't you tranq them before they jumped me?"

"I figured they'd sober you up for me."

"Humph." Oleg scowled at Titus. "And you think I'd really partner with you now? I could've been killed, Titus!"

"If you would've been sober, you could've handled them yourself." Titus flashed a broad grin, visible in the streetlights. "It ain't easy learning we're getting older."

"You're not exactly winning me over." Oleg wiped his bloody face with the handkerchief then offered it back to Titus, who rejected it. "What do I have to do with you for COIL?"

"There's plenty for us to do, but first we have to be moving in the same direction. In God's direction."

"You don't really want me, Titus. I'm all used up."

"Well, I'm already in Russia, and I don't know any other ugly Russians who'll tolerate me."

"So you're saying you want me sober by morning?"

"This is about more than being sober. '*The night is almost gone, and the day is near.*'"

"When did you become a poet?"

"It's not poetry. It's the Bible. I know all about living in darkness. Jesus Christ is returning soon, brother. The day is near and we need to be a lot more than legal or sober to be acceptable to Him."

"Religion's never been much use to me. You know that."

"Me, neither. But realizing what our purpose is for the Creator isn't about religion. It's not time to get right; it's time to be *made* right. And we're going to do it together."

"Are you about to convert me on this Moscow street?"

"It ain't easy facing your dead and lost condition, old friend, but I wouldn't be here if this weren't important, for you and for me."

Oleg closed his eyes. A reformed criminal was about to teach him about God? He scoffed at himself. God was just who he needed right now. The bottle certainly wasn't the answer.

"All right. My way obviously isn't working. Go ahead. Give it to me straight."

"That's the only way I know it, Oleg."

Titus pulled him to his feet, and the two walked shoulder to shoulder down the street.

CHAPTER ONE

Arctic

*"And He came and preached peace to you who were far away,
and peace to those who were near."* Ephesians 2:17 (NASB)

~

Rudolph Caspertein opened his eyes to darkness. The air was so cold, it burned his lungs. He tried to move his arms, his legs, but they seemed paralyzed. No. They were cast tightly into snow pack. But how deep?

When he moved his head, he discovered a pocket of air had been trapped above him. Squirming upward, his skull hit solid ice. He settled his mind, trying to fight the panic. Ten minutes of air. Twenty, tops.

Suddenly, a loud grinding sound rumbled through the snow pack around him. Everything shifted and threatened to crush him as the pack slid and dropped a few inches.

He grunted against the settled snow. His air pocket was now smaller, but the grinding sound ceased. Everything was still again. Was it possible to find peace at the moment of death? Rudy prayed for mercy, or at least a quick death without pain.

Rudolph "Rudy" Caspertein was a seismologist in Barrow on the northern coast of Alaska, three hundred miles north of the Arctic Circle. When he'd hiked back to the Point from the Meade River Station, the last thing he'd expected to find was the vanishing of the Point Barrow Peninsula. The whole land mass had sunk into the Arctic Ocean!

The snow blizzard had distracted him, he remembered now. He hadn't even felt the ground tremble. But a snow blizzard in July? Stranger things had happened in Northern Alaska.

Even as Rudy realized he was about to die, he mentally tallied how many had already met death from the freak occurrence. The town of Barrow had a population of almost four thousand. Most of those people were support staff for the Naval Arctic Research Laboratory. Now, they were all gone.

Two days earlier, the tundra had been green, budding white flowers. The day before, small snowflakes had begun to fall. The town of Barrow was under-supplied and not prepared for an early snow, so he'd hiked north from the station over sixty miles. Thirty miles a day through fierce conditions was nothing for the six-and-a-half-foot tall mammoth, as his friends often called him.

When he'd stood where the peninsula was supposed to be, he'd peered off a cliff at the Arctic waters. And then, without warning, the peninsula stump had crumbled beneath him. Instead of landing in the water, he'd landed on glacier ice—maybe a drifting iceberg. Then a mountain of snow had fallen on top of him, leaving him buried alive in an ice coffin.

Scratching reached his snow-filled ears. Scratching?

The sun shined twenty hours a day during the summers. Perhaps even though it was nighttime, someone had seen him fall. But no. This scratching wasn't human; this was an animal digging. A bear, most likely. Maybe a Kodiak. The carnivore would eat him alive, starting with his head, while the rest of his body was braced and immovable.

"Get outta here!" Rudy screamed.

The scratching and digging stopped for a few seconds, then started again more furiously. Any amount of screaming after that only heightened the ravenous beast's digging.

Rudy wiggled his right arm. It moved no more than an inch at his side, just enough to feel his antler-tipped harpoon and its three-foot shaft under his ribs. The short harpoon was his tool of choice in the Arctic and everyone in Barrow knew him for it. If he could free one arm . . .

Gray light poured into his tiny air hole. The animal stopped digging. The top of Rudy's head was exposed. He could feel the night air. No, that wasn't the air. It was the creature's wet nose sniffing his shaggy hair, licking him, tasting his humanity and fear!

Throwing his head back and forth, Rudy beat his forehead against the snow pack in a raging growl. Then he lay still. The beast dug around his head, deeper. Only a very demented Kodiak or polar bear would want his prey to see him before he ate him alive!

Twice, the animal's claws scratched his ear and forehead, drawing blood. Every twenty seconds, the creature stopped digging to sniff around Rudy's head and lick his blood. The beast was toying with him!

"No!" Rudy screamed. To be eaten alive was unthinkable. He prayed for calm in his last seconds. In a moment, he would be with his Lord Jesus Christ. With regret, he realized he would die without forgiving his younger brother, Titus. It had been easier to live in his hatred for the family outcast.

A tongue licked Rudy's forehead. An eye was finally free of snow to see this devious predator.

"Kobuk?" Rudy gasped and gagged on loose snow. He struggled to breathe past his own sobs of relief. "Kobuk, dig! Good girl! Dig!"

The two-hundred-pound St. Bernard was well-known in Barrow for begging scraps from its citizens, though she was well cared for by the Search and Rescue personnel. But during each of his visits to Barrow, Rudy had made a point of spoiling the big dog, whose affection seemed sufficiently earned now! Kobuk obeyed Rudy's command and dug deeper around Rudy's neck and shoulders. Rudy gazed skyward. He was five feet below the snow pack surface. The sky looked clear at the moment—and never more beautiful!

"Good girl, Kobuk. Good girl!"

Closing his eyes, Rudy prayed his thanks to God. So often, Rudy had thought of God as a distant Being, but no longer. God was with him and caring. Why had the people of Barrow perished? He didn't know, but the dog had been bred in the Alps of Switzerland to have a sense of smell and burly strength, ideal for search and rescue. Helping Rudy was in Kobuk's blood. But it was God Rudy attributed with placing Kobuk in the right place at the right time. Perhaps she'd even fallen onto the same icy ledge as Rudy, to rescue him from death.

Rudy pulled an arm free and assisted Kobuk. Every few minutes, Kobuk paw-shoveled the loose snow behind her and out of the shallow tunnel. Finally, Rudy was able to kick his legs loose and push upward.

"Up, girl. Go back."

Kobuk refused to abandon him as she found his caribou coat collar and dragged him to the surface. Rudy rolled over the mounds of snow. Devotedly, the bear-sized dog licked his face and whined.

"Good girl." Rudy clung to her thick coat. "Thank You, God. I'm alive . . ."

Rudy struggled to his knees, then stood. The night's brief darkness was settling in. It would last four hours. Though he could still see, he didn't want to believe what his eyes told him.

He shook the snow from his body and stepped from his chilly coffin. His strides were over a yard in length. Even in his early forties and at three hundred pounds, he was still agile, though he rarely did anything hastily. But he suddenly wondered if he were better off dead under the ice.

Instinctively, he touched his right hip. His harpoon was still there. Kobuk trotted beside him. Together, they crossed a short expanse of snow pack to its edge. Ice water lapped gently against the snow. Quickly, he stepped away before it crumbled beneath his weight. Then, he turned in a slow circle. As far as his eyes could see, there was only water. No, wait. There were spots of floating ice and islands of drifting snow pack like his own, but no land. He was on a flat iceberg a quarter-mile in diameter.

Kobuk whined and looked up at him.

"We're not going anywhere too soon, girl. Just sit tight."

As a scientist, Rudy combed the island on foot by sections. The earthquake had caused the land's peninsula to fall off the mainland, but the ice and icebergs made little sense—unless they came from farther north. Icebergs from the north and earthquake tremors in the south? The snowstorm from the Bering Sea topped off the phenomenon. Somehow, the underwater Beaufort Shelf had collapsed.

The iceberg was clean. There was no debris or sign of life. Rudy shook his head in disbelief. Four thousand dead and missing in the Arctic. It could be a week before Search and Rescue arrived. No one, not even himself, could survive that long if another storm blew in.

Rudy eyed Kobuk. He would have to kill Kobuk for food by the following night. She could feed him for a couple weeks, long enough until he was rescued. His eyes narrowed. Kobuk seemed to be sizing him up as well.

He sat down in the middle of the berg on the snow piles Kobuk had dug. Scratching at his full beard, he contemplated his chances of survival. No food. His pack was gone. He had a watch on his wrist, but no matches, knife, or freshwater. They could eat ice and snow for fluids—that was freshwater. He could survive a week on that, but no more without fuel against the cold.

The polar ice mass rotated clockwise due to polar, easterly winds and westward currents. Already, he could be on his way toward the northern coast of Siberia. No one would find him after another week. No one would expect any earthquake survivors to be floating on an iceberg drifting west around the Arctic.

As Kobuk watched, Rudy began to pile up the loose snow to make a shelter. His caribou skin clothing would keep him warm and dry, but shelter through a storm was mandatory. An igloo was out of the question since the berg was mostly snow, and not packed too solid at that.

Then, Rudy paused. Mostly snow? Not ice? Since the berg was primarily snow, it would melt so much faster than a true iceberg. The wind shifted, and a southern breeze transferred subpolar heat toward the pole. A warm wind. The iceberg was melting. Melting or not, Rudy couldn't swim toward land he couldn't see. He continued to build his shelter with his hands. His right hand was missing its pinky finger, and frostbite scars on his cheeks marked other memories of hardship and survival. This wasn't Rudy Caspertein's first tangle with the Arctic.

CHAPTER TWO

Azerbaijan

Wynter Caspertein tapped the underwater vacuum with her gloved hand. Her flashlight danced over dusty rocks and—There! She shut off the vacuum tube and adjusted her face mask to see in the dimness. Shedding a glove, she fingered a gold plate on a rusted metal cord. She was close!

Trembling in her scuba gear, Wynter turned the vacuum back on and sucked up the gold plate and cord. Rocks, dirt, and vegetation disappeared up the ribbed hose connected to her platform boat above.

Her heart skipped a beat and she stopped again. She tapped on a bronze case, a twenty-three-hundred-year-old trunk dating back to the Greek Empire. It was here!

She squealed with enthusiasm into her demand regulator. Pushing off the bottom, she surfaced thirty feet above. Her head bobbed next to the boat anchored in the Mingechaur Reservoir in Western Azerbaijan. She tugged off her face mask and unstrapped her rebreather apparatus to hand to Gamal, her interpreter and guide while in the Asian country. Gamal was nineteen, and Wynter, who was nearly twice his age, had been patient with his boyish infatuation. Wynter was an experienced underwater archaeologist, but little was known of Gamal. She and her partner, Ingram Thatcher, had rented the platform boat, and Gamal, a tall, heavy-set youth, had been available.

Gamal lifted the rebreather onto the platform, then offered his hand to pull Wynter up. But she was already on her feet crossing the deck. Growing up in Arkansas with two rowdy brothers, Rudy and Titus, independence was her way.

"I need cable, Gamal. Cable and the winch system." She looked around the deck. "Where's Ingram?"

"Gone to beach. Lunch." Gamal pointed at the north shore. "He bring lunch. I tell him where to go."

"Ingram!" she punched her palm. He was always thinking of his stomach! Even though they were engaged to be married, that didn't diminish the frustration she sometimes felt with him.

"You find treasure, Miss Wynter?"

"I found something, Gamal, and that's Miss Caspertein to you, remember?"

Gamal nodded with diverted eyes. Wynter studied the shore. Nothing moved. Ingram wasn't even in the small boat headed back to them yet. Maybe he'd only told Gamal he'd gone to lunch to cover for his true ambition while in the Muslim country. Ingram made a habit of sharing the gospel with the locals wherever he traveled.

"He could be gone for another hour, and I need him now!" She threw her weight belt against the vacuum pump. "The sediment I removed could settle in again."

"I help you, Miss Caspertein. What you need?"

"I need an experienced diver."

"I dive."

"You've never dived before, Gamal." She wagged her finger. "We've gone through this already."

"But Mr. Thatcher has gear I use." Gamal held up Ingram's scuba outfit.

"No, I need you on the winch. I guess . . . we can start without Ingram. You want to help?"

"Yes. I here to help."

Wynter scooped up her weight belt again. She shrugged into her rebreather straps and stepped to the edge of the platform.

"When I tug on the cable three times, Gamal, you start the winch. If it gets caught or stuck, stop the motor and wait. It might need some adjusting. I'll guide it up."

"Yes. I do that."

"Good." Wynter sealed the face mask around her eyes and nose. "Go ahead. Let the cable out." Inserting her demand regulator, she stepped off the platform.

She didn't like raising an artifact alone. Ingram was always criticizing her for working too hastily without precautions. But she was too excited to stop now! The sonar had been right. If she hurried, she could have it all on deck in time to surprise him. The Etruscan Jewelry was here after all!

Wynter reached the chest and tapped it with her knuckles. It felt solid. Folks in the bronze era had made things to last. Lifting one end of the chest, she found it to be about ninety pounds—ninety pounds of over two-thousand-year-old treasure. It was the find of the century!

But she wasn't thinking about the riches enclosed in the bronze case. Such artifacts—exactly where she'd tracked Alexander the Great—showed that the Greeks had ventured west into Italy instead of simply east to conquer the Persians. The Caspertein family was already wealthy. Wynter was ecstatic only for the history to be found inside the chest.

When she spotted the cable from above had reached her depth, she swept her arm in an arc to grasp it. Pulling it tight, she fit it across the bottom of the chest by lifting each end in turn. Coupling the cable, she crossed it perpendicular across the bottom a second time, then hooked the cable to itself. Ninety pounds. It would hold. She hoped.

The cable was snug around the chest, but in case it slipped a little on the way to the top, she would swim up with it. No problem. She yanked three times on the cable. Nothing happened. Yanking again, she checked her air gauge. There were twenty minutes left on a system that managed a total of over two hours breathing time. The upgrade from standard air tanks to the rebreather system had changed her career since she was able to stay underwater longer without the distortion of hundreds of bubbles with every breath.

Looking upward, she saw the shadow of the platform boat. She was about to tug on the cable again when her mouth gaped and her regulator slid from her mouth. Wynter shoved off the lake floor toward a vague shape floating on the surface ten feet from the platform boat. Though there were no sharks in the reservoir, her first instinct was to look for the man-eaters—especially when she saw a floating body. She wore an oceanic shark's tooth on a chain around her neck to remind her of a close call she'd had in Argentina. Even now, her gloved hand touched the tooth. That day off Argentina, Someone had been watching over her. She prayed He was still looking on her now.

Wynter reached the body and sighed with relief when she found it wasn't Ingram. But it was Gamal—wearing Ingram's scuba gear. She turned Gamal's body face-up on the surface and towed his limp form toward the boat. Her mind flipped through the pages of diving safety. This youth knew nothing of scuba diving!

She arrived at the boat and reached for the edge. Instead, another hand grasped her own. Thankfully, it was Ingram.

"What happened?" Ingram was an Englishman from Birmingham, tall and athletic. He dragged the body from the water.

"He tried to dive while I was below!"

Climbing onto the platform, she stripped Gamal of his gear as Ingram started mouth-to-mouth. She touched her shark's tooth.

"Come on, Gamal!" She was angry at herself as much as at the youth. "God help us. Ingram, we're in so much trouble!"

"Check the gear," Ingram said. "See what he did."

Wynter turned over the rebreather, which recycled air, removing carbon dioxide with chemical screeners, adding oxygen as needed. One of the dials was closed.

"He turned off the oxygen, I think. He has carbon dioxide poisoning."

Neither spoke as Ingram continued mouth-to-mouth for five more minutes. Finally, he sat back. Wynter leaned over the boat and vomited.

"How long was he suited up?"

"No more than ten minutes." Wynter wiped her mouth. "He was supposed to be running the winch. Oh, Ingram, he was just a kid!"

"Not just a kid." Ingram pointed at Gamal's still chest. "Look."

Wynter crawled closer to the body and pulled up Gamal's shirt to expose his bare chest. Around his neck hung a medallion of a crescent moon and a star in gold, with Arabic writing.

"It says 'Soldiers of Mahdi'." She felt like vomiting again. "The terrorist group? Mahdi. The Muslim messiah?"

"If he's anything of the sort, we just summoned about a million Muslims to jihad." Ingram put his hand to his mouth. "I don't know what to do. A medallion like that—he must be the son of one of the leaders in the Soldiers of Mahdi, but I thought they were in Iran."

"Maybe he just stole the necklace."

"No, I've heard of this sort of thing. If his father is some sort of imam, he might be in hiding up here in Azerbaijan in case his father is assassinated by Sunni Muslims. That could make this boy next in line. He wouldn't be wearing that medallion, otherwise. The gold and artistry—it must've been worth a fortune. They perpetuate jihad, trying to usher in their version of the end times."

Wynter stood and peered toward the shore.

"We've been here a week, Ingram. Everyone around here knows he's been coming out here with us." She fought a sob, and reached for his hand. "I should've been more careful. Now we'll never get out of Azerbaijan!"

"The sat-phone's back at the hotel. We can make a call and—"

"What if the call is intercepted? No, we can't call from inside this country. The same applies for emails, or we're finished."

"One thing for sure," Ingram said as he stripped the rest of the scuba gear from Gamal, "the first doctor who examines him will see how he died: carbon dioxide overdose. In a country with a Shiite majority, we'll find no justice sticking around here. Pull up the anchor. We need to get out of here on the first flight tonight!"

"But the cable!"

Ingram knelt and touched the taut cable.

"What are you talking about?"

"The trunk! I found it. We found it, Ingram!"

"It doesn't matter. Leave it, Wynter. News flash: sacred dead boy. There won't be a trial for us. There'll be a ceremony—a beheading ceremony. Then, they quarter us. Get it?"

"We have time." Wynter crossed her arms. "Nobody's missing him right now. Nobody knows he's dead. It'll take an hour, no more, to get that trunk on board!"

"Seconds count. It's afternoon already. Turn in the boat, check out of the hotel, and drive to Baku. There's a chance we won't even get a flight out tonight. Think about it, Wynter! Someone may have seen all this from shore. We're done hunting. We're on the run now!"

"We'll never be able to come back for it." Wynter stared at him angrily. "The government will never let us return—probably no Westerners ever again."

"That's your brother's department, not ours. You're always telling me he's a smuggler. Let him come back for it."

"Titus is a thief! I would never tell him about this find." Wynter scowled. "If he came for the trunk, we'd never know what's in it. He'd melt it down and sell it. Besides, nobody's seen or heard from Titus in years."

Ingram dug into a tool bag and pulled out a pair of bolt cutters. He offered them to Wynter.

"Cut the cable, Wynter. Seconds count!"

"We'll never get this chance again, Ingram! The sediments will settle. We'll need sonar equipment all over again and another week to find it."

"You're going to kill us both." Ingram frowned. "Cut it."

Wynter gritted her teeth and wrenched the bolt cutters from his hand. Instead of cutting the cable, she snatched up her face mask and an inflatable life jacket.

"What are you doing?" Ingram stepped in front of her, but she shoved him aside. "We don't have time for this!"

"Then leave!"

She grabbed a handheld oxygen canister, took a deep breath, and dove into the water. She swam ten feet down the cable and cut it. Above, she saw the cable snap back so fast onto the boat that Ingram had to jump back to save his leg from being lashed.

Next, she tied the cable to the life jacket, then inflated the jacket. She dropped the bolt cutters and the air canister to the bottom. Holding her breath, she took one last look into the murkiness below. The trunk wasn't visible in the dark water. The cable would hold, she hoped, until she returned to the lake—as long as the reservoir didn't recede ten or more feet to expose the hastily-created buoy. It was a gamble. But in examining the shoreline that week, she knew the water level was at its lowest point in years. Most likely, it would only rise. Instead of bringing sonar equipment next time, she could use a GPS and drag the area for her marker.

Resurfacing, she climbed onto the platform and threw her face mask on the deck.

"Can we go now?" Ingram had covered Gamal's body with a blanket.

"Should we dump the body or let them find it on board?" Wynter pulled on warm clothes.

"If we dump it, they'll think we kidnapped their sacred son. If we let them find him dead, they'll see he died in our company. Either way, they're coming for us."

"Fine. Put him in the hold under the gear." Wynter checked the shoreline. "I'll start heading to shore, but if anyone saw us, we're already dead."

Arctic

Rudolph Caspertein looked at Kobuk and she looked at him. They were both hungry. If Kobuk's loyalties shifted to satisfying her stomach, Rudy hoped his harpoon edge was enough to defend himself.

Standing, he surveyed the surrounding water again. Day two on the iceberg. The water around them seemed endless, with more ice floating nearby—chunks from his own melting berg and other bergs in the distance. By now, he was sure the current had pushed them north and west, past Russia's Wrangel Island. They were moving swiftly.

A taller iceberg was closing on them slowly, drifting faster than their own. For the rest of the day, Rudy ate snow and watched the other berg with Kobuk. Just maybe this new berg carried debris from the lost town of Barrow. Food or wood to burn for a signal would be an answer to prayer.

When the approaching berg drew close enough, Rudy could see it wasn't only taller than his, but also much larger. He decided if the two bergs collided, he would jump onto the other. There was nothing on his present berg. Their chances for survival could only get better.

Then the symptoms began, but Rudy noticed his mistake too late—solar retinopathy, the beginning stages of snow blindness. Nothing but whiteness around him had reflected the sun's rays into his eyes for nearly thirty hours. Quickly, he cut a strap off his jacket, sliced two holes for his eyes, and tied the blindfold around his head. But the damage was already done. His vision began to blur more and he knew it would go rapidly now. Kobuk seemed to sense something was wrong and pawed at his leg. Familiar with the symptoms, he guessed he had one hour left until he was fully blind. Healing would require two days, maybe more, and even then, he would see only red shapes when his vision did return.

Stupid! Of all the trips in the Arctic he'd guided for beginners, he'd made the simplest of mistakes.

Then, the neighboring berg bumped his own. It was so gentle, Rudy barely felt it. He jumped to the other berg. Kobuk followed him, and their old berg was nudged to the side as the larger, swifter one was swept ahead on the westerly current.

Rudy wanted to explore the new berg. It was monstrous. But his eyes were too far gone. In his last moments of sight, he thought part of the iceberg had shifted or moved. Had it cracked? He was still barely seeing what lay before him. Yet it wasn't until Kobuk made a deep, guttural growl that Rudy realized it wasn't their berg that was shifting.

There, again. It moved. White on white. Kobuk growled again. Rudy's vision was spent. He turned the blindfold eye-slits to the side of his head so he wouldn't try to use his eyes even if tempted. He needed to heal for a couple days. The Arctic had its rules, and he'd broken them. For two days, he'd have to wait—if he survived that long.

But Rudy knew he and Kobuk weren't alone on that iceberg.

CHAPTER THREE

Azerbaijan

When Wynter Caspertein had arrived in Azerbaijan, she and Ingram Thatcher had done everything through Gamal—hotel reservations, the boat rental, document translations, and visa paperwork. Now, upon leaving in haste, they were nervous and confused. They assured the hotel manager, who spoke very little English, that they weren't leaving for good, only fetching other archaeologists and returning in a couple days.

But at the airport in Baku, over one hundred miles from the reservoir, customs officers escorted them into a waiting room while an interpreter was found. The government didn't have them scheduled to leave the country, per their new regulations.

"Do you think they found the body already?" Wynter whispered to Ingram without moving her lips. The room was bare except for three chairs and a table, but the country was experiencing a technological revolution since the new railroad had come from the West. She was afraid there might be listening devices in the room.

"I hid it, but anyone could go into the hold. We rented the boat for the week, so hopefully no one will go aboard until after that."

"How important is it that we didn't line up our departure date? I've never run into this before."

"Every Islamic country is different when dealing with us infidels." Ingram shrugged. "You've traveled more than me. Just play ignorant if we get separated."

"They won't separate us." Wynter fingered the shark's tooth. "They can't. I'll just die!"

The door opened and three men entered. One was a customs officer in a diplomat's suit. Another was a military guard with a sidearm. The third introduced himself in English.

"I am Tawfiq al-Siddiqi." He didn't offer his hand. His eyes were dark but showed boredom. "These men . . . they ask me to question you."

"Of course." Ingram nodded slightly. "Anything you need."

Wynter smiled and nodded, though they seemed to ignore her, since she was a woman. She hoped Ingram didn't seem anxious to them, but she could see he was. They'd been together in nearly a dozen countries, and both their nerves were now overloaded.

Months earlier, they'd left an archaeological team to search for artifacts at their own blistering pace. But as Christians, they'd approached their relationship more slowly, even staying in separate hotel rooms since they weren't yet married. Wynter knew her trade, but she relied on Ingram to guide her, settle her, and even slow her down at times.

"You're not scheduled to leave today." Tawfiq flipped through copies of their travel documents. "You arrived with ninety-seven kilos of equipment and luggage. Now, you leave with twelve kilos of clothing and hygiene articles?"

"Yes, sir. We've left our equipment behind because we'll return in two days to continue our work."

"Two days? That's not scheduled, either. Why do you leave without notice? You make these men, this office, very suspicious. This is not America. You may not do this."

"This is our first time in Azerbaijan." Ingram scratched his head like an oblivious foreigner, but Wynter didn't think they were buying it. "We weren't aware of such customs."

"They are not customs. They are rules, laws," Tawfiq said. "These laws you received in English translation just in case you did not speak Azerbaijani. You both read English?"

"Yes, we do. Might I ask, sir, if we've left our kilos of equipment behind, we'll obviously return here to spend time and money, so why the attention to our departure?"

"We have many Armenian enemies, besides the pagan Sunnis. You come and go without notice. It's against policy. It's suspicious."

"Perhaps we could leave a deposit to assure our return?" Ingram offered. He pulled out a thick billfold.

Tawfiq turned to the customs officer and spoke in Azerbaijani. The officer pointed to Ingram, then Wynter.

"He says, one of you may go, but one of you must remain here," Tawfiq explained. "That's a deposit we will accept. You may choose which one will go and which will stay."

Wynter inhaled slowly. This was what she didn't want: separation.

"Are you arresting the one who stays here?" Ingram asked.

"No, but that one will be monitored until the other returns. You have stated that is your intention, anyway. After that, a scheduled departure will be allowed for both of you. We are doing our best to accommodate you."

"I will be the one who stays behind," Ingram said.

Tawfiq nodded his understanding, but Wynter stepped forward.

"Will you leave us for a few minutes, sir?" she asked. "We need to discuss this decision."

"There's nothing to discuss," Ingram said.

"We'll return in a few minutes." Tawfiq informed the officer and guard of Wynter's request, then the three left the room.

The second they were gone, Wynter turned to Ingram with a scowl.

"You are not staying here, Ingram! This is my fault from every angle! I hired Gamal. I turned my back and let him put on your gear. I'm the one who—"

"Stop it. This isn't about blame. This is about life and death, Wynter. Now, listen to me. You're the famous historian. People know you. They don't know me; they won't even listen to me. If I leave you, people won't rally behind me like they would if you were out there. Whoever stays behind will be arrested as soon as the body is found, or whenever someone notices Gamal is missing. Besides, as a woman, you have no chance in a prison here. People around the world will listen to you. They know your family and respect their accomplishments."

"This isn't a time for chivalry." Wynter gritted her teeth through tears. "We both know whoever stays behind is likely to be tried and executed."

"Well, when you put it like that . . . !" Ingram laughed nervously. "No, seriously, Wynter, I'm staying. I just stated all the reasons. At least with you getting out of the country, we've got a chance at working together again. Besides, what kind of man leaves his bride-to-be in a strange country?"

Wynter crossed her arms and turned away. She hated to be out of control. One minute, she'd found the treasure of a lifetime—two lifetimes. The next minute, she was running for her life.

"What if we both stayed?" she asked. "We could make a call from the hotel and contact the embassy. My oldest brother, Rudy, has friends in Washington, D.C. They could help us."

"There's only one airport. And we don't want this to become an international incident. If you leave now, at least one of us will go free. You can still get in touch with Rudy, but I think this is a situation for Titus now, if you can find him. From what you've told me, he may be a crook, but this is his territory. The British and American governments can't help us now. Find Titus."

"Anyone but Titus!" She hugged Ingram. "Okay. I want you to believe me when I say I'll do everything I can to help you. I'll hold people hostage. I'll hire an attorney. I'll—"

"You'll need a black ops team to get me out of here." Ingram sighed. "This boy who died could've been the next *imam* of the *Soldiers of Mahdi*. If you can't get me out within a couple days . . ."

"Don't say any more. I'll handle it. I will. Go back to the hotel. Maybe . . . hide or something. Will that work?"

"They said they'd be watching. It's okay. Let them come. We didn't get a chance to walk down the aisle yet, but this last year with you has been the best year of my life. Together, we touched lives where we worked. Christ used us. I don't regret a moment with you, Wynter."

"God will watch over you."

"I'll see you in the air, if not before." He kissed her on the lips. "I love you, Wynter."

"Don't stop hoping, Ingram. Promise me!"

Tawfiq entered the room.

"Did you decide? The plane is waiting."

Egypt

Titus Caspertein had never worn a woman's *hijab* before, but it seemed the only way to make contact with a mysterious woman who led the Christian underground in Egypt. As women assembled around him, chattering excitedly, he bowed his veiled face lower, and stooped, so as to disguise his six-three height.

The women's retreat had been announced in Cairo's Khan el-Khalili Friday Market. It was disguised as a celebration of Egyptian woman-hood, but Titus had learned to read certain Christian undertones during his past year with COIL. The retreat was actually a meeting among Christian women leaders in Egypt, but Titus wasn't the only one with intentions of crashing their party.

Deep in one of the gardens within the Kharija Oasis in east-central Egypt, the women greeted one another like long-lost sisters. Pools of water surrounded by grass sparkled in the sunlight, and palms moved gently in the comfortable breeze. Titus stood off to one side near an investigative peacock that seemed to suspect he might have something edible in his robe. He nudged the peacock aside with his boot, but the pest wasn't being intimidated away from a possible treat. Finally, Titus decided to ignore the brilliantly-colored bird. There were more threatening things afoot than pesky birds.

"Ladies, please! Let us begin!" A young woman, perhaps in her twenties, raised her hands as she spoke Arabic. Her accent wasn't Egyptian, but it was familiar to Titus. "We have so much to cover today. Please, I know you're nervous and excited. So am I! Let me open in prayer to our Lord."

The crowd of about sixty women finally hushed their twittering. Some stood to support the elderly. Others remained seated with heads held low, their Christian experience much more secretive than the tradition of the bolder women.

"Gracious Father," the woman prayed, "we are Your daughters . . ."

In his heart, Titus prayed with his sisters in Christ, but he didn't close his eyes. Rather, he swept the edges of the garden for the threat he knew was coming. Stepping over the peacock, he angled closer to the leader dressed in a light green *hijab*. His work for COIL wasn't confined only to protecting threatened believers. He was also to network with them. Though the woman in green had attracted a bad element in the days leading up to the retreat, she seemed to have remarkable resources to draw so many underground followers. Renting the garden for the weekend must've been costly. Who was she?

When finished praying, the woman folded her hands and smiled warmly at her guests.

"If I could send you one message in these two days," she said, "it is that you are not alone. You are not alone in your silent suffering. You are not alone in your fear. You are not alone in your hidden worship of Isa."

Women openly wailed. A few clapped and mumbled prayers. Isa was the name the Koran used for Jesus, and it was the name by which they knew their Savior. Titus was tempted to fall to his own knees and weep in celebration with these courageous souls, but he held his posture, his right hand poised near his tranquilizer handgun. He prayed he would remember every detail of the secret Christian meeting to tell Annette, his wife of just over a year. After living a life of evil, Titus craved gentler moments now that Christ lived in him.

A flash of movement beyond the palms! From under his robe, Titus drew his sidearm, a customized nine-millimeter, loaded with gel-tranqs. The women on the grass were too focused on the speaker to notice the approaching gunmen—three from the entrance, two more from the back.

The peacock chose that moment to fan his tail to flaunt his beauty, brushing against Titus' knees. There seemed no alternative to getting rid of the nuisance except to reach down with his free hand and pluck a lengthy tail feather from his backside. It squawked in such alarm that the speaker paused to acknowledge Titus behind his costume. Several women glared critically at him for causing the interruption. He cringed behind the veil in guilt and dropped the tail feather on the grass and bowed humbly.

"My apologies," he said, chirping in an Arabic falsetto voice. It wasn't yet time to blow his cover.

But the leader didn't have the opportunity to continue her discourse. The five gunmen emerged from the perimeter foliage and froze, automatic weapons leveled. The women were surrounded. Several cried out and lay flat on the ground, wailing louder than before, as if they knew the brutality they would now endure. The female leader approached the nearest gunman and demanded an explanation, but he slapped her with the back of his hand, sending her to the ground.

"You are all under arrest!" the violent man said. "If you move before processing, you will be shot!"

Titus met the gaze of one gunman, a short Russian who stared back at him with amusement in his eyes. Sighing, Titus knew he'd never live this stunt down. Sure, Oleg Saratov had seen him in disguise at other times, but never in a woman's *hijab*.

Before anyone else was harmed, Titus set a foot under the frisky peacock. Maybe God had designed the bird to bother him for a reason. When he briskly lifted his foot, the bird flapped its shrieking annoyance into the sky. Every eye in the garden went to the angry fowl. It was all Oleg needed to distract his fellow Muslim officers. He dropped his automatic weapon and drew from under his suit two identical COIL pistols. The bird was still in flight when he fired at the two gunmen toward the front of the gathering.

As the armed men nearest Titus hesitated in their confusion between the peacock and Oleg's treachery, Titus tranquilized each of them with a round to the chest. Oleg leaped onto a one-thousand-year-old marble podium above the woman leader as she regained her composure and rose to her feet. From his vantage point, Oleg commanded the terrain inside and outside the garden.

Tossing off his veil, Titus stepped away from his discarded *hijab*. Many of the women cried out for a second time at this latest wave of potential danger. He waded through their crumpled, praying bodies to reach the leading woman. Her lip was cut and bleeding from the strike. Offering her a handkerchief, he faced her audience while at her side.

"You're safe, sister. We were tailing some Muslim Brotherhood agents when we came upon your plans for today. We're here to protect you." Titus gestured to Oleg. "He infiltrated their group last week and participated in the sting. Oleg, is everyone accounted for?"

The stout Russian, years older than Titus, slapped his knee.

"How am I supposed to look at you with a straight face ever again?" Oleg shook his head. "I'm risking my life with these wolves, and you're playing dress-up?"

"Ignore him." Titus rolled his eyes, shrugged, and smiled at the leader. She wiped her bleeding lip and offered the cloth back to Titus. "Keep it. Listen, we have to relocate this little party. A bus is waiting in the parking lot. The accommodations at the next place won't be as nice, but I can promise it'll be safe for the rest of the weekend. We also brought a suitcase of Arabic Bibles."

"You're really disciples of Isa?"

"By His blood, I'm saved. By His life, I live by faith. Your accent—is it Saudi?"

"Yes." She lifted her glowing face. "My father is Prince Abdul."

"Oh!" Titus holstered his sidearm. "I believe I sold a gold-mounted hand mirror to a Prince Abdul two years ago. He's a collector, your father?"

"He likes to show off to his rich oil friends." She blushed. "Shall I tell the women what's happening? The only men they know restrict any kind of worship of Isa. With both of you around this weekend, maybe I won't be the only speaker for our retreat?"

"We're here to serve you all." Titus bowed his head. "We have much to discuss."

"As long as this weekend remains about the women, right? They have risked their lives for this day."

"We'll stay out of your way, sister," Oleg assured. "As sure as my partner wears a beautiful veil, you're to continue without interruption—after this interruption."

Prince Abdul's daughter explained the situation to her group, and Oleg hopped off the marble mount next to Titus.

"Can you drive the bus?" Titus asked and gave Oleg the keys. "I'll clean up here and leave a false trail of evidence toward Cairo for when our Muslim Brotherhood friends wake up."

"I'll see you at the other oasis?"

"In a couple hours."

Oleg backed away.

"Hey, the peacock was a nice touch. But the veil—you know I'll have to tell Annette."

"Of course you will!" Titus faked a scowl, then laughed with Oleg as he departed with the women.

Titus remained behind in the garden, standing in its peacefulness for a moment. With the excitement over, his own mortality rushed back to mind. He'd asked his wife, Annette, to forward an oncologist's report to him as soon as it came in. Even if he was in the field, he wanted to know what poison grew in his body. But no matter how advanced the cancer was, he was a child of God now, and he would trust Him for the outcome!

Ever since he'd led Oleg to Christ six months earlier on a Moscow street, they'd been risking their lives for God's people. But moments like this—basking in the might of God's saving work—was worth it all. A Saudi prince's daughter was a believer? And not just a believer, but an organizer in the Christian underground!

Before he was summoned by the COIL office to the next mission, Titus hoped to set up a system for operatives to network with the prince's daughter. The family of God worked together, even secretly.

CHAPTER FOUR

Arctic

Rudy tensed as Kobuk's entire body trembled from a growl. Rudy's first instinct was to rip off his blindfold and face their adversary, but he fought the urge. He was still snow-blind. Instead, he gripped a fistful of the thick coat on Kobuk's shoulders to feel the movements of the dog—her wariness, her guidance.

He felt rather than heard a footfall twenty yards away and remembered his last blurred vision before his sight had completely faded. White on white. He wondered how large the polar bear was.

More than anything else, bears hated dogs. More than anything else, Rudy disliked bears. He disliked them even when he could see them. Facing a hungry polar bear as a blind man wasn't on his list of adventures to try before dying, or while dying.

Standing tall and moving his arms above his head, Rudy growled and snarled, doing his best to mimic Kobuk's ferocious sounds. Then, the bear roared for the first time. The roar lasted twelve seconds. Rudy counted as the iceberg vibrated under his feet. But both man and dog stood their ground. Nothing was getting through Kobuk to her companion. In an instant of reflection, Rudy chastised himself for ever contemplating making a meal out of Kobuk.

He could hear the bear retreat a distance, but not too far. The iceberg was larger than their last, but it still had its limits. Rudy felt Kobuk's body relax as the polar bear left their immediate area, probably behind a shelf of ice or pile of snow. Kneeling, Rudy massaged Kobuk's back muscles while she licked his sightless face.

"Good girl, Kobuk. Good dog! Man's best friend. They weren't kidding!"

For now, the bear would leave them alone. But Rudy knew a time would come when all three berg occupants would grow irresistibly hungry. No less than two days until Rudy could see again.

"Two more days, Lord," Rudy prayed. "Please just hold that bear off for two more days."

He tapped his three-foot-long antler-tipped harpoon against his leg.

Like an ancient Eskimo hunter, he was ready for battle, blind or not.

Armenia

Wynter flew into Yerevan, Armenia, that night. She was only two hundred miles away from Ingram, but it felt like a thousand. During the flight, she turned her face toward the window and wept. Deep down, she knew Ingram was lost. She wouldn't see him again in this life. Always on the move, romance had seemed impossible. Ingram had shared her faith in God and her zeal for history. Now, she'd be alone forever.

The hop across Azerbaijan's border to neighboring Armenia would've seemed far too close to the Shiite population, but the two nations were enemies. Since the 1990's, a land dispute, then a railway conflict between the two peoples, had erupted in violence. Over four hundred thousand Armenians had fled Azerbaijan, and two hundred thousand Azerbaijanis had fled from Armenia. For now, Wynter felt she was safe.

She went straight to the US embassy and dialed a secure phone. The first and only person she called during any crisis was an old family friend in Little Rock, Attorney at Law Arlin Skokes.

"This is Skokes," a deep booming voice said. "What's your business?"

"Arlin, it's Wynter. Can you hear me?"

"Hey, girl! Yeah, I hear you. Still treasure hunting?"

She imagined him seated behind his massive oak desk, chewing sunflower seeds behind an even bigger belly. Arlin was a bit of a scavenger. He prided himself in getting anything from anywhere and putting it somewhere else more practical.

"Big problems, Arlin," Wynter said. "I'm in Armenia at the embassy in Yerevan. I was diving in Azerbaijan for some artifacts when our guide, a nineteen-year-old boy, tried to follow me down in scuba gear he'd never been taught how to use. He died, Arlin."

She told him about hiding the body and leaving Ingram behind. When he didn't know what an *imam* was, she explained.

"When Muhammad, their prophet, died in AD 632, a controversy started over who would be the earthly spiritual leader—the *imam*, or the next caliph, if you're a Sunni Muslim. Today, twenty percent of

Muslims are Shiite. That's about forty million people. About one million of those are part of the *Soldiers of Mahdi*, devout Shiites who are willing to kill or die to bring in their messiah, the *Mahdi*, the Twelfth *Imam*.

"The boy who died was probably the son of the present *imam* over the *Soldiers of Mahdi*. We figure the boy was hiding in Azerbaijan because the top Sunni caliph is always trying to assassinate their enemies. Worse yet, leaders like this are believed to be protected by Allah from sin or error, and continue as the source of divine guidance for the world—as Muhammad incarnate. That's what we're dealing with. Are you getting all this?"

"And this, uh, Gamal, he was your porter and guide?"

"Yeah, and interpreter. I should've known something was up when he said he spoke Arabic and Azerbaijani, as well as English."

"Okay, are you in danger right now?"

"No, not right now. I talked to the US ambassador here, though he's off to bed now. They'll put me up. But Ingram can't stay in Azerbaijan, Arlin! They'll find the body. We're already infidels to them. Gamal's death was an accident, his own fault, but they won't care. They'll charge Ingram and justify the execution of an Englishman. We have to act now!"

"Okay. I'm thinking. My wheels are spinning . . ."

"We have twenty-four hours, probably no more. Any longer and Ingram is history."

"Promise me one thing, Wynter. Don't return to Azerbaijan. Promise me! Any execution Ingram may receive would look like a hill compared to the mountain your own imprisonment would cause, along with a parade in front of all the online cameras."

"All right, all right. I promise."

"Okay, now, the only route I have to helping Ingram is by diplomatic means. I'll call London, then put pressure on our government to move."

"We've got to do more. It's urgent, Arlin! They're keeping him in the country until I return and line up a scheduled departure."

"We have to think about possibilities besides diplomacy as well, something under the radar, maybe. I need to talk to a contact and see what he's willing to help us with, a friend at the FBI."

"That's what I wanted to hear, Arlin."

"And Rudy as well. I'll see if he's near a phone and find out if he has contacts in Azerbaijan."

"Just get him out, Arlin! Ingram Thatcher."

"I got it."

"And Arlin?"

"Yeah, girl?"

"We left a fortune behind."

"Oh, no. What are we talking about?"

"Eight figures. A high eight, is my guess."

"Who else knows about it?"

Two quiet clicks reached Wynter's ear. A chill passed up her spine. The clicks were slight and distant, but real.

"Ingram knows, of course, and you, and whoever else is listening."

"Yeah, I heard that, too. You're at the embassy?"

"Yeah. Why?"

"Tell them someone's tapped into their secure lines. Get out of there, out of Armenia. Somewhere safe only you know. Watch your back. Call me in twenty-four hours. I'll work on Ingram, I promise. Leave now. People are making plans for your eight figures right now. Lose yourself, girl. I'm praying for you. You've got to run for your life now."

"I'll call you tomorrow night."

Wynter checked her watch. Almost midnight. On a piece of paper, she scribbled a note to the ambassador about the breach in the phone line. She left the secure booth and gave her note to a night watchman to deliver to the ambassador's office mailbox. Once back downstairs, she entered a conference room where an enlarged map of Asia Minor hung on the wall. Tracing with her finger, she followed several routes across the Little Caucasus Mountains. The highways branched out of the capital in all four directions. She was in danger. Getting trapped inside a foreign embassy wasn't her idea of safety, and an airport was no place for her to spend the night. She'd have to hit the road. Fortunately, her bags were in the hallway.

She touched her shark tooth. Where could she go? So much depended on who had heard her phone conversation with Arlin Skokes in Arkansas. It wasn't necessarily anyone local. Small wars had been fought over eight figures. It would be irresponsible to expect anything but a full assault by someone. Ironically, she'd left Ingram inside Azerbaijan so she wouldn't be in danger. Now, she was in just as much danger.

Frustrated with her lack of options, she left the conference room map and went to her luggage in the hallway. Picking it up, she signed out of the embassy. Though it was raining outside, she hailed a taxi. She didn't know who to trust or who she could turn to now, since whoever she turned to would be in just as much danger for helping her. So, she would trust God alone to guide her. It was only twenty miles to Turkey's border. Depending on her new enemy, it was possible the border could be closed to her if someone were watching for her, but she had to try.

For the sake of the taxi driver, she pointed to a tourist brochure of Armenia and its western border with Turkey, and gave him a handful of *drams.*

"Take me here."

Mediterranean Sea

Titus sat shoulder to shoulder and knees to back amidst six hundred Asian and African refugees on a seventy-foot boat meant to carry a maximum of forty souls. He wore a hood over his head, his Egyptian *burnoose* still on his back, hiding his features as best he could. There were other foreigners on board—Lebanese, Eritreans, and Syrians who sought illegal entry into Europe, even though they'd launched from Libya.

Oleg sat across the boat from Titus. The ugly, scarred man was Titus' only backup on board the human trafficking boat, a boat of death, since it was unlikely they'd ever reach Italy so overloaded. It was these kinds of risks for others that had taught Titus the true meaning of sacrifice. With Oleg beside him, they'd learned in six months what would've otherwise taken six years to learn.

The two made eye contact, then Oleg looked away. Normally light-hearted, even on missions, they had no reason for amusement on this day. Their relationship needed to remain a secret until the smugglers abandoned the immigrants to die at sea.

The boat rocked against waves, and bodies shifted awkwardly on deck. If the boat capsized, Titus doubted he'd survive the ocean unless he swam straight down to get away from the mass of humanity.

Glancing again at Oleg, he saw him share his *couscous* bread with men and women around him. The steamed, cracked wheat was received with thankfulness. Titus drew his own lunch from under his robe. Since he daily gave his life to others, sharing his food wasn't a struggle.

With one hand, Titus offered *couscous* to the men behind and beside him, and a woman who sat against his legs in front of him. He dared not turn around to look at the armed men at the back of the boat. They'd ordered everyone to face forward. The smugglers didn't want to be identified later, if someone happened to live long enough to be rescued by the Italian Coast Guard. Nevertheless, Titus kept one hand on the trigger under his robe.

Upon joining COIL, Titus had met with engineers and designed a new non-lethal weapon series, as well as other technology. The new non-lethal rounds could be fired from a regular firearm of the right caliber. With Corban Dowler overseeing, Titus had arranged for .22 caliber, nine-millimeter, and .308 cartridges. Thus, Titus carried a nine-millimeter handgun, customized with a twenty-round magazine and a built-in silencer.

The tranquilizer ammunition carried a heavier punch than the old NL series of pellet ammo. Each new round had a gelatin base, with a half-inch tack inside the gelatin, and was shaped like a regular bullet. On impact, the gelatin toxin flattened against the skin of the target, and the tack was thrust forward to puncture the skin. The results were a bruise and an hour of unconsciousness. Using guns and ammo that saved lives was a long way from Titus' selfish days of gun smuggling and radioactive weapons deals.

Morning stretched into afternoon. A child cried behind him, but Titus still didn't turn around. The single motor hummed, propelling the derelict vessel northward, probably toward a predetermined GPS coordinate. The smugglers would leave the boat soon, when they were picked up by another. It would happen before Italian authorities could apprehend the extortionists and murderers.

Some of the refugees had been searched before boarding, but Titus and Oleg had boarded early and scowled threateningly. The three smugglers, two with rifles, hadn't bothered them. Weaker people hadn't been as fortunate, but Titus hadn't reacted. His cover was required to put a stop to the dead bodies washing up on the shores of Europe and Africa.

"You English?" the man on his right asked. He was black and wore a t-shirt and khaki pants.

No one else seemed to be talking on board, but the weeping and churning of the sea covered their guarded words.

"Yes, I speak English."

"I translate for tourists in Asmara." He gestured at the woman against Titus' knees. "My sister. This is my family now. Wife, children, all dead."

"Famine?" Titus asked.

"Prison. Killers of Isa followers. Most of us here are believers. You follow Isa?"

Titus browsed the people around him without moving his head. He'd been with COIL for only a year, so he often came face-to-face with grave truths he'd never heard of before. A boat full of Christians, fleeing persecution? No wonder COIL had arranged for a couple operatives to shut down the dangerous smuggling ring. Corban had told him how smugglers were killing hundreds each year once the immigrants paid their fare, which was as much as fifteen hundred dollars per person. It made Titus' own concerns about his cancer seem small in comparison.

"Yeah, I'm a follower. For one year now."

"It is hard today." The man bobbed his head. "Soon, Isa must return."

"I pray so."

Titus wasn't sure whether he should rejoice or grieve over meeting his Eritrean brother. This man truly had no home. He would reach Italy, because Titus and Oleg would make sure the boatload did, but then what?

Plastic jugs with water were passed around. The smugglers yelled a warning in Arabic that there would be no more water until the morning, but Titus knew the smugglers had only loaded four jugs. There would be no more water at all, unless some of the immigrants had their own water, which was unlikely since those who carried anything on their person carried only their belongings.

Night fell, but Titus didn't join his neighbors in sleep. He kept his head low, as did Oleg, hoping not to draw the smugglers' attention.

The watch on his wrist vibrated. Hiding his arm in his lap, he pulled up his sleeve to read a text message from COIL tech Marc Densort: "Boat. ETA: 20 min."

Titus tapped the touch-screen of the watch. It blinked to GABE, or Gabriel mode. Three stealth UAVs seventy miles overhead watched over him with high resolution cameras. Circling his finger on the screen, the view zoomed in on his location, closer and closer. His boat was a dot on a field of black sea. To the southwest, another single white pixel raced toward them.

He zoomed in on the racing pixel, larger and larger, testing the limits of the new COIL overwatch system—until he could see the speedboat approaching from Tunisia. Switching to thermal imaging, he saw two glowing signatures identifying two humans on board.

With the necessary intel gathered, he covered his watch and coughed loudly into his hand. A few yards away, Oleg lifted his head—a shadow against the dim horizon.

"Two!" Titus sneezed. "Two!"

Oleg clicked his tongue twice. Message received.

Again, they waited, listening for the faintest sound of a motor in the distance. Having known Oleg for some time, even before they were friends, Titus knew he could count on the trained agent. The man had been lethal as an Interpol officer, but now as a Christian, with the Spirit of Christ compelling him, Titus trusted Oleg with his life.

There! The speedboat motor revved and faded in and out, bouncing over the waves. Titus drew his handgun from its shoulder holster as he turned around. Leaning on his free arm, he aimed and fired three times, tranquilizing two smugglers. Oleg fired twice, taking out one more. The three men slumped to the deck as Titus jumped to his feet, nearly fell over from a thigh cramp, then stumbled through sleeping refugees to the stern where the motor hadn't changed its pitch.

Oleg met him there as they assumed the position of the smugglers. Titus used his foot to scoot the two dropped rifles to the side of the deck. He reached down, grabbed both rifle slings, and tossed the weapons overboard.

No one on deck stirred.

"Hey," Oleg called over the rumble of motor. "You think we'll ever get tired of doing this?"

"For these people?" Titus shook his head and smiled. "Not a chance."

The speedboat pulled along the starboard side. Oleg leaned over and fired five times.

"Done," he said, and started to reload. "Two down."

"That's a nice boat. Are you just going to let her drift away?"

Oleg gazed after the other vessel as it dropped into the wake of the larger boat.

"I'm not jumping in."

"You're the one who shot them before they tied on. Use their radio to call in the Coast Guard."

"Use your watch."

"We're getting father away . . ."

"I'll have some choice words for you when I return." Oleg stripped off his *burnoose* and thrust his gun into his holster. "You know I don't like to bathe more often than you. It makes you feel inferior."

Titus didn't get a chance to respond before Oleg dove overboard and swam for the idling speedboat now one hundred feet off their stern. Instead, Titus prayed he remembered moments like these, not only for himself, but to share with Annette and other Christians in America. He tried to return to the States every few missions, but the demand for his expertise was high. When he could be home in New York, he cherished his days with Annette, however short they were.

COIL operatives everywhere, for the sake of Christ and His sheep, had to make sacrifices.

CHAPTER FIVE

Arctic

Rudy knew his habitat was about to become water. Since the iceberg was melting so quickly, it probably wasn't age-old ice, but seasonal snow pack like the last berg they'd been on.

The polar bear had only approached Kobuk and Rudy twice in the last twenty-four hours. Somehow, Rudy had refrained from pulling off his blindfold. His retinas needed complete rest for what lay ahead. And thankfully, the bear had retreated each time to what Rudy assumed to be the opposite side of the berg.

But that wouldn't last much longer. Rudy's hunger pangs had long subsided. Now, he was starving. Two days without food. Kobuk was feeling it, too, he could tell. The huge St. Bernard had nuzzled him roughly in search of edibles within the folds of his clothes. Rudy had cut off a piece of his caribou skin coat and fed it to the canine. Kobuk had gulped the hide and fur down in one swallow. At least Kobuk would have a little strength if the bear attacked.

Only two things were sure and inevitable in Rudy's mind. The first thing was that the iceberg was melting. Chunks of the edges were falling, calving into the water every few minutes. The mountain was becoming a mole hill, which forced the second inevitable fact: that the bear would attack.

The more the iceberg melted, the closer the three mammals moved toward one another—a bear, a dog, and a man. And of the three, Rudy knew he wasn't the strongest or the fiercest. He was the weak link in the island's food chain.

"Tomorrow, girl," Rudy whispered to Kobuk. "Tomorrow, we need to stand together."

Turkey

Wynter left her taxi at the Turkey border. From there, she paid a Turkish border policeman for a ride to the city of Igdir fifteen miles inside the country. Regional tension was high, and no one seemed to pay her any mind as the Kurds fought ISIS a short distance to the south. Global attention was on the Turkish boundary and the war against terror. As Wynter slipped into Turkey with her head covered, she prepared for the next step in her flight to safety.

In Igdir, she reduced her luggage to one suitcase, then paid a country barber to cut her brunette hair like a man's haircut. The barber swore he'd never cut a woman's hair before, but he'd cut men's hair, so he cropped it short as she insisted. With a touch of make-up, she created her desired effect of darkened eyes, hollowed cheeks, and a crooked nose. Even Ingram would have trouble recognizing her now, she guessed. At the thought of him, she teared up and gazed to the north. He was back there somewhere, alone, giving his life so she could live.

She rented a car and drove west. It was nearly one thousand miles across Turkey to Istanbul. All she could think about was running, getting away, surviving, and she prayed Ingram was surviving, too.

But her money was dwindling and her hope was running short. Now totally alone, she prayed for preservation. In a careless moment on the water, her life had been reduced to one of flight. With the enemies she now had, she couldn't imagine a future where she would ever be safe again.

Azerbaijan

Imam Nasser al-Hakim stalked into the police station coroner's office in Baku, Azerbaijan. A parade of followers accompanied him. He was the leader of Iran's most powerful militant Shiite faction, the *Soldiers of Mahdi*.

Nasser was forty-nine years old, bearded with a beaked nose that would shame the boldest falcon. He was six-three and nearly three hundred pounds. As an Iranian soldier, he knew strife, loss, and war. But when he saw his son, Gamal, lying on the sheeted coroner's table, he wanted to kill. Kill anybody. Kill everybody.

"How did he die?" When Nasser spoke, he stuttered, not from sorrow but from a speech impediment since a child in Tehran.

"Carbon dioxide poisoning."

"Poisoning?"

"There were two Westerners. We have one of them. His name is Ingram Thatcher."

"Infidels? They killed him?"

"Gamal was accompanying them as they explored the reservoir for historic articles."

"Take me to this man."

The doctor shrugged and led the way from the basement to a holding cell on the first floor. The doctor and two policemen humbly tried to bar Nasser from entering the cell, but Nasser was the *imam* of the *Soldiers of Mahdi*, sinless and holy. He pushed past and opened the cell door himself. Ingram Thatcher stood from his cement bunk. His scalp had a fresh scab above the left ear, and dried blood dotted his shirt collar.

Nasser turned to one of his followers, who shoved a pistol into Nasser's hand. With fury in his heart, Nasser turned back and leveled the barrel at Ingram's forehead. Ingram froze with his mouth open as a bullet tore through bone and tissue. For two seconds, he remained standing, terror in his eyes. Then Ingram's body crumbled to the floor. Nasser turned to his followers.

"My son will be buried within our borders!" He glared at his men. "Give me two days. While I'm gone, find the second infidel. But I want to see him die myself!"

"It's actually a woman, Great *Imam*," the doctor said. "This man, this infidel was with a woman. She fled. She flew to Armenia. We think she's in Turkey. I knew to send agents after her."

"No, turn the investigation over to my men," the *imam* ordered. "This is beyond the jurisdiction of Azerbaijan now. By Allah, I will find this woman myself! But first, I will grieve for my son."

Cyprus

Rashid al-Sabur was a treasure hunter. Most of his fortune had been made from communication intercepts—like the one he'd heard from the US embassy's secure line in Armenia. The phone call from someone codenamed "Winter" had connected to someone in America named Arlin. This had Rashid rushing for information.

Alone in his office, Rashid reviewed the phone tap. The man had called himself Skokes, then the woman had called him Arlin. Later, Arlin Skokes had called her Winter. Rashid wrote these names down to file into his computer later. He could care less about the *imam*'s dead son, Gamal. A scuba accident? So, that meant they were in water—either the Caspian Sea or the reservoir.

But what really intrigued Rashid was when Winter had said she'd left an eight-figure fortune behind. *Eight figures.* Rashid wrote eight zeros on the paper and circled it eight times. The hunt would begin. This fortune needed to be found by whatever means necessary.

Rashid "The Saber" al-Sabur was Egyptian. No one knew him. He lived a life of solitude, of silence, rarely speaking. Ironically, he was a communications expert. But even though no one knew him, Rashid knew himself. He was a ruthless killer, a thief, and he worked alone. After all, if he worked with anyone, he'd have to share the treasures he found. And sharing wasn't an option.

His offices were in Nicosia, Cyprus, the wedge-shaped island west of Lebanon's coast in the Mediterranean Sea. Cyprus was the center of everything, Rashid claimed. Just a few hours of flight time, he could be anywhere inside the borders of any of three different continents.

On his computer, he typed the name Arlin Skokes. Nothing came up. No big deal. His specialized database consisted mostly of targets and competitors the world over. Next, he typed in the name of Winter and scanned the results, but found nothing helpful. Unless . . . He tried different variant spellings and received seven results. He froze on the fourth result. It was an article about a woman named Wynter Caspertein, an archaeologist who'd been involved in a shark attack off the coast of Argentina.

Caspertein. Thoughtfully, Rashid laced his fingers behind his head and sat back in his office chair. *Caspertein.* Yes, he knew the name well. He'd crossed paths with Titus Caspertein many times, the latest just a couple years earlier. Both treasure hunters had tried to steal the same diamond shipment from a Johannesburg security company. Titus was the smart expert and had gotten away with the prize. That was Titus' specialty, it seemed—transportation, smuggling, escape, and evasion. Rashid was a thief and killer. No disguises, no mercy, all greed.

Rashid wasn't afraid of Titus. Well, maybe a little. This Wynter Caspertein was certainly a relative. He would need to be wary. Stealing from common civilians was a daily venture, but the family of Titus Caspertein? The danger of crossing the renowned professional caused him to consider skipping the job altogether.

But eight figures? He could retire on that! All he had to do was find the woman, Wynter. A few minutes alone with her and he'd know where the treasure was that she'd left behind.

As an Arab atheist, religion and gods and crosses and prophets—Rashid never saw much use for any of it. His faith was in himself. Besides, religious people all died, equally and easily, once he got what he wanted out of them.

With a sneer at the photo of Wynter Caspertein on his computer screen, Rashid left his office to pack a bag. He was going treasure hunting!

Arkansas

Arlin Skokes chewed on another handful of sunflower seeds, a habit his dentist wished he'd break. Arkansas in July—the heat was torture. He gazed at his wall calendar. Where had the years gone? His best friend and business partner, Richard Caspertein, had died after a heart attack. A year before that, Lucy Caspertein had died after a long battle with breast cancer. The parents had left behind three untamable children—Titus, Rudy, and Wynter. Arlin was far from a father figure, but he was happy whenever one of the three called to ask for help, to send him a client, or simply to visit. Wynter had been the closest to him. He managed her accounts with the museums in Washington, D.C., and—

His eyes twitched from the calendar to the wall clock. It was time to make the call. He dialed a number he rarely dialed. This number was for emergencies only—or for planning fishing trips.

"*Hola*. Speak to me," a voice answered.

"Hey, Lee. It's Arlin Skokes calling from Arkansas. How's the world of international crime?"

Lee Stambler was a US-based FBI agent, operating out of a D.C. office. Arlin had met him while fishing in Crooked Creek, and the Fed had been thankful when Arlin showed him the best fly-fishing holes in Arkansas. Over the years, Arlin had kept in touch, even leaving messages when the agent was in the field. From stories Lee had told him, Arlin gathered he was a patriot and a cowboy—a perfect combination to go up against a million *jihadis*.

"I'm well, Arly, but international crime has my fingers worked to the bone. Wish I was back in the Ozarks with you. What's up?"

"I've got a problem outside your area, but I was hoping for some advice, if not some assistance."

"Shoot it, Arly. I'll do what I can."

Arlin smiled. Lee had called him Arly since the day they'd met on the banks of the river.

"An American archaeologist named Wynter Caspertein was in Azerbaijan when a local kid got himself killed using her scuba gear. The kid was some *imam*'s son. No, scratch that. He was the son of someone involved in the *Soldiers of Mahdi*."

"Hmm . . . Azerbaijan's been leaning toward the extreme lately. This Caspertein woman's in deep, huh?"

"If a million radicals is deep, then yes." Arlin spit out seed shells. "She got out of Azerbaijan to Armenia's embassy, then she called from there to tell me she's on the run, but I heard a few clicks on the wire."

"Maybe a faulty wiretap. Probably as ancient as the Soviet's old systems. Infrastructure hasn't been rewired in much of that part of the world."

"Well, as a scientist, she uncovered some . . . valuables, to put it lightly. She'll be wanted for the Muslim boy's death, but also for her underwater find probably worth a pretty penny."

"And she left it behind?"

"Well, what she left behind that most concerns me is an Englishman named Ingram Thatcher. The authorities made him stay in the country. If the *imam*'s son is found any time soon, this Ingram fellow is history. I've talked to half of Parliament in London, and now I'm talking to you."

"Okay, I'm kicking out a memo as we speak. It'll generate some additional pressure to at least inquire about the Englishman. What's the archaeologist's full name?"

"Wynter. Wynter Caspertein."

"And she's on the run?"

"Yeah. Somewhere in Asia, I guess. The wiretap—she couldn't be specific about where she'd go next."

"I understand. If she's smart, she went west from Armenia. Does she have people she can call in Turkey?"

"She stopped carrying a sat-phone a few years ago. I can't say for sure who she knows over there. But she'll call again, I'm sure. Can you give me someone I can tell her to go to? Someone trustworthy?"

"I'm no handler or principal, Arly. I don't have the authority to direct an agent with express or implied orders. Thus, I can give you nothing sanctioned. Like I said, I'm passing the word along to the higher-ups. She'll have to get to Istanbul, though. Tell her that. Besides that, um, I'll monitor all data coming and going. Phone calls, news reports, everything that crosses land or air. I'm on it."

"Good, good, Lee. Thanks. Istanbul. I'll tell her when she calls."

"Arly, why don't we talk soon. Call tomorrow."

"Thanks, Lee. Next time you're in the Ozarks, I'll tell you about the fishing hole I've never shown anybody."

"You better, Arly. You better."

The two hung up. Arlin opened a world atlas and located Azerbaijan, Armenia, and Turkey. With a heavy sigh, he prayed that Wynter was already on her way to Istanbul.

Algeria

"Oleg?"

"Titus."

"I love you, brother, but it ain't easy trying to sleep while you're clipping your nails in my ear!"

Oleg set the fingernail clippers on his knee and folded his hands. Titus sat next to him in the shade of the hangar. Their Piper PA-31P Navajo jet-powered plane sat out on the dusty runway.

After their Mediterranean smuggling mission, they'd reached the coast of North Africa to rest and refuel the jet. Next, they planned to fly into Nigeria by way of Mali, following the Niger River to Kumo.

"I never thought I'd see ten thousand MP3 players in one place," Oleg said, referring to the cargo they'd recently taken aboard. "You think people back in civilization understand what we do out here?"

"In America, everyone has access to a Bible." Titus flicked a beetle off his arm. "Instead of celebrating that kind of liberty, they live any way their self-designed gods dictate. They insist they control their own destinies. Most can't imagine there are people who would give their lives to serve Jesus Christ. That's how I see it in America."

"Wealth in Russia has made us weak as well. Comfort has a way of feeding the flesh, but starving the soul."

"If there were more workers, these digital Bibles could've been delivered weeks ago. The number of devoted seem to be getting fewer and fewer." He smiled. "I guess that just means we'll be enjoying the Lord that much more since we're doing a little more of the labor."

"Makes me wonder how much we missed when we were running around the globe all those years, thinking only of our careers. You ever think of that?"

"Yeah." Titus shook his head. "Makes me sick knowing I could've been saving lives. Corban helped me see all that. I was so selfish."

"When you put it like that, I don't mind all those MP3 boxes filling up the plane, forcing us to nap out here for a change." Oleg climbed to this feet and stretched. "We have a circus ahead of us. I'll check the weapons. You want anything?"

"Yeah, a week with Annette back in the States!" She worked for COIL a week each month, usually on humanitarian aid runs into safe countries, so he didn't know where she was right then.

Titus watched Oleg walk to their plane. A lesser man might've complained, but not Oleg. They'd come from different sides of the law, but they both agreed they'd each previously lived worldly, worthless lives. God had opened their eyes to His truth, and there was no going back. They had tasted the presence of God, and now all they wanted was more—more of Christ in their lives.

The sunny afternoon in Algeria reminded Titus of Arkansas, of a family day as a child when his parents were still alive, and he and Rudy were still friends. What he would give to be at peace with Rudy. Or to see Wynter again. Corban had given Titus space to reconcile with his family, but that had only ended with Titus not knowing how to reach out to his two siblings.

"I miss them, Lord." Titus closed his eyes, drifting off to sleep. "And I miss Annette so much . . ."

His watch vibrated. Before he thought to brace himself for the incoming text from North America, he browsed the message forwarded from Annette. The skin growth they'd done a biopsy on was malignant. The oncologist wanted to do a full body scan to see if more than a few lymph nodes were affected. It may have spread.

Titus turned the screen off. So, the cancer was more serious than just some superficial spot on his back. He realized he'd have to tell Oleg and Corban Dowler at some point. His energy level, he felt, was already waning. But by God's grace, he had to finish the next mission!

CHAPTER SIX

Arctic

Rudy knelt on the snow of his iceberg. Kobuk sniffed at his sightless face. For the last hour, the polar bear had been growling and roaring, low and deep. It was hungry. The giant animal was less than two hundred feet away.

"This is the moment of truth," Rudy whispered to Kobuk.

He kept his eyes closed as he slid his blindfold back to its original position where the eye slits were over his eyes. Slowly, he opened his left eye with his hand over his face. Light!

Flinching, he closed his eye again. It was so bright. He tried again as his retinas adjusted, then both eyes. There was light, but he also saw red. Vaguely, he could see shapes in shades of red and gray. Seeing red was the first step in healing from snow blindness.

Kobuk growled beside him. Rudy looked up in time to see a red mass of fur moving toward him. Red equals white, he reminded himself. Gripping his antler-tipped harpoon, Rudy stood. The polar bear didn't stop. Kobuk snarled, her neck hairs bristling.

"Let's get him, girl!"

The bear started to run, a lumbering pace that made the iceberg shake. The king of the Arctic was used to intimidating its prey. Rudy ripped off his eye-slit bandana completely. He needed to see everything.

As the bear closed in, Rudy braced himself, balanced on the balls of his feet. When the bear was twelve bounds away, it slowed to a fast walk and moved in for the kill.

At that instant, Kobuk crossed in front of Rudy to the side of the bear to attack from behind. But the bear was wise. Arctic wolves had probably tried a similar strategy.

"That's it, Kobuk!" Rudy shouted.

Spinning on its heels, the bear snapped at Kobuk, and Rudy took a few quick steps to plunge his harpoon into the beast's ribs. Faster than Rudy expected, the bear swung back and swatted him with the back of a monstrous paw. Rudy flew through the air and landed hard ten feet away. The bear jumped toward him, but Kobuk ripped a patch of fur from the bear's tender backside.

With empty hands, Rudy scrambled to his feet and looked for his harpoon. He circled clockwise around the bear as Kobuk antagonized it relentlessly. Rudy spotted his harpoon still stuck in the bear's side! With a lunge, he ran forward, gripped the harpoon shaft, pushed it in farther, twisted, and pulled it out. The bear roared and turned on Rudy, but Kobuk was ready. The St. Bernard sunk her teeth into the tendon behind the bear's front left paw.

The beast limped toward the berg's edge. In the past, the bear may have found refuge in the icy waters. Rudy would've never hunted the giant if his own life hadn't been at risk. Now, the bear was confused since its prey was much deadlier than it had assumed. Its white coat dripped blood from its side. The harpoon had ripped a lung when Rudy had pushed past the ribs with the harpoon. And every step left a bloody paw print where Kobuk had slashed its tendon.

Kobuk sensed victory and targeted the tendons on the hind legs. Rudy saw an opening, a vulnerable point in the bear's labored stride. He ran alongside and thrust the harpoon upward and forward into the bear's chest cavity. At the same instant, Rudy slipped on the snow and fell underneath the bear.

A heavy foot stepped on Rudy's shoulder, but he pulled out the harpoon and rolled away as soon as the foot moved forward. Running four paces to the side, he darted past Kobuk and turned to face the bear before it could enter the water. It stood still, unable to breathe. The massive animal waivered on its feet, eyeing the water just feet away. Kobuk looked up at Rudy.

"Good girl, Kobuk." Rudy ruffled her head. "Give me a half-hour, and we'll be thanking the Lord for bear steaks! Raw, but it'll have to do."

The bear fell over, kicked once, then lay still. The snow soaked up the polar bear's warm blood.

Turkey

Wynter licked her chapped lips as she stared at the rental car's engine. She was on the side of a rural road in Turkey with the hood propped open. But she knew next to nothing about vehicle engines. Cars had been her brother Titus' hobby. She kicked the rusty bumper.

It creaked and groaned, then one end fell to the ground.

She stepped into the middle of the road, which was a mess of pot-holes and rutted pavement in both directions. To the east, where she'd been, there was only danger. No doubt, danger awaited her to the west as well, but she didn't know where to find help otherwise. At least in Istanbul she could find a phone and Westerners to help her. There had to be news about Ingram's status by now. For months, they'd been inseparable, and now this!

The Black Sea was somewhere north of her over the Pontic Mountains. She knew there were villages along its shores, but there were no roads leading north. She'd grown up in the Ozarks, but she didn't have even half the gear she needed to hike across the sub-continent.

Wynter climbed into the car and opened her bag. It was time to reduce her belongings again since she couldn't carry luggage along the roadside. It was July and the sky was clear. If she had to, she could spend the night on the rugged steppes a short distance off the highway.

She bundled a few necessities inside a towel—a hairbrush, one change of clothes, an address book, and a wallet. She'd never owned a purse.

With a yank, she tied a knot with an extra shirt around the towel and used the sleeves to tie her burden diagonally across her front. Wincing, she realized she had no food, but she had a water jug with a picture of Mt. Ararat she'd bought back at the border. Her shoes were in good shape and she was an experienced hiker. Though obstacles were nothing new to Wynter, anything beyond basic survival made her anxious. Even during the shark attack off Argentina, there'd been people in boats nearby.

Setting off to the west, she walked on the side of the road. Barely holding back the tears, she prayed for help. If she understood what God was teaching her, she thought it might help if she could trust Him. But the fear of what men would do to her if she were caught distracted her terribly.

It was that fear that caused her to look over her shoulder at the empty highway. Her enemies were surely on her trail by now.

Rashid al-Sabur, treasure hunter and thief, flew from Cyprus to

Istanbul that afternoon. He rented an apartment on the outskirts of the city on the west side of the Bosporus Strait, with the narrow crossing in sight. The apartment had a back room with a cement wall. This was mandatory for him—a place that could insulate the screaming when he questioned victims for information.

He set up a high-powered telescope in the window that faced the strait. Beside the window on the wall, he taped a photograph of Wynter Caspertein. With his brow against the scope, Rashid gazed through the lens at the strait. Yes, there were a number of ferries now, connecting two peoples with two continents, the city split between the two land masses. And most importantly, connecting Wynter to Rashid. That's what he was counting on. But even if she didn't use a ferry, no one came to Istanbul without visiting the coastline or seeing the strait where Europe lay. Using the scope, Rashid could see the wrinkles on a man's face all the way across the water. He would find Wynter and the secret of her riches!

Iran

The Shrine of Ali Mosque was the noisiest it had been since the last suicide bomber had targeted its doorway. Hundreds of the *Soldiers of Mahdi* wailed at the top of their lungs over the loss of Gamal, *Imam* Nasser al-Hakim's nineteen-year-old son. The boy would never become their *imam*.

Out in the streets, men stood vigil with rifles over their shoulders. They had all sworn *jihad* against an enemy about whom Nasser had only told a few. But inside the mosque, where no guns were allowed, the wailing was the loudest and most fervent.

Nasser beat on his chest and screamed vengeance at the high roof of the mosque. He wanted blood, and he knew whom to send to get it: Serik Tomir would do the job. Serik never failed to kill anyone Nasser sent him to kill, inside or outside Iran.

Nigeria

Titus and Oleg unloaded the ten thousand MP3 players, with airport officials in Kumo watching from across the tarmac. Beside the plane, Oleg climbed into one of the two ATVs that were each attached to a trailer on which the boxes of digital players were piled under secured tarps.

"Give me five minutes," Titus said, and Oleg nodded, content to watch over their cargo. Oleg had left Interpol because of bureaucratic upheavals so he'd shared that he was more than happy to leave their travel assignments and intelligence communiques in Titus' hands.

Crossing the tarmac, Titus unclipped his belt buckle, which was literally his satellite uplink and Wi-Fi station for his watch. His belt acted as an antenna. The technology was COIL's design, and it was advanced in comparison to what the civilized world owned, but it was especially new to Titus. For years, he'd avoided carrying even a cell phone, since some of his black market buyers or contacts were certain to be government officials, waiting for him to slip up. The threat of an enemy tracking his phone had limited Titus to brief burner phones or landlines.

COIL had changed all that. Now, he used the secure Gabriel sub-orbital satellites—essentially drones seventy thousand feet above—to bounce signals around the world.

He logged onto a message service in Tel Aviv. With a glance over his shoulder from years of paranoia, he typed in his username: *Swain*. It was the name of a mountain west of where he'd grown up, but dozens of contacts worldwide surely thought it was his real name. Next came the prompt for his password.

One new message awaited his attention: *"Swain, Ashanti Empire artifacts. Some gold. 1600s. Talk to me. Bemba."*

He typed a response: *"Bemba, Ashanti must be in demand, buyer in place. For now, not interested. Thanks. –Swain."*

The Ashanti Empire had thrived during the 1700s. They'd conquered areas around the Ivory Coast and Togo, West Africa. Of the sixteen thousand museums on his database, less than one thousand would be interested in something so recent. Besides, the merchandise was no doubt stolen, or he wouldn't have been notified to move it. Titus erased the message.

He logged off the message service and instant-messaged Marc Densort, his COIL contact who maintained the Gabriels fulltime. *"In Nigeria. Headed into bush. Armed and ready. Nothing new to report."*

With his mission status addressed, he left Annette a brief message about his health—the first message since receiving her text from the oncologist.

"Ann, I understand the urgency to get the body scan. I can't take the time off right now. It'll have to be during my next break. Pray for us.—T."

Returning his buckle to the belt, he tightened his watch strap as he walked back to Oleg. It would be a bumpy ride to the north, and there was sure to be conflict ahead. Their plane would be safe left there in the city, but they were leaving the city with their load. Boko Haram, the Islamic militants, regularly killed non-Muslims who traveled in the bush.

Oleg handed Titus a heavy gym bag as he climbed onto his own ATV. Titus set the bag on his lap, then drove away. The contents of the bag rattled against his leg. Their new COIL artillery needed to remain hidden until they reached the rural area. God's people expressed the mercy of Jesus Christ, but that didn't mean they were unarmed.

Arkansas

Arlin Skokes dialed Agent Lee Stambler's number as expected twenty-four hours after their first contact.

"Any news?" Arlin asked.

"Some. Nothing too positive, though, Arly. Looks like the Englishman, Ingram Thatcher, won't be a problem to bring home."

"No? That's a relief! Wynter will be so—"

"I'm sorry, Arly. I was trying to ease into the news. They killed Ingram. I found a little footage about the body on a Shiite website. They say he died from a shark attack."

"Well, they were diving."

"Maybe they were diving, but it says a shark attack in Mingechaur Lake," Lee said. "Mingechaur Lake is a reservoir. There are no sharks there. It's fresh water. And in the picture, Ingram is clearly shot through the forehead. It's not too far off to assume they're taunting us. They surely know someone will be trying to help the second person involved—Miss Caspertein."

"Well, finding her just became a lot more urgent for me, now that we know they killed Ingram."

"I hear you, Arly. I've also gotten a report from the Iranian division about a funeral for Nasser al-Hakim's son. He would've been the next *imam* of the *Soldiers of Mahdi*. Nasser is the one who's after Miss Caspertein. Apparently, they already returned Gamal's body to Tehran."

"Okay, what's done is done," Arlin said. "I still haven't heard again from Wynter, though. Are you able to do anything more to help her?"

"You have to understand, relations with all these factions are real touchy right now," Lee said. "I wasn't able to get any state-sanctioned agent involved, but I did get permission from Director Harcoff at The Hague to activate a sleeper agent we've used before."

"Sleeper agent?" Arlin frowned. "Is that like a sleeper cell?"

"Sometimes sleeper agents do more than we expect from them. Sure, occasionally they're criminals or foreigners, but they're usually better at what they do in their own areas of expertise than our domestic agents. They're naturals at what they do best for the right amount of money."

"Who do you have in mind?"

"Well, it's tough to say who these sleeper agents are sometimes, Arly. All I've got are message accounts anymore. Some phone numbers. Everything's digital. I have a codename. I pitch the request across the wire and hope for a response."

"Actually, that sounds a little sketchy. Wynter needs bona fide assistance. She's all alone out there."

"I worked with a sleeper agent extensively last month in China. They file reports because they want their weekly stipend. The guy Interpol suggested has produced before. I believe we can trust him."

"So Interpol will foot the bill for this operation?"

"Oh, no. They're just giving me the green light to confidentially use one of our mutual agents. Sorry, Arly, but you'll have to come up with the money. There'll be a bill and everything, but it'll come from a dummy corporation. You see, if this blows up in our face, I've been ordered to disassociate from it all, and you and I never had this conversation. The State Department wants to maintain good relations with the Shiites. ISIS in Syria has everyone on the run. Between you and me, we've been pacifying the extreme Muslims in Iran for a long time."

"While our own people are getting slaughtered. You feel good about moving forward like this?"

"It doesn't matter how I feel, Arly. It's all I have to work with. We make a difference how and where we can with the resources the politicians allow us to use. Listen, the sleeper agent I'm going to try first—this person, or team has been used before. They've always gotten the job done, but their identity is unknown. It works as a system of trust. Almost old fashioned, but it does work."

"Okay, well, tell me when someone confirms the operation, will you, Lee?"

"Absolutely. As soon as I get word."

"Good. This girl's like a daughter to me. Her safety's a priority, and right now, she's alone. I can feel it."

"I'm on it, Arly. Just give her my number if she calls, and make sure she goes to Istanbul."

Arctic

Kobuk was patient as Rudy gutted the animal, tossing the innards into the ocean. He kept the stomach and bladder so he could clean and dry them to use as waterproofed bags. Then Rudy began to cut into the polar bear carcass, giving the St. Bernard the first steak, but not too big. They hadn't eaten in three days.

Rudy chewed on his raw meat slowly. The last thing he wanted was to be sick on a floating iceberg somewhere in the Arctic Ocean. While he ate, he contemplated his next steps. Now they had food. At least they would have full stomachs before they drowned when the berg melted. All the other snow pack islands that floated nearby were mere icicles compared to their own berg. Still, as the heat beat down on them, Rudy figured they had about a week until they were standing on a piece of ice about the size of a car.

His eyes scanned the horizon for land. They needed to bump right into it. The water was far too cold to go swimming.

As he skinned the bear of its hide, Rudy wished he had a second blade, even though one edge of the harpoon was sharpened into a razor. It was still cumbersome work. When the bear was skinned, which took three hours, Rudy stretched the hide out on the snow to dry. Next, he cut into the back and ribs, stripping the bones of all the meat, then buried the meat in the snow. Kobuk watched him with curiosity. She cocked her head and whined. Rudy stopped working.

"Good idea, Kobuk." Rudy cast a glance heavenward then tied his bandana blindfold over his eyes to preserve his sight. He could see through the eye slits to do everything he needed to do. "God's not done with us yet, girl."

As he worked, an idea began to form in his mind. A Russian named Fabian von Bellingshausen had sailed around Antarctica in 1821. An American named Matthew Henson reached the North Pole in 1909. Men had survived with less knowledge in the coldest regions of the earth for a couple hundred years. Rudy had read about their exploits in the Barrow library.

"If they did it, Kobuk, we can do it, too!"

But Kobuk just whined and cocked her head.

CHAPTER SEVEN

Nigeria

Titus checked the coordinates on his watch, then stopped his ATV on a dirt road in northeast Nigeria. A village lay ahead. While he waited for Oleg to catch up, he guzzled water and sprayed some on his dusty face. He prepared spiritually to face the condition of the village and probable diminished health of the villagers. The whole region lived in terror. Doctors and medical supplies were rarely transported out there, due to Boko Haram antagonists.

"Let me check it out first," Oleg said as he drove his ATV past Titus. The trailer hitched behind his ATV rattled some, but their vehicles had otherwise made the journey into Adamawa State without difficulty. Of course, that would change if Oleg insisted on placing himself in danger before Titus could observe the Gabriel cameras for what lay ahead.

Far ahead, Oleg disappeared behind white-washed buildings with thatched roofs. Titus let his ATV engine idle and listened to his radio in case Oleg called for help. Now in the bush of northeast Nigeria, they could bring out their weapons. There were magistrates in the rural villages, but no one was armed enough to take on what he and Oleg appeared to be: foreign mercenaries.

Boko Haram militants could be anywhere. He unzipped his bag of gear. Over his head, he slung the NL-X2, which was a .308 caliber battle rifle, effective up to six hundred yards. It fired gel-tranqs, same as his sidearm, and held the standard thirty rounds in a stubby magazine.

The secret behind the NL-X2 was its compact design. The barrel was eighteen inches, the casings ejecting from the stock rather than in front of the pistol grip. Its ugly, snub-nosed appearance had earned it the name of bullpup around the world, but COIL's gel-tranq ammunition made it a unique, non-lethal problem-solver, no longer than a man's arm.

"We're clear, Titus," his comm announced in his ear. "No sign of our Boko Haram friends."

"Roger. I'm coming."

But Titus took another minute to check his watch. In thermal imaging mode, he zoomed in on his own position first, then zoomed out slowly. Two hundred or so warm bodies were in the village. He could see smaller hot spots on the edge of the huts—goats. With his finger, he drew a digital perimeter on the screen a mile outside the village and turned on the proximity alert. If a warm body crossed the perimeter, the Gabriels would alert him. It was also comforting to know Marc Densort was back in New York watching over them, using the same Gabriel view Titus occasionally tapped for a heads up.

When Titus arrived in the village, Oleg was already distributing the MP3 players with pre-recorded files of the Bible. Nigerians spoke English, so the purchase of the digital Bibles had been easy. But distribution required careful attention by trained operatives. Even then, COIL had lost men and women to anti-Christian militants in Nigeria.

An elderly man approached the trailer as Titus pulled back the tarp to expose his half of the MP3s.

"We have prayed for today." The elder gestured to a group of slender youths who stood expectantly nearby. "These men are prepared."

"Prepared for what?" Titus wasn't surprised the local Christians had been praying. He'd often arrived in towns or villages where people who owned no phones or computers had expected him. As sure as God's peace was with them, they trusted God to provide for them in His time. "Everyone in the village may have one, my friend."

"No, you do not understand." The elder stepped closer. "The Word of God does not need armed men. These runners, not you, will deliver the rest of the Bibles to other villages. These young men have been training for this day."

"Oh!" Titus glanced at Oleg, who shrugged. "We're thankful for the help, but these are non-lethal guns. They don't kill. They won't even draw blood."

"No death?"

"No death." Titus grinned and patted the bullpup slung across his chest. "The bad guys fall asleep, then wake up, thankful they didn't die. Just maybe their thanks will be directed toward God, and they'll repent of their sins because they'll see God's grace through us."

"I do not believe you." The old man held his head up higher. "We will deliver the Bibles ourselves. We do not want you making trouble for us beyond this village."

"Well, I won't argue with you, sir." Titus scratched his head. Normally, people begged them to keep them safe, but here, the man was asking that the village men be placed in danger to protect the testimony of Christ.

"It'll save us a week," Oleg said. "I wouldn't mind a free week."

"With COIL, there are no free weeks." Titus chuckled, and moved aside with Oleg. "Very well. You're God's messengers now."

The runners unloaded the trailers and distributed the boxes to the youths. Large sheets, as thick as canvas, were spread over the ground and piles of MP3 players were bundled evenly. Grinning, each runner picked up a bundle, threw it over his back, and jogged out of the village.

"We had in mind to deliver to a couple villages in Cameroon, too," Titus said to the elder.

"Cameroon or Nigeria—there are no borders here." He waved his hand at his own people as they excitedly inspected their personal devices. "The men know which villages will receive them, and which villages will destroy them. And which villages have Muslim spies."

"Boko Haram spies?"

"They are everywhere, killing anyone who objects to their Islamic Law." The elder walked away. "Come. You will eat with me. You can tell me of God's work in other countries."

Oleg elbowed Titus as they fell in behind the elder, a crowd surrounding them to escort.

"I kind of like the sound of a week off, some good food, and some Christian fellowship, huh?"

"Yeah." Titus moved with the flow of the people and checked his watch for activity along the perimeter of the village. The first runners were already passing the mile perimeter setting, but no one was approaching the village otherwise. "Just remember what he said. Boko Haram is everywhere."

Turkey

Imam Nasser al-Hakim stood on the balcony of one of his houses in Istanbul, Turkey, and peered eastward across the Bosporus Strait at the

Thrace side of the city of Istanbul. Here, in the district of Uskudar, the strait was no more than two miles across. Ferries moved to and from the port of Besiktas where the coastal highway could be accessed.

The *imam* was a wealthy man with houses, planes, servants, and cars on every continent, even North America. The Americans, to his delight, were blindly welcoming his soldiers, and Nasser was exploiting their ignorance to his beliefs. It would be to their capitalistic doom.

He loved Istanbul and this house. It was one of the first houses he'd purchased when he'd made his fortune through the oil industry in southern Iran. Again, he owed the Americans for financing his family's continued *jihadist* efforts.

A tall, cold-hearted man stepped onto the balcony next to Nasser. Serik Tomir was the only man Nasser admired and treated as an equal. The man handled Nasser's most sensitive work within the *Soldiers of Mahdi* network. It was sensitive because Nasser needed to maintain a certain appearance as a holy man for the Muslims of the world. Of course, his closest followers knew he was something altogether different, but it was the rest of his people, and the West, that he needed to convince. The mercenary had killed and tortured numerous men for Nasser. Nasser had lost count of how many they'd maimed together in the name of Allah. And since the Koran justified such treatment of Allah's enemies, Nasser's conscience was clear.

Serik Tomir was a slender snake with a goatee trimmed to a point. And he never went anywhere without his cane. It had a spring-loaded sword inside its length that extended to a total length of eight feet. The sword was Serik's weapon of choice as Nasser's right-hand man, and Nasser rather enjoyed the idea of vanquishing enemies with a sword. The prophet Muhammad would approve, he imagined.

Behind the two powerful men, a dozen Islamic loyalists stood waiting for a command from Nasser or Serik.

"What's her name?" Nasser asked in Persian.

"Wynter Caspertein," Serik said.

"And you're certain she'll come this way? Through the two land masses?"

"One way or another, yes. My cousin found her rental car abandoned far east of the city. But she was coming this way. She seems to know no one and she's afraid. We'll catch her. No one will help her in Turkey. If they do, we'll kill them."

"The fact that she is running further proves her guilt." Nasser smiled, appreciating simple reasons to exact final justice. "Tell me, Serik, how will you catch my son's murderer?"

"The men are already spread throughout the two halves of the city, especially at American gathering places. The bridges and ferries are covered. And men at the airport are loyal to us."

"And what orders will your men follow when she is identified?"

"They'll abduct her, or follow her until she can be abducted. I haven't limited their methods, so she may be injured upon capture. I'll be notified as soon as she is seen. We'll bring her here for you to deal with . . . personally."

Nasser smiled again, almost contentedly. He would feel better after he'd turned the American woman over to his men. After that, he would circle her throat with his own hands. Then he would be content, fully content.

"Thank you, Serik. You have shown your love for Allah this day."

Washington, D.C.

Agent Lee Stambler sat in his FBI cubicle and stared at his screen. His right trigger finger twitched at the thought of representing American interests around the world. He was a patriot, after all, yet so often he was assigned to tracking war criminals or American fugitives. Desk work!

But now, he'd been approved to help in the Caspertein case. Lee was still new to the idea of acting as a principal to an agent in the field. Interpol was backing him up, which showed his superiors that his ten years of loyalty had impressed even other agencies. Certainly, a promotion was in order if he handled the Caspertein situation well!

Slowly, he typed a message to the sleeper agent who'd been selected in the Middle East to help Wynter Caspertein reach safety. He'd read hundreds of Interpol memos. How hard could it be to draft one? For this memo, all he had was a codename. Hopefully, this person or people could indeed help Wynter. He'd promised Arly he'd do his best.

"*To Swain,*" he typed. "*Urgent emergency . . .*"

Nigeria

Titus sat upright on his sleeping mat in the Nigerian village. His watch vibrated on his wrist for the fourth time since midnight, the perimeter alarm alerting him over inconsequential breaches. But not this time. This time, the heat signature one mile away wasn't a goat. He tugged on his boots and grabbed his rifle on the way out the door. The next cottage had no glass in its window, only a worn curtain.

"Oleg! Thirty seconds! We've got company!"

"At this hour?" Oleg muttered, his belly probably as full as Titus' since they'd been treated so well by their hosts. They'd shared about God's work late into the night. "Unbelievable timing!"

Titus didn't wait for his partner to stumble out of his host's dwelling. They'd already rehearsed crossfire positions, and Titus jogged west through the village to a small rise. Goats silently scattered before him, certainly as bothered by the pre-dawn interruption as Oleg.

"I'm on comm, Lazy," Titus said and dropped to his belly. "Where you at?"

"I'm in position." Oleg sounded winded. His position was on an elevated feed platform east of the village. "Two Land Cruisers pulling in. I count . . . six predators with rifles."

"Roger." Titus yawned and shook his head. These moments were difficult to judge. Engaging the enemy in a firefight wasn't difficult, but Titus and Oleg didn't live in the village. Boko Haram had been known to shoot people indiscriminately during firefights. Knowing their brutality, Titus didn't want to make the local people's lives any more difficult than they already were. "I have no one in sight yet."

"They went into the elder's house," Oleg said, "like they've been here before. I have three visible outside."

"Don't engage unless—"

A gunshot interrupted the night.

"They're dragging the elder outside! He's been shot, Titus. Looks like a belly wound I'm engaging. Titus?"

"Roger. Engage!"

Oleg's canon opened fire, the caliber too large to silence, but its muzzle flash was suppressed in the darkness east of Titus. Still, Titus could see no one since the six enemies had remained at the other end of the village.

"I'm repositioning!" Titus wasn't anxious to leave the high ground, but he had to get eyes on the militants to watch over Oleg.

"Two down!" Oleg shouted over his gunfire. "They weren't expecting resistance. Reloading!"

Titus came up behind the militants as they hid behind the cottages. Instead of using his loud bullpup, he drew his handgun and tranqed two quietly in the back. Farther away, the final two militants were returning fire at Oleg. Advancing down the middle of an avenue, Titus holstered his sidearm and held his rifle against his shoulder.

"Titus, find some cover!" Oleg yelled. "You're out in the open!"

One then the other gunman noticed Titus walking up on them. As they dove for better cover, Titus shot one, and Oleg got the other.

"Six down." Titus knelt over the elder. "Hang on, old man. Oleg, get down here. You were right. It's a bad one."

"Our daughters!" The elder clawed at Titus' arm. "You're already here. Get . . . them . . . back!"

Titus moved away as Oleg dropped to the man's side, a medical kit falling open in the dust. The whole village was there, and the family of the elder gathered around Oleg and the grandfather.

Dawn peeked over the horizon as Titus flex-cuffed the wrists and ankles of the six militants, and loaded them onto the back of the ATV trailers, three men on each bed. Next, he searched the two Land Cruisers and found a map that he showed to a middle-aged man with no teeth.

"What are these marked towns?" Titus asked.

"Christian." The man pointed to each of the eleven marked on the map. "Christian. Christian. And Christian. All Christian towns."

"What's this blue dot?"

"The school. It's closed now. All the girls from Christian homes were kidnapped, do you remember?"

"I remember. The whole world remembers, but remembering and caring enough to respond are two different things."

"More are taken all the time."

"The daughters." Titus folded up the map and stuffed it into his pocket. "Thanks, friend. How many daughters were taken from this village?"

"Twenty, I think. They have no family, those twenty. The girls were taken, then the families were killed. Such courage you've never seen. I became a Christian after that. Someday, it will be my turn. I won't deny Christ, either, and I used to be Muslim."

The man walked away. Titus was alone for a moment, reflecting on his own faith. Someday, it might be his turn for Jesus. Oleg approached.

"I lost him." Oleg used red dirt from the ground to wash his crimson-stained hands. "At least he was with loved ones. He was a believer, so now he's with God."

"Want to go Boko Haram-hunting?"

"We have a free week. What else do I have to do?"

"I told you," Titus slapped him on the back, "with COIL, there's no time off."

At the ATVs, Oleg checked the restraints of the six militants.

"Titus, you know as well as I do that any girls these crooks kidnapped are held only long enough to abuse, kill, or send off for a Muslim marriage. We won't be able to find them."

"Vengeance is the Lord's." Titus started the engine of his ATV. "But you said the world court has some of these guys on file for crimes? We can catch a few. I'm up for a little justice. How about you?"

Both men surveyed the village again. Boko Haram would continue to torment Christians across Western Africa because it would cost too much money for a country to root out the real problem. The poorest of Africa were alone.

"Let's at least put a little dent in the operation Boko Haram does for their Allah."

"I was hoping you'd say that." Titus smiled and nodded at the road leading out of the village."It ain't easy being hunted by COIL."

CHAPTER EIGHT

Turkey

Wynter waved to the family inside the Volkswagen. For the last two hundred miles, they had given her a ride west. They didn't speak the same language, but Wynter had slept most of the four hours, anyway. At least with the family, she'd felt safe for a few hours.

She was now in Istanbul, a place she thought she'd never reach alive. Finally, she was safe even if she was cold and tired. Nothing a warm meal, shower, and bed wouldn't cure. But first, she needed to find a phone to call Arlin Skokes for money and a flight home. The first travel agency she could find would do the trick!

Since she'd been in the Bosporus area before, she didn't take time to note the Islamic art and aged architecture. She worked her way through the city to the waterside shops and suburbs along the eastern shore. Blending well enough in the district of Uskudar, Wynter watched for a person in the evening crowd she could ask to use their cell phone. The city was a melting pot of peoples, countries, and even continents. At five-eleven, though, she was one of the tallest women around. Her short-cropped hair drew more attention than she wished, and her makeup disguise had long since worn off.

Using a shop window as a mirror, she pulled out an extra shirt from her bundle and draped it over her head, tying it in a headscarf fashion used by many Muslim women. She needed desperately to blend in.

Suddenly, she froze. In the reflection, she saw two men observing her from the cobblestone sidewalk behind her. One was pointing at her as he held up a piece of paper. The paper was transparent enough for her to see it was a photograph of her. They'd found her!

Acting as if unaware of her admirers, she smoothed down her headscarf and continued along the shoreline. She rounded a corner, then ducked into a dark alley. Running down the alley, she stepped into a busy street. Halting, she looked back. She'd lost the men near the shops, but others on the busy street pointed and came toward her. Pocketing only her address book and wallet, she threw her clothes bundle aside. Without the bundle, she could move faster.

Wynter walked quickly away from the shore. The farther uphill and inland she journeyed, the more she stood out in the residential neighborhoods, but it seemed the men pursuing her were on the shore below. Sadly, she realized if they were after her like this, Ingram had surely been arrested in Azerbaijan. Someday, she hoped to be back at Ingram's side, and she'd never leave him behind again!

She zigzagged through the streets until she reached the poorest and oldest section of the city. It seemed her only refuge, but she still needed a bed and a phone.

When no one seemed to be looking toward her, she picked up a piece of concrete shaped like a banana. She swung it to test it as a weapon. With her jaw set determinedly, she headed back into the city. Though she was alone and afraid, she told herself she wasn't abandoned. God was still with her. And He could deliver her.

Nigeria

Wearily, Titus took his time reloading his rifle even though Boko Haram militants fired nonstop in his direction. Occasionally, a chance round thumped into the ground near him, but their AK-47s couldn't match the range, and certainly not the accuracy, of the bullpup. Oleg was three hundred yards to his right, a distance either man could cover to watch over the other on the sub-Saharan plain.

Before Titus could settle in to take another few shots, the gunmen not yet tranquilized jumped up, ran to their vehicles, and drove away.

"They'll think twice the next time they set up a roadblock on the open highway," Oleg said over his comm. In the distance, the Russian stood up. "I received those images from The Hague of wanted criminals. Shall we see who we netted?"

Titus met Oleg at what had been the roadblock where seven men had been tranquilized, but left for dead by their fleeing companions. Oleg held up his sat-phone and snapped images of the militants' sleeping faces.

"There's one." Titus patted the cheek of an unconscious man. "It ain't easy having your face on a wanted list."

"Look who's talking!" Oleg moved to the next man. "Your mug would pay enough for me to retire twice if I turned you in!"

"Twice, you say?" Titus chuckled and held up the head of the next militant as Oleg checked Interpol's database. "I've seen you eat. You'd better not settle for retirement before you have a fortune to keep you alive."

Together, they cut loose the men on their trailers who Oleg's contacts said weren't yet wanted for human rights violations. But they kept two men from the village and one from the roadblock. As Oleg disassembled the militants' rifles and threw the pieces across the grassy plain, Titus checked his messages in Tel Aviv.

He had two new texts. The first was an offer to smuggle a looted truckload of artifacts out of Syria. A truckload? Impossible to do with the small jet he'd been using. Though he needed to maintain his old identity, some jobs were too involved or too immoral to accept. Responding, he turned it down.

The second message was from someone named Einsteinium. Titus sighed. It was someone he'd done a few jobs for in the past, someone from the US or Britain. He tapped the screen to read the message: "*Swain, Urgent emergency. American in flight. Shiite radicals in pursuit. Subject needs assist. Istanbul. Confirm attention. –Einsteinium.*"

Titus guessed it was a US contact. This Einsteinium used him sometimes, and he usually had no problem agreeing to their requests, as long as Corban Dowler remained updated. Einsteinium was a username some agency handed down who knew that Swain was reliable in the Middle East and Africa, willing to take a job if the money was good.

Kneeling in the grass, Titus looked back at Oleg. They had a few days off, but that didn't mean he wanted to spend it chasing ghosts for the CIA or MI6. Yet, he'd been racing around Africa for a day and a half with only three wanted men to show for their labors. Maybe it wouldn't hurt to fly up to Istanbul to help an American on the run.

He punched the reply button: "*Einsteinium, send details. Will check mail in 12 hours. –Swain.*"

"Something new?" Oleg asked as they climbed onto their ATVs.

"I might have something up in Istanbul. Some Muslims chasing an American."

"How's the pay?"

"It's Muslims chasing an American." Titus shrugged. "They'd have to pay me not to intervene. Besides, we're not making much of a difference down here, not since we handed off the MP3 Bibles."

"Go ahead to the plane. I'll get these boys to the capital. They just love our mysterious gifts left on their doorstep for Interpol. I think it makes Nigerian officials feel like a legitimate government."

The two drove away in separate directions. Titus turned to look after his partner. They'd parted so casually, but each of them lived dangerous lives. They could be killed at any time for their work. Before Titus turned back toward the airport, he prayed for his newfound brother to remain safe, until God chose to take him home.

Turkey

Wynter tiptoed into a Turkish coffee shop. It was nearly closing time. A Turk with a baritone voice belted out an eastern folk song. He was too busy at a sink to notice Wynter pick up his counter phone and trail the cord behind a display rack. What she would do for a satphone! Without difficulty, she connected with Little Rock.

"It's me," she whispered when Arlin Skokes answered. "Trace this line and call me back as soon as you can."

"It won't be me," Arlin said. "It'll be a contact."

Carefully, she hung up the phone and set it back on the counter. Walking across the floor, she admired a sweetened pita bread display. The Turk watched her. She flashed him a smile and nodded while pointing at the display. Continuing to browse the store, she prayed for the phone to ring. Her fingers fondled the shark tooth necklace. She was back in the Argentine waters with the shark circling, but that shark's Creator hadn't forgotten her then. He wouldn't forget her now.

The phone rang. The Turk answered in a language she couldn't identify. He argued for several minutes, then hung up. The Turk rattled off a curse at the ceiling, then Wynter jumped when the phone rang again. The owner answered with a snap, then softened as he listened. He glanced up at Wynter and waved her to him.

"You . . . Vinta?"

"Yes, I am Wynter."

Handing her the phone, he stepped away from the counter to give her space—all of two feet. The connection crackled.

"Wynter Caspertein?"

"Yes, who's this?"

"My name is Lee Stambler. I'm with the FBI."

"Oh, thank God! Are you guys coming for me?"

"It's not that easy. You've made a lot of enemies in a region where we have very few friends anymore. Even if you made it to an embassy, you'd be in danger. You understand?"

"Yes. I need an escort of some type, and flown out of here."

"We're working on that. How are you?"

"How am I?" She gasped. "I'm cold and hungry and dirty. I've run halfway across Asia only to find out when I got here, there are people already waiting to kill me! How do you think I am?"

"Right now, are you safe?"

"No, I'm not safe! I'm hiding in a coffee shop. Some Turk is undressing me with his eyes. I had to sneak in here just to use the phone. All over Istanbul, the Asian side at least, there are thugs trying to get me. I saw like four of them with my picture. They must've known I'd come this way."

"Perhaps. It was logical. Listen, I'm sending someone to you as soon as I can, an agent, or a team of agents. Where can they rendezvous with you?"

"Um . . ." Wynter smiled again at the coffee man. "I think there are some ferries that cross the strait a few times every day, right?"

"Multiple crossings, many times a day." The man paused. "Okay, I'm looking at a schedule right now."

"All right. At twelve in the morning and twelve at night, I'll board the ferry, and ride it across to the European side, then back again."

"Okay, every twelve hours you'll ride the ferry. We can work with that. It's a public place. Even if it takes a couple more days, I'll get someone to meet you on the ferry. Just be there!"

A couple more days? Wynter frowned. It wasn't what she was expecting. She had no clothes, little money, less hope . . .

"As soon as you can, Mr. Stambler."

"I don't need to tell you to stay out of sight, right? I mean, I'm being realistic. Just because you're in a group of people or around other Americans, that doesn't mean you're safe. These people will be looking everywhere they expect a Westerner to go to feel safe."

"I understand."

"And I'd better tell you now so it's not a shock later."

"What is it?"

"They killed Ingram Thatcher two days ago."

"Oh, no . . ." She closed her eyes. This wasn't real! "Ingram . . ."

"Find somewhere safe, Miss Caspertein. We're going to get you out of there. I'm personally working on this. Someone is coming!"

Mali

Titus was somewhere over Mali, flying on a wide northwesterly heading toward Europe. From his years as a fugitive, he'd learned to misdirect his pursuers by making broad gestures that had no relevance to his true intentions. Now, as an agent for Christ, and legally absolved through Corban Dowler's government contacts, Titus still misdirected potential enemies.

On autopilot, he opened his Bible and read from the Gospel of Luke. From Galilee to Jerusalem, Jesus taught what it meant to be a true disciple. Every few verses, Titus paused to consider Christ's words for himself. He was astonished at how impossible living obediently was for anyone. But then he realized, that was the point of Jesus' whole ministry. Without Christ moving in and through His people, the courage to live obediently, even the motivation to love, was impossible.

"This life of dependence on You ain't easy, Lord," Titus prayed as he closed his Bible, "especially since I'm the independent type."

His mind went to a subject he often avoided—his family. God had been tugging at his heart to seek them out. He sensed God wanted him to begin by talking to Rudy and Wynter, to begin some kind of dialogue. At least something! But every time he imagined how those conversations would go, he became discouraged. Reconciliation seemed impossible. How could the injuries and pain he'd caused ever be mended? A miracle would have to happen, he decided. But to believe such a miracle could happen, he'd been faithless. He'd given up before he'd even tried.

That brought the cancer back to his mind. God seemed to be weakening his flesh to pay closer attention to spiritual matters and relationship priorities. If the cancer killed him sooner rather than later, it wouldn't be right to pass into eternity without reconciling with Rudy and Wynter.

Repentantly, Titus confessed to God his weak faith. But as God's son, he cried out for God to be his strength, and to heal the relationships of the past. Wynter and Rudy didn't know his wife—or that he was even married. When Titus was finished praying, he believed his sovereign Lord was already active, moving, and orchestrating for the highest good in the Caspertein family.

"Thank You, Lord," Titus said, then sighed, a restful confidence sweeping over him. He sensed God's care, though he knew God expected him to respond obediently when the door opened.

On a laptop, he wrote a mission report to Chloe Azmaveth, a report he knew would be copied to Corban Dowler. He detailed the Boko Haram military action after the MP3 Bible delivery, and the death of the elderly Christian man. Toward the end of the report, he admitted a helpless feeling regarding the lack of closure while addressing the Boko Haram militants. Sure, Oleg had taken three wanted criminals to Abuja for processing, but many hundreds of Christian young women had been kidnapped and dispersed by the hands of wicked men, to be wives in demanding Muslim families. How was God in this? Titus confessed he didn't know what else to do but to trust that the Lord was still loving and still just, and that He would turn what men meant for evil into a glorious result.

Regularly, Titus witnessed Christians in the worst conditions, and yet, those same Christians proclaimed Jesus from the strongest hearts. It was a phenomenon Titus wanted to explore more. The suffering of the flesh seemed to unlock Christian beauty in the heart of many true believers.

After uploading his mission report, he connected to the server in Tel Aviv. It had been twelve hours. He had one new message from Einsteinium: "*Swain, details: subject is riding Bosporus ferry at noon and midnight, crossing every 12 hours until you intervene. Muslim hostiles on heels. Recent photo for ID. Wynter Caspertein. Confirm involvement ASAP.—Einsteinium.*"

Titus stopped breathing as he read his sister's name. Initially, he felt an ambush had been laid for him by authorities who refused to throw away old warrants for his arrest. But then he remembered his prayer. God was already answering, opening the door he was supposed to walk through.

Clicking on the attachment link, he stared at his sister's photograph. He hadn't spoken to her in about twelve years! Choking on a swallow, he touched the screen. She was obviously older, but still stunning as she smiled broadly in her passport photo. *His little sister!*

Responding, he wrote: *"Einsteinium, I'm on it. Will be in Istanbul inside 24 hours. –Swain."*

Titus set aside his laptop and plotted a new course for his plane—to more directly approach Turkey. *He was going to help his little sister!*

CHAPTER NINE

Arctic

Rudy ignored the splashing sounds in the water as chunks of his melting iceberg fell into the ocean. He was racing the sun, which set only four hours each night, racing to remedy his desperate situation, racing for his life. The odds were against him, but his faith wasn't placed in luck. He believed in a God who worked beyond the odds of nature and man.

With so much polar bear meat, he was eating more than a normal man ate. Kobuk was content as well. Burying the meat kept it fresh in the snow for now. The bear had been as large as a draft horse, nearly two thousand pounds. There seemed no end to its ribs and other bones that Rudy had stripped clean of sinew and fat.

Now that all the bones were bare, Rudy had quite a collection. The massive, waterproof hide had dried some. The bladder and stomach were clean, elastic, and ready for the next step.

Standing with his hands on his hips, Rudy looked down on the mess he'd made over the last two days. The snow was stained crimson all around him, as were his boots and knees. On the right, he'd lined up the rib bones, which were still attached to the backbone. He wanted those intact. Next to the spine and ribs were the leg and shoulder bones.

Kobuk looked at Rudy. The dog's jaws were also stained red from eating the crimson snow. She whined and studied the bones of the beast she and Rudy had brought down. Scratching his head, Rudy knew the iceberg was melting too fast. They had mere days to rig up some sort of raft or canoe before they were standing in slush. Years earlier, Rudy had seen pictures of Eskimo kayaks and umiaks. He knew them to be made from seal and caribou skins, and he'd seen Eskimo boots made of polar bear skin. The skin was waterproof, but his tools were limited.

He knelt to arrange the spine and ribs in the shape of a boat frame. The ribs would need to be reinforced to the backbone with scraps of hide and tissue. Already, he'd trimmed his own coat down to a vest.

Fortunately, Kobuk didn't mind snuggling, sharing her body heat at night.

Rudy had also been watching the stars during the short period of darkness each night. He wasn't sure where they were. By his watch, he knew what time it was in Alaska. With Perseus reaching its zenith so early, he knew his longitude was somewhere above the Siberian coast. Maybe as far west as the Laptev Sea. It didn't matter where they drifted, though. Any voyage southward would take him to land.

But the currents would be a problem. The currents generally cycled away from the northern coasts, unless he was within a few miles of land.

Snow blindness and fighting the bear had been difficult, but he warned himself that the worst was maybe yet to come. For Kobuk, too.

Turkey

Serik Tomir of the *Soldiers of Mahdi* noticed Wynter Caspertein in the crowd that was about to board a ferry. He nodded to *Imam* Nasser al-Hakim's other soldiers and waved them back a distance. There were too many witnesses to pick her up. They would wait until she was more isolated.

Wynter boarded the ferry and found a seat on the upper balcony amongst a dozen other tourists. Serik sat three rows behind her. He rested his deadly cane on his knees. Patience was one of his strengths. While staring at the back of her head, he was stunned at the degree of hatred he had for this woman. She was an infidel, so she automatically deserved to die. But more so, because she'd killed the next *imam*. Deep down, Serik could feel Allah himself quaking on his throne.

In his fury, Serik lost track of time. They reached the other side of the Bosporus, the western division of the city as ancient as the eastern. He followed his target off the ferry onto the street of European Istanbul, heading toward Gulhane Park. Waving at his men, they closed on their target.

Serik pressed the lever on his cane and the sword blade extended to its full length. No one seemed to be taking notice of him. Most other tourists from the ferry had headed in the opposite direction toward the Egyptian Bazaar. He wouldn't kill Wynter Caspertein. He'd only cripple her and take her back to *Imam* Nasser.

He stepped close behind her. His men bunched up with him, ready to pounce. With a sweep of his sword across her heels, he sliced through her shoes and Achilles' tendons. Serik tackled her, kneeling on her back to hold her down. With a firm hand, he covered her mouth before she could scream, and fought the urge to snuff out her life altogether.

£

Rashid al-Sabur, treasure hunter from Cyprus, stared all day through his telescope. When he wasn't watching the bridges, his eyes were on the ferries, studying faces. Fortunate for him, there were only so many ways to cross the water between the land masses. For a woman who had few resources in the region, the ferries were the most likely.

Finally, around noon, when his eyes burned from lack of sleep, he noticed a familiar face. He checked the picture on the wall. Yes. It was her face, but her hair was different. She'd cut it, obviously to throw off those who were chasing her. Rashid wouldn't be so fooled. He watched Wynter board the noon ferry and seat herself on the top level with a group of Europeans. The ferry started across, and for twenty minutes, he watched Wynter draw nearer. Soon, he would have her in his sound-proofed room to find out what treasure she'd abandoned in Azerbaijan.

Suddenly, Rashid's heart beat faster. Behind Wynter were a number of hard-looking men, jostling for seats on the ferry. Their obvious disdain for Wynter gave themselves away, along with their clutching at weapons hidden under their jackets. They had no style, making faces at one another and jutting their chins at her from behind. They hadn't been fooled by her change in appearance, either, but they were fools to think she was theirs.

With narrowed eyes, Rashid felt certain these clumsy hunters were loyal to *Imam* Nasser al-Hakim, the father of the deceased who had started the chase. There was little Rashid could do but watch. The Muslims were closest to her on the boat. He would have to wait for an opportunity to steal her back, after they captured her. Stealing what others had already stolen was not unfamiliar to him, so he wasn't worried, even though he didn't have a plan yet.

He massaged his temples for a few seconds, then looked back at the ferry—nearly to the European side now. His eyes swept the top of the ferry. Wynter had disappeared. No, there she was on the top balcony, and the Muslims were still—

Rashid looked closer. No, Wynter was gone. Purposely or by accident, she had sat down next to a fair-skinned tourist with hair like her own. From the back, the Muslims might be mistaken. But from the front, as Rashid could clearly see, it was the tall, young tourist with brown hair.

He scanned what he could see of the ferry, but the other levels were shadowed and hidden. The ferry docked at the shore. Rashid studied the passengers as they disembarked down a narrow ramp. The fair-skinned young man stepped off the boat alone. Sure enough, mere steps behind him, the Muslim gang hustled along with death on their faces. Their zeal to kill had blinded them to their enemy's wiles.

Smiling, Rashid adjusted the telescope to see the shoreline street in focus. The Shiites followed the young man toward the park, crowded behind him, then attacked.

In seconds, the hunters realized their mistake. Rashid swung his telescope back to the ferry as it departed. There, on the second level, leaning out over the rail, was Wynter. She hadn't even left the ferry!

Again, Rashid narrowed his eyes in thought. This woman was very clever. She knew she was pursued by dangerous people. Crossing the strait in the daylight and riding it back to Asia? It could only mean one thing: she was meeting someone, perhaps waiting for a contact.

Rashid turned from the window and grabbed his leather jacket. Under his arm, he carried a pistol. A dagger was on his calf. Wynter Caspertein was in Istanbul. He had to get her before she met anyone who could help her!

Serik Tomir cursed as he realized the person he'd attacked wasn't Wynter Caspertein at all. His victim was merely a boy with a similar haircut! He'd been outsmarted by a woman! He'd beaten women for less. And he would beat Wynter, the deceitful, murdering, American infidel!

Spitting on the boy, Serik withdrew his sword. He turned away, his men with him. A second time, he cursed. The ferry was leaving, their prey still on board taunting them.

They had lost Wynter Caspertein.

Italy

Titus refueled in Salerno and took an hour-long nap in the cabin of the Navajo. When he woke, he connected by instant message with Oleg to find that his partner had left Nigeria and flown to Syria for an ISIS confrontation. A militant army was closing in on a small village in western Syria where Christians were hiding. Oleg invited Titus to come die with him when he was done playing around in Istanbul.

Without explaining all the details, Titus messaged that he'd be at least another day and night before he reached Syria. It was impossible for Titus to commit too much when Wynter was his priority for the next couple days.

He checked the engine and wings, then taxied down the short, private runway. Once in the air, he pointed the nose eastward toward Asia. Hopefully, he wasn't too late for his sister.

Turkey

Wynter took one last look around the ferry before stepping off—just tourists coming and going. No one had approached her to help her. *No one!* Where was the contact who was supposed to escort her to safety?

She left the ferry and hurried away from the shoreline into the district of Uskudar toward Bagdat Avenue, wherein she'd spent much of her time hiding in the back alleys of the upscale shopping hub. The Shiites were all over the city looking for her. Sitting next to the look-alike on the top deck had misled them once. They had followed the tall boy with a similar haircut off the ferry, but they would realize their mistake in no time and continue hunting for her. And the trick wouldn't work against them again.

With caution, she worked her way back to the coffee shop. She stepped off the street to the side of the building and climbed into the garbage where she'd spent the previous night. With fading hope, she pulled a cardboard box over her legs and an old coffee bean sack over her upper body. Wandering the streets, looking for food, help, or shelter, was simply too risky.

Wynter checked her watch. Ten more hours until midnight. She'd nearly paid for the first ferry ride with her life. The midnight one could be her last. Where was the agent?

If she survived until morning, she would be surprised. She fell asleep praying for a guardian angel.

Rashid al-Sabur hunched his shoulders around his neck. The Black Sea's chilly breeze rolled across the Turkish coastal towns every night about this time. Until then, Rashid had forgotten why he hated the Bosporus. Now, he remembered. The temperature changed too quickly and too often for his liking.

He stood next to a coffee shop and looked up and down the street. The *Soldiers of Mahdi* were all over the city. None of them knew Rashid and he'd never seen many of them before, but he knew beginners at a glance. Beginners or not, he still had to find the Caspertein woman before they did. Just because they had no professionalism didn't mean they wouldn't steal his fortune if he didn't keep a step ahead of them.

Walking into the coffee shop, he thought about asking the owner if he'd seen an American woman who looked like the picture in his pocket, but he decided the chances were too slim. Besides, he liked to keep his affairs to himself. He bought a coffee with cream and left the shop.

Again, he stood on the street. Two men emerged from an avenue, paused to study Rashid, then continued out of sight. They were beginning to see each other too often now, and they'd soon figure out he was also looking for Wynter Caspertein. The risk involved kept Rashid's adrenalin flowing. He was outnumbered but she was prey worthy of his skill as the hunter.

Rashid tapped his fingers on the butt of his gun. Just a few minutes with Wynter and he'd know where all eight figures were hidden. But at the moment, he was torn between whether to keep an eye on the *imam*'s men or search for Wynter himself. They had more eyes around the city, but they could also be spotted at a mere glance as they waved her photo around like a pamphlet!

Sighing, he headed south. He hadn't checked the Kadikoy area yet, the southwest coastline of the Asian part of the city. Maybe she was sleeping on the doorstep of some wealthy Turk. He was running out of time.

Titus flew his Navajo jet low over the Rhodope Mountains, almost scraping the tops of the chestnut trees as he lined up with the runway torches below. Everywhere he flew, he used the smallest and most out-of-sight runways. He'd called ahead and asked the man to light four barrels of oil at the four corners of the strip.

Six months earlier, the farmer just west of European Istanbul had charged him one hundred dollars a night to leave the plane in the field behind his barn. On that occasion, Titus had smuggled out a Christian convicted of converting Muslims. The believer had been in the hospital, watched by only two security officers. Titus had rescued him as soon as COIL got word about his desperate plight.

Opening the door, he greeted the farmer in his native Turkish. He counted out five hundred dollars cash.

"I need a car for one night, Brost." Titus nodded at the farmer's wife who scowled from the kitchen window. She certainly objected to her husband's risks. "If I'm not back by dawn, I'll give you another five hundred."

Brost scratched his head under a straw hat. The old farmer would've blended in well in Arkansas.

"Last time, you returned my car without a bumper, and the right side of the car had to be hammered out." Brost looked toward the house where one light still glowed. "My wife doesn't like that, Titus. She kicks me under the blankets, and she kicks hard! In the mornings, she—"

Titus waved another two hundred dollars in front of his face. Brost smiled and dangled the keys in his fingers until Titus snatched them.

"I'm in a hurry, Brost. Maybe we'll talk when I get back."

Stepping around the man, Titus started off the field.

"Hey, you mean before the police chase you here again and you fly away, or after you steal us a nice painting from the Chartres Cathedral?"

"You don't even speak French, Brost. What do you know about Gothic art, anyway?"

"Okay. Then how about some tobacco from the city?"

Titus laughed and waved. He climbed into a heavy, black Lincoln that had served him well in the past. Now, to Istanbul!

CHAPTER TEN

Arctic

In July, inside the polar isotherm region of the Arctic, the average highs were around forty-seven degrees. The night lows in the summer were generally about thirty-four. That was normal. Rudy was certain it was in the fifties. The iceberg was rapidly becoming a puddle. Every time he collapsed to sleep, he woke soaked from the melting of his diminishing island.

Kobuk yawned in the sunlight and rolled in the snow. From her back, she watched Rudy work.

Rudy stretched another section of the dried bear skin over the rib cage. Using a sharpened toe bone, he hooked the edge of the skin, punctured the hide under the rib end, and fastened it like a button into place.

He stepped back and admired his work. Bone buttons lined the umiak's sides far above where the water line would reach. The ends of the boat were another story. Already, he guessed he'd have to stretch the bear's massive stomach lining over each end to make the hide watertight along the folds.

Perspiring, he wiped his brow. It was dangerous to sweat in the Arctic. If the temperature dropped suddenly, as it had been known to do, his sweat would turn to ice within minutes. With nothing to burn for fire to heat his core temperature, he would die in hours. Death surrounded him on every side.

Turkey

Wynter snuck through Asian Istanbul like a cautious mouse with rat traps and hungry cats on every street corner. She glanced at her watch, afraid she'd miss the midnight ferry to the west. Quickening her pace, her shoes made a whisper on the two-hundred-year-old cobblestone. The ancient walls of the city seemed to crowd her, the shadows hiding potential enemies.

Checking over her shoulder, she saw a tall man in a suit about a block behind her. With a cane, he walked toward her. It was too dark in the lamplight, but she thought he looked like one of the men who'd been on the ferry the previous afternoon.

The ferry came into sight and she ran toward it. But others emerged from the shadows and ran as well. They couldn't all be late arrivals for the ferry! The closest man charged directly and reached for her. Instead of running away from him, she stopped short and backhanded him on the mouth, then kicked him in the knee. That stopped him for the moment. Then she was running again.

The ferry's green light changed to red as she dashed down the loading ramp onto the ferry's lower deck. She looked back. Four of her pursuers had made the ferry as well. One was the man with the cane. Those who hadn't dared the final leap hailed a taxi to probably cross the Bosporus by bridge. Her breath trembled as she realized they—whoever they were—would be waiting on the other side.

The horn whistled and the boat nudged from the shore. Wynter circled the first deck and mounted the stairs to the second deck. She pondered approaching someone for help. No, that wouldn't stop these men. That would only get more innocent people injured or killed. Besides, the ferry was nearly deserted at midnight.

The second deck had only two people near the bridge. Sitting down, she looked behind her. Two of the four men had ascended the stairs to the second level as well. They saw her. Standing, she started toward the forecastle, the front stairway. Where were the other two? She wasn't waiting to find out. Reaching the stairs for the third deck, she froze on the first step. The man with the cane was at the top. His goatee was shaped to a point, like a picture of the devil she'd seen once. He smiled and started down toward her.

Wynter spun and dashed to the front stairwell to descend to the first level again. Halfway down the stairs, the fourth man lunged at her. She grasped the stairway rails and kicked with both feet. The man took her two heels in his chest. He did a backflip to the first level. She ran past him, around the engine room, and ducked into a small room surrounded by windows, probably meant for women or children in extremely cold transports across the strait. Slamming the door shut, she braced her shoe in front of it as a man she hadn't noticed before pressed himself against the glass. He wore a leather jacket, looked eastern, but he hadn't been with the others. Still, he gazed at her in a chilling way. From his pocket, he drew a small piece of paper and held it against the glass next to his crazed face. The note was written in English, and read: "Azerbaijan. Eight figures. You tell me, Wynter Caspertein."

She gasped as the leather-jacketed man stuffed the note in his mouth and chewed it. *How did he know about the eight figures in Azerbaijan?* He drew a knife from his pant leg, then swung it to crack the glass. Again, he struck the window, harder, causing tiny shards to shower over Wynter.

Stepping away to shield her face from her attacker and the glass, she saw the leather-jacketed man suddenly pause and look to his right. The four other attackers were approaching quickly, one of them limping severely. Scowling at Wynter, the leather-jacketed man disappeared toward the back of the ferry. Not once did he speak to her.

Wynter refused to be trapped again. She broke out the last fragments of glass with her shoe and climbed out of the booth. Behind her, the man with the cane shouted and ran at her.

After dashing to the stairs in the stern, Wynter climbed to the second deck. She didn't hesitate there; she continued to the open air of the third deck. Looking toward the eastern shore, she wondered if she should risk going overboard. Though she could probably swim better than her pursuers, the Bosporus was like ice—too cold to swim for the thirty minutes it would take to reach shore.

The men climbed the stairs below her. Their panting was loud. She'd given them a good chase, but it was over now.

She looked around the deck. One man stood near the bow, his back to her, and she ran toward him. Now cornered, she fought panic. The four men had to be *Soldiers of Mahdi*, she guessed, as they arrived on the deck. They came toward her. There was no escaping, nowhere to go but overboard, or into their hands.

Wynter drew near the lone man at the bow. He wore a jean jacket, faded and torn at the elbows.

"Excuse me," she said breathlessly, but the man didn't acknowledge her. She looked over the rail at the dark water. It was better than becoming a captive. Maybe she would survive the swim after all . . .

The four men closed in on her, and spread out to discourage any further escape. The one with the cane held up his hand to the others. They stopped.

Wynter glanced at the lone man to her right. Would they kill him, too? By the dim ferry lights, she could see he was blond with no facial hair. Maybe he was a Westerner. The Shiites seemed to ignore him.

"Come, Wynter," the man with the cane said in rough English. "You must come with us now." With a flick of the wrist, he extended his cane to double its length. The bottom half became a sword that gleamed in the moonlight. The sword tip was aimed at her throat.

The wind gusted fiercely as the lone stranger turned to face the Shiites. Wynter could see only his profile, but he seemed very calm. He was tall with high cheekbones, like the face of a Scandinavian. But with dread, she wondered if he were one of the Shiites! Why wasn't he as afraid of them as she was?

"Leave us, friend," the man with the cane ordered in Turkish. "This is personal."

"This is personal to me, too," Titus said in Arabic, now certain of the identity of his sister's pursuers. His hands remained tucked inside his jean jacket pockets. "Is this how you show a couple of infidels a good time in a foreign land?"

Titus glanced at his sister. She didn't seem to understand either language as she studied each of their faces and kept one hand on the rail as if she were about to jump the thirty feet into the water.

The man with the cane pointed his sword at Titus.

"You know our tongue. Who are you?"

Titus drew his hands from his coat. In one hand, he held a grenade. In the other was his COIL nine-millimeter.

"If you are a man of knowledge, then you already know me by my trade name."

"And? What is your trade name, infidel?"

"I am called . . . *the Serval*."

The sword-wielding man narrowed his eyes. The three others looked at one another with obvious concern. Titus had hoped to cause them some hesitation. They'd probably heard of the man of Africa and Arabia who ruthlessly stole and sold arms and artifacts, but they also had the look in their eyes of men who wouldn't easily abandon their path of an honor killing.

"You're not the Serval. The Serval is an African."

"How would you know, sand-under-my-shoe?" Titus asked. "You and the Serval have never met. All you know is my legend."

"What's this woman to you? She can't matter to you. She has desecrated Allah's holy name. We're dedicated to her demise. You dare to stand between us?"

"I'll do more than stand between you." Titus held up his grenade so it could be seen better. "It ain't easy bringing a sword to a grenade fight, huh?"

He tossed the flash-bang grenade into the air and caught it again. The man with the sword shoved one of his men toward Titus. Titus dropped the grenade and pulled Wynter by the elbow to the side. The explosion flashed through the night and echoed across the strait. The coughing from the killers brought them to their knees. Since Wynter seemed partially paralyzed, Titus guided her down the deck.

"You're safe now," he said in English, but in looking back, he saw the leader was already recovering, feeding the sword into his cane.

Wynter clung to Titus's arm, jogging to keep up as he hustled to the stern.

"Are you one of the agents the FBI sent for me?"

"Yeah." His eyes were busy watching the deck for more danger. He thought he'd seen a fifth suspicious man in a leather jacket board the ferry. "I'm not just one of the men they sent for you; I'm the only one."

"I want to see some identification."

Still, he continued to walk briskly. She couldn't see his face now, but Titus wondered when she'd recognize him, or at least his voice.

"Agents like me don't carry identification, but if it helps, here's this." Peeling off his fake nose and bushy eyebrows, he offered them to her. She didn't accept them, so he dropped them to the deck floor. He reached the stern railing of the ferry where a rope was tied to an inflatable raft with an outboard motor. The raft bumped and trailed in the wake of the ferry.

"What's this?" Wynter nodded as she apparently understood. "Okay, this is good. At least tell me your name."

"You know my name." He climbed over the rail and stood there, with their faces inches apart.

"What, that thing you said to the Muslims about being the serval? A cat in Africa? Are you saying that's who you are?"

"So, you know a little Arabic. If a serval isn't tamed while it's young, it's wild for life—untamable. Now you know who I am. Come on. We'll have time to talk later."

He clutched the rope and lowered himself hand over hand down to the inflatable. Wynter shoved her wallet into the waist of her pants, then climbed over the railing and down the rope to join him. She sat in the middle of the raft. Everything was wet and cold, but Titus wasn't worried about her now; she was a tough Arkansas girl. He sat in the back of the raft and handed Wynter a knife.

"Cut us loose and hang on."

She sawed briefly at the rope connecting them to the ferry until it fell away and the ferry moved ahead.

"What you did back there," she said with a scowl, facing him, "I don't approve of violence. You could've killed those men."

Titus started the motor and steered it on a parallel course with the ferry to the European side. He noticed the man with the cane on board the ferry, watching them withdraw into the darkness of the sea. Above the cane man on the second level stood the man in the leather jacket. He waved, but Titus didn't wave back. There was something familiar about him. And dangerous.

Imam Nasser al-Hakim glared at Serik Tomir with distaste. Serik stared back, his sword-cane balanced on two fingers as he rolled it back and forth over his knees.

"How could you fail me, Serik?" *Imam* Nasser repeated for the fourth time. "You . . . had her on the boat and you let her get away!"

"I know you're disappointed, Nasser." Serik looked away. "It would've been impossible to get her tonight."

"But you had her on the boat, Serik!" Nasser turned and struck the wall. He cried out in pain and frustration. "Most *Soldiers of Mahdi* would've died rather than to shame me!"

Like lightning, Serik extended his sword from the cane and swung it toward Nasser's neck. With perfect control, he stopped the blade against the *imam*'s vital artery. *Imam* Nasser didn't move; he saw the fury in Serik's eyes, and he understood he'd pushed his most trusted man too far.

Serik relaxed and rested the blade on Nasser's shoulder. Nasser was still as Serik closed the distance that separated them until he was so close to Nasser that they shared the same breath.

"You think I didn't try, Nasser? I didn't shame you; I shamed myself!" Serik spoke low, almost a whisper. "I was more of a father to Gamal than you ever were. You're the *imam*. You have greater responsibilities than raising children. I loved Gamal. I hid him in Azerbaijan. He died where I hid him. Don't ever accuse me of not trying, Nasser. Besides, she had help on the boat tonight. Wynter Caspertein had help we didn't expect."

He slid his cane from Nasser's shoulder and sat down, retracting the sword into the cane.

"What kind of help?" Nasser's voice was more respectful now. "Who could've helped her here? No one with any power."

"A Westerner, perhaps. He defeated the three worthless men you gave me from Tehran. We had her trapped, then he appeared out of the night. I'm reminded of the dream I've been having."

"Forget your nightmares! An infidel helped her here? A Westerner?" Nasser searched Serik's eyes for an answer. If he didn't know better, he would guess he saw fear on Serik's scowling face. "This Westerner—did you speak to him?"

"In Arabic. He knew it fluently. I spoke to the woman first in English, then he interrupted. It was as if he wanted to impress upon me who he was. That's when he said he had a personal interest in this Wynter Caspertein, and he said his name."

"His name? What is this man's name? I must know! I'll hunt him down, and for Allah, massacre his family before his own eyes!"

Serik raised his hand.

"I've already spread his name afar, but killing him won't be easy. He has many powerful friends, some of them our own allies, and some of them our enemies."

"Well, who is he?"

"The Serval."

Nasser felt his mouth gape.

"*The Serval*. I've heard of this man, an African, it's said. You're certain he was the Serval?"

"He was ruthless and unafraid, even against many of us. He spoke our tongue without an accent and spit in our faces with such treachery that Allah must now be in a violent rage. No mere Westerner would be able to do these things. Only the Serval could be so . . . untamed."

"But, can you kill him?" Nasser asked.

"He's just a man. Yes, I'll kill him. Then I'll get Wynter Caspertein."

"The Serval of Africa. We go to Africa, then?"

"As soon as we have intelligence on where the Serval has been operating. He's a thief and smuggler. Allah is against him. We'll hunt him down. I swear it!"

Treasure hunter Rashid al-Sabur ripped off his leather jacket and threw it on the floor of his rented apartment. He drew his pistol and emptied his magazine at the jacket. The gunshots echoed in the room, but the noise didn't bother him; he was too angry.

Whoever the man was who'd helped Wynter on the ferry had ruined Rashid's plans! He'd hoped to allow the *Soldiers of Mahdi* to capture her, then he'd intended to kill them and flee the ferry with her.

But, no. The tall American with the fake nose and eyebrows had saved her! Rashid had found his discarded disguise on the ferry floor. It wasn't by chance, Rashid knew. The man had arranged to meet her there at that time. It had been staged, he was sure.

Rashid moved to the window and packed up his telescope. He was done in Istanbul. Wynter Caspertein was probably far away by now. The Muslims would know where, eventually. He could monitor the *imam*'s movements. They wouldn't stop hunting for the killer of the one who was to have become their next religious leader. Rumor had it, *Imam* Nasser had no other male children.

Suddenly, Rashid stopped packing. *Caspertein.* He repeated the name in his head. Of course! He smiled wickedly. The tall American was Titus Caspertein. And why wouldn't she call her infamous brother? Rashid had hoped he wouldn't show, but a great reward was never easily won.

A chill passed up his spine. Titus Caspertein was a man of men, one with whom to be reckoned. After all, he had beat Rashid at his own game in South Africa, and nobody ever beat Rashid.

Nodding, Rashid continued to pack. It was like a game again—him and Titus, with Wynter in the middle. The prize was eight figures. Now, if he didn't die trying to reach that prize . . .

CHAPTER ELEVEN

Arctic

K obuk whined with uncertainty as Rudy tested his foot inside the floating umiak.

"Look, girl." Rudy laughed. "It floats!"

Rudy put more of his weight on his foot. The small craft sunk into the water a few inches. The ribs and backbone flexed slightly under the pressure, but no water leaked through the bottom. And on the ends, the bear stomach lining seemed an adequate seal—for now.

He shook his head. His eyes measured the vessel's size against his own frame and Kobuk's two hundred-plus pounds. There would be no room to move once they piled in and shoved off. If Kobuk moved suddenly, the whole craft could roll.

But leaving Kobuk behind wasn't an option. Kobuk was like family now. Taking the massive canine on his trip south was the only honorable thing to do.

"At first light, Kobuk," Rudy said. "At first light."

It was almost sundown. First light was four hours away.

He dragged the umiak back onto the iceberg's melting bank. They needed to leave soon. Twice, Rudy's foot had plunged through soft spots in the snow to watery depths beneath.

Through the slushy snow, Rudy dug to find the last of their meat. He needed everything ready for the voyage south. Rather than leaving the meat as steaks, he cut it into strips. Any extra movement inside the umiak would be risking death—even straining over the simple act of cutting meat.

Rudy watched the sky as the first stars twinkled to life. Vega was already overhead. Arcturus was cruising northwest. Altair would soon be directly south, if his mental compass was right. The sun would always be south during the days, along its path, and the North Star, Polaris, should remain at his back during the nights. The constellations of the Zodiac would appear within degrees of the sun's ecliptic. He hoped these simple observations were enough to guide him southward. But if the sky became overcast, he would be lost.

He settled into the snow on his back to nap for a few hours. With a yawn, Kobuk lay down next to him.

Rudy drifted off to sleep, a sleep that could be his last for many days.

𝄢

Turkey

Titus drove recklessly up a winding road west of Istanbul. Cottonwood trees loomed on both sides and blotted out the early morning starlight. Wynter sat in the back seat, rocking wildly back and forth with every swerve of the Lincoln.

"Where are we going?" Wynter asked.

Titus hit a pothole so large, the whole car rattled.

"To a friend's place." He studied her in the rearview mirror. "My friend is safe, right? I don't need to blindfold you, do I?" He felt twelve years old again, teasing his sister.

"No!" Wynter scowled. "I would never betray someone who helped me. You saved my life!"

"So, tell me, why are the *Soldiers of Mahdi* after you?"

"You don't know? I thought you agents knew everything."

"Nah, I'm not that connected. I'm just a grunt. A minnow in an ocean of whale sharks."

"That's not a very good analogy," Wynter said. "A whale shark is hardly the carnivore people think. They only eat plankton."

Titus laughed and shook his head, but she frowned.

"What? Are you laughing at me?"

"Oh, I'm just glad to see you're the same old Wynter as always. Still correcting everyone. Of course, if I'd been attacked by a shark, I'd be an expert on them, too."

"So, you do know about me." She touched something around her neck, but Titus couldn't see what it was in the mirror.

"A little bit. But since you're not giving it up, I'll have to give ol' Arlin a ring to find out what you've gotten yourself into."

Wynter dove into the front seat next to Titus. A huge grin of disbelief covered her face. She studied him for a few seconds.

"No . . . way!" She leaned farther forward, the back of her head against the windshield to see his face straight-on. "I don't believe it!"

She smacked him with a bracing left hand that made Titus taste blood.

"What was that for?" Titus held his cheek and felt his lip begin to swell.

"For lying, you coward!" Roughly, she crossed her arms and settled into the front seat.

"Coward? How am I a coward? A minute ago, I was your savior."

"A coward for lacking the nerve to do anything honest!"

Titus drove in silence for a minute. His jovial mood at their reunion was declining by the second.

"I see," he said finally. "This isn't about tonight. This is about, well, everything else."

"Good guess."

"Have you heard from Rudy? How's he doing?"

"If you cared, you'd find out for yourself."

"You're right. I'm a coward. We'll just go back to pretending we're strangers. We are, after all."

Titus took a sharp left through the woods onto the farmer's property. He parked in front of the one-story house. To the right, on the edge of the long field, his plane was hidden behind the barn, but one of its wings was still barely visible. A light was lit in the front room window of the house, and Brost's face poked out the door.

Opening his door, Titus waved at Brost, then turned to Wynter as he transitioned from brother back to protector.

"I bring shipments through here occasionally. But just because I use these people doesn't mean I necessarily trust them. On the other hand, if they're found out to have helped us, they could die a painful death. Act like the cargo you are and don't leave an impression. And here, put this on. You're Muslim now. Don't speak at all!"

Wynter tugged on a light *haik* with a sewn-on headscarf to cover her clothes. Titus stepped out of the old car and greeted Brost in Turkish. Wynter climbed out of the vehicle and stood nearby, listening, but Titus figured she didn't understand. He gave Brost more cash. Brost went back into the house and Titus approached Wynter.

"You're staying here tonight. His wife will help you get cleaned up and give you a bed. Don't speak to either of them. They can't know you're American. Got it?"

"Okay. I'm mute. Where are you going?"

"Back into the city."

"You're just leaving me already? Maybe we should call—"

"No. Don't involve anyone. I can keep you safe, but you have to do what I say."

He turned away, but she grabbed his arm.

"Wait, Titus. I can't believe it's you. I've prayed for you for years. Sometimes I thought I'd meet you on some distant shore, maybe trying to dig up the same artifacts. Other times I thought you were dead or in prison."

"Wynter, I—" He took a deep breath and rested his hand on hers where she still had hold of his arm. Though he wanted to tell her everything, about the cancer and his relationship with Jesus Christ, it still wasn't time. Besides, his faith was something she'd have to see for herself. "I'm not the man you think you know, not the brother you remember. I'll be back in the morning."

He climbed into the car, but didn't start the engine right away. In the low light of the early morning, he watched Wynter as she wiped at tears. In a perfect world, he would leave everything and go back home to Arkansas. But those in need demanded his skills, so he couldn't simply walk away. His past made him what he was now, and with the help of Jesus Christ, he would live in the newness of that life. He was bound to it.

Washington, D.C.

The phone rang in Agent Lee Stambler's office. He answered on the third ring to hear Arlin Skokes' voice.

"Please tell me you have good news," Arlin said.

"As good as we're going to get right now." Lee gazed at a message on his computer screen. "But we're not out of the woods yet. My agent just sent me a text from Istanbul. It's night there right now, so they're hiding out."

"So, Wynter is safe! What's the message?"

"Just that. She's safe, but the *Soldiers of Mahdi* probably aren't done yet. He doesn't want to risk extracting her all the way to the US quite yet, so they'll stay in hiding while we sort all this out. Then he signed out and that's all I know."

"What does he mean he can't risk extraction yet?" Arlin sounded frustrated. "The US is the safest place for Wynter! Either here or a US military base."

"Arly, he knows what he's doing. He understands the sensitive nature, so he can't involve diplomacy. And he can't simply fly her home on a commercial flight, either. She's still got a million extremists after her. That's not only in the Middle East, Arly. See what I'm saying? That's Asia, Europe, Africa, even here. Don't get me started on how many fundamentalists we have living in the US in the name of peaceful diplomacy with Muslim nations, even radical ones. This agent is doing what he should be doing: hiding out."

"You still don't know who this guy is?"

"I don't, but I'm not opposed to the way he seems to be handling the situation. The US can't be implicated, or there could be international reprisals. This is big, Arly."

"All right. Well, at least she's safe. I'll sleep a little better now, but I'll still be restless until I see her for myself."

"I understand. I've got an alarm to deal with in Europe, Arly, so I've got to run."

"Lee, thanks for everything. I owe you."

Arctic

Rudy balanced carefully on one foot in the umiak. He knew as soon as he sat down, he wouldn't be able to move until he found another iceberg or land to resituate himself.

To sit, he had two options. He could set his legs out in front of him to the end of the bear ribs and backbone. But then Kobuk would have nowhere to lay except on his feet and legs. The dog was too heavy for that position over a prolonged period of time.

His other option was to sit cross-legged. He thought he might cramp that way, but at least Kobuk would have space to lie down. For Rudy, kneeling wasn't an option since he needed to distribute his weight low in the boat.

He put his other foot into the umiak, then crossed his legs and sat down. The rib and spine joints spread but held. Then came the hard part. Kobuk pranced excitedly in anticipation, as if she sensed a journey was afoot, and she would simply not be left behind.

Rudy braced an arm on the iceberg's melting shore. He gripped Kobuk's mane with his other hand, holding her back.

"Nice and easy, girl. Let's go."

Kobuk touched a paw on the edge of the boat. She didn't seem to like the way it moved.

"Come on, girl. Gently now . . ."

The big dog lunged. Rudy grunted as she landed in his lap. He steadied the boat.

"Sit, Kobuk!"

She sat down facing him, her ears perked for the next event.

With his left hand, Rudy reached for his paddles: two bear hip bones. He could paddle with only one at a time, but it never hurt to have a backup. If he'd had anything extra resembling a canvas, he would've rigged a sail. Though if the wind blew in the right direction, he could brace the two paddles upright and stretch his caribou coat over the paddles. But the umiak had no rudder and very little that resembled a keel, so the wind would have to be directly at his back before he risked such a maneuver.

Shifting his weight, he shoved off from the iceberg. It had been their home for a week. They left behind hardly more than drifting slush, much of it still red from butchering the bear. The sun rose in the southeast. Rudy aimed south and Kobuk watched him paddle gently away from their berg. After a few minutes, she stretched out and lay down, her nose on Rudy's crossed legs. With one hip bone, Rudy paddled smoothly and deeply, careful strokes without rocking the boat too much.

"That's good, Kobuk. Get comfortable. It's going to be a long trip. We're in God's hands, which has worked so far."

Kobuk whined at his words, as if she knew what lay ahead.

Turkey

Titus arrived back at Brost's farm after dawn.

"The woman hasn't moved since she rested her head," Brost informed in Turkish. "She's really a Kazakhstanian princess?"

"There's a story of a power-hungry man who wants to kill his sister, so he can have the throne for himself."

"I didn't know Kazakhstan had royalty such as this." Brost lowered his voice. "She's beautiful, Titus! Of all the treasures you've smuggled through here, she's the most precious."

"We must leave now, Brost. Here, I got this for you in town." Titus tossed him a can of the richest eastern Turkey tobacco he could find.

"And this is for your troubles, and for your mouth."

"My mouth?" Brost accepted a wad of cash.

"Your silent, closed mouth."

"Ah. I am as a mouse, Titus."

"A mouse squeaks, Brost."

"Then I am as the worm, simply plowing the land without another care."

"For your own sake, I hope so. Please tell your wife to wake the princess."

Titus waited on the porch for fifteen minutes, praying for wisdom as the sun rose. He needed coffee since sleep would have to wait for now.

Brost brought Wynter to Titus. She was clothed in the Arabian *haik*, but it did nothing to disguise the dark rings under her eyes.

"You need anything, Titus, I'll light the runway, yes?"

"Very well. Goodbye, Brost."

Titus hooked his arm under Wynter's elbow and walked her toward the barn. She looked weak and tired, but they needed to move.

"Where are we going now?" she asked when they were a distance from the house. "Do you have another car?"

"You'll see."

They rounded the barn and her eyes widened at the sight of the Navajo.

"This is yours?"

"It is. Come on. We're in a hurry."

He opened the cabin door and lowered the steps. She climbed up first, then he followed. The cabin originally sat six passengers, but four seats had been replaced by two mounted cots. With torn upholstery, and oil and coffee stains, it was obviously a bachelor pad, but it was otherwise in order. Titus pulled up the steps and shut the door.

"We'll be in flight for a few hours." He nodded at the cots. "Plenty of time to sleep."

"When do you sleep?"

He shrugged, too tired to say anything witty. Ducking into the cockpit, he strapped into the pilot seat. Surprisingly, Wynter sat down in the copilot seat. They looked at one another.

"Is this okay?" she asked.

"Sure. Just thought you were tired."

Starting the engine, he measured the fuel. They would need to refuel in a few hours at another small airfield. Pressing down on the throttle, he taxied into the field. A moment later, they were airborne and locked onto a flight path.

Next to the pilot seat was a thermos with two-day-old coffee. He took a swig and offered some to Wynter. She shook her head like she'd already tasted it.

"I had a bite at the house."

Titus downed the remainder of the coffee, wondering how much he should say to his sister. Since she'd disapproved of him for so long, he had to give her time to discover who he really was now.

"Look, Titus, I didn't mean to be so hard on you last night." She stared out the windshield at wisps of clouds. "Everything came together all at once. I just lost somebody over this whole mess, and I'm trying to process it all. Somehow, I knew I'd see you again, but I never knew how I'd react. You hurt a lot of people over the years, and the pain people felt was always directed at us, your own family, since you've always been on the run."

"I've been thinking about it all night, too. Most of what you said was right. I don't blame you for anything you said. I ran away from you and Rudy, even God, before anyone ever turned their back on me."

"God hasn't disowned you, Titus. He's still waiting for you." When Titus didn't respond, Wynter continued. "So, we're going to Europe? We're flying northwest."

"Just a touch and go near Slovakia. We're actually headed to Africa. I have a few hideouts down there."

"Africa. Wow. I haven't been there for awhile."

"Really? When were you there last?"

"Um, two years, I guess, this August."

"Where?"

"Al Qusiya. There's this—"

"Tel el Amarna," Titus said. "It was once Akhetaton. That was some dig, huh?"

"Yeah." She smiled. "I forgot we're in similar fields."

"Similar."

The two laughed lightly.

"What were you doing there?" he asked. "Working?

"Playing, working—same thing to me." Wynter settled into her seat and ruffled her short hair free from the head covering. "Someone found an emblazoned mask they wanted out of the Nile. Some diplomat from Aswan."

"Yeah? You got it out of the area for them?"

"Yeah." She grinned. "I got it out for this guy, showed it to him, he paid me, then I sent it to Oxford University. Cairo had me deported the next day. They were furious I didn't let them keep it."

"That's my sis." Titus shook his head. "Stirring it up with every Arab in the realm. I tell you, it must be in the Caspertein blood."

"And now we're going back to Africa?" She sighed. "I guess that means this nightmare isn't quite over."

"It ain't easy being a Caspertein."

CHAPTER TWELVE

Artic

Rudy paddled south. It wasn't long before he realized he'd made a potentially grave error. He had to relieve himself, but standing in the umiak, or even moving much, was an impossibility. It wasn't simply a choice of humbling himself and going in his drawers. It was life and death. At night, in thirty-two-degree weather, any moisture would freeze. Even more, Kobuk had her own business to handle. Some dogs were more private than they were given credit for.

Right away, Rudy searched the horizon for an island of ice on which to climb, then continue their journey. He had snow water and plenty of meat in the bladder skin pouch, but still, stopping on another iceberg would give them a chance to get more water as well as a chance to answer nature's call.

It was noon before Rudy spied a large enough snow pack island on which to visit. But it wasn't buoyant enough for both man and dog to stand on together. One at a time, Kobuk first, then Rudy, exited the boat. It wasn't as much a relief to Rudy as it was a necessary annoyance. Instead of traveling due south now, their journey would be dictated by the next visible drifting island of snow, which wouldn't necessarily be southward.

Carefully, Rudy and his companion continued their voyage. The farther south they went, however, the fewer icebergs they would cross.

"And this is just the first day, girl." Rudy smiled at Kobuk and she whined through a yawn. "We wouldn't know how to live without a challenge to face, would we?"

Hungary

In Hungary, while refueling in Miskolc, Titus hitchhiked into town for food. At a small cafe, he bought several sandwiches for the foreseeable meals, then outside the café, he connected with Oleg.

"It's bad here, Titus," Oleg said on his sat-phone. "Maybe the worst we've ever seen. No electricity, food, or water. The whole village is hemmed in by ISIS fighters. I found some regional evangelists who had a chance to leave with me, but they refused to leave the villagers behind."

"Let me guess: you stayed with them?"

"Hey, what do I get paid for?" He chuckled. "I can't get back to the airfield east of town. Militants everywhere."

"Has ISIS located your position?"

"Not yet, but I'm ready for them. The bullpup has them outgunned, but these ISIS boys have small artillery and mortar rounds. When they do find us, we're finished."

"Did you call Corban?"

"Yeah. The other COIL teams are spread too thin in their own mud. He said you're our best option. You finished in Istanbul?"

"I'm in Hungary now, but I have cargo, the priceless sort. Enemies are circling me as well."

"I see." Oleg sounded like he'd been awake for a couple days. Titus knew how bad choices could be made when people had little sleep. Lives were depending on him.

"It ain't easy being needed in two different places." Titus winced. Maybe it wasn't time for wit. Oleg didn't laugh. "I have your coordinates. I'm coming to you now."

"What about your cargo?"

"She might enjoy the adventure."

"We'll pray you get here in time. I'd say you have until noon tomorrow before they take the town from local militia defenders. You might consider a plan along the way."

"Why would I do that? Wouldn't want to break from my tradition of winging it!"

"Titus, if you can make it in, bring those Arabic Bibles in the hold. This whole town has only a few pages they have to share."

After disconnecting from Oleg, Titus found a message from Annette: "*I know it's against protocol, Titus, but call me. I'm worried about you. How're you taking this news?—Ann*"

He typed her a quick text: "*Ann, All in stride. God is still good. I have obligations and lives besides my own to consider. Hope to make it home soon. I really love you and miss you!—T*"

When he returned to the plane, Titus didn't wake Wynter. Noon tomorrow, Syrian time, wasn't much time to fly over one thousand nautical miles, but he'd never make the trip or do any good when he got there if he didn't sleep a little himself.

Next to his sister, he fell asleep on the second cot, remembering his childhood. Life had been less complicated then.

Egypt

Imam Nasser al-Hakim went back to Iran as Serik Tomir and the other Shiites flew down to Alexandria and Cairo, Egypt. These two cities, their contacts told them, were the stomping grounds of the Serval. If the man on the ferry had truly been the Serval, they would see him come back to his home—Africa. Then they would get Wynter Caspertein.

Nasser tried to focus on battle reports at his office in Tehran. ISIS and its own factions were still threatening Syria and the many militia groups who looked to Nasser for spiritual guidance. Of course, as one of the region's prominent *imam*s, his influence spanned farther than the spiritual realm. The only reason he received battle reports was because he offered strategic advice to military commanders, financed and equipped by US and European governments. They listened to him, though, lest their eternal rewards be revoked.

But there was no focusing on the field of battle for Nasser. He wanted revenge. He wanted to kill. He wanted the head of Wynter Caspertein!

Arctic

Rudy felt like he was playing connect the dots on a giant canvas of icy water. They were on their second day at sea, having stopped on six different snow islands. They'd found the largest floating island the previous night, and together, he and Kobuk had collapsed on the snow to sleep for six hours.

But they were awakened by a quiet splash. Rudy snapped to attention. Gripping his harpoon, he saw a small ringed seal two feet away with an expression on its face that matched Kobuk's look of surprise. The seal had probably never seen a human. It barked at Kobuk, who didn't seem to know whether to attack or stand guard for her master.

Since they would need the food, Rudy made the decision for them both. He stabbed his harpoon into the breast of the seal. Kobuk understood this signal, and lunged forward.

"No, Kobuk! Sit!"

The seal was already dead. They needed the fur with as few puncture holes as possible.

The ringed seal was the smallest of seals. They could weigh up to two hundred pounds, but this one was barely one hundred. Rudy began to skin off the creature's soft fur. Its meat would be Rudy's food for now since the polar bear meat was beginning to rot. Kobuk could eat the rotting meat, since her stomach could handle it, but Rudy wasn't too excited about eating the seal meat, either. Normally, it was used for animal food. Eskimos ate it sometimes. The meat had such a strange flavor that eating much of it at once was difficult—and that was when it was cooked! But Rudy was surviving one day at a time. He couldn't be picky over what the Lord provided.

Unfortunately, catching and killing the seal didn't mean they were near land. Some seals stayed at sea for eight months at a time, swimming and hunting for fish over hundreds of miles.

When the seal was skinned and its meat was stored on the umiak, the two loaded back into the boat. A north wind started blowing, so Rudy braced the two hip bone paddles behind Kobuk and draped the drying seal fur over the paddles. Rudy had no way to steer, only to run with the wind. They moved along at about four knots in a southern direction.

After a few hours, Rudy searched the horizon for an iceberg on which to take a break, but none were in sight. There wasn't even any slush in the water. Rudy swallowed hard as he realized the inevitable. They weren't leaving the umiak until they reached land. To Rudy, this was a worse realization than when he'd noticed he and the polar bear were on the same iceberg. At least with the bear, he knew what to do, how to kill it, or try to kill it. He'd had no options then.

He didn't know how to survive the next week, sitting cross-legged in a short, narrow boat with a giant St. Bernard in his lap.

Syria

Titus descended the Navajo plane to three hundred feet over the desert area of Northern Syria. Eucalyptus trees flashed under the fuselage, and brown, rolling hills were a blur from the cockpit window.

"If you're trying to keep me safe," Wynter said, gripping the copilot seat with white knuckles, "Syria hardly seems the right place to be."

"I told you, it's not about where you are, but who you're with." Titus thought about the spiritual principle of that statement, but he wasn't about to tell Wynter he was a Christian yet; she would see it when God opened her eyes. "Besides, Oleg needs us."

"Oleg, the Interpol agent who you said became a smuggler with you?" She scoffed. "You haven't changed a bit. I'm sorry, but you're still manipulating and corrupting people, Titus. My rescue has left a bitter-sweet taste in my mouth. Guess who gave it the bitter part."

"You don't feel safe with me?" He pulled the plane into a steep climb to avoid a low mountain range. The whole plane shook, then he leveled off. "Up until the last twenty seconds, I mean."

Wynter gasped, caught her breath, and checked her seat belt.

"You seem to know what you're doing, but honestly, Titus, no. I don't feel safe with you. Especially, not morally. You're making me some sort of accomplice with whatever you and Oleg are stealing or smuggling out of Syria. Of course, I don't feel comfortable with that!"

"Well, just hang tough with me until we can sort out your Muslim dilemma, then you're on your own."

"There's no sorting out my Muslim problem."

"You'd be surprised. I'm resourceful."

After checking his coordinates, Titus circled a wind-swept stretch of desert and landed the plane. He taxied around to aim the nose into the wind for a hasty take-off later.

"It's providential you're with me today." He flipped off switches and unbuckled his seat belt. "I have lots of gear to take in to Oleg's location, and you get to help me carry it."

"Wait—gear? I'm not going with you, Titus! You said he's under siege in this village. What if ISIS saw us land?"

"Exactly. You don't want to be with the plane when they show up. Find a *burnoose* in the overhead compartment and wrap up your face. Anyone who sees us should see two men with backpacks. We leave in five minutes."

"I think I was safer in Istanbul."

"Maybe." Titus chuckled and ducked his head as he left the cockpit.

"It ain't easy taking orders from the likes of me."

Egypt

Treasure hunter Rashid al-Sabur waited all day for some sign of Titus Caspertein in Africa. Electronically, he monitored the movements of his Arab counterparts also hunting the Casperteins.

Unfortunately, he couldn't watch for Titus in Egypt as well as he could if he were at home in Cyprus. Besides, there were other locations the smuggler might take his sister. Abandoning Egypt, Rashid bought a ticket that afternoon. He was going home to Cyprus.

With concern, Rashid realized Titus had other sanctuaries besides his normal African haunts. What if he took Wynter directly back to the United States? Rashid wanted to re-analyze the original phone tap he'd recorded from the Armenian embassy. It wasn't Titus whom Rashid was after; it was Wynter. And if he needed to, Rashid would go to Arkansas himself to get her. That was something most of the *Soldiers of Mahdi* wouldn't do.

Laughing at his greed, Rashid appreciated the lengths he would go to claim the riches he desired. Even the blood he was willing to shed.

Syria

Oleg lifted the head of a child and offered her the last drops of his canteen to her cracked lips. The child's head was wrapped in a rag, her eyes and much of her scalp had been burned from some sort of shrapnel during the overnight bombardment from Islamic militants. The night before, there'd even been the smell of chemicals in the air as ISIS employed chlorine gas to root out their enemies.

The situation for the civilians was further compounded since a small contingent of Jordanian soldiers, working with a mix of local militia, were attempting to hold the town. ISIS fighters were killing civilians while trying to kill the Jordanian troops. But without the Jordanian troops, the town would've been overrun already.

"Brother?" A bruised and beaten woman half Oleg's age offered him a cracker. She had survived the last "cleansing" of non-Muslims, and had recently come to believe in Christ. "This is our last food. Do us the honor of eating it."

Oleg took the cracker and surveyed the faces of the men, women, and children in the dim lighting. They had been hiding in the only building with a basement in the whole town.

The woman's face was peaceful, resigned to die, if necessary, without denying her Savior Jesus Christ.

The others watched him expectantly. How could he not eat the cracker? With tears, he set the cracker on his tongue and did his best to chew. He was dehydrated and his saliva was thick, so he chewed for over a minute, the others watching his face. They'd given him the last of their food. If he lived beyond this day, he would celebrate them for the rest of his life. To celebrate them, he would better resemble and testify of Jesus Christ, who had given them such hearts of love.

"Brother, tell us about the Letter of James," a young man said.

Oleg cleared his throat, still hindered by cracker, and recalled what he knew about the Book of James. The villagers had been Christians for less than a year, and their Bible consisted of only a few pages of the Psalms and most of the Gospel of Matthew. Yet God had given them a heart to believe—repenting from false beliefs and turning to Jesus. They didn't need to know everything about God, only the right thing: salvation in Jesus could be theirs through belief in the truth of His justice and love for them.

"The Letter of James is about our walk of faith. Will we be religious, or will our faith pour freely from our changed hearts upon those around us?"

As Oleg taught the Scriptures, he kept an eye on his sat-phone. Only Titus could task the overhead Gabriels' systems for his own use, but COIL agent Marc Densort had made sure Oleg's position was known and his sat-phone was always operational. On Oleg's phone, a blinking dot to the southeast showed Titus was in Syria. From the speed of the moving dot, it seemed Titus was on foot.

But if he didn't make it before nightfall, another bombardment from ISIS could kill the last survivors in the town.

"Chapter one of James is about God's goodness," Oleg said.

He'd never felt so much joy. If he were to die now, he would be content. Desperate strangers surrounded him, but they were brothers and sisters in Christ. Some of them had believed longer than he had, but since he'd studied the whole Bible with Titus, it was his responsebility to pass on the truth of their Lord. And in that truth was a correcting word regarding any remnant hatred toward the Muslims that were trying to kill them. For those listening, he encouraged a Christ-like attitude.

"One of Satan's tricks is to make us fear and hate the Muslim people. If we fear and hate our enemies, then the message of God's love will not reach them. But we are wise to Satan's schemes. God does love them. And we will love them as well. Given the opportunity, we will love them to the truth."

New York

Ex-assassin Luigi Putelli had a bad habit, and it wasn't his gum chewing addiction. That was actually a good habit, much better than the cigarettes that had nearly killed him years earlier. No, this bad habit was a remnant activity of his old life of stealth. He had a bad habit of surprising people at night, sometimes when they slept securely in their American dream homes.

Now that he worked full time for COIL, he was expected to file daily activity reports with a senior field agent or case worker. But after failing his responsibility with three case workers at the COIL head office, Corban Dowler had finally taken the Italian under his personal supervision—which had been what Luigi intended all along. But that didn't mean he'd become consistent in filing his reports daily, or even weekly. He filed when it was convenient for him, enjoying the autonomous nature of his assignments, primarily in America, while quietly courting Heather Oakes, who now worked for COIL as well.

Feeling especially mischievous one evening, Luigi slipped inside Corban Dowler's home in Queens before the man on crutches set the house alarm for the night. Janice Dowler was home, and Jenna was already in bed, but the couple ate a late dinner together and talked softly as Luigi stood in the darkness of their coat closet.

An hour later, Luigi heard Corban set the night alarm. The possibilities for Luigi were endless. Corban insisted Luigi report in more often, but he never indicated how, exactly. Luigi contemplated eating a midnight breakfast, loudly rattling the dishes until he drew Corban's attention. Or simply reclining on the couch until they found him in the morning. Whatever he chose, he hoped to impress Corban. Of course, it would seem he'd already circumvented the sophisticated alarm system.

The house was silent. Luigi waited another hour, knowing Corban sometimes stayed up late at the dining table to pray and read his Bible.

Finally, Luigi brushed past several coats, careful not to rattle the hangers, and gripped the door handle. It turned without a squeak. But when he pushed on the door, it wouldn't budge. It had closed so easily, but now— He put his shoulder into a firm push. Still, nothing.

In the darkness, his fingers explored around the door handle. Was he even pressing against the door, or merely a wall? No, this was the door. Puzzled, he jiggled the handle as much as he dared, hoping the noise wouldn't draw Corban from his bedroom down the hall. There seemed to be no lock, no deadbolt. And yet, the door was—

"Corban," Luigi spoke softly at the door frame, "are you there?"

"Yes, Luigi. I'm here."

Luigi's enjoyment evaporated. Now, he appeared to be an intruder rather than a cunning friend intent on surprising his peer, showing off his craft.

"How did you know? I always fail to outsmart you."

"We have shag carpet. I wear size ten loafers. Janice's feet are smaller than mine. You left tracks straight to the door, Luigi."

"You . . . tracked me indoors?" Luigi unwrapped a piece of bubble gum and stuck it in his mouth. "You won't let me out?"

"How else will you learn that even friends must respect one another's boundaries?"

"I see. I have offended you, my brother."

"We've been needing to talk, anyway, Luigi. You're about the worst COIL agent we've ever had. I haven't heard from you for a week, and we're not even in the middle of an operation! You should have plenty of time to file a status report."

"But I've been monitoring domestic operatives, growing wiser to COIL ways, just as you instructed."

"How would I know that? You never report in anymore. And I'm your handler. You know better."

"There's been no danger."

"Do we coordinate our communication only when we're at conflict with enemies? No. Luigi, it's because we are well-trained in communication—with God and one another—during peaceful times that we're ready to work together when war comes."

"Are you firing me from COIL?" Luigi closed his eyes, dreading the conversation he'd have with Heather to explain all this. "I have nothing else, Corban."

"No, I'm not firing you. But I'm reassigning you. As well as you know me, get to know Titus Caspertein. Watch his back. Listen for chatter. Whoever might be looking for him probably means to harm him and us. I release you from normal COIL protocol to return to your old style—within limits."

"That's it?"

"Isn't that enough? Titus is COIL's central muscle right now, and Satan knows it. I'm sure the devil will be throwing some weight against him. I want to know who's closing in. And one more thing—I like them over-easy."

"Over-easy?"

"So does Janice. But Jenna likes hers scrambled. Since you're sleeping on the couch for the night and fixing breakfast in the morning, that's how we'd like our eggs."

Luigi heard him remove a brace from the door—presumably one of Corban's crutches—and the man hobbled softly away. Slipping out of the closet, Luigi scuffed his size twelve boot at the shag carpet. He never could get one over on Corban, but the joke was still on the old spy; Luigi didn't know how to make over-easy eggs!

CHAPTER THIRTEEN

Syria

Wynter hefted the heavy backpack farther up onto her shoulders. To her left, Titus hiked with a larger pack, yet he walked with ease across the rocky desert.

"You're gonna kill me, Titus," she said, though she didn't stop her trek for fear she wouldn't be able to start again. "We've been walking for hours."

"Just three."

"How much farther?"

"About two more." He studied his wristwatch. "We'll be there about sundown."

"What do you have, a compass on your watch or something?" She winced as something rigid in her pack poked her shoulder. "You sure look at it a lot."

"A compass, GPS, and some other functions." He stopped and looked back. "How're you doing?"

"Not well." She paused next to him. "I'm not afraid of hard work, but I'm not a mule for smuggling contraband to your illegal contacts."

"I told you to look in the pack." He smiled, and she scorned the amusement in his eyes. Why did he have to taunt her now? "It might help you carry it if you knew what you're carrying."

"And I told you, I want deniability if I'm ever questioned about what I trafficked for you into Syria."

"I didn't remember you being such a complainer."

"I'm not a complainer. I'm moral. You saved my life, so I'm helping you, because I never saved your life. After this, believe me, we're even!"

"You know that's not true." Titus offered her his canteen, which she refused—partly because she had her own canteen, and partly because when he lifted his arm, she saw the rifle under his robe. "Don't you remember when we were swimming out on Norfork Lake."

"You want to talk about memories? How about Mom's funeral? Or Dad's? There's some memories for you! Where's Titus? On the run, somewhere in some country, stealing, killing, maiming, terrorizing."

"As I was saying, Norfork Lake. You, Rudy, and I pulled up that dock anchor out in the middle of the lake. The rope must've been thirty feet long. It took all three of us kids to pull it up. Rudy wasn't even ten yet. We got the anchor up and we were resting when Rudy shoved the anchor back over the edge of the dock. I froze, scared to death, as the anchor line zipped over the edge, because it was all tangled around my legs. Rudy was too carefree to think about reacting quickly. You were the one who clawed at my skinny legs and freed me of that rope before it dragged me under. You did that."

"Oh, yeah." Wynter frowned. "Well, don't flatter me with your sentimentality, all right? I know you have that giant gun under your robe."

"That's right. I do have a giant gun to continue to protect you."

"Mom and Dad would never approve."

"Some things aren't what they appear, sis."

"Except with you, Titus, we get what we expect, don't we? Which is nothing."

Titus concluded their rest and conversation when he turned and walked away at a faster pace than before. Wynter wondered if she'd said too much. Her words hadn't seemed to sting him as intended, so she'd gotten more confrontational. For twelve years they hadn't spoken, and this was her thanks? No, she decided. He wasn't going to guilt-trip her now. She wasn't the criminal. He was!

But, that thought didn't seem right, either. The FBI had called on Titus to help them rescue her in Istanbul. It didn't make any sense! She guessed he was misleading her about something.

Gazing to the south, she wondered if she could find her way back to the plane. Anything to avoid another hour with Titus! Since he had a rifle under his *burnoose*, it was just a matter of time before he killed someone. How would she ever explain to investigators that she'd accompanied a killer? Her archaeological work could be tainted forever by his company!

"If you're thinking of going back, don't." Titus didn't look back at her. "Women are kidnapped and worse in this region."

"Then you're an idiot for bringing me here."

"With me, you're safe."

"Yeah, right!"

He turned on her so quickly, she almost ran into him. For a moment, she thought he might slap her.

"You know who I was, Wynter, but not who I've become. Stop sniveling. Open your eyes, and pay attention. Yeah, your brother was a jerk and mistreated everyone. Well, this jerk is the only one standing between you and a few bloodthirsty Muslims. Do you see anyone else out here? How about that night on the ferry? Do you really want to go back to the plane?"

"Actually, yes."

"Then drop the pack and get walking. Go. Just follow our tracks. Won't take you long."

"But you said if I went alone—"

"Don't worry about what I said. Anything's better than continuing with me, right? Go ahead. I'm sure you'll make some nice Muslim friends along the way. Maybe pick up a new husband for Allah. Hopefully, he won't beat you too much. Go on."

"No, Titus, I—" She lowered her head. His words weren't nearly as cruel as hers had been, she realized, but they still hurt. She hated it when he was right! "I'll go with you."

"You sure? What about your mouth? Is it coming, too? Because you're depressing my otherwise determined stability. What's it going to be?"

"I'll . . . keep my mouth shut."

"You want to talk, then talk. But don't run me down, and I won't run you ragged. Got it?"

"Yeah." She shrugged, still not meeting his eyes. "Sorry. It's just . . . so many years of thinking about what I'd say, and now this. It's all coming out wrong, I think."

"I know. It ain't easy."

"You still say that just like Dad used to, huh?" She chuckled. "Reminds me of him."

"Me, too. That's why I say it. Come on. We've got to get to Oleg."

Titus imagined the three Gabriel UAVs flying seventy thousand feet overhead giving him every angle of the ground ahead. With one Gabriel, he had a two-dimensional map on the terrain. With two Gabriels active, he was afforded a three-dimensional image. But with all three providing high-resolution, real-time feed, he could triangulate his own position and the position of every hotspot around him.

"I see a way into town." He pointed down a shallow draw. "See it? We'll have to keep our heads down."

"Why would we want to join the ones in the siege?" Wynter leaned against a boulder, trying to shift the weight of her pack. "ISIS is all around. Can't you hear the gunfire? Why are we risking our lives in this battle zone?"

"If I can get us in, I can get us out, okay?" Titus lifted his *burnoose* and drew out the bullpup. "Stay close to me. If you have to talk to me, give the chickadee whistle."

"Chickadee?"

"Really? You don't remember the black-capped chickadee whistle Rudy taught us at family camp?"

"Oh, that."

"And one more thing. If we come under fire, you can take off your pack and hide behind it."

"Seriously? Don't you have incendiary devices or claymore mines in this meat sack?"

"No, you'll be safe. They'll stop a bullet. They're Bibles."

"*What?*"

Oleg leaned out a doorway with no door and watched the sun disappear into the western haze. From his basement vantage point where the Syrian Christians were hiding, he could see the last mortar round the ISIS militants had fired. It was fifty yards away, stabbed into the ground, undetonated. It probably wasn't the first armament that Russia and other weapons dealers had sold cheaply to ISIS in years past.

After all the months Oleg had spent risking his life with Titus, he'd never felt so helpless. He clutched the bullpup, COIL's most advanced, non-lethal assault rifle, yet he couldn't fight an army alone. Down the street, the Jordanian troops struggled to hold the city. But ISIS wasn't after territory. They sought to shock the world by their radical zeal when they killed the local Christians in a gruesome way.

A mortar shell landed behind the building, exploding and sprinkling ceiling dust on Oleg's head. Muffled cries and whispered prayers drifted to him from the darkness. He'd come as their deliverer, but he'd become one of those needing to be saved.

"Brother?" One of the young men set his hand on Oleg's shoulder. "Come away from the door. It's not safe. Join us."

"There's a time to pray," Oleg said, "and there's a time to move."

"You just quoted from the Book of Exodus." The man gestured to Oleg's phone fastened to his jacket pocket. "Is your friend near?"

"Near enough." Oleg held up his phone to show the dot that showed Titus' position. "We're here, and this is my partner, Titus."

"How will he come through the fighting? It's too dangerous."

"It would be impossible for you or me, but this man is . . . protected." Oleg chuckled and glanced at the darkening sky. "God has given him a special protection to succeed in what he does. We can stay here and die, or we can go out and meet him."

"But this is our home."

Oleg nodded. Another round exploded down the street. Gunfire drew closer. This wasn't the first time persecuted Christians had declined to flee. Some had an earthly claim to territory that would be their ruin.

"You're a pilgrim in this world, brother." Oleg braced his rifle against his shoulder as he noticed two militants in cover formation creeping up the street. "You can die for land and possessions, or you can live for Christ in another land. We're forty miles from the border of Turkey. You'll be safe with the Kurds. Well . . . safer."

Stepping from the doorway, Oleg leveled the bullpup. The two ISIS militants seemed surprised to see him. He fired two gel-tranqs into their chests before they raised their AK-47s, then he ducked back into the doorway.

"I'll discuss it with the others," the man said, and returned to the interior of the basement.

But ten minutes later, the discussion had still reached no consensus. Outside, the mortar rounds stopped completely, and Oleg's heart sank. There could only be one reason the shelling had ceased—the Jordanian troops had been pushed back entirely, and ISIS militants were now searching house to house. They would burn books and destroy century-old architecture. Men, women, and children would be rounded up for questioning. Anyone who couldn't quote the Koran, or anyone who professed Christ, would be executed immediately. Except for young women. They would be forced to marry loyal Islamists.

"The time is upon us, Lord." Oleg sighed, his eyes still on the street.

He intended to protect the Christians as long as he could remain standing in the doorway. "Thank You for Your saving grace. I've enjoyed the last year living for You."

Titus used his watch to navigate through the crumbled buildings and blocked streets. Darkness had fallen on the town, and the silence was more than disheartening because it meant death. The siege had broken, but only because ISIS had won.

Three hot spots on his screen made Titus pause. Wynter bumped into him from behind. Since he'd told her she was carrying Bibles on her back, she'd been quiet. Titus guessed she was reassessing her judgment of him.

"This way." Titus nudged her to the left, away from the three soldiers on his screen. Oleg's own physical hotspot was invisible since he was probably indoors where his body heat couldn't be detected. But his digital signal, the ping from his sat-phone, was strong.

Finally, down one street, a shadowy bulk stepped from a building. Titus and Oleg gripped forearms briefly, then moved aside for Wynter to enter the doorway. Inside the building, but near enough to the door to watch the street, they crouched on the floor, their heads together.

"You know how to make a Russian nervous!" Oleg laughed nervously. "What's the plan?"

"ISIS has taken the town. They're blocking roads in and out, but I'm guessing they're waiting for daylight to search more carefully for survivors and captives."

"You mean victims."

"Right."

"Who's the woman?"

"My Istanbul errand." Titus glanced over his shoulder. Wynter had crept deeper into the building toward the sound of hushed voices.

"She's the American you— Wait. Is that *Wynter, your sister?*"

"God has a funny way of healing relationships, huh? He forces us to deal with one another." Titus handed Oleg his canteen and an energy bar. "How're things here?"

"Better with you here. The elders are deciding if they want to stay and die, or run and live."

"I can get us through the checkpoints." Titus wiggled his bulky watch. "But we need to leave within the hour, before ISIS gets better established around the town perimeter. Right now, there are still gaps."

"The people are weak."

"Then figure two days instead of one to reach Turkey."

"I mean, they're *weak*. They may not want to leave at all on account of their lack of faith. And then there's these guys." He pointed down the street. "I tranqed two ISIS boys down there forty minutes ago. In twenty more minutes, they'll be waking up."

"Okay, watch the door." Titus ducked his head under several rafters to reach a huddled crowd of fifty men, women, and children. They were gathered around a single candle where four men were leading a discussion. He reached Wynter who was standing on the outskirts, not yet noticed by the others. "Pass out the Bibles. Can you?"

She shrugged off her pack and unzipped it for the first time. Titus gently pressed his way through the bodies to reach the candle at the center. He took a knee with the four men and they stopped talking.

"My name is Titus Caspertein, sent by God to rescue your people from death or Muslim conversion." He spoke Arabic and gazed up at their frightened faces. "God has blessed me with the opportunity to save the lives of Christians around the world, so this is not my first flight from danger. I know the choice you must make. Many others have had to make it before you. This is your opportunity. I can get you safely into Kurdish territory."

"But we will be refugees forever!" A man shook his fist. A young boy clung to his shoulder.

"Your alternative is to remain here and face what Satan has for you through his ambassadors. Both ways will be hard. It's forty miles to Turkey."

"We have elderly men and women!" another said.

"I understand." Titus bowed his head, more fully digesting the fact that he might not be able to save everyone. "Those who can walk, I will take to safety. You have ten minutes to decide and gather for instructions at the door."

Titus' last instructions were interrupted by the Bibles as thirty of them were passed from hand to hand. Literacy was above eighty-percent in Syria, so he knew the Arabic Bibles wouldn't be wasted, only cherished.

He returned to Oleg at the door as Wynter and her gifts became the center of attention, rather than the discussion to leave or not. The volume of their voices and wails increased, but neither Titus nor Oleg moved to hush them. The people were rejoicing and praising God; how could they interrupt them?

From his pack, Titus drew two dozen containers of fluids high in protein and potassium, and a bundle of one hundred energy bars.

"A feast before we leave?" Oleg asked.

"No, a meal as we leave. With their mouths full, they won't be quick to talk as we sneak out of here. I'll take the lead. You pass this stuff out to whoever goes. Leftovers to those who remain, if there are any. You bring up the rear."

"There's at least one bedridden woman." Oleg clucked his tongue. "How do we leave her?"

"I don't have the answer to that." Titus closed his eyes, a prayer for help on his lips. "We save who we can. Those who can't or won't march know the score. We can pray for people, but we can't force anyone."

Wynter returned to the door, a small child's head peeking over her shoulder from her backpack.

"The people are ready."

Titus saw the line of people behind her. Some held a few belongings in their hands, and others clung only to their new Bibles.

"No talking," Titus said. "As soon as we're in the desert, we'll stop and rest. Oleg, tell everyone as they come past. I'll see you in the desert."

"You got it." Oleg held drinks and energy bars ready to pass out. "See you in the desert."

CHAPTER FOURTEEN

Cyprus

Treasure hunter Rashid al-Sabur worked for an hour before he could hack into Arlin Skoke's phone service system. All it had taken was a call in English to the Arkansas Development Commission. The Commission handled all requests for information on the state's manufacturing and industrial services.

From there, he called one of Little Rock's cellular phone systems as Arlin Skokes, seeking personal information to enhance his phone coverage.

Thus, Rashid discovered Arlin's two business addresses. He called the first one. No one picked up, so he dialed the second one.

"This is Skokes. What's your business?"

"Hello, Mr. Skokes. This is Brad with the Department of Parks and Tourism. It's Arlin, isn't it?"

"Sure is, Brad. How can I help you?"

As Rashid spoke on the phone, his fingers flew over his laptop keyboard. He needed the line open for at least thirty seconds to install a digital bug.

"We're taking a quick poll with the businesses in your area. Will you be attending next month's Watermelon Festival in Hope?"

"Hmm. I like watermelon, but I've never gone. Probably never will."

"How about the Fiddler's Championship in Mountain View?" Rashid asked. "It's in August as well."

"I like fiddling. Mountain View, you say? There's good fishing around there."

"Yes, sir," Rashid checked his algorithm. It was almost ready. "It's the county seat of Stone County. It's about, oh, eighty miles north of us here in Little Rock."

Almost done . . .

"Yeah, why don't you put me on the list for that one, Brad."

"Done, Arlin. Well, those are the only two events we're checking for this month. Thank you, and have a nice day."

"All right. Take care."

Click.

Rashid didn't smile or even celebrate his success. He'd made hundreds of similar calls in a dozen languages. It was usually the only occasion he chose to speak to people.

After a moment, he cleared memory on a parallel drive to record any incoming or outgoing calls to and from Arlin Skokes' business office.

If Wynter called him once, she might call him again, wherever she was. Rashid would be the first to intercept her call.

Egypt

Serik Tomir wiped the moisture off his forehead. Every time he thought of his dream, he broke out in a sweat. No, it was a nightmare! It seemed so real. A creature—some sort of avenging angel—was attacking him. He couldn't help but think it was related to his hunt for Wynter Caspertein. But why such a creature? It was part man, part bear, and part dog. A giant dog. And the bear wasn't just an ordinary bear, either. It was a polar bear. If the spirits were trying to tell him something, he refused to accept the warning, even if it meant he'd one day face such a creature.

The Serval didn't seem to be returning to Africa with Wynter Caspertein. Thus, Serik resorted to other means to locate them. *Imam* Nasser al-Hakim would thank him later.

As Serik paced behind a man typing at a computer, he mopped his brow again, and twirled his cane like a baton.

"Next, say this," he dictated to his clerk, "'Don't kill her, just capture her. Capture her, hold her, and wait for the *imam*'s instructions. In so doing, you will be honored among Allah's disciples for completing his justice. The infidel who ruthlessly murdered our next intended *imam* will pay the price for her wickedness. Do not think of her as a woman. Think of her as a devil from the West who has slain our most beloved.'"

"The world will see this in mere minutes, Serik," the scribe said.

"Post the modified picture at the top and bottom of the notice, then send it."

Serik admired the modified picture of Wynter. He instructed a

Shiite graphics artist from the university to enhance the photograph with Wynter's latest features, namely her short hair.

The world would know her treachery. The article would be on the radio, television, and Internet for the entire Shiite population to help in the hunt. They would find her soon. The *imam*'s followers were everywhere!

Syria

Wynter had never been so energized and weary at the same time. Far out in the desert darkness she marched in the line of Christian refugees, following her brother, Titus. Every time she thought about the reality of what he was doing—saving lives—her eyes began to water. Was Titus truly a Christian now?

She didn't know how he'd done it, but Titus had led them in a zig-zag route out of the village. Twice, they'd passed silently below ISIS camps and sentries. Wynter had seen gunmen standing so close, but Titus had delivered them! Through rubble and darkness, they'd followed him—*her brother*—the prodigal son, the exiled criminal, the scorn of Crooked Creek, Arkansas!

As promised, Titus halted the procession thirty minutes outside the town. The way the people collapsed, Wynter didn't know how they'd ever continue. She set the child from her backpack onto the rocky ground and went to Titus, who shared his canteen with a circle of youths. They seemed drawn to him as he told a story about King David's fighting men who had fetched him a drink of water at the risk of their own lives.

"What now?" Wynter whispered to him when they had a moment alone.

"Thirty minutes rest, then we go again." He glanced at his watch, always the watch. "We're still in sight of the town. Come daylight, we need to be over the horizon."

"Can you call someone to pick us up? Trucks or something?"

"Not out here. We can't ask anyone to make themselves a target on such short notice. This is ISIS country."

"Right. Of course. I'm . . . trying to trust God." She watched with Titus as the tail of the refugee line reached them. "But these people won't make it through two days of walking."

"They'll make it."

"Some don't even have shoes."

"Then we need to wrap their feet."

"Why are you doing this?"

"Why do you think?"

"Well . . ." She shrugged and shook her head. "I'm a little confused, to be honest. If you walked down Main Street in Yellville, they'd probably arrest you. I personally know there are warrants for your arrest. Really, every time I go back home, people remind me."

"It ain't easy being wanted." Even in the dimness of the night, Wynter saw his bright, flashy smile.

"A double meaning, obviously. You're some sort of agent, but everyone thinks you're a fugitive."

"Oh, don't be fooled, sis. They don't know half the crimes I've committed. But I've been more or less exonerated due to particular skills I seem to have. Certain contacts have assured authorities I'm to be trusted. And I've made a commitment to God."

"Exonerated? Well, why didn't you come home, then?" Wynter scoffed. "Everyone thinks you're still a crook. Me included!"

"I guess I just got busy out here. It's not that I haven't wanted to come home, but there's more involved than a plane ticket if I return to Arkansas. Is that Oleg?"

Titus moved around her to reach for Oleg as he fell to his knees. From his arms, Titus took and cradled an elderly woman as frail and light as a child. A boy of about two was tied to Oleg's back. Wynter untied the boy and let him run free. Several of the children with them seemed to now be orphans.

"You trying to kill yourself?" Titus shook his last canteen. Barely a swallow remained, but he gave it to Oleg.

"I couldn't leave anyone behind." He swigged the water and licked his lips. "They said they'd all come if we could bring everyone."

"Everyone came?" Titus observed the weary crowd, then elbowed Wynter playfully. "Kinda makes our little problems in the world seem smaller, doesn't it?"

"How?" She elbowed him back, but harder.

"You know, just to see how God is going to preserve these people. We're out of food and water, but God will provide."

"Don't let him fool you, Wynter." Oleg rose to his feet and

stretched his back. "He's just building suspense. He actually knows this desert."

"How do you know a desert in Syria?"

"Oleg, put some sand in that big mouth of yours!" Titus shook his head, then addressed Wynter. "When he was an Interpol agent, Oleg used to track my arms deals. Yes, I sold to militants. I've driven across the Euphrates River Valley a few times. But it'll still be God who delivers us, whether we use my knowledge to live or not. I certainly didn't create pools of water in the desert."

"Pools of water?" Even Oleg leaned forward. "Where exactly is this mirage?"

"Can I use your phone?" Titus asked, and Oleg gave his sat-phone to him. A moment later, he had typed in coordinates and returned it. "You'll find food and water there. Water, at least, and food if ISIS left the fueling station operational. They probably did. From what I can see from the sky, there's no one manning the station."

"Why are you giving me the coordinates to find it?" Oleg shifted on his feet. "Why do I get the feeling that we're parting ways again? Right in the middle of an adventure, Wynter, and this guy is constantly running off."

"Wynter and I need to head back to the plane." Titus checked his watch. "We need to think about her safety now."

"I'm going to continue, Titus." Wynter touched her necklace. "We can't just abandon these people."

"We're not abandoning them. Oleg started this. He can finish it."

"They need my help! I'm not going back to the plane. Not yet!"

"Wynter!" Titus stood over her. "You won't be safe in Turkey. Would you listen to me? You can't go right back to where you said all this started for you!"

"You risked my life this far. Let's all finish it."

"Well, I have to get the plane." Titus slapped his hand against his side. "It can't fall into ISIS hands. How am I supposed to keep you alive if you insist on being reckless?"

"Must run in the family." Oleg chuckled. "Now you know how I feel, Titus—constantly!"

"Thanks, Oleg. Are you gonna keep her safe from those radical fellows?"

"I don't even know what's going on with you two." Oleg raised his hands defensively. "But I'll bet she can tell me the story as we walk. Actually, I'd like to hear some other stories, too. It must've been quite an adventure growing up with this wild child, huh? Calling him a serval is no accident."

"You have no idea!" Wynter shook her head.

"All right, all right." Titus held up his watch and bit his lip. Wynter wondered what he was always checking. "You two get everyone to Turkey. I'll get the plane and meet you both at Kobani. We can refuel and get out of the Middle East by tomorrow night."

"Kobani, it is." Oleg shook Titus' hand.

"Wynter, stay close to him."

"Stop worrying, will you? I haven't felt this safe in days."

"Well, safety is like the desert," Titus said. "Conditions can change really quickly with a little wind and sun."

New York

Corban Dowler rode alone on an elevator deep into a mining shaft in New York's Catskill Mountains. The mining shaft was two hundred years old, but the elevator was new. It ran by voice command, and required a biological identity scan just to get on the car.

A half-mile underground, the car stopped gently and the door opened to a steel blast door, capable of withstanding a ten kiloton nuclear blast. Using his forearm crutches to walk, Corban approached the side of the door, and offered his hand to a palm sensor and his eyes to a retinal scanner.

"Welcome, Corban Dowler," a computerized voice said, and the heavy door clicked, then lumbered open on hydraulics the size of a man's arm.

The first thing Corban noticed were the plants under artificial sunlight. He moved into the jungle-like interior as the vault door closed with a hiss behind him.

"Corban!" Marc Densort waved from a computer console fifty feet away. "Welcome to my lair!"

"Isn't this an electrical hazard?" Corban pointed one crutch at a leafy vine that grew toward a cooling fan. "The kudzu is getting out of control."

"I know." Marc laughed. "I have to trim her back every few days.

Obviously, I've planted a few more since you were here last."

"Did you really just call this plant *her?*"

"Hey, it gets lonely down here. It's only me, the computers, and the plants. Come on over here."

Marc spoke with a Middle Eastern accent. Though Israeli-born of Jewish parents, he'd turned against Zionism as a youth in exchange for Hamas ideals. Corban had found him years later, laboring in the basement as a Muslim bomb-maker, building suicide backpacks to detonate amongst Jewish settlers.

"Titus has had me up for almost two days straight." The forty-year-old COIL technician turned one flat screen toward Corban. "He's still in Syria with Oleg, though they split up."

"What about the militants?"

"ISIS factions seem oblivious that we just stole fifty Christians from the village. Oleg is taking them to Turkey, almost straight north. Titus called me thirty minutes ago. He's almost back to his plane."

The screen, with three frames of different angles—each view from the sky—showed images of Titus walking southeast across a parched land.

"Okay, send him this." Corban handed Marc a piece of paper. "They're coordinates for a medical run in Iraq. A couple kids came up-on a minefield while playing soccer. They need immediate transportation to Haifa for surgery."

Marc typed away on his keyboard.

"Done. He'll respond in a minute."

"Thanks. So, how's prison life treating you?"

"Better than what I deserve." Marc left his chair and picked up a water sprayer to mist a plant near a server rack. A twin-sized bed, desk, and bureau were arranged behind a low partition. "As a Christian, I know we don't have to do penance to cleanse our past sins. That was handled by Christ on the cross. But I do appreciate you allowing me to make a difference for Christ while I serve my sentence here."

"It's all part of the arrangement with the Israelis. You have ten years to do, but they can be productive years. What's the Lord been teaching you lately?"

"Maybe this is simple, but I've been learning about the God of the Bible." Marc picked up his leather-bound Bible, frayed around the edges from use. "The wrath and justice of God are seen in the Old Testament. The grace and love of God are most seen in the New Testament. Always the same God, but I've had to ask myself, why do I just see certain sides of God?"

"And what's your discovery?"

"Jesus!" Marc threw up his hands. "Jesus' life and words explain the God I want to know better. He explains who God is. Jesus explains why COIL and other Christians are free to show compassion and forgiveness to the wicked around the world, and why we don't kill the enemy."

"So, why do we show the enemy favor they don't deserve?"

"Christ died in anticipation of mankind hearing the truth and giving themselves back to their Creator. Christ paid my sin debt, so the way is open for peace to enter my life. But I must believe to receive the full blessing of eternal life."

"So, why don't COIL agents kill their enemies?"

"You're testing me, huh? Okay, the simple answer must be because with Christ's love, we love our enemies. But our theological answer must be—where Christ showed us grace, we show others grace, expecting, praying, and laboring for men to repent from their unbelief."

"You've turned into a theologian down here, Marc."

"Hold it. Titus is calling." Marc hit a few keys and turned a volume dial. "Speak, Serval. Marc-ed for Christ is here."

"Tell Corban I can get over to Iraq, but I need some shut-eye first."

"He's right here."

"In the vault?"

"Hi, Titus," Corban said, trusting the Gabriel encryption system to allow them to speak frankly. "Oleg is twenty hours from the Turkey border still. Take your time."

"You get my earlier report? The sister situation?"

"I got it. And I'm concerned." Corban moved closer to the mic. "COIL needs your identity to remain intact, Titus. If, while protecting Wynter, you show yourself to be connected to COIL, your access to Christians inside aggressive countries will dry up."

"I hear you, Corban, but my options for keeping Wynter safe are limited. Under certain religious freedom laws, even America has opened the floodgates to politically-connected Muslim fundamentalists like the *Soldiers of Mahdi.*"

"This may not be an animal you can fight." Corban admired the Gabriels' three-dimensional imaging of Titus as he reached his Navajo plane. "Maybe we can help Wynter diplomatically, if she were to return to the States. If we blow your cover . . ."

"Honestly, Corban, I don't even know the whole story yet. But I do know we're not up against a diplomatic issue. That's one of America's problems fighting terrorism. It's not a battle to be fought in the flesh. This is a spiritual issue."

"I couldn't agree with you more, but we have to protect both ends—your sister and your cover. Lives depend on both."

"No one knows the evil I'm working against better than me." Titus stood outside his plane. "How can I send her back to the States where she'll be in as much danger as if she were in Tehran or Azerbaijan?"

"So, what's your plan?"

"To start with, to lay low in Africa. But Corban, the head of the snake needs to be cut off. We've got to go to the top. I need to. And I need to deal with this personally. How? I don't know for sure, yet."

"Let's stay in prayer, Titus." Corban set a hand on Marc's shoulder. "Keep updating Marc as often as you can. Remember your limitations. We'll be in touch."

"You got it, Boss. And I'm on the Iraqi run to Haifa, Israel. Then I'll fetch Oleg and Wynter in Turkey. If you can, tell Annette I'll be back in two weeks, Lord willing."

"Don't worry about your wife." Corban chuckled. "Several of the COIL wives are up to their ears in African aid packages. They're flying them to Botswana themselves. They may have forgotten we even exist."

"It ain't easy being insignificant and forgettable." Titus waved at the sky. "See you in the clouds, if not before, if you know what I mean."

CHAPTER FIFTEEN

Arctic

Rudy couldn't feel his legs. He hadn't straightened them in the umiak for sixteen hours. After he'd fed Kobuk a few pounds of bear meat, he then dumped the rotting meat into the sea. He needed to use the bag for their toilet. Kobuk almost tipped the small vessel as she climbed on top of Rudy to escape her own odor.

"Sit down, Kobuk! You've forgotten you're an animal, girl. Those boys back at Barrow have been obviously spoiling you!"

They continued south almost directly now, without detouring toward icebergs since there were none in sight. The current had changed, which encouraged Rudy. A current change meant they were probably within two hundred miles of Siberia's coastline. The current nearest the shore rotated counter-clockwise unlike the rest of the Arctic waters.

It would be somewhere around three days before they'd even hope to glimpse land—if everything went perfectly. Two hundred miles, Rudy measured, while paddling about three knots per hour.

Rudy pulled his paddle out of the water. He rested it on his knees, which were numb. *Three more days?* It was a lot to ask of himself. Deep inside, he felt hopelessness welling up. Partly, he was surprised they'd made it this far without dying. Another part of him didn't care if they made it all the way or not. The challenge had kept him going. They'd gone farther than most humans ever could.

There was something still inside Rudy, though, that forced him to dip his paddle back into the water. He still cared that everyone on the mainland thought he was dead. But he was alive! And if the Lord willed it, he would win this battle as well. He and Kobuk would win together!

Turkey

Wynter felt supercharged. For two days, she'd marched through the desert, rescued Christians from execution, and now had arrived safely in Turkey. Exhausted, but still excited, she imagined a life committed to such work. What a thrill it would be to live for God like this!

As an American citizen, she'd crossed the strict border security fence without much incident, even without a passport. A quick search online had shown her face and identity. However, the refugees she'd escorted from the village had been detained at the border for processing. Soon, they'd be housed in a refugee camp, and when employment was arranged, permanent status would be granted as legal immigrants of Turkey.

North of the border town of Kobani, near the new airfield that had been bulldozed extra-long for heavy NATO planes, Wynter found phone access at a military outpost. Though in Turkey again, she was hundreds of miles from Istanbul and Azerbaijan. Oleg had stayed back at the border with the refugees. It was a perfect time to call Arlin. He answered after the first ring.

"Wynter! Where are you? I've been worried out of my mind!"

"You wouldn't believe it, Arlin! The things I've . . . Let me just say that God's been teaching me even more than I can fathom or express right now."

"I've been waiting for your call. I have something to tell you."

"Just wait till we're face to face, Arlin. I don't think I should even say it on the phone—who I've been with the last few days. It's just . . . too much right now. I'm overwhelmed by God's work in our family!"

"Wynter, slow down. Are you safe? I need to tell you something."

"Yeah, I'm safe. I'm back in Turkey, but I'm safe. Why? What's going on?"

"It's about Rudy. Are you alone?"

Wynter felt the blood drain from her face. She touched her shark tooth, remembering the words she'd just said about God's goodness. Whatever it was, God was still there, still watching.

"Yeah. I'm at a military installation, but no one's in the garage with me. What is it?"

"Rudy's been up at Barrow, researching and helping out at the facility. You know Rudy—involved in everything."

"Arlin, just get to it."

"There was an earthquake. Four, uh, four thousand were lost. The whole research facility."

"*What?* That's . . . impossible! Well, last I heard, Rudy wasn't even staying in Barrow exactly."

"He had returned. People south of the facility confirmed it. He and everyone else. They're gone, Wynter. They just . . . dropped right into the ocean. There's been some weather up there, so news has been scarce for the past week."

"When did this happen?" Wynter sat down slowly on the oily floor of the shop. "I haven't been near a radio in weeks."

"Almost two weeks ago. It's so remote, no one really understood what the silence meant. Look, I'm arranging a funeral up in Yellville. We'll bury him next to your parents. When can you get back here? Wynter? Are you there?"

Wynter stared, unseeing. God had given her Titus again, but taken Rudy? It wasn't fair.

Giant Rudy had always been a lonely man, distant, consumed with his expeditions. Even as children, she and Titus had often stood against the big kid, just to level the playing field, and he preferred it that way. But once Titus had run away after high school, Rudy's friendship had become more important to her. When they'd both had a pause in their travels, they met at home and compared their adventures abroad, boasting and laughing, sometimes late into the night. And they always remembered how the family had once been—their perfect childhood in the woods near Crooked Creek.

"Yes, I'm here. I wish I hadn't called." She wiped at her tears as men in uniform walked past. "I'm waiting for . . . a pilot to come pick me up, then we'll fly home."

"Who's this *we?*"

"You'll see. Maybe it'll help us grieve, knowing he's here with us now."

"Uh, I don't understand."

"Just trust me." Wynter closed her eyes, the pain washing over her. How would the pain ever pass? "When I arrive, it'll be with good news. I think we could use some of that right now."

Arctic

Rudy hadn't paddled for an hour, maybe longer. His arms were too heavy. Kobuk blinked at him lazily as the sun beat down on them yet another day. Nodding forward as he dozed, he suddenly woke as his face fell onto Kobuk's hairy back. He'd meant only to take a short break from paddling. Thankfully, Kobuk remained still under his weight as he carefully sat upright so as not to rock the boat.

Even though he'd done periodic pressure releases, his legs were still numb. If he bumped into land now, he'd have to roll the boat over to flop out like a seal since he wouldn't be able to stand or walk.

He'd always been callused with tough skin, but Rudy looked at his hands now to find that the bone paddle and salt water had rubbed his palms raw.

Picking up the bladder pouch, he saw their seal meat was nearly gone. After eating to maintain his strength and body heat, he was sure he'd gained a few pounds of muscle on the trek. But muscle would break down first once starvation set in. Muscle always went before fat.

There was a squeak on the wind. He reached for his harpoon. Three times the previous day, a family of seals had drifted with him to the south. It was migration season for some animals, so Rudy appreciated the confirmation that he indeed was on a southern heading. But that was yesterday. Today, he needed more meat. He searched the water for the creature that had yelped. Then a shadow passed over him. Looking into the sky, he shielded his eyes. A white-bodied bird with a black head studied him briefly, then moved ahead of Rudy's umiak.

An Arctic tern! Rudy grabbed his paddle and began paddling, peering after the bird on the horizon—a mere dot already. He measured his strokes—two on this side, two on that side.

The Arctic tern migrated farther than any other bird in the world. A migratory champion, some called it. And one thing about the tern— it nested on land!

Rudy paddled with renewed determination. A little encouragement had come to him when he needed it most.

"Please, get us home, Lord," he prayed. "I have unfinished business with my family."

Israel

Titus sat in the cockpit of his plane, which was parked on the tarmac of a Tel Aviv runway. He needed to get back to Turkey to pick up Oleg and Wynter, but there was the small matter of the tank blocking the runway.

He leaned forward to gaze out the window. Yep. The tank was still there. And a hundred crack IDF soldiers held rifles at their shoulders.

From his pocket, Titus drew out a harmonica and leaned back.

"It ain't easy being stranded in Israel," he said aloud to himself. He thought of his father as he placed the harp to his lips and played a few bars. Playing the harp always made him melancholy, which was why he usually played while alone. After all, the little instrument had belonged to his father.

"Mister Caspertein!" A man called from outside. "Mister Caspertein! Titus, come to the door!"

Titus left the cockpit and lowered the steps to the runway.

"Colonel Yasof. Shalom." Titus waved, though he didn't dare show himself too much. Israeli snipers were known for their accuracy. "Care to join me? It's definitely cooler in here."

Kalil Yasof spoke to his armed escorts on the tarmac, then climbed the steps. He wore a black beret, which gave the fifty-something commander a sharp look. He shook Titus' hand.

"You're a wanted man, Titus. I thought I told you to stay out of Israel!"

"Now, you know COIL only goes where we're needed." Titus noticed a new medal on the colonel's uniform. "Forward command has been good to you, huh? Seems I had a little something to do with you getting that medal last year."

"You put me in a real spot here, Titus. You're a wanted man, and you show up at the most secure airport in the world?"

"I thought I was a friend of Israel."

"Sure, you've helped us in the past, but look at it from our point of view. You've also armed terrorists all over the world—against the Jewish people. Do I really have to say anything about the weapon you nearly sold to Hamas?"

"What about the two children I just brought you? Did they get to Haifa? That's all I'm here for."

"Yes, they arrived safely by ambulance." Kalil scratched at an old war wound on his hand, a testament of the soldier's involvement in Israel's ongoing defense against aggressors. "Is that really all you're here for?"

"Yep, that's it."

"You wouldn't allow customs officers on board. Do you have contraband?"

"No. You know I'm a Christian now, Kalil. I work for COIL. My life belongs to the Lord."

"Israel doesn't forget her enemies easily, Titus. Our survival depends on it. Don't return!"

"I can't guarantee that." Titus grinned. "But if I do return, I'll count on you and me catching up again."

"Well, it's my job to warn you, even if I do enjoy our brief talks." Kalil shook his head and exited the plane. At the bottom of the steps, he turned and looked up. "How's Corban?"

"He's partially paralyzed, but you know Corban. Nothing will slow him down as long as the Lord has work for him to do."

"I won't forget what he did for Israel, even if it officially never happened."

Back in the cockpit, Titus started the engine as the tank rolled off the runway. Even if Israel was humane with her prisoners, Titus wasn't interested in an Israeli prison cell. He taxied onto the runway and flew out over the Mediterranean Sea, carving a wide swath around Lebanon toward Turkey.

Cyprus

Rashid al-Sabur couldn't leave his island of Cyprus as long as his surveillance system continued to report rapidly changing circumstances in Wynter's life. The latest eavesdropped call between Wynter and Arlin Skokes had informed him of the death of Rudolph Caspertein. In photographs, Rashid found the dead man to have been of considerable size. One less Caspertein to worry about. And anything that isolated Wynter more, as far as Rashid was concerned, was good for his plans.

Finally, Rashid approached his bureau full of false identities. It was time for a trip to America. He imagined the unguarded opportunities he'd have to abduct Wynter while she grieved. Small-town Arkansas seemed like the perfect place to blend in and get close enough to complete his job. During the flight, he might even consider seismography as a connection to Rudy—to act the part of a colleague of the man many in newspapers were calling a gentle giant.

Of course, Rashid wasn't as worried about a dead giant as he was about a giant treasure. The last item he shoved into his luggage was a double-bladed dagger. He almost wished he believed in God right then so he could pray that abducting Wynter would go smoothly. After all, she still had one more brother who seemed to be hanging around . . .

Arctic

The weather had been very nice for Rudy. It was bound to get nasty sooner or later. And it did as darkness settled in around the two lonely umiak occupants. Clouds drifted over them from the west and a cold wind came and went from the northeast.

Rudy hugged his coat around his midsection. He'd cut so much material from his coat tail, it was barely more than a long-sleeved belly-shirt now. Keeping his head low to protect his neck, he paddled onward, trying to keep the sinking orb of the sun on the southwestern horizon always to his right. With the clouds moving in, even the stars would be hidden and his bearings would be lost in a matter of minutes.

A gust of wind wobbled his balance and he gripped both sides of the umiak. A capsize now would mean certain death. There'd be no swimming to shore or getting dry. But he realized his error an instant later and plunged his hand into the icy water for the bone paddle. It was long gone, sunk to depths where even the blue whales shivered.

The umiak rose and sank suddenly. The waves were getting bigger as the wind continued to blow stronger and steadier.

Rudy didn't have time to mourn the loss of his paddle. He picked up the other one and paddled, propelling the boat forward with each thrust. Again, a wave rose on the right side of the umiak. Rolling with the swell, he continued to stroke. Momentum would help them stay upright. Though he was weary to the bone, if he stopped, they would surely die.

Kobuk howled at the wind. As she sang her song of death, Rudy prayed.

CHAPTER SIXTEEN

Arkansas

Oleg remained with the plane and luggage while Titus and Wynter embraced a chubby, short man whom Oleg had never met, but knew to be Arlin Skokes. It was a bittersweet homecoming. From past conversations, Oleg knew Rudy's death was hitting Titus harder than even Wynter knew. Throughout their missions, Oleg had prayed often with Titus about his family, as to how God would bring about reconciliation. Now, Rudy had died without knowing Titus was a child of God. He'd died without the opportunity for Titus to repair the injuries from the past.

As Oleg finished unloading the plane—a jet they used for trans-Atlantic flights while the Navajo remained in Paris—his sat-phone rang. He set a duffel bag of civilian clothes on the tarmac and answered his phone. It was Corban Dowler.

"How're things in Arkansas?" the COIL founder asked. "I'd come to the funeral, but I'm up to my neck in something."

"We just arrived." Oleg watched Titus, Wynter, and Arlin Skokes walk arm in arm toward a waiting suburban. "As Titus would say, sometimes it ain't easy coming home."

"How are you holding up, Oleg?"

"Well, our unscheduled trip to Arkansas is a welcomed rest. Syria was a real challenge. I thought I was about finished on that one."

"It'll get worse for Christians before Christ Himself restores order in this fallen world."

"Without you and Titus, I'd still be on the other side of the issue." Oleg sighed. "Tired or not, I'll be ready for whatever COIL needs me to respond to. For now, that seems to be luggage porter for Titus."

"Well, I hate to do this to you and Titus, but he's going to have to see to his own luggage, Oleg. I need you in Washington on the next plane. Your Interpol experience will be invaluable as we wade through this thing."

"What exactly are you talking about?" Oleg waved at Titus who was signaling to him that it was time to leave.

"Seems Wynter has pushed the Caspertein name into the minds of some powerful people. I'm talking White House powerful."

"That's good, isn't it?" Oleg sensed a ray of hope for Wynter's situation. "If the president is behind her—"

"No, it's the other way around. Azerbaijan is crying foul. They want the US to extradite Wynter so she can answer to murder charges. They're insisting on it. Now that Titus is involved, his own checkered past is under the microscope. All of COIL is under the squeeze of the State Department."

"They can't be serious!" Oleg dismissed Titus with another wave as he called him to get a move on. "They'd never send Wynter back to Azerbaijan, would they?"

"That's what they're proposing. Relations with Muslim-dominant countries are on the rise, Oleg. It's right out of the Bible—nations uniting over evil for a final purpose."

"Titus'll never allow it. I pity those who go up against him."

"Well, Titus doesn't need this on his mind right now. I'm sorry, Oleg. You two are partners, but maybe let him grieve for his brother for now. He doesn't need to hear about this quite yet."

"Yeah, maybe you're right. I'll tell him you need me up there and I'll leave tomorrow."

"Make it tonight, my friend. I need your counsel now. And just so we're clear: COIL isn't abandoning the Casperteins. I'm fighting this all the way, even if it ruins us. That's just how we do things. We're all in with everything we've got, which is a dwindling amount in these last days."

"God won't let COIL implode. I don't believe that." Oleg felt an anxiety in his stomach that told him hard times were ahead. "We may be attacked. We may even take some punches. But we're not ever abandoned by our Father."

"Who taught you that?"

"Titus." Oleg laughed. "Who else do I spend every waking moment barely tolerating?"

"He taught you well. I look forward to seeing you, Oleg."

Arctic

Rudy shivered as he paddled through a wave that splashed over the side of the umiak. Ice clung to his clothes and coated the inside of the boat. His beard was heavy with crystals. Rain blinded him. Freezing water from the ocean took his breath away. He couldn't remember ever being this cold.

The sky had been dark for over thirty hours. The fact that Rudy was one of the largest, strongest men alive meant nothing to the ruthless mid-summer ice storm. Kobuk lay in the bottom calmly. She watched Rudy, surely sensing his desperation, his fear. But she couldn't help.

A huge wave swept the boat onto its side. Ocean water filled the umiak to the rim. Rudy righted the vessel while simultaneously sitting up to his belly in water, but he'd lost their last paddle. It was gone.

Kobuk raised her head to breathe, but still, she lay on the bottom of the umiak. Even underwater, her coat and fat would keep her warmer than Rudy ever hoped to be again.

Rudy caught at the waterproof bear bladder as it floated around his knee. His hands were so cold, his fingers barely worked. He dumped the remaining seal meat into the sea, then plunged the bladder-pouch into the umiak's water and dumped it overboard. Bailing water frantically, he knew he had only minutes to survive at that temperature. Up until the boat had rolled, his caribou skin coat had kept at least his upper body relatively dry. But now he faced hypothermia. Cold to the core. Lost in the Arctic. In a flooded umiak with no paddle.

Five minutes later, Rudy had bailed all but a shallow puddle from the boat. He turned his face to the dark sky. Torrents of rain were already filling his boat again. There was no chance for warmth in the near future. Soon, he would die. And he was ready to die, ready for the struggle to be over, ready for the warmth of the presence of Jesus Christ. In moments, he would be with his Savior. The wind stole his tears and froze them as they were blown from his face.

"Please, God, not like this. At least, spare Kobuk . . ."

Kobuk howled at the wind. She seemed to know their doom as well. When she stood in the boat, Rudy didn't command her to lie back down. She stepped toward him and rested a heavy paw on his chest, then on his shoulder. Then both front paws. With his hands, Rudy manually lifted his legs to straighten them out in front of him. He still couldn't feel them due to lack of circulation from his posture. Scooting his backside forward, he reclined the best he could in the boat. With

Kobuk's paws on his shoulders, she lay on top of her master. She howled again at the wind as she covered him with her body, her warmth.

Rudy wrapped his arms around the dog that nearly smothered him with her weight and coat. She rested her head on top of his. He closed his eyes and waited for death. It was the only peace he could imagine now.

There was no surviving this. They had fought, but they had lost. Nevertheless, he was glad to have experienced the battle. Together, man and dog, a team to the death. Wynter, his bold sister—he wouldn't see her again on this side. He hoped she continued to unearth ancient relics and their secrets. And Titus, if he was still alive, he hoped he found what truly mattered in life. Rudy had hated him, but in his moment of death, before God, he forgave Titus for hurting him, for hurting their family.

"Mom and Dad," he whispered in his delirium, "I'll see you soon. God, thank You for even this much warmth . . ."

The umiak rocked like a cradle in the sea.

Iran

A short drive south of Tehran, Serik Tomir sat at the feet of a renowned professor of Islam, Ali Sabouk. The seminary, one of fifty in the city of Qom, was even named after Ali's family. All leaders of Shiite Islam had studied in Qom, many at the Sabouk Seminary. It was where Serik would have enrolled Gamal, if the American Wynter Caspertein hadn't murdered him.

As Ali considered Serik's question, Serik fought the urge to finger his sword-cane. Weapons weren't allowed in the mosque-like class-rooms, but Serik enjoyed the secret pleasure of the hidden sword, the sword he would use to kill Wynter, if he were given the chance.

While Serik waited, he reminisced over the night he'd spent in Tehran in a women's prison. He visited the prisons as often as possible, enjoying their treatment of him, since he was the right hand of *Imam* Nasser al-Hakim. Serik would've felt guilty about the women prisoners he demanded to have relations with, except Sharia Law sanctioned such treatment. How else would the women in political custody earn money for small living improvements? All the mullahs had blessed the system of prisoner prostitution, and Serik boasted in having fully exploited their hospitality.

The prisoner he'd selected the night before was a Christian, imprisoned for nine years for multiple offenses of converting Muslim women and children to Christianity. In fact, her file said she continued to preach her lies in the women's prison. When she wasn't in chemically-induced interrogation and torture sessions, the prison officials made her available for *sigheh*, or temporary marriage, for the sake of men willing to pay the price as well as leaving their victim a small gift.

Serik had been especially frustrated over the failed capture of Wynter, and he sensed he'd been particularly abusive to the woman overnight. He'd left her the obligatory gift and said his prayers to Allah that morning, so his conscience was clear, but he wouldn't be fully satisfied until Wynter was in his hands.

"Don't go to America." Ali opened his eyes, and Serik sat up straighter. "That is my first advice. Allow Allah to bring the woman of the Great Satan to you."

"Why would she come to me, Teacher?" Serik frowned. "She knows we hunt her. We must go to America."

"Allah must be avenged, but not on Satan's soil. This woman—she's a well-known archaeologist, you say?"

"Yes. She's written many papers and studied at many sites in many countries."

"Then what was she doing in Azerbaijan?"

"Hmmm. When she left the country, she abandoned many possessions. I can have it analyzed to find out what she was searching for."

"After a time, if she thinks she's safe, she may return to finish in Azerbaijan what she has begun. Americans are proud and they have short memories of the dangers in the Middle East. Consider their recent political maneuvers. We are sworn enemies because of their homosexuality and other immorality against Allah. And yet, they now openly make treaties with us, against Israel. Yes, this woman is no different, I reason. Her same optimism will bring upon her a similar defeat. That's when you'll capture her, if Azerbaijan's demand for her extradition doesn't work."

"Azerbaijan." Serik grinned. His grip tightened around his sword-cane. "Of course. I'll recruit men to ambush her, men who know the country, men who are loyal to the *Soldiers of Mahdi*."

"But first, you must make her feel secure. Remove her picture from the computer screens. Cease advertising her destruction. Become silent. The gazelle will graze. But you, the leopard, will leap without warning. It is the Persian way. Will this serve *Imam* Nasser's desires?"

"You've been most helpful, Teacher. Allah be praised!"

Siberian Arctic

Rudy was frozen. Rather, his coat and clothes were frozen around Kobuk. Somehow, his body preserved some heat. Somehow, he was still alive.

He was conscious now. Earlier, during the harshest period of the storm, he'd fallen asleep, a graven sleep. But he was awakened later as Kobuk barked loudly in his face. Now, the rain had ceased. Though he was conscious, he waited for death. At any moment, one of the small waves would roll the umiak over to a watery grave. He was too exhausted to sit up, and Kobuk didn't seem willing to let him. They drifted like a ghost ship with no direction or hope.

In what seemed like slow motion, the umiak tipped to its side and spilled out its two passengers. Kobuk slipped out of Rudy's frozen embrace and swam away from him.

Barely conscious, Rudy saw Kobuk climb onto a barren shore of seedless soil and rock. Shaking herself, raining icy droplets of water all around, she barked at her master as he rolled over to float face down. His head bumped against the shore, and Kobuk sunk her teeth into his collar on the back of his neck to drag him onto perpetually frozen mud.

Rudy opened and shut his half-frozen eyelids.

"Good, Kobuk."

A low growl emitted from a throat behind Kobuk. A bark sounded from another angle, then a yip. Kobuk turned as five Siberian timber wolves closed in for the kill. Rudy rolled onto his back, too weak to sit up or crawl any farther. The wolves were starving, the rare northern storm surely limiting their hunt for other game. Their slender gray muzzles showed teeth accustomed to tearing, and their discernible ribs fully pronounced their intentions.

But Kobuk wasn't starving. Up until twelve hours earlier, Rudy had fed her well. She wasn't cold or weary. And though she was out-numbered, she weighed more than the largest of the wolves by one hundred pounds.

"Get 'em, girl," was all Rudy could say, and she seemed to sense his desperate state. As a sow protects her cub, Kobuk waded into the wolves with fury in her eyes. As a Search and Rescue canine in Barrow, she'd fought the Alaskan malamute sled dogs. These wolves didn't frighten her.

Kobuk stepped on one and closed her massive jaws around the skull of another. She turned and ripped a limb half off a third. The fourth tried for her flank as the first recovered and the fifth closed for a bite.

She spun in the air as one wolf ripped hide from her hip. Tackling it angrily, she tore into its back and ripped open its spine. The uninjured two skirted away, took a lasting glance at their dying companions, then fled up the black shore now basking in morning light.

Rudy welcomed her tongue on his face as she trotted over to receive his praise. He thanked her with barely coherent words. In his hand, he still gripped his harpoon, but he hadn't had the strength to help her fight. If Kobuk hadn't done the job, he would've died.

However, the victory against the wolves only prolonged his death. There was no surviving the cold. He would receive no mercy from the barren land of Siberia. At least, Kobuk would live, he thought. Then he slept.

CHAPTER SEVENTEEN

Arkansas

A t the airport in Little Rock, Titus walked toward Annette the instant she appeared on the exit ramp. There were no words at first as she dropped her carry-on bag and wrapped her arms around him. She'd left her COIL work in New York where they lived now so she could be with him at the funeral. The two clung to one another as their pain was expressed in sighs and wordless restraint. Passengers floated past them to more joyous reunions, but Titus remained locked in Annette's embrace until the ramp was empty of strangers.

Finally, he released her and picked up her bag. Annette swept a dark strand of hair from her wet cheek and linked her arm around Titus' elbow. They walked toward the exit.

"How do you feel?" she asked. "Any symptoms? The doctor said they might hit you all at once."

"Just weariness, in bouts and waves." He forced a smile. "Nothing that a little time with my wife won't cure. There's too much happening right now for this weekend to be about me."

"Please tell me Rudy's death had nothing to do with Wynter's Muslim enemies."

"No, I don't think it does." They boarded a bus to taxi them to short-term parking. "Not unless Muhammad appeared to someone and revealed earthquake secrets to the *Soldiers of Mahdi*."

"You're terrible!" She slapped him on the shoulder. "How can you joke at a time like this?"

"If I didn't joke, I'd fall apart." He nodded at a suited man near the back of the nearly empty bus. The man didn't nod back. "Sometimes, it ain't easy being a Caspertein."

"Well, I came as soon as I could. How's Wynter? I can't wait to meet your baby sister!"

"She's in pieces. Arlin took her up to Yellville to Mom and Dad's place." Titus browsed the three other passengers on the bus. No one suspicious, except for the suited man . . . "Oleg was called back to the East Coast. Corban's hiding something from me."

"You're paranoid. I'm sure Oleg wanted to be here for you. But while you're here, the world's crises don't stop. Oleg can fill your shoes for a few days, can't he?"

"Yeah." He smiled. "Sure he can. Give me a minute, will you?"

Titus released her hand and approached the suited man at the back of the bus. Instead of confronting him directly, he plopped down in the seat next to him, their knees nearly touching. Since he wasn't disguising his interest, Titus noticed the suited man's posture became more rigid. He looked to be in his forties with careful eyes and a white strip around his blond hair, telling of a recent haircut.

"What agency?" Titus asked, aware of Annette shaking her head at him.

"Excuse me?" The Fed glanced at Titus, then looked out the window as the bus arrived at the short-term parking. "You have me mistaken for someone else."

"Come on. You have no luggage. Nobody travels in this weather with their tie that tight. And you're alone."

"So? Maybe I work in the airport."

"Not unless you're a security officer." Faster than the man could react, Titus held down the man's right arm and reached into his suit jacket to draw a .45 semi-automatic from a shoulder holster. Titus released the magazine and checked the chamber, which was empty, then offered the weapon back to the startled agent. "Just so we're not wasting any more time, for my next trick, I'll take your wallet to check your identification. Do you believe me?"

"There's nothing subtle about you, Titus Caspertein!" The man yanked his gun from Titus' hand and holstered it, but didn't bother reaching for the magazine. "I'm FBI, since you must know. Agent Stambler. Believe it or not, we have a mutual friend who got me involved."

"That would make you Einsteinium, and our mutual friend would be Arlin Skokes. Relax, Agent Stambler. You're not the first government official I've disarmed in public. You've helped Wynter, and that means a lot to me. But you're not here for Wynter now, are you?"

"You're so sure of yourself." The agent scooted to another seat to face Titus. He seemed distracted by the gun magazine Titus fiddled with in his left hand. "You may have a sense of immunity, but the wind is shifting. You still have powerful enemies."

"True. But I have even more powerful friends." Titus glanced at Annette, who rolled her eyes, as if she knew too well his antics. "If you're a friend of a friend, then we can talk as friends."

"Your friends are running to the shadows. The Caspertein family is about to take a fall. Do you feel it coming?"

"You're not a very nice man, Agent Stambler, even if you did help my sister."

"That was before I knew she was *your* sister."

"Very well. I'll be nice for both of us." Titus stood and offered the agent his ammunition. "Get yourself a pair of jeans to fit in. If you've got to follow me around, try to be invisible. I'll take it personally if you upset my family. Got it?"

The two held their gazes for a few seconds. Finally, Stambler accepted the magazine and thrust it in his pocket, without a word.

When the bus stopped, Titus moved to Annette's side and picked up her bag.

"That confirms it, hon. There's something happening. If I make myself scarce this week, just stay next to Wynter, okay?"

"What else would I do at my sister-in-law's house?"

"I have a .22 loaded with gel-tranqs in the car. Don't go anywhere without it.

Siberian Arctic

Somehow, Rudy stumbled a mile down the coastline. Kobuk plodded ahead of him and scouted for danger. By the second mile, Rudy came upon a hunting shack. The St. Bernard investigated the area as her master drew near. It was the first time Rudy had seen signs of humanity in . . . He couldn't remember how long. A week on the iceberg. Almost as long in the umiak? Maybe longer.

"Thank You, God . . ." he whispered, but he knew they were still very far from being rescued.

The shack was made of plywood—a single layer of wood, with no insulation. Rudy's hands were too frozen to open the door latch, so he broke through the door with one kick. The hide hinges dangled free. Inside, there was standing room for two men, but sleeping room for only one.

Rudy didn't care about the size. Right now, he cared about warmth and getting dry, but there wasn't a stove inside the shack. However, after a moment of clawing through empty food cans and a mouse-infested blanket, he found matches and a lantern, though no firewood.

Outside the cabin, he stood with the match box and lantern. Kicking at the corners of the shack, it crumbled into a rugged heap of wood splinters. He tossed the largest piece of plywood over his shoulder, then he cracked the lantern on the pile until the kerosene leaked onto the wood.

Shivering, Rudy struggled with the matchbox. The anticipation of warmth was torture, nearly causing him to sob. His fingers refused to grip a single match. But he could make a fist. He took a handful of the matches and bent over the woodpile, then struck fifty matches at once over the plywood.

Fire leaped at the cold air. The plywood blazed suddenly and Rudy forced himself to step back. He dropped the rest of the matches before he realized his error. A part of him wanted to fall into the crackling warmth, but he remained a stride away as his matches were consumed.

Kobuk was familiar with fire, but she kept her distance even when Rudy urged her closer. She was apparently warm enough, yet her stomach caused her to look across the empty land restlessly, then look back at Rudy. Rudy waved his hand at her, and she seemed to understand. From the shore, she turned inland to the south. There wasn't a forest for a hundred miles, but there had to be other animals around besides the ravenous timber wolves.

Rudy held his hands up to the growing flames. Heat! He began stripping off his icy clothing to lay everything on the frozen earth to dry. Naked, he rotated in front of the fire. Ice from days of cold fell from his beard and chest. Droplets of water evaporated within minutes.

His fingers were stiff, but the pain slowly subsided. He reached down and turned his clothes over and held some of them up so the heat could attack their dampness directly.

He noticed Kobuk was already out of sight. Hopefully, she would return soon. Somewhere, he'd lost his antler-tipped harpoon, maybe down the coast. But he was warm, finally, and dry. God had preserved him for another day, maybe even to see his siblings again. Maybe even to see Titus and tell him he still loved his little brother. The thought choked his throat with yearning.

Writing on the empty food cans in the shack had been in Russian. He recognized the letters from when he'd visited with Russian settlers still living in Sitka, Alaska, and other settlements. His fears were confirmed: he was in Siberia, an unforgiving land.

Arkansas

Past several state parks and rivers, Rashid followed Titus northward to Crooked Creek, eventually reaching the small community of Yellville, population of twelve hundred. Rashid had never been to the Ozarks, but he guessed the town was growing by a couple hundred strangers that weekend for the funeral of Rudolph Caspertein, so Rashid felt his identity was sufficiently secure.

The funeral was set for the following day, but Rashid wasn't particularly interested in the funeral. As it turned out, the funeral wasn't a nuisance but an aid to his intentions. Without even trying, he could now get close to Wynter, and maybe even Titus. By the time he was done in Arkansas, there might be three Caspertein caskets to bury!

Once through town, he distanced himself from Titus' car as he and a woman from the airport drove onto a county road surrounded by thick elm and oak trees. Rashid was about to park and explore ahead on foot when he came upon a two-story house set back in the trees. A dozen cars and trucks were parked along the sides of the driveway, so Rashid pulled off the county road and parked his rental behind a truck with a gun rack in its rear window. Though he didn't have a firearm, he wasn't intimidated by American hunters. His double-edged blade had shed more human blood than local rifles had shed deer blood.

After applying a light brown mustache to his upper lip, Rashid approached the Caspertein house. No matter where he ventured in the world, he prided himself in his ability to deceive others. No one knew him. As far as he knew, no one had ever photographed him during a job. In loafers and slacks, the first two buttons unbuttoned on his shirt, he was confident he would find entry. All he needed was five minutes alone with Wynter, then he could leave. And now he knew she was here—safe, sheltered, vulnerable . . .

Titus knew almost everyone in his parents' house, but he still felt like a stranger. Hesitantly, several men shook his hand, while others acted predisposed, suddenly studying the rafters, or darting out the back door to discuss the level of the creek. Wives moved into another room, and the children were corralled elsewhere, away from the international fugitive. Annette gave him an encouraging smile, then went immediately to the kitchen where she could be of use.

"Welcome home, Titus," an elderly man greeted. "Sorry this is what brought you home."

"Thank you."

It didn't help that Titus had long forgotten the man's name, but the neighbor had helped his father with firewood when Titus was a boy. Even though he was a child of God now, his two decades of criminal enterprising had left him ignorant of the old community. Not once, in all those years, had he checked on any of the neighbors, old classmates, or even Arlin, who approached him next.

"They'll warm to you, son." The heavy man pumped Titus' hand. His face was redder than normal, probably from the emotional reunion of so many. "They'll see who you are, eventually."

Behind him, the open front door was filled with the shape of a mustached stranger. His head barely cleared when he stepped into the living room, an appropriate somberness to his face, and a half-wave to the mourners. Arlin, having assumed the place of family liaison, approached the stranger immediately. But Titus wasn't so fooled. In fact, the chilly welcome he'd received from past acquaintances was forgotten as he recognized Rahsid al-Sabur, an old smuggling rival. With a dash of amusement, he imagined the man in a leather jacket, and realized he'd seen him a few days earlier on an Istanbul ferry.

"Rudy was my friend." Rashid frowned for the room of people as Arlin shook his hand. "Seismography was our occupation, but kindness was that big man's identity. My name's Jared Volkan."

The room accepted the tall stranger's words, and Arlin guided him to a platter of triangle sandwiches. From the corner of the room, Titus stared over a cup of punch at Rashid, or Jared, trying to recall everything he knew about the imposter. He was certain the man was the killer he knew, many of his jobs having left evidence of that fact. But Titus, being the American cowboy, had often plowed through competitive heists, in and out of cities with the loot, while more sophisticated smugglers, or thieves like Rashid, took their time. Specifically, Titus recalled a South African diamond heist he'd taken from under Rashid's nose, knowing full-well Rashid had been in town for the ice, as diamonds were sometimes called. What a display of arrogance for the killer to show up now at his brother's funeral!

"Are you back for long, Titus?" a man asked. Titus recognized him as a cousin about Wynter's age. He wore a fly-fishing hat and rubber boots, as if he and Arlin had plans for Crooked Creek as soon as no one was looking.

"No real plans." Titus glanced at Rashid. The criminal had to be there for only one reason. Where was Wynter? "I don't want Arlin and Wynter to be alone right now, dealing with everything. Would you excuse me? Wynter needs me."

He found his sister in their mother's sewing room next to the kitchen, looking at a photo album with Marilyn, Arlin's daughter. Wynter looked up.

"There's the woodsman himself." She held up a page. "Just looking at this picture Mom took of us playing cowboys and Indians in the woods. You never did cooperate."

"I remember." Marilyn rose to her feet. "You and Rudy would always get distracted and go hunting for squirrels when us cowgirls wanted to attack you Indians!"

"It was the only time Rudy and I weren't fighting each other." Titus nodded and held out his arms. "Hello, Marilyn."

They embraced, and Titus realized this wasn't the time to upset Wynter, endanger Annette, or cause a scene. Rashid al-Sabur was his problem. If Oleg were there, he would've been good backup, but his partner was with Corban. That fact reminded him there was much more happening than he knew.

Leaving Wynter and Marilyn, he stepped into the bathroom under the stairs and drew his .22 revolver, loaded with gel-tranqs, from his ankle holster. Someone like Rashid was definitely armed, though Titus wouldn't have guessed he had so many contacts in America. The man usually operated out of the Mediterranean somewhere. He replaced the revolver and closed his eyes.

"Wisdom, Lord. I'm here to remember Rudy. Please don't let this weekend become about me. How do I handle Rashid? Why is he here?"

Before he could finish praying, he had an answer—not audibly, but just as clearly as if it had been. As a Christian, he was to address Rashid as Christ would if Jesus were in Titus' shoes. That was the answer to his prayer. Christ would show Rashid grace.

Instead of arguing with God, Titus left the bathroom and stepped into the living room. Rashid wasn't there. He picked up a plate of cheese and crackers and walked into the kitchen where he found Rashid kneeling in front of the open fridge. Shoulder to shoulder with Annette, the two were selecting a soda for themselves.

When Rashid rose to his full height and turned, his eyes met Titus' face. Titus wasn't accustomed to looking up to meet the gaze of another.

"Hey, hon," Annette said, popping the top of her soda. "This is Jared from Turkey. He worked with Rudy in Asia a few years ago. Jared, this is my husband, Titus."

Holding the plate with his left, Titus smiled and shook Rashid's hand with his right.

"Jared, is it? A friend of Rudy's is a friend of mine." He held up the plate. "Cheese?"

"Thank you." Rashid's eyes were anything but kind up that close. The man's mustache had been too hastily applied, the underlying epoxy smudged and glossy next to one nostril, but Titus guessed he was the only one who would notice. "What line of work are you in, Titus?"

"I'm between jobs right now."

Rashid slowly chewed on a piece of cheese, glaring down at Titus. Maybe it was the tension. Maybe it was the thought of wrestling with Rashid if he misbehaved. But Titus couldn't hold back a grin. *The nerve—to come into his house!*

"Uh, guys?" Wynter backed away toward the sink where two women from church chatted. "Am I missing something? You guys know each other?"

"Sure." Titus slapped Rashid on the shoulder, making him flinch. "We've crossed paths over similar interests. You have a place to stay, Jared, or did you just get into town?"

Titus vaguely recalled there may have been a vehicle that had followed him from the airport, but he'd assumed it was the Feds keeping tabs on the notorious Serval.

"I just arrived." Now, Rashid looked nervous, realizing he'd been recognized.

"It's settled then. We'll bunk upstairs together in my old room. You take the bed, huh? I'll take the floor. I bet a couple blow-up mattresses are still in the basement from our camping days. You need somewhere to stay for the funeral, right, Jared?"

"Uh . . ."

"Oh, it's no problem." Titus was enjoying himself now—and the man's obvious discomfort. "You're a guest of the Casperteins."

Rashid was cornered, and not only against the cupboard and fridge. His face contorted through several expressions until he attempted a smile, but it came out as a pale grimace.

"Thank you, old friend. I am . . . grateful."

CHAPTER EIGHTEEN

Siberian Arctic

Rudy backtracked to the east along the frozen coast to where he'd emerged from the water half-frozen. Yes, there was his harpoon. Picking it up, he checked its antler edge. Still sharp. Then he lifted his head and searched for the polar bear umiak that had brought him across hundreds of ocean miles. But the little ark had washed out to sea. A small sadness touched Rudy's heart. The sea had claimed so much recently. He prayed that God would give him a few triumphs for a change.

Gazing south, he studied the Siberian tundra. He hadn't seen Kobuk since the previous day, after he'd burned the shack for warmth. Kobuk was gone, but where would a giant St. Bernard go? Depending on where they were on the coast, Rudy knew there were Chukchi Indian tribes who raised reindeer along the coastline, but he'd seen no sign of anyone outside the abandoned hunting shack. He hoped Kobuk hadn't come upon the Arctic peoples who might capture her as a stray. They wouldn't eat her, but they'd surely use her for labor.

The timber wolves that Kobuk had killed the previous morning had been torn into by other wolves, the flesh entirely consumed, and their large paw prints then tracked east. The stain on the frozen ground reminded Rudy of the continued danger. He gripped his harpoon tightly and started back to the west, his eyes searching for game. Once he found food, he would head south. There would be more game along the Arctic coast than south in the heart of Siberia, but he would have a better chance at running into a settlement to the south.

A big part of him mourned the absence of Kobuk. At the same time, he knew Kobuk needed her freedom. She had reason to leave. When she was ready, when she'd perhaps eaten, she could find him easier than he could find her.

The weather had lifted. It was late July. In that region, it would be fall in a few weeks, and darkness would consume the land. But for now, it was nearly fifty degrees, and it felt good.

Rudy wasn't unrealistic about being rescued or reaching humanity any time soon. He was possibly hundreds of miles from civilization or safety. The weather could turn and he could be dead in hours. And the wolves—there was always the possibility of more wolves showing up.

He was in God's hands.

Washington, D.C.

Oleg leaned against the wall in the office waiting room. Seated next to him was Corban Dowler, the aging man's forearm crutches lying across his knees. There were few people in the world who actually impressed Oleg, and Corban was one of them. Corban glanced at him, and Oleg realized he'd been staring at the veteran agent.

"Maybe I should've worn a suit, too." Oleg tried to flatten the wrinkled front of his button-up shirt. "People are always whispering how I look like a Russian slob."

"You're fine, Oleg." Corban smiled warmly. "Your reputation precedes you. You could've worn shorts, and people would still nod with respect. People who know about you, anyway."

"Titus should be here. This is more about him than me."

"He'll come when the funeral is over." Corban fit his arms into his crutches as a tall door opened to the main office. "This is us."

An administrative assistant stepped forward and folded her hands.

"Gentlemen, Deputy Secretary Gaultridge will see you now."

Oleg didn't ask Corban if he needed help to his feet. He just grabbed the older man's left arm in a bracing grip and yanked him upright. It wasn't a matter of thinking less of his boss, but honoring him enough to not let anyone see him struggle on his own.

Deputy Secretary of State Emily Gaultridge was a tall redhead with shoulder-length hair. Her teeth shined from over-bleaching when she smiled and shook Corban's hand, then Oleg's. Oleg definitely felt underdressed now, especially in the lush office with oil paintings on the wall and photos of international heads of state on the broad desk. This was no junior office assistant, he realized. Maybe he and Titus had been in the Middle East too long. No, he decided. He'd been a slob even working for Interpol. It was hard to care about his wardrobe when he didn't care for the people who expected him to dress differently. Mentally, he considered praying about this attitude later.

The two seated themselves in front of the desk, Gaultridge in her great chair, which seemed like a throne in front of a window that faced a courtyard garden.

"This will be a brief meeting," she stated, addressing Corban with an emotionless stare. "It's a preparatory appointment for the meeting tomorrow morning. You have an appointment with Secretary of State Baxter at nine o'clock."

"That's short notice." Corban frowned. Oleg guessed he was thinking about how he wished Chloe Azamveth were handling the bureaucratic issues for COIL. "Why the urgency?"

"As stated in my email, the president is no longer able to give COIL free reign as it once enjoyed. The world has changed since you founded COIL, Mr. Dowler. The US has new enemies and new allies."

"By allies, I assume you're speaking of Azerbaijan?" It was Corban's turn to sound cold and disconnected. "They've become a Muslim fundamentalist state, intent on the destruction of Israel and America. Their hostility toward Christians is known around the world."

"Relations are fragile all over. This doesn't need to become an international crisis for COIL or America. A young man is dead. We are determining the validity of Azerbaijan's request to extradite Wynter Caspertein to face murder charges."

"She's a US citizen, Deputy Secretary." Corban was composed, but clearly frustrated. "Even a cursory examination of the body of Gamal al-Hakim would show how he died. Have you asked for a coroner's report?"

"Of course not. That would be paramount to calling them liars as to how the youth died."

"Isn't that the point?" Corban smiled. "We know they're lying."

"Based on the word of Wynter Caspertein?"

"No, based first on a Christian's word, on the word of a world-respected archaeologist. It seems your objectivity is being clouded, young lady, by your ambition for a working relationship with Azerbaijan."

"I beg your pardon!"

"My sources say this regards the pipeline combined with the country's western railway." Corban cocked his head. "You forget my credentials, young lady. If lucrative deals are more important than just dealings and a woman's life, then say so. You're willing to have Wynter Caspertein executed to save a diplomatic agreement over oil and rail access. What will it be next time Azerbaijan makes demands?"

"Perhaps you forget *my* credentials, Mr. Dowler!" She was ruffled, and Oleg didn't blame her. Corban had addressed her as a young lady twice! "Clearly, you haven't balanced two countries toward peaceful relations. We both know this is about much more than just an archaeologist. This also involves that archaeologist's brother, an internationally wanted criminal for nearly twenty years."

Corban nodded at Oleg.

"Until a year ago, Deputy Secretary," Oleg said, "I worked as a senior Interpol agent in pursuit of Titus Caspertein. Not only the US, but also the World Court, have dismissed all charges against Titus due to reparations which continue to this day—and his ongoing involvement in police actions worldwide."

"We're aware of Mr. Caspertein's change of heart. But some of his crimes have no statute of limitations. For instance, smuggling nuclear devices to known terrorist groups for the purpose of sale. There are several murders from over a decade ago—all with Mr. Caspertein's name on them."

"Again," Corban said, "the courts have ruled on those charges."

"The president wants to revisit the subject."

"I see." Corban lifted his head. "Perhaps the president could use a reminder as to why Titus Caspertein was originally exiled from the US. It was detrimental to the safety of the US and its allies to take him down. His arrest would've upset a balance of power that would've impacted whole nations. After all, we're not talking about a mere art thief, but an arms dealer, as you yourself have said, who trafficked in the highest quality of merchandise."

"But you said he's not that man anymore."

"As influential as he was as a crook, I assure you he's much more influential as a man of God, as a servant of Jesus Christ, and as a partner of COIL. The US doesn't want to go head-to-head with the Casperteins."

"Perhaps you've explained the position yourself, Mr. Dowler." Gaultridge rose to her feet. "The president won't be bullied by powerful rogue organizations on matters of international importance. Tomorrow, you may meet with Secretary Baxter. I assure you: he won't be as patient as I've been today. Consider your words carefully."

Oleg moved to the door while Corban exchanged pleasantries and a handshake. As they passed through the waiting room, Oleg glanced at Corban.

"These people really want to take on COIL? Is that wise?"

"It won't be the first time an administration has made a fool of itself. But we both know this is a spiritual battle at its very root. COIL is under attack." They reached the hallway and Corban paused to touch his forehead with a handkerchief. "As easily as I could once manipulate the gears of governments, Titus has twice the resources and imagination in a broader network that spans the globe and a dozen markets."

"What are you saying?"

"The president could be receiving bad advice from his advisors—people like Ms. Gaultridge. They think they can take COIL down a notch, but COIL is comprised of individuals who serve God, with His purposes in the forefront of our minds. COIL can be dismantled. I can be crippled. Titus could be arrested. But God Almighty? Last time I read my Bible, He won't be moved."

"Well, I'm not moving, either. And as long as I'm alive, I'm standing with you and Titus."

They moved down the hallway again.

"That's the point, Oleg. COIL's success to them is measured by worldly means, like pieces on a chess board. But God plays with the kingdoms of the world on a multi-dimensional level, and He's playing all sides, for the good of His own people. We all need to remain immoveable. As long as we stand with God, we will fill whatever capacity He desires, not what anyone else decides."

"How do you think Titus will take this? I mean, this woman's talking about turning Wynter over to Azerbaijan and taking him into custody."

"I highly doubt this is Titus' first time under pressure. After all, he's known as the Serval by a billion people, isn't he? Why is that?"

"Because he's untamed." Oleg chuckled. "I see what you mean. Every time an untamed man of faith is backed by God's power in the Bible, the earth shakes."

"And giants fall."

"Seas roll back."

"Stones roll away."

"With that in mind," Oleg said, "I wouldn't want to be in their shoes."

"I think I know just the man who can better advise the president." Corban winked. "But first, let's call Titus."

Siberian Arctic

Rudy used his harpoon to carve a hole out of the ground for himself. He curled up in the fetal position with a piece of plywood salvaged from the shack leaning against his back to block the cold wind. It was a harsh place to sleep, but his options were limited. Restlessly, he slept, but somewhere deep in a dream, the wolves prowled closer.

There were seven wolves in his dream. They were larger than the starving timber wolves from down the coast. It was warmer now, and these had feasted on ermines and lemmings for the last day. Thus, they were patient about their next kill. They sniffed Rudy's camp with caution, but there seemed no danger.

One daring wolf stuck its muzzle next to the plywood and against Rudy's neck. Another nipped at his booted foot. Rudy kicked at the creature, then woke suddenly to find it wasn't a dream! He erupted from his hole in the ground, knocking the board several feet away.

Withdrawing a few yards, the wolves circled. Rudy counted them. So, he hadn't been dreaming. Seven. He spotted the wolf pack leader with a sliced ear, determining to keep his eye on that savage.

Rudy picked up the plywood board in one hand and held his harpoon in the other. The board was four-by-six feet with weathered cracks and splinters running its length. It wouldn't withstand much abuse.

But before the wolves attacked, they apparently wanted to study him more, to circle and test him, find his weakness. Their hesitation allowed Rudy to move casually to the frozen bank of the sea. With his back to the icy water and holding the plywood as a shield, his defenses made a triangle.

The wolves moved in. They snapped at his knees with their ears back and hair standing on end. He let them close in as he held his harpoon high like a lance ready to thrust downward. Then, they did the unexpected. They attacked in pairs. Two at a time, they lunged at his legs, slashing with fangs two inches long. He stabbed at them but they were quick. The first two retreated as two others attacked, side by side. One leapt for Rudy's chest as the other bit at his boots. Rudy shifted the board and stabbed the leaping wolf in the shoulder. He ripped the harpoon out as the wolves retreated, regrouped, and studied him again.

Rudy looked at his harpoon tip. The sharp deer antler had gray hair on it. He'd gotten one of them. Before they killed him, he hoped to get a few more. It was all he could do without Kobuk.

Arkansas

Rashid gripped and regripped his knife handle. Lying on the twin-sized bed, he held the blade at his side, listening to Titus Caspertein breathe from where he slept on the floor below him. In two bounds across the room, Rashid guessed he could kill the greatest smuggler in the world—the only real competitor Rashid had ever considered an equal.

But he didn't attack. Was it curiosity? Was it respect? Maybe it was fear.

The Caspertein house was silent. The gathering from that afternoon had dispersed near midnight. Those who lived locally had departed, and those who had arrived from afar were offered a bed, as Rashid had been. No sleeping in his rental car while on surveillance, as he'd expected.

He wondered where Wynter slept. Titus hadn't left his side all evening, so he hadn't explored the house or even spoken to Wynter as he'd intended. How close he'd been to kidnapping and killing her! And now—*welcomed?* It made no sense! The Titus he knew would've taken him into the woods and shot him. That was the Serval, not this man sleeping below him on the floor.

Rashid remembered the way Titus had even put his arm around him that evening, when all the men had gathered to pray, the local assembly's elders calling on God in turn. Had Titus welcomed him like family? It seemed so. Maybe that was why Rashid was struggling with visualizing Wynter's death and Titus' demise. He'd never been part of a family. Yet, here he was with the Casperteins.

"I'm a friend of Titus Caspertein," Rashid mouthed silently, liking the way it warmed his heart. "Titus Caspertein is my friend."

Perhaps what shocked Rashid the most was that he knew he didn't deserve an ounce of kindness. Titus knew exactly who Rashid was, too! And still, Titus had handed him a corncob that evening, and Rashid had held it as his enemy salted it for him. All while they listened to neighbors share tales of Rudy's great blunders and achievements. Even Arlin Skokes, a man he'd deceived on the phone, had given him the last of the ice tea, rather than take it himself.

Rashid drifted to sleep, wondering what was happening to him. Though he'd spent a life in total control of his environment, he was now out of control, but content about it. Maybe this was Titus' secret to his power. He welcomed people into a friendship, then he owned them as part of his network. But no, the Serval wasn't manipulating him. He was genuinely . . . *friendly!*

A presence touched Rashid's shoulder. Death seemed imminent. He lifted and thrust his knife, twisting it as he stabbed at a figure above him. The blade sunk into flesh and tendons, and he felt hot blood pour across his hand, but an instant later, he was pinned down, a hand over his mouth. He couldn't move!

"Hold still!" a warm breath whispered in his ear. "Relax. I'm leaving for Washington right now. You're coming with me. Can you get ready without waking the house? We'll take your car to the airport."

Rashid nodded his head, his mouth still covered by Titus' hand.

"Okay. Let go of your knife."

Releasing his blade handle, Rashid then watched in the moonlight from the window as Titus held up his left hand, the steel having passed clean through the palm. Sitting up, Rashid expected severe reprisal. He'd just stabbed his new friend!

Instead, Titus gasped as he tugged the dagger straight out of his hand, then dropped the knife onto the bed. Rashid wiped the blade on the blanket and pulled on his clothes. Titus left the room, then returned with his hand wrapped by the time Rashid was ready, his backpack of belongings over his shoulder.

Together, they crept through the house, past a sleeping duo on the hide-a-bed in the living room, to arrive outside.

"My boss wants me in Washington for a meeting." Titus opened the passenger door and tossed in a bag of his own. "You don't mind being my traveling partner for a while, do you?"

"Not ten minutes ago, I stabbed you!" Rashid shook his head, conflicted between anger and attachment to this strange man.

"Sure, but you'd take it back if you could, right?"

"Yes. But I held the knife by my side. I drew your blood. You have no reason to—" Rashid took a deep breath. "At any time last evening, you could've attacked me. You know who I am. Why are you playing with me?"

"I'm not playing with you, Rashid. This is my life, as ridiculous as it may be. The man we're going to meet gave me the opportunity to choose peace instead of wrath. Do you want the same opportunity?"

"I am Rashid al-Sabur of Cyprus. I don't know what peace is."

"Get in the car. I'll tell you about the Man who shed blood for both of us, so we could all have peace, if we believe it was actually for us."

CHAPTER NINETEEN

Siberian Arctic

Since ancient times, the Arctic served as a dramatic source of food. Rudy was certain he would become the main course if he didn't think of something quick. One wolf lay dead at his feet. Another injured wolf had limped away—but not too far so it could partake of the coming feast. The other five wolves attacked in rotation. Such a strategy never gave Rudy rest. They were wearing him down as they rested in relay.

Rudy's harpoon arm had dropped to his waist over the past hour, but he still remained on guard. The plywood board still acted as a shield, and he moved it to and fro, depending on the angle of each wolf attack. But tiny splinters dug into his hand, lengthy slivers he couldn't take time to remove.

Finally, for the first time, the wolves withdrew together, though only a few yards. Rudy stretched and flexed his shield arm. He better understood the fitness demanded of the Romans and other warring soldiers. And his plywood shield was light in comparison to theirs.

He checked the sun. It was only mid-afternoon.

"Lord," he prayed, "You kept me alive this long, against all odds . . ."

The wolves sat or lay down to watch him. Their eyes never left their prey. They were patient. Some of them took turns to pad down the shore twenty yards to gnaw at the frozen chunks of fresh water.

Ah, the water. Rudy backed up a little farther. Thus far, the shore and the water's edge at his heels had been a defense. But it was just a matter of time before the wolves realized how shallow the ocean was near the shore. When they did notice, they would attack on all sides. He would be finished.

What he lacked most of all, he decided, were weapons. His three-foot-long harpoon had proven its deadliness, but the wolves were accustomed to his thrusts. He needed to change his strategy before they changed their tactics.

Rudy looked at his plywood shield, then shook it, rattling loose sections six feet long along the grain of the wood. It wouldn't last much longer, but those loose sections could be used, maybe. He eyed the wolves. They were beginning to gather for possibly their final assault. It could be his end.

Quickly, he tucked his harpoon into his belt. The wolves perked their ears curiously. Using his free hand, Rudy tore the loose and splintered sections off the plywood. He was left with a couple six foot long shafts, roughly pointed on one end. When he balanced one in his hand, he guessed it might work as a spear.

Dropping the first couple of lengths on the ground, he tore more lengths off the shield, shrinking the shield, but increasing his arsenal. If his plan didn't work, he was through. This was the wolves' last assault; it was his final stand.

When they finally charged him, he had nine spear lengths ready. He turned his diminished shield sideways so it was six feet tall, though only eighteen inches wide. The wolves didn't know anything was different until the first wolf missed a step and fell dead. Two wolves investigated their leader. A six-foot wooden shaft was sunk into its chest.

The other wolves attacked, and Rudy threw another spear and grazed a wolf. It yelped and danced away. He kicked the other wolf with his boot as he reached for another spear on the ground.

"Come on!" he screamed.

They paced in front of him, some of them wounded, but still determined.

Next, they attacked his shield. Two of them wrestled it out of his hand and dragged it away from the shore. Rudy dropped to the ground and snatched up the rest of his spears. Five remained.

He hurled one that ripped a wolf's stomach from rib to hip. The other three pressed him in formation and Rudy backed into the cold water, holding one spear high overhead. They sensed the object was dangerous, but when he threw it, they were too close to react in time. He put his muscle behind each throw. Years of hardship. Months of rugged Alaskan survival. Weeks of endurance in the Arctic. Days of discipline on an iceberg. Hours of paddling a handmade umiak made from a polar bear corpse. The wolves didn't stand a chance!

Arkansas

The overcast weather wasn't helping Wynter's attitude as she sat in the folding chair at the funeral. Like statues around her, people clothed in black stood vigil as a young woman with tears read a poem in honor of Rudolph Caspertein.

Four chairs sat empty next to Wynter, one of which should've been occupied by Titus, but he'd disappeared sometime before sunrise. Sure, he'd left them a note saying his boss had recalled him for something—but *this was Rudy's funeral!*

The other two chairs represented their mother and father, Richard and Lucy Caspertein. The first had passed of a heart attack, and the other from cancer. They lay a few feet from Rudy's empty casket.

The young woman finished her poem and one of the local assembly elders stepped to the head of the casket. Wynter recognized him from her years in the Yellville youth group, but she couldn't remember his name.

"Jesus Christ swallowed up death in victory," the elder said slowly, his voice carrying as the patter of rain began. "And yet we here are mourning a child of God passing to the other side. Rudy was one of God's own, and his involvement in the life of those around him proved he was a follower of our humble Servant. The Apostle Paul reminds us to rejoice rather than weep, because we will soon see Rudy again, as sure as we will all see our risen Lord . . ."

Arlin held an umbrella over Wynter. Marilyn ignored the symbolism of the empty chairs and sat down to hold Wynter's hand. Wynter tried to focus on the preacher's words, but her anger at Titus kept rising up. *How could he abandon her like this?* Though she'd spent much of the evening with Marilyn and a few other women from the community, she'd noticed Titus with a tall Eastern-looking man. He had a familiar face, and when Wynter had noticed his eyes on her before the late-night supper, he'd looked away. His face had betrayed something more than concern for her loss. Yes, he was someone she sensed she should know. But now, he was gone with Titus, and not even Annette knew their whereabouts, but she hadn't seemed too bothered. In his defense, she'd assured Wynter if Titus wasn't there, he'd left for a very good reason, maybe even a life or death reason. But Wynter wasn't buying it. She chalked it up to more of her brother's antics. Maybe he wasn't as reformed as she'd given him credit for.

Siberian Arctic

Like a mighty soldier of the north, Rudy knelt on one knee to rest. He'd won the battle. His foes lay dead around him, slayed by his medieval weapons. The five-hour standoff had tired him, and he thought he'd succeeded unscathed until he noticed a gash on the outside of his right knee. Initially, he believed the wound was self-inflicted. He'd been a wild man with the harpoon and plywood spears. But on closer examination, he pulled an incisor out of the clotting gash. A fang nearly two inches long had been ripped from a wolf's diseased gums. The tooth itself looked rotten, much like the meat it had probably torn into over the years.

Rudy's feet were already wet, so he waded into the ocean and scrubbed at the wound.

Rolling up his pant leg, he discovered the gash was as long as the tooth and almost to the bone. He ignored the pain and pressed deep as he cleansed it.

He looked around the Siberian tundra. What he really needed to do was sear the wound with fire to avoid infection. But there were no trees for fuel as far as the eye could see to the south. The last of his wood had been burned in the hunting shack.

But no, he still had the plywood shield and spears. Limping back to shore, his knee grew stiff. With effort, he collected the spears and what was left of the flimsy shield. It wasn't much, and he wasn't an expert on wolf bites, but he was fairly certain he was on the right track. The wound needed to be closed.

While some boys learned it in Boy Scouts, Rudy and Titus had been taught how to start a fire with sticks by their father in the Ozarks of north-central Arkansas. Fire was essential for survival in the great outdoors. And starting a fire with only sticks had also been essential for the two boys before Richard Caspertein had allowed them to hike alone into the mountains, valleys, and dense forests of their great Natural State.

Rudy knelt to the earth with his back to the western wind. He broke one spear in half, and half again, then split the shield into smaller pieces. With his harpoon tip, he peeled out a deep grain of a plywood shaft. This rut would work as a guiding groove. He held the rutted wood at an angle toward his fuel as he began to smoothly slide another spear point up and down the rut. The key was to produce heat from the friction.

After five minutes, he stopped. The plywood wasn't getting hot enough. He prayed for help. Everything was simpler when he was eight years old, trying desperately to prove to his father he could light a fire faster than his scrawny brother, Titus. But now, the Arctic wind blew at Rudy's back. The frustration of the ongoing struggles to survive plagued him. And Kobuk had left him.

Again, he bent his back into the pressure on the plywood, except this time he used the blunt end of his harpoon shaft. It was hickory, and would hold heat longer until a spark formed.

It worked. The first few sparks missed their mark, but finally, one caught on the plywood and bore a hole. Rudy cupped his hands and blew gently. He fed slivers of wood into the flame until it became a small blaze. Quickly, he used the other wood to shelter the small blaze from the wind.

With his harpoon, Rudy hastily cut open a wolf. He wished he would've done the butchering before his fire was already burning, but he was fast about tearing a shoulder flank off the brute. Already, he could taste the flavor of cooked meat, which would be a rarity after all the raw meat he'd been eating.

He cooked it low over the fire on a plywood spear. Twice, the lean meat fell into the fire and he plucked it out with quick fingers. When the meat was blackened and his fire was burning well, he cut off more meat, another shoulder, and cooked it in its own juices. No more raw meat, if he could help it!

When his fire was low and his fuel was nearly spent, Rudy selected a red-hot coal from the fire. He rolled up his pant leg and mentally cheered his fear into bravery. With two plywood sticks, like chopsticks, he picked up the coal. Reminding himself that his life depended on his next act, he exhaled all the air in his lungs so his scream didn't disrupt his doctoring.

He pressed the coal into his wound. His leg went into spasms. His mouth opened in a silent scream. Biting down on his harpoon shaft, he rolled the coal lengthwise down the gash, pressing hard to ensure a perfect cauterization.

In agony, he dropped the coal and his harpoon. He ripped off his bandana-blindfold he'd used against snow blindness and tied it in a hurry around his knee, with the knot over the wound and under his pant leg.

He took a breath of air and relaxed. Mission accomplished. Then he passed out next to the coals of his dwindling fire.

Washington, D.C.

Titus gave Corban a reassuring nod as they waited in the otherwise empty press room of the White House. Rashid al-Sabur stood against the wall nearby, seeming a little cagey inside the secure wing. During the plane ride overnight, Titus could see Rashid glancing at Titus' hand more than once. It was swollen and it burned as if steel were still twisting inside his wound, but Titus was praying the killer learned from the mercy he was being shown.

"You look a little tense," Titus said to Corban. "It ain't easy putting everything on the line, huh?"

"And you're not tense?" Corban chuckled. "Of course, you're not. You're in your element, aren't you? The more tense, the better. I haven't forgotten how we met in Gaza. It was like a playground to you."

"God allows a little pressure to teach us who we really are. It tones us for Him. You taught me that."

Titus could've faked anxiety, but he didn't bother. He really was enjoying himself. For the first time in years, his life was transparent. For a solid year, he'd placed his life on the line for God's people. His degree of confidence in his Lord was immeasurable, so he welcomed what fierceness the kingdoms and rulers of this world threw at him. God would fight his battles.

The white door near the podium and presidential seal opened. Two Secret Service agents checked the room a few seconds before Secretary of State Barry Baxter walked briskly inside. He was a thin man with small eyes in a deeply serious face. Corban and Titus rose to their feet, and the powerful man first shook Corban's hand and then Titus'.

The Secret Service agents took their positions, one behind the Secretary, the second across the room from Rashid. Even Titus admitted the man from Cyprus looked suspicious. He'd only been allowed entry on the word of Corban that he was part of the COIL delegation, and Corban knew only from Titus that Rashid was a Nathanael situation. Nathanael was a code name COIL operatives used after Christ's disciple Nathanael, who had to see for himself the Christ before he confessed his faith. Since Titus knew some of Corban's own Nathanael subjects, like Luigi Putelli, he knew why Corban had asked no questions about Rashid, and simply included him in their delegation.

Once seated, Secretary Baxter crossed his legs and analyzed Corban, then Titus.

"I may be one of the most powerful men in the world right now," Baxter said, "but seeing you two together makes my knees weak."

Titus resisted the urge to smile. So, the Secretary did have some idea as to the strings COIL could pull, under threat, to protect itself for God's work. They'd even arranged for Oleg to remain in hiding until their meeting was over, in case the meeting was an ambush.

"But that won't stop me from arresting you, Titus, or your sister."

Titus bit his tongue, considering his words. Wynter had barely escaped with her life, then ran across all of Asia Minor from *jihadis*. Now, she was grieving Rudy's death. Did she have any idea the risks he was going through to secure her safety? Hopefully, she understood why he wasn't at the funeral. According to Baxter, her very life was in the balance.

"If I've broken some law or policy," Titus said calmly, "I'll gladly submit to whatever justice you deem appropriate."

"That won't be necessary. Yet. The president isn't so sure about you guys, but I've vouched for you. You have one week to resolve this Azerbaijani mess, and then we extradite your sister, Titus. The president's hands are tied. Relations with Azerbaijan cannot be damaged at this important juncture. If either of you interfere with said extradition, you will be arrested—or hunted down until you're caught, along with all who aid you."

Titus had a choice word for the man's threat, but Corban raised his hand.

"But we have one week to first resolve the murder charges in Azerbaijan?"

"Yes. One week. That's all the president will allow. And that's all I can stall with the Azerbaijani government." The man stood. "All right, gentlemen? I have to get to a briefing. It's been a pleasure."

He shook their hands and left the room, his security detail following him out.

"I'm not sending Wynter to her death," Titus said. "She won't get a trial in Azerbaijan. How can the US turn its back on us like this? This isn't justice!"

"We have a week." Corban accepted Titus' help to stand. "That's more than enough time to do something. God will lead us, somehow."

"You have a plan?" Titus' temperature cooled, feeling a little foolish that he was now flustered and Corban was the calm one.

"No, I don't have a plan. But I bet Wes Trimble does." Corban took a deep breath. "It's time to start calling on our friends."

Iraq

"One week!" *Imam* Nasser al-Hakim cheered. "Allah be praised! The Great Satan will deliver my son's murderer to us himself!"

"But a whole week?" Serik Tomir slid his hand down his cane. "What are they up to?"

"It's perfect." Nasser walked across the living room of an immaculate marble palace in Tehran, once a seasonal residence of an honored *ayatollah*. He used a water container to spray mist on a cactus plant. "It's all been handled diplomatically by the faithful in Azerbaijan. You can focus on other things now, Serik."

"The Serval doesn't need a week to hide Wynter Caspertein. The man is a ghost himself, and he can whisk her away if we don't act now!"

"Bah! He's just a man. What did your contact in Washington say again?"

"His name is Titus Caspertein, the brother of Gamal's murderer."

"And you trust this infidel spy we have? This woman?"

"Emily Gaultridge. She came to us." He shrugged. "She's the Deputy Secretary to the President of the United States. It seems the Serval has made enemies in America, though I would've never guessed he came from America. All of this makes me nervous."

"Your dream again?"

"It's not just a dream, Nasser! The demon is a prophecy. It haunts me. Perhaps you can't understand such a premonition."

"I understand my most fearless friend and beloved soldier of Allah is needlessly afraid. Wynter Caspertein will soon be in my hands. We have won. She can't imagine the misery we'll cause her for Allah. There were others before her, and she won't be the last."

"Of course, but my dream—it's about something still out there."

"A bear-dog-man? Ridiculous!"

Siberian Arctic

Rudy gnawed on a mouthful of wolf meat. It wasn't the best-tasting, but it was cooked, so he was thankful. After catching a few krill in the icy waters, he was enjoying the first feast he'd had in weeks!

Suddenly, he stopped chewing. Far to the south, on the Siberian tundra, a mass moved. Over the next minute, he wondered if his eyes were playing tricks on him, but no. This was no trick of the eyes or a mirage. The thing was growing larger as it approached him directly. And it wasn't Kobuk.

"Oh, Lord, not another one!"

Rudy gathered the cooked wolf meat and tucked his harpoon into his belt as a lumbering brown bear sniffed in his direction. The scent of dead wolves had surely drawn the monstrous sow, Rudy understood, so he didn't believe she had come for him. Giving ground, Rudy walked down the coastline, as the bear advanced, sniffing at the carcasses. She wasn't as large as the polar bear, but she was still over four hundred pounds.

With a frown, Rudy stared south. He didn't like the thought of leaving the coast. It had his only source of fresh water, even if it was in the form of melting ice. But he couldn't stay there indefinitely. Nor could he expect help from humanity. He could very well be on a stretch of coastline where hunters only frequented once a decade or so. Without fuel for fire and shelter through a storm, he would die.

But he could die traveling south as well. It was as dry as a desert, and treeless for hundreds of miles. He wasn't sure when he might come across a road, or how far that road might be away from a settlement.

Holding three sides of a wolf skin together, since he had no way to sew an actual pouch, he placed chunks of ice into the skin. The remainder of the wolf meat hung off his hip. Then, he started walking toward the sun. As he walked, he contemplated how his life had never truly been under his own control. If he'd thought he controlled his own life, it was merely an illusion. His very heartbeat was by the grace of God. The molecules of his body were held together only because God tolerated this fallen world, created through Jesus Christ.

With these considerations, Rudy took one step after another with renewed assurance, believing he wasn't alone, nor forgotten by the God he'd committed his life to as a youth. Though Rudy had had his times of rebellion, God never abandoned his children. And God wouldn't abandon him now, even if he were walking to his death.

CHAPTER TWENTY

Virginia

CIA Agent Wes Trimble, Deputy Director of the Pacific Rim Security Division, wasn't new to taking extra precautions when arranging a rendezvous. Nor was he a stranger to COIL's unique situation in the States, and its impact around the world. Even with only one eye—and a green silk patch covering the other empty socket—he appreciated the confidence the Agency continued to have in him.

Off Washington Boulevard, Wes parked his Trans Am and walked into Arlington National Cemetery. He'd been told to come alone, and to watch for surveillance indicators. Since Wes was familiar with top secret surveillance technology, he knew he wouldn't necessarily notice anyone within sight. Stealth drones and laser listening devices could pick up whispers from miles away. However, he paused at a tombstone along his way to the Rough Riders Memorial on the west side of the cemetery, and studied the edges of the vast lawn for suspicious tails.

If someone were spying on him, that didn't mean he would automatically know who it was. The part of the world for which he was responsible—the Pacific Rim—had its share of problems, attracting an assortment of enemies and allies, any of whom could hire people to watch him, investigate his habits, and catalogue his interests. There were certainly domestic-based monitors on him occasionally, possibly even from his own agency, just keeping tabs. Even COIL hadn't ignored him, if his senses over the past year were accurate. One of COIL's covert agents, Luigi Putelli, had lurked nearby, perhaps even tapping his phones at home on occasion. Before Wes had become aware of Luigi's attachment to Corban Dowler, he'd tried to have the Italian arrested and prosecuted for past crimes. The intelligence world was always watching one another. It wasn't the watching that worried Wes, however. It was the motives of the watchers.

Behind the memorial, he stopped in a shadow. His hands were in his pockets, but he could still draw his Desert Eagle .45 from his hip in an instant.

"Heard you were with COIL now," Wes said to the tall blond man ten yards away. From where Titus stood, the memorial blocked him visually from multiple angles. The two didn't approach one another. "They still mention you on the wire from time to time, telling us to watch out for you."

"And do you?"

"I've known Corban Dowler for a while now." Wes browsed what he could see of the cemetery. A dark-skinned man stood out of earshot, but was visibly watching them. "I know how you guys operate. You maintain a cover of evil to blend in to places no one else can access. Is that guy over there with you?"

"He'll signal us if he notices someone approaching." Titus shifted his feet. "You heard about my sister? We need to set up a coat-of-many-colors for her in Azerbaijan. The boss said you'd be on board."

Wes studied Titus. He didn't look forty years old, but some intel was off by a few years. It was a thrill to know the Serval was now a Christian, asking for help by using coded Bible references.

"That wouldn't be impossible. Maybe we can use the media that's already picked up on her situation. The exposure will help convince her enemies."

"Corban said to follow your instructions, that you're the best."

"Well, she has a million enemies, all of them dedicated *Soldiers of Mahdi*, from what I'm hearing. Is she prepared to pay the price?"

"If she wants to stay alive, she'll have to die. I'll make sure she understands."

"Okay." Wes considered the coat-of-many-colors request. It was just like Corban Dowler to propose the staged death of Wynter Caspertein to throw the Iranian *jihadis* off her trail. "We'll need a killer."

"My guy here will do." Titus nodded at the spook nearby. "He's one of the best and works alone."

"And we'll need a body, someone that looks like Wynter." Wes adjusted his eye patch. "I'll take care of that end. Lastly, we need a location."

"My sister has unfinished business in Azerbaijan. It's not unreasonable for her to return there."

"That's their backyard. Risky for us, but better for the strategy." Wes thought for a moment. It wasn't the first time he'd worked closely with men whom the world had otherwise condemned. He'd found that the truly repentant, saved from the brink of hell, served God more faithfully than lukewarm Christians who'd been professing Christ for twenty years. "Take care of the aftermath. She can't be popping up in Little Rock in two months, alive and well."

"Understood."

"You really live in New York now?"

"Married and resting in God's grace."

"That's good to hear." Wes backed away. "We'll be in touch. Usual channels for contact."

When he reached his car, Wes realized he'd been humming on the walk back. It was good to be working with God's agents again! Not that the coming operation would be any easier because of it . . .

Siberian Arctic

She was a Kodiak bear, a predator. So ancient were her tactics and so vicious her stealth that even the wolf packs in the region sensed her as a threat and steered clear of her. She slept where she wanted, ate what she took from lesser animals, and killed anything that even remotely stood against her. Oftentimes, she killed with no intention to eat, leaving a carcass only to bait other carnivores who followed her trail of carnage.

But more than other bears or wolf packs, she preferred to kill humans. The wounds they had inflicted upon her over her decades were still tender during the fiercest weather changes. Their guns were only dangerous if their dogs sensed her coming. Thus, she had attacked small camps of humans, approaching from downwind, killing anything that didn't flee in her rampage.

As far as she was aware, no lone human had crossed her and lived, not in her territory. And yet, here was a human who had not fled before her. Investigating the dead wolves, she sensed danger in this human, more than any other. He hadn't eaten the wolf carcasses. His scent had the remnants of another bear and a dog as well, and all these elements combined enticed her onto the human's trail. Southward, she tracked his path with ease, aware of the direction of the wind and the closing darkness in which she would kill him.

New York

In COIL's Manhattan headquarters, Titus gathered Rashid al-Sabur, Oleg, Annette, and Wynter in the small conference room adjacent to the bunk room, where layover operatives often slept. He closed the door and waited for the wall panel light to click to green. They were clear of bugs and free to talk openly.

"Oleg, please open us in prayer." Titus stood at the head of the table with a map of Azerbaijan laid out before them. "Let's remain aware of the spiritual forces drawing us away from our primary goal of protecting God's people so the gospel can be spread unhindered. Oleg?"

His Russian partner nodded and prayed briefly, mentioning their gratitude for their trials and their dedication to submit to God's will as they proceeded. When he concluded, Titus studied the faces that waited for him to begin. His wife, Annette, appeared eager for adventure, even after an afternoon spent on a chartered jet, arriving with Wynter from Arkansas. Wynter looked haggard in contrast, perhaps from mourning Rudy's death. Upon her arrival, Annette had whispered to him, "She isn't happy about this."

"She doesn't know enough to be unhappy, yet," Titus had whispered back. "She should wait until she has something to be unhappy about."

Rashid sat at the far end of the table as a quiet student of all that Titus included him in. When the two were alone, Titus had advised Rashid on the COIL machine and its objectives for God, which explained why the Serval hadn't killed the thief and killer from Cyprus.

Next to Rashid, stout Oleg sat picking at his teeth with a toothpick as he leaned back in his chair. His dark hair was disheveled and his polo shirt looked like he'd slept in it for a week, which he might've done. Like Titus, he wore a shoulder holster over his shirt with a COIL nine-millimeter tucked inside.

"We are here to save Wynter's life."

"*My* life?" Wynter asked with a gasp.

"The president has given us six more days to remove Azerbaijan's interest in her, or the US will arrest her and anyone who helps her. Wynter is meant to stand trial in Azerbaijan, after which she'll be executed, probably publically—and a lot more gruesomely than how Ingram Thatcher was executed, is my guess."

Wynter's mouth gaped open, and Annette reached over to grip Wynter's hand.

"We have one shot, as best we can figure, and that's to kill off Wynter ourselves so the world thinks she's dead. There are details to this operation that are miles away from being sorted out, but we're trusting God to provide the necessary components, one of which is a dead body that can double as Wynter."

"Please don't tell me you're going back to Azerbaijan!" Annette said. "Wait. I'm not going, am I?"

"You're too quick for me, Annette. No, hon, we'd like you to stay here at the COIL office and relay communications. We have several parties involved and Corban says other COIL personnel is stretched too thin. Besides, we need Wynter's disappearance to remain very quiet, or word will get out that she's still alive. Can you handle the comm?"

"How come you ask her so nicely?" Oleg elbowed Rashid. Titus hadn't seen Rashid smile or participate in their jesting yet, but that never stopped Oleg. "All we get are orders, huh, Rashid?"

"No, I don't mind." Annette shook her head at Oleg. "Someone needs to stay behind and pray Oleg's mouth doesn't get him in trouble."

"I can't believe what I'm hearing!" Wynter threw up her hands. "We're on the verge— I'm about to be—"

"Take a breath, sis. We have a pretty good plan here, and a few surprises the *Soldiers of Mahdi* don't know about."

"Like what?" Wynter pouted. "Your fancy watch?"

Titus smiled patiently. His sat-watch wasn't a matter he discussed publicly, but he couldn't expect Wynter, in her grief and selfishness, to grasp the sensitivity of such secrets. From Annette's warning, he'd gathered that Wynter had thought he'd skipped out on the funeral for his own reasons.

"Wynter, you need to tell us all what you left in Azerbaijan, because we need an excuse to go back there—enough of a reason that *Imam* Nasser al-Hakim's people will believe we'd risk everything for whatever it is."

"I'm not telling you guys!" She laughed. "You've got to be kidding. That's my life's work!"

"If you've been paying attention, then you'd know your life is over as you know it. We've got one shot to keep you alive. We have COIL and CIA resources involved, not to mention whatever Rashid can throw in."

"I'll contribute all I have." He nodded curtly.

"Wait. I thought his name was Jared." Annette glanced from Titus to Oleg. "And wasn't he wearing a mustache at the house? Who is he exactly?"

"I came to kill Wynter." Rashid's face was as stone as the others waited for him to continue. "Now, it's my honor to keep you alive, Miss Caspertein. I'd like to take this opportunity to tell you I'm sorry for chasing you in Istanbul."

"That was you on the ferry!" Wynter pointed at him. "I knew it! You wanted to know where the eight figures were. It was you who listened to the phone in Armenia!"

"Wynter, he said he was sorry." Titus raised his eyebrows. "What else do you want from the guy?"

"How are you so nonchalant about this?" She scowled at Titus. "There's no way I'm telling you guys what I left back there! It could be the only thing keeping me alive!"

She pushed back her chair and marched out of the room. Titus started after her, but Annette caught at his arm outside the room where they were alone.

"Why are you being so tough on her?" Annette crossed her arms. "She's your sister, a scientist, and she's scared. She's not one of your hardened operative buddies."

"Well, she thinks she's better than us. You can hear it in her voice. I'm just trying to crack her a little."

"So you're treating her like an enemy?" Annette lowered her voice. "This is your sister. You don't have to break her. She's already broken. That's what you really hear in her voice. Just be her brother. Do I need to remind you that you don't know how much longer you'll be around to be her brother?"

Titus growled and squeezed the bridge of his nose. But that only made him flinch at the use of his wrapped hand.

"So, I'm a jerk?"

"A little bit of an abrupt one." She kissed him. "You can't do this without her, right?"

"She's the centerpiece."

"Then help her understand you're doing this for her, not to spite her."

Wynter found herself in an empty, darkened office suite—empty of people but not empty of computer terminals and racks of secure servers with hard-wired connections. She knew enough about tech in the office to know a high-security environment when she saw it, rather than a Wi-Fi system that could potentially be intercepted. Next door, through a glass partition, was another similar suite, filled with actual operators at their stations.

She heard Titus enter the room behind her. Instead of being bothered as expected, she found herself comforted.

"My big brother is always coming after me." She faced him, feeling the fight leave her. "So what's this room for?"

"Case workers." He indicated the adjacent suite. "Just the night crew is needed right now. They monitor COIL field agents where it's still daytime. In the morning, both offices will be filled and bustling."

"Which one's your case worker?"

"He's off-site. Corban has Oleg and me running special operations, a little more technical than those who need a home base to report their needs to."

"That's my brother." She heard her voice break and felt her eyes water before she realized she was crying. "You can never do anything ordinary. Only spectacular."

"Well, that goes for my mistakes, too, unfortunately." He sat on the edge of a desk. "My mistakes are spectacular and devastating."

"Maybe." She wiped at her eyes. "Maybe we just read you wrong. I was thinking you were being self-absorbed again, missing Rudy's funeral. But you were out here, trying to clean up my mess."

"Your mess, but not your fault."

Wynter closed her eyes, wishing all the pain and fear could be erased. As a Christian, she knew faith was always the answer to a crisis, but how was trusting God supposed to make everything go away?

"So, my life will never be the same again. I get that. But you can keep me alive? Like when we were in Syria?"

"This is a lot riskier than Syria, I think."

"This Rashid guy was really sent to kill me in Istanbul. How am I supposed to believe he's on our side now?"

"First of all, no one sent him. He was acting on his own. He always works for himself. As for why he's joined us, all I can tell you is what I know, then let you judge for yourself.

"I was casing a shipment of gold bullion out of Turkmenistan about ten years ago. A tough hijack to do alone, so I brought in a small army of mercenaries from all over the map. They were hungry for a half-million each, and I was taking in twenty times that. We were about to jump when I saw Rashid for the first time. He took out five Turkmenistan soldiers before they knew they were under attack. My men and I stood down as we watched from the roof of a warehouse while the shipment we were about to steal was stolen out from under us.

"Singlehandedly, Rashid took apart the soldiers guarding the gold, but he wasn't finished. He still had to access the bullion vault. For the next hour, he convinced one of the soldiers to talk, to open the vault. My men and I couldn't move, or we'd be detected, so we were forced to listen to this. . . animal work on his victim."

"Why didn't you interfere?"

"Honestly? I was a little afraid of what Rashid would do to the men I had. I'd just seen him attack a whole company of guards. That's when I realized wherever I went, there was a killer out there, someone who was willing to commit the unthinkable to win his trophy, to get his treasure. We crossed paths a few times on several different continents since then, but I avoided him every time I knew he was around."

"And this is Rashid, this guy? Why would you want him anywhere near us?"

"That's just the thing. He's not the same man. He could've done us a lot of damage by now. He's had plenty of opportunity, but he hasn't. I've even been sharing the gospel with him."

"Maybe he's just waiting to find out where my treasure is."

"Maybe. So tell him. There'd be no reason for him to stick around us if that's what he's really after. But I think Christ has touched him, softened him."

"Through you?"

"Isn't that our job as Christ's ambassadors?"

Wynter couldn't hold back a chuckle.

"It sounds so weird to hear you say stuff like that. Rudy wouldn't believe you caved in to the call of God!" She sighed. "So, before we go back in, how's this all supposed to work?"

"Rashid is a known killer. He'll take the fall for your murder when you, Oleg, and I sneak back into Azerbaijan to recover your treasure. Because it'll be Rashid "The Saber" al-Sabur, the Muslims won't question your death when he says he killed you. He has a frightening reputation. They'll just parade the body we'll provide in front of the cameras. All we have to do is keep you alive in Azerbaijan for all that to happen."

"And the treasure?"

"That's up to you. Is it recoverable?"

"With scuba gear, yeah. But it'll take a plane to get it out of the country."

"Is it that important? You can't claim it as your find, you know. You'll be dead. The world can never know."

"You can turn it over to the museum for me." She grinned. "That way it'll still have the Caspertein name on it. But what'll I do?"

"Become someone new. Anyone you want. I think Annette may have had a long lost sister once. Maybe she makes contact again, becomes part of the family after being distant for so many years."

"You have it all figured out, huh?"

"Just the outline. There are always unknowns in something this dangerous."

"I guess all that's missing is the location of the treasure." She exhaled loudly. "Do I tell you here, or everyone at once?"

"Let's join the others. After all, we can't do any of this without everyone doing their part."

As Janice Dowler rode the elevator deep into the mine shaft in New York's Catskill Mountains, Corban described the two-hundred-year-old history. Knowing how old the shaft was, and that they were a half-mile underground, didn't help settle her nerves.

"I've been in a lot of places with you," she said as the elevator lurched to a stop, "but this place makes me feel the most . . . edgy."

"Edgy?" He moved to the steel blast door and offered his palm to the sensor. "You're safer here than in your garden at home."

The door swung open and Janice gasped at the kudzu vine that crawled across half the floor and filled the room where Marc Densort sat at his computer monitoring station.

"I see why you're talking about gardens!" Janice stepped into the room. She carried a box of supplies and a backpack of gear. "Maybe jungle is a better word."

Janice had met many COIL technicians over the years, but she sensed Marc Densort was the most single-minded. As Corban introduced him, he kept sneaking glances at his flat screens as if twenty seconds of neglect would've crashed the system. The instant after Janice shook the tech's hand, he was back in his seat at his station.

"Forgive him," Corban said. "He's been down here for months without much human contact."

"I heard that." Marc shook a finger at Corban without looking back at him. His Middle Eastern accent was distracting. "I just don't want to miss a moment of this playing out. Titus, Oleg, and Wynter are on their way."

"What about Rashid?" Corban sat down in a chair next to Marc and stowed his crutches against the wall. "Titus said to be praying about the new guy."

"He has the sat-phone Titus gave him, so we can track him."

"Does Rashid know we can see him?"

"Titus thought it best if we're transparent, so, yeah, he knows." Marc shrugged. "The man's a surveillance expert, according to Titus. He probably would've found the bug himself if we hadn't told him, and then he'd be upset."

Janice sniffed at an unwashed bowl in the kitchenette sink and opened a refrigerator that hadn't been cleaned in what looked like months. As her husband and Marc spoke anxiously about the mission to Azerbaijan, Janice half-listened as she got to work. She loved accompanying Corban on trips, but she wasn't one to sit idle. For what could be a five-day monitoring venture, she'd asked Corban if he wanted company. After all, they'd been together the night the Gabriels had been launched to monitor one of COIL's most elite operatives yet—Titus Caspertein. Other COIL technology was already in development as well, and her participation in the covert happenings gave her an added sense of service for their Lord.

Of course, her service wasn't always cleaning dirty dishes and speculating on ways to trim back kudzu vines. Normally, she was at COIL headquarters in Manhattan where she oversaw their medical relief branch. Many of the operatives' wives had participated in overseas missions of their own, even if it was to spend a week administering malaria vaccines in the Congo, or nursing AIDs victims in Uganda.

Corban hadn't always included her. During his CIA years, Janice had wept herself to sleep through many lonely nights. She hadn't even known he was an agent, only that he was gone, traveling, and apart from her.

But now, he excelled in the world's modern-day women's liberation movement. He didn't blur gender lines or fabricate COIL personnel gender equality stats. Rather, by the Word of God, Corban celebrated women's participation, not their competition or exclusion, in as many operations as he had volunteers to send. COIL had women in deep cover venturing where men couldn't go, and men undercover where no female operative could survive. There were husband and wife teams, like Memphis and June, or Nathan and Chen Li. And then there were married women who worked individually, like Chloe Azmaveth. Corban understood the biblical family unit, as it pictured the church, and he insisted that the Body of Christ inside COIL live faithfully and morally to exemplify Christ.

It was all a wonderful dream, Janice considered. Their daughter, Jenna, was now in high school, staying with a friend for the week. Even she, as a teenager, was considering ways to be involved in ministry efforts. COIL had never had its people in more countries, and Janice was able to watch it all over the shoulder of the man whom God had used to pull it all together. With a sense of righteous pride, she recalled what had started Corban down the COIL path in the first place—she'd led him to Christ!

"Janice!" Corban called. "You have to hear this. Titus left his watch-mic on as they're traveling, and Wynter is telling a story to Oleg about Titus. I don't know who's interrupting more—Titus, who's denying he really had a turtle for a best friend as a child, or Oleg, who can't stop laughing. Come listen."

Janice dried her hands and shook her head with a smile. If COIL agents loved anything, it was their incessant teasing. As serious as their jobs were, she didn't blame them for craving the camaraderie and comedic relief. And from what she could already hear over the speaker, the Caspertein brother and sister were getting enough of both.

CHAPTER TWENTY-ONE

Siberia

Kobuk trotted south on the trail of a bear—the same bear that was on the trail of her master. In her jaws, she held the haunch of a reindeer, carried fifty miles to feed her master. With her mouth full, she panted through her nostrils, inhaling the scent of the bear with every breath.

Suddenly, the St. Bernard stopped. An ermine scrambled into its burrow ten feet away. Kobuk glanced south, then again at the ermine hole. Finally, her maternal instinct drove her southward. There would be other ermines to hunt later. The bear trailing Rudy seemed to be a much more dangerous threat.

Germany

Agent Wes Trimble stood in a basement coroner's office in Stuttgart at the US European Command Center. He'd used his official CIA credentials to access the facility as a personal favor for COIL, but not breaching Agency protocol by doing so. Because of Wes's lengthy history of acting in the interests of US safety and justice, the director of the PRS Division gave him uncommon liberty to make his own decisions. Since COIL participated in countless aid operations worldwide, oftentimes represented by US civilians, the CIA had a vested interest in lending COIL operatives certain support from time to time. This was regardless of the opinion of whoever occupied the Oval Office at the moment. Additionally, Wes had begun to make moves to join COIL himself, and to resign from the Agency. Many Christian field agents had gone before him, following Corban Dowler into the lion's den for the sake of Christ.

Facing Wes, the coroner tapped on his tablet with a dirty fingernail.

"Ah, here's one." The small man who wore a waistcoat over a t-shirt walked down a hall of metal doors and stopped at one. "A service woman from Belarus. But her family is claiming her body in two days."

"Too bad." Wes stood back as the man slid out the table with a sheeted corpse on it. Holding up a photo of Wynter Caspertein, Wes compared the faces. "Not even close. The bone structure's all wrong. You have anything closer?"

"I have one more. She came in two nights ago. Unclaimed, but died on the base. Probably an illegal."

"Let me see her."

"You know how much trouble I can get in for losing a body?" The man slid another table out.

"This one's better. The bone structure's closer. Hmm. About the same height. Hair color is close. Can you cut her hair short like this picture?"

"Do I look like a mortician?"

"Fine. Do you have some scissors I can use?"

The man didn't move.

"You spooks have no respect for the dead." The man walked away, shaking his head.

"That's because all of our respect goes toward the living."

Wes studied the dead woman closer. She was younger than Wynter by ten years, but that couldn't matter now. His next hurdle, now that he had a body, was to get it to Azerbaijan. He had contacts in Russia on the Caspian Sea, but he still needed someone daring enough to operate inside Azerbaijan on behalf of the Casperteins.

"Lord, I'm trusting You to provide. Lives are in the balance."

Wes squinted his one eye as he was handed scissors and he began trimming the deceased woman's hair. He thought of Wynter's identifications in his pocket. If he didn't come through all the way, the real Wynter would be exposed and in danger. They had one chance to make her disappear and convince the *Soldiers of Mahdi* that she was dead. Wes felt the pressure. *He couldn't fail COIL!*

Western Asia

"Two days hardly seems like enough time to plan this." Wynter sat in the copilot seat of the Navajo. "We have basically no intelligence for what we're walking into."

"Are you kidding?" Oleg knelt behind the seats in the tight cockpit. "Titus hardly ever has intelligence. You should see him, running into gunfire, explosions on every side, bullets nipping at his heels. Total ignorance. No intelligence whatsoever!"

"No intelligence? Really?" Titus pushed the plane's controls forward into a dive. "You want to badmouth the pilot's intelligence as he's flying the plane?"

"Okay, okay!" Wynter slugged her brother's shoulder. "Quit playing around!"

"Hey, it does take a certain amount of intelligence to crash a plane!"

"Only Titus could so artfully put those two words in the same sentence." Oleg chuckled with Wynter. "Crash and plane."

"Here's a few more words for you two hecklers." Titus switched off the external lights. "Prayer and seatbelt. We're over Armenia right now. The border is sixty seconds ahead. Once we're past the peaks of the Lesser Caucasus Mountains, I'm dropping her into the Kur River."

"You've done this before, right?" Wynter checked her seatbelt.

"Oh, you mean crash a perfectly good airplane into a river in the dark inside the borders of a terribly hostile country?"

"Yeah, that."

"With no landing gear, and with explosives on board?" Oleg strapped himself into the front cabin seat. "Hey, don't forget the explosives, Titus."

"Once again, Oleg, it ain't easy flying this plane with your over-whelming support."

Titus felt the updraft of the mountains, an invisible mass in the void below, but then the plane dipped again, indicating they were over the highest ridges. Rather than use the plane's instruments, he checked his watch and the Gabriels' point of view. He steered east, then banked left, lining up with the river.

"I'll try to put her on the north bank, but if not, grab the gear and swim for it. There's no way to know how swift the current flows here."

"Is it too late to cancel all this, and run for the rest of my life?" Wynter asked.

"Yes, it's too late. Brace yourselves! Oleg, any last comments?" He glanced over his shoulder. "Nothing from you?"

"Quiet. I'm praying you remember your flaps from your elevators."

"Maybe you should be flying, because I thought they were the same thing."

"Please, you two!" Wynter clutched her seatbelt straps. "Titus, just focus!"

Titus checked his altimeter and guessed they were below the nearby forest line. He switched on the landing lights and resisted the urge to pull up the instant he saw water directly below him. The team had ruled out a float plane simply so they could bait their enemies closer in for the ruse. It was a dangerous game—a game that was costing Titus one of his planes.

The belly of the plane skimmed then bounced off the surface of the river.

"Hold on!"

The fuselage caught as the belly suctioned onto the river. Titus growled as he clung to the controls, fighting to steer to the right where the north bank flashed past. Suddenly, they faced a section of rapids and rocks. But they'd lost too much speed to pull out. The starboard wing caught on a boulder, then the nose hooked under the surface.

Suffering a sudden stop, the plane flipped over and landed upside down. Titus lost consciousness for a few seconds, his brain rattled, then he felt the bruises over his collarbone from the seatbelt. Several fuses in the control panel sparked.

"It ain't easy being a crash test dummy." He unclipped his belt and fell to the ceiling. "Everyone okay?"

"Titus, I feel the plane moving!" Oleg yelled. He dropped to the ceiling and sat upright. "We're in the current!"

"I don't think so." Titus moved to Wynter. "There's mud oozing through the windshield. We're on the north bank—at least partially."

"This wasn't your best landing ever, I hope." Wynter moaned and reached for Titus as he unhooked her belt. She fell into his arms. "How are we supposed to hike two days to the reservoir if I'm sore all over?"

"You're a Caspertein." He patted her cheek. "Gear up and get onto the shore. Our timeline starts now."

Azerbaijan

Rashid hung up his sat-phone. Annette Caspertein from COIL headquarters had just called to tell him Titus had landed in south-western Azerbaijan. Perfect timing, too. Though Rashid had never worked with covert operatives—and Christians, no less—he was impressed with their expertise, even through their informality. Of course, he reminded himself, he was working with the Serval.

Outside the airport in Baku, Rashid dialed a memorized number.

"Peace to you," Rashid spoke in Persian. "I am searching for Serik Tomir regarding Wynter Caspertein."

There was a moment of silence.

"Who is this? How did you get this number?"

Rashid laughed, his hand covering the mouth piece. People really had no idea what he was capable of doing. However, it felt oddly satisfying to use his skills for the preservation rather than the destruction of others.

"My name isn't important. What is important is that I'm hunting for Wynter Caspertein, and I've tracked her to Azerbaijan. She's here, but I can't catch her alone."

"You lie. Wynter Caspertein is in America."

"I watched you chase her around Istanbul. You still carry your cane with the hidden blade, I presume?"

"What do you want with her? How can you be certain she's really back in Azerbaijan?"

"She left a treasure behind when she departed in a hurry. That's all I want. The treasure. Then, you can have her, or I can kill her for you. But I need your help to flush her out."

"I want only vengeance! The enemy of my enemy must be my ally."

"Then we have a deal? I'll tell you everything I know."

"Where do you want to meet? I'm in Tehran right now."

"How fast can you get to Azerbaijan? Wynter Caspertein is already here. I'll wait for you at the Ma'a Salama Lodge."

Rashid heard Serik curse as he hung up the phone. The bait had been set.

Azerbaijan had experienced drastic changes in a few short years, all because of fundamental Islam. Bibles were restricted and Christians had been hunted and forced to convert. And now Rashid was working with Christians. He reached for his knife blade for reassurance, but felt nothing under his leather jacket. Then he remembered—he had no weapons. The mission before him was dangerous to approach without arms, though it wasn't the first time he had to rely only on his mind.

But it was the first time he'd worked with Christians to meet a goal. The thought intrigued him, and also confused him. How exactly had Titus manipulated him to this point?

With amusement, Rashid shook his head and rented a car for the four-hour drive to the far end of Mingechaur Reservoir. The Serval hadn't manipulated him. Rashid was simply tired of being alone. And if he could prove himself, he'd never be alone again. The Serval was his friend.

Siberia

Rudy didn't remember falling asleep, but he woke shivering. For an instant, he thought he was still in the umiak, freezing to death. Then he felt the cold, hard earth beneath him. Siberia.

But that wasn't all he sensed. He lunged to his feet, holding his short harpoon like a lance. Somewhere in the darkness, predators were fighting. Their growling and roars terrified him, forcing him to pray to the Creator of such beasts for protection. With no fire and very little starlight on the overcast night, Rudy faced the black expanse and slowly backed away, his heart thumping, his hands shaking.

The previous day, he'd seen no movement on the horizon. And now, when he could see nothing, there were nightmarish creatures within hearing.

Then, there was silence, and he wondered if that was worse! At least with their noisy fighting, he knew where they were.

"Where is the God of David, the shepherd boy?" he whispered as the sound of heavy paws approached. If only he could see, he would have a fighting chance. "Give me courage, Lord . . ."

The shadow of a creature moved toward him. He started to plunge his harpoon, praying he struck true, when the animal gave a familiar whine.

"*Kobuk?* Kobuk!"

He collapsed to his knees and buried his face in her mane. As in the past, she knocked him over and climbed on top of him, covering him with her heavy coat, leaving him gasping and laughing under her weight. Tears ran down his weather-beaten face.

In the morning, he woke to the featureless landscape of perpetually frozen earth. Rudy traced a ghastly odor to the rotting hind leg of some sort of deer that Kobuk had brought him, but he couldn't imagine eating it since he still had a couple days of cooked wolf meat in his skin pouch. He tore the raw meat into bite-size pieces and fed them to Kobuk a scrap at a time. It was better than throwing the leg away, after she'd traveled and apparently fought something for the morsel.

Their march south resumed, now side by side, but only until they approached the trampled ground of a thousand hooves. Rudy studied the tracks that led west as the sun peeked through the gray mass above.

"We may survive this yet, old girl."

Kobuk barked and seemed to rally Rudy's own determination as she trotted in search of the reindeer herd. Rudy picked up his pace, more concerned that he'd lose Kobuk than the tracks.

That afternoon, Rudy's exhaustion was replaced by exhilaration. The herd of over three hundred reindeer gnawed at the tundra moss. They were two hundred yards away. A few of the deer had noticed him, and several aimed their antlers in Kobuk's direction, but Rudy still licked his lips optimistically while Kobuk whined.

"I hear you, girl." He gripped her mane, then shoved her hard toward them. "Get 'em, girl!"

Kobuk lunged to the right as Rudy jogged to the left. He hoped something in Kobuk recalled a time when her ancestors hunted together. As soon as she was on the opposite side of the herd, she charged, and Rudy waited. Some of the reindeer had seen him.

Rudy realized his potentially fatal plan when the reindeer stampeded toward him. Rather than be trampled from Kobuk's too-effective hunting skills, Rudy sprinted out of harm's way as the herd swept by him. Somewhere in its midst, Kobuk barked, having an exhilarating time chasing such majestic creatures, and Rudy ran along the edge of the fleeing herd, gradually falling behind them.

One deer dropped back, limping, and Kobuk trotted up to Rudy, obviously proud at having hamstrung the deer.

"Good girl." Rudy embraced her briefly. Gone were the days when he merely patted his friend's head.

The deer limped after the herd, but Rudy caught it easily. He measured the best approach, gripping his harpoon with confidence, when a gunshot pierced the afternoon and the deer dropped in front of them.

Rudy plunged to the ground and lay falt. Kobuk growled, her fanged muzzle pointing northeast. Slowly, Rudy rose to his feet to see three natives, obviously of the fabled Chukchi tribe, with rifles and five husky-like dogs.

"I thought we were just good hunters, girl." Rudy stowed his harpoon in his belt. "But I think you hamstrung someone's pet."

The men approached directly, their dogs circling Kobuk with reverence, partly because her head was low and her ears were laid back, and partly because she outweighed any two of them together.

Rudy raised his hand in greeting. The three men did likewise, then they stopped a few yards away. They studied his appearance for a moment. Unlike the reindeer ranchers, Rudy wore a beard as thick as wool, and he was filthy, his skin coat stained with blood—his own and that of various animals. His pants were ripped, and at almost seven feet tall, he was reminded that not many men had seen anyone his size.

"Rudy." He touched his chest, then pointed at his companion. "Kobuk."

"Kobuk?" One man asked, and spoke Russian to the others. Maybe it was a familiar word to them since Kobuk was the name of a river in Alaska where many Russians had settled.

"Yes!" Rudy smiled. "Uh, do you have a telephone?"

He made a gesture that they understood instantly, and waved for him to join them. One man produced his cell phone from a deep pocket in insulated trousers. But after a few minutes of the four men huddling over the phone, Rudy realized all the device could do was take pictures and play hip-hop music. Of course, there were no cell towers in the middle of Siberia. Rudy congratulated the owner of the phone for the fine family of sons and daughters in the photos by slapping him on the back and laughing. The terrible offense of hamstringing the herders' reindeer seemed to be forgotten.

Untying his remaining wolf meat, Rudy tossed it to their dogs. They snapped and snarled for a bite, but Kobuk ignored them and fell in beside Rudy. A moment later, the other dogs caught up, but submissively trotted behind their new alpha, Kobuk. They evidently knew their place.

CHAPTER TWENTY-TWO

Azerbaijan

Titus crouched under thick evergreen brush in southwestern Azerbaijan. The dark landscape around them was unnerving. He scrolled through a text on his watch as Wynter and Oleg caught up.

"Annette says Rashid is on track." He eased his pack onto the ground. The early morning was damp and cool. "None of this works without him."

Wynter and Oleg also set their packs under a tree. But this stop wasn't for resting. They'd been walking for only twenty minutes since leaving the plane at the river. Hastily, they reorganized their packs and straps for serious hiking.

"How long until—" Wynter started to say, then a distant explosion reached their ears. "Never mind."

Titus gazed south as an orange glow rose above the tree line.

"It ain't easy blowing up your home." Titus clucked his tongue and shook his head.

"Sure it was." Oleg snapped his fingers. "Ten pounds of Czech TNT will sink any plane. Easy."

Wynter retied her hiking boots then helped Titus into his heavier pack of rebreather equipment for diving the Mingechaur Reservoir. Her own pack contained their lighter gear of food, tarp, and fresh water. Oleg's was the same as Titus' pack with a second rebreather.

"We'll rest every two hours once the sun rises." Titus flinched under the weight of his burden. "At sundown, we'll make camp. But if they start to close in on us, our timetable will move up. Ready?"

"Just keep an eye on that watch." Oleg pointed at Titus' wrist, then selected a sturdy walking stick. "Even if I'm to be taken prisoner, I'd rather know they were coming."

"Well, know it already—they're coming." Titus turned north. "This only works for Wynter if they're really coming."

"I've risked my safety during some excavations," Wynter said as she started after Titus, "but never my life. I still don't know how we'll get that trunk out of the country."

"Wes Trimble will come through." Titus eyed his watch again, hoping for a text from the agent, though it hadn't vibrated. "If all else fails, we'll drop the trunk and head straight into Russia on foot. We'll be all right."

Titus waited for someone else to comment, but no one did. They all knew the risks. And they also knew no one would be safe until they were back in the sky, flying safely away from the region, with Wynter supposedly deceased.

With Wynter's safety in sight, Titus knew he'd have to finally start thinking seriously about returning to the oncologist. If treatment was necessary to enjoy more time with his wife and sister, then so be it. He'd have to face chemotherapy like God had taught him to face other struggles in life as a Christian—sigh prayerfully, then take the next step.

Since they wanted to travel light, fast, and inconspicuous, they'd opted to leave their COIL rifles behind. Titus and Oleg carried only their sidearms in shoulder holsters under their jackets. And the tranq handguns were only useful for close-range contact. If cornered by gunmen with rifles, their options would be limited. They had no backup. Since Christianity was restricted in Azerbaijan, they couldn't safely appeal to the Christian underground without endangering more lives. They were on their own.

Russia

Rudy arrived by truck to the Siberian town of Verkhoyansk, which he'd learned was known for extremely low temperatures and was a center for raising reindeer. He waved his thanks to the driver and Kobuk trotted protectively next to him as he sought an address written on paper by one of the reindeer herders.

On the three-hour truck ride into the town, Rudy had expected to sleep away his exhaustion, but he was too excited to announce his return to life. In most respects, he was in good shape. He was tired and somewhat malnourished, but the herder village had revitalized him as he'd stayed a full day until the mail and grocery truck arrived with supplies. His worst injury from his ordeal was the wolf bite near his knee, but it had closed without infection after cauterizing, though his knee was a little stiff.

Since he didn't know where Wynter was exactly, he decided to call

Arlin Skokes first. The heavy-set jolly man would surely appreciate the news of his survival. After all, he was back from the dead! Rudy couldn't wait to tell his story of God's provision. What a month!

But it wouldn't be an entirely painless return. His multiple brushes with death had caused much reflection. He didn't want to enter eternity with animosity still in his heart toward Titus. After he found Wynter, he would set about locating Titus, if the rogue was still alive. Maybe he was in prison in some distant country. Even better! Rudy could reconcile with his younger brother while he was a captive audience. If an opportunity opened up, he might even help him get released from prison, if the foreign courts approved. He would do anything to win back the brother he'd ignored, and who'd ignored him, since high school.

Finally, Rudy located the house and offered the note to a plump woman in her sixties.

"English? Yes, I speak a little. Come in." She read the note as Rudy left Kobuk outside. "Ah, yes. My brother. He says here you have some adventure. Rudolph from America. I am Galina."

"It's a pleasure, Galina. Yes, I've had a big adventure!" Rudy laughed and shed his tattered coat. He leaned his harpoon against the wall. The woman lived modestly, a photo of her grown children and husband hung on the wall. "Your husband?"

"Long dead. Uh, war. Yes, Afghanistan."

"Oh, I'm sorry."

"I am a nurse at hospital."

"Wonderful." Rudy stood for a moment, anxious to make his phone call, but also content to finally be in the company of someone who spoke English. Conversation with Kobuk had been rather one-sided. "You have a fine home, Galina."

"You stay, or . . . ?"

"The note didn't say? Your brother didn't explain?"

"No. He only say, 'American Rudolph. Great adventure. Speak no Russian.' You want tea?"

"Yes, please. Wait. I really need a phone. I have to tell my friends and family I'm still alive."

"Phone! I thought all Americans have cell phone."

"Not this American, and not where I've been."

She showed him to a landline and went to make tea. Rudy dialed Arlin.

"This is Skokes. What's your business?"

"Hello, Arlin. How're the fish biting?" Rudy couldn't hold back a burst of laughter when there was no response. "Seriously, Arlin, it's me. Hello? You still there?"

"Rudy?"

"Yep. It's a long story, but I'm in Russia right now. God has kept me alive. I can't wait to tell you about it, but right now, I could use a little of that money you've been holding all these years. I could use a plane ticket back to the States, too."

"Rudy! We had your funeral!"

"Really? Oh, this is going to be fun!" Rudy slapped his knee. "Was it a good crowd? Lots of tears?"

"Yellville doubled its population for a few days. Titus was here, too. Oh, boy, do you need to get back here!"

"Titus came home? For my funeral? Wow. I'm shocked."

"And that's another long story. Wait. You're in Russia?"

"That's right. God has a funny way of preserving us sometimes. How's Wynter? Can I talk to her?"

"Listen, Wynter's in hot water, Rudy. I've got to cut this short with you. You need to call Annette, uh, Titus' wife, right now!

"Titus got married? What's going on?"

"Wynter and Titus are in Azerbaijan. It's a big mess. A real emergency. You might be able to help, but I don't know all the details. Call Annette!"

"Okay, okay." He wrote down the number Arlin gave him. "But listen, Arlin, I have no money, and these people in Russia have been helping me and my . . . friend."

"I'll wire some funds to you right away, Rudy. Be sure to give me your info before we hang up. You say you have a friend with you? So, there are other survivors from Barrow?"

"Oh, I didn't mean to mislead you. A Search and Rescue dog named Kobuk is with me. We've been through it all, Arlin."

"Well, don't do anything else until you call Annette."

"Annette, Titus' wife. Got it. Wow. What am I supposed to say to her?"

"Son, you don't need to say anything. Just listen."

Rudy gave his contact info to Arlin, then hung up and accepted tea from Galina.

"They are happy?"

"They are. My friend is wiring money here, okay? You can give some to your brother for his help. He gave me shelter and food."

"It is no bother." She waved at the air.

Rudy prayed he had the words to say to Titus' wife. He dialed her number, considering how God had brought Titus back home by Rudy's supposed death.

"COIL headquarters. This is Cheryl," a woman answered. "How may I direct your call?"

"COIL?" Rudy frowned. "The Christian relief people?"

"That's us. How may I help you, sir?"

"I'm supposed to connect with Annette . . . I guess, Caspertein?"

"Please hold."

"What's Titus up to now?" Rudy mumbled to himself as he waited.

"This is Annette. Hello?"

"Hello. Um, my name is Rudy Caspertein. I guess that makes you my sister-in-law? Arlin Skokes told me to call you right away."

"Seriously? Rudy Caspertein? Rudy Caspertein died in Alaska, like, two weeks ago."

"More like three or four weeks, but yes, this is me. I've been drifting through the Arctic, and now I made land in Russia. You really married my little pest?"

"Yes, I married him. Is this really Rudy? What's Titus' middle name?"

"Bartholomew."

"This is amazing. Titus is going to flip when I tell him!"

"Don't you tell him! Sorry, I mean, I just want to surprise him."

"The novelty of you being back from the dead will wear off as soon as you hear what's happening south of you in Azerbaijan."

Rudy listened quietly, his scientific mind organizing the details of Wynter's flight from Azerbaijan, Titus' involvement with COIL, and the plan to kill off Wynter back where it all started.

"You need to talk to CIA Agent Wes Trimble," she said. "The whole operation hinges on this body getting placed in Azerbaijan. Trimble has been praying that God would provide someone to take care of the body. No one—*I mean no one*—ever thought it could be you!"

"Okay. I understand." Rudy felt a chill like Arctic ice creep up his spine at the thought of Muslim extremists chasing his little sister. "Titus is really a Christian?"

"For about a year now. He can tell you all about it."

Rudy hung up the phone and paused before he dialed Wes Trimble. *Titus was a Christian.* Something rotten in Rudy ached in his gut. For years, he hadn't even prayed for his little brother, disgusted with his hopeless lifestyle. *Hopeless?* Meanwhile, Titus had been working for COIL while Rudy was floating around on icebergs?

"I have dinner," Galina announced. "You know Spam?"

"Spam? Yes, that sounds great. I love Spam."

Rudy pulled back the window curtain to see Kobuk standing sentry on the porch.

"Well, old girl, looks like our adventure together isn't quite over." As if she heard him, Kobuk turned her head and looked at him through the window. "Don't worry, I'm not leaving you behind."

Azerbaijan

Serik Tomir gripped his sword-cane as he hopped out of the helicopter provided by *Imam* Nasser al-Hakim. A rescue crew was already at the plane crash site. A barge in the river was blasting the diminishing flames with two streams of water.

"Keep the chopper running!" Serik yelled at the pilot. "This won't take long!"

With a wicked grin, he turned his back to the helicopter. He didn't mind making Nasser pay for a little more fuel. His secret loathing for Nasser was brought to the forefront of Serik's mind by the hunt for Wynter Caspertein. *A holy man?* Serik knew his friend better than anyone, and he knew Nasser was far from holy. Maybe thinking of the man in that way meant he wasn't his friend at all, but only a mutual associate, each taking what he wanted in an immoral world.

Five lethal *Soldiers of Mahdi* exited the chopper behind Serik and together they stalked toward the bank of the river. Floodlights from the shore crew shined on the charred fuselage of the plane. Serik guessed he looked like an official because an emergency supervisor jogged over and briefed him.

"It looks like it exploded on impact, sir. We're looking in the river for bodies. Nothing is easy or safe in the dark. Four men have already slipped into the river. We'll know more in a couple of hours, maybe by dawn."

Serik nodded and the man left. From years of observing wreckage—some that he'd caused himself—Serik saw the bent metal in the fuselage and identified the effects of explosives. That puzzled him. If Wynter Caspertein really was in the country, why not enter quietly across the southern border? Instead, she'd blown up her plane. Now, she'd have to leave another way, by train, or by plane from the only airport in the country in Baku. Agents were already watching the rails east and west. Whatever she'd risked her life for would need to be transported one way or another.

"Serik?" One of his soldiers approached him with a flashlight. "There's a clean trail heading north. About three people."

"Follow them. Take all the men. I'll supply you with gear by dawn. Go."

The killer signaled the four others and they traipsed away from the river wreckage toward the chopper.

"Whatever you're doing, Wynter Caspertein," Serik said into the night, "you won't leave Azerbaijan unless you're in my hands. By Allah, I swear it!"

Returning to the chopper, he ordered the pilot to fly to the lodge near the reservoir. It was time to meet with the man who'd tipped them off about Wynter's arrival. Something about the whole situation seemed off, and Serik wasn't suspicious just because his nightmare had persisted to haunt him. If the Serval was anywhere near, nothing about the hunt would be predictable.

CHAPTER TWENTY-THREE

Germany

Agent Wes Trimble realized he had the authority to mobilize troops and crumble small countries. Maybe that's why he was so amused that he was rolling a crate across the US military base to a cargo plane near the runway.

One of three men loosely saluted him as the other two took the crate and pushed it up the ramp of the cargo plane. Wes handed the pilot a sheaf of papers.

"There's your flight plan, the one you file, and here's the one you actually fly."

"I love you guys." The pilot smiled and flipped through the forms. "The Ukraine didn't give us fly-over permission. No surprise there. We'll cross the Black Sea. Fine. The Caucasus Mountains. And then we dump the package in the Caspian Sea?"

"No, you drop it. It's precious cargo. No dumping. It needs to float down at those exact coordinates."

"Okay, the boys'll rig it with a parachute." The pilot folded the papers and tucked them into his flight suit. "I follow orders, sir, but sometimes it's nice to know what kind of a difference I'm actually making. I usually don't ask. Usually."

"Off the record?"

"It'd be nice to know this time."

"You're dropping a dead body who looks like someone so that someone else can exchange the body for the one who is the look-alike." Wes chuckled. "Is that enough knowledge?"

"I'd rather save a life than take a life, so that works for me. We'll hit your mark on the map, sir."

Wes stood on the tarmac holding his eye patch so it wouldn't flap in the wind until the plane taxied up, then rumbled past.

He was still reeling at how God had provided Rudy Caspertein, back from the dead, to deliver the corpse that would save his sister's life. He'd reported back to COIL headquarters that the body would be in place at the scheduled time, but Rudy had insisted to everyone that he wanted to be the one to first show himself to his brother and sister.

"That'll be some meeting." Wes sighed, wishing he was more involved with COIL, but realizing God obviously still had him in the CIA where he could be used like this—where no one else could respond.

With his hands in his pockets, he walked away from the runway. Maybe his part in the latest COIL situation was over, but he knew there would be another one. God's people were always under attack. And, Lord willing, Wes hoped he'd be available to serve his brothers and sisters again.

Azerbaijan

Titus hated to admit it, but they were surrounded. In the darkness, he couldn't even tell Oleg a few yards away how bad the situation really was. Two minutes earlier, his watch proximity alarm had vibrated him awake, and he'd crept into the bushes with his handgun to ambush the enemy. However, the enemy numbered as twenty hotspots in thermal imaging mode. Twenty enemies were too many!

He lay flat on the dewy ground. Dawn was two hours away. After marching all day, they'd stopped to sleep before midnight. But now, with so many adversaries surrounding them in the thicket, he guessed it was best if Wynter and Oleg were taken alive, then he could try to free them as they were marched out of the woods. But twenty enemies at once? Entering Azerbaijan by crash landing suddenly seemed like an amateur move. They'd underestimated the *Soldiers of Mahdi's* ability to mobilize a search party.

Bushes rustled nearby, a subtle crunching sound coming from the nearest man who stood nearly on top of Titus. He didn't understand how the soldier hadn't noticed his prone shape, even in the dimness.

"Titus?" Oleg moved closer and kicked the boot of Titus' left foot. "You aren't sleeping out here, are you?"

Before Titus could answer, a wet nose nuzzled his head, then nipped at his jacket collar. He lunged back and sprang to his feet, his sidearm aimed at . . . a sheep.

"Those are the ugliest sheep I've ever seen." Oleg roughly jostled the nearest animal and tugged on lengths of wool tangled like dreadlocks. "Must've gotten loose from somewhere."

Titus calmed his heartbeat and slowly holstered his gun.

"My watch alarm went off. I thought we'd been had. It ain't easy being attacked by a flock of woolly varmints."

"What's going on?" Wynter stumbled up to them, her boot laces untied. "Those sheep—they're all over the country. They wake you guys up?"

"Titus thought the Shiites were disguised in sheep's clothing." Oleg muffled his laughter. "You almost tranquilized that sheep! All she wanted was a little affection."

"This isn't good." Titus stepped away from the growing flock of curious grazers. He touched his watch, analyzing angles of their position in Azerbaijan. "I was counting on the Gabriels to keep us updated on our Iranian friends' positions. The sheep have the same heat signature as a human. They're everywhere. I can't guide us like this."

They stood in the darkness for a moment, the tiny screen illuminating Titus' face.

"Rely on movement," Oleg said. "They may look alike from the sky, but people move differently than sheep. Track backwards along our trail. What do you see?"

"Okay . . ." Titus guided the Gabriel viewpoint southward. "Okay. There's a strange sheep formation about eight miles back. Or a perfectly-ordered hunting party. Ten in line on our trail."

"My bet is, it's our search party." Oleg laid a hand on Titus' shoulder as he moved past him. "Eight miles isn't far, not if they're moving fast. Good thing your ugly guard-sheep woke you, Titus, or we'd be waking up in an Azerbaijani prison cell."

Oleg and Wynter gathered their gear as Titus knelt next to the sheep that had nuzzled him.

"Don't listen to him, Woolly. You're not that ugly."

Wynter guffawed and helped Oleg into his pack.

"How long will it take them to cover eight miles?"

"No more than two hours at the pace they're traveling." Titus calculated on his watch. "They could even beat us to the reservoir. We hadn't planned on entering the water for another night."

"So, we're on schedule." Oleg picked up his walking stick. "And they're ahead of schedule. What's the plan?"

"Rashid made sure we got their attention, and now they're on our trail. They could send another hunting party from the north to intercept us. I can try to anticipate it, but it won't be easy with the sheep all over the place. There are hundreds ahead of us, too."

"Call Marc and Corban. They can see what you see, but they can study on a larger screen what's ahead and behind." Oleg started out of camp. "Come on, Wynter. I promised Titus I'd never forget the day he wore a woman's *hijab* to go undercover. To set the scene, I have to tell you first about this peacock . . ."

Titus dialed COIL tech Marc Densort back in New York.

"Hey, Marc. Listen, are you seeing these sheep? Yeah, they're sheep. I need your help to guide us forward . . ."

Caspian Sea

Rudy sat in a twenty-foot motorboat, feeling the roll of the waves, remembering a much more tumultuous time of boating only two weeks earlier. Kobuk lounged on one of the seats near the bow. She lifted her head once when the sun first rose over the eastern horizon, then relaxed again.

He'd rented a boat from the western coastal town of Russia's Makhachkala. Agent Wes Trimble had arranged gear for a fishing trip into the Caspian Sea, complete with extra fishing rods and bait to catch giant sturgeon. At the boat landing, Rudy had played the part by asking other boaters how best to prepare Caspian sturgeon caviar.

But besides fishing gear, he'd loaded several auxiliary tanks of fuel to cover the two hundred miles necessary to reach Baku, the capital of Azerbaijan, after trolling far out to sea according to Wes's precise coordinates.

Kobuk lifted her head again and perked her ears. Rudy sat up and reached for his GPS. They hadn't drifted far from the instructed coordinates, but Rudy started the engine anyway, then searched the sky for the noise that had alerted Kobuk. There, in the west, was a plane at about fifteen thousand feet. It seemed the plane barely reached his coordinates, when it banked north and flew out of sight.

Rudy shielded his eyes from the sun. A square object floated toward the sea, its parachute a transparent blue, almost invisible to the eye unless he looked closely. He motored slowly to the west, following the package as it drifted on the sea breeze. Kobuk stood and licked her jaws, watching the incoming delivery like it was expected venison.

It splashed down off the bow to starboard. Rudy cut the engine and checked the sea around them. Only one other vessel was visible, a freighter far to the east, steaming steadily toward Iran.

Leaning overboard, he pulled in the parachute, wadded it into a ball, then grabbed the watertight casket. He loosed the clasps on the ends and side, then threw up the top. Since he expected the smell of a decomposed body, he instinctively covered his nose, but Wes Trimble had placed the young woman in a plastic bag.

She was a little younger than Wynter and had shorter hair, but she wore jeans, boots, and a vest with extra pockets, exactly like Wynter might wear on an excursion.

He hadn't seen Wynter for a few months, but up until the Barrow incident, he'd spoken to her on the phone every few weeks. With his own hardships recently, and now Wynter's situation, he couldn't help but express gratitude to God for preserving them thus far. Where separation seemed to have governed their lives, God had orchestrated a yearning in him to now be together.

Kobuk nudged against him, and he realized he'd been reminiscing about his sister. Rudy grasped the shoulders of the deceased woman and pulled her easily into the boat. Kobuk barely investigated her presence before Rudy covered her with an oily tarp that stunk like fish.

Beside the boat, he stuffed the parachute into the casket, flooded it with water, then let it sink to the dark depths of the Caspian Sea.

Azerbaijan

"Titus, the hunting party of ten behind you has picked up its pace," Marc Densort said through Titus' wireless ear comm. "And on the west end of the reservoir, from what we can see here, the village has doubled in heat signatures. There's a small army waiting for you guys."

"Thanks, Marc. Keep us posted."

The noon hour approached as Titus, Wynter, and Oleg crouched in the bushes west of the village, a two-street settlement that had once been a resort town at the end of the reservoir. Exhausted, they were thankful for the rest after hiking all morning without a break.

"So, it's come down to this." Titus kept his voice low and one eye on his watch face. They'd covered sixty miles in a day and a half. "We have the option to run to Baku where we can finish this operation. Wes Trimble says he has a guy waiting for us at the capital. Wynter, a body is being positioned there to take your place. Everything is on track."

"What about the trunk?" Wynter asked. "We're so close!"

"Now may not be the time to be an archaeologist," Oleg said. His hand remained near his sidearm. "It may be time to think about survival. The enemy knows we're here. We can end this safely right now."

"I'm all for survival." Titus didn't bother to hide his grin. "But as a former smuggler and mover of precious cargo, I'm inclined to fetch the trunk."

"Why am I not surprised?" Oleg shook his head. "Just tell me what you want me to do."

"It ain't easy backing up us Casperteins." Titus laughed and shoved Oleg playfully. "At exactly 2200 hours tonight, Wynter and I will enter the water from the north. That'll be the easy part. After we get the trunk, we'll exit the reservoir on the south side, where the old industry scaffolding stands. Oleg, set our diversion in the woods here, and maybe farther north, for 2330 hours. With explosions going off in this area, we might be able to exit the water without anyone noticing. The soldiers are our biggest obstacle."

"An hour and a half to swim the width of the reservoir and find the trunk?" Oleg glanced at Wynter. "Is that possible?"

"It's not even a half-mile across where we're going. As long as the water hasn't risen too much, the buoy I left should be easy to find. It should be enough time."

"Then find a vehicle and meet us on the south shore." Titus slapped Oleg on the shoulder. "While we're taking a comfortable swim, splashing about, you get to do all the hard work. Unless you want to be the one who takes the dip with Wynter."

"Not a chance. That water must be fifty degrees." Oleg set his rebreather pack in front of Wynter. "I guess this is yours now."

"The forest is clear." Titus looked up from his watch. "We have a few minutes before we separate. We're here for Wynter because of the spiritual battle spanning the world. Ultimately, this is about Jesus Christ. We're needed in the field, but we're here defending ourselves against an evil that will last until Christ's return. I want to pray we remain true at heart, and guarded from hating those who may wish the worst for us. We might have a plan, but we can't be so proud to think we can do all this on our own."

"Are you going to preach or pray?" Oleg asked.

"Are you two ever serious?" Wynter jabbed Oleg on the shoulder.

"Only when we have nothing else to do." Titus chuckled, then bowed his head. "Dear Father, we should be running scared to Baku right now, but we'd rather settle our anxieties by placing them at Your feet . . ."

CHAPTER TWENTY-FOUR

Azerbaijan

Serik Tomir impatiently tapped his sword-cane on the balcony outside the Ma'a Salama Lodge on the north side of the Mingechaur Reservoir. The lodge had been built as a memorial of the day the country had bid a violent farewell to American cooperation. No longer did US troops and other infidels use Azerbaijan as a strategic transit point to attack Allah's precious souls throughout the Middle East. The village at the end of the reservoir hadn't seen a steady stream of tourists for two seasons, but Serik didn't miss the Westerners. Now, when he wanted a break from Iran, it was easy to get a cheap room; there were no infidels or their money in Azerbaijan.

Through the window of the lodge, Serik peeked at the man who'd driven from Baku to meet him. A stranger, and yet, somehow familiar, as if he'd seen him somewhere, in the background, moving in the shadows.

His phone rang and he studied a text with an attachment of a photo of the man who waited inside. Serik frowned as he read, his finger subconsciously caressing the switch on his cane.

Exiting his message screen, he took a deep breath and rubbed his eyes. It was after sundown. He'd been up for two days, but the hunt was nearly over. With a prayer to Allah, he entered the lodge.

The lodge interior was as warm as the late summer air outside. The great room smelled like cinnamon. Exotic animals, poached from Africa's most-restricted parks, had been stuffed and mounted on the wall by an acquaintance of Serik's. Only one attendant was in sight, besides the man Serik approached. Serik sat down in a soft chair across from the steely-eyed stranger. The sword was within Serik's reach, should he need it.

"I arrived as soon as possible." Serik crossed his legs. "There was a plane crash site I had to visit. It was a unique experience. Usually, I make them fall from the sky in small pieces. But this one fell in one piece for no apparent reason."

"Wynter Caspertein."

"Yes, I deduced as much." Serik frowned as the man sipped steaming tea from a mug, then rested the hot mug on his knee. It had to burn, but Serik knew other men like this one. They didn't feel pain the same as other men. "So? What do you know?"

"The Americans let her go instead of arresting her as agreed."

"They'll pay for that later. But I want to know about Wynter Caspertein. Tell me more about why she's here."

"It's something in the water. She left it behind. Something valuable that I want. You can have her, or I can kill her for you. But I want the artifact."

"That's not your decision to make."

"I've been hunting her for weeks. Unlike your men, I've seen her up close. I can identify her, even if she's disguised."

"So what? I can, too."

"And I know the Serval."

Serik sat up attentively.

"Titus Caspertein? I saw him in Istanbul. By Allah, tell me how to kill him. He shamed me. It's my right to destroy the entire Caspertein family."

"If he's with Wynter Caspertein now, you'll need my help to stop him. He's afraid of me."

"You? Why is the Serval afraid of you?"

"You must know who I am." He sipped his tea. "Isn't that why you lingered on the balcony? You were debating whether to come in to meet me or not. You've been in Azerbaijan for two days, preparing an ambush for Wynter, and only now do you meet me?"

"Rashid al-Sabur. Yes, I know who you are. The British call you the Saber, but they're not sure what you look like. The Russians used you against a Chechen general. They had your photo, but it's grainy and old."

"How resourceful you are. So, you know what I'm capable of. I want what Wynter Caspertein left behind. I'll destroy anyone who gets in my way. Anyone."

"I believe you." Serik wasn't usually inclined to make alliances with dangerous assets who weren't already in the employ of Nasser al-Hakim, but Wynter had evaded him long enough. And if the Serval really was still around, Serik wasn't willing to face the legend, even if he really was a Westerner. "Once I have Wynter, I'll allow you ten minutes with her before we board the plane to Tehran. Nasser al-Hakim wants his son's murderer."

"And if I catch her first, I will give her to you. Of course, after I'm finished extracting the information I require."

"Agreed." Serik nodded once. "I have fifty men posted around the village. This is where Wynter and her Englishman were diving. Ten men are on her trail now."

"If I'm not needed here, I'll return to the airport, in case she slips through your net. I have a few traps of my own to lay."

"It's unlikely she'll get that far, but whatever suits you. Without your intel, we wouldn't be on her trail at all."

"There is a chance," Rashid said, "that Wynter won't come easily, especially with the Serval in the vicinity. Are we agreed she may need to be killed outright?"

"Nasser al-Hakim wants her alive." Serik considered the possibility of a face-off. "Of course, I won't risk my life to keep her alive. Do what you must."

"Very well. But it serves us both if she's taken alive." Rashid raised his mug in a subtle salute. "May we all achieve our goals."

With that, Rashid stood, gathered a leather jacket, and left the lodge.

Serik didn't move for a time, considering their conversation. Nasser would be glad to hear such a vicious ally had joined them in the hunt. As he walked onto the lodge balcony, he texted Nasser in Tehran to update him on the hunt. The noose was tightening around Wynter Caspertein.

Virginia

US President Cliff Pantrow woke to darkness and fear. His first thought was that he was in hell. This was the afterlife! Such loneliness. Sweat soaked his clothing. The choking blackness caught at his throat. He wasn't bound, but his terror held him captive as he sat against a hard wall. Now in hell, he realized he'd failed to seek out the true God and place his life in His hands. Something else had always come first, but now . . .

A presence stirred nearby and his senses began to return. That smell—was he in the cellar? Yes, he was in his home in Virginia. He'd been communicating via Skype with his vice president, then he'd gone to bed around midnight. Or had something else happened?

A penlight clicked on. He squinted at the LED brightness, then observed his surroundings. Yes, the wine cellar. Where was his security team? His thought of hell lingered, even though he was thankful he wasn't there, yet.

"You're safe, Mr. President." The man's voice was soft with a foreign accent, maybe Italian. "I needed to be alone with you to talk privately. It's a matter of international and eternal importance. Are you coherent?"

"My wife—" His fear was only slightly abated.

"She's upstairs asleep in your master bedroom. I tranquilized your security detail for a few minutes. That's all we'll need, then I'll leave your estate without incident."

"You . . . tranquilized the Secret Service?" The president felt his tension give way to amusement. "Who are you?"

"My name is Luigi Putelli. I'm not an enemy of yours, but I've carried you down here in a most irregular fashion. I have a gift for you and a warning. Which would you prefer first?"

The president sat up straighter, noticing a few features of the gaunt man in front of him, and the chomping of the man's mouth, as if he were chewing a wad of bubble gum.

"If you're not an enemy, then why all the subterfuge?"

"You have an enemy near to you. I'd rather you handle that enemy without alerting her that you know she's a traitor."

"Her? Who are you talking about?"

"Very well. You've chosen the gift I have for you first. Extend your hand. This is a recording of Deputy Secretary Emily Gaultridge's secret phone conversation with leadership within the *Soldiers of Mahdi* to destroy the Caspertein family."

"The terrorist group, SOM?" He accepted the recording and held it tightly in his fist.

"That's correct. And now for the warning. She's manipulating you for her own ambitions, which is currently to ruin the Commission of International Laborers."

"COIL? Is that what this is all about?"

"There are dark hearts at work here, Mr. President. Publicly, you've claimed to be a Christian. However true or false that claim may be, it will be proven by your subsequent actions regarding COIL. They are God's personal servants in this world. If you hold them close, you'll be blessed. If you try to hurt them, you'll be both unsuccessful and cursed. Would you prefer God to be for or against you?"

"Why would Emily try to manipulate me? She's a family friend. She's sleeping upstairs a few doors away from my wife!"

"COIL submits to the authority of the land, but they are ambassadors of a heavenly kingdom first. Ms. Gaultridge can't control COIL. And she hates Christians. This is one way she can promote her liberal agenda. It's all in the recordings. COIL has received private agency authorization assigned to them in years past, and hasn't broken any laws. Ms. Gaultridge is conspiring with known terrorists for the demise of a US ally."

"Okay." The president was actually finding the conversation interesting now, however irregular it was. And his fear was gone. "I'll listen to the recording. That doesn't mean I'll necessarily respond the way you want. I've been briefed by Emily about COIL's powers overseas and domestically. Maybe it's time to check that strength."

"Check it all you want, Mr. President, as you might observe any other ally. But if they are found worthy of the powers bestowed, then let the blessings of having COIL nearby be the advantage God intends them to be for you."

"What advantage?"

"COIL wields its skills for good, for Christ's sake. They're overflowing with goodness from God. That goodness will make anyone near them look good and favorable."

"I appreciate the warning, Mr. . . . ."

"Putelli. Luigi Putelli. I live in New York."

"Okay, Mr. Putelli. So, what if I don't acknowledge your warning? Does this become a threat?"

"Does it need to become a threat? Perhaps the threat is implied. I'm confident enough to tell you my name, and show you my face. I've tranquilized your entire security detail. Your embedded locator chips are meaningless if everyone is asleep. It's only when a friend is unrestrained to do evil that he shows himself truly to be a friend. You have enemies, Mr. President, but COIL is not one of them."

"So, you're with COIL?"

"I'm with Christ now, and so is COIL. That means I'm a partner of COIL's. I watch over its people who are vulnerable to the more sinister adversaries."

"Like Emily Gaultridge?"

"Unfortunately, she's made herself what she is now. She is responsible. You and I alone know this." Luigi rose to his feet, and the president realized the man had been seated cross-legged before him. "I must go."

"Wait. What if I have more questions for you?"

"Hold COIL close to your heart, Mr. President, or distant contacts will mislead you."

The penlight clicked off. There was a whisper of movement, then President Cliff Pantrow sensed he was alone. He would've been outraged if he weren't so intrigued.

A moment later, he heard faint footsteps on the floor above, and there were shouts for the president's whereabouts. So, his security team was now awake. He climbed to his feet and tucked the recording into his pocket. It was time he became intimately familiar with COIL.

Azerbaijan

On the north side of the Mingechaur Reservoir, behind a magnificent lodge constructed of imported wood, Titus lay on his belly next to Wynter. The sun was down and stars twinkled high above. The village lights, though few, provided enough illumination to see shapes moving between the village and water. The hike through the gullies and thickets that day had wearied him, so he knew Wynter was near exhaustion, but neither seemed able to sleep.

The ridge on which they lay provided a view of the entire western end of the reservoir and half of the village below them. Wynter kept a small set of binoculars at hand, occasionally studying the expanse of water or movement in the village. Titus used only his watch, zooming in and out, using the thermal imaging mode, examining the people in the village from different angles.

"When you were here a month ago," Titus asked, "were there this many gunmen?"

"I don't remember seeing a single one."

"Then they're definitely here for us." Titus watched a pair of men in civilian clothes sit on the porch of an apartment building close to the shoreline. "Have you figured out where we need to enter the water? If you can't, then we're better off heading for Baku."

"The lodge below us—see the driveway? About fifty yards down the highway to the right. If we enter the water there, we should be able to swim straight across and find the buoy I left."

"How's the water level?"

"It's gone down maybe a foot or two. My buoy was low enough. I tried to gauge for that possibility. You think Oleg is okay?"

"We'd see more activity below if he wasn't." Titus focused his Gabriel view on a stand of trees far out in the western woods. "If I can't find him from the sky, our Muslim friends probably can't find him on the ground."

"Well, I doubt they're confusing sheep for people."

"Ah, touche." He chuckled. "So, tell me: you haven't said what you'll become after all this."

"I've barely had time to think about the death of Wynter Caspertein and the new birth as someone else. How many times have you died to disappear?"

"Oh, several times, in the early days. But those were for evil reasons while good people chased me."

"I've been to a lot of archaeological sites around the world, and even surfaced some remarkable artifacts, but you know what has touched me the most in all my years?"

"What?"

"Those two days on foot in Syria, helping those Christians run from ISIS." She sighed. "I don't know if I'm qualified, but I've been considering applying for a spot in COIL. You think I could handle it?"

"You qualify if you're born again, sis. There's a place for everyone at COIL. Not everyone is flying planes—"

"Or crashing them?"

"—or running from gunmen, or designing false identities. There are prayer chains around the world that keep apprised of COIL needs, elderly women in retirement homes, disabled men living at home, even children in schools—they're all part of the network."

"You sound like COIL claims every Christian as their own."

"Aren't we one Church like that, though? Call it whatever you want, but every Christian is part of one big team, fighting one big enemy, in one big conflict for one big prize. An eternity with Christ is worth it all. Of course, there's your husband to consider as well."

"What? What are you going on about now?"

"I can't think of a better place to meet your future husband than from somewhere inside the COIL family. I may have a couple prospects already picked out for you."

"Oh, now you're arranging marriages? I think the Serval has been hanging out in the Middle Eastern culture too long!"

CHAPTER TWENTY-FIVE

Azerbaijan

O leg set the timer on the last distraction device underneath a log, then backed away. It was after sundown and soldiers were as thick as the sheep in the woods west of the reservoir. He knew all it would take was one soldier to spot him, and the whole local force would descend on him. Maybe the *Soldiers of Mahdi* would hold him prisoner for ransom demands, but he wasn't worth as much as Wynter or Titus. He guessed his captors would kill him within a week, maybe even before Titus could organize a rescue.

Smiling at the idea, Oleg belly-crawled through low tree branches. He almost wanted to test Titus' ability to perform such a rescue, or show the extremists they weren't the supernatural force they thought they were. The armies and religions of the world would rise and fall, but only the faithful born of the true God, through Jesus Christ, would overcome the things of the world.

Reaching the edge of the woods behind a boat rental agency, Oleg pulled a broken tree bough over the top of him. Two soldiers were in sight, and he could move no farther until the distraction devices were ready to detonate. Next on his list was to get a vehicle. The escape from the reservoir to Baku had been more or less outlined, but none of them knew how to get out of the capital city with the cargo Wynter insisted on retrieving. Their final departure and mission conclusion rested in the arms of Agent Wes Trimble, a man Oleg had met, but he didn't like to put all his dependence on one man. And he doubted very much that Titus liked remaining ignorant of all the details, either.

Another soldier joined the first two, with rifles over their shoulders. Two sat down in the boat yard and passed out food as the third poured liquid from a thermos. Of all the places for the search party to have a meal, they had to camp out a few yards from Oleg! He slipped his nine-millimeter from its holster. The muzzle had a factory silencer built into it, but taking on three men at once was only foolish enough for Titus to attempt. Or maybe Titus was rubbing off on him.

Careful not to rustle any plants, Oleg eased the weapon forward to aim at the three men taking a break. It was a little early to make rash decisions, but darkness was on his side, and Oleg needed to begin his search for a vehicle before it became too late. Besides, three men with food in their hands weren't as dangerous as three men with their fingers on their triggers.

He rose suddenly and threw off the tree bough. From his knees, he aimed and fired three times. Couscous bread and tea spilled onto the ground as the men toppled over. Oleg lunged to his feet to bind the unconscious men and hide them in the forest.

Once Oleg had cleaned the scene, he dialed Titus. He imagined Titus' watch vibrating on his arm before he answered in a whisper.

"I just put three to sleep for an hour. They're gagged, but they'll be found eventually."

"And I have a feeling your three won't be the last to be tranqed tonight. It has begun. Stay safe, brother."

Serik Tomir used his binoculars to scope the dark shoreline of the reservoir below. Few vehicles drove on the narrow highway that separated the town from the water, as if the whole country knew to avoid the vicinity of the hunt.

Something was wrong, and Serik knew Wynter Caspertein was to blame. Three men hadn't called in, searchers who'd been assigned to the western woods. The canyons and ridges were dark and rugged, but not treacherous enough to swallow up three veteran trackers. It was as if a force was moving against him, and Serik pondered his continued nightmare. Was Allah giving him a warning? For almost a month, his entire life had revolved around the hunt for Gamal's killer. Perhaps his psyche was falling apart and he was going crazy. By Allah, he prayed, he would capture Wynter before he went completely insane! And he'd do it here, in sight of the very water where Gamal had been murdered.

Cursing, Serik punched redial on his phone and connected with one of his lieutenants in town.

"The water," he said. "Get boats and patrol the water. It's not enough to search the edges of town. She's already here. I feel it!"

When he'd hung up, he touched the lever on his sword-cane to spring the blade to its six-foot length. Yes, Wynter Caspertein would pay!

"There's a search party coming up behind us!" Titus helped Wynter shoulder her rebreather gear. "We have to move now. It's dark enough."

"Maybe it's just more sheep!"

"Not unless sheep know cover formation strategies. We have less than two minutes to get across that road."

Titus didn't bother to pull on his pack; he merely slung it over his shoulder. In his right fist, he clutched his firearm and led the way down the ridge behind the quiet lodge. Skidding on his heels down the slope, he plowed into a tree and hit his wounded hand. To make matters worse, Wynter collided into him from behind. It took all his effort not to cry out as nerve pain from his pierced hand screamed through his body. The ledge loomed on their left.

"Someone's there, Titus!" Wynter pointed at the front balcony railing now in sight from their new vantage point.

On the corner of the balcony twenty yards away was a tall man, his silhouette against the starry sky. He held binoculars to his eyes and a staff under his arm.

"Rashid said the *Soldiers of Mahdi* are led by a man with a sword-cane," Titus whispered.

"That guy was in Istanbul!" She elbowed him in the gut. "Titus, he was on the ferry!"

In the woods on the ridge, the search party was making no effort to disguise their advance as they talked amongst themselves, breaking branches loudly under their boots.

"We have to get in the water!" Wynter nudged Titus forward. "Do something!"

Titus eased his pack to the ground and crept closer to the lodge. His wounded hand trembled in pain, and every footstep intensified it, but his gun hand was steady, aimed at the dark figure on the balcony. Finally below the man, Titus stopped, then lowered his gun. He looked back, but he couldn't see Wynter; he guessed she could see him, though.

"*Alma'derah*," Titus interrupted the man's concentration with the binoculars. "Any progress finding the infidel woman?"

Since he spoke Arabic rather than Azerbaijani, Titus hoped the man took him for a fellow searcher rather than a local.

"She can't escape this time." The man leaned over the railing. "Where's your team? Why are you alone?"

"The Serval doesn't need a team to beat you." Titus raised his pistol and fired a silenced gel-tranq into the man's chest. "It ain't easy losing to a few Christians, is it?"

The cane dropped from the balcony to the ground at Titus' feet. He bounded up the porch steps and hooked his hands under the arms of the unconscious man. Before anyone from inside the lodge noticed, Titus dragged him down the stairs and into the woods. Since the man was as large as himself, Titus was winded by the time he reached Wynter and his pack.

"What have you done?" Wynter slugged his shoulder. "Now they'll know we're here!"

"We couldn't get to the water past this guy. You told me to do something, so I did. Relax, sis. He'll be out for an hour."

With his gear, Titus moved below the balcony, picked up the dropped cane, and briefly inspected it. The lever triggered the spring-loaded sword, making Titus flinch.

"Come on!" Wynter hustled to the pavement of the highway.

Titus glanced back at the ridge. The *Soldiers of Mahdi* were advancing quickly, but once they found their leader, that might cause them to pause. Now was the only chance Titus and Wynter had to enter the water undetected.

With a sharp crack, Titus broke the blade over his knee and tossed the sword into the woods. He felt the weight of the remaining cane sleeve, then hurled it onto the balcony.

Wynter waited for him across the highway, crouched behind a sign announcing the entrance to the lodge. Lights from the buildings reflected and shimmered off the glassy water.

"It's too exposed!" Wynter gasped. "Look! The whole village will see us!"

"Let them see us. We don't have a choice. I doubt anyone will be able to follow us, right?"

He jogged down to the water, over rocks once submerged when the reservoir level was higher.

"Why do I think you're enjoying yourself?" She joined him at the water's edge as they stripped off their loose clothing, down to their dry suits. "Look at you. You're actually grinning!"

"Aren't you? I never thought we'd make it this far." He chuckled. "Come on. Adjust everything in the water."

Leaving their clothes behind, Titus picked up his gear and painfully carried Wynter's flippers with his own in his sore hand. Wynter fit her demand regulator into her mouth and submerged in waist-deep water as Titus was still searching for safe footing in knee-deep water. Finally, he fell forward with his gear and swam out to her. Without talking, they finished donning their weight belts, rebreather straps, then their flippers. Titus felt a little panic as he sucked on his demand regulator and nothing came out. Wynter adjusted something on his back, then patted him twice on the head.

His last view before he submerged was of floodlights playing across the water. Boats were patrolling toward them! Wynter took his left wrist, which held his watch, and guided him at a sharp descent along the bottom of the reservoir. The water was dark and murky, giving Titus a sense of fright a second time until he felt Wynter's hand still on his arm. He had dived a few times, mostly for pleasure along exotic reefs in tropical waters, but this was her environment. Settling his nerves, he submitted to her direction as they kicked into the nearly half-mile-wide expanse of the reservoir.

But all Titus could think of were the floodlights above. Boats were now on the water, hunting them down. There would be no surfacing if there were boats above. They were trapped under the water!

🦂

New York

Janice leaned forward in her chair as she watched one of three flat screens. The Gabriels were providing live views of the events in Azerbaijan. Marc Densort, the Gabriel tech, sat on the other side of Corban, adjusting a viewing angle every couple minutes, toggling between the three Gabriel UAVs seventy thousand feet above Titus.

"Well, this is a little unnerving, huh?" Corban squeezed Janice's hand and she realized she hadn't taken a breath for several seconds. "It's all right, hon. They can't see them under the water, even if we can."

Janice nodded, but she had trouble imagining that Titus and Wynter were actually safe as motor boats slowly cruised across the surface of the reservoir, sometimes directly above the hotspots of the two swimmers.

"How deep underwater are they?" she asked.

"Wynter would know not to go below thirty feet, which would cross into the third atmosphere." Marc tightened a cable connection to diminish the static from one feed. "They have to stay relatively shallow since there's no decompression chamber they can step into when they get out."

Janice held her breath again as another boat slowly traveled over Titus and Wynter. Their swimming figures glowed brightly through the water, changing course occasionally, perhaps disoriented in what Janice had been told was polluted, dark water.

"What if something goes wrong?"

"Here's Oleg right here." Corban pointed at a solitary bright spot on the screen, moving at the edge of town. "That's how Titus and Oleg work. One always covers the other. We've had some exceptional COIL operatives before, but nothing like these two. That's why we need them back in the field so desperately. They can do what few others ever could for persecuted Christians around the world."

"I've listened to these two men for six months straight." Marc cleaned his thick glasses. "They don't have to be on a mission to make a difference for Christ. The attitudes of everyone around them improves even when they walk into a grocery store."

"That's mostly Christ in them." Corban smiled at Janice. "And partly because they're natural clowns who never grew up."

Janice felt a lump in her throat and hoped she didn't burst into tears—from her worry for Wynter, from her righteous pride for God's people, and from the loneliness she felt for the operatives so isolated in the distant land of Azerbaijan. What amazing people God had allowed her to witness working for Him!

Azerbaijan

Wynter gritted her teeth against the cold and terror of the debilitating swim. She had dived in waters all over the world, and the shark attack off Argentina's coastline had been a life-changing experience. But no archaeologist expedition could ever compare to this.

She checked her depth gauge on her wrist by biting the illumination button. Since the water was so murky, she dared not release her hold on Titus' wrist. If she did, they'd have to find each other only by surfacing, and that was out of the question.

A beam of light barely pierced to their depth of thirty-two feet, and the growl of a motor filled her ears as the boat soared over them, like a vulture circling its prey. There was a certain safety in the water, but it could also be their death. In a couple hours, their rebreathers would be depleted of carbon dioxide scrubber-chemicals. If they couldn't find the buoy in time, and get out of the water safely before daylight, they'd be caught and certainly killed.

Once the boat motored past, Wynter yanked on Titus' arm. He'd learned the cue. Holding his satellite-watch close to her face mask, he illuminated the GPS mode. They were so close to the buoy!

Turning Titus away from her, she tugged a length of nylon rope wedged between Titus and his rebreather. The line was thirty feet long, and she thrust one end into his left hand. As much as they'd rehearsed this dive during the flight over, nothing was easy in the blinding water, without the ability to communicate, as killers zigzagged above them.

Wynter took the other end of the line and shoved away from Titus, then she swam ahead, hopefully southward, as Titus presumably swam parallel to her.

A moment later, Titus was clearly disoriented as Wynter's end of the line tugged contrary to their heading. Following the line, gathering the length as she swam, she reached Titus sooner than expected along its length. Frustrated, she tried to calm his frantic gesturing to instruct him to swim in a southward direction. But it was no use. Since he couldn't see her arm movements, he didn't know which way to swim. And in all the confusion, Wynter believed she'd gotten turned around as well.

The surface seemed safe, so she ascended, pulling on his arm as she went, but somewhere along her rise, she'd dropped the rope. She prayed Titus still had the other end, or finding the buoy would be nearly impossible.

She surfaced with caution, the warmer night air a welcome sensation on her numb face. Fog rose in wisps from the water. Spitting out her regulator, she eyed the hunting boats at a distance, the nearest a quarter-mile away. Some were a mile or two down the long lake.

Titus surfaced with a splash, and Wynter reached for him to reassure him she was there. He may have been an untamed serval around the world, but in the water, he was just a clumsy tomcat trying to swim. Once he located the search lights, he pivoted toward her. His mouth still held his regulator.

"We need to swim south." She pointed. "See? We need to drag for the buoy, remember? You still have the rope?"

He spit out his regulator.

"Why do you want to swim south without the treasure?"

"We need to—" Wynter frowned, then turned in a circle, checking her dead-reckoning landmarks on shore. She'd never dived in the reservoir at night, but after Gamal had died, she'd taken note of the shoreline. "You found the buoy?"

"I'm not this excited because I'm cold. We ran right into it a few seconds after you gave me the rope!"

"Okay, let's bring it up."

"Wait." He toggled the modes of his watch, the illumination shining on his face. "Look at the south shore. Oleg's already there. He left a message. We're right on schedule."

Wynter was tempted to tease him with another sheep joke, but a search boat had turned back toward them.

"Okay. Get ready to inflate the inner tube. Let's finish this."

CHAPTER TWENTY-SIX

Azerbaijan

Serik Tomir woke in the lodge. His first instinct was to grasp for his sword-cane. His men must have presumed as much since they'd lain it at his side. He sat up on a divan in the great room and several men came to his side.

"I'm fine!" He touched his chest, finding a fierce welt, swollen and painful. Vaguely, he recalled the man who'd shot him, his voice, his confidence, his casual familiarity . . . "Give me a status report!"

"They're in the water. We're sure of it," one man said. "We found two sets of clothing at the water's edge."

"If they're in the water, then they're ours for sure! Greedy Americans! Our boats?"

"We have three in the water, we're bringing four others out of dry dock, and ten more are coming from farther up the coast."

"How could they get past you to the water?" Serik stood and pointed his cane at the soldier. He relished the fear displayed on the man's face. Everyone knew the deadliness hidden inside his cane. "The whole town is surrounded. No one could possibly avoid all our men. Someone must be helping them! Is it you?"

"Serik, by Allah, I swear it! The men are loyal. We are at your command!"

"Get away from me! Someone bring me a phone. You fools! The clothes by the water could be a diversion!" Then, under his breath, he said, "That'd be just like the Serval—to misdirect me. The coward!"

Oleg parked the Lexus he'd acquired on the southwest side of the reservoir, and cut the engine. He'd driven without lights from town to avoid detection, but now in place for Titus and Wynter, he felt exposed and vulnerable. Remnant scaffolding and towers of drilling platforms stood around and above the vehicle. It was a cemetery for Azerbaijan's brief capitalistic era, before Sharia Law permeated the government, policies, and eventually infected its people and industry.

"This is Oleg. Can you hear me?" he spoke aloud for his ear piece to pick up his audio, wirelessly communicating with his sat-phone. "Mark my present location. The car for Titus is here. The shoreline is extremely exposed. I'm looking right at it."

"We hear you, Oleg." It was Corban. "How exposed? What do you see?"

"I can see the water. There are about six boats on patrol now. From the shore to the car, there's no cover."

"Titus has been in the same location for twenty minutes, so they must've located the trunk. Stand by for their arrival."

Oleg spotted a slow-moving vehicle on the southern highway.

"I don't think I can stay here. It's just a matter of time before the search parties shift their focus to this side of the reservoir." He checked the time. "The diversions will blow in a few minutes. The Serval needs to hurry up."

"He can't hear us or read our texts while he's underwater." Corban spoke softly, but Oleg could still hear the anxiety in his voice. "Stay in place, Oleg. The Serval will need you as soon as they hit the beach. They'll probably need help carrying the package."

"They won't need me. They need the car." Oleg set a hand on the leather-trimmed interior. The hypocrisy of the *Soldiers of Mahdi* was sickening. They condemned the West while they imported the best the West had to offer. "The car I found should work. I'll walk back to town and find another car. It's best we're not all in the same vehicle for our exit plan, anyway. Corban? You there?"

"Yes, Oleg. We're here. We're watching a party of four men on foot approaching your area. They're three minutes out."

Oleg climbed out of the car and closed the door softly.

"I can lead them away. That's the Serval's only chance at a clean water exit and getaway."

"Negative, Oleg. Tranquilize the four and remain in place. You cannot miss your airport exit with the Serval."

He saw the flashlights approaching. They were searching the shoreline.

"If I tranq these guys, more will come, and the Serval isn't even on the beach yet. Besides, I can't take four without them firing a warning shot. But I can lead them away. I'll go southwest, toward our crashed plane. Maybe I can reach Armenia."

A moment passed. Oleg realized his window to even flee west was diminishing.

"Oleg, keep your phone on you. We'll track you and arrange an evac as soon as possible."

"It's my turn to say negative, Corban. If I'm captured, COIL could be compromised if my phone is analyzed. I've got to go now if I don't want them to see the car. I'm destroying my phone now. Pray for me."

Oleg plucked out his earpiece before Corban could object further, and drew his phone from his pocket. A distance from the car, he used a rock to loudly smash his phone, then he dropped the shattered components into a barrel of smelly rainwater. The searchers had heard his racket. He drew his gun and fired two rounds in their direction. Even silenced, the gel-tranqs had the velocity of normal bullets, and the men must've realized they were being shot at since they immediately returned fire.

A metal beam was leaning against cabled oil rigging nearby. Oleg heaved against it until it slid with a crash onto the ground. He hoped the clatter was enough to convince anyone of his whereabouts.

Bullets whipped past his head as he ran. Behind him, he heard yells and more gunfire, some of it directed at him, and some not, as confusion ensued. At the highway, he paused to allow the chasers to locate him in the darkness, but he failed to see two men already on the highway until it was too late. One raised his gun and fired. A bullet tore through his right shoulder. His gun fell to the pavement.

Oleg crossed the road, his left hand holding his seeping wound. He wouldn't get far now with a bleeding wound. But Titus and Wynter didn't need much more time. A brief distraction was all—

A flash was followed by a loud explosion in the north. The first detonation had gone off. The *Soldiers of Mahdi* were surely receiving all kinds of confused instructions now, perhaps thinking the town was under attack while they chased him.

"Get them to the airport, Lord." He prayed for Titus and Wynter, then crashed loudly through the woods, his pursuers not far behind.

As soon as Titus dragged the Etruscan trunk onto the polluted pebble beach, cradled in an inflated inner tube sling, Corban was in his ear.

"There's a vehicle thirty yards south of you. Oleg left it. He's drawing the enemy southwest."

"Roger that."

Titus kicked off his flippers. He and Wynter had already released their rebreathers in the water. Using a knife from his thigh, Titus stubbed the inner tube to deflate it.

"The car's right over there." Titus nodded at Wynter. "I hope this is worth it."

Wynter crouched at one end of the trunk, Titus at the other.

"One, two, three, lift!"

Together they lifted what Titus guessed was seventy pounds. Water was still pouring out of the cracks of the ancient trunk. They reached the car and heaved the artifact into the trunk. A boat planed onto the beach behind them.

"Where's Oleg?" Wynter shrieked.

"Get in!" Titus opened the driver's door as he drew his sidearm and fired three times at the men who piled out of the boat. He saw two fall before he suddenly felt a shock to his skull.

His last awareness was weakly collapsing backward into the car. Wynter clawed at his body and legs, drawing him into the car and climbing over him. Then he passed out.

New York

Corban watched the scene unfold. Next to him, his wife whispered a prayer. Marc Densort placed a digital trace on the hotspot that marked Oleg as he struggled through the wilderness of Azerbaijan. Titus wasn't answering, but at least he and Wynter had escaped in the car Oleg had acquired. Whether Titus or Wynter was driving, Corban didn't know. For now, at least, the car was heading east toward the capital and airport, a four-hour drive.

Things had unraveled, especially with Oleg in the wind. Corban didn't like to leave anyone behind, but at least Oleg was an operative. He knew what to expect if he were captured, and he'd die without betraying the One to whom he'd entrusted his eternal soul. Corban believed it was better for a COIL agent to be left behind rather than an untrained believer. An agent's job was one of intentional sacrifice, substitutionary if necessary, but anyone left behind was a wound to Corban's heart.

"Keep trying to raise Titus." Corban pushed the mic towards Marc, who was normally the one who communicated daily with Titus. "I need a few minutes."

Gathering his crutches, Corban shuffled across the vine and cable-strewn dwelling that was Marc's habitat. He sat in a chair that faced the cement wall. A mural was on the wall, one of several, that depicted a scene from the Bible. The murals were meant to add character and a human touch to Marc's drab existence underground. This particular mural, painted by a COIL associate, Joshua from Kentucky, depicted a scene Corban had yet to figure out. It showed a man running from a crowd of hostile people, their faces in a rage. Maybe it was Paul or Stephen, or a general story of persecution from Acts, since the people wore first-century clothing.

"I don't like to run away, Father," Corban whispered, staring at the pain on the painted man's face. "I don't know what's more painful—the shame of running away, or the agony of these people making them-selves enemies of Your love, Lord." He bowed his head. "I hear You. It's okay to run. It's okay to flee. I'll trust You to recover what's lost, the things we can't affect right now. Please help me shed my yearning to fix everything. I need Your discipline, Lord."

A moment later, Corban returned to stand behind Marc.

"Oleg has just been captured." Marc used a cursor to magnify the situation where a cluster of hotspots converged on one. "I don't know what they're doing to him. Without daylight, we can't—"

"They just attacked him." Corban sat in his chair next to a tearful Janice, and held her hand. "That doesn't mean he's dead. His body heat will diminish as a signature if they kill him. Marc, dedicate Gabriel One to track Oleg indefinitely. Follow his every move. If he's still alive, they'll hold him somewhere. Because we're dealing with the *Soldiers of Mahdi*, they may not keep him in Azerbaijan at all. Janice, are you okay?"

"I was just thinking how none of this would've been necessary if our president wouldn't have threatened to extradite Wynter to Azerbaijan in the first place."

"The president may have made the final call, but intel has it he received some bad advice to side against us. All that's being sorted out." He squeezed her hand. "Marc, keep the other two Gabriels on

Titus and Wynter. And keep calling them. We've got to get through, or they'll never know what to do once they reach Baku."

Azerbaijan

Serik Tomir approached the captured foreigner. He used his sword-cane to whack tree branches and bushes aside to reach his men.

"That's enough! I want him alive." Serik used his cane to lift the infidel's huge head, as his men held the dark-haired man's thick arms. "What's your name? Where is Wynter Caspertein?"

"Are you the leader of this wilderness experience?" The prisoner spoke fluent Arabic. "I want a refund. I don't like this vacation package."

Serik jabbed him in the gut with his cane. He wasn't surprised when the man passed out. His men had already beaten him terribly before he'd arrived, and his shoulder was wounded from a gunshot. But Serik was surprised to find this man instead of the one he knew to be the Serval.

"Four men take him back to town. The rest of you, search the woods. And someone find my car!"

Wynter was startled awake by the chill in the car. It was daytime, almost noon. She'd parked the Lexus off the highway and out of sight down an access road. A sign nearby with an emblem of an oil drilling derrick marked unfenced property that Wynter guessed belonged to a mining company. The writing was in Azerbaijani, and gave Wynter no indication as to how far she was from the airport or the capital city. The reservoir was far behind, and in the daylight, she couldn't risk traveling alone in the increasingly rigid Islamic country.

Well, almost alone. In the passenger seat, Titus sat unconscious, not even moaning. From the backpack of gear Oleg had left, Wynter had torn a spare shirt and wrapped Titus' head wound, but it was still swelling and bleeding. The bullet had passed above his left ear, shattering his skull, and splintering pieces of bone into his hair, some even embedding in his ear. She'd picked out what she could, but guessed his internal injuries were of greater concern.

To make matters worse, somewhere between the lake and the car, perhaps when Titus had collapsed, he'd disabled his sat-phone. Wynter knew it communicated wirelessly with his watch and the earpiece she'd taken from his bloodied ear, but the watch was dark and the earpiece was silent.

She held Titus' cold hand and prayed. He still had a pulse, but she couldn't imagine he would live without modern medical attention. His traumatic brain injury had surely caused swelling that needed to be relieved. Wynter's own medical experience was too limited to treat more than his bleeding, and she certainly wasn't taking him to an Azerbaijani hospital!

The treasure in the trunk of the car hardly seemed to matter any longer. Sure, it had provided a viable excuse to return to Azerbaijan and set up her supposed death, but now it all seemed to be a loss. Titus couldn't possibly survive, unless a miracle occurred. And she was right back where she started—in Azerbaijan, alone, running for her life. No Oleg. No COIL people.

And the car fuel was low. She wasn't sure she could make it to Baku without refueling.

Exhausted from the hopelessness, she drifted to sleep again, not especially caring if she woke around sundown to continue toward Baku or not. Perhaps God would let her pass away right there, she pondered. In her despair, without Rudy, and without Titus, she couldn't imagine ever being happy again.

Rashid stood tensely against the outer wall of the airport in Baku. Three *Soldiers of Mahdi* had been assigned to him or for him. He wasn't sure Serik Tomir meant to watch him or help him in his capture of Wynter Caspertein. Whatever Serik's suspicions of him, Rashid had fallen into his comfortable routine of silence and alertness. Due to the present company, he hadn't been able to check in with Annette Caspertein for an update, but Titus' plan was solid, and Rashid had only to play his personal part in its brilliance.

Dusk approached, and his level of anxiety increased since this was the night of their departure. Where were Titus and Wynter? Though since Arkansas, he hadn't felt any tendencies to take the treasure for himself, he was curious about what Wynter may have actually recovered—what he'd been chasing her for around the world to take as his own.

Taking the treasure now hardly seemed valuable in comparison to being a companion of Titus Caspertein. How could he have misread the Serval so dreadfully? The man was actually pleasant company. Titus had done most of the talking when they'd been together in the US, but that was how Rashid liked it. The Serval was a genuine mystery to the world, but Rashid now knew the man behind the facade. The Serval was his friend. Very few in the world had such a powerful friend.

Three speeding vehicles turned into the airport entrance and passed the parking lot without stopping at the armed checkpoint. Rashid guessed that all the police in the country knew not to get in Serik Tomir's way. Though Rashid had firmly entrenched himself in the man's favor, he wouldn't trust the one who carried the sword-cane.

"Has there been any word?" Serik asked as he exited the SUV at the curb. "There's nothing west of Baku. No sign. Wynter must be in the city."

"There's been no sign of her here." Rashid gestured to his three attendants. "No one has entered the property without us inspecting them. The customs officers inside scrutinize everyone. Wynter would be a fool to come here. But if she does . . ."

Rashid drew his thumb across his throat, causing Serik to frown.

"I want her alive. I captured one of them, but Wynter is still here, probably with the one we know as the Serval."

"Where's the one you captured?" Rashid contemplated a new plan, wondering if he could free their captive without compromising the plan to clear Wynter's name. They probably had Oleg. "Let me talk to him. I have a unique ability to make people talk."

"No, I want you here. You know Wynter better than anyone. The harbor is monitored. The railway is funneled through several checkpoints, and we are here. There's no escape. She's finished! Believe it or not, I think she's responsible for the theft of my car. By Allah, I will see her bleed!"

CHAPTER TWENTY-SEVEN

Azerbaijan

Serik Tomir walked away from Rashid al-Sabur, happy to distance himself from the chilling, strange killer. He was just glad the man was on his side, but he still didn't trust him. Allah wanted vengeance for young Gamal's death, but Rashid seemed to have no righteous zeal, only greed. Greed was unpredictable. If Rashid couldn't make Wynter talk, Serik guessed the man would kill her, regardless of their deal to take her alive. Serik wasn't stupid enough to cross such a dealer of death.

Even though Serik had the authority of a prince in the land, he doubted he'd be successful in capturing Rashid if the man became contrary. Already, the *Soldiers of Mahdi* had been whispering about the tall man from Cyprus. Rumor had it, the quiet killer had murdered a thousand people over the years. But that was just rumor, Serik knew. Rashid was a thief, and the file from British intelligence had documented only forty murders.

At the far end of the airport driveway, Serik turned and observed the parking lot, wishing for better lighting. He tapped his cane on the pavement, trying to think like the Serval would think. How would he escape Azerbaijan with whatever they'd recovered from the reservoir? Wynter was an adventurous woman, but she was after all just a woman. How could she possibly elude Allah's chosen avengers again? Impossible!

Suddenly, Serik froze. The cane fell from his fingers and rolled across the pavement. He vaguely noticed his men hesitate to retrieve it for him, since everyone knew it was his most prized token of authority. Instead, Serik's gaze searched the other end of the airport, nearest the hangars where private planes and jets were parked.

He'd seen the creature from his nightmares! It was just a glimpse, but it had been there. Sweat poured from his skin and the welt on his chest throbbed with every racing heartbeat. It couldn't be, he told himself. The demon couldn't be real, moving across the land in public. Had no one else seen it? Was he to be haunted while awake and not only in his sleep—for his inability to capture Wynter? Allah was surely tormenting him, he guessed, for his ineptitude.

Then he saw him clearly. The bear-dog-man moved past Rashid, exiting the parking lot, approaching the private hangars. Serik rubbed his eyes. A man so large, and a dog the size of a pony—it wasn't possible. It had to be a demon. But what did it mean?

"Serik!" Rashid shouted and pointed at the parking lot. "There she is! She's right there! It's Wynter Caspertein!"

Picking up his cane, Serik ran toward Rashid.

"Where?" He frantically studied the parking lot of cars and a few trucks. Two tour buses sat off to the side. "I don't see her!"

Rashid was gesturing toward the third row of cars, when the parking lot exploded. Along with everyone in the area, Serik fell to the pavement. Glass sprinkled over them like hail. Molten metal landed on his men. Other cars erupted in fire. Men screamed and flames leapt. Serik climbed to his feet and watched Rashid run toward the flames. *Was the man insane?* Only then did Serik begin to grasp that the explosion had something to do with Wynter. And the bear-dog-man creature. And the Serval. His mind couldn't tie the connections, but it was all in front of him.

In the parking lot, he saw Rashid shield his face from the heat. Such was his determination to get one moment with Wynter to discover the location of her treasure. Then he stomped away, back to Serik. Nearby, Serik's men regained their composure, but Serik didn't know what to tell them to do. First, the bear-dog-man, then the explosion . . .

"My device malfunctioned!" Rashid spit on the pavement. His face was smeared with soot. "It was Wynter! I'm sure of it. She was there, in one of the cars!"

"What device?" Serik shifted his cane from hand to hand. He'd never been more confused—or haunted. "You had explosives out there, and you didn't tell me?"

"I wanted her first!" Rashid shook his fist, forcing Serik to back away. The tall killer's face twisted with hatred. "I could've had her! Stupid Russian wiring!"

Rashid turned and shoved three men aside as he marched away. Serik let him go, beginning to make sense of the situation. A fire crew from the tarmac area reached the scene and shot foam onto the five burning cars so they wouldn't ignite other vehicles or structures nearby. He moved closer, hoping Wynter had indeed died in the explosion so his torment could end. It was much easier to hunt defenseless Christians in Iran, where bear-dog-men didn't haunt him and the Serval didn't outsmart him at every juncture. If Wynter was dead, then Allah could rest.

Wynter drove slowly into the airport entrance. The timing couldn't have been better, it seemed, with a fire incident burning far to the left. Emergency vehicles were still arriving at the scene, lights flashing, crowds gathering. It was her incident, she suddenly realized. This was no accident! This was for her, to keep her alive, somehow.

She hit the brakes as a scowling man crossed the road in front of her. He glanced up at her. It was Rashid! He carried a backpack over one shoulder. Wynter reached for the door lever to call for him when he signaled subtly toward the east. An instant later, he walked beyond the pavement and entered the airport's main building.

Easing up on the brake, she steered to the right where monstrous shadowy hangars stood off to the side of the airport property. A gate with only a padlock blocked her path, but it had razor wire coiled on top. Glancing over her shoulder, it seemed no one was watching. The parking lot flames were extinguished. She only had seconds before onlookers turned her way again.

With a little extra gas, her bumper pushed through the fence with a loud snapping of metal. The car body squeezed through the too-narrow gate, making her wince at the screeching sound. An instant later, she'd passed beyond the fence and turned off the car lights. Rashid had gestured here, but where exactly? Everything was dark.

She parked next to the nearest hangar, blocked from advancing farther by a rusty fuel truck.

"Now would be a great time to wake up," she mumbled to Titus. "Oh, Lord, what do I do?"

Serik Tomir sneered as his men pushed their way past emergency personnel and dragged a charred body from one vehicle. They would have no respect for this one. The flames were gone, yet the stench of burnt flesh and pungent fumes drove many back. But Serik wanted proof. He had to take something back to Nasser in Tehran.

"I think it's a woman, Serik!" one of his soldiers called. "But it's hard to tell."

"Look for her papers, identification, something." He pointed. "Search the car!"

Holding their breaths, two men leaned into the car most damaged from the explosion. Serik didn't understand how Rashid had intended to threaten Wynter to talk with such an explosion, but the killer had clearly planted enough explosive to wipe out anyone even remotely near the vehicle.

"This may be it!"

One of the men choked on the fumes as he emerged from the car and handed a leather pocketbook to Serik. He knelt and set his cane on the ground to gently open the burnt leather. Three men held flashlights on the item. The identifications inside had been fringed by heat, but they were intact.

"*It's her,*" he whispered. "Wynter Caspertein." He thumbed through a driver's license and passport and half-burnt business cards for businesses in Arkansas, America. "It's her! Allah be praised! Gamal is avenged! The blood of the chosen one can rest! The infidel will suffer for eternity!"

Paramedics and other rescue workers looked on as Serik and his men cheered and danced. After a moment, Serik excused himself and dialed his phone.

"*Imam* Nasser? It is finished."

"You have her?"

"I have her body. Unfortunately, she was killed, but it was in a gruesome fashion. Your son is avenged. Your honor is restored."

"Thank you, Serik. I never doubted you would return triumphant. May Allah bless you and your faithfulness."

When Serik hung up his phone, he looked up and saw the strangest sight. What appeared to be his silver Lexus was parked one hundred meters away in the private hangar sector of the airport. He jogged away from the crowd, through the broken fence, and approached his car. The driver's door was open. Serik held his cane level, his finger on the lever, and eased up to the passenger window. The shadowy figure of a man sat stationary. Was he dead?

It was the Serval! Serik opened the door and checked the man's neck for a pulse. His hand came away wet with blood before a pulse was detected. What a day! First Wynter, and now her brother, the Serval!

A clang from inside the hangar made him pivot, his cane ready to slay his enemy. He crept with stealth along the side of the hangar. Whoever had accompanied the Serval in his car—he could kill him with his own blade. Serik felt invincible. All of his recent enemies vanquished in one day—and the recovery of his car! It was a glorious day!

§

Wynter peered around the outside corner of the hangar, the massive door ajar. She expected to see a plane, but instead was met by a growling dog, its head as high as her waist.

"Easy there, puppy." Wynter's mouth went dry. She had no food in her pockets to toss the monstrous canine. Her hand went to her shark's tooth. God was still with her. "Nice little pooch."

She backed away one step, but guessed running away wasn't the answer. Then the dog took a step toward her.

The sky seemed to darken, and Wynter glanced up to see the tail of a small jet drift silently past her from the hangar. The dog, which Wynter now realized was a St. Bernard, turned to watch the jet as well. Wynter was tempted to flee while the dog was distracted, but running away wouldn't help her or Titus.

The jet continued to emerge from the hangar, and finally the nose. A single man leaned against the forward landing gear, pushing the jet out onto the tarmac. The St. Bernard turned and trotted after the hulk of a man who seemed to push planes around like toys.

Wynter hesitated. Rashid had guided her to the hangar, and now here was a man who used his own brute strength to move a plane, rather than use a tarmac vehicle, which would've created noise and drawn attention.

"Excuse me," she said in English, wondering if she should've used Arabic. But anyone who Titus had lined up to meet him probably spoke English. "Hello?"

The man stopped guiding the plane and turned. The wheels of the turbo-prop eased to a halt.

Suddenly, Wynter gasped as a man's arm circled her neck and hot breath panted in her ear. Her eyes widened at the shape of the man who'd pushed the plane out. She knew that man. *But it couldn't be!* Rudy was dead! What was happening?

"Stay back!" the man who held her yelled in Arabic. With his other hand, he held out his cane, the end pointed at the St. Bernard. His thumb pressed repeatedly on the cane, but nothing happened. "Stay away from me!"

"I don't know what you're saying, pal." Rudy's voice was unmistakable. "But that's my sister you've got there."

Rudy lumbered forward. Wynter realized the man who held her was the Muslim who'd hunted her for weeks—the man with the sword-cane, from the Istanbul ferry, and from the lodge two nights earlier! Except she'd watched Titus break the sword off, so she knew his sword was no threat.

Pumping her arm, Wynter jabbed backwards with her elbow. She'd wrestled enough with Caspertein boys growing up to know how to at least get a brief edge to run away. Her elbow struck the man's ribs once, twice, making him cry in agony. His grip around her throat weakened a fraction, and she pushed his arm over her head and dove to the tarmac.

"Get 'em, Kobuk!" Rudy ordered, and the St. Bernard charged, followed immediately by Rudy.

Wynter jumped to her feet as the dog closed its jaws around the cane and wrestled it out of the man's hand. Rudy was next, his arms spread wide to tackle him.

Then, as if the bizarre night wasn't strange enough, the Muslim man spun around and ran screaming into the hangar. Rudy stopped beside Wynter, and Kobuk nuzzled Wynter's hand for attention. From the midst of the hangar, in the darkness where twilight couldn't reach, the man whimpered Arabic prayers that Wynter couldn't quite hear but every few words.

"Maybe he didn't like my beard?" Rudy shrugged.

Wynter chuckled and tried to remember how she used to embrace this oversized brother since her head barely reached his chest.

"I can't believe you're alive!"

"Arlin said it was a nice funeral." He bent down and embraced her, pulling her off her feet by a foot. "Sounds like God's been throwing all of us some curve balls lately."

"Put me down, Rudy. We can talk later." He set her down. "Titus was shot. He's in the car. We've got to get out of here, or all our planning is ruined."

"So, my explosion worked?"

"That was you?" She led the way around the side of the hangar. "I don't know what Titus planned next. And Oleg's missing."

"His COIL friends are tracking him from the air, or something. I called Annette a few minutes ago. You know Titus' wife? I'm new to all this, but his people seem to know how to respond to these kinds of things."

They reached the car and Rudy went to Titus. Wynter saw the back of the car open and she ran to the trunk. The treasure was gone! She gazed toward the airport and saw a tall figure carrying her trunk on his shoulder.

"Rashid!" She punched her palm.

"Grab everything." Rudy said. He held Titus in his arms like a child. As large as Titus' frame was, he appeared only half the size of Rudy. "We're out of here. You have what you need?"

"Yeah, that's everything, I guess." Wynter followed him to the plane, a smile creeping onto her face at the sneakiness of Rashid. The man had saved her life, but he'd taken the treasure. It seemed a fair exchange. And Rudy was still alive? It was hardly the time to complain about a trunk full of artifacts!

"Is this your plane?" Wynter pulled the steps down.

"Nope. I arrived by boat a couple days ago. We'll tell them they can get their bird back from Turkey after we land. You don't think Azerbaijan will mind, do you? Come on, Kobuk. Up you go!"

Wynter followed her brothers up the stairs. Instead of joining Rudy in the cockpit as he ran diagnostics, Wynter changed the bandage on Titus' head. Kobuk investigated the wound with her wet nose until Wynter nudged her away.

"Your dog is kind of nosy, Rudy!" She laughed.

"Here we go!" he announced. "Hang on to Titus. I might be a little rusty here . . ."

"Just take us home." Wynter held Titus' head in her lap. "Just take us home."

New York

Corban hobbled on his crutches to the blast door, then turned back to Marc Densort.

"Do your best to track Oleg. I know it won't be easy."

"I'll stay on it." Marc waved without looking away from his computer screens. "Have a safe drive home."

"Maybe you should stay a little longer?" Janice carried a bag of their belongings over her shoulder. "I can come back next week to pick you up."

"No, we'll let Marc handle things for now." Corban frowned at the vast mine shaft room now consumed by tech wires and vines. "Besides Oleg, there's other important issues at hand. COIL needs to continue doing what it's designed to do. We'll rescue Oleg somehow, someday, but we also need to focus on other pressing missions. Besides, we haven't seen Jenna in almost a week. Let's go home."

CHAPTER TWENTY-EIGHT

Washington, D.C.

CIA Agent Wes Trimble was guided by Secret Service into the Oval Office of the White House. President Pantrow rose from his desk and offered his hand. The Secret Service left the two alone.

"Agent Trimble." They shook hands and the president offered Wes a seat on one of the two facing settees as he took the other. "I've been wanting to meet you for some time. Your reputation would be unbelievable, except your peers and superiors assure my people you're for real."

"The honor is mine, Mr. President."

"Oh, don't patronize me, Trimble." The president leaned forward with a grim face and his distinctive bulging eyes, of which media cartoonists had taken full advantage. "We both know we've had our differences. Someone with your history and connections, you surely know I've recently opposed certain extracurricular activities of yours."

"Ah, I see. We're talking about COIL." Wes grimaced. "Seems I'm not the only one with some intel."

"I don't know exactly how you did it, but Azerbaijan seems content. That's good enough for me. And we don't have to go to war against COIL by extraditing one of its acquaintances."

"Everyone wins, sir."

"Even the *Soldiers of Mahdi* win, it seems. That's what they think, right?" The president smiled knowingly, but Wes couldn't guess how knowingly. The last he'd heard, Wynter's staged body had done the trick. "I like your style, Trimble. And that's why I'm concerned to hear that you might be resigning from the Agency. I'd like you to stay."

"Mr. President, I love this country and I've enjoyed my career. But occasionally I receive an assignment that contradicts with my priorities. I'm a Christian first, sir. God, then country."

"That kind of uncompromising zeal might bother me if I didn't know you coordinated much of what happened last week in Azerbaijan."

"Sir?"

"Which assignments conflict with your faith?"

"The Bible, God's inspired Word, is the final authority for me on right and wrong. It's absolute truth to me."

"So, what's the Bible's policy on patriotism?"

Wes considered his words prayerfully.

"Give to Caesar what is Caesar's. And give to God what is God's. Caesar should never demand what God has prohibited, or what God alone should receive."

"I think I understand." The president sat back on the sofa, studying Wes. "Do you know this Corban Dowler?"

"As well as anyone could, I suspect."

"Someone recently contacted me, urging me to work more closely with him. Are his beliefs the same as yours?"

"He's counseled me before, so I can say yes with certainty."

"Then he's a friend of the United States? Without question?"

"Because he's a genuine Christian, sir, Corban Dowler is the best friend the United States could have. COIL makes America look good, besides the blessings from God that come as this country provides COIL a base of operations."

"Yes, I've heard something like that before. If you believe that, that's fine. My job is to protect the American people, and if that means I have in my pocket a moral agency that's as powerful as COIL, I'll be the last one to diminish her capacity to operate within every available outlet I can authorize."

"But, Mr. President, haven't you been against COIL? Wasn't that your recent stand?"

"I've seen the light from a rather dark perspective. Leave it at that."

"Well, thank you, sir. Corban Dowler will be glad to hear that."

"I don't want him to know. I'm sure Dowler will sense my new policy in favor of COIL, but this is between you and me."

"I'm sorry, I don't understand." Wes shook his head in perplexity.

"I want you to stay with the Agency as a cover. But really, you're my inside man at COIL. You're the Executive Branch's new liaison with COIL. Top secret."

"Honestly, sir, I won't spy on COIL for you."

"No, I don't want a spy, only assurances, and a two-way line of communication. Don't worry. I'll give you a grade so high to operate that no one will get in your way. I want COIL to get the most out of us, so we can get the most out of COIL's reputation, if they're as amazing as you and others claim."

"I'll do it on one condition: Corban Dowler needs to know. It wouldn't be right if he didn't, and it'll protect me from being dishonest toward both you and him."

"You're the genuine article, aren't you, Agent Trimble?" The president shook his head. "I didn't think they made guys like you anymore."

"God developed me into what I am today, sir. Thank Him."

"I'll agree to your terms, but no one else is to know except Dowler. You remain Deputy Director of PRS, stationed at the Pentagon. I'll call you in monthly for Agency reports, which you'll give me, but I'm especially interested in COIL's activities. They had a relationship with this office in the sometimes-shaky past, before my administration. I want to restore that. My intentions are entirely selfish, of course, since COIL can make this office look good without all the bureaucracy."

"That, I understand, Mr. President. And thank you."

"I'll be in touch, Agent Trimble. I look forward to working closely with you."

Iran

Imam Nasser al-Hakim walked through the sterile halls of Ana Bakhair Assylum. His followers trailed him with two of his youngest wives. Finally, he stopped at a sealed door, a speaker about chin level set into the cell door.

Through a thick door window, Nasser pitied Serik Tomir, once his finest assassin, now diminished to a wailing lunatic. Who would've known hunting down Gamal's murderer would've brought the great man to his wit's end? Perhaps it was worth it, Nasser considered. Wynter Caspertein's death had given him peace, but it had cost him his friendship with Serik, if that's what they'd truly had.

"Nasser!" Serik rushed the door, his nose smashed against the window glass. "Is it you? It's me, Serik! Did you see it? Did you kill it?"

"Kill what, Serik?" Nasser snickered with his followers. In two weeks, Serik's beard was untrimmed and his clothes were soiled.

"The demon! My sword. You see?" Serik danced around, holding a sword that wasn't really there. "I had it, but they took it! Then the bear came. The dog—it was huge! I don't know, but Wynter Caspertein knows! She was there. The man pushed the plane out, then I ran for my life!"

"A man pushed a plane and a bear came. Well, I had to see you for myself, old friend. I see you're in a world that you have created. I hope you are happy."

"Happy? Allah be merciful! There won't be any happiness until we catch Wynter Caspertein and avenge Gamal, our son! But avoid the bear. Nasser, please, promise me. The bear will devour us all!"

Serik mumbled more, then curled up in the far corner to cry. Nasser recalled Serik's recurring dream of a bear-dog-man beast. The pressures had ruined him, but thankfully, not before he'd taken Wynter Caspertein's life. Nasser had burned her charred body in a pit of pigs' bones near the sea. She was no more.

"Let us leave this place!" Nasser led his followers out of the asylum.

Oleg managed his breathing under the hood that covered his head. The hood smelled like vomit, surely from some past victim imprisoned by the *Soldiers of Mahdi,* but Oleg remained focused. He'd been deprived of sleep, and the marches down cold corridors for painful interrogations were haunting—but he wasn't alone.

In his misery, Oleg sensed his safety in God's loving arms. After all, Oleg had entrusted his eternal soul to the Father's mighty hands. No one could separate him from such love. And though this eternal reality was sufficient to carry him through the present anguish, his cup ran over with the thought of another reality. Titus, the Serval—the untamed man from Arkansas, the man who'd led him to Christ on a Moscow street corner—would not leave him to rot. Soon, Titus would come for him. COIL needed them. Oleg couldn't wait to see what God would do next!

New York

When Titus opened his eyes, he recognized his bedroom at his house in upstate New York, but he couldn't remember how he'd gotten there. The last thing he could remember was the chill of Mingechaur Reservoir.

He sat up dizzily, vaguely focusing on Annette's voice in another room.

"That's not the worst haircut you ever got."

Rudy sat motionless in a chair beside the bureau. Titus touched his head and felt half his scalp bald and stitched, while the other half was still covered with his hair.

"It ain't easy seeing dead people. How hard did I hit my head?"

"By the look of you, it's not the first bullet you thought you could stop with your Caspertein courage, either."

Titus stared at his brother for a moment. *This was real. Rudy was really there!* The mammoth himself, indeed. His beard was thick and his shoulders were built like an ox's.

"Did you have something to do with me making it home?"

"You're not the only Caspertein who can pilot a turbo-prop." Rudy chuckled. "You'll get the whole story eventually. Just know that Wes Trimble and I connected."

"And Wynter?"

"She's good. Someone dropped off a treasure chest on the porch, so she couldn't be happier. And right now, I suspect she's in the kitchen teaching your wife some of Mom's casserole recipes."

"That could be good, or it could be bad, depending on which casserole." Titus smiled when Rudy's big shoulders shook at the memory of their late mother's attempt at certain dishes. "Rudy, there was a guy, my partner. Is he—?"

"Oleg. No, he didn't make it back. Corban Dowler says he's still alive, though. The *Soldiers of Mahdi* have him in Iran."

"How long?"

"Two weeks. A private doctor kept you asleep until your brain de-swelled."

"*De-swelled?* Is that how seismologists refer to a decrease in cranial mass?"

"You always were better with words."

"Well, a smart mouth doesn't necessarily equal a smart man."

Titus bowed his head. They had a lifetime of history to plow through, but he'd prayed for this moment. God had brought his brother back to him. Oleg was missing and needed to be recovered, but right now, Rudy was priority. He lifted his head and held out his hand.

"It's good to see you, Rudy."

"You, too, little brother." Rudy gripped Titus' hand. "You, too."

DISTANT FRONT

BOOK TWO

The COIL Legacy

D.I. Telbat

A note from the author

Dear Reader,

In this age when truth is often taken for granted, I want you to know what is fiction in this *Distant Front* story, and what is fact.

Hudie Valley is a fictional rice paddy valley. The terrain north of the Huang River is desert, as this book indicates, but rice is generally cultivated in China south of the Chang River. However, the secret prison in Hudie Valley typifies China's actual ongoing antagonism against biblical Christianity. Reports of real re-education labor camps and prisons where Christians are held or have been held in the past are common knowledge.

The Gabriel sub-orbital, solar-paneled spy drone technology is currently being developed by Titan Airspace. The combat drone, which COIL calls the DRIL, is actually undergoing flight tests right now by the Department of Defense.

The sub-net technology developed by Steve Brookshire was modeled after actual Dark Web browser software. A special browser is required to access certain servers. The "Deep Web" is estimated to be 500 times larger than the surface web we commonly know of. The Deep Web offers nefarious goods and services, like an online black market, with goods such as cryptocurrency, unhackable web-hosting services, crimeware, hitmen, explosives, forged papers, drugs, and human organs.

Shanghai Tower really is 2073 feet high, and its elevators are the fastest in the world, about forty miles per hour.

COIL's satellite watch (sat-watch) technology that Titus Caspertein wears is years old in reality. IGZO has a display resolution of 498 pixels per inch, many times sharper than iPhone's version.

Red Light Districts in Kathmandu really do have safe houses run by Christians, and beauty salons meant as outreaches to women trapped in prostitution. These ministries rescue women and sometimes babies born in these districts, which much of the world turns a blind eye toward, due to the promise of commerce.

Akita, Japan, really was a Samurai hotspot in the ancient Orient. Preserved houses remain for tourists to visit in this old NW town.

I hope you enjoy reading *Distant Front* as much as I enjoyed writing it. May God use it to enrich your relationship with Him!—*David Telbat*

Dedication

To the Christian Persecuted Church in China,
whose sacrifice and suffering
is beyond our Western minds.
Yet God sees. He knows.
Your reward awaits you in heaven.

Iran – Present Day

Titus "The Serval" Caspertein stood on a mountain ridge in Northern Iran. The haze of the Caspian Sea lingered to the north and Mount Damavand rose behind him. A wet wind whipped at his parka as he donned a pair of glasses to protect his eyes.

The dull throb of a combat drone reached his ears before he noticed the massive machine flying above the sparse forest terrain, climbing in elevation to his position. It was the latest technology developed by the Commission of International Laborers to aid persecuted Christians. But since the drone with a forty-five-foot wing-span was unmanned, Titus had to duck as it flew dangerously low over his head, then circled and swooped in for a landing.

COIL had called this drone the DRIL, or Drone Resupply Insertion Lander, and Titus was still getting familiar with its stealth capabilities. Landing fifty miles inside Iran was certainly COIL's most courageous mission yet with the machine, especially since its top speed was only two hundred and forty miles per hour. It would be an easy target for Iran's fighter jets, if the DRIL happened to appear on radar.

"Okay, shut her down, Marc," Titus shouted into his watch, communicating with technician Marc Densort in New York via their suborbital satellites called Gabriels.

The roar of the DRIL's two-ducted fans, each nine feet wide, powered down as it came to rest on its chopper-like runners. The two five-blade propellers hadn't stopped spinning before Titus approached the detachable payload bay, which was capable of carrying over three thousand pounds.

Using a keypad on the dark green fuselage, Titus communicated with the onboard computer, then the bay opened its cargo door to reveal forty duffel bags, each weighing precisely seventy pounds.

"We have a touchdown here." Titus lifted the first bag and carried it awkwardly toward a suburban parked on a dirt access road. "Give me about twenty minutes."

"Roger that. Hey, how was my landing this time?" Marc Densort was an ex-*jihadist* from the Middle East, now serving Jesus Christ with his skills rather than building bombs for Hamas. "Was it nice and smooth?"

"It was your best yet." Titus reached the suburban and set the duffel bag in the back. With all but the front driver's seat removed, there was plenty of space for the rest of the bags. "Maybe next time, you could deliver me a forklift to unload all these Bibles. It ain't easy doing Oleg's half of the labor."

"Maybe by next week's shipment, you can watch him carry his own share."

Titus returned for another bag. The capture of his partner, Oleg Saratov, was a sore subject on his mind, but it helped to chide the man in his absence. Iran's extremist group, *Soldiers of Mahdi*, had captured him during a previous mission into Azerbaijan, and Titus wasn't leaving the country until he recovered his companion in Christ. His surveillance on the SOM's compound east of Esfahan was only interrupted by Bible shipments into the country where it was still too dangerous to print Bibles.

Thirty minutes later, Titus closed the empty cargo hold of the DRIL and patted her fuselage as if she were a loyal shepherd.

"Off you go, Marc."

"You know, you could catch a ride back to the mothership if you want." Marc referred to a COIL tanker far out in the Caspian Sea that returned to Russia between supply runs. "Corban Dowler has been calling me daily, wondering when you're returning to normal mission status."

Titus stood back and shielded his face as the DRIL's two helicopter engines roared to life. A moment later, the green beast rose a few feet off the ground, then swooped down the mountainside. Avoiding the populations of Nowshahr and Amol, it disappeared out to sea.

"You can tell Corban I may not even be in Iran for next week's shipment." Titus climbed into the suburban. "Once I free Oleg from his little vacation resort, we'll probably be leaving Iran in a hurry."

"Okay. You should probably tell me what you have in mind. When exactly are you planning to extract Oleg?"

"I'm dropping the Bibles at the safe house in Tehran, then I'm returning to Esfahan."

"All right, so what's your extraction timeline? I'll need a couple days to set up some support for you. The more the better, of course."

"In last week's drop, you left me all the toys I need."

"You're still not answering my question, Titus, which makes me nervous . . ."

"Tonight. I'm getting Oleg out of prison tonight."

CHAPTER ONE

Hong Kong – Two Years Ago

Steve Brookshire touched the gash in his right shoulder as he held his breath underwater. With his goggles, he peered upward through Hong Kong's murky seawater. Training for the next Ironman Championship to be held in Kona, Hawaii, had suddenly become a swimming hazard.

From a depth of twenty feet, Steve gazed up at the undersides of two boats. As a Christian operative in China, he knew there were risks in the communist country, but there'd been no warnings that someone was moving in on him. A part of him wanted to surface and gulp a breath of fresh air—then demand an explanation for this attack. But they'd already wounded him with a spear gun. These men couldn't be reasoned with. What nightmare was occurring on board the boats idling above him?

In the smaller of the two motor boats, his fiancée, Lisa Kennedy, had been piloting beside him as he swam far out into the sea east of Hong Kong. As a citizen of China, he was often recognized on the streets of the city and honored as one of their own athletes. Steve welcomed their attention, hoping it secured him a little more safety to work covertly for Jesus Christ.

As for the other boat, a giant cruiser, Steve could imagine who was in it. There were dark forces inside China's government who would do anything and hire anyone to shut down his work. They'd used a spear gun rather than a firearm this time. Even in Hong Kong's turbulent waters, gunfire would've brought the marine authorities and police investigators.

The spear gun also meant something else—they intended to injure him and take him alive. If their next shot was more accurate, they could reel him in to the boat and take their time questioning him. He knew they wanted to discover his secrets—the keys to his network in the underground church that spanned the country of China. Hundreds of thousands of lives were in danger.

Steve felt his lungs begin to burn, forcing him to determine a plan. He couldn't rescue Lisa, if she were still alive. Without COIL's non-lethal weaponry, he was defenseless to fight them. His morning training swim had rapidly turned into an operation of desperation.

If he surfaced unexpectedly, he wondered if he could sneak a quick breath of air then dive underwater again and continue to out-wait his attackers. Once darkness covered the waters, he could swim ashore. However, because of his shoulder wound, he figured the blood loss would hasten his fatigue. As a triathlete, he could compete against the finest athletes in the world, but here, he needed to dodge spear gun projectiles and hold his breath indefinitely.

He could only see shimmering images through the murky water above, but he guessed that those leaning over the cruiser's deck didn't realize who they were dealing with, or they would've killed him out-right. He'd never talk. And if he found his way to a phone, Corban Dowler would send the most skilled COIL agents in the world to sort out the situation.

But more than that, Steve was a Christian. God was his Father—a Father who never abandoned His children. And since God was already watching, Steve tried to settle his mind about Lisa's life now in the enemy's hands. He loved her, and he wanted her back, but this was now about the countless Christians who used Steve's secret network for safety, communication, and resources for spiritual growth. Those men, women, and children were a priority, their lives in Steve's safe-keeping.

It was now time to call COIL.

Iran – Present Day

Titus Caspertein drove a silver Mercedes up to the walled com-pound used by the *Soldiers of Mahdi* outside Esfahan in central Iran, and parked outside the front gate. Using a Russian accent, he'd already called ahead, so his late-night arrival to the extremist training center wasn't a surprise. He presented a manufactured Russian identification to a heavily-armed Persian, then a sturdy door swung open to allow him entry.

There was a small flutter of fear deep in Titus' gut. He didn't mind dying for Christ, or being captured by a million-strong apocalyptic *jihadi* group. Rather, he felt anxiety over the possible failure of rescuing Oleg Saratov. After all, the ugly brute had been captured because he'd sacrificed himself so Titus and his sister could escape during the previous operation. Oleg had offered his life for Titus, and Titus could imagine doing no less for Oleg. It was probable, Titus guessed, that Oleg was wondering what was taking him so long. It'd already been two months since the Azerbaijan operation!

Parking next to a row of transport vehicles, Titus glanced in the rearview mirror to check his disguise. He'd dyed his blond hair dark and donned a salt-and-pepper beard. Many of the *Soldiers of Mahdi* knew him, but he hoped his hasty disguise adequately hid his identity for the next hour.

"It ain't easy being this foolish," he mumbled to himself, then climbed out of the car. He adjusted his suit and buttoned his jacket as two soldiers approached and greeted him in Arabic, which indicated they were foreign recruits to the cause, since they weren't speaking Persian. He held his arms wide for the customary frisk, but he hadn't worn any obvious weapons, particularly his non-lethal sidearm that would've instantly announced his COIL affiliation. This wasn't his first meeting with a powerful—and deranged—religious leader.

He was led into a concrete building, down a corridor, and up a flight of stairs. Though he had gunmen before and after him, he remained focused, comparing in his mind what he'd seen of the compound in images he'd studied from the three Gabriel UAVs flying at seventy thousand feet. He'd also seen the compound directly outside its walls the night before as he'd scouted around and planted distraction devices.

The compound perimeter was four miles around, complete with barracks, shooting range, and an urban warfare training arena that resembled a modern Western city. Though less than ten percent of Iranians took Islam seriously, the leaders and the elite were devoted. They believed the *Mahdi*, their messiah or prophet, would return only after followers of Allah caused unprecedented carnage against all infidels. Then, the *Mahdi* would descend from heaven. Titus wasn't sure exactly when, but in some religious writings, the extremists believed that Jesus Christ would worship and serve the *Mahdi*. He didn't mind single-handedly showing the extremists that they weren't as supernaturally powerful as they thought. But his

his priority was essentially to spread the Word, and preserve those who were also active in sharing the gospel of Jesus Christ. That priority didn't change just because he was on a rescue mission.

His escorts directed him into an inner office that was lit by candles but smelled like opium. Titus had trafficked enough contraband over his rebellious years without Christ to know Iran was the world's leading user of heroin. After all, Afghanistan, the largest producer of heroin, was its immediate neighbor to the east.

Imam Serik al-Hakim swiveled in his office chair toward Titus. He was an intimidating man, in size and glare, with a beard that added to his air of authority. Gesturing to a leather chair, the man didn't otherwise welcome Titus.

Titus seated himself and briefly touched his breast pocket under his jacket where he carried two pens. He felt a trickle of sweat along his spine as he realized he should've placed each pen in a different pocket, because they each had their own purpose. What if he grabbed and clicked the wrong pen at the wrong time? This was what Corban Dowler and Marc Densort were always worried about, he realized. Planning out all the details of a mission didn't cross his mind until he was in the middle of an operation.

"Y-you are Yevgeny Zimyatov?" Serik spoke accented English with a stutter, but it didn't diminish his powerful presence. "I didn't know we had acquaintances still in Moscow."

"Whether we are called acquaintances, or friends—" Titus hoped his exaggerated Russian accent could be understood, "we can always do business, da?"

"Business is in a true Persian's blood." Serik smiled, showing teeth stained from smoking too much opium. "Your call intrigued me. You say you have information that could lead to the capture of the man called the Serval."

"This is true. The Serval is in a very vulnerable position at this very moment." Titus casually turned his head and nodded at one of the *imam's* renowned bodyguards. Ercan Sanli was a Kurd built like a linebacker, and carried a sawed-off shotgun on a sling. He was on an Interpol watch list for the assassination of a pro-Israel journalist, but Titus reminded himself he was only there for Oleg, not to make arrests for Interpol. The two other gunmen behind Titus had their own flavors of intimidation with machine guns in hand. "I'm happy to provide you with the information necessary to capture the Serval, if you act quickly—yet I have a request for you as well."

"I see." Serik frowned. "So, you don't contribute to the efforts of Allah's holy ones without conditions?"

"Perhaps business is in my Russian blood as well." Titus raised his palms and smiled. "We are both men who have much wealth already. Some business is perhaps accomplished for the entertainment value."

"Hmph." Serik grunted and picked up a walnut. He made a show of crushing the shell with a nut cracker, then eating the demolished nut piece by piece. "What is your request?"

"Not long ago, a man named Oleg Saratov joined the Serval. The two have been a smuggling scourge upon the earth." Titus never missed an opportunity to bolster his rogue cover. "Before he joined the Serval, Oleg was with Interpol. He and I have a history. I can give you the Serval's precise location, but I want Oleg Saratov for myself. And you have him."

"Impossible." Serik dismissed the idea with a wave of his hand. "I'm saving Oleg to execute in front of the Serval, when I have caught him. It will be an honor killing in a blood feud."

"May I be present when this execution is carried out?" Titus wondered if he'd thought of enough contingencies if things didn't go as planned. "I must see for myself when this man dies."

"That's easy. Give me the Serval, and you may see Oleg Saratov's painful execution."

"If I may not take Oleg for myself, may I at least see him before he dies?"

"Just see him?"

"I am one who appreciates the look of defeat on an enemy's face."

"Are you sure you're not Persian? You have the mind of one." Serik smiled again, and Titus chuckled gruffly. "Go. Now. See Oleg for yourself. That's as much as I can do, but you will deliver the Serval?"

"With certainty, I can tell you where he is at this very moment."

Titus rose, and two escorts led him from the office and farther down a corridor. When they picked up a third escort, Titus glanced at his watch to confirm they were indeed moving toward where Oleg's body heat signature had been tracked and observed for two months.

He just hoped Oleg was in condition to run for his life.

Hong Kong – Two Years Ago

Steve Brookshire surfaced for a breath of air between the two boats. The shimmering shapes he'd seen leaning over the side of the larger boat had been gunmen. He guessed even if the gunmen on board saw him, they wouldn't risk shooting their own multi-million-dollar cruiser.

He panted for several breaths, then dove again. As if the gunmen suspected his strategy, the rental boat that had been previously piloted by Lisa Kennedy sped away and turned in an arc toward the shore. Only the cruiser remained, its fifty-foot length a dark shadow in the midmorning sunlight above.

Two splashes near the bow drew Steve's attention. As the bubbles ascended, Steve saw two men with face masks, and each held a spear gun aimed at him! He was contemplating surrender, possibly to preserve himself as well as to assess Lisa's condition—when both men fired.

Steve dodged one spear about to stab him in the torso, but the lower spear pierced his right calf. Blood clouded the water and Steve screamed through the pain as he struggled toward the surface. But something was wrong, much worse than merely being shot in the calf. He looked down. The spear was connected to a thin cord, and the shooter was reeling him in like a captured tuna! The second shooter recovered his spear and aimed it at Steve.

Together, the three rose to the surface. As soon as his head bobbed in the air, Steve's arms were grabbed by strangers, who dragged him on board. He was punched in the face and kicked in the gut. Instinctively, he tried to curl into the fetal position to protect his vitals and head, but the cord attached to his calf hindered his movements.

The beating stopped. Dazed, Steve exhaled shakily and lay still on his back, his eyes half-open. The sun shined through the smog of Hong Kong, but he felt no comfort, no security, no warmth.

"Help me," he prayed, remembering that the ocean, like the world, was often unpredictable, but God was no less present. God had preserved him through countless ocean swims; He was just as trustworthy out of the water.

Someone flipped him onto his belly and wrenched his arms behind him. A knee pressed on his spine as his hands were tied. Only then did he feel someone tend to his calf wound. His body convulsed when the dart was forced the rest of the way through his muscle, then yanked out.

A hood that smelled like diesel was thrust over his head then tightened around his neck. Next, his ankles were bound. Finally, he was left alone. Before the hood was put on, Steve had sensed as many as a dozen men on deck. He fought panic by focusing on one truth: God was aware.

When they spoke, his confusion grew. They spoke Japanese, which he didn't know. From Hong Kong, he'd operated across China, as far as Golmud in the west. Christianity was legal in Japan. They had no reason to kidnap a Christian missionary in China!

"Hey." A shoe nudged him in the shoulder. The speaker spoke softly, now in accented English. "Your life is over. Your girlfriend is dead. The sooner you talk, the sooner we end this."

Steve was about to respond when he was roughly picked up by two men and carried away. The little bit of light that showed through the hood disappeared, and he guessed he was below deck. Men's footsteps echoed off close quarters, and Steve was jostled against a metal door. The man who carried his legs was none too gentle about the wound, bringing tears of pain to Steve's eyes.

Suddenly, he was dropped onto the cold floor, his brow hitting the hard surface. He fought to retain consciousness. Nothing was right. *Lisa was dead?* They wanted him to talk, but they stowed him below deck. *Lord God, what is happening?*

Partially from the choking diesel fumes and partly from the blow to the head, Steve mercifully passed out.

Iran – Present Day

Titus was feeling the jitters. The *Soldiers of Mahdi* compound had three thousand faithful followers on site—one hundred of them women, called *baseige*, devoted to a militant lifestyle of the worship of Allah. These soldiers had passed various stress tests and memorized the entire Koran. They were Islam's *Shiite* elites, and their proudly-worn armbands boasted as much.

The detainment cells in the subterranean level were built of steel with modernized electronic locking mechanisms. Five cells lined the wall on the left and five on the right. Titus' three escorts stopped at the second cell on the left and pounded on the door. One soldier, with an Iranian rifle over his shoulder, opened a small metal slot in the door and Titus crouched to see into a dark interior.

Slowly, his eyes adjusted. There was a very dim ceiling light, covered in grime, barely illuminating the cell. A cement bunk and a hole in the floor seemed to be the cell's only amenities. A mountainous mass moved under a small blanket on the bunk.

Titus nodded at his escorts.

"I must speak to this cursed man in Russian. It's our native tongue. For him to hear it—his death will feel much more bitter. Do you approve?"

The nearest escort shrugged and stepped back. Titus knelt on one knee, his mouth at the edge of the slot.

"Get out of bed!" Titus' gruff voice reverberated off the walls. "It's disgraceful to catch you snoring while there's work to do! Come over to the door, you filthy Russian!"

Oleg rolled off the bed, then made his way to the door, the blanket over his shoulders.

"Did you make an appointment with my interrogator?" Oleg's voice sounded weak, but Titus wanted to shout for joy at the unbroken man's wit. "I'd hate to miss a scheduled torture session just to visit with you."

"Don't worry. They're keeping you alive to be executed in front of the Serval, as soon as they capture him."

"Then I'm flattered you came to witness the occasion." Oleg coughed into his meaty fist. "Actually, I wouldn't object to a little COIL attention. A measure of warm sunshine and pleasant company might do me some good. Sooner rather than later. Not that I'm dissatisfied with the hospitality here."

"Don't let me interrupt your vacation." Titus tucked his right hand into his jacket. "There's something about suffering that brings us closer to God. I'd hate to get in the way of your communion."

"Would you get on with it?"

"It ain't easy putting up with my mouth, huh?" Titus felt the two pens in his pocket. They felt the same. He had to pick one. "Maybe I'm stalling for a reason."

"What would that reason be?"

"There are three bulls out here, and three thousand more nearby. And my plan is a little sketchy."

"That never stopped you before. I thought that's the Serval's motto: a sketchy plan is better than no plan at all."

"The silver Mercedes out front is armored. A bullpup is hidden in the back seat."

"Roger that."

"Help me out with one of these bulls, and I'll handle the other two."

"Open the door, and I'll handle all three."

Titus chuckled and roughly slammed the metal slot as if he were angry.

"Enough!" he shouted in Arabic and threw his hands into the air, holding a pen in one. "This infidel has no honor. Take me back to the *imam*. It's time I told him where to find the Serval!"

They started up the corridor, two in front, and one behind Titus. When they reached the stairs, Titus pivoted and kicked the soldier behind him in the chest. He grabbed the one directly in front of him by the back of the belt and yanked him backwards. The first soldier turned to see what the commotion was, but Titus was already on him. The pen flashed like the hidden syringe it was, stabbing superficially into the man's thigh muscle. Two heartbeats later, the tranquilizer took effect.

Titus slammed a fist over the electronic control that released the second cell door. Oleg emerged while the two fallen soldiers were still tangled by their own limbs, trying to level their rifles. With more strength than Titus expected from Oleg, the Russian plucked one soldier off the floor. He ripped the rifle out of the man's hands and hooked an elbow around the soldier's neck in a choke hold.

With ease, Titus tranquilized the second man and dragged him into the open cell.

"Anyone else in these cells we need to take with us?"

Oleg dropped his unconscious soldier and punched the right wall button that opened the fifth door.

"He's the only other one down here." Oleg moved to the fifth door as Titus dragged the last unconscious soldier into Oleg's vacated cell. "Titus, meet Brother Abib."

"Introductions later." Titus nodded at a wiry, middle-aged Iranian who looked like he'd been imprisoned and starved for months. He hit the cell buttons to close all doors. "You got it from here? I have to go say goodbye."

Oleg supported Abib, nearly carrying the malnourished man, and shook his head at Titus.

"Let it go, Titus. For once, no games. You said an armored carriage awaits."

Titus gave Oleg the tranq-pen.

"It ain't easy putting up with my antics, I know, but this is important for the Kingdom."

Oleg and Abib shuffled down the corridor toward the front of the building, but Titus marched up the stairs, back to *Imam* Serik al-Hakim's office. Two soldiers stood outside the door.

"Muhammad told me to return to talk to the *imam*." Titus pointed behind him with his thumb. "The prisoners are acting up. Muhammad said you guys would know what to do."

"Which Muhammad?" One of the guards frowned. "Achmed?"

"Exactly. Achmed."

The guard seemed satisfied and knocked lightly on the door before opening it. Titus entered the office where Ercan Sanli, the shotgun bodyguard, was alone with the bearded *Imam* Serik al-Hakim. The door closed behind him, and Titus seated himself solemnly in the leather chair. Ercan glowered, one hand on his shotgun, but Titus focused on Serik, who pushed a laptop aside.

"You spoke to Oleg Saratov?"

"I did, and I am satisfied. My work here is nearly complete, with exception to my promise to you: the exact location of the Serval at this moment."

"You can guarantee it?" Serik shared a glance with his bodyguard. "The Serval has many tricks. Some say he's not even a man, but I want to see for myself how he bleeds."

"I can guarantee his location. But it comes with a warning."

"Warning?"

"Yes. You see, the Serval serves the true God, and therefore, he is literally in the watch-care of the Almighty, until God Himself calls him home."

"Yevgeny Zimyatov, you are a guest here, so I will allow this slight against Allah, but we have discovered the Serval is a Nazarene. A servant of Isa! He has no protection from Allah!"

Titus nodded, understanding the designation for Christians across the Middle East, and the name Isa, as the Koran called Jesus.

"I understand your hesitation to believe me, but it is because the Serval serves Isa that he desires kindness for you, not harm. You have said it yourself: the Serval is very crafty. If he wanted to, he could cause you harm. But his compassion for you, because of the true God's love for all people, even the sinful—has provided you with time to repent from your hatred. Love is stronger than hate. It is the love of Isa."

The *imam's* mouth was open in shock. Ercan's hand shifted on his shotgun grip. Surely, no one had ever spoken such words to the supposed holy man.

"Blasphemy! How dare you!"

"The Koran says this." Titus held up his hand. "In Surah 5:110, that Isa raised the dead by miracles, and in Surah 6:36 and 22:6, the Koran says that whoever raised the dead is God. Isa did raise the dead. I think this is important to remember. Isa raised the dead, and He is alive today. Isa is God."

"Shut your mouth!" Serik shook with rage, his stutter more pronounced. "Tell me where the Serval is before I behead you here and now!"

"Very well. I will tell you exactly where the Serval is. He's in your office."

"What? Which office? In Tehran? Istanbul?"

"No, your office east of Esfahan."

"East of— That's this office!"

"You got it." Titus winked. "You're not real swift, are you?"

As his words sunk into their minds, Titus drew out the second pen and rested his thumb on the clicker.

"Remember my words about Isa. His love for you will bring peace to your life, but you must open your hearts and believe."

He pressed his thumb down. The explosion was far away on the other side of the compound, but it still shook the floor. Then, the next explosion detonated in a chain of planted ordnance. The buried explosives had been planted against the wall the night before. Titus' surveillance of the compound over the weeks provided him easy access to plant packages all the way around to the front gate.

The detonations grew closer. Ercan's eyes grew larger, and he started to level his weapon.

"Tough love is still love," Titus stated, and from his seat, he jabbed the bodyguard hard in the solar plexus, and tore his shotgun away from him. Before the man recovered, Titus opened the door where the two guards were about to enter. "Stay at the door! Protect the *imam* with your lives!"

Titus slammed the door then crossed the office to Serik. The confused *imam* backed away. Receiving a hard right hook to the chin from Titus, the *imam* slumped to the floor. Seeing movement on his right, Titus turned in time to brace himself as the bodyguard tackled him. After a forearm brace, Titus tossed the larger man over the desk. The explosions outside shook the building as Titus jumped on Ercan's back.

From his back pocket, Titus drew what looked like a baby pacifier. Riding Ercan like he were an ostrich, Titus shoved the applicator into the man's mouth, then pressed a plastic release. Together, they smashed into a bookshelf, but Titus hung on, his hands covering the bodyguard's nose and mouth.

The brute spit out the applicator, but its contents were already in his mouth. With one hand on the man's nose, and an arm around his throat, Titus forced his adversary to swallow the tracker that would eventually lodge harmlessly in his intestinal tract.

Finally, Titus allowed himself to be thrown to the floor. Dust from the ceiling sprinkled on them as they recovered their breaths. Explosions on the perimeter wall were close now. Titus picked up the empty applicator and stuck it in his pocket. When the bodyguard seemed ready to continue, Titus held up his hand.

"Wait a minute. I have one more thing to say. I know you're willing to die for your god. But Isa was and is God, and He was willing to die for you. You won't find greater love than that. Get your hands on a Bible, Ercan, and find out for yourself. You won't be disappointed."

With a roar, Ercan charged. Titus leaped back and swung open the door. The two guards had fled or had run to join what sounded like an attack on the compound. One more explosion shook the walls, throwing Titus and his infuriated pursuer to the floor. Barely out of

Ercan's grasp, Titus bounded upright and dashed up the corridor toward sunlight shining through an open door.

The parking lot was a fray of armed men in various states of dress. They seemed so determined to defend the walls against an outside attacker that no one bothered to stop Titus as he raced past several cars in the parking lot. Oleg was in sight, leaning over the silver Mercedes with a bullpup in his hands. The .308 caliber, short battle rifle was loaded with gel-tranqs—the latest in COIL's non-lethal arsenal.

"Down!" Oleg's voice boomed in English, barely audible over the chaos.

Titus dropped to his belly, scuffing his palms as he slid a few inches on the blacktop. The bullpup roared overhead, and the bodyguard dropped mid-stride, coming to rest on top of Titus' feet.

Kicking free, Titus lunged for the Mercedes as Abib threw open the driver's door for him. Oleg hopped into the passenger seat, the bullpup in his lap, and Abib climbed into the back seat. The engine was already running. As intended, the last explosion had knocked the front gate off its hinges. Since the detonations were planted outside the compound, no one inside had been harmed, only shaken.

Titus plowed the armored car through what was left of the gate and raced down the desert highway toward the city of Esfahan.

"You have a little something right there." Oleg pointed to Titus' cheek.

"I can always count on you, Oleg." Titus peeled off what remained of his beard disguise. "Feel like a midnight run over the Zargos Mountains?"

"Abib here has a place in Shiraz. Might be a good place to hole-up for a day or two. You mind telling me what was so important that you had to light that hornet's nest on fire?"

"Had to preach a short gospel message and force-feed a giant." Titus plucked the plastic applicator from his pocket. "I made the *imam's* bodyguard swallow a time-release beacon on a five-minute ping delay. Even if they scan him, it's unlikely they'll detect a ping. We can keep track of the *imam* now. I don't think we've seen the last of the *Soldiers of Mahdi!*"

CHAPTER TWO

Shanghai – Two Years Ago

Steve prayed through what he guessed was the night. His leg wound throbbed and his hands were numb from the tight binds, but he'd witnessed God's might and love for too many years to believe the Lord had abandoned him now. This was China, where thousands of Christians resided in prisons, where only house churches in hiding preached the true gospel, where miracles occurred daily to bring souls to Christ. That was his mighty God's work!

"Thank You, Father," Steve whispered through swollen lips, "for counting me worthy to suffer for You."

As a professional athlete, his body was toned like few others in the world. Steve's resting heartbeat was barely fifty beats per minute, which may have saved his life since he received so little oxygen through the fuel-soaked hood. Athletic or not, he'd been reduced to an invalid from the injury and the beating on deck. Thus, his mind remained on the spiritual realm for strength and comfort. He was a triathlete only secondarily. His identity was as a child of God.

"They may take my body, Lord, but You hold my spirit." Tears leaked from his shut eyes. "You are trustworthy. Let me be true to You, I pray. . ."

The cruiser went silent, the vibrating motor cut abruptly. Steve listened for noises, footsteps, or even Lisa's screams. Was she really dead? Operating inside a country hostile to true Christianity was always dangerous, but nothing about the situation made sense yet. How were the Japanese involved?

Boots stomped on the platform outside. They were coming for him. Steve's heart beat faster, like it did at the beginning of a race.

A door opened and he was picked up by two men. The hood was removed. A third man shined a flashlight in his face and spoke more Japanese.

Steve didn't struggle as they hauled him up a corridor and companionway to the deck. The sky was dark, but it gave Steve no indication as to how long he'd slept. Across the deck, he noticed a dozen other men, each of them armed. His captors carried him across the gangway to a pier and shipping yard, then into a large metal shipping container. Halfway inside the container's length, the two men set him on the cold floor, then backed away.

The heavy door slammed shut and Steve was alone again. At least they hadn't placed the hood back over his head, he thought. He realized that his stability through the coming hours or days would depend on him recognizing the small witness God was leaving him to remember that his Lord was good and caring. There was light even on the darkest night.

His mind drifted to the possibility of rescue. To expect immediate relief was unreasonable, but he was a COIL-trained and COIL-supported operative. Through weekly encrypted reports, he'd kept his case worker in New York apprised of basic events. As soon as he didn't report in, his file would be handed to a COIL administrator, maybe even Corban Dowler himself. Then, a field agent or a whole team would be tasked to follow the trail. But would there be any trail to follow? Rescue was unlikely.

Steve fought despair at the idea of enduring senseless torture for the secrets he held. There were chemicals and powerful drugs that might make him talk as well. Resistance in some cases was futile, but dependence on God to guard his tongue was a reliable thought.

"Lord, see me now," he prayed. "I need You. Keep me going, please. Don't let me despair. Hold me from faltering. This is for You . . ."

Shanghai – Two Years Ago

Lisa Kennedy lay handcuffed on a bed. For what seemed like days, she'd stared at a ceiling with water stains. Now, suddenly, her reasoning returned and she enjoyed moments of rare clarity. At gunpoint, she'd been captured, bound, and gagged before she'd been able to warn Steve of danger. She'd been his spotter while he swam in the ocean, and now he was—where?

The bed frame was metal, and the handcuffs were attached to the corner posts and to each wrist. Her ankles were free now, but she seemed to recall them being bound at some point. This wasn't a normal kidnapping for ransom, or even a human trafficking abduction. This was about Steve. She knew now she'd merely been in the way. Steve was the real Christian operative, she knew—the one they wanted.

A sore on her left arm was festering. And there were a dozen needle marks there from violent punctures into her veins, as if her abductors wanted to intentionally leave needle marks. One of the drugs they'd given her was familiar—heroin. And something else to keep her sedated and complacent. Heroin wouldn't have been familiar, but she'd had a past, a past she hadn't even told Steve about. Those two years on the streets of San Francisco had been a whole other life, another nightmare. But she was a Christian now. She was dead to that old life.

The flimsy, wooden door opened, one that Lisa wouldn't expect to hold a prisoner. The lamp in the corner offered enough light to see the painted face of an elderly Chinese woman. With a syringe held visible, the woman approached Lisa.

"Please, no!" Lisa was tempted to kick the woman to keep her at bay. "No, I don't want any more! I'll be good. Please!"

"I know you be good." The woman said in choppy English then smiled and patted Lisa's cheek. Lisa had seen her type all over Hong Kong, particularly in the red light districts. Retired prostitutes sometimes became managers of brothels. "This is for you arrest. I get you ready. Here."

Lisa wiggled and kicked, but the woman finally won through the violence. As the poison flooded her veins, Lisa tried to process her tormentor's words. *For her arrest?* She was being prepped for something else!

"God, help me . . ." She whimpered as her body relaxed and her mind slipped into an escaping void she both loved and hated.

"No God here," the woman cackled, then retreated from the room.

Lisa's eyes fluttered. The oblivion of past days returned. Her gaze settled on the ceiling, on a water spot that looked like a funnel. Or a whirlwind. Elijah and a whirlwind. Yes, there was something distant and comforting there. It was enough to give her hope as her tears ran.

Pakistan – Present Day

Titus crossed his arms and felt his silenced nine-millimeter holstered under his jean jacket. Deep inside unpredictable Pakistan, he hoped his zeal for God rose above his weariness. He still had a few scratches and bruises from Oleg's rescue in Iran, but this wasn't the first time he'd pushed himself this hard with cancer coursing through his body. Before rescuing Oleg, the results had been sent to him by Annette, his wife. He was in stage four. The dye test had shown cancer cells infecting even his bone marrow.

He could see his operative status for COIL was coming to a close as his cancer spread.

"Three Philistines on site," Oleg reported on his comm, drawing Titus from thoughts of his secret condition. As of yet, he hadn't told anyone inside COIL about the disease eating away at his insides. His broad-shouldered Russian partner walked hastily up the street, past a Christian safe house. "What do you want to do?"

"What we get paid the big bucks to do." Titus stepped from the cover of a factory building and walked toward the entrance of the safe house. It was a duplex apartment, a residence on one side, and an electronics repair shop on the other.

"Wait," Oleg said, now out of sight around a corner. "We get paid for this? What's been happening to my paychecks?"

"It ain't easy laying up that heavenly coin, brother." Titus chuckled, realizing he'd be seeing heaven sooner than his partner. He pushed through the shop's front door. "I'm inside. We'll talk about your wages later."

Oleg didn't respond, which told Titus his partner was probably in the process of incapacitating the first of three police watchers outside. All across Pakistan, Christians were being targeted and falsely accused of crimes against the Koran. COIL had been able to help a few individuals, but only a few.

"Jimmah?" Titus called to a slender man in his fifties. The contact was behind the counter, glasses on the end of his nose, hunched over what appeared to be a hair dryer. "The Fisher of men sent me."

"I'll get my family!"

The man disappeared up a staircase that led to the next door apartment. Titus didn't know how instrumental the electrician was to the cause of Christ in Pakistan, but he didn't need to know. Any believer in danger was reason enough for him to risk everything.

"Report, Oleg." Titus checked the window.

"Three down, but we have bigger problems."

"Explain."

"A unit just showed up. Eight total. All armed. Two cars and one empty van, like they're here to pick up Jimmah!"

"We're too late!" Titus clenched his fist. "Suggestion?"

"I'm really good at distractions." Oleg chuckled. "Say the word."

"Is the back alley clear? I'd rather you didn't turn yourself in to get tortured again so soon."

"Negative. The back alley is blocked by a wall. You'll have to bring him out the front."

"Okay." Titus closed his eyes for a few seconds, trusting the Spirit inside him to be his guide. "Okay, Oleg, find an elevated place to hide and back me up. Let's hope your aim is as sharp as your tongue."

"Please, no bluffing, Titus. There are eight of them!"

"It ain't easy, brother, but we're in a pickle here." Titus heard Jimmah's family descending the stairs. "How much time do I have?"

"Thirty seconds, I'd say, and they'll be walking in that door." Oleg sounded winded. "I'm on someone's roof. Your visitors are about ready!"

Titus turned from the window's limited view to greet Jimmah's family. It took a few seconds for Titus to actually count all the family members. *Fourteen!* It took restraint for him not to laugh. God was always doing this to him—testing the limits of his faith and dependency. The family appeared to be four generations strong. An elderly couple clutched bags while two younger couples held backpacks and children, the youngest no more than two years old.

"Jimmah, this is your whole family?"

"Yes, my father operates the press. My mother is a book binder. The rest of us are learning the trade. It's a family trade. The electronics store is just a cover."

"You print Bibles?" Finally understanding, Titus held up his hand. "Never mind. Tell me later. Keep everyone here until I return and tell you it's safe."

He walked outside and approached the Pakistani police officers as they started toward the electronics shop. As a tall, blond foreigner, Titus expected to draw their attention, so he wasn't surprised when a mustached lieutenant halted his two sergeants and five officers, all burdened with handcuffs and leg chains like they were familiar with the number of law-breakers inside.

"Lieutenant?" Titus spoke English rather than Urdu, the official language. English was the language of the elite and government officials inside Pakistan. "A cautious word before you make your arrests, please?"

The balding lieutenant who Titus led aside was no hardened policeman. He appeared to be some kind of office manager, occasion ally called out to arrest trouble-making though peaceful Christians. His shoes were new and his uniform buttons were still shiny. Nearby, his officers grouped idly in the narrow street.

"You need to know I'm here for Jimmah's family." Titus stopped against the factory building where he'd stood ten minutes earlier. "It happens that you're here for the Jimmah family as well. You and I are peaceful men, men with families, right? There's no need for gunfire."

To emphasize the gravity of the situation, Titus set his hands on his hips, which opened the front of his jean jacket enough to show the grip of his concealed sidearm. The lieutenant took a step back, but Titus quickly closed the gap between them.

"We're not enemies, right, Lieutenant?"

The officer glanced at his companions, who seemed no more familiar with interruptions in their peaceful religious arrests than the lieutenant.

"You are interfering in a police action!" The man did his best to appear ruffled, adjusting his uniform, then nervously unbuckling and buckling the sidearm on his belt. "You need to stand aside, sir!"

"Listen very carefully." Titus lowered his head a little. "I'm not alone. I have a shooter, and you're in his sights. I'm leaving with the Jimmah family. This will turn into a bloodbath unless you and I reach an agreement."

"Where are your men?"

"A better question to ask is, where are your own three men? You left three on the street, watching the electronics store. They're already down. Do you want to be next?"

"You sympathize with criminals?" The man struggled for control of his fear.

"Lieutenant, I am a criminal. I'm threatening you. You've already lost three men. Don't make it more. This is Karachi. We are modern men. Give me a bank account, and you can walk away. Tell your superiors you were too late."

"I could lose my job!"

"Better than your life!"

The man's eyes darted as he searched for another argument. Finally, he drew out his phone.

"I must never see you again!"

"If you do, it'll be because you've been persecuting my Christian friends."

Titus punched a dollar amount into his own phone and transferred five digits into the lieutenant's account. They both waited for confirmation. It wasn't the first time Titus had used his bankroll from his wicked past to purchase the lives of God's righteous people.

"I don't think you would really shoot me," the lieutenant said, "not if you are a true Christian."

"And I don't think you really want to bother peaceful Christians."

"Charges were filed. The offended must be appeased."

"You should be more worried about Jesus Christ taking offense at the persecution of His loved ones. It's God's wrath against sin that needs to be appeased, not some complaining neighbors. Eternity is waiting, my friend."

"You *are* a Christian! Now I know you wouldn't hurt me." His phone chimed. "There it is. That's . . . Is this a joke?"

"Maybe it's time to find a job where your conscience isn't burdened. Is that enough to send you on your way and us to remain friends?"

"This is six years' wages for me!" The man couldn't look away from his phone. "What is this family to you?"

"To God, every soul is important, even yours." Titus took the man's phone and punched in his information. "You know now that I'll do anything to help people in trouble. When you want to talk more about Jesus, the Messiah, you call me. I'm always looking for committed people to be my friends."

"I won't forget you."

They shook hands and parted ways. Even if it was money that had brought them to an understanding, Titus prayed he would actually hear from the lieutenant someday—before or after he retired on the small fortune he'd just received.

"We have lives in the balance," Oleg said in his comm, "and you're making contacts in the Karachi police department. How much did you pay him?"

"Whatever it was, it kept us from testing your marksmanship today, didn't it?" Titus waited until the two cars and the van drove away, then he returned to the electronics shop. "The car we have to relocate the family to Islamabad won't do. We'll need a van of our own."

"Tell them to leave their luggage behind."

"It's not their luggage that's the issue. Corban didn't tell us this family had fourteen souls."

"*Fourteen?*"

Shanghai – Two Years Ago

Steve was still laying on his side when the shipping container door creaked open. Daylight poured in, making him wince. Men moved toward him, casting foreboding shadows in the empty space. His only security from injury at that moment was the reminder that they needed him alive if they wanted information from him. Before they became too rough, they'd try to coax the secrets out of him. The real pain would come later, after he resisted their enticing offers.

The binds were removed from his wrists and ankles. The agony when his captors moved his limbs made him cry out. His joints screamed and the renewed blood circulation to his extremities tingled like fire.

A knife sliced his one-piece wetsuit down the spine to his hip. Naked, he was forced to his feet by two men as a third man used a portable water pump to spray him clean of three days of filth. A plastic chair was placed against one wall, and he was roughly pushed into it. He doubled over while his body continued to adjust to the freedom without restraints. Loose cotton pants and shirt were tossed at him. Weakly, he struggled into the clothes, his skin still damp.

Another chair was deposited into the container, followed by a long-necked lamp with an extension cord stretching outside. The lamp was flipped on and aimed to shine in Steve's face. A plastic table appeared next, placed several feet away, with a carton of juice, a bottle of water, and a tray of spiced rice set on it. He could smell the rice.

A man sat down in the opposite chair, facing him. Steve clutched his midsection and did his best to sit upright. His calf wound throbbed and the chill of his wet skin made him shiver. He'd been in more misery during triathlon races, he told himself. This wasn't impossible to endure.

"My name is Song Sakana." It was the same soft voice he'd heard before—the man from days earlier on the cruiser. "Do you know who I am, Steve Brookshire?"

Steve peered past the lamplight at the suited figure, a man in his forties with thick arms and a small body. Sakana was a name not taken lightly in Hong Kong. Though extortion and money laundering were the Japanese family trades, for the right price, they might do anything, even this.

"I know the name." Steve lifted his head and looked around.

"Good. Then we know one another. We can move on to the business at hand. Why are you smiling?"

"This reminds me of a studio apartment I had when I first moved to China. This might even be larger."

Song Sakana's face was expressionless.

"I don't care about your activities in China. I don't care that you're a Christian. I've been hired because I'm effective. My family likes that about me. My enemies hate it about me. But I don't care. This is not an American movie situation. Understand? Here, you have no hope. Here, you talk or we move immediately to misery. My surgeon is especially skilled at keeping people alive under the most brutal circumstances. Did I mention that I'm very effective?"

"I recall that about you."

"Good. Your girlfriend is still alive."

Steve tried to hide his reaction. Lisa, in this savage's hands—there were things worse than death!

"She doesn't know anything." Steve flexed his injured calf. There were four men at the door of the container. The air smelled like the ocean. If he could charge past those men and get to the water— "We can talk this out. Someone hired you. I can arrange for Lisa's freedom."

"The price for her freedom is the key to your electronic sub-net. That's all I want. Give me entry to the sub-net, and you and Lisa can walk away."

"On the boat you said she was dead and my life was over."

"Intimidation." The mobster shrugged. "You understand there's a process to these things."

"She's alive?"

"For now."

Steve took a deep breath and prayed for mental clarity. Abductions of Christians worldwide were so frequent, COIL taught a complete class on it at their Mexican camp where he'd met Lisa. Kidnappers always sought an edge, something to use to break their victims, leverage. COIL pressed their agents to be so grounded in Christ that no vulnerability could be detected or used.

"You should know that my faith matters to me more than life itself." Steve smiled at the water and food on the table. "I've fasted longer than this while seeking God's will in certain matters. If Lisa's alive, then release her. But I think you already killed her or you'd be using her against me by now."

"Would that have made you talk?"

"The sub-net protects thousands from your employers—presumably someone in the Chinese secret police. Lisa knows I can't talk. She would gladly die for Jesus Christ and those we protect in His name."

"I guessed as much, Steve Brookshire." Song Sakana grinned. "You're right. I've gotten rid of her, precisely as my employer requested. Very unfortunate, too. Such a beautiful girl."

"I'm resigned to die. There's nothing more to say."

"Not so quickly." Song Sakana wagged his finger. "In your weakness, you would die too soon. Eat. Rest. Consider your career as an athlete. Without your foot—how will it go for you?"

Steve didn't get a chance to respond. Song Sakana exited the container. His men removed the lamp, then slammed the door closed. For a moment, Steve didn't move, but not because Sakana's words haunted him. He stayed still and prayed for God's presence to remain tangible, to comfort and strengthen him.

Then, with sorrow over Lisa's confirmed death, he scooted his plastic chair closer to the table of food. In the inky blackness, he felt for the water bottle first, and took a sip. If Sakana had his way, then Steve knew he'd be in unthinkable misery soon. When Steve began to eat and drink his meal, it wasn't for the strength to endure the torture ahead, but for the strength to testify of Christ.

A sure way out of this predicament was to lead Sakana to Christ, he realized. And soon, since Steve's calf wound was beginning to fester.

$

Venezuela – Present Day

"Titus, you have no idea how dangerous this jungle is!" Rashid al-Sabur piloted a fiberglass canoe up a river toward the Colombian-Venezuelan border. The motor droned so loudly that Rashid needed to shout. He was a sizeable Cyprian, taller than even Titus when they stood side-by-side. "If the rebels don't kill me, the mosquitoes will!"

From the front of the canoe, Oleg slapped a mosquito on his neck, then turned to look at Titus in the middle seat.

"Russians and jungles, Titus." Oleg scowled playfully. "When you said 'tropical paradise,' you could've mentioned the humidity and insects."

Titus smiled, lost for words as he prayed for what to say to the communist faction they were about to meet. For weeks, he hadn't been certain his health would be stable enough to even make the Venezuelan meeting, once Rashid had set it up. How was he supposed to reach the hearts of killers and soldiers and outlaws—who spoke a language he didn't know?

"This is insane," Rashid said. He was a treasure hunter, recruited by Titus as an asset only two months earlier. The man wasn't yet a Christian, so Titus didn't expect him to understand the unreasonable risks Christians sometimes took for Jesus Christ. "We could be stopped by the army at any moment. They patrol out here, too. Or other communist groups—the FARC, or the ELN. I don't even know what those names mean! Why am I out here, Titus?"

"It's where I needed someone I trust with this important work," Titus said. "You have no idea how grateful I am that you've risked so much, Rashid."

That stopped the Middle Eastern man's complaining. After all, Titus knew Rashid's recent reform from his murderous treasure hunting was primarily for the prospect of friendship with the renowned Serval. Titus didn't take the man's need for friendship lightly, though. Nor did he want to abuse the Cyprian's newfound loyalty.

A few minutes later, Rashid steered the canoe underneath a tree that hung over the river. The three men ducked under several stringy branches, then Rashid beached the canoe onto a narrow dirt landing, and cut the motor. From the river proper, they would be hidden. The men gathered their gear. Titus and Oleg carried small packs and their .308 bullpup rifles. Rashid wore only a standard handgun in a shoulder holster.

"What do they know about me, Rashid?" Titus asked now that they could speak without yelling over the motor.

Rashid guided them onto a bush trail.

"I had only a month to do as you asked. You wanted an audience with a guerrilla faction? I got you an audience. They trust me only a little since I sold them that army surplus food so cheaply. What do they know about you? I told them the worst things I know about you, like you wanted. My Castilian is terrible, but I think they understood enough to meet with you. The leader speaks good English. These people love violence. It's about all they respect."

"And what about Oleg?"

"I didn't know much to tell them, so I may have improvised."

"What'd you tell them?" Oleg growled, panting as he kept up with the two men with longer legs.

"I told them you don't like to be touched. You go crazy about people being too close to you. Then I made up some tales, making you sound paranoid about people being in your personal space."

Titus stopped in the trail and faced Oleg.

"That's actually not that bad of a cover." Titus jabbed Oleg hard in the chest. "Does that bother you?"

"Actually, it does." Oleg drew back a plant from their trail and let it spring into Titus' face. "Some might say being near you makes me a little crazy."

The two laughed and continued down the trail after Rashid. They waded across a river then climbed a mountain with switchback trails. When they descended into the forest again, it was nightfall. Below a ridge where a stream cascaded, the trees and bushes suddenly came to life. Men and women with rifles swarmed upon them.

Rashid shouted in Spanish, identifying themselves, and the dozen ambushers backed away. Camp was a quarter-mile farther, Rashid told Titus, and the party continued. Five guerrillas accompanied them, but for some reason, the soldiers kept their distance from Oleg.

Shanghai – Two Years Ago

Steve sat in the plastic chair with his hands folded and legs crossed.

Song Sakana sat in front of him. For the moment, only the two of them occupied the metal container. Though Steve was anything but relaxed, he was spiritually and mentally prepared for whatever was to come, and he knew it would be horrible. The time he'd spent alone in the container had given him the opportunity to focus his mind on the spiritual rather than the worldly. When he imagined the misery to come, he wasn't discouraged. His circumstances in the container were separate from his salvation reserved in heaven.

A laptop sat on the plastic table at his elbow. Three Japanese men in black suits stood at the entrance of the container, but they seemed at ease, as if they knew no one would attack their boss, especially not a wounded Christian. Two days had passed since Sakana had been there last, but Steve hadn't gone hungry. They'd fed him twice more, whole meals. Except for the fever that had set in from his infected calf, he felt remarkably revived in contrast to the previous days of starvation.

"It's time, Steve," Sakana said. He wore a purple suit that day. The sunshine through the open door gave the fabric an oil-like sheen. "I need the key to the sub-net you use across inland China. Now."

Sakana gestured at the laptop, and Steve knew he was out of time. The key Sakana wanted—for the Chinese government—was actually a whole browser platform that could only be installed by another system that already had it, one cloning the other. Steve had designed it as a safety measure, though his present situation was an extreme instance of its necessity. He couldn't give Sakana what he wanted, even if Steve wanted to. Which he didn't. But even that much intel was too secret to expose. If Sakana knew another browser was required to initiate the sub-net protocols, he would simply hunt down a Christian in the underground church who used the program. It would be a start, at least, toward breaking into the system Steve had created.

"Because I love the people who are protected by this system— because Christ loves them—I can't tell you, Sakana-san. But I'm praying that God softens your heart so you can see this truth for your-self. I know this is business to you. I don't hate you. In the days or weeks to come, when you think back to these moments, don't let it burden you. I forgive you for whatever you're about to do to me, only because I have also been forgiven much by Jesus Christ. The bad things we do are not so irredeemable that God can't still move on our behalf."

Sakana didn't move for almost a minute.

"I was raised Buddhist," he said. "I have found that the first Noble Truth is the most practical in my work: life is full of suffering. It's a fact, Steve. And I have perfected the suffering of humanity to achieve my goals. I'm effective this way."

"There's a Buddhist belief," Steve said in response, "called *anicca*—that nothing in life is permanent. In Christianity, we view this as well. Nothing in this life is eternal—except our souls. We're responsible for what we say and do and believe. One day, you and I will stand before the one and only perfect God and give an account. In death, there's an end to suffering. It's a gift of an eternally good life with the Creator—if a person receives His gift of forgiveness. The guilt, even suppressed, burdens us in this life— God gave His Son, Jesus, to take away our shame. No one was like Jesus, Sakana-san. He was perfect, even when He suffered injustice and died so you would be provided with this gift. This moment, this opportunity, was seen from eternity. Will you repent from your sin and trust in Jesus Christ?"

"No, Steve." Sakana leaned forward. "The question is, which foot shall we amputate first? Since you're a forgiving man, you'll forgive me that we don't provide pain killers. Of course, pain is the point. I want you to focus on the pain. It can go on and on until you talk. Talk, and it's over."

Sakana stood and left the container. The other men entered. Two gripped Steve's arms and threw him face down on the floor. They sat on top of him while the third and fourth men poked and prodded his legs. They spoke in Japanese, then conferred with Sakana.

"It seems we'll be amputating below the knee instead, Steve," Sakana said. "Your wound has become infected. Without modern medical attention, we can only amputate. It's for your best. Forgive me, won't you?"

From a bag, the doctor spread metal tools on the floor, clattering them loudly, probably for his benefit. Steve closed his eyes and tried not to visualize the bone saw he'd glimpsed. He didn't fight the men who sat on him. To his amusement, their combined weight on his back and spine made breathing impossible. Lacking oxygen, he blacked out before the doctor started cutting.

CHAPTER THREE

Colombia – Present Day

Titus strolled into a muddy camp covered by camouflage netting. Several cooking fires illuminated the haunted faces of young and old, men and women, and the rifles on their backs. Those who hadn't joined the communist rebel unit voluntarily, had been lured by riches and grandeur, Titus guessed. Some had been kidnapped and indoctrinated. Escape was punishable by death, if caught.

The camp appeared to be fifty strong. Ironically, Titus realized, that was exactly how many gel-tranq rounds he'd brought into the country for his bullpup. One tranquilizer bullet for each communist rebel—if all went wrong during the night. But that was his fear talking. He was there for Christ, not himself.

"It must be a hundred degrees still." Oleg wiped his brow. "But there's a coldness in their faces. You sure about this?"

Titus nodded at a passing trio of soldiers laden with rifles and grenades, but they didn't nod back.

"Just pray for open hearts while I'm speaking. The Holy Spirit is inside us, ready to work through us. Last resort, we rendezvous down the Orinoco River. Rashid already laid the groundwork. Let's bring it home."

"What's your watch show?" Oleg adjusted his rifle on his shoulder. "Any other camps we need to worry about?"

"Nothing for thirty miles around. Go mingle, will you?"

As Oleg wandered off, Rashid approached with three soldiers. The eldest was obviously the leader. He wore a red beret and carried a six-gun strapped to his thigh.

"Yevgeny Zimyatov!" The man greeted, his arms wide and his smile wider. "I have heard a great deal about you! Welcome to my camp, brother. I am Lazaro Franca. Your motherland is not the same as it once was, is it?"

"It's changed a lot since I was a child." Titus used his best Russian accent and mentally reminded himself to change his Russian cover name the next chance he got, since he'd burned the Yevgeny one in Iran. But Lazaro Franca didn't seem to have any connections to the *Soldiers of Mahdi.* "I'm honored to visit and speak to your proud people."

"Socialism is dying, comrade." The short, bearded man frowned. "But we are alive. With bullets and brains, we will change the world, huh? Together!"

"Together!" shouted those in earshot.

Lazaro led Titus to a cooking fire and they ate beans, rice, and snake meat, with chopped fruit mixed in—a delicious combination. The women forced to labor in the guerrilla camps did much of the farming on stepped hillsides, as well as the latrine digging and fire-wood fetching. Between bites, Lazaro boasted of how organized they were, and how many local officials he'd threatened and Christians he'd killed up and down the banks of the river.

"Christians are like rats." Lazaro spit into the fire. "Shoot two, and five more are born. They take our pride, amigo. They change our way of life, our principles. They're takers. We have to build together, not live for imaginary beings. You understand."

"How many Christians have you killed, approximately?"

Titus had difficulty swallowing a bite of snake, perhaps because he was so aware of the snake standing next to him.

"At least a hundred. But they were—*como se dice?*—nobodies. Insig-nificant. But the army? Now from them we have taken real trophies!"

"When would you like me to speak to your soldiers?"

Titus had never felt more aware of his desire to run from a fight in his life. Across the camp, Oleg tapped three times on his comm. He'd heard every word Lazaro had said. *They'd killed a hundred Christians!*

"Tonight," the man answered. "Let the people eat first. When their bellies are full, we will assemble. For days we have waited for you. We need what you will say to us. It may give us new words to recruit new members. There is much work to do!"

Shanghai – Two Years Ago

Commander Peng Zemin of the Chinese Secret Police, Shanghai Division, was lounging in the Yong Yi Ting Restaurant inside the Mandarin Oriental Hotel in Shanghai's Pudong Financial District. He prided himself in the financial dependence that secured him the five-star establishment's luxury treatment. The host and even some of the patrons knew who he was, but no one ever approached him directly. That might have been because of tall Tond-zu, who overshadowed him constantly.

"Quit yawning, Tond-zu." Peng pointed a bejeweled pinky at a chair. "Sit down and eat. It's not the same Yong Yi Ting, but the food is still good."

"I'd rather be on the streets, Commander, not here." The security officer was missing the teeth in the left side of his mouth, giving his face a caved-in appearance. "And I prefer to stand."

Peng wiped chicken grease on his pants and reached for another platter of rice pudding. If he were soon fired by President Win-chou from his appointment, he was going to enjoy the pleasures while he could. Unless Song Sakana came through for him.

At that thought, the room seemed to darken as a procession of fierce-looking men moved through the patrons and tables, past mosaic murals under elegant lighting, to reach the remodeled and elevated VIP tables. Peng refused to stand to greet the Hong Kong mobster. He had his dignity. After all, the Sakana family were Japanese.

"Commander." Song Sakana bowed his head slightly, speaking English.

"Sit. Sit. No need to make a scene. I ordered enough for everyone."

"I have an update on Steve Brookshire."

"Business later. I'm eating."

"This won't take long." Sakana held out his hand. One of his escorts, who wore dark sunglasses, handed him a thick envelope. "I'm returning your deposit. I have been unsuccessful with the American."

"Excuse me?" Peng wiped his mouth and threw down his napkin. "You're Mr. Effective, aren't you? Break that dog! I need to know how to access the Christian sub-net! I told you the stakes. I paid you for results. You think I have time for these meetings? Speak!"

Sakana's face was emotionless, which infuriated Peng even more. He was used to intimidating people with his power and presence.

"I warned you about this combination of subjects." Sakana folded his hands in front of him. "Steve Brookshire is an athlete—in the most elite condition. Do you know what it takes to compete in a triathlon? Or even to train for one?"

Peng felt his temperature rise as the Japanese party seemed amused, exchanging glances. Of course, Peng was overweight and had never competed in a triathlon. He slammed his fist on the table. The Japanese men quickly recovered and their faces became once again like granite.

"So what? He's just an athlete."

"His mental discipline is extraordinary. Such athletes endure unspeakable pain. They train for it. The one who tolerates the most pain wins the race. But that was only half the problem."

"I thought your drugs could destroy any man's resolve. I need those codes!"

"We tried four combinations of the best serums, once we amputated."

"*Amputated?*" Peng gagged on his food. "What did you cut off? Only a finger or toe, I hope. We need this troublemaker alive!"

"We removed his right leg below the knee. It was gangrene, anyway. The point is—you waited too long to contact me for help. The man's resolve as a Christian is too strong. Even in delirium, with his mind gone, he gave up no secrets. His will is too strong."

"Well, keep trying. It's only been two weeks."

"I gave his girlfriend to the people you requested. For days, I interrogated him personally, off and on. It's not worth my time and money to continue trying to make him talk. I have a business to run. You're paying for results. There haven't been any. Here's your money. My apologies."

"Well, you're as worthless as a—" Peng rose to his feet, spilling a glass of wine. The Japanese men reached into their suits, whether for blades or guns, Peng wasn't sure. Tond-zu moved to the side of the table, ready to protect the commander. "Easy, gentlemen. Just because you couldn't finish the job doesn't mean we have to kill one another, yet. You returned the money. Now return Steve Brookshire. I assume he's still alive?"

"He's still on the pier, but he won't survive without medical attention." Sakana sneered at Tond-zu. "There's no honor here. You may have power in Shanghai, Commander, but you'd better not come to Hong Kong, ever."

Peng watched the Japanese mobsters leave. Their honor, their order, their fancy suits—he hated them. He gestured to Tond-zu.

"The hard part was abducting Steve Brookshire." Peng returned to his seat and picked up a pork chop with his fingers. "It's safe now for us to deal with him ourselves. Take some men. Get to the pier and move him to one of our warehouses, a safe place no one will discover. We have to make him talk. Our futures depend on it. Arrests against instigators have to increase in Shanghai. We need that sub-net!"

Colombia – Present Day

Fifty soldiers assembled with socialistic precision as Titus stood at a podium that may as well have been a pulpit. The lanterns in the communist camp were turned low. Lazaro Franca straightened his red beret, adjusted the six-gun on his hip, and cleared his throat.

"We are one people!" he shouted in Spanish. A translator had been provided for Titus and Oleg. "We are a united people! And we are a courageous people! Our guests have come from far away, but they have the same heart as you. They are our brothers, our comrades!"

The soldiers applauded. Lazaro turned and gripped Titus by the shoulders. The communist was a little shorter, so Titus had to accommodate, but the man succeeded to kiss him on both cheeks. The applause died down, and Lazaro took a seat in the front, squeezing shoulder to shoulder with others on low benches, which were split logs with legs. Oleg stood a few feet away on Titus' left. The broad-shouldered Russian held Titus' rifle and pack while he spoke, both of them ready to disappear into the jungle if the soldiers reacted badly to his words. Rashid al-Sabur stood at the back of the gathering, his own escape from the camp just as important, but the man had expressed to Titus his own plan to disappear and catch up to Titus down the trail. The Cyprian was a master hunter, having hunted treasure all over the world, and he certainly had resources on every continent, resources that Titus didn't know about. Titus guessed the whole scene at the communist camp was strange to his new friend, but he was glad Rashid was with him and no longer his enemy.

"I'm a man like you all," Titus began. He steadied his trembling hand and raised his head in confidence, knowing God was with him. "I need you and you need me. Designed within us is a need to belong, and we often find that necessity satisfied by gatherings such as this. But I'm here to challenge you to reach beyond merely belonging. Belonging isn't enough. So, I challenge you to seek out that which delivers you from the dread of evil in this world and within yourselves."

Lazaro clapped enthusiastically, and the others joined in. Oleg and Rashid remained in their places, amusement on Oleg's face, nervousness on Rashid's.

"I have traveled the world, and have spoken to the most powerful leaders of the most influential people movements from Japan to Morocco, from Belarus to Tanzania. All of these leaders have told me a secret in private, and I share that secret tonight with you: they have a fear that the meaning of life is found not in man, but above man; not in the power of arms, but in the arm of where power itself originates. We want to change the world here tonight, tomorrow, and next year. But we must first be changed in our hearts!"

Again, Lazaro applauded with gusto, the people with him. Titus glanced at Oleg, who shrugged as if in response to Titus' curiosity—*were the people even listening or hearing the meaning of his words?*

"The need to feel significant has been designed inside us all. You as an individual have a desire to be recognized as important by your fellow comrades. You want your dignity affirmed. But for this thirst in your heart to be truly satisfied, you must not look to others who are broken. You must not seek this recognition from man. You must look above man. What has made man have these desires? What Greatness has designed within us this same yearning? If we are all the same—all in a state of need—then we can't hope to look to what's lacking for the answer of greatness. We must look to that which is complete and final, that which has the promise of deliverance from the dread of evil, that which we may see as the beginning of all and the end of all. Your heart cries as mine once did. *Deliver me from myself!* Attach me not to the greater good, but to the Majestic Source of goodness Himself!"

Lazaro clapped, but Titus noticed a frown on the socialist's face. He could see the man trying to unfurl Titus' veiled undermining of communistic ideals.

"We look around us here, and we see objects of security. We have weapons—rifles and RPGs and landmines. What security we should feel! But instead, we cower from a darkness within us. And that darkness is a virus that spreads the longer it goes untreated. Security from the fear about eternity cannot be remedied by man's bullets. We boast in our pride. We show the trophies we've claimed from killing the unarmed. Your purpose is being questioned this very night.

"The man who leads you is a man of great strength. Lazaro, please stand." Lazaro's look of concern was replaced by a smile as he stood and tightened his belt. Titus turned him to face the audience, his arm around the man's shoulder. "Even this great man of power needs your courage to state plainly what your hearts plead within you. A general may make plans to wage a war, but a wise man once said that victory is achieved by an abundance of counselors. Express your hearts—by action or words, and your leaders will listen. Thank you, Lazaro."

Titus shook his hand as the people applauded, and their leader sat down. Looking again at Oleg, Titus nodded and took a deep breath. This was the moment of truth.

"My words tonight have been veiled so that the hearts of you who are longing for deliverance from darkness may respond with caution. You desire to belong, but not to this." Titus spread his arms, indicating the camp. Lazaro's face showed shock. He now understood his entire command was being attacked. "You desire to be recognized as a significant person, but not like this. The security meant for you tonight is a matter of the heart, not of the gun. Where is your commitment? Are you longing for more than the pride of a jungle hide? Have you looked into the emptiness of your soul and cried out, '*Why am I here? What is my purpose among my comrades? How can I live to meet my potential if my longings are restless?*'"

Stepping around the podium, Titus pointed at Lazaro, who mopped his brow with his handkerchief.

"This man, or men like him, have recruited you in times past. Lazaro Franca and I are friends, so I know he agrees with me when I say very strongly—what you do in this life must be done with great zeal, with an inner passion that is expressed by your actions and devotion! Lazaro, is this true? Total commitment or we live in misery!"

"*Adalante, hermano.* Onward, brother," the man said, urging him, though Titus could see his lack of enthusiasm now. "*Adalante.*"

"Tonight, you are at a crossroads. I have meant my words to speak to your hearts, so I plead with you to respond now, without hesitation, if you have heard my own heart. If you desire a refreshing of the soul, a fulfillment from your emptiness, and a deliverance from the dread of evil, stand up and come forward now. I want to embrace you as your comrade and speak to you privately. Stand. Respond! Never will there be another night like tonight!"

At first, no one stood. Heads swiveled, and Titus, from the depths of his heart, prayed for a single soul. Had he spoken too cryptically? Had no one really understood? Were the people so brainwashed that they couldn't feel their soul's desire for healing from sin?

"This is your moment," he encouraged. "We're waiting. Has no one a heart for change? For deliverance? Come forward."

"Me." A man moved in the shadows at the back of the assembly. Titus squinted, then realized it was Rashid! The Cyprian walked down the outer edge of benches. "You spoke to me, brother."

Titus embraced Rashid, suspicious of his motives, but pleased, nonetheless. Was he responding merely to break the ice with the men, or because his heart was indeed touched? When Titus had first met Rashid, he'd spoken to him plainly about the gospel of Jesus Christ. Now, though the message was veiled and meant for others, was he responding?

Next, a man in the second row stood and came forward. Then, two from the middle. Then, a dozen all at once, four of them women. After an embrace with each, Titus waved at Lazaro to join him with Oleg and the responders.

"Lazaro, you've been a gracious host. This is an important moment for these people who came forward. I would like to speak to them separately to address their confessed state of heart. I'll be just a few minutes. When I'm finished with them, they'll be discernibly new people."

"Hmm." Lazaro scratched his chin. "You want to take them?"

"For a few minutes, just outside the camp. They'll be remarkably more zealous about life when I'm done with them."

"Okay. We're done here, then? Already?"

"We are. Thank you." Titus shook Lazaro's hand firmly. "Your army won't be the same after tonight. I guarantee it."

The responders had heard Titus' words, so when he led them into the jungle, they followed. Oleg crashed along the trail to catch up to Titus.

"You could've told me this was your plan. An altar call was really your plan?"

"Plan?" Titus shook his head. "You know me better than that. If you could feel my heart beating, you'd know I didn't plan any of this part. It just came out that way!"

"Well, what do you want me to do?"

"Just keep praying. This night isn't over yet!"

Maryland – Present Day

One-eyed Wes Trimble, deputy director of the CIA's Pacific Rim Security, walked into The Grill. The basement offices of the PRS worked around the clock. Nothing happened from Tasmania to the Bering Sea that his twenty-four agents didn't log into the massive Department of Defense database.

The Grill got its name from the Cold War Days, when Wes's predecessor worked his agents to death, like hamburger on a grill.

Now, the analysts were his. But Wes didn't know how they got any work done—all the noise, all the activity. They'd even pushed the cubicle dividers against the walls so they could mingle—impromptu think-tanks popping up day and night. A digital printer hummed out false IDs in the corner. Three analysts argued about a lost Malay tanker. A bag of popcorn popped in the microwave on a tray that had once held bulky server drives.

His people. Even though he was their superior, they paid him little mind as he wandered aimlessly through The Grill. He preferred it that way, to remain unnoticed in the shadows. But secretly, he was always in control with more authority than anyone in the Pentagon knew. As deputy director of the PRS Division, he could mobilize hundreds of agents for any number of crises, some of them foreign agents. But as the president's direct liaison with COIL, Wes felt he didn't need hundreds of agents. He simply needed open doors for COIL Christians to continue their work for Christ.

He approached one of his top Grill techs, David Weinbaum. The young genius adjusted his glasses almost as often as he touched the spacebar while he typed. He was an Orthodox Jewish young man from Brooklyn, famous inside the Pentagon walls for creating database patches that streamed misinformation packets to intruding hackers who were testing the DOD's security.

"Hey, Bossman." David didn't look up.

"I've got my eye on you, David."

"Frankly, sir, we have a pool going in the office that you wear that eye patch just to justify your dry, ocular humor."

Wes laughed and pulled up an office chair next to David's desk.

"How're things?"

"I'm tracking the Malay tanker by an Indian satellite while those three are arguing about its disappearance."

Wes turned his head to listen to the analysts across the room. They were the best at their jobs, but if they didn't work out their problem soon, he knew David would tell them he was already tracking the wayward tanker.

"Listen, David, I need you to check on the Eleventh File."

"Whatever you say, Bossman."

David closed one application and jumped to another window. Wes barely followed the young man's cursor movements as he accessed an NSA sniffer program. Wes had set up the project to listen to international chatter on missing COIL field agents. Sometimes Christian operatives were quietly executed behind closed borders, but that didn't mean Wes wouldn't keep looking for some sign of them.

"Here's something, Bossman." David highlighted a cryptic report. "Brookshire. You know the name?"

"No, I don't. Pull it up."

"Okay, Steve Brookshire. Hmm. Disappeared about two years ago. Hong Kong area. Ring any bells?"

"Not yet, but that doesn't mean much. I wasn't keeping an eye out until recently. Why did we get this alert now?"

"Stacy!" David called. "Japanese translation!"

A twenty-something blond with pigtails pushed off her desk and spun her office chair to collide into Wes's leg. She leaned toward one of the three screens on David's desk.

"Okay. One guy is asking how to file a report on a missing American. The other guy asks the man's name. Brookshire, he says. Then the guy says he knows all the missing Americans in Japan. There are two, and neither of them is named Brookshire. Then the guy says it wasn't in Japan; it was in China. Then the second guy says he doesn't deal with China's problems. That's it."

"Can you transcribe a translation?" Wes asked Stacy.

"No prob." She twirled back to her desk, pigtails flying. "Send it to me, Davey."

Wes reached for his suit jacket.

"David, send everything to my phone. This is big."

"You got it, Bossman. Stay safe."

At the door, Wes looked back at his team. They were the CIA's stepchildren, too unorthodox to reside at Langley. But they didn't complain about the drafty Pentagon basement office. The lives they'd saved were innumerable. Whoever Steve Brookshire was, Wes hoped he was another life they could save—if the missing American was still alive . . .

Shanghai – Two Years Ago

Lisa Kennedy fell out of the car, rolling twice before coming to rest on wet pavement. Her elbows and knees were scraped raw. Vaguely, she heard the vehicle rush away. They'd actually freed her!

Her head hung as she rose to her hands and knees. The drugs that had been forced on her still swam in her system, but she had enough sense to know she needed to get to the police. She had to call her mother. And COIL—Steve's secure contacts in America. They'd know what to do about Steve, and come help her.

Lifting her head, she saw a building sign in Chinese and English announcing a police precinct. Intentionally or accidentally, her abductors had helped her! With a sob, she forced herself to her feet and trudged toward the police station. Maybe Steve had been released as well. Her nightmare was over, but she wouldn't rest until Steve was found.

Staggering, she pushed through the office door and collapsed in the arms of an officer. They asked questions in Mandarin, which she didn't know, since she'd lived only in Hong Kong where Cantonese was the spoken language.

"I'm an American," she said in English.

"Passport?"

Two others picked her up and set her in a chair. A female officer searched her clothing. As those present gasped, Lisa opened her eyes to see what they'd drawn from her pockets—a large baggie of heroin from each pocket!

"No!" she said. "It's not mine!"

But the officer grabbed one of her wrists, twisting it to expose the inside of her arm. Lisa stared with them at the ugly needle tracks, a couple of them infected.

"No, please!"

They wrestled her out of the chair and onto the floor. As her wrists were cuffed, she remembered her previous handcuffed location. They'd done this to her. This was their way of—what? She wept as she was carried to a cell. Since she was so drugged, her emotions were more extreme, and the less she was able to express herself. But no one would listen.

Alone in a cell, she curled into a ball on a soiled mattress. Satan was in this business. He was the accuser. But God was bigger, she believed. God was the Creator. Nothing escaped His loving care. Maybe Steve was thinking the same thing that very moment.

Shanghai – Two Years Ago

Steve was conscious, but he kept his eyes closed in case someone were watching him. He concentrated on a steady breathing rhythm, then he began to process what he knew. Days of delirium had passed. The torture from Song Sakana and his doctor had nearly killed him. But the amputation of his right leg had been a real trauma. Nothing about his body felt right. He felt unbalanced, even as he lay on the bed.

At the present, his resting heartbeat had slowed its pounding in his ears, which meant the IV he felt in his arm was hydrating him. And his chills were gone now, the fever with it. If anyone were monitoring his vitals, his facade of continued illness would be short-lived.

His leg was gone. He'd seen them throw it away after flaunting it in front of him. That memory in the metal container was sobering now. A whole chunk of his body had been removed and disposed of. But it was just his body, he told himself. His body was just the shell God had placed him in to function and serve Him. But his soul had been entrusted securely in God's loving arms. The sooner he passed away, the sooner he would be with Christ—and he'd even see Lisa again in heaven.

"You are awake," a man stated in English.

Steve opened his eyes, realizing his breathing had probably given himself away. He was in an empty warehouse, lying on a bed next to a saline bag attached to his arm. Beside him, a lanky oriental man yawned. He wore a silk shirt and a shoulder holster with a sidearm.

"Where am I?"

"Nowhere special." The man's English accent was Chinese, not Japanese this time.

"Song Sakana?"

"We rescued you from him. You're safe now."

Steve tried to relax, his eyes studying the metal trusses on the ceiling. No, he wasn't safe, yet. Something was still wrong. He frowned at the man.

"Who are you?"

"You can call me Tond-zu. My employer told me to sit with you, to help you."

"Your employer?"

"Commander Peng Zemin. Do you know about him?"

"Yes." Steve scoffed. "So, I'm in the hands of Shanghai's secret police now. The commander thinks he can do better than the Japanese mob?"

"No, we're not your enemies, Steve. We want to work with you. For the sake of the people of China, we want to partner with you to help organize the Christian population."

"You mean monitor and restrict." Steve smiled weakly. "I'm not new to this game, Tond-zu."

"The people know what's best. You're just one man. Don't carry this tremendous responsibility on your own."

"What responsibility?" Steve stretched. "I'm pretty comfortable. And I'm willing to talk."

"Are you?"

"I feel compelled to tell you about the love of Jesus Christ."

"Tell me about the sub-net you designed over the last few years."

"I'd rather tell you about—"

Tond-zu suddenly dragged Steve off the bed. Steve gasped as his IV was tugged out, the needle ripping off a patch of tape and skin. He covered his head as the tall Chinese man commenced to kick and stomp on him. The blows weren't excessively hard, though they were definitely bruising. But then his captor kicked Steve's amputated stump. Pain screamed through his whole body and he gripped his stump, holding the bloody wrappings for the first time. The blows continued, but Steve's mind went somewhere else. Far away, he was swimming through the ocean. The chill of the water was kept at bay by his wetsuit. The day was perfect for a swim. Lisa was motoring in a boat next to him, a lily stem tucked into her hair that was blowing in the wind. Every time she thought his ears weren't submerged, she whistled and cheered for him to continue, to endure, to be victorious.

It was a perfect day.

CHAPTER FOUR

Venezuela – Present Day

Titus gathered the guerrilla responders in the darkness of the jungle shadows. The moon wasn't out, but the stars were bright, offering enough visibility to distinguish people from trees. With Oleg posted as security, Titus focused on the seventeen yearning people before him.

"From the talk we just had in camp, each of you should know that it is God who is pulling at your hearts right now. He is calling you to Himself." He paused as a murmur spread through the group. So many of them had been indoctrinated by communistic ideals for years. The mention of God at work was certainly foreign, even forbidden. "The searching in your soul, the emptiness you want filled, the guilt and shame you need erased—these things are answered by opening your hearts to the love of Jesus Christ.

"I know some of you have killed Christians. Now is the time to turn from the evil things your conscience has told you are wrong—and trust in God to give you a new life. It's a historic fact that Jesus died on a cross to pay the penalty of death that you and I deserve for the evil deeds we've done. God is pure and holy, so He must condemn all workers of evil. But He's also compassionate. He provided God the Son to make provision for you to be set free from your burdens of sin.

"Right now, God is calling you to respond before it's too late. Place your eternal soul in His hands. He loves you. I've risked my life to tell you these things. Hiding and killing isn't God's desire for you. God made you to enjoy Him and to live lives of light, not lives of darkness. Here are some papers. Pass one to the person next to you. This has everything I've said written on it, as well as several radio frequencies where you can hear the Good News for yourself. You don't need to live in fear about eternity any longer. Are there any questions?"

Several people spoke at once. Finally, they settled down and took turns.

"I know a Christian in my village," a woman said. "My boyfriend convinced me to come up here and fight. That was ten years ago. Lazaro won't let me leave—none of us."

"That's why I'm here. You're welcome to leave with the three of us tonight, but it may be too dangerous to ever return."

"Where would we live?" a man asked. "Fighting in the rebellion is all we know. Some of us are fugitives from the government for fighting in the resistance."

"The evil things man has used you for, God desires to use those things for good. You're all survivors. You farm out here, raise animals. You have skills that many in society don't have. With some imagination, you'll learn to trust God to lead you to a life of peace and livelihood."

A man pushed roughly past Titus.

"I'm telling Lazaro!"

Oleg must've been ready for a disturbance since he swung his hand at the man's thigh, then caught him as he fell. Titus guessed Oleg had held a gel-tranq cartridge in his fist and had slammed it into the man's leg muscle.

"He's just tranquilized," Titus said to the others. "He'll wake up in an hour. There may be others who want to tell Lazaro. That's fine, because we're leaving now."

"But we have so many questions!" A man stepped closer, his rifle slung over his shoulder. "How will we live new lives?"

"The radio frequency I've given you will tell you how to get a Bible of your own and how to transition to a life of peace. Many other rebel fighters have given their lives to Jesus, too. They've never regretted their decision. But it's a decision you must each make for yourselves. Now, who's leaving with us right now, and who is staying?"

Ten said they were ready to leave. The others wanted to return to camp and think about the offer. Since the soldiers weren't allowed to have many personal possessions, what they owned of value was already on their persons.

"I scouted a way east," Rashid said. "We'll be deep into Venezuela by dawn, and to the river by noon. Once we get to the river, anyone who follows us will fall back. Venezuelan troops are a major risk to invaders."

"Lead us out, Rashid." Titus patted the taller man on the shoulder. "Oleg and I will bring up the rear. Our work here is finished."

The thirteen—four of them women—slipped down a jungle trail the very next minute. One-fifth of the guerrilla camp had chosen to run away. Titus couldn't wait to tell prayer warriors back in America and elsewhere that their prayers had been effective.

New York – Present Day

PRS Agent Wes Trimble walked into an art museum in Midtown, Manhattan. The Frick Collection of paintings, and even collectible furniture, were of no interest to the one-eyed spy, but he gazed at the displays with feigned interest, as if the mansion's worldly-valued items mattered more than the under-valued lives he often saved from the jaws of tyranny and death.

In one hall, Wes sat on a sofa below the painting of a house, and gazed across the expanse at another painting of an elderly couple.

Wes moved his feet aside as an old man shuffled a walker far too close to be an accident. The man wore a sparse white beard and dark glasses—as if his vision were impaired—and braces on his legs.

"It's always an adventure meeting with you." Wes played with a museum brochure in his hands as Corban Dowler, in his elaborate disguise, seated himself. Since the man was known to be a paraplegic, the walking, old man costume was completely disorienting. "This secrecy is necessary, even in our own country?"

"For your sake, and for mine." Corban spoke normally, their shoulders inches apart. "Your relationship to the president needs to be protected. And COIL doesn't need what comes with the politics of the State Department."

"The Lord certainly has arranged things in a unique way." Wes chuckled. "The whole country has turned against Christian morality, and yet, here we are with the government's favor to affect change around the world."

"Amen." Corban shifted his walker closer. "Your message was cryptic. What've you found?"

"One of the names you gave me to keep an eye out for, Steve Brookshire. You know him?"

"He reached out?"

"No, someone in Japan was looking to file a report on him. A phone intercept is all we have through NSA channels. We analyzed the voices. The inquirer was Song Sakana, once a lieutenant in the Japanese Sakana Crime Family out of Hong Kong. Seems he's back home in Japan now. And the second voice was the assistant to the US ambassador in Tokyo. A real gem, this guy. Told Sakana to go talk to someone else about the missing American."

"This is an answer to two years of prayer." Corban turned and looked into Wes's eye to convey his emotion. "Steve Brookshire was China's Christian underground's primary organizer. He disappeared two years ago. We kept it quiet, waiting for demands that never came. The only thing we know for sure is that his girlfriend popped up weeks later, charged with drug distribution. Lisa Kennedy."

"I remember her!" Wes growled to himself. "Back then, I excused it as a legitimate arrest because I ran her name and saw she had drug priors in the US."

"One other thing: Steve Brookshire never talked. From everything we know, not a single asset has ever been compromised in China. We still use the sub-net he designed to organize house churches, their meetings, and contacts. Arrests have continued to decline rather than increase across China."

"How do you want me to handle this Song Sakana guy? He used to be mob, now he's back in Japan living what seems to be a normal life."

"For now, let COIL run with that. I'll keep you posted. This is a perfect mission for Titus. He used to smuggle artifacts in the Orient, so I know he has some resources and hidden airfields he can use. Right now, he's playing guerrilla in South America. As soon as he gets back in a day or two, I'll send him to Japan."

"Well, I'm glad I could bring you good news for a change."

"It gives us some hope, Wes. Thank you."

"What about Lisa Kennedy?"

"She disappeared after her trial in Shanghai. Her charges seemed legit, sure, but she and Steve were together when they were abducted. It would've been easy to set her up. Satan enjoys destroying Christians, using their pasts against them. A lead on Steve might be a lead on Lisa as well. We'll bring them both home, Lord willing."

"Say the word, and the president will shake a few trees."

"For now, it's enough to know he's got our backs—to a degree."

"Well, he's after anything that makes himself look good. I've been witnessing to him. His eyes are on his ratings first, and the country second. God isn't near the top of his priorities, yet, but the gospel has a way of wearing down stubbornness."

"Sounds like the right guy's on the job." Corban waited for two young art-lovers to pass before he continued. "I'd hate to miss an opportunity to pray with you, Wes. I know you stick your neck out for COIL. We certainly need to stand together against the realm of darkness. I've found that prayer sets in order whatever else is meant to follow."

"Dear Father, this news about Steve Brookshire is exciting, but we want to honor You right now. You are worthy of our loyalty, for You alone have the power to preserve us and put down what evils intend to ambush us . . ."

Shanghai – Two Years Ago

In the shadow of Gensler Shanghai Tower, Commander Peng Zemin rode an elevator to his fourth-story office. Since everyone in Shanghai knew his identity, he changed offices frequently, and at times altered the way his hairdresser cut his hair so he wasn't as recognizable.

As the city's primary religious infraction authority, Peng preferred a little anonymity. In his younger years, he'd posed as a Christian convert as often as possible, bringing down the destabilizing religious house church movement everywhere he went. He missed those exciting days of rapid-fire arrests, which he'd instigated, but the imprisonments and executions of Christians today was just as satisfying.

When he stepped out of the elevator, he clutched at his chest at the sight of yawning Tond-zu waiting outside the door.

"How about some warning?" Peng stalked into his office. Two secretaries stood to bow as he passed them. "I know you don't like cell phones, Tond-zu, but you have to get used to modern communication."

Once in Peng's inner office, Tond-zu closed the door and sat down. He yawned as Peng shed his jacket and puffed on an inhaler. Shanghai smog was worse than ever. What Peng needed was some time out in the country air, away from the city.

"You'd better have some good news for me." Peng turned on his laptop. "And quit yawning! Act like you give a care."

Tond-zu stared at him in silence, but Peng turned away. Peng knew his security officer had a neurological disorder that caused him to yawn excessively—but the man could at least disguise the annoyance!

"Steve Brookshire isn't talking," Tond-zu said.

"By now, he must be giving at least false reports we can look into."

"No. He's not even bothering to lie." Tond-zu yawned without covering his gaping, deformed mouth. "I thought about bringing the girlfriend back, using her to make him talk, but I don't think even that would work at this point. Besides, she's in a Shanghai jail now, awaiting a hearing."

"How long until the information that Steve knows becomes insignificant?"

"It won't expire, if that's what you're asking. As long as the Christian sub-net remains uncompromised, they'll keep using it."

"So, there's no sense in killing the criminal, yet." Peng checked his messages. "In every city, Christians are multiplying. The Party is destabilized, and we've never been less effective."

"Tell me what you want me to do."

Peng stood and looked out his window. He cursed as he admired Shanghai Tower, one hundred and twenty-seven stories of beautiful engineering, complete with the world's fastest elevators, indoor pressurization, and filtration. Meanwhile, he stood in the squalor of a fourth story. What he'd give to climb a little higher in the Communist Party's *Shanghai Clique*. It wasn't about money, anymore; he had plenty. He wanted to provoke jealousy from his peers, especially those who visited from Beijing.

"We need to attack our Christian problem in another way. Can we hide Steve Brookshire until he's ready to talk?" Peng asked. "The usual place?"

"Hudie Valley? I don't see why not."

"Make him comfortable. Don't let him die, and make sure he's watched by Party friends at the prison."

"I'll call on them. Steve won't be going anywhere very fast, not since the Japanese cut off his leg."

"Disgusting!" Peng shuddered. "Tell Steve his usefulness expires as soon as we break the sub-net ourselves. I'd like nothing more than to execute him myself."

"Very well." Tond-zu yawned and stood. "And the house church problem?"

"Increase stakeouts and abductions. Someone else must be able to get us into the sub-net!"

Shanghai – Two Years Ago

Lisa lay in her Shanghai jail cell, her eyes dry. She had no more tears left after four weeks of isolation. In the cell, her mind had imagined the worst scenarios mounting from the drugs she'd been found with. The word despair hardly described her depression. And it seemed her worst fears were coming true.

Officer Wu seemed to hate her. His English was good, and every time the detective called her out for questioning, he stated plainly her charges, complete with a witness who said he'd bought drugs from her. It seemed Lisa had no case, and nothing with which to argue her innocence. Any claims of her abduction and forced drug-taking were easily batted aside by reminding her she had a history of the exact same drug use in America. "Did America force you to take the heroin, too?" the detective often asked, mocking her.

She wore grey pajama top and bottoms. Except for her pale skin and five-ten height, she was like the hundreds of other inmates held inside the massive facility. That's how they intended to break her, she guessed, by taking her identity. They wanted a confession, and then they'd put her away.

It was getting harder to trust God the more she examined the uselessness she felt. How could God use this? She wasn't even around other prisoners to witness to them—not that she would've been much use while going through detox, but still! If Steve were there, he would've had some wisdom for her, some encouragement. He'd always been her strength. Where was he?

Patience, she told herself. COIL wouldn't let her rot in a Chinese prison, and her mother would certainly not stand by as the government railroaded her daughter. They had to be searching for her!

Lisa guessed the modernized jail was better than the old dungeons she'd heard about, but her cell still seemed to be something from the Dark Ages. The mattress on the cement slab was soiled, and her toilet was a hole in the corner. There was no sink, just a faucet of cold water that dripped constantly into the hole.

The noises at night were chilling. Cries from down the cement corridors were enough to make her tremble. Sometimes she tried to pray, and other times she visualized a happier time, something from her childhood. Her mother kept a nursery with every type of flower imaginable. After school, caring for those flowers would occupy Lisa for hours, her mom beside her, teaching her how to nourish and water and love the colorful plants to grand maturity. The lily had always been her favorite, its tiny flowers like little trumpets yearning to squeak to announce their place in the world.

After such memories, Lisa always slept. Except this night. Something dreadful seemed to loom over her, a shadow that had no equal, intent on suffocating her in its choking embrace.

New York – Present Day

In upstate New York, Titus repositioned a step ladder to reach the rain gutters. After three weeks on the road, he hadn't expected to return home and relax, even with the illness coursing through his body.

"Corban wants to send you out already?" Annette asked, an iced tea in her hand. They'd been married for over a year after meeting in Gaza during a Mid-East crisis. "You have to tell him about the cancer, Titus. You can't keep pretending you're not sick. You need to slow down. Stubbornness alone won't beat this. I thought we were visiting my parents this weekend."

He flicked wet leaves out of the gutter and climbed down to move the ladder again.

"I've been wanting to get to know your dad, Annette, but this can't be helped. I have to go to China."

Titus never knew how to respond to Annette's urgings to fight the cancer. One side of him wanted to fight, while the other didn't want to spend his last months alive focused on a disease that would inevitably win.

"My parents haven't seen us since the wedding. Living across the country as we do, we may not get another opportunity like this, Titus."

Nodding, Titus understood what she was saying, without saying it. He would die soon. Anyone they were going to see together, they needed to see while he was still able to travel.

"We have a lead on two missing COIL people in Asia." Titus took off a glove and received the tea from her. He took a gulp and handed it back. "I don't know how to say no to that. You want to go on ahead to California yourself? If I finish early, I can join you there in the sunshine instead of returning here to more leaves in the gutter."

"I'm assuming Oleg is going with you." She sipped the tea. "What about Rashid?"

"He's already on his way."

"You think his conversion in South America was real? You've witnessed to him before."

"Something seemed to click inside him that night in the jungle." Titus grinned as he reminisced. "I've never been so uncertain of myself, and so certain of God. I want more of that."

She held the ladder with one hand as he set it on uneven ground and ascended again.

"Sometimes you ask me to go with you on missions, but not this time?"

"There's a Chinese government element to it, hon." He grunted, accidentally flinging leaves onto Annette. "Sorry. It ain't easy tolerating a husband who cleans these only twice a year."

Annette plucked the leaves out of her hair.

"China can't be that bad. America has all kinds of trade agreements with them."

"The US has trade agreements with some of the worst human rights violators in the world—Saudi Arabia, Iran, Egypt—so that's no longer a gauge for safety. In China, any ideal that detracts from communist power is viewed as a threat. Putting God first, as we teach, threatens the Communist Party, who wants to be first. There are hundreds of thousands in re-education camps in China under bogus political charges, all for owning Bibles, converting others to Christ, or teaching in a house church. I won't be able to focus on the mission if I have to focus on keeping you safe in that kind of environment. This isn't a go-and-see mission. This sounds like a go-and-get-out-quick one."

"In a perfect world, I'd have you all to myself. Who knows how much longer I'll have you at all?" Annette gave a pouty frown. "I guess I'll have to settle for the occasional conversation around the rain gutters."

"The world may not be perfect, but that's why God gave me a perfect wife who understands these things." He pulled her into his arms. "I want to be with you. Oh, I want to!"

"What would the world do without Titus Caspertein?" She laughed, touching his face. "Come on. Give me a, '*It ain't easy.*'"

He held her at arm's length.

"It ain't easy putting up with a wild boy from Arkansas."

"Just straighten China out while you're over there, will ya?"

"The whole country?"

"Why not? You're the Serval, after all!"

"In that case, why not the whole world!"

"One step at a time, babe." She pinched his cheek and kissed him. "Then maybe you'll be ready for my parents!"

China – Two Years Ago

God was allowing this, Steve repeated to himself. And if his good, loving, and holy God were allowing this to happen to him, then he could anticipate a good result, even if the circumstances at the present were uncomfortable.

On his belly and under a blanket, Steve lay bound on the back seat of an SUV. He was certainly uncomfortable. The torturer he knew as Tond-zu was driving. They were alone in the vehicle, on day three of traveling. On the first day, Steve had thought he was being taken out to be strangled once and for all. His body was raked with scars, scabs, and bruises from the interrogations. He hadn't told them anything except the truth of the Cross. Since he was uncooperative, he wasn't sure why they were keeping him alive.

The SUV stopped. Steve shifted his head under the blanket. He guessed the blanket was meant to keep him hidden from civilian eyes. After all, even in China, kidnapping was illegal.

The blanket was suddenly whipped off and Tond-zu uncuffed one wrist.

"Sit up."

With difficulty, since he'd been in one position for hours, Steve shifted to his side. Every movement felt awkward without his right leg. Once seated upright, Tond-zu cuffed Steve's hands in front of him, then the man faced forward and continued driving.

Steve blinked through tears of gratefulness. Praying facedown under a suffocating blanket had been adequate, but this? This was paradise! The brown landscape rolled past him as Tond-zu raced the

SUV down the paved highway, somewhere deep in China's interior. A glance at the afternoon sun's position told him they were traveling westward. The countryside was occasionally covered with rugged hills, then fields, some of them cultivated. Rarely, there was a patch of green vegetation, perhaps crowding a lonely spring of water or seasonal stream.

"At any moment," Tond-zu said, glancing at Steve through the rear-view mirror, "you may tell me about the sub-net—how to access it. That's all I want from you."

"I was just thinking about how we plan out our lives and protect our reputations." Steve took a deep breath and watched a distant flock of birds soar above the fields. "In a moment, everything can be stripped away, and all we're left with is our faith. What do we depend on? What truly matters in life? If I were someone who depended on fragile ideas and fleeting things, I'd have talked to you about the sub-net days ago, because I'd have lost hope. If I believed in nothing real, there would be no point in remaining silent. But my faith is evidence of the things we can't see, the things of God."

"What hope could you have now?" Tond-zu shook his head. "You have no idea the isolation you will now experience. I'm taking you to hell, to Hudie Valley."

"Whatever it is, my dependence upon my God is only as strong as He is to sustain my spirit. Apparently, He's pretty strong. Tell me, Tond-zu, have you ever tortured someone as much as you have me?"

"I've tortured people to death."

"But for so many days without results?" Steve clucked his tongue. "If I met a man with the strength inside him to endure like that—I'd try to find out everything I could about that strength. Are you ready to receive it yet?"

"I already know. You've been telling me for days. You want me to pull out another tooth so it hurts to talk, or do you want to go back under the blanket?"

"I'll be quiet." Steve smiled. "But I'm still going to pray for you. I haven't stopped, you know. How about this? When you want to talk again, you initiate it. I'll wait for you, just like Jesus is waiting for you."

Tond-zu scowled in the mirror, but Steve needed some game to entertain him. He wondered how long Tond-zu would hold out, since the man surely had allowed him to sit up to keep him company.

The highway dipped into a valley where a small town nestled, then rose again through a low mountain pass. The otherwise empty landscape reminded Steve that this was how God intended all His children to be filled up. No one could be absolutely ready for what God had for him to do until he'd died to all the things the world wanted from him. Empty. God had allowed even his own mobility to be taken, only to be better used in some way without his leg. And Steve couldn't wait to see how God would do it!

Hong Kong – Present Day

Treasure hunter Rashid al-Sabur rode in a taxi away from the Hong Kong shoreline. He may have been residing in Cyprus for years, but he was no fool concerning the Orient. The Dark Web had kept him connected to resources and competitors that had led him to countless Eastern treasures over the years. Of course, he'd stolen those treasures as quickly as he'd identified their value and locations. It seemed like another life now, someone else's violent pursuits of insignificance.

In Rashid's arsenal was knowledge far beyond even the common brigand of the day. His software could reroute signals across thousands of servers to hide the origin of inquiries. But hiding his digital footprint was no longer Rashid's objective. This time, he intended to sniff out a trail that no one else could find. And he was doing it for Jesus now.

Rashid guessed if all his sins could be measured against the next most sinful man, he would still deserve hellfire ten times more. His whole life, he'd been an atheist. What good could God be if a man couldn't see Him? But there were needs in Rashid's heart he hadn't known or seen—until Titus had told him the truth about his condition. That strange night in a Venezuelan jungle would always stand as the moment he'd died. And yet, he was still alive. His reading of the Bible had confirmed not only his previous state of hopelessness, but also his present state of anticipation in the eternal.

His first task before him—to find Steve Brookshire—involved the Sakana Crime Family. Not many Japanese families were strong enough to thrive where the Triad underworld criminals reigned on Chinese soil. But the Sakanas had earned their place by ruthlessness and craft. The terrible deeds the locals weren't willing to do, the Sakanas had accomplished with precision and Japanese loyalty. No one had found a weakness in the Sakanas since the father, Lin Sakana, had established his presence in Hong Kong twenty years earlier, with his two sons, Chin and Song.

The taxi arrived at a gated residence and Rashid climbed out to press an intercom button.

"You have a visitor," Rashid said into the system.

He waited a few seconds. Through the gate he acknowledged several armed guards on the lawn and porch. They couldn't possibly know he'd recently come from the United Sates, and carried with him an offer from the president's most secret operative, Wes Trimble.

"Your name, please?"

"Rashid al-Sabur."

The gate buzzed and he pushed his way through. It clicked closed behind him as he walked toward the gunmen, leaving the taxi behind. One of the men intercepted him on the rock walkway and frisked him.

Inside the front door, he was led onto a patio that doubled as a greenhouse. Birds fluttered nearby in the humid enclosure. A frog croaked and insects buzzed. Rashid made note of a garden rake and hoe within reach. Six bodyguards protected Lin Sakana, a white-haired man whose back popped when he stood from a shallow koi pond.

Rashid, with his hands at his sides, bowed from the waist, held it a moment, then straightened. He may have been outnumbered, but he wasn't afraid. And he was a head taller than anyone present. Lin Sakana had surely checked Rashid's name against a criminal database, so his curiosity had given Rashid an audience with the crime boss. Lin wouldn't try to kill him until after he learned what Rashid wanted. By that time, Rashid hoped he'd sufficiently impressed upon his host to let him live. It was the kind of gamble Titus would take. After all, he was happy to be part of Titus' inner circle now.

"Is this your first time in Hong Kong, Rashid?" The old man's English was unaccented, confirming everything Rashid knew about the man—that he'd learned English some time ago in America. Lin's fingers delicately lifted a plant and touched the soil beneath.

"No, sir. I've visited a few times before."

"What is it that I have that brings the infamous Saber to my home?"

"As my request to meet you stated, I desire information, not treasure."

"Oftentimes, those two are the same." The old man pulled up several small weeds and tossed them onto the walkway. "What information do I have?"

"Almost two years ago, your son, Song, returned to Japan. If you tell me why, I will tell you what you want to know."

"Young man, you cannot possibly know what I want to know."

"I know you once lived in America. I know you worked for the government. I know you were charged with espionage, and you fled the country. You lived under the name Sid Sanko then. You ran away, but as a man of honor, you've always wondered about redemption. That's why your browser history shows you have searched for legal leniency through NATO channels. But there are no channels for espionage, even though you continue to seek redemption."

Lin briskly approached Rashid, and his bodyguards closed in.

"What would Rashid al-Sabur know about redemption? You dare to dishonor me in my own house?"

"I dare to honor you with answers no one else can provide. Since I'm not worthy to give you anything, Sakana-san, I offer an exchange."

"And place my son at risk?" The man's mouth trembled. "What is Song to you?"

"Your son reached out to us. But I must know why."

Lin's face softened.

"You mean him no harm?"

"I am Rashid al-Sabur. If I meant your son harm, I wouldn't speak of it with his own family. I simply must know his intentions before my associates visit with him."

Lin backed away and turned toward a plant with a beetle crawling on a leaf.

"How did you know I was Sid Sanko? My own sons don't know what I was before they were born."

"None of us became what we are today without having past imperfections. Perhaps the true test of a man is that he doesn't stop until his worst is in the past."

Rashid almost scoffed at his own words. Titus had truly infected him with the wisdom of God. He was even speaking like a Christian already!

"There is no redemption for me, Rashid. As you know, I've looked for it. Japanese spies for China receive no mercy from Americans, even if I truly became an American patriot while I was a spy there."

"If that is your answer, then please permit me to leave."

"A man who knows I was Sid Sanko—you cannot leave. Not yet." Lin faced Rashid again. "What happened to my son two years ago? That's what you want to know?"

"That's all."

"Song became a family . . . liability. But he is my son."

"I see." Rashid looked at the floor of the greenhouse. He understood now why Lin hesitated to share the news. Song had disgraced his father, somehow bringing him shame. "May I ask how?"

"Is it important?"

"To me, it is. It may help me understand why he tried to meet with someone."

"Your associates?"

"Yes."

"And who are you working with? Rumor has it, the Saber never works with anyone, not without killing them afterward, anyway."

"Neither of us are who we once were."

Lin grunted and nodded.

"Song became a Christian," Lin stated.

Rashid held back a guffaw. Was God reaching the most lost and despicable people in the world, first him and now Song Sakana?

"That's . . . unexpected news. Who directed him to Jesus Christ?"

"I don't know. You can ask him."

Nodding thoughtfully, Rashid wasn't sure yet how or if this news related to Steve Brookshire.

"Thank you for your trust." Rashid bowed his head. "Now, for my promise. You are not beyond redemption. A man in Maryland named Wes Trimble is waiting for your call. He's an honest man. He'll help you sort out your past charges in America."

"You spoke to him about me? You're a confident man, Rashid al-Sabur. Do you always get what you want?"

"I used to." Rashid felt himself smile, which was a strange feeling. "Now, I receive what God gives me. I'm a different kind of treasure hunter now, Sakana-san."

CHAPTER FIVE

Shanghai – Two Years Ago

"Wake up!" A female prison guard banged on Lisa's steel door. "Visit! Twenty minutes!"

The meal tray slot in the door slid open as Lisa sat cross-legged on the floor. On the opposite side of the door, her mother, Marie Kennedy, crouched down and peered inside. Their eyes were inches apart. Lisa noticed surprise on her mother's face, as if she didn't immediately recognize her own daughter.

"Mom!" Lisa reached through the twelve-by-four-inch hatch, to touch her mother. "Oh, Mom, you came!"

The guard pounded on the door with a baton.

"No touching! No passing!"

Trembling, both women withdrew their hands. Marie wept in great sobs. Lisa did her best to hold her brokenness inside, to be strong for her mother. There would be time to weep later. Maybe it was her imagination, but she thought her mother smelled like the flowers she cared for back in America.

"I wasn't sure you knew what had happened to me."

"No, no. Everyone knows. It's been on the news." Marie blew her nose on a hanky. "It's been in all the papers. Well, last week, it was. And on TV."

"That's good! Is anyone doing anything?"

"What do you mean it's good? Lisa, it was drugs. They have you on camera, coming into that police station. You couldn't even walk, you were so high. All those drugs . . ."

"No, Mom, they weren't mine! Is this why no one from the embassy has even come here to see me yet? I was kidnapped! You've got to believe me, Mom, please!"

"There's a woman outside. Chloe. She said to tell you they're working on things."

"Chloe? From the embassy?"

"No, from that COIL organization."

"Chloe Azmaveth?"

"Yes, that's it. They wouldn't let her in since she's not family. She said you'd know they won't leave you behind. But Lisa, I can't imagine anyone standing with you now. Drugs again?"

Lisa shook her head, her throat choked by anger and fear.

"Is this what you came for? To discourage me?"

"No, Lisa. You're my daughter. I will always love you. Tomorrow at court, I'll speak on your behalf, if they let me."

"Court tomorrow?"

"That's what they said. Jason Allison, the American embassy attorney. He didn't give me details, but he said to keep your hope alive. He'll shoot for the shortest sentence possible."

"Sentence? Mom, I'm here working for Jesus Christ! I shouldn't even be in jail! I was set up, Mom!"

"I never wanted you to come here in the first place! It was your attachment to that Steve—always secretive. Now we know what he got you into." Marie's tone hurt Lisa more than the news she'd brought. She took a deep breath. "Do you have a message to tell Chloe?"

"Yes. The Japanese kidnapped me and Steve while he was training east of Hong Kong."

"Japanese? What do they have to do with any of this? They're drug dealers?"

"Please, just tell her. They have to find Steve."

"I'll tell her. Anything else?"

Lisa shook her head, saddened at the bittersweet reunion with her mother. It hadn't been encouraging at all.

"If they sentence me, I don't know what I'll do. I mean, I don't know how to face prison. I've heard they have work camps."

"I don't want to hear it." Marie closed her eyes. "You did the dope. Now you have to bear the consequences. I'd rather have you home, but you're a grown woman. Maybe while I'm here I can get some magnolia seeds. They have the most beautiful trees just outside the entrance. There's nothing like them in San Francisco. It might open up a new market."

"That's . . . nice, Mom."

"We'll know more tomorrow. After the hearing. We'll find out what's to become of you."

Japan – Present Day

"We just got a text from Rashid." Titus read through the message in a mumble as Oleg parked their rental car in a middle class neighborhood in Akita, Japan. "Okay, it says—you're not going to believe this— Song Sakana became a Christian two years ago, and Sakana Senior wanted him out of the family business."

"Two years ago . . ." Oleg studied the residence out his window. "That's about the time Corban said Steve disappeared. Coincidence?"

"With God," Titus chuckled, "there are no coincidences."

"If Song is retired, that explains why there's no security around this guy's house. It looks like every other house on this street, maybe even less tidy." Oleg drew his sidearm from his shoulder holster, checked the safety, then replaced it. "Still want me to go around back?"

"Actually, no." Titus climbed out of the car. "Rashid's message fills in the blanks we had in our intel. I think we can approach this head-on."

The two strolled through an open gate and knocked on the front door of the modern house. A small elderly woman answered the door, the top of her head reaching no higher than Oleg's shoulder. Titus bowed, with Oleg an instant behind him.

"*Konichiwa.* My name is Titus Caspertein. This is Oleg Saratov. We're looking for Song Sakana-san, please."

The woman nodded and held the door wide, pointing to the floor, where other shoes had been neatly lined. Titus and Oleg knelt together to unlace their footwear.

"It ain't easy wearing combat boots everywhere we go, huh?" Titus elbowed Oleg, knocking him off balance. "I hope you wore your best socks."

"Speak for yourself." Oleg shoved Titus harder than was necessary at the sight of Titus' big toe protruding from his stocking. "Now whose face is red?"

Both men rose to their full height to realize the woman had been watching them the whole time.

"I'm sorry for my friend." Titus bowed again.

The woman's face was blank, then she turned away and spoke a single Japanese word.

"I think that means to follow her," Oleg said.

"Or to wait here." Titus folded his hands. "I think we should wait."

"Are you sure?" Oleg leaned closer. "Or are you just ashamed of that ugly toe sticking out?"

The woman turned back and gestured for them to follow.

Beyond a living room and kitchen, they reached a sliding door onto an enclosed porch where a man in his forties sat at a wooden table. Two books were open before him. The woman bowed, then returned to the house.

"Song Sakana?" Titus bowed, noticed his bare toe, and straightened upright. "My name is Titus Caspertein. My partner, Oleg Saratov."

"My father said to expect visitors." The Japanese man stood and shook their hands. His voice was soft, his hand firm. "You are friends with a Middle Eastern man known as the Saber?"

"Yes. Rashid al-Sabur spoke to your father yesterday. We had to know who you were before we followed up on a conversation you had with the American embassy."

"Apparently, that wasn't a waste of time after all. Please, sit."

They sat across from him.

"As you can imagine, we're a little shocked to hear that anyone would report on Steve Brookshire's whereabouts." Titus spoke slowly, studying the ex-mobster. Intel said the youngest of the Sakanas had been the most brutal. "Especially Song Sakana saying something."

"We take many paths in life." Sakana closed both books in front of him. They were written in Japanese. Titus guessed one was a Bible, and the other some sort of commentary. "But only one path leads to life."

"Well said. You're indeed a Christian now?"

"Without reservation, even though it has isolated me from all I once knew." He raised his hand to acknowledge the house. "My wife is now dead. I care for my mother-in-law, who is ill. We have no care and no steady income, except what my father sends me. But I am a son of God now. We host three Bible studies each week here. Someday, I hope to teach, but for now, I'm a student."

"The best teachers never stop being students," Titus said.

"Well said." Sakana smiled, but there was pain behind his smile. "And you both?"

"We're your brothers, as was Steve Brookshire."

"Of course." He diverted his eyes. "My work in the family was a source of pride for most of my life. We ruled Hong Kong for years. Not so much now. We are weaker. My father blames me."

"Perhaps your stand will help him see the light." Titus folded his hands. "Our Middle Eastern partner is a Christian, and your father will soon talk to another brother in the Lord we have in America who can help him further. We'll pray for your father."

"Thank you. It's so . . . strange. This joy I have inside, and yet such agony that my family is still lost."

"I understand." Titus closed his eyes for a few seconds. Thirty hours ago, he'd been cleaning leaves off his roof as his wife dropped hints about spending time with him before he died. Now, he was listening to an ex-mobster speak of Christ and His love for the lost. He didn't want it to end, but he'd come to Japan for a purpose. "How did you cross Steve Brookshire?"

The man hesitated. Perhaps he'd been willing to talk to the US embassy in the past, but now the words didn't come easily.

"I was responsible for taking him in Hong Kong. A man named Peng Zemin hired me. He was—still is—Shanghai's commander of the secret police. Your faces show that you know of him?"

"We know of his victims." Titus glanced at Oleg. "His hatred for Christians goes unmatched, I would say, at least across China."

"Commander Peng has a security officer named Tond-zu, known for his yawning."

"Yawning?"

"Yes, but he's fully alert. His face is deformed from a gang fight during his youth. He's missing teeth. He's the muscle for Peng, but both are vicious, deadly men."

"Tond-zu. Got it."

"They didn't want a Chinese official connected with Steve's abduction and disappearance. I was an effective operator, so Peng hired me. Not just to take him, but to make him talk."

"You mean torture," said Oleg, who quickly lowered his head. "Sorry."

"No, you were correct. It was torture." Sakana's face was grim. "For days, my men and I kept him alive. I hired a doctor to monitor his health. We'd never seen anyone so strong. No one ever lasts that long. We cut off . . . even his leg."

"His leg?" Titus looked away. It was another mission that would end in disappointment. They were two years too late. "But he never talked?"

"Only about Jesus." Sakana bowed his head and muffled a sob under his hand. "I'm so sorry. It's my fault. The only thing I can understand is that God wanted me to see his strength. The whole time, you know what Steve kept telling me?"

"What?" Titus tried to be angry at the broken man in front of him, but it was impossible. He'd seen God use suffering too often to touch hard hearts; he couldn't doubt the new Christian across the table.

"He kept telling me he didn't hate me, that he wasn't angry, that he was praying for me. It was several weeks later that it all rose up inside of me. I couldn't look away any longer. My need inside was too great. I found a Bible and started reading. When I told my father, he removed me. But I don't regret what Jesus has done inside me."

"That's a testimony I will tell everyone," Titus said, "not only those who knew Steve. We won't let his death or your sacrifice be in vain."

"His death?" Sakana lifted his head. "No, I don't think he's dead."

"He's still alive?" Titus gasped. "After everything? I mean, you cut off his leg!"

"He was my first unsuccessful contract, ever. I was ineffective. Tond-zu took him back. Steve's strength was beyond what a normal human could endure. I refunded Peng's money before I walked away. That man is still commander in Shanghai, only he's more powerful now. I've made inquiries into what may have happened to Steve, but the Sakana name has diminished, and it was in Hong Kong where we were most feared. Nothing has turned up."

"Where would Peng or Tond-zu hold Steve all this time? What kind of place could keep that a secret?"

"Maybe not in Japan or America, but in China, people disappear all the time. Maybe they're dead, maybe they're alive. Maybe in a prison hospital, or a work camp. Wherever it is, it's inland, far from the population centers. They still want what I was supposed to discover: the key to the Christian sub-net."

"He's still out there!" Oleg elbowed Titus. "We need to have a little chat with this yawning Tond-zu character pronto!"

"Let's back up." Titus held up his hand. "You said you took Steve. What about Lisa Kennedy?"

"Her as well. Peng wanted her out of the way. I took her to a brothel in Shanghai where they gave her heroin, then turned her over to the police. There was a hearing or trial, but then she disappeared."

"That's all we know, too." Titus sighed. "Our colleague and Mrs. Kennedy visited Lisa, but later, she vanished. Sounds like more of Peng's handiwork."

"Anyone could disappear in China's interior, even a foreigner. There are prisons that are pits in the earth. Nothing ever leaves, not even garbage. Whole families have been murdered out there, then forgotten."

"We need to start looking. Can you point us to some possibilities?"

"There are too many prisons." Sakana shook his head. "And you'd never gain access to search. These prisons aren't even supposed to exist. They have no regulations, no human rights oversight. They are little kingdoms, and the wardens have absolute power. Somehow, you have to make Peng talk and tell you where he sent Steve and Lisa."

"The commander of the secret police?" Oleg frowned. "I've got a better chance of going to prison myself and looking from inside."

"Don't get yourself arrested quite yet, Oleg." Titus clenched his fist. "We have a few tricks up our sleeves, not to mention the Christian underground to help us, if need be."

"The sub-net?" Sakana raised his eyebrows. "You know about it? Who exactly are you guys?"

Titus sat back in his chair as Sakana's mother-in-law served them tea.

"Sakana-san, we have much to talk about!"

Shanghai – Two Years Ago

"Stay calm, Miss Kennedy."

Lisa couldn't stop shaking as she sat beside the American embassy attorney, Jason Allison, who didn't appear any calmer than she felt. He had a distracting eye twitch that made Lisa wonder if anyone would take him seriously.

"There's no jury!" her mother, Marie, called from the front row behind Lisa. "Mr. Allison, where's the jury?"

"It's not that kind of hearing. Now, please! An outburst could sway the judge in the wrong direction."

Lisa risked a peek over her shoulder. Fifty cameras clicked simultaneously from the back of the room. The international press wasn't missing a juicy detail regarding the American heroin addict's proceedings.

"Don't worry." Mr. Allison patted Lisa's hand, and she tugged at her pajama sleeves. The needle scars on her arm hadn't faded. "This judge will decide if your case needs a closer look. I'll push it as far as I can. But you have two strikes already against you: you claim to be a Christian missionary, which is illegal, and you have drug priors in America. Everyone has Google now, Miss Kennedy. Your whole life is known to the world."

The judge entered the room. He was a stone-faced fifty-year-old in a black robe. Lisa tried to make eye contact, maybe flash him an optimistic smile, but he didn't look up from his throne. The hearing began. The Communist Party presented its condemning evidence first—video and still photos of Lisa's arrest. Everyone spoke in Mandarin. Then Mr. Allison was given the floor.

Right away, Lisa sensed the judge's impatience with Mr. Allison's halting Mandarin. He paused often in mental search for words, which Lisa herself couldn't understand. Finally, Mr. Allison seated himself.

The courtroom was silent as the magistrate studied digital transcripts on his laptop. Finally, he began to speak, and Lisa felt her body go numb. She could tell by the man's tone that he was declaring bad news.

"He says he sees no reason to go to trial," Allison translated in a whisper. "The evidence is without controversy. But he cannot give you the maximum sentence, because it wouldn't be fair. Nor can he give you the shortest sentence, since the world is watching, and China cannot appear weak against narcotics, especially foreign ones. Now, he's determining the years, something in the middle . . ."

"What?" Lisa blinked rapidly, hyperventilating. Would no one stand up for her? "What's he saying, Mr. Allison?"

"I'm sorry. We can appeal. I didn't think it would be that much."

"How much?" Lisa ripped her arms away as two guards reached for her. Her eyes were filled with tears. "What's my sentence, you incompetent fool!"

"Fifteen years re-education. I'm sorry. The evidence was just too much to argue against."

Lisa was cuffed as the camera flashes popped. Her mother's hands were covering her face. Before Lisa was led out of the courtroom she glanced back, but her mother wouldn't even look at her.

Shanghai – Present Day

Rashid al-Sabur set his Bible aside and walked to his hotel window in Shanghai. A storm had swept across the East China Sea overnight, dropping rain, washing away the street grime and smog. He could see Shanghai Tower in the distance, which was rare. In two days, the pollution would return and there would be no long-range stalking of his target, the brutal Tond-zu of the secret police.

Bibles themselves weren't illegal in China, only restricted. Customs had allowed him to enter with the personal one Titus had given him to study since their Venezuelan mission. Rashid's heart was in turmoil at the spiritual state of mankind. Could the Bible truly be right? It had to be. It had already told him the truth about his own desperate heart. The history of mankind and the fate of the world was too shocking for Rashid to fully grasp. If the truth was right there, in the Bible's plain words, why weren't more Christians involved in the effort to save souls?

Gazing above the city, Rashid saw the smoggy haze already threatening to blanket the steel towers. Maybe that's how sin was. Lukewarm Christians got a little nightly washing off once in a while, but the pollution of their own passions held them back from seeing the needs of others. A day or two after an experience with God, lukewarm believers returned to their smog-laden state of busy-ness and self-centeredness. In a notebook, Rashid jotted several questions to ask Titus the next time they spoke. Primarily, he wanted to find out how he could remain sensitive to God's call each day—to be as genuine as Titus and Oleg were. This was a matter Rashid felt necessary to uncover. He didn't want to be what the Bible called lukewarm.

The work before him was dangerous, he thought as he left his hotel room, but there was too much power in the words of the Bible for him to doubt what power God was willing to wield for him. With God watching his back, he realized he could boldly approach a plan he'd devised himself, to achieve all that Titus had presented to him as their problem: finding Steve Brookshire.

At street level, Rashid climbed into a taxi and rode to Shanghai

Tower. The spear into the sky was over a quarter-mile straight up. Because Rashid was a careful researcher, he'd learned everything about the tower, in case he needed to escape from the building in a hurry. His target resided in the tower, so there was no avoiding going inside. Perhaps at one time, Commander Peng and his right hand, Tond-zu, had been simple knights in the authority structure of Shanghai, but now they were kings. Tond-zu himself was no longer a thug of the secret police, but a lieutenant with agents under him, all tasked with the ruthless demise of anyone who threatened the Communist Party.

Inside Shanghai Tower, Rashid rode the elevator up the spine of the building. At forty miles per hour, the force on his midriff threatened the contents of his stomach. The fastest elevator in the world was about to embarrass him in front of Shanghai's elite. The business men and women in the elevator with him chatted casually as if they had no idea the local cuisine was about to splash all over their shoes.

But Rashid kept down his breakfast, chastising himself for not easing into the colorful food more slowly. Sometimes he was in a rush to acclimate to a region when he knew he'd be in a country for a spell, searching for treasure.

The elevator chimed and he stepped into a lobby decorated by pale marble floors and glass chandeliers. Still queasy from the ride, he didn't tempt vertigo with a look toward the outer window and quarter-mile-high view of the city. He approached a reception desk.

"My name is Rashid al-Sabur. I'm here to meet with Tond-zu."

"Enter, please, Mr. Al-Sabur." The young woman indicated a vaulted door. "He is expecting you."

Rashid walked down the marble floor. *Tond-zu.* The man had only one name. Chinese names were already strange enough, their family name listed first, and their personal name last. What was Tond-zu, he wondered, first or last?

A camera in the wall apparently saw him coming, since the door opened automatically. Though he'd seen several photographs of lanky Tond-zu, Rashid wasn't prepared for the fierceness in the face of the deformed man. Even with all his riches, Tond-zu hadn't paid for artificial teeth or reconstruction work to repair the left side of his jaw, top and bottom. But to his satisfaction, Tond-zu's face reflected a grimace at Rashid's presence. Growing in Jesus Christ, Rashid hadn't considered until that moment that his own countenance might have softened. Since this operation for COIL required an impression of the coldest heart possible, he fixed a sneer on his face and thrust his hands in his pockets.

Tond-zu dismissed two aids but didn't offer his hand of greeting to Rashid after seeing his reluctance to approach the desk, which was decorated with one grotesque figurine on the corner.

"You like it?" Tond-zu picked up the figurine. "I'm a collector. It's the refuse of capitalists after they've been crushed under the foot of labor."

Rashid tilted his head, wondering if Tond-zu truly appreciated the disgusting sculpture of skeletons, tortured beings, and hammer-wielding workers—or if he kept it to shock his guests.

"There is a simplicity in brutality." Rashid drew an upholstered chair aside to sit down. "We may have more in common than I imagined."

Tond-zu sat down behind his desk.

"Then I'm glad we're meeting. Your exploits internationally are . . . notorious." Tond-zu smiled, the missing half of his teeth offering a gaping hole that Rashid likened to an abyss. "Like minds are meant to cross paths. It's a Chinese proverb."

"You came recommended for what I have in mind."

"The Great Saber has come to Shanghai. I'm intrigued. What treasure have the ancestors left for you to take before I get my hands on it myself?"

"There may be enough for both of us to receive the—" Rashid paused, recalling the poetic words of the Bible. "As laborers, we reap what we sow. I'm willing to reap after I sow. Together, may we both receive what we justly deserve."

"If I held a glass of champagne, I'd raise my glass to such words. How can I play a part in whatever you're plotting?"

Rashid stood and walked to the window. For a lifetime, he'd manipulated fear and built suspense in the hearts of men and women to get what he wanted. He felt suddenly unclean in the presence of a man who so reminded him of his old nature. Indeed, Tond-zu felt a kinship to what he perceived in Rashid, though Rashid guessed most of what attracted the man was from his reputation across the Dark Web as a blood-chilling treasure hunter. Now, as a Christian, Rashid knew he had to continue that facade for the sake of Steve Brookshire.

"I need something, but someone stands in my way."

"That's easily resolved." Tond-zu joined Rashid at the window, standing shoulder to shoulder. "That hardly seems like something that would stop men like us."

"He's an official in Shanghai. It's why I'm here. I need him gone, but in a rather precise way."

"Officials are not invincible."

"I don't want him dead. I want him accused."

"Oh." Tond-zu laughed and clapped Rashid on the back. "You and I are too alike. An accusation is—"

Rashid shoved Tond-zu on the shoulder so hard that Tond-zu stumbled away. His gaping grin disappeared through a yawn.

"Don't touch me again." Rashid lowered his head, glaring at the monster. "I'm not here to bond with you. I'm here for treasure. You're instrumental, that's all. There are unearthly riches at stake beyond our imaginations. With riches, comes power. You're a man of precision. Can I count on you?"

"It depends on what you're talking about." Tond-zu drew no closer. "Who am I supposed to accuse, and of what am I to accuse him?"

"Someone close to you recently acquired a coal-bearing zone in the Xinjiang Uygur autonomous region. He took the property for himself from a businessman in Kuqa. A Christian."

"So? We take from Christians all the time." Tond-zu licked his lips. "You could say it's a Party hobby."

"Understandably." Rashid shrugged. "They're just Christians. But the man who took the property in secret didn't share it with you. He's about to have you removed."

"No one can remove me." Tond-zu's fists clenched. "Who is this?"

"You know my abilities. I'm able to intercept encrypted texts and unfold their mysteries with the world's most powerful computers. You're about to disappear while he grows to new heights. You threaten his future. You know his methods. There's too much blood on his hands with you still around. The land he took—he won't share it. But if we proceed carefully, you and I can take it for ourselves, and put him away without anyone else ever knowing. He certainly won't say anything himself, since it would incriminate him even further."

"Who is this? Don't play games with me!"

"You know who it is!" Rashid faced the window. "You've trusted him for years. Now, at the moment of his ultimate crowning in the *Shanghai Clique*, he will set you aside. He has used you, and now you are nothing."

"Peng!" Tond-zu punched his palm. "I suspected he was up to something!"

"Forty-percent of China's proven coal reserves are in Xinjiang. It's worth billions."

"How would you and I split it?" Tond-zu lifted his head. "There are corruption committees. We have to be careful."

"I'll work out the financial details for us. You focus on Peng Zemin's accusation as a Christian. Poetic justice, yes?"

"He's been like a father to me. And now you want the hunter of Christians accused of being a Christian?"

"You doubt my intel? The man is about to do the same to you, maybe worse, just to make you go away."

"I don't doubt it." Tond-zu scowled. "I've seen it coming." He walked to his desk. "You're right. Peng's disappearance in death won't do. I'll devise a trail of fabricated Christian contacts leading to him. It'll take time to make it convincing. How much time do we have?"

"I'd like to be finished in China in a matter of weeks. I can't move until you complete your work and place Peng in a secure place, somewhere isolated, where he can't contact anyone who matters. But keep him alive in the event we need him for something."

"I know just the place. It's far to the west. He'll never return. No one ever does. He'll regret the day he ever turned against me!"

China – Two Years Ago

Steve accepted a pair of crutches from Tond-zu, and hobbled away from the vehicle. Their trip into the heart of China had left him exhausted, ready for sleep. He was also starving; Tond-zu hadn't fed him in two days.

"This is the Hudie Valley, discovered by an ancient Japanese warlord during his invasion. You'll live here. You'll die here, unless you find your tongue and speak about the sub-net."

Weakly balanced on his crutches, Steve stood with Tond-zu at the top of a ridge. *Hudie* meant butterfly in Mandarin. The rugged desert of inner Mongolia surrounded them, but here, north of the Huang River, was a green and cultivated oasis. The dirt road they'd taken north from the river highway ended there at a dirt parking lot where they'd found a few vehicles. Down in the valley, sloping up to the east, were a number of dirt paths, a few cottages, a stone fortress, and terraced rice paddies.

"This is the extent of your freedom." Tond-zu swept his arm across the scene, from trees in the west to the rice fields, from the decrepit fortress to a scum pond. "Every day you will go to the prison gate for food."

"That's a prison? You're not putting me inside?"

"Shut up and listen. The men at the gate will expect you each morning. You'll receive your daily food rations from them. If you don't go, you won't eat."

"And my walls are these . . . mountains?"

"If you leave, you'll be killed. The peasants below are all spies. They have family members in the prison. They'll inform on you in an instant if it means a shorter sentence for their loved one in the prison."

Steve watched several farmers working in water only a few inches deep. They were spies? Of course, where could he go, anyway?

"Home," he said softly. The valley was springing with life. They'd killed Lisa, kidnapped and crippled him. But Steve saw a mission field before him. "Thank you, Tond-zu. But why aren't you putting me inside the prison?"

"It's full of lepers. You're of no use to us dead. When you're ready to talk, let the guards know at the prison gate. The warden will call me. We're old friends. I've warned him that you're not to be trusted. He knows if anyone helps you or shows you favor, that person will meet a painful death."

"I understand."

"Of course, I may get tired of waiting for you to talk. Or we may discover the sub-net access key ourselves. You won't be necessary after that. I'll call Warden Fongdu Jen, and he'll send guards to kill you in the night. You can try to sleep with that thought."

"My God has given me a clear conscience, Tond-zu. I'll sleep fine every night, after I pray for you."

"Someday, I will kill you, Steve Brookshire. Then your other leg will become my trophy." Tond-zu kicked at Steve's stump, knocking him to the ground. "Your misery is your own fault."

Steve blinked the tears away as he held his stump. The shooting pain took minutes to subside. Blood soaked through the soiled cloth protecting the healing tissue.

Tond-zu returned to his SUV and drove away. From the ground, Steve stared after the vehicle. Dust boiled from the dirt road that was as dry as the surrounding terrain. He was miles from the river. Could he hobble to the Huang and float down river without anyone reporting him? He guessed it was impossible on crutches. Maybe if he found a bike, he could peddle with his one leg and coast down what looked to be mostly downhill slopes to the distant river.

But then he'd need a boat at the river. Or a phone. He hadn't seen any cell towers, but there had to be landlines. Tond-zu had said he'd called ahead. One call to Corban Dowler, and a team of COIL agents would be there in hours. There was still hope.

"Thank You, Lord."

He strained upright and leaned against his crutches, already praying for Tond-zu. Still unfamiliar with the crutches, he shuffled around to turn his back on the empty road, then faced the terraced valley that was now his prison.

"Home," he said again, and with a heavy heart, he moved onto the nearest path.

CHAPTER SIX

Shanghai – Two Years Ago

A female guard pounded on Lisa's cell door.

"Li Ken! Li Ken!"

"Not this cell!" Lisa yelled back and willed herself back to sleep. Sleep was the only escape she received from depression.

"Li Ken, transfer! Up now!"

"Not this cell!" Lisa sat up. "I'm Lisa Kennedy, not Li Ken!"

The door opened and the guard raised a baton.

"Oh, help me, Jesus!" Lisa gasped and dove into a corner, but her cell was small. The lead-weighted baton landed twice on her leg and back, striking a nerve and paralyzing her leg. "Okay, okay!"

Limping, she was roughly escorted down a corridor and out a back door to a city street. She was handcuffed and forced to stand against the wall, her nose to the cement. The night was cool and she shivered in her thin pajama top and bottoms.

A moment later, four men wearing the same drab clothing were cuffed and told to stand next to her. She stole a couple glances. The men were older than her, two of them with grey hair and bowed backs—either from hard labor or from age.

"No talking!" a male guard shouted and jabbed his baton into Lisa's ribs. She twisted in pain, but quickly recovered and faced forward. "Stay still. No moving!"

Minutes passed. Lisa closed her eyes, praying she could endure whatever came next. Did God even hear her anymore? It didn't seem like it. Her sentencing had occurred without a hint of mercy or understanding. COIL knew she was there, but her past drug use as a teen had discredited her too much. Her Chinese adversaries had pulled all the right strings, threatening to wipe out her very desire to live. She hoped Steve was standing stronger than she was.

Two hours later, Lisa's shivers had turned into spasms. The men beside her were fairing no better, their teeth chattering. All that time a male and female guard stood a few feet behind them, sharing cigarettes and speaking Mandarin, which Lisa still couldn't understand.

Finally, when Lisa felt her legs about to collapse, a government truck with an extended cab roared into the alley. It parked behind the prisoners and the doors were opened. At baton point, Lisa was the first to board, shoved from behind into the back seat of the truck. A seat meant for three was quickly filled with all five prisoners. The doors slammed. An official drove, and another with a compact rifle in his lap sat in the passenger seat.

Lisa, squished to the far left, was in pain, her hip pressing against the plastic exterior. She shifted sideways and the man next to her lifted his cuffed hands and grabbed her arm. Panic caught in her throat. The surprising strength from the man, much smaller than she, forced her to lean over his lap. The next thing she knew, the second man drew her farther down to the third and fourth man. In two breaths, she'd been man-handled across their laps to end reclining on her back.

Underneath her, the four men repositioned themselves to claim the extra space she'd left. As they settled, Lisa relaxed. These men were veterans. They knew how to work together to be as comfortable as possible in such an uncomfortable position. With her on their laps, they all had more room, not to mention the body heat that would keep them warmer on the cold night.

Down her body's length, their cuffed hands rested on her. Lisa was strangely comforted by their simple act of decency, even if it was for mutual relief. She was being given an opportunity to sleep. Not wanting to waste a moment as the truck roared down the highway, she sighed and drifted away while praying for Steve. Maybe God hadn't abandoned her after all . . .

Shanghai – Present Day

PRS Agent Wes Trimble crept into a Shanghai apartment, his Beretta sidearm drawn. The COIL safe house should've been occupied, but instead, he found it empty, the lights and two computer screens still on. A police raid might've been the cause of the vacancy. Titus and Oleg weren't exactly able to disguise themselves in the Orient. Titus was an athletic blond, and Oleg was a broad-shouldered brute. Neither had probably ever been mistaken for being low-profile.

After sweeping the two-bedroom apartment for enemies or signs of a struggle, Wes approached one of the computer screens. In bright green letters, someone had typed, *"Gone fishin'."* That was probably Titus, Wes guessed. The Arkansas man was always jesting, though Oleg was his close sidekick. Not for a minute did Wes believe the two had actually gone fishing, not after arriving in China from Japan a day earlier. They'd gone fishing for souls, evangelizing, or perhaps prowling the city for other believers. Those two never rested!

Wes frowned at a ridiculously large poster on one wall praising the Communist Party. How would Titus ever allow such an eyesore while they were there to search for Steve Brookshire? But the poster seemed to be a facade, too. Wes unclipped its top hooks and turned it over. Sure enough, their operational schematics were detailed in code on the backside. There were many unknowns about the current mission, so there were empty spaces in the diagram.

Finding Song Sakana was worthy of praising God, and Wes had an appointment in Hong Kong to meet with his mobster father in two days. Since US President Pantrow had made Wes his personal COIL liaison, Wes was taking full advantage of his governmental credentials to further the gospel with COIL—as well as protect God's people.

"Where's Titus?" someone asked behind him.

Wes turned, his sidearm leveled.

"Luigi!" Wes holstered his weapon at the sight of Luigi Putelli, the COIL superspy who was shadowing Titus and watching the COIL agent's back. "I could've shot you!"

"It took me by surprise when Titus came to China." Luigi strode into the room past Wes to examine the schematic on the wall. "I had to come up with another identification before entering the country. Then I followed you from the airport."

"Yeah, right." Wes chuckled, then realized the gaunt spook was telling the truth. He had to stop underestimating the expertise of the team Corban Dowler kept in the field. "You're probably looking for Titus, huh?"

"In the flesh when not digitally doing so." Luigi returned the poster to its former position. "A lot is riding on him. Corban says he still has many enemies. You certainly know it doesn't hurt to keep another eye on the Serval."

"Eye. Yeah. That's funny, Luigi." Wes adjusted his eye patch, a blue one that day, as he watched Luigi survey the apartment with care.

"Titus has his shadows, and Corban has his. Is there anyone on me?"

"You're close enough to the president that someone's always trying to tail you." Luigi ran his fingers under the edge of the kitchen counter. "You have to watch out for your own government people, or enemies trying to find something to use against President Pantrow. But you're usually too slippery to follow. No one else followed us here."

"You know I work for the president?"

"I keep an open line on all COIL personnel who are in regular contact with Corban, and now Titus. I picked up a whisper about you and the president. Someone else might have, too."

"Things are much simpler in my basement office with my computer geeks." Wes waited until Luigi had sufficiently inspected the apartment. "Say, Titus and Oleg are pretty much just detectives right now, waiting on Rashid to turn up something about Steve Brookshire. Can I borrow you in two days for a Hong Kong meeting? It loosely relates to this."

"You want me?" Luigi looked up sharply. "I wasn't sure you ever got over that time you arrested me in Oregon, and Chloe had me released."

"That was a long time ago, Luigi. You're a Christian and I'm in the COIL loop, now. Yes, I want you. Is that belt of yours still what it used to be?"

Luigi hooked his thumb in his waistband as if he might demonstrate he was still as agile as he was years earlier. Wes knew the belt buckle contained sharp shards dipped in falaco tranquilizer. More than a few enemies had felt the lash of that buckle since Luigi had given up his lethal weapons for the cause of Christ.

"I'll be available in two days." Luigi drew out a piece of gum, unwrapped it, and threw the wrapper in the corner. "Leave that for Titus so he knows I'm local."

"You got it." Wes was about to give the mysterious man more details about his Hong Kong plans in two days, but Luigi exited the room, his bubblegum chewing louder than the whisper of his feet on the floor.

Checking the refrigerator and cupboards, Wes started to cook dinner. It was getting late. Wherever Titus and Oleg were, they'd be hungry when they returned. Chicken, dumplings, and rice were on the menu.

❦

Hudie Valley – Two Years Ago

Lisa fell to her knees as she was dragged from the transport truck. For three days and three nights, she'd resided on the back seat with the four other prisoners. No speaking. Eating and drinking only when their two transport officers offered them rations. Exiting the vehicle only every few hours when they'd stopped to answer nature's call.

On the back seat, they'd rotated through seating arrangements each time they were unloaded and loaded for bathroom breaks. The fifth prisoner was always allowed to lay across the laps of the other four. It was the most comfortable, and maybe the last comfort Lisa would experience, she guessed.

The morning was crisp as she struggled to her feet, stretching her cramped legs alongside her Chinese companions. The two officers leaned against their truck, neither seeming concerned about their cuffed prisoners. And it was no wonder, Lisa thought as she turned in a circle. The land around them was desolate. Except for the valley below the ridge where the truck had stopped at the end of the dirt road.

Curiosity moved Lisa and the others with her to study the valley below. Hudie Prison was situated in picturesque greenery, the stone structure with creeping vines and mold perhaps as old as the rice paddies themselves. Over the last day, the two officers had talked between themselves, partially in English so Lisa could understand, instilling fear in the listening prisoners as the guards described the horrors awaiting them in the valley prison.

"We will die here," one of the prisoners said in Cantonese, of which Lisa understood a little. It was the first words that Lisa had heard him or any of her companions speak.

The fortress-turned-prison below was dug into the opposite ridge, its walls rising thirty feet, and higher where the towers were erected. From her height, Lisa could see into the courtyard, also of stone, except for a green lawn in the very center of the keep.

Three guards with bamboo batons walked up a worn path from the prison toward the ridge where the prisoners stood. As the guards drew closer, the two transport officers unlocked their handcuffs. Lisa rubbed her raw wrists, which she knew were scarred for life.

"God won't let us die here," Lisa said in English for the other prisoners, hoping they understood. "We have to keep hope."

Her words surprised her, since her own level of hope was so miniscule. But in such a place of desperation, brought so low and without earthly hope, she sensed the Spirit of God reminding her that she wasn't completely forgotten. Whether she'd been transferred purposely or accidentally as Li Ken, even if she were lost to everyone in her past in this vast barrenness—God was able to see and comfort her.

The three prison guards visited with the two Shanghai officers for a few minutes, then the guards directed the prisoners down the path into the valley. Lisa watched her footing, but she kept stealing glances at their surroundings. This could be her last view of the outside world so she wanted to hold a snapshot of beauty in her mind.

A cluster of cottages were scattered along the northern edge of the paddies. From the officers, Lisa knew those dwellings were occupied by peasants who labored in the fields to provide food for the prison population. Farther up the valley, there was a single cottage on a patch of dry ground in the midst of a sloping rice terrace. Outside that cottage a quarter-mile away, a man hobbled on crutches. Though he was some distance from her, Lisa thought he might be a white man. That rang true with what she'd learned about Hudie Valley. It was a prison for political prisoners who'd not yet received a death sentence. But inside the walls of the prison, many had died of disease and despair, even suicide. The government didn't seem to care, if the government proper even knew the hidden valley existed at all.

Before she'd received her fill of the view, Lisa followed the others through the prison gate. The smell of feces choked her senses. The sewage system was literally a pond outside the eastern wall.

At the edge of the courtyard lawn, the five prisoners stopped in a line. A hunched Chinese man issued a tin cup and a thin blanket to each prisoner, then one at a time, the prisoners were escorted away, through a dark archway in the corner of the courtyard. Lisa was last. She clutched her cup and blanket as she was led into a musty tunnel that twisted down a stone stairway to a number of steel doors covered in peeling rust. After one door was unlocked, she ducked inside before one of the male guards shoved her.

The door slammed closed behind her. She stood for a moment as her eyes adjusted to the darkness. Only one source of light existed in the small cell: a glass-less archer's window, narrow and tall, with a view of the east end of the valley. All she could see was sky, the refuse pond, and the surrounding hills.

A woman spoke Mandarin Chinese, then another. Six women were gawking at her. One raggedy-haired woman who sat on the floor pointed at a mat in the middle of the room that was currently unoccupied, large enough for a small child to lie upon.

This was her place. Her mat. Her territory. Her home.

She fell asleep thinking of the stranger on crutches up the valley. If she wasn't the only white person in Hudie Valley, she wondered if she could get word to someone, anyone. After all, COIL had promised not to abandon her. But did they even know where she was? Oh, she missed Steve.

Hong Kong – Present Day

Agent Wes Trimble strode into a private garden on the northern edge of Hong Kong's sprawling mass. Luigi Putelli walked a step behind him with cadet-like posture. This wasn't the first time Wes had allowed an operation to be interrupted to promote Christ with a potential government asset or Christian convert. Lin Sakana may have been king in Hong Kong, but something inside him had responded to Rashid al-Sabur's offer to set his disgraceful past in order. And if Wes got his way, he intended to see the Japanese mobster set his eternal future in order as well.

Crossing a wooden bridge over a pond, Wes reached a small island where ducks waddled ignorantly between the legs of Lin Sakana's six bodyguards. The stone-faced men wore black suits and dark glasses. Wes glanced at Luigi. The two had a complicated past, some of it on opposite sides of the law, but since Luigi was a Christian now, Wes felt sufficiently supported in the hostile environment—spiritually and martially.

A few yards from Lin Sakana, Wes stopped and bowed his head slightly to show honor, but not low enough to concede his stature as a high official.

Lin mirrored the gesture, showing he wasn't willing to give much ground, either. Out of the corner of his eye, Wes saw Luigi take up a stance facing the three bodyguards on the right. That meant if things got messy, Wes was responsible for the three on the left. No one's weapon was visible, but the bulk inside their suit jackets indicated the bodyguards carried mini-submachine guns, maybe on slings. It was a classic mistake, Wes judged, against his smaller handgun, which he could draw quickly from where it was concealed high on his hip. He'd already unclipped the holster. And Luigi? Wes had heard enough about the efficiency of the man's skills with his belt to know Lin Sakana hadn't brought enough men.

"It's an honor to meet the renowned Wes Trimble," Lin said, "even if your exploits are unknown by most in America."

Wes smiled. The Japanese loved to show off, but with class. The man was implying he had an arm, or contact, in the US government sufficiently informed on even Wes's covert activities along the Pacific Rim.

"My old bones prefer the comfort of an office chair," he said, "but I couldn't miss a meeting with you, Lin Sakana."

"Your associate last week said you're fair and just. That was quite a compliment coming from the Saber."

"I know justice only by the justice I've been shown—by God."

"*God?*" Lin seemed surprised at the mention. "You're religious?"

"I always failed at the do's and do not's of religion, but I have a close relationship with Jesus Christ." Wes shifted his feet. None of these meetings went the same. He had to indeed rely on what he sensed God wanted him to say. "The legal vulnerabilities of your past in America as Sid Sanko have certainly weighed heavily on your soul. I believe the two of us meeting now is divinely ordained."

"I wondered if you would arrive to arrest me. You Americans aren't known for your judicial mercies."

"It depends on the person, I suppose." Wes smiled. "The heart experiences changes over time. Your days as Sid Sanko were long ago. I'm a man who believes in the right medicine for the current malady, not a cure for an ailment that no longer exists."

"I didn't expect such wisdom from a CIA man." Lin paused, his remaining concerns showing in his weary eyes. "When I ran from America, I entered this life. I have become powerful. But the weight you speak of—I know it well."

"Redemption is costly." Wes considered the spiritual reality of the statement. "Your trespasses against the United States are worthy of death. You sold secrets to Chinese scientists. You used those secrets to secure your safety here in China. Some might say all this is unforgivable. But God has placed me in a position to see you forgiven, to pay for your redemption myself."

"I don't understand. My crimes . . ."

"Let me be your advocate. No one will touch you without going through me. And no one will pierce the authority I have to secure your redemption today."

"You would do this for me? You would accept this cost?"

"I'll accept the cost upon myself. You've come here today. I acknowledge your gesture . . . of confidence. But the choice you make comes with a cost as well. It'll cost everything you have."

"What do you expect in return for this proclaimed reprieve from a death sentence in your courts?"

"I expect actions consistent with your gratitude. If you are serious about the death of the old Sid Sanko, then get serious about the new Lin Sakana."

"Reform?" Lin's head tilted with amusement. "I'm a Sakana, *the* Sakana. Thousands bow at my feet."

"Well, no one's forcing you, but before you is a choice. You can continue as you have been, and your life will bear fruit of the darkness you sow. Or, you can sow seeds worthy of a new nature."

"My enemies would see me as weak. They would kill me for leaving."

"Then, it may be time to trust your advocate. You wouldn't be the first prince of crime I've guided toward a new life, hidden away somewhere."

"I have to set things in order first."

"I'm leaving Hong Kong tonight."

Lin sighed and looked away. The sounds of the garden were gentle and soothing, but Wes knew that the decision before Lin could be equated to a war raging inside the aging mobster.

"What would I do?"

"That's not in focus right now. Leave it in God's hands." Wes scratched his jaw and turned his head toward Luigi to mumble two words: "Get ready."

Luigi's thumb, however, was already hooked inside his waistband.

The bodyguards either didn't understand English or were too professional to express concern over their boss's words.

"I would need to leave everything," Lin said. "I could never return."

"You've considered the cost?" Wes tried not to move his hand toward his sidearm. If the bodyguards could sense his readiness for what was about to happen, they would've already reached for their weapons. "Are you ready to walk away now?"

"I almost wish you'd arrived to arrest me." Lin frowned and gestured to his bodyguards. "These men have sworn to protect me. They'll never leave me without—"

Those were the words Wes had been waiting for. He lifted his jacket and drew his Beretta in an instant, leveled at the first of three men on his left. For only a few weeks, he'd been using COIL's non-lethal ammunition. Now, he was grateful he was ready to respond without lethal force. The gel-tranq hit the first bodyguard in the chest. On his right, he sensed Luigi responding with his belt.

In two seconds, Wes tranquilized the three bodyguards, then he turned toward Luigi's three. The last one was lifting his machine gun when Wes dropped him as well.

Lin stood frozen, his empty hand slightly raised. Luigi let his belt hang loosely after whipping the buckle at the first two bodyguards.

"They may have sworn to never leave your side," Wes said as he holstered his weapon, "but I doubt you swore to never leave theirs."

"You want me to leave with you right now?" Lin leaned over to examine his men. "These were the finest in Hong Kong. They'd been with my family for over a decade."

"They're still fine men." Luigi fed his belt back into his belt loops. "They're just sleeping."

"I'm in your debt." Lin bowed to Wes, this time twice as low as the first time. "I'm ready to leave China."

"Let's start by leaving Hong Kong, my friend." Wes threw an arm around Lin's shoulders as if they were old buddies. "We actually need to stay in China for a few more days. I've got to get back to Shanghai for a little meeting. Don't worry. It's nothing public. A little disguise will keep you safe. Besides, we have lots to talk about."

"And that is?"

"Your redemption. You didn't think I'm smart enough to come up with this whole idea on my own, did you?" Wes chuckled as ducks scattered in front of them on the sidewalk. "The only reason I know to risk my reputation for others is because of a Man who gave His life for me. Your son, Song, knows this Man. I think you're going to love this story . . ."

✺

Hudie Valley – Two Years Ago

Steve sat upright in his bed and listened to the night noises of Hudie Valley—frogs and insects. Far away, some mammal shrieked, and a bat outside his door-less cottage squeaked as it probably chased a moth.

This was the beginning of the second day in the valley of his captivity. It hadn't begun well. The first day, he'd woken too late in the morning. By the time he'd made his way on crutches to the prison gate, he'd been too tardy to receive his daily rations—so said the morning guard. They'd sent him on his way with an empty tin cup and a blanket that smelled like mildew.

But now, he was determined to arrive on time. The sun wasn't even up yet. Gathering his crutches, he left his empty cottage that contained a bed mat and a counter sink with no faucet. Outside, the night noises seemed amplified. The air was cool, but when he gazed toward the prison, he wasn't sure whether he shivered from the fall air or the misery he imagined residing inside those stone walls.

A narrow, raised path cut a track through the sloping rice paddies, barely wide enough to plant his crutches and swing his one-and-a-half legs forward. A canal trickled water from one terraced level to the next. He maneuvered over it carefully. The water was only a few inches deep there, but without a second change of clothes, falling into the mud would be a messy affair.

Several rice paddy levels later, he stopped and looked back at his cottage. It seemed so lonely, but he knew God placed His people where they could best mature and share His gospel.

"Lord, give me a heart for the people here." He looked toward the prison. "Even if I'm here to reach the guards. Just use me, Lord. Don't let my journey be in vain. I know it won't be. I'm here for You."

One hundred yards later, he stopped again and studied the only other cottages in the valley. A dozen dwellings sat dark on the northern edge of the rice paddies. Those families, mostly women and children, were in as much captivity as their loved ones. They worked for the prison. Steve guessed they'd arrived from all over China to live there. When a prisoner died in the prison, he wondered if the family was evicted to make room for another family. It was a sorrowful existence that he hoped to impact in some way.

By the time Steve reached the prison gate, his arms felt as heavy as lead. He hadn't eaten in three days. If they refused to feed him today, he wasn't certain he had the strength to return to his cottage where he'd regretfully left his blanket.

He sat down on a patch of uncut grass to wait for dawn. Below and to the right, the stench of the pool fortunately was blowing away from him at that hour.

Looking at the sky, he smiled, thinking of God's sovereign hand and how his life had been so drastically altered by evil. For years, he'd played the tourist and athlete in China, when secretly, he'd been securing the underground church in a way that discernibly reduced arrests of Christians. God had seen fit to allow his kidnapping, torture, and leg amputation. But Lisa's death was an ache that he'd only barely begun to feel. Could he have been more careful in Hong Kong? Was she dead because of him?

And his suffering wasn't finished, he knew. When he'd become a Christian almost twenty years earlier, he'd counted the cost, expecting opposition from the kingdom of Satan since he was now a citizen of the Kingdom of Heaven. Seeing the persecution against Christians in China, he'd not shrunk away. Rather, he'd charged forward, involving himself, learning languages, and joining the fight to save souls from hell's eternal separation from God. His Lord had suffered in this world, so he expected nothing less as a true disciple who'd cast aside his own safety to secure others for an eternal inheritance.

Somewhere in the prison, a door or cage slammed shut—steel on stone. It was a haunting sound.

"Lord God, someday, let me reach the tormented souls in those walls." Tears suddenly flowed down his cheeks. "Open these doors. Let me see the God of Joseph. Show me the One who sets captives free. Please don't let me live out here without sharing in their sufferings inside this place."

Mist came with the dawn, blanketing the landscape in a low, drifting fog. The prison gate screeched open on rusty hinges and a guard approached Steve before he could struggle upright.

"You're strong enough to come here for two days?" Everyone at the prison spoke Mandarin. "Then you're strong enough to work! You take more than your share and the warden will have you beaten. We're watching you!"

The guard turned away.

"Wait. You want me to work? Doing what?"

"What do you think?" The guard waved his baton at the foggy field. "What does everyone else do here? Work!"

The gate slammed closed. Steve leaned heavily on the crutches, his head hanging not because he was bowing to pray, but because he had no energy to hold it up any longer.

For long minutes, he labored over the words of a prayer—laboring because his flesh was complaining, but his spirit was relishing the opportunity to trust God in the face of hardship.

"Man doesn't live by rice alone," he whispered weakly as he turned toward the rice paddies. In the fog, shadows were moving as the farmers trekked into the fields to begin their day. Normally so independent, Steve accepted the fact that he'd need to rely on the kindness of strangers to keep him alive, more than on the tolerance of the prison guards to keep him fed.

He was about to become a rice farmer.

CHAPTER SEVEN

Shanghai – Present Day

"**Y**ou don't need to worry about this making you any uglier," Titus said, examining Oleg's cheek wound. They'd returned to the Shanghai safe house to find Wes Trimble and an elderly stocky Japanese man sitting at the dining table. "I don't even think a bullet did this."

"Not a bullet?" Oleg rolled his eyes as he was held captive by Titus stitching the cut below his cheekbone. "How do you think it happened, oh, wise Hole-In-Your-Sock?"

"Maybe you ran into a wall or something?" Titus laughed at his own joke and paused his stitching for a moment. "Seriously, I picked some plaster out of the wound. Some of those bullets zipping past us may have kicked some wall debris at you. An inch higher, and you'd have lost an eye. It wouldn't be easy fighting Wes over his last silk eyepatch."

"Hey, don't drag me into your brawl." Wes squinted his eye at Titus' work on Oleg's cheek. "Huh. That's the first stitching I've ever seen in the shape of a heart. Is that a thing in Russia, Oleg?"

Oleg shoved Titus and Wes away from him as they roared in laughter. Holding up a mirror, Oleg checked the perfectly straight stitches Titus had sewn.

"How was he wounded?" the Japanese man asked. "I don't understand. Was it a bullet or did he run into a wall?"

The room went silent, as if Titus and Oleg noticed the stranger for the first time.

"Titus Caspertein," Wes said, placing a hand on Titus' shoulder, "meet Lin Sakana."

"I've heard of you, sir." Titus shook the man's hand.

"The things you've heard were certainly not good things." He frowned.

Oleg stepped around Titus to shake Lin's hand.

"Each one of us ran wild against God for years, Mr. Sakana," Oleg said. "If you're looking for a fresh start from a bad past—you're in good company."

"Don't listen to him, Mr. Sakana," Titus said. "We're the last people in China you want to be around—unless you don't mind being hunted, arrested, interrogated, and imprisoned. It ain't easy being around a few of the most wanted people in all of China—if they only knew what we were up to!"

"You actually operate like this?" Bewilderment covered the mobster's face. "Are you ever serious?"

"About the things of God and people's lives, yes, we're serious." Titus put away his first aid kit. "But the things of the world? Since coming to Christ, we just can't take the world seriously anymore, and keep a straight face."

"I'm taking Lin to Japan to see his son," Wes said, "then it's off to the US mainland for a new life."

"Mr. Sakana, we're happy to have you." Titus shook the man's hand again. "But I need to steal Wes and Oleg for a little business." He elbowed Oleg in the gut. "If I'm done sewing up your blunders, we can actually get some planning done while Wes is here."

A moment later, the three men sat on the kitchen floor, their heads close to touching. The water in the sink ran loudly to distort their voices for any listening devices that may have been planted.

"First," Wes said after praying, "are you going to tell me how Oleg caught a bullet in the cheek?"

"We slipped through a police station's back door." Titus shrugged. "Figured while we're in China, we may as well help out the Christians, see what kind of intel the secret police have on the local churches."

"A couple of officers came into the back office where we were trying to get onto a computer." Oleg shook his head. "I'm not sure we've ever had a dumber idea. We barely made it out alive with them shooting at us! Our faces were covered, so they won't be rounding up all the Caucasians in Shanghai, but we're still intent on making a difference here."

"Okay." Wes said, his fingertips touching in the shape of a steeple. "We have a rule in the CIA. Maybe it's foreign to you two. When you're on a mission, you stay on mission. Breaking into a police station? Am I wasting my time looking for this Steve Brookshire or what?

Are you trying to get arrested and find him yourselves by visiting a few re-education camps? I hear their pajama uniforms are all the rage."

"Lesson learned," Titus said. He guessed if his wife, Annette, were there, she would've agreed with Wes. Sometimes his methods were just plain obnoxious. "We'll stay on mission. Now, tell us what we know so far."

"Two years ago, Song Sakana took a Chinese contract and abducted Steve and Lisa together. The contract was sponsored by the Shanghai commander of the secret police, Peng Zemin. Lisa was drugged and handed over to the police as a heroin addict and trafficker. Initially, Chloe Azmaveth followed her court proceedings, but Lisa disappeared at some point—transferred, killed, or smuggled into the flesh market, perhaps. Personally, I'd like to recover both her and Steve Brookshire."

"Agreed." Titus bowed his head, aware that his righteous anger against such evil had a tendency to get the better of him. He understood how Peter could've drawn a knife and attacked those who arrested Jesus in the garden. "Okay, take us forward to the info about Steve."

"Steve was tortured for information, according to what you found out from Song Sakana, now retired. Steve didn't talk, so Song gave Steve back to Commander Peng. Song believes Steve may still be alive, perhaps in the hands of a henchman named Tond-zu."

"That takes us to Rashid," Oleg said, then flinched as his skin pulled against the stitches. "We heard from him last night."

"Right, but it wasn't an operational update." Titus chuckled. "He sent a back-channel text to ask about a Bible passage he's confused about. '*What is the filling of the Spirit?*' he asked. I answered him that it's the Person of God consuming his attitude and influencing his actions by the reading of God's Word, the sword of the Spirit. He's chewing on the idea of a Person living inside of him."

"I couldn't have explained it better," Wes said approvingly, which Titus appreciated since Wes had been a believer much longer. "But what about Rashid's subterfuge against Tond-zu? Is his plan working?"

"That's just the thing," Titus said. "From Rashid, I think we can assume no news is good news. He's on track to divide the enemy, to turn Tond-zu against the commander, Peng."

"Titus, this is a crazy idea Rashid came up with." Wes shook his head. "You know him best. You sure he's up for this type of tension?"

"The man's the coldest and most brutal person I've ever known. At least, he was. If anyone can fake a scenario to entice Tond-zu, it's Rashid. He saved Wynter's life in Azerbaijan, I'm sure we all recall, and he took me and Oleg through South America without flinching. Everything about the guy seems genuine."

"Rashid will come through." Oleg placed his palm on his stitches to hold the skin together as he spoke. "He's probably already met with Tond-zu. Rashid's old reputation could bait another evil heart. When I was at Interpol, it was a foolproof method to draw out criminals: send in the supposed worst criminal we could find, and the other monsters would flutter to the flame."

"You mean the moths flutter to the flame," Titus said.

"What moths?" Oleg looked to Wes. "It's an American expression, right—like monsters to a flame?"

"Monsters aren't attracted to flames," Titus argued. "Name one monster that's attracted to a flame."

"Insects fly toward an open flame." Wes frowned. "What are we talking about?"

"Hole-In-Sock was correcting my English."

"Try getting your foot into your sock without holes!" Titus tugged off his boot and wiggled his exposed big toe in Oleg's face. "Ventilation is good for the skin."

"Only stench needs ventilation!" Oleg grasped Titus' ankle. "Now, I know why I had monsters on the mind!"

Titus wrestled his ankle free and cleared his throat for seriousness as Wes waited patiently.

"Sorry, Wes. It ain't easy putting up with a couple of circus clowns, especially one from Russia."

"I think I've grown immune to your Caspertein antics," Wes said, "but only because you two somehow get results. Somehow."

"That's Russian engineering," Oleg said, "not Caspertein antics."

"I'll be leaving with Lin." Wes glanced over his shoulder to see the bedroom door still closed. "With what you guys are doing next, it's probably best I'm not around to draw attention. A few diplomats know me as a government man. But this is my terrain, boys. Don't keep me in the dark. I can't help you if I'm the last one to find out how bad things could get."

"We'll keep you informed." Titus tapped his sat-watch. "If you're going back to the States, maybe I should tell you that my sister was asking about you."

"Wynter?"

"That's not her name anymore, but yes, Wynter. After you helped save her life in Azerbaijan, we brought her back as Annette's long-lost sister, Nicole. Nicole Sheffield is now a COIL trainee in Qatar, putting her Arabic to use."

"What's she want with me?"

"It'd better be a question about some clandestine protocol in the Middle East." Titus shook his finger at Wes. "You better give me a heads-up if we're about to have a one-eyed Agency man as part of the family."

"I'm not— There's nothing—" Wes held up his hand and took a breath. "Seriously, I didn't even know where you hid Wynter. Nicole. Your sister."

Titus nudged Oleg.

"I think his face is getting red."

"There's more to this than meets the eye," Oleg said, emphasizing the last word.

All three men laughed at Wes's expense.

But in the recesses of Titus' thoughts was a growing dread for Steve Brookshire and Lisa Kennedy. Two years was a long time to survive the brutality of anti-Christian sentiment in China. Titus prayed they would be able to at least bring one of the two home.

Hudie Valley – One Year Ago

A year had passed since Steve had been kidnapped while swimming near Hong Kong. During that year, Steve had heard nothing from grim-faced Tond-zu who'd left him there, so Hudie Valley hadn't been the place of misery he guessed his abductors intended it to be.

He gripped his crutches and hobbled outside the cottage. It was a pleasant fall day that greeted him, along with the little Chinese boy who'd watched and followed him for the last few weeks. Steve had become part of the rice cultivation—laboring to plant, transplant, then harvest mature rice—but not too busy to attempt to cultivate simple relationships as well. Besides being a strange white man who spoke several Chinese dialects, Steve had realized that word had been spread, probably by the prison guards that he was to be avoided. But the misery amongst the farmers was at such a desperate state, that even threats hadn't hindered the love of God that Steve had for his fellow workers. By working hard, Steve had tried to show his kindness for them as he helped them farm and produce rice for their loved ones in the prison.

The boy's name was Wu-Li. His mother was Shek-jai, one of the principal people who'd taught Steve how to grow rice. She was no older than thirty, with eyes full of sorrow, except when she looked at Wu-Li. Then, her face brightened, perhaps remembering a happier time when she hadn't been forced to feed someone in the prison. Her rice-farming instructions had been curt and in a strange Cantonese dialect, but further conversation had been fruitless. Only Wu-Li seemed to completely ignore the ban to associate with the one-legged captive of the paddy fields.

Steve did everything he could to show his appreciation to his fellow workers. They were many times more productive than he was, though he no longer tried to use his crutches when he worked in the water. The first days of falling in the mud were fresh in his memory, before he'd abandoned the crutches on the dry mid-paddy paths. Now, he crawled on his knee and stump through the mud, transplanting seeds, rebuilding containment walls, or clearing irrigation troughs. Regardless of his dedication, he was still clumsy, sometimes ruining work the farmers had already completed. And yet, they shared their rice with him each day, though usually without talking to him at all.

Secretly, Steve had involved young Wu-Li in his plan for the valley. Though Wu-Li didn't speak to him, Steve spoke to the ever-present boy. After several weeks of hinting to the child that Steve wished he had paper and pencil, Wu-Li had finally brought him a single sheet of notebook paper. Next had come a pencil, more paper, then another pencil. Steve didn't question his little bandit's source, but he certainly wouldn't waste what had been provided.

In characters learned from years of hidden Bible studies across China, Steve had begun compiling a book of Bible stories and verses in standard Mandarin. Some of his loose pages contained mere events from the Old Testament. Other pages bore complete quotes from passages Steve had memorized, like Psalm 23, John 1, and I Corinthians

13. Though he didn't share his project with anyone, he prayed daily that God would use it somehow. He felt he had so little to contribute to the farmers' lives, otherwise. But he believed the Lord hadn't allowed him to enter the valley merely to die an anonymous death.

The winter rice harvest was nearly complete. As the seeds had matured, the water level was decreased until the terraces were dry, which made for an easy harvest. But his fellow farmers had been clear that they didn't want Steve to participate in the harvest itself. He was to maintain the fully exposed containment walls and irrigation ditches. Since the water wasn't flooding the paddies for this process, the water flowed without diversion from the western spring, straight to the prison refuse pond.

With the year's work less urgent for him, Steve had intended to explore the valley. He hadn't strayed from his work for a year. The guards, sometimes visible on the prison ramparts, had surely kept an eye on him. Having gained some trust, he guessed he could move about without drawing too much attention, beginning with exploring the edges of the paddies all around.

The prison sat in the east. Beyond his own cottage, there was a belt of trees that grew thick along the ridges that blocked the view of desert ground beyond.

"Wu-Li!" Steve called, then tossed the four-year-old a tiny soldier made of twisted and tied grass. In the figure's hand was a short stick, like a sword.

The boy admired the soldier on his palm. He grinned broadly, then ran into the paddies where his mother was working. In another year, Wu-Li would be transcribed into the work force, like the valley's other children. Two hundred yards away, Shek-jai paused to adjust her pointy woven hat and acknowledge her son's figurine. She turned suddenly, and gazed in Steve's direction. Steve waved. He wasn't the boy's father, but maybe some masculine attention was good for the child.

Shek-jai didn't wave back, but Steve didn't expect her to. He headed to the east, smiling to himself and swinging his crutches forward. Wu-Li would come running any minute, which was perhaps one of Steve's more practical abilities to help valley farmers—keeping Wu-Li out of mischief!

Where the path forked—one led to the prison, and the other to the farmers' cottages—Steve paused to catch his breath. Behind him,

Wu-Li ran a zig-zag pattern after him. Steve laughed and knelt, then held out his arms to receive the child.

Wu-Li stopped suddenly, held up the tiny soldier, and rattled off some rapid Chinese that Steve didn't completely catch. But finally, the boy was speaking to him!

"I don't know what that means," Steve confessed in Cantonese, "but I think it's a start." He waved his hand at the cottages. "Let's go. Show me where you live. Come on."

Steve led the way north, ever aware of the looming prison wall fifty yards to his right. Nearly to the doorway of the first cottage, he was greeted by an awkward-stepping puppy that appeared crippled in the spine or hip. It sniffed at Steve as Wu-Li pet its black and white coat.

"Wong-wei," Wu-Li said. "Wong-wei."

The dog scampered off sideways and Steve continued to the cottages that were identical to his own: bleached brick and earth with thatched roofs. He was reminded of his prayer-walks when he'd first arrived in China, visiting remote villages, seeking God's heart and intent for the people of China. As he hobbled past these cottages, he was distinctly aware of a lingering thought: *God may have put him through all the turmoil simply to plant him in Hudie Valley because there was no other way to reach the farmers with the gospel of Jesus Christ.* But how could he get them to listen? They wouldn't even talk with him!

In front of one doorway, several elderly women sat on short stools. They were busy with what looked like a basket-weaving contest and paid little attention to Steve as he paused. No doubt they'd seen him from a distance, but Steve had never seen these four women out in the paddies. Apparently, the grandmothers were too old to work in the fields, so they tended to the homes and cooking.

Wu-Li pointed to his cottage. Steve poked his head inside the one-room abode. A hat and shirt hung on a wall hook. The counter with a faucet-less sink held a clutter of personal belongings: a wooden hair brush, a mirror, and chopsticks. They seemed no wealthier than Steve after he'd lived there a whole year.

He returned to the basket-weavers and sat down on the ground to watch them. First Wu-Li and then Wong-wei joined him, but to watch him, not the weavers. Suddenly, Steve's mouth gaped in wonder at the weavers. Crawling a little closer, he watched how they weaved the baskets. He gazed up at the ridge where prison personnel occasionally came and went from the valley. Sometimes they brought supplies or new prisoners. But nothing really left Hudie Valley. He'd never seen a prisoner ever released, either. But maybe there was a way . . .

A plan began to shape in his imagination. The basket-weavers were the key. He would escape Hudie Valley come spring—if Tond-zu didn't have him killed first!

Hudie Valley – One Year Ago

Little had changed in the past year in Lisa's surroundings—her world was still a crowded cell with the same seven women, including herself. She'd lost more weight, but she didn't feel unhealthy. The women around her were shorter and more petite, perhaps the outcome of malnutrition over years of captivity, but so far, Lisa wasn't starving.

Since the prison housed primarily political prisoners, her cellmates were mostly educated women. Fifty-year-old Ghuning from the southern coast near Hong Kong ran the cell. She decided who received which food portions, and which rags of clothing, when thrown to them. She spoke boldly to the guards for certain requests or reminders, like receiving their complete food rations, or their promised fresh air once a week.

Ghuning was also the headmaster of education, not only for Lisa, but for the others as well. She kept the women active and their minds positive. They had a few tattered sections of a Beijing newspaper they took turns reading, even memorizing. And it was Ghuning who'd begun to teach Lisa the Mandarin vocabulary that the guards spoke. Likewise, Lisa had found some purpose in teaching English to the others. The cell was their whole world.

In the silent nights when Lisa attempted to pray while the others snored softly next to her, she wept. For a year, she'd been discarded. There'd been no word from her mother or from COIL operatives. The reality of her past life seemed to be a fading memory—the happiness of her childhood in California, the afternoons spent at her mother's nursery, the joy of coming to Christ at a summer retreat, the excitement of meeting Steve at the COIL boot camp . . .

It all seemed like another life now. Or a life that had never really happened. In her cell, the women were healthy, but they lived under the threat of being found unhealthy, at which time they'd be moved to another cell for the diseased, the dying, the lepers. Health inspections occurred weekly during bathing, but their health wasn't the concern of the prison administration, it seemed. The containment of disease was their only response to illness. Two women had been removed from Lisa's cell in the year before her arrival. Everyone whispered fearfully, worried they would disappear next.

On some days, Lisa was optimistic. Her Mandarin was improving, and with it some hope to proposition the guards to be a trustee. But such an idea came with the dread of assault. The guards hadn't touched them, but if she became a trustee, she might become prone to attack, as she'd seen elsewhere in the prison. Though she desperately wanted more sunlight than only during the weekly bathing, she wasn't sure the little activity outside the cell was worth the risk. The best scenario would be to find a job working in the rice paddies up the valley, but she kept these ideas to herself. To survive, she had to think first of herself. She felt she wouldn't last for years in such a cell, not like the other women.

Sometimes, Lisa considered escaping. When led out to bathe, she and her cellmates were marched single file outside the gate to the pond, which was runoff from the rice paddies. Nearest the stream, the water was cleanest, but the whole place reeked of sewage. No one actually bathed, especially in front of the leering guards. But they were allowed to stand in formation for one hour, admiring the valley. During this time, Lisa had begun to study her surroundings, considering an escape.

The southern ridge up the trail was the biggest enticement. Where the truck had first dropped her off, she vaguely recalled the Huang River winding a few miles south of them. Perhaps being shot in the back while escaping would be better than dying of leprosy in a crowded, damp cell.

Such disparaging thoughts kept her Christian hope absent from her lips, and the year had passed without ever sharing her faith in Jesus with her fellow prisoners. Having turned inward, she saw no route to relief except by changing her circumstances. Depression was always under the surface. God didn't seem to be moving for her good, and even if COIL were looking into her abduction, she guessed their priority was Steve. Her hope faded with each passing day.

Shanghai – Present Day

Rashid al-Sabur zipped up his leather jacket against Shanghai's afternoon breeze. After two weeks in the city, his plan to crumble Commander Peng and Tond-zu's empire within the secret police was ahead of schedule. Their hunt for Christians was ruthless and rabid, but their greed was greater than their hatred. Turning Tond-zu against his boss had bought a short reprieve for underground believers, but the persecution would return if Rashid didn't tighten the noose completely. Removing Peng as commander wouldn't solve China's overall anti-Christian policy, but Rashid needed to focus on his immediate mission. Peng Zemin could lead him to Steve Brookshire, and yawning Tond-zu would be the one to make it happen.

In central Shanghai, Rashid walked along the storefronts on a street bustling with noisy traffic. The world's oldest trolley bus system serviced the world's largest city. Shanghai Metro rumbled through the underground subway, and an elevated expressway spewed racket that amplified the city's already deafening din. In all the organized chaos, Rashid would've missed the man who was following him if he hadn't used the reflection of a window to spy on his back trail. Amongst the rushing and commotion, a lone, stationary man stood out.

Entering a department store, Rashid calmly walked down an aisle of knock-off American designer clothes. Near the back wall, he shifted a display of action figures to hide behind them. Crouching, he waited, only his eyes exposed to a potential enemy.

A moment later, Tond-zu himself walked into sight. Rashid crouched lower. The greedy lieutenant was probably becoming suspicious of Rashid's plan, and the delay to take the Xinjiang property that Peng had supposedly confiscated from a Christian owner. Of course, there was no coal-producing property, but Rashid's plan only worked if Tond-zu believed there was. That Tond-zu was spying on him in person meant Rashid's plan was moving too slowly. Titus wanted Steve Brookshire located and rescued *now*, but without everything in place, the plan wouldn't work at all!

Rashid moved silently from behind the display. As Tond-zu's back was turned, Rashid drew a COIL tranq-pen and stabbed the man below his ribs. With his free hand, Rashid caught the lieutenant and dragged him through a back exit door into a smelly alley. An overweight rat scampered aside as Rashid lay Tond-zu on the damp pavement. With a glance, Rashid saw that both ends of the alley were blocked by metal barriers to deter through-traffic, so no one would likely be interrupting their conversation.

With twenty minutes until Tond-zu woke, Rashid searched the man's pockets and took pictures of his identification. There would be a time when Tond-zu's wickedness would lead to his downfall, but that time wasn't yet. Without regard to Tond-zu's expensive suit, Rashid dragged the Chinese man through a puddle and leaned him against a stained brick wall. Moments later, the lieutenant stirred and his eyes slowly focused on Rashid.

"What's going on?" Tond-zu examined his alley-soiled suit. "What have you done to me? Oh, I don't feel well. Did you drug me?" Tond-zu yawned and shook his head, but remained seated.

"Yeah, you may have fainted. But, you were following me and I don't like being followed." Rashid drew a decorative knife. The weapon, purchased at a flea market, was intended as an intimidation prop for such an occasion. The blade was polished and serrated on one side. "I'm a treasure hunter. I travel the world looking for treasure. You know that. And I remove anyone who gets between me and my treasure. Are you getting between me and my treasure, Tond-zu? Why are you following me?"

"You haven't returned my messages."

"I've been busy. You should be busy, too, setting up Commander Peng's fall as a Christian collaborator. With him in the way, we can't get to the property—the treasure."

"Everything's ready. False reports, doctored surveillance photos, even a couple witnesses who will testify that Peng gave away Bibles with anti-Party literature." Tond-zu climbed shakily to his feet and wiped his hands on his filthy pants. "The trap is ready, but now I find you coming out of the Communication Bureau. You're up to something that you're not telling me!"

Rashid cackled with laughter.

"You fool! I told you I'd set everything else up. We need the Communication Bureau to run the right press release the instant the news breaks about Peng. Public opinion will ruin him before you even arrest him as a collaborator. I've seen it happen in America. People don't have to be guilty to be convicted any longer."

"As long as that's all you were doing there . . ."

"Just tell me where you're going to hide Peng after he's sentenced. You'll be the acting commander. I don't want any problems."

"I told you, I have a place in the west." Tond-zu twisted and turned, trying to reach a hand to the back of his ribs where he surely felt a bruise. Rashid prayed that the man would simply tell him where he was sending Peng, then the whole mission could shift out of Shanghai entirely. "I don't trust you. How soon can we conclude this business?"

"You're holding all the keys, Tond-zu. Once Peng is removed, I'll hand you the confiscated property deed. I'm a foreigner. But you'll have authority to reap the benefits. The question is, can I trust you?"

Rashid pointed a bony finger at Tond-zu. After years of treasure hunting for himself, Rashid realized he was adept at counter-accusations and drawing attention away from the actual situation. To defeat the enemy, he would remain harmless as a dove, but sly as a serpent.

"You'll get your share!" Tond-zu sneered. "Just answer my question. How soon? I have investments, houses, planes, and women I need to see to. This transaction needs to happen now!"

"You've told no one?"

"No! I'm no fool!"

"Then, tomorrow the news will break. Peng will be arrested and isolated. His contacts will withdraw from him. Freeze his assets. Seize what you can. Get him through the courts as fast as possible, shipped off to whatever place you have for him."

"Maybe it would be easier to just kill him, like the others I've done something similar to."

"And risk a departmental investigation? No, you don't need that kind of attention. Dead bodies draw attention. Let Peng fade away as an accused Christian. No one will listen to him, and you and I will become wealthy men."

"And I'll be commander. Arresting him will be big news for me. It'll show my power. Any ethics committees will stay away from me after this. I'll be able to do anything I want. Just do your part."

"Tomorrow, it begins." Rashid looked away and prayed that Titus and Oleg were ready as well. All of his planning would be for naught if they didn't follow Peng to Tond-zu's hiding place for prisoners.

CHAPTER EIGHT

Hudie Valley – One Year Ago

Steve was a quick learner. A week after he'd watched the old women weave baskets, he was crafting containers well enough to hold water. They weren't the best baskets, and the women clucked their criticisms openly, but it gave his mind and fingers something to do other than adding to his Bible story book and working on rice paddy retaining walls. Besides, it was the most direct contact he'd had with the people all year. With his escape plan formulating, he didn't see why he couldn't share Christ with these women before he left, if only by his presence.

In the back of his mind, there was a ticking clock. He remembered what Tond-zu had last told him: if the Christian sub-net access were discovered, keeping him alive would fade as a priority for the Communist Party. At any time, guards from the prison could visit his cottage in the night and kill him. Or put him in the prison to die.

He gave his first three baskets to the women. They set his simple creations aside as if they were complete failures. But Steve wasn't discouraged. He made three more improved ones, with some jabbering critiques from Wu-Li, and gave them to Shek-jai. The woman seemed to be shunned by the others since she spoke such a different dialect.

A couple days later, the women nodded approvingly at Steve's work. Wu-Li took one basket Steve had made, donned it as a helmet, and marched around the cottage grounds with his soldier figurine in his fist, with Wong-wei nipping at his pant legs.

But Steve's new hobby with the women wore on Wu-Li's patience. The boy's Cantonese was indiscernible most of the time, but Steve understood the boy would rather be doing anything other than basket-weaving. With his plan on hold, Steve set aside his flattened reeds and followed Wu-Li and Wong-wei back up the central path of the valley.

Steve's pace was slow. Wu-Li ran ahead, then ran back to his side. Wong-wei ventured in curiosity away from the cottages for the first time.

Wu-Li led Steve west, beyond his own cottage on a small path that Steve had hobbled on many times, but always for upkeep or cultivation purposes. Women and older children were still in the fields, collecting the second harvest that autumn before the ground froze.

The three explorers reached the far end of the path where the wooded ridge rose steeply above them, giving Steve a true sense of captivity. But between the end of the path and the ridge lay the irrigation pool, the source of water for the paddies. The spring that fed it had flooded in decades past, bringing the containment walls close to eroding completely. A steady flow of water bubbled now, running down the valley to the prison refuse pond.

The boy climbed over rotting boards, rusting iron, and rocks in the dam wall to splash with Wong-wei at the edge of the pool. Steve picked up a pebble and tossed it in. Most of the pool was about two feet deep, but in the center, from where the spring rippled, the depth was measureless, seeming to flow from the heart of the earth. With a little rebuilding of the walls, Steve guessed he could raise the water level to increase the flow and water pressure. The higher paddies that didn't get much water could receive more, if he engineered a trough to the north. More water meant more food. Finally, he could possibly contribute something meaningful to the farmers' work!

Though Steve now had his mind set on leaving the valley in a matter of weeks, he'd spent a year relying on the kindness of his fellow farmers. To please them by improving their irrigation system was a small gesture he intended to make, even if the farmers continued to avoid him.

It was midday when Steve disrobed and hopped on one leg into the water. His objective was first to clear the pool of debris that he could use to rebuild with later. Old chunks of iron and pieces of wood were tossed aside, some for potential use in his basket-weaving project. Rebuilding the wall with a canal to the north would take several days for a man with two legs. But for a man with only one leg, even as capable as Steve was, the job would take a couple weeks. Between basket-weaving and writing his Bible story book, he was happy for the water project.

Several days passed. His reed weaving was improving with determined mastery, and the farmers in the fields had shown interest in the development of the irrigation pool. But they only watched from a distance. As the banks were strengthened and heightened, the water level rose. And as the water rose, Wu-Li grew increasingly more wary.

Standing in the water, Steve waved for Wu-Li to join him. Wu-Li would have no part of it. He knew if he fell in now, the water would be well over his head. Steve continued his work, and gave up trying to convince the child that he wouldn't let him drown.

The day Steve finished the wall, the water rose high enough for someone to swim across the small pool, about the span of a volleyball court. Since the afternoon sun was fading, Steve determined to test the new swimming hole the following day—and try to swim with only one leg. Escaping the valley might require the knowledge to swim, so this was his opportunity to learn.

The next day, however, swimming was put aside as he sat down with the women and began to construct another basket, this one shaped to fit like a sleeve over his leg stump.

A couple hours later, with schoolboy-like glee, he set down his work and hurried with his crutches back to the irrigation pool. For a few minutes, he picked through the pile of debris he hadn't used to rebuild the dam wall, and soon found a twisted piece of flat iron. He guessed it was an old piece of farm machinery, or maybe from an ancient war vehicle. It was two feet in length and twisted like a mild S. Weighing around ten pounds, the construct and shape was the durable design Steve had in mind for a prosthetic. Until recently, he'd lacked a method to attach an artificial limb to his leg just below his knee.

When he returned to the weaving party, several women set their own work aside to move closer. With interest, they watched as he measured his stump with reeds and constructed a sleeve with which to mount the iron. After two hours, he fit the basket-cup snuggly over his stump all the way to his knee. It was tight enough that he had to wrestle with it to tug it off, then pull it on again.

Finally, he weaved a second cup, this time attaching it to the iron, then intertwined it with the first cup. The first basket was attached to his stump, and the second one brought the iron and first cup together.

His fingers trembled with excitement as he finished the second cup a little after noon. He held it up for the women to inspect. They nodded, one even clapped, her face a toothless grin.

It was the moment of truth, and Steve glanced toward the prison walls. Was someone watching him from one of the towers? For days, he'd been weaving baskets. Now, he'd made a device that changed the dynamics of his captivity in the valley. Would they come for him now that he was mobile enough to walk away on his own two limbs?

Steve twisted and struggled to fit his stump into the cup. It was tight and uncomfortable. He guessed he'd eventually need a piece of cloth to separate his skin from the reeds to avoid chaffing. Using a crutch and one of the elderly women's shoulders, he stood with uncertainty. Gradually, he applied pressure to the artificial limb. The iron seemed the right length. With a little flourish, Steve cast his crutch aside as if God Himself had regrown the missing limb. His crutch hit the ground and he raised his arms. The women all clapped and nodded this time.

Grinning at the attention and triumph, he took his first step—and fell flat on his face. The women were breathless with laughter. Steve spit earth from his teeth and winked at Wu-Li who crouched low to inspect the damage. But Steve's hopes weren't dashed. Walking on the iron leg would require new balancing skills, new coordination.

Again, he stood, this time without the aid of crutch or woman. He tested the leg, feeling adjustments he could make inside the cups, but it held sure. With arms raised to the sky, tears streamed down his cheeks. God had given him this moment, and he honored Him with hands raised toward heaven.

Steve Brookshire had two legs once again.

Shanghai – Present Day

Commander Peng Zemin was shoved into the back of a police van. The cheek of his fat face lay on the cold floor of the vehicle he'd used himself to arrest Christians over the years. Now, his expensive suit was spattered with the spittle of Tond-zu, his own lieutenant, as the yawning man had shouted his charges loud enough for the state media cameras. *This was impossible!* He had raised Tond-zu, given him a career of luxury, included him in all his sinister schemes to retain power in the government. *Not Tond-zu!*

Peng rolled over to sit against the van wall as photos were taken of him through the back windows. Those he'd trampled so he could remain on top in Shanghai were certainly enjoying themselves now. The sting of his collaboration charges were made that much more painful by Tond-zu's remarks of him being a Christian. *He hated Christians!* But Tond-zu had planned carefully, perhaps for weeks, to fabricate evidence against him. Peng had used similar tactics against others, suspected Christians or not, to destroy them with anti-Party suspicions. The number and magnitude of his own devilish tricks were the only things that hindered his clenched teeth from crying foul, or unfair! No, this was justice, and now as his sobs shook his jowls, he knew he deserved every lash. Tond-zu would feel justice one day himself, but for now, Peng was the recipient of well-planned deceit and treachery.

He fell against the back door as the van lunged forward. His brow began to bleed, ruining his suit even more. But his thoughts weren't on his wealth, which had undoubtedly been seized already. The sordid pleasures of the recent past were suddenly gone forever, but even these he didn't waste tears over. Rather, Peng gasped at the idea of being treated as a Christian collaborator. If he were indeed a secret convert and Bible smuggler, someone of his prestige and standing would receive no mercy from a judge. He would be shamed, mistreated, and ridiculed through the entire legal process, which could last days or years, depending on Tond-zu's intentions. Or he could be strangled in a jail cell, a further shame in death, and described later as a suicide. Again, Peng had used such tactics against suspects when he had little evidence to convict them in the courts.

To be arrested in China for religious conspiracy was trouble enough for a common civilian. But Peng was from the communist elite, and Tond-zu was no standard police officer. The yawner was greedy and resourceful, able to convince media and peers alike. The few friends Peng did have would shrink into the shadows lest they be suspected by Tond-zu. The jackal might even keep him alive, Peng considered, hidden away in his private prison in the west, cut off from human rights groups, thrust forever into the weak company of Christians and other despised prisoners he'd made disappear over the years.

Peng wondered what it was like to go hungry, to starve to death, for his flesh to shrink against his bones as his stomach rumbled for a bowl of rice. He'd never gone hungry before. The privileges of his secret caste had guarded him from ever missing a meal, from ever sleeping on anything but a soft mattress with silk sheets.

He knew that would all change now. And he hated his adopted son, Tond-zu, for it all!

Shanghai – Present Day

Titus checked his sat-watch for an overview image from COIL's Gabriel drones. One thermal imaging hotspot approached his position on the coastline docks. This was Shanghai Port, the busiest container port in the world. Before the figure reached his location, Titus peeked around the body of a loading crane.

"This isn't why we're in China, Titus." Oleg passed his partner an NL-X2 rifle and two extra magazines for the bullpup. "We're supposed to be downtown watching for Peng Zemin's transfer. Any minute, Tond-zu could send him to the same place he sent Steve Brookshire."

"It ain't easy smuggling wanted Christians out of China." Titus grinned and jutted his chin at the shadows. "You telling me you'd miss a firefight to protect a bunch of refugees?"

Oleg stepped closer and Titus saw his Russian friend's resolve soften at the sight of fourteen men, women, and children, their bundled belongings at their feet.

"We have one shot at finding Steve. Why'd you drag me off Peng's surveillance?" Oleg sighed. "What's their story?"

"These are second and third generation offenders for being Christians—running house churches, printing and distributing Bibles, circumventing the government's regulated churches. They want to leave China."

"Let me guess—you've been putting this together since we arrived." Oleg shook his head and rested his bullpup over his shoulder. "Does Corban know about this? Worse yet, does Wes Trimble know? He's got a lot riding on this hunt for Steve and Lisa, too, you know. Rashid's out there as well, putting in work for us."

"Hey, this was already in action before I promised Wes that I'd stay on mission. Look at these people. They couldn't finance their own escape to South Korea. These are families. I'm not going to let them all go to re-education camps. That's not happening."

"So, ship them out. Let me get back downtown."

"It's not that simple, Oleg. When I was putting this together, I didn't know there was a rat in their midst until some of them started to get arrested. I lost five of them earlier today, and then I sniffed out the rat." Titus cleared his throat uncomfortably. "These fourteen believers made it here, but now the rat knows about this rendezvous point. And I can't get them on board a ship until the weekend."

"Are you crazy?" Oleg walked to the water's edge and studied the lights across the harbor. "You're telling me there could be secret police out there right now, waiting for us to move these people? Maybe even Tond-zu himself?"

"The rat didn't know which ship I bought them passage on, just that this was our staging point. We should be fine."

"So, we're like China's dumbest smugglers, maybe on video right now?" Oleg waved at the dark reaches of the shoreline. "Hello, I'm the one you're about to arrest. I swear, Titus, could you put us in a worse position in the middle of an operation?"

"Look, I cancelled their transport tonight. I just need your coverage as we get them safely away. Can you do that?"

"I'm here, aren't I?" Oleg tightened his bullpup sling. "Where are we taking them?"

"I don't want to endanger other believers in the city. Fourteen is a lot to take in."

"Titus, no."

"The safe house is the best place. We'll call in COIL help if we can't get them smuggled out in a week or two."

"That's sixteen living in our two bedroom apartment." Oleg looked to the dark sky as if for help on high. "All right. With my Volvo Wagon and Crossover, can we do this in one trip?"

"If we go caravan, bungee-cord-style, and you don't mind three or four people sitting on your lap as you drive."

"Is that all?" Oleg walked into the quiet shipping yard. "Give me five minutes to find a cover angle, then get them loaded up."

Titus smiled as he watched his friend disappear down a container alley.

"It ain't easy teaching him to tolerate me, Lord," he whispered. Without the friendship he had with Oleg, he would've found being away from Annette much more difficult. The mission had already run longer than expected. He purposed to call Annette in the morning, to pray together at least, since he couldn't yet give her a date when he could return.

Nearby, the refugees waited in silence. Titus knew they'd come from the west, some following the Grand Canal as stowaways, fleeing persecution that had reached intolerable levels. Foreigners who were Christians were merely denied entry when they were found to be contrary to China's religious laws. But citizens of China were treated without remorse, pressured to recant their faith, or imprisoned to hard labor until they reformed, if they perchance survived their sentences. Many chose to flee instead of face death or the camps, especially with whole families relying on them.

Titus waved the refugees toward him, and they came with hushed movements. They surely sensed the danger in the night as they crowded close together. They had no one else. With his bullpup leveled, Titus regretted not being fully equipped for properly defending the refugees. Under similar circumstances, he and Oleg preferred to maintain radio contact with full support and over-watch by Gabriel tech Marc Densort secured in a mine shaft in upstate New York. But Titus' spontaneous missions didn't allow anyone preparation, not even himself.

A proximity alarm rang on Titus' watch—they had company.

Halting the refugees, Titus peered around a dry-docked ship. Their two vehicles were in sight eighty yards away. Since China now owned the Volvo Company, renting two four-doors—a Wagon and a Cross-over—had seemed the two perfect vehicles to blend into Shanghai's middle class. But at that time of night, both cars were suddenly the objects of eight of Shanghai's finest secret police. In the headlights and flashing lights of three response vehicles, the eight suited agents used flashlights to inspect the rental cars. From the shadows of the ship, Titus sighted on the closest agents, hoping Oleg was somewhere near, doing the same.

The night erupted in gunfire when Titus fired first. The distance was only eighty yards. He dropped two agents before the others scattered for cover. But then Oleg's rifle boomed from some unseen height, and the agents were squeezed into a crossfire without cover, outgunned by COIL weaponry. Titus withdrew behind the ship, joining the refugees on their knees. Using his watch, he observed four of the eight agents flee from their vehicles and run toward the warehouse district. The other four lay still, presumably tranquilized.

The gunfire ceased. A hotspot on his watch told Titus that Oleg was on the other side of the vehicles, above the scene, commanding the battlefield.

"*Qing! Qing! Please!*" Titus pleaded to the refugees, hoping his simple Mandarin was enough to hustle them forward.

They reached the vehicles in a hurried tumult. Titus gestured to the rentals, but the refugees piled into two of the police cruisers as well. Two of the men jumped into the driver's seats and waited for instructions.

Oleg slid down a cable and jogged to his rental car. With a nod at Titus, he climbed into the driver's seat, the other seats filled with refugees, and drove away. The two police cruisers pulled out behind Oleg, and Titus hung back a moment. Four officers were down, lying on the ground, their sidearms drawn. It hadn't been his intention to pick a fight with the local authorities. Now, the secret police would be on a rampage. No known Christian would be safe in Shanghai.

Titus drove away, praying his botched smuggling attempt didn't blow up in his face.

⚓

Hudie Valley – One Year Ago

Lisa stood on the road outside the prison gate as a senior guard read from a communist manifesto. The women beside her stood at attention, half-heartedly receiving the indoctrinating words that constituted their re-education. Since Lisa was taller than the others, she could see over her fellow female prisoners to admire the valley. It was her favorite time of the week.

To her right, the rice paddies stretched for a quarter-mile. Farther back to the north were a number of houses belonging to the farmers. At the far end of the valley, at its highest point against the perimeter ridge, a tall man hobbled with such a horrible limp that Lisa could see it from that distance. Maybe he was the man from the year before who'd used crutches to move around. Beside him, a child dashed back and forth, chasing a small dog. The crippled man settled Lisa's heart. Perhaps he'd once been a prisoner, but now he was lame, forced to work in the fields with the women and children. Without them, the prisoners wouldn't be fed. Secretly, Lisa thanked the awkward-walking man and wondered if he wasn't a past inmate of the prison at all, but a relative of a current prisoner, maybe of one of the women in the cell with her. No one had said anything, and it didn't seem to be a subject of conversation. Occasionally, someone was pulled out of the cell for an interrogation. Lisa hadn't told her own story, either, so that no one else could be questioned about her. She guessed others had their own secrets to keep as well.

But her contemplations of the valley were disrupted by a sharp jab from a bamboo baton—the preferred weapon of the guards. She joined the procession of the women down to the refuse pond. Time to bathe.

As she walked down the path a few yards with Ghuning and the others to the stagnate water, barely freshened from the paddy irrigation stream, her eyes strayed to the ridge above. Even if she could get over the ridge, she knew little of that region of China. Besides, if she did escape, she'd be a white woman in an Oriental land. The ocean was hundreds of miles to the east, Mongolia and Siberia to the north. The Huang River was somewhere to the south, and to the west, deserts and mountains.

That day, no one bathed. No one ever bathed. Some had in the past, and the diseases they died from were warnings to those still alive. Now, they stood at the water's edge, thankful for a view that wasn't a cell wall, until the guards marched them back inside.

As Lisa's Mandarin improved, she hoped to learn more from Ghuning. She couldn't fantasize about escape—by foot over land, or on boat down the river—until she knew more. What surrounded the valley? What would they do to her if she escaped and were caught?

She wished Steve were there. He'd always known how to approach challenges, to triumph over adversity. As a triathlete, his mental discipline to endure was one of the things she'd loved about him. It had become a phenomenal tool in his missionary work, trekking on foot across China to reach remote villages where even the police didn't go. Without him, Lisa didn't know how to persevere on her own. Deep down, she felt her resolve slipping. She was close to giving up. How much longer could she live like this?

Shanghai – Present Day

Pounding on the safe house apartment door made Titus sit upright from his sleeping place on the floor and reach for his bullpup. It was noon. He wasn't expecting visitors. The fourteen refugees occupying the apartment froze at the noise. Titus pointed at the nearest bedroom door. They calmly and silently gathered their bedrolls, food bowls, and clothes, and in seconds had disappeared into the back room.

The pounding shook the door frame again.

"I'm coming!" Titus called and hid his rifle in the sofa cushions. He drew a tranq-pen from his pocket and opened the door. "Rashid? I thought you were the police!"

Rashid al-Sabur shoved his way into the apartment and stopped. Titus checked the hallway, then closed the door. He stowed the tranq-pen and gestured to a dining chair.

"You want some lunch?" He noticed several food containers on the counter and a cupboard door was ajar. "Wasn't expecting you."

The man observed the apartment for a moment longer, not responding.

"Where's Oleg?" Rashid finally asked.

"He's watching the police station." Titus sat on the arm of the couch. "I'll spell him in a couple hours. As soon as they transfer Peng Zemin, we'll follow him wherever Tond-zu sends him. Lord willing, he'll lead us right to Steve, and we can bring him home. That scheme of yours—I'm sure glad you're on our side now."

"But are you on *my* side?" Rashid took a step closer to Titus.

"It ain't easy following your thoughts, Rashid." Titus stood and took a step back, not comfortable looking up at the taller man, especially with ice daggers in his eyes. "What's the matter?"

"I've spent days and considerable risk to set up Peng so Tond-zu would arrest him. Tond-zu has moved up as acting commander, one of the most powerful men in Shanghai, if not all of China. And you've thrown all of our work away. Now, we may never find Steve!"

"What are you talking about?"

"It's in the news. Men with non-lethal weaponry attacked a squad of secret police about to make a number of criminal arrests. Where were you and Oleg last night?"

"Rashid, relax." Titus smiled. "It was something I put together to get some Chinese Christians to South Korea. It fell through, but we handled it. I brought the refugees here."

"Oleg was with you?"

"Yeah, just for two hours. What's the problem?"

"Recall Oleg." Rashid walked into the kitchen and took a glass of water from the sink. Only then did Titus realize the treasure hunter appeared disheveled, as if he'd been living on the street for days. "We're done in China. Your lack of professionalism has cost us more than we can calculate right now. Tond-zu couldn't be more dangerous. My bluff was fruitless. We have to leave right away."

"What are you talking about?" Titus chuckled, his nervousness mounting. "Stick to the plan. We're not in any real danger."

"Now you want to stick to the plan?" Rashid's face was filled with fury. "Why didn't you think of that before you went on another mission last night? When Peng was being transferred out of Shanghai in the middle of the night!"

Titus blinked.

"Oh. He's gone?"

"Tond-zu made him disappear. He shipped Peng off, and now he's texting me for a meeting. You and Oleg were supposed to be alert, ready to follow him."

"We didn't know he'd left." Titus' shoulders slumped. Since it was safe, he walked over to the bedroom and opened the door. "I'm the one who pulled Oleg off the station. It's my fault. I blew it."

They watched the refugees emerge from the bedroom and resume their activities, though they cast furtive glances toward the scowling Rashid. Several women fixed food in the kitchen. Three men huddled around Titus' laptop, set up with a Bible program in Chinese. Four children played a card game on the carpet.

"Would Steve approve?" Rashid nodded at the people. "Would he give his life for all these people?"

"I guess that's the decision I made for him." Titus ran his fingers through his hair. "It wasn't intentional, but these people were in trouble and I reacted. If the trail to Steve is really gone, then it's my fault."

"I can abduct Tond-zu and try to make him talk." Rashid licked his lips. "Maybe we can find out where he sent Steve two years ago."

"Even if that were our style still, a guy like Tond-zu wouldn't talk."

"You and Oleg need to get out of China." Rashid moved to the door. "There were traffic cameras between here and the docks. The police are looking for footage to see who ambushed them. Leave China before your photos are on the news. I'll cover your tracks. Maybe I'll cause Tond-zu a little frustration as we pull out. We gave the worst possible person the whip and reins of the secret police. I need to monitor the situation. Maybe we can come back later."

"I'm sorry, Rashid." Titus held out his hand. "I didn't consider the consequences."

"Tell that to the thousands of lives relying on Steve's sub-net. If he talks now, their blood is on your hands, Serval."

Rashid left the apartment without shaking Titus' hand. Titus dropped his hand to his side. He would have to explain himself to Corban Dowler and Wes Trimble, two men he admired more than any others.

But it was Rashid's words that hurt the most right now. Titus felt as if he'd lost a brother. Then his thoughts drifted back to his cancer. His time on earth was limited. He'd botched this mission entirely, and now, what might have been his last mission for COIL, was a complete failure. This would be his legacy, he feared—letting down his friends and mentors. Not wanting to alert the refugees, Titus walked calmly into the bathroom, closed the door, and wept.

CHAPTER NINE

Hudie Valley – One Year Ago

Steve walked out of his cottage with a sense of newness about life. Something in the valley was about to change for him. It already had changed! He was walking without crutches and the farmers were interacting with him like never before. His prayers to be an effective resident in the valley were being answered!

The children of the valley seemed just as pleased as he was that the irrigation pool had been turned into a swimming hole, which was where Steve marched that morning with Wu-Li and Wong-wei. He counted sixteen children splashing about—seventeen, counting Wu-Li, who rarely drew closer to the water than getting his toes wet. Steve sat next to the now five-year-old as the child looked on with envy at the braver children. Later, their mothers, who were working nearby, would surely demand double labor for this ruckus of free time.

Easing himself into the shallow side of the pool, Steve patted his shoulders and back, motioning to Wu-Li.

"Come on, Wu-Li, climb on."

Hesitantly, Wu-Li climbed onto Steve's back, then Steve waded into deeper water, feeling for stability with his one foot and one prosthetic limb. Wu-Li clung to Steve's neck like a rat to its mother. Wong-wei wasn't about to be abandoned on shore as everyone else was playing. The little dog leaped in and paddled circles around Steve and Wu-Li. The other children laughed and splashed Steve as he reciprocated, then someone started a game of tag that left Wu-Li shouting orders to Steve that he didn't understand.

Two of the children, a boy and a girl, were new to the valley, though the other children seemed to avoid them. Both were about ten years old. Steve assumed the prison had added a recent prisoner—their father or mother—and they were subsequently subjected to the valley of labor as well. But today, they were children, not slaves. And they joined in the game.

After half an hour, Wu-Li tugged on Steve's hair to direct him to the shore so he could dismount his sea monster. Steve relaxed on the bank beside Wong-wei and cheered a younger child in the pool as he tried to tag the others. Since not all the children knew how to swim, there were plenty of tag-targets in the wading depths along the shoreline. Every child should know how to swim, Steve considered. That was another thing he could offer the families of the valley before he left.

Suddenly, as Steve was measuring each child's swimming ability, his mouth gaped. A child floated face-down in the middle of the pool, where the underground spring deemed that area the deepest spot!

Steve pushed himself up to stand on his iron leg.

"Hey!" he shouted in the most general Mandarin. "Help him! Get the boy!"

The other children pointed at a limp reed floating on the surface, and someone yelled "snake!" They screamed and evacuated the pool within seconds. Steve looked down at his leg. Iron leg or not, he was the only one who could save the boy. He dove in.

He stroked powerfully forward with triathlon speed as his arms remembered their practiced motion. His legs, however, were another story. His good leg kicked vigorously while his prosthetic leg was clumsy and heavy at the end of his stump. But he didn't have time to take the iron off.

When he reached the boy, he tried to tread water, but only sank below the surface, the heavy iron like a deadweight. His lungs screamed for air. Using only his arms, he surged back to the surface and gulped air.

The children on the shore had realized the true emergency, and their screams filled Steve's ears. He rolled the boy onto his back on the water, then cradled his head as he paddled toward the shore. Already, he was discovering how to compensate for his right leg's clumsiness.

He reached the bank and dragged the boy onto the muddy land. He was one of the two new children to the valley. Steve started mouth-to-mouth as the children huddled about, some weeping, and a few running down the valley to their mothers. With a prayer between breaths, Steve called upon the God of Elijah who alone could restore life into a child's still body. The dread of a child dying on his watch was unthinkable!

The boy convulsed, vomited, and gasped. Steve held the child and wept with him as the boy clung to Steve. The other children patted Steve on his shoulders, consoling and praising him. He acknowledged their contact after so many months of avoidance, and sent his gratitude to God for sparing the child's life. His relief was immeasurable.

Looking up at the sound of a man's sharp voice giving orders in Mandarin, Steve stood with the boy still clinging to him. The man was dressed in a People's Republic of China military uniform, and beside him were two PRC guards with bamboo batons—guards from the prison! They were being led to the scene by the new girl to the valley.

The man in uniform yanked the boy from Steve's arms, and struck Steve on the side of the head. The child's wailings were transferred toward the man, who Steve now guessed was his father. Using their batons, the two guards forced Steve backwards. Abruptly, one of the guards drew his sidearm while the other clubbed the back of Steve's legs, driving him to his knees. The muzzle of the gun was pressed to his temple.

Steve surrendered resolutely to death an instant away. With his hands at his sides, he closed his eyes and turned his face heavenward. This was acceptable. It would be quick. He was ready.

Small arms encircled Steve's neck. He opened his eyes to see it was Wu-Li. Wong-wei cowered below the legs of the guards, but not so far away that the little dog had abandoned his boy-master altogether. Wu-Li jabbered Cantonese at the guards, and by their faces, Steve wondered if they understood the boy's dialect any better than he did.

When Wu-Li had finished speaking, the uniformed official analyzed Steve more curiously, but the pistol remained pressed against his head.

"You!" The man pointed at an older child from the valley. The child, one of the swimmers from the group, stepped forward rigidly. "What happened here?"

"We were swimming, playing a game. Your son was drowning. He looked dead. The *Bao'r* brought him back to life."

"The *Bao'r?*" The official set his son on his own feet. "What do you mean by that?"

"Him. The American with one leg. We call him *Bao'r* since he wears a handbasket on his one leg."

The official waved his hand and the boy melted into the throng of children who kept their heads bowed.

"Put the gun away." The father ordered and stepped close to Steve as his guards moved aside. "Everyone leave us, now!"

In an instant, his son, the guards, and the children marched away. Even Wu-Li, in all his boldness, withdrew with the other children a short distance. Steve remained on his knees at the water's edge.

"You Americans are vermin."

The hatred in the man's voice was palpable. He appeared to be in his mid-forties, and Steve noticed one of his eyelids sagged a little.

"Yes, I'm vermin."

"But you rescued my son? My only son."

Steve looked down the valley. The two guards were escorting the man's two children back to the prison. While most of China had been under the one-child policy, the Communist Party official had apparently received permission to raise two children, even before the policy had been changed.

"It's an honor to be used in some way. I'm not a very good farmer."

"My son and his sister aren't to play with these peasants. My children aren't vermin like you and these others."

Steve felt as if the man were testing him. He could take the insults, but now he sensed more than hatred in the official's voice.

"I could teach your son to swim so his life is never saved by vermin again."

"You'd teach him to swim here?" He eyed the pool. "It's filthy."

"But it's fun for the children . . . and vermin."

The corner of the man's mouth twitched upward slightly.

"I'm Fongdu Jen, warden of Hudie Prison."

"I'm Steve Brookshire." Steve offered his hand up to the man. "But my friends call me Vermin."

"It would seem your friends actually call you *Bao'r, the Hand-basket*." The warden accepted Steve's hand, but instead of shaking it, he helped Steve to stand upright. "Since you saved my son's life, I may not get away with calling you Vermin any longer."

Standing tall, Steve realized he was more comfortable looking up at the shorter man. Now, he awkwardly looked down at the official.

"The man named Tond-zu, a party official friend, has sent me prisoners for years. He pays me well, so I take them. I never dreamt one of you would save my son's life."

"It was my honor, Warden." Steve bowed his head.

"Your Mandarin is excellent. I know a little English. My father was an engineer in Canada. You know Edmonton?"

"Yes, I've heard of it."

"I know everything about Edmonton—malls, radio stations, parks, everything."

"I'd like to hear about Edmonton sometime."

"You like your house?" Fongdu Jen pointed with his thumb at the cottage. "I built it many years ago."

"It's very nice. Thank you."

Fongdu nodded, then looked around as if he didn't know what else to say. Finally, he gestured to Steve's leg.

"This was smart. A woven basket."

"I'm learning to walk like a child again."

"How did you lose it?"

"Tond-zu's friends."

"Hmm." He frowned. "I'm returning to the prison now."

"It was a pleasure meeting you, Mr. Fongdu. I would be honored to serve you further, if you require it."

"Maybe you could teach the children to swim?"

"As you wish."

"Good."

And Warden Fongdu Jen walked away, leaving Steve standing by the pool. As soon as Fongdu was a distance away, Wu-Li led the charge of children and dog back to Steve's side. After a moment of praise for Steve, they all entered the muddy water again, playing as if nothing had happened, as if Steve's life hadn't just been drastically altered.

But Steve knew—nothing in the valley would be the same now. He'd saved the warden's son.

New York City – Present Day

Oleg gently set Titus' sat-watch on the meeting room table in COIL headquarters. Outside the two-suite offices, beyond the double-plated, soundproof, and bulletproof windows that faced Times Square, the material world seemed to hustle about its pursuit of finding the good life. But inside the conference room, there were solemn faces, subdued voices, and uncertain glances.

"Titus gave it to me before we were supposed to board the plane out of Shanghai." Oleg pushed the bulky watch into the middle of the table, as if it carried a contagion. The other three people in the room didn't reach for it, though it carried the top secret might of COIL's authority and capabilities on earth. "Then, he just walked away."

Oleg looked at Corban. The paraplegic man was now in his early sixties, but his eyes were as vibrant as a young man's, and when he spoke, his words were as wise as those of an older man. Chloe Azmaveth, one of Mossad's prized agents of the past, and now Corban's right hand, cracked her knuckles against the edge of the table. Wes Trimble sat at the opposite end. He was the CIA's one-eyed wonder-agent with a secret past with the president that wasn't so secret anymore. His connections had earned him a seat at the table that night. Besides the fact that China fell inside his Pacific Rim Security territory.

"If Titus Caspertein doesn't want to be found," Corban said, "then we won't find him. He has more tricks and a better imagination than I did in my prime."

"Well, if Titus has gone rogue," Wes said, clucking his tongue, "maybe the president should know."

"He hasn't gone rogue," Oleg stated, daring anyone to argue with him. "He thought he was doing a good thing for the Chinese refugees. We both did. Losing track of Commander Peng Zemin wasn't intentional."

"But that was Rashid al-Sabur's only lead to Steve Brookshire." Chloe traced her finger on her digital tablet. "Speaking of which, Rashid hasn't reported in, either."

"Rashid's an animal." Wes shook his head. "Titus is one thing, but the Saber on the loose is a complete—"

"Rashid's a believer now, Wes," Corban said, "and so is Titus. We need to slow down with our speculations. We can cause panic in others if we draw the wrong conclusions. All we know is that Titus was distraught about messing up the hunt for Steve Brookshire. It's a little unsettling that he turned in his watch and disappeared, but we can give the guy a little space if he needs it. Chloe, if his wife calls, don't lie. Tell her we haven't heard a report from him regarding his return. Wes, say nothing to the president, yet. There're too many government agents out there with trigger fingers who'd love to go up against Titus or Rashid if they thought our guys had gone rogue. I believe both men can handle themselves against a superior force, but don't stir the pot."

"I'll keep it quiet." Wes nodded once. "You want PRS resources in China? It's steaming hot with Tond-zu in charge of Shanghai now, but I'll continue looking for Steve, Rashid, and Titus."

"Follow your gut on leads, Wes." Corban sighed. "Go where God guides you. We just want our people safe and supported. Oleg, what are your thoughts on this? You know Titus best."

"He's never done anything like this before. He's probably feeling inadequate after blowing the op. We've been moving pretty hard and fast for a year—with the exception to my Iranian vacation. I'm not sure, but I've suspected a health issue slowing him down. Maybe an old injury. But right now, he's probably just doing some soul-searching."

"I believe a Christian goes through numerous times of breaking." Corban leaned forward on the table, peering into each of their faces. "Our outer man must be broken in new and fresh ways, refining us to be purer vessels for God's work. Since we know that's what God does, we can pray confidently that Titus submits and trusts God's hand in his life right now. We may never find Steve Brookshire. That was always a sad possibility. And that's Titus' burden. We don't need to add to it. Just praise God that Titus will be learning this lesson to be an even more effective operative in the future. Maybe a little less self-confident and a lot more Holy Spirit-dependent. Sometimes, the most devoted of God's people undergo the most difficult breaking. We can all learn something from this."

The room was silent for a few moments. Oleg received Corban's words, and prayed in his heart that he would hear God's plain voice for direction, lest he be dragged through too many painful lessons himself.

"What do you want me to do, Corban?" Oleg asked.

"Wes, Chloe?" Corban smiled at them. "Oleg and I need a moment alone." They both collected their things and left the room. As soon as the door clicked shut, Corban faced Oleg. "I'll let you know as soon as Titus resurfaces. In the meantime, I'm teaming you with Luigi Putelli. Though you may never see him, he'll shadow you overseas. It seems your Iranian friends are on the move."

"The *Soldiers of Mahdi?*" Oleg tried to suppress a shiver. His captivity and torture were fresh on his mind, and his scars were still sensitive. "I might be a little too close to that group to go up against them."

"We need someone who was close. Before Titus extracted you from the SOM compound, he made the bodyguard of their head *imam* swallow a gastro-tracker. No doubt you remember Ercan Sanli. We thought it'd be a good way to track the *imam's* movements. Who doesn't want to keep tabs on an apocalyptic terrorist group, right?"

"So, what are they up to?"

"Ercan Sanli wants a meeting."

"No way. It's a trap. Titus destroyed that compound as we exited. Of course they want to meet—to kill us!"

"Maybe. It's even probable that's what's going on. But we're Christians. We pray for spiritual impact when you guys go into these dark haunts. And we make ourselves vulnerable to create opportunities for the lost to hear the message of hope in Christ."

"Titus did share the gospel with the *imam* and his bodyguard." Oleg shook his head. "He told me that later. He went back to *Imam* Serik al-Hakim's office to talk to them all. He spoke the Word to them, then detonated his mines along the wall as a heavenly exclamation point."

"Well, talk to the bodyguard. If it's a heavenly call, bring him in. If it's a trap, get out alive. Luigi will watch your back."

"I'm up against *Soldiers of Mahdi*, and all you're giving me is Luigi?"

"He's the best, and he's invisible—until you need him most." Corban chuckled. "I know this from experience. But no, that's not all. Take the watch. You'll have Gabriel coverage until Titus returns, which I'm confident he will."

"Well, he can wrestle this thing off my wrist when he does." Oleg grinned as he strapped the band to his arm. "He shouldn't leave his toys laying around if he wants them back!"

Japan – Present Day

Song Sakana rose from his knees at the persistent knocking on the front door. After three hours in prayer, his stiff back and joints creaked as he approached the door. When he opened it, he smiled up at Titus Caspertein.

"You don't look surprised to see me," the big American said, a bag in his hand that told Song he'd have a house guest for a spell.

"And you don't look as though the search for Steve Brookshire has gone well." He stepped aside to allow the Christian agent to enter.

"I've been talking to God. He helps me anticipate what would normally be unexpected—like you."

Titus kicked off his boots and Song tried not to frown at the same worn socks Titus had worn three weeks earlier when he and the big Russian had first visited. Though Akita, Japan, had its formalities in ancient traditions, Song welcomed the familiarity of an informal brotherhood.

"Sorry about that." Titus wiggled his exposed toe. "Not very samurai of me."

"The samurai have been gone a long time from Akita. Now we have men who wear sagging pants, pink hair, and shirts with vulgar writing on them. An exposed toe is probably the least of my worries if you've shown up alone with an overnight bag."

"Am I being too presumptuous?" Titus appeared as if he were about to weep, or had been weeping already. "I need a quiet place to just—"

"You came to the right place." Song gestured for them to move into the house. "As long as you don't mind Kaori's calls for help now and then. My mother-in-law has her spells. She doesn't move around as well as she used to."

"I'll help however I can." Titus dropped his bag on the living room floor and plopped into one of three low-to-the-ground soft chairs. "The truth is, Song, I messed up in China, and that's just the tip of the iceberg, I feel. We were on Peng's trail to Steve, but then I had to be the hero and, bam! We lost Peng."

"I see." Song sat in an adjacent chair, thinking about how God so uniquely moved in the lives of His people. One day, not long ago, he'd been a mobster. Now, the secret agents of Christian organizations were coming to him for spiritual counsel. "Actually, I don't see. Tell me everything. In my prayers, God may have given me an idea how to help, but I need to know what has happened."

Titus expounded on his Shanghai operation as Song served tea. Kaori wandered into the room midway. But Song knew she was interested only in their company, not in the family's criminal past or the consequences that had led Americans to their doorstep twice in the same month. The old woman had been a godsend, Song reflected, helping him endure the past two years. Providing for her had allowed him to focus, to keep him selfless, and to give him a purpose that was no longer criminal or violent.

"So, Tond-zu is in charge of Shanghai now?" Song nodded thoughtfully when Titus finished briefing him. "That's most unfortunate. Peng was ruthless, but lazy and gluttonous. Tond-zu is a brutal man with endless zeal. I see I'm not the only one who's made a mess where Steve Brookshire is concerned."

"You said you might have an idea?" Titus covered his mouth through what sounded like a sob. "I'm dying for ideas right now, Song. I'm not exactly feeling right about going home without first fixing my mess."

"I've learned, Titus, that I don't fix my messes." Song held out his hand. "And you need to know, you're not fixing this, either. Let's pray to the only Fixer I know. In Akita Prefecture, we can't climb Mount Chokai unless we first go down into the valleys and canyons of brokenness. Give me your hand."

"You should know, also," Titus said, "that I have only months to live. Cancer. I'm stage four, Song. It's all through my body, even the bone marrow."

"And you're not in a hospital? What are you doing on a mission?"

"I want to finish strong, like this, out in the field."

"Hmm." Song frowned. "It seems we may have different ideas as to what measures strength. Let's begin by presenting everything to our Master."

Song prayed for Titus. He felt the man's discomfort, but in the second hour of pleading, Titus wept, and Song knew a time of refreshing was ahead. Perhaps, even a time of healing . . .

Hudie Valley – One Year Ago

For the next several days, Steve worked on the rice paddy containment walls. There was also topsoil to be carried in a wheelbarrow from the bottom of the valley to the top, where the water could transmit nutrients adequately when the season approached for flooding the fields. Since he was an able man with two legs again, the peasant women had an endless list of tasks for him to tackle—or fields to walk through to repair walls. Wu-Li hiked with him everywhere, mumbling complaints, Steve guessed, about their lack of play. The two children from the prison hadn't been seen since the near-drowning incident, and the other youths from the valley had been as busy in the fields as Steve was, rather than swimming at the pool.

One afternoon, Steve was using a broken shovel to load a wheelbarrow with topsoil. His mind was reviewing escape possibilities, especially since his walking was improving daily. Soon, he might even be able to run! But ideas weren't falling into place, almost as if it weren't God's will for him to run away from the valley at all. Didn't God know Tond-zu could order his death at any time? Didn't God have other work for him to do outside the small valley? Didn't God know he was lonely without Lisa?

"Hey, *Bao'r!*" A man called to him in Mandarin.

Steve dropped his shovel and looked up at the prison wall. He recognized Warden Fongdu Jen in his PRC uniform.

"Come to the gate!" he ordered, then disappeared from the rampart.

Steve's heart beat faster. Maybe he should've already escaped during the night, hiking south toward the river, searching for a phone until he could call COIL. It was his own fault, he decided. Building the iron leg had made him a flight risk. They simply had to house him inside a prison cell now.

Discouraged, he walked down the path to the gate of the prison. The Bible story book was back in his cottage, nearly completed. His work seemed all but wasted now. Wu-Li stayed back from the smelly prison wall, Wong-wei with him.

The gate squeaked open and a guard appeared, carrying a cage with three chickens inside. He set the cage on the ground and retreated back inside the prison. Steve stared at the chickens—two hens and a rooster. The prison received occasional supplies by way of the ridge above, but he'd always been up the valley, too far away to see what came. Apparently, the prison had received three extra chickens!

He picked up the cage and carried it away, praising God for such an unexpected blessing. How weak was his faith! The chickens had to be from Fongdu for saving his son.

Stopping at the cottage of the four basket-weavers, Steve set the cage down and crossed his arms proudly, feeling like a school boy showing off a prize.

"Would someone like to fix chicken stew tonight?"

One of the elderly women who could understand Steve's Mandarin, shook a crooked finger at him and scowled.

"If you kill those chickens, you fool, you won't get any eggs!"

"Eggs?" Steve felt sweat on his forehead. He'd almost killed the chickens for one meal, when he could feed the chickens for one thousand eggs! "Thank you. I'll keep them myself."

Returning to his own cottage, he used discarded boards to build a house and roost for his new feathered friends. He guessed by feeding and caring for the birds for a couple weeks, he could open their cage and they'd remain nearby during the day, feeding on their own. And once or twice a day, he'd have eggs to eat and share with the farmers.

Steve knew that God was in even this moment. But what did the arrival of the chickens mean? He couldn't take the birds with him when he escaped the valley. What was God trying to tell him?

Turkey – Present Day

Oleg arrived alone at a mountainous rendezvous point in windy, southeastern Turkey overlooking an arm of the Ataturk Reservoir. The rugged passes and shivering heights of steep ridges gave Oleg a sense of isolation, but wearing Titus' sat-watch was of some consolation. And from somewhere near, Luigi Putelli was supposed to be monitoring the situation, he hoped.

He climbed out of his rental car, having driven from Karakus, Turkey, and checked the sat-watch. A vehicle with two people was approaching on the narrow highway from the east. The bug Titus had made the man swallow weeks earlier was blinking with clarity. It was expected that the bodyguard from the *Soldiers of Mahdi*, Ercan Sanli, would approach from the east since the Iranian border was a short distance away, but the man's intentions were still a mystery.

A large refrigerator truck came into sight. Oleg was more comfortable backing up Titus while the Arkansas native used his craftiness to charm a contact. But Oleg trusted God now to give him the words, if not the wit, so he wouldn't blunder the situation for COIL, even if this were an ambush. He didn't like the idea of returning to the hands of the *Soldiers of Mahdi*, especially with Titus missing and unable to rescue him right away.

Two men climbed out of the truck's cab. The passenger was Ercan Sanli, his height and girth intimidating enough without his sawed-off shotgun carried on a sling. The other man wasn't familiar to Oleg, but he carried an Uzi and glared hatefully at Oleg. Ercan approached Oleg directly while the driver monitored the desolate highway a few yards away.

"I expected the Serval," Ercan said in rough English, "not you again! I need the Serval!"

"Everyone needs the Serval. I was sent in his place." Oleg kept his hands in his pockets, not offering to shake the giant's mitt. How could he even touch the man who'd tortured him a few weeks earlier? "The last time you and I met, I was chained to a table and you were playing electrician. My heart still flutters when I hear your name."

Ercan glanced at his partner, barely out of earshot.

"The Serval and I fought in *Imam* Serik's office. While we were there, the Serval said some things about Isa. You call Him Jesus."

"Oh." Oleg nodded, his body relaxing. Corban had been right. This wasn't an aggressive rendezvous after all! "The Serval has been known to share the love of Jesus even with his enemies. That's why you're still alive today. Jesus has changed the Serval's heart."

"I considered that. Now I'm alive to respond as well." He looked again at his partner, then back to Oleg. "I was trusting the Serval to arrive and understand my need for . . . discretion and privacy."

"I can be discreet." Oleg waited a moment, but Ercan only stared at him, one eyebrow raised, as if expecting something. Suddenly, Oleg understood. "Oh, I'm sorry! The Serval is a little quicker than I am."

From his shoulder holster, Oleg drew his sidearm and shot Ercan's partner in the side. The silenced round and gel-tranq impact made the man jump, turn halfway, then collapse on the edge of the highway.

"Thank you." Ercan stooped to his partner and dragged him over to the truck. "I didn't want to kill him, but I know you have non-lethal weapons. I have much to learn of this Jesus."

Oleg followed him to the truck and helped load the unconscious man into the passenger seat.

"I wasn't sure why you wanted to meet the Serval, but know this: if you're talking about following Jesus, the Serval will be sorry he missed this meeting!"

Without thinking, Oleg laughed and slapped Ercan on his oversized shoulder. The man jerked back and his hand brushed his shotgun.

"Whoa! Easy, friend!" Oleg raised his empty hands. "I meant no offense, really. I've already forgotten the whole electrocution session a while back."

"I'm very nervous." The man held up his hand to show he was shaking. "If *Imam* Serik finds out about this, I'm dead. He's already suspicious why I'd want to travel with a shipment of weapons to fighters in Syria. I simply had to meet the Serval alone."

"You're stuck with me, Ercan. You've risked a lot, but I'm your guy. Tell me how I can help you."

"I just need to know. I don't know what to believe." Ercan stepped uncomfortably close to Oleg. "Is Jesus alive?"

"Oh, yes! He's alive!" Oleg laughed and slapped his thigh. "Absolutely, Jesus the Messiah is alive. He rose three days after His crucifixion, defeating sin and death once and for all. His power—His Spirit—lives in me, so I know it's true, just as the Bible says."

"Okay." Ercan took a deep breath and looked up at the cloudy sky. "Then He really is God. He's the One I need. Now I know what to believe."

"Let's sit in the car out of this wind and talk." Oleg rubbed his hands together. "I'll tranquilize your friend every hour if I have to, every ten hours, if we need to talk for ten hours."

"We cannot talk for ten hours!" Ercan walked towards Oleg's car "There's another reason I needed the Serval. Seven years ago, I quietly sold my sister to a brothel in Nepal. I was ashamed that she was a Christian. I have to get her back. The Serval—I've seen that he's an escape artist."

"You're right. We might need the Serval for that!"

CHAPTER TEN

Hudie Valley – One Year Ago

Steve felt he was getting mixed signals from God. Initially, he believed God wanted him to escape Hudie Valley and return to America. Why else would he have learned to walk and begin to run if not to escape the threat of being murdered by men sent by Tond-zu?

But now, there were the warden's children splashing in the irrigation pool. It changed everything, as if maybe God were testing Steve's loyalties. Was freedom more important to himself than preaching the gospel to the valley inhabitants? Was his safety an idol before God's desire to touch the warden's heart through his children?

"Keep your feet moving!" he cheered as Lijia and Zou, the daughter and son of Fongdu Jen tread water. "Like a bicycle. Peddle!"

"Peddle!" Wu-Li ordered more strictly from the shoreline, his toy soldier in his fist. "Peddle!"

"Okay, okay, take a break." Steve waved the children to the bank. "Come on. Rest."

He watched proudly as they doggie-paddled to shallow water, then splashed ashore to collapse. Nearby, the other children of the valley worked in the fields next to their mothers. Occasionally, they looked up wistfully toward the pool, and Steve waved at them. They, too, wanted to play rather than work, of course.

The night before, Steve had overheard the basket-weavers talk of the change in the valley. As he'd delivered eggs to Wu-Li's mother, he'd lingered in the doorway to hear more. Indeed, the farmers were talking about his new relationship with the warden and his children. If the warden's heart could be softened toward *Bao'r*, the *Handbasket*, couldn't it also be softened toward their captive brothers, husbands, and sisters in the prison?

Steve had left without comment, but the thought remained with him. The value of this opportunity with the warden was far greater than escaping the valley for his own safety. Yes, he was in danger of Tond-zu having him killed. Yes, the discomfort of captivity was restricting. Yes, Lisa had been killed, and no one from COIL knew where he was. But he'd prayed long ago for the God of Joseph to help him, and now he had the warden's favor! Would he now demand his freedom by escaping, when he could enter the door God had opened wide?

The rice farmers were alert to the fact that he could affect the situation in their favor as well. He couldn't do that for them if he ran away, leaving behind people who needed his care, his skills, and his favor translated to them.

"Two lessons, and you're already treading water." Steve tucked a piece of grass in his mouth. "It's good, but life is more than swimming and exercise."

"We do our school work each morning," Lijia said, "now that we live in the fortress. Zou, pay attention to *Bao'r!*"

She was a year older than Zou, who tolerated her mothering bossiness in silence. Quietly, he released a frog and wiped off his hands.

"School work is good, but life is more than knowledge as well." Steve touched his chest. "I'm talking about our spiritual health, finding peace with the Creator, even though we are full of faults."

"Father said we came from the earth and we return to the earth." Lijia poked her brother. "But Zou almost returned to the water last month!"

"Our bodies come from the earth, but our souls are made from unseen things," Steve said. "Our souls are eternal, from God. I have evidence there is a God who cares for us."

"Evidence?" Zou lifted his head. "Like what?"

"Countless things. Let's consider me and you, to start with. Before I came to Hudie Valley, I was a famous athlete, a competitive swimmer."

"Even with one leg?" Lijia frowned.

"I had two legs one year ago. Then I came to this valley. You almost drowned in the pool, Zou. But I knew how to swim to rescue you, and I knew how to revive you to deliver you from death. The evidence of all those events working together points to the hand of a Designer."

"A Designer." Zou tapped his muddy hand on his chin in thought. "What else?"

"We exist. The world exists. Look around us. Beauty and complexity. Everything comes from somewhere. An egg comes from a chicken.

Rice comes from a seedbed. Who is the Source of us? It's God."

"Prove it," Lijia said."

"You're the proof." Steve smiled. "Does a frog change its ways? Does it care about wrong or right?"

"No, he cares only for eating more insects." Zou grinned.

"Exactly. But we have a conscience. Where did it come from? Who wrote good and evil in our hearts so we know right from wrong? It's something we're born with, but it's only in humans, not frogs." Steve picked up a flat rock. "If I turned over this rock and your names were on the other side, would we suppose the rock wrote your names on itself? Of course not. The order and complexity we see around us must be attributed to a Maker."

"Who wrote on my heart?" Zou leaned forward for the answer.

"Maybe I shouldn't say." Steve tossed the rock into the pool. "I know Him very well. He doesn't like to be doubted."

"You know the Creator?" Lijia crossed her arms. "I don't believe it."

"I have a book you could read. I wrote it from memory of man's experiences with the Creator. It'll change your life, if you believe it."

That afternoon, Steve sent the children back to the prison with more than weariness from their swimming lesson. Zou carried under his arm the book that Steve had bound in rice paper, full of Bible quotes, stories, and whole passages. As he watched them walk down the valley with his work of the past few months, he prayed with anticipation. If he didn't take risks for God to work the miraculous, then he couldn't trust God to perform the miraculous. The Word of God had been turned loose into the hands of a ten year old and his bossy sister. Anything was possible now!

Qatar – Present Day

Agent Wes Trimble sipped lemon-flavored water as he stood on an apartment balcony in Qatar. Thirty floors below and as far as his one eye could see, the Persian Gulf stretched in dark blue-green water to the north. An oil tanker moved on the horizon, a ghost in the haze many miles away.

"What are you thinking?" a woman asked.

He turned to see Wynter Caspertein wrap a scarf around her head and toss the end over her shoulder. Even half-covered, she was a beautiful woman. Wes couldn't believe she was interested in him.

Actually, he wasn't completely certain she was interested in him. His work in the CIA had occasionally attracted women for the wrong reasons, but he liked to think Wynter wasn't hunting for his occupational leverage.

"Just wondering if it's wise for a woman who's supposedly dead— hiding from Muslim extremists—to be living in plain sight in a country run by Wahhabi Sunnis."

"Would you rather have me out of sight, like this?" She lifted the scarf to cover her face, all but her blue eyes visible. Wes was reminded of Titus, her older brother, since they had the same eyes. "Is that better?"

"Now you're mocking me." He wagged his finger. "Remember, I'm the one who arranged for your disappearance in Azerbaijan, uh . . ."

"Nicole. You call me Nicole, now. I'm Annette's sister. And yes, I remember what you did for me a few months ago."

"Right." He smiled, turning to the ocean again. "What a world we live in now, huh?"

"What do you mean?" She joined him at the balcony railing. "Isn't this what you spooks live for? Living in the shadows, secret names, and disguises? Soldiers for Christ sharing love where soldiers of Sharia Law demand obedience and submission."

"Yeah. Some life."

"Hey, I'm loving it. Really."

"You are?" He looked into her eyes. "What exactly are you loving? You're no longer the archaeologist you spent half a lifetime becoming."

"Really? I'm not even forty yet and you're saying half my life is over?" She jabbed him on the shoulder. "Come on. I'm giving you a hard time. Do you expect anything else? Look who I grew up with! Rudy and Titus never stopped playing games."

"So, you're happy?"

"More than ever." She nodded at the distant water. "I'm serving God. I'm still in training with COIL, but I've already seen women secretly come to Christ. Last week, I went to a baptism in a woman's home. We had to use the bathtub, you know. Her husband didn't even know that while he was at work, a bunch of underground Christians celebrated his wife's salvation. That's my life now. So, yeah, I'm happy. How about you?"

"I'm content." He shrugged. "I always have a restlessness that keeps me moving, but I'm enjoying myself."

"Does your restless life leave any room for a girlfriend?"

Wes choked on his lemon water, then he wiped his mouth with his sleeve.

"You are definitely Titus' sister—always direct."

"Answer the question, Agent." She smiled, obviously enjoying his squirming.

"I'm here, aren't I? I mean, I'm in a place with the PRS Division that I can write my own schedule. I mentor a few young Christians on the side, and helping COIL keeps me attached to the global action."

"It doesn't hurt to have the president in your corner, either."

"Does everyone know about that?" He rolled his eye. "How do you know?"

"Titus said you stopped talking about leaving the CIA, and Rashid called and said you've been at the White House a lot lately."

"You talk to Rashid still?" Wes sipped his water. "Must be strange after he spent weeks trying to capture and kill you."

"I think we've all seen his heart for Christ, now. He feels indebted to Titus, too, or he worships him—I don't know which. But he's lonely. Yeah, we talk every week or two."

"Huh." Wes steeled himself. "Did he say what he's been up to lately?"

"Something in China with Titus and Oleg. Hey!" She gave him a little shove. "You're pretty crafty at changing the focus. I'll be finished with my training soon. Should I request a COIL assignment along the Pacific Rim, or not?"

"Just focus on the best place for you, Wynter. No one speaks Arabic on the Pacific Rim. You have plenty of options here in the Middle East."

"Then, how will I see you? You're part of the Pacific Rim Security."

"Well, naturally . . ." He took her hand. "When I check on you for COIL every few weeks, we'll see each other then."

"What if it's in the heart of Africa in some mud-hut village?"

"Then I'll grab my spear and grass skirt and fly into the bush. I have a baobab eye-patch just for African safaris. It's all the rage on the savanna."

"Oh? Among all the one-eyed warriors?"

"We stick together, us one-eyed warriors—pairing up so we have depth perception for the hunt."

"I see." She gripped his hand with both of hers. "Maybe if we were a pair, you and I could stick together instead."

"Are we still talking about Africa?"

"Just go with it, Agent Trimble." Then she kissed him. "You don't need two eyes for that, do you?"

"You Casperteins are going to be the end of me." He led her to the door. "But not before I eat some spicy Qatar food. You'll show me the best restaurant?"

"That's what I promised, and then afterward, Chloe Azmaveth wants someone besides me to know where I set up a COIL safe house in the city."

"You set up a safe house?" Wes closed the door behind them. "COIL doesn't waste any time moving its new recruits into the field, do they?"

"There aren't many of us, so we can't afford to move too slowly. These are the last days, I believe. Even one-eyed men and Arkansas girls are needed out here."

Hudie Valley – One Year Ago

Lisa was sick. It had been her worst fear—falling prey to a strange virus in a strange land. She had a fever and suffered from dehydration, and even bouts of delirium. Sometimes during the long nights she didn't even recognize Ghuning, who was the only woman brave enough to tend to her shrinking form. Convulsions and abdominal pains had brought screams to her lips, but Ghuning had tried to smother her noises lest the guards come and take her away permanently.

However, at the next weekly bath, when Lisa was too weak to stand, Ghuning conceded to help three other women carry her pale, limp body out of the cell. There was no use in one prisoner passing her sickness on to the others. Lisa didn't object, mostly because she had no strength. On the cold corridor rock, she lay and wordlessly watched her cellmates file outside.

This was it, Lisa thought. She would die soon. At least it wouldn't be much more painful. Now, she would just drift to sleep, and wake in the presence of Jesus. There was comfort in that thought, but regret as well, knowing she hadn't lived the past year as a faithful witness amongst her cellmates.

She remembered Steve's unabashed courage to witness wherever he went, handing out tracts even in villages where police had told him to give nothing to the people. Tears of happiness welled at the thought of him. Somewhere, he was serving God. If he was a prisoner as well, Steve would find a way to share Christ's love. He would tell Bible stories and offer arguments to defy any suffering Buddhist or weak communist viewpoint of life and eternity. And he would do it with care and courtesy.

Sometime later, the women returned from their time outside. The guards instructed them to pick up Lisa and carry her up the stairs to the courtyard. Lisa watched passively as hands lifted her feverish body, their grips slipping on her moist skin, and carried her up the spiraling stone steps.

Sunlight hit her face, and for an instant, Lisa smiled. This was the light of Christ, she imagined. Well, soon enough. On the courtyard grass, they set her down and backed away as guards hovered. Only Ghuning hesitated, her hand on Lisa's forehead.

"We will miss you," the older woman said, then she was gone.

"Get up." A booted foot roughly nudged her arm. "If you get up, we'll feed you."

Lisa didn't even try to rise. Food wasn't on her list of desires after vomiting for more days than she could count. Why prolong the misery by eating more?

"One of the Americans," someone said in Mandarin. "From cell eight on the bottom, sir."

A figure stepped close and blocked the sun. Lisa opened her eyes and noticed a middle-aged man in a crisp uniform. She'd seen him before on the courtyard balcony when they'd been marched out for bathing. Ghuning had described him as the warden of the prison, and his two children lived upstairs. He'd been a colonel in the military, which made him the highest-ranking Communist Party official in that part of China.

"Name?"

"Li Ken. Her file says drug trafficking."

"Li Ken," the warden repeated. "One of Shanghai's cases?"

"Yes, sir. Do you want us to put her in the corpse cell? She won't last long. The afternoon trustee crew can bury her."

"She's only been here a year, hasn't she?" The warden crouched next to her. Lisa stared into his eyes a moment, then her lids closed. It was too much effort to keep them open. "No, better take her down to the clinic. If Shanghai calls, I don't want to report her death this soon. Take her yourself, and bring her back alive."

"Yes, sir."

A few minutes later, Lisa felt a cloth stretcher under her. Tears trickled from her eyes. She wanted to die, to end the misery. But they were keeping her alive to suffer more. It didn't seem fair.

The gentle rocking of being carried away put her to sleep.

Japan – Present Day

Titus strolled beside the Omono River, which ran through the center of Akita, Japan. For three days, he'd been communing with God, detached from the rest of the world. He likened himself to taking a vow of silence, as some did there in the ancient Orient. Sleeping on a hard mat on the floor in Song Sakana's house, and caring for his ill mother-in-law, Kaori, had actually taught him about God. It was all being used by God to convey Titus' deep need for more of Christ in his life. The Spirit's gentle voice was breaking through his hard heart as he yielded completely. Even the wearying effects of the cancer had diminished since he'd been resting and praying with Song. For the first time in his Christian walk, Titus was learning what it meant to minister to God while he fasted and waited on His moving.

Meanwhile, Song had suggested his mobster brother, Chin, who was still in Hong Kong, could help them find Steve. But hearing back from the busy man in China was taking time, leaving Titus in full sponge-mode—to soak up the rest in his soul, a rest he didn't realize he craved so much.

"Hindus pray ritually," Song had counselled two days earlier. "Buddhists meditate with practiced devotion. Muslims humble them-selves to five mandatory prayers a day—minimum. And what about the Christian? A moment before a meal and a thought before rising in the morning?"

"We serve the true God." Titus had said, nodding thoughtfully. "Yet we're neglecting Him and taking Him for granted."

"We shouldn't only petition Him," Song had continued, "we should remember our Lord yearns to commune with us. We should take time daily, as much time as is necessary, to listen to His petitions for us as well. Your soul is thirsty for Him. A dedicated servant of His cannot serve without receiving from Him. Let Him nourish you. Just rest, Titus. Rest in Him. Nothing else."

And so, Titus had been resting. There would come a time when he would call Annette, communicate with Corban, and partner up with Oleg again. Every time he looked at his empty, pale wrist, he was reminded he'd cut himself off from his friends and family. But this time was about centering himself back on Jesus Christ. His carelessness in Shanghai had been regrettable, but he'd dealt with that guilt before God's throne. Now, he was about the business of finding more secure closeness to Christ. Song had counseled him toward a path that Titus prayed would develop into new life habits, as long as he was alive. These were lessons he could learn only through the trials of failure and understanding his daily need of Christ. He felt a deep desire to share his recent discoveries with Annette, as soon as God signaled it was time to return.

"Hey, are you an American?"

Titus paused on the sidewalk as a drunken crowd of tourists streamed by. Some visited the samurai sites during the day, then binged on *sake* at night. The speaker was a youth in a university hoodie, a paper cup in his hand and a glassy-eyed blond on his arm.

"Yeah," Titus admitted freely, though normally when he ran into Westerners in foreign lands, he spoke to them in Russian until they left him alone. "I'm from Arkansas."

"No way! I'm from Oklahoma!" He burped. "You want a swig? This stuff is amazing. They say you don't even get a hangover. I could drink all night, and not even regret it the next day!"

The blond on his arm vomited on the young man's shoes, but he didn't notice.

"Oh, I think you'll regret it." Titus chuckled. "At least at some point, you'll regret it. It ain't easy smelling like puke."

"Hey, are you all alone?" The drunk gestured to the west. "We're going to the coast. They say Oga needs to be seen in the light moon."

"The moonlight?"

"Yeah, that's what I said. Come with us. You shouldn't be alone."

"Is that right?" Titus considered the youth's words. Was God telling him something through a drunkard's mouth? He'd used donkeys' mouths to communicate to stubborn souls before. "Not tonight. But thanks for the message. You guys go on without me. And be careful."

Titus returned to Song Sakana's house, praying as he walked. He noticed Song helping his mother-in-law with her shoes when he walked in the door.

"I think God is telling me it's time to leave," Titus said as he closed the door. "I need to get back to work—after I call my wife."

"That's good timing." Song stood up. "My brother just sent me a text. He said we can meet him in Hong Kong. He'll receive me."

"You think he has something on Steve?"

"He has something, or he wouldn't accept a meeting. I'm taking Kaori to a church friend. We leave for Hong Kong tonight!"

Nepal – Present Day

Oleg followed a step behind Ercan Sanli's bulky frame down yet another Kathmandu street. For two hours, they'd zigzagged through the city's red light district, searching for the brothel Ercan had given his sister to seven years earlier. The streets seemed all the same to Oleg: littered, smelly, and provocative. But Ercan was committed, even though they'd traipsed up some streets twice.

"There it is!" Ercan finally blurted, then ducked his head to whisper. "That's the one. The last earthquake toppled many structures, so I didn't recognize it right away. See the young men with cell phones outside that business? It looks like a hotel. I've never been so ashamed of myself than at this moment."

"Wait just a second. We need a plan." Oleg grabbed Ercan's arm to hold him back. There was no physical danger, but Oleg had learned there was a spiritual sense to consider as well. "I've heard about these neighborhoods. I haven't been a Christian much longer than you, brother, but I've learned a little something about God in my travels with the Serval."

"What is it? What do you see?" Ercan browsed the intersection of filth and three-story establishments. "Is it security? You have your tranq-gun."

"No, I see no security." Oleg couldn't read Nepali, but many of the signs above the businesses were in English, inviting Western tourists to sample their wares. "I'm looking for— There! The presence of God."

"The presence of God in a place like this?" Ercan shook his head. "You must be joking. That's a beauty salon. I'm telling you, I left my sister in that brothel over there. What do we need with a beauty salon?"

"Come with me and see." Oleg started across the street, traveled only by bicycles and pedestrians.

"I'm not going into a woman's beauty salon!"

Oleg was too awed by the actual presence of the salon to pay Ercan's Middle Eastern sensitivities any more mind. He reached the door of the salon and traced his fingers on the stenciled letters of a fish symbol, followed by the Bible reference: John 8:11.

"What does that mean?" Ercan asked when he caught up. "Is it a code? A Christian code?"

"In the Bible, there's a traditional story of a woman caught in adultery. When the people brought her to Jesus to be stoned, Jesus said the one without sin should throw the first stone. When no one threw a stone, Jesus told the woman that He didn't condemn her, either, and she should sin no more."

"This story is in the Bible you gave me?"

"It is. Come. We need to meet these people before we rush blindly into that place to help your sister."

Inside, Oleg was choked by the scents of nail polish and burning candles—a combination that seemed explosive, but at least it masked the odors from the street.

A Nepalese girl about the age of ten rose from a desk, jabbered a greeting, then dashed behind a beaded doorway. Oleg waved casually at two female customers whose nails were being tended by two beauticians.

"Say hello." Oleg elbowed Ercan, as he would've done to Titus if the two had been together.

"I think I'm going to be sick." Ercan covered his mouth with his hand. "I can't believe I would do this to my sister. Did you see the kind of people out there in front of that brothel? What scum!"

The ten-year-old and a woman about Oleg's age emerged from the beaded door.

"Good day to you. English?" The woman smiled pleasantly, a warmth about her that Oleg could feel almost physically. "May I help you?"

Oleg usually followed Titus' lead at these junctures, so he imagined what the Serval would say.

"My friend and I are friends of the Fisherman." He glanced at the salon customers, not wanting to get the salon owner in trouble, even if she did have a cryptic Bible reference on her door. "May we speak somewhere?"

"Of course. Come into my office."

"Oleg!" Ercan tugged on Oleg's jacket. "How can a child be forced to work in a place like this?"

The girl returned to her desk and the owner held the beads aside for them to enter.

"Do you know how many girls in this city are thrown away?" Oleg frowned at his companion. "They either beg on the streets or go to the brothels to survive. A few get taken in. A beauty salon hardly seems to be a bad place for a girl to work, not that you're in a position to judge where young women are found working!"

Behind the beads, Oleg squeezed onto a tiny bench in the corner as the woman prepared tea for them from a kettle on her crammed desk. Ercan stood next to the door since there was no room to sit, which seemed fine with him since he was so cagey.

"You may call me Rikta. I'm from India." She offered a tiny porcelain cup of tea to Oleg, using two hands, then to Ercan. "Forgive me for not being better prepared to receive you. We don't have many men come here."

"Thank you for your hospitality. My name is Oleg. It's a beautiful salon. I've heard there were Christians who run beauty parlors in the red light districts of Nepalese cities. We found yours at a providential moment." He sipped his tea. "We couldn't leave without visiting."

"Oh?" Her tone was suddenly cold. "You have business in this neighborhood? What kind of Christians are you?"

Ercan's mouth gaped at the accusation, but Oleg only smiled. He'd been accused of worse.

"The business we came for does regard a brothel up the street." He set the cup down after draining it in two gulps, which he hoped wasn't impolite. "We're here to rescue a forced prostitution victim who was dropped off here seven years ago. She was disowned and abandoned, since she'd become a Christian. We were hoping, in your outreach to the women here, that you might know her."

"What is her name?"

"Irem Sanli." Ercan looked at the floor. "She is my sister."

"I don't know anyone by that name." Rikta's eyes pleaded her apology to Oleg. "There are other streets you could try. I can give you the address of other Christian salons in the city."

"Actually, she was left at that brothel right there." Oleg pointed through the beads as Ercan moved aside. "We know she was here seven years ago."

"Yes, okay. I know the owners." Rikta's eyes darted nervously. "Some of the brothels, I'm allowed to go inside to care for the women in private. I share the hope of Jesus with them. That's what saved me from that life. Now you see my daughter. God has been good."

"You mean you were a—"

"Ercan!" Oleg stopped the man's mouth. "Mind yourself or I will gladly tranquilize you!" He shrugged at Rikta. "Forgive my new Christian friend. The Lord is still training his mouth how to speak in the presence of a beautiful woman of the King."

"Yes," she said, "I was a prostitute. There are thousands in this city. Very few, if any, of them are so by choice. The brothel you pointed to is one of nine on this street. A father and son own and run it. They're very cruel. I'm never allowed inside that one, but I witness to the workers when they're allowed to come here. I've heard they have two rooms with locks upstairs where they keep new arrivals. The women say there's been a foreigner in one of those rooms for a long time. It could be her—your sister—but it's unlikely after so much time."

Oleg nodded. *Now what?*

"This father and son—how will we recognize them?"

"They're the only men who run the brothel. Any other men you see in there will be customers." She looked up at Ercan. "I pray your sister hasn't been locked up for seven years. But it would mean she hasn't cooperated."

"Then I'm proud of her." He lifted his head.

"Prepare yourself. She has still seen customers, no doubt, though by force. Even if she has cooperated, you should still be proud of her.

She's a woman, and your sister. And she needs your love."

Ercan hung his head again.

"Will you pray for us before we go in there?" Oleg asked. "In Russia, we have a saying: a fox is about to upset the chickens."

Rikta smiled shyly.

"I will pray for you, but remember this one thing: if you run out the two owners, the women will have nowhere to go but to another brothel where their loyalties will need to be proven yet again. It's a very sad balance, I fear, but there's no remedy on this side of Paradise."

"Maybe . . ." Oleg looked at Ercan, and chuckled. He was truly beginning to think like Titus now. "If there were another salon in this neighborhood, would you run it?"

"There's no more salon space on this street. I've looked."

"How big is that brothel?"

"Oleg, it looks like a hotel," Ercan said.

"Scratch the additional salon idea." Oleg held his arms wide to emphasize his idea. "Imagine a whole building that bears the presence of God, not just a salon. Could you run your salon and a hotel?"

"A hotel?" Rikta's eyes widened. "Oh, no, you can't turn the brothel into a hotel. Other brothel owners wouldn't allow it. They'd be afraid I would ruin them next. I could never run it. I would be targeted constantly."

"What if you had a man to protect you?"

"In this neighborhood? There are no such men who would do that here."

"What about a man his size?" Oleg nodded at Ercan. "And I'd make sure you had a little more money so the girls can stay in your hotel for cheap, maybe free, until you train them to be beauticians or seamstresses or something."

"Is he as strong as he looks?" Rikta sized up Ercan, who frowned as if he wasn't sure how to properly object yet.

"He was the bodyguard for an *imam* in Iran. A few weeks ago, he was torturing me. Now, Jesus Christ is his Master. I'm happy to place him in your charge."

"Absolutely not!" Ercan finally blurted. "Oleg, I'm taking my sister out of here!"

"And go where? *Imam* Serik has a million *Soldiers of Mahdi* who'll fry you alive if they find you back in Iran, Iraq, or Syria. Sometimes the choices we make have consequences to them. You need to lay low, brother, and this woman needs your expertise. Besides, if that locked-up girl is your sister, she needs Rikta's help to recover. I've rescued these kinds of girls before. We need to think about your sister and these other girls. Right?"

"I'm willing to take the risk," Rikta refilled his tea cup, "if you can provide everything you say. Everyone I care for will be ten times safer with a man watching over us."

"Oleg!" Ercan's fists were clenched. "Have you smelled the street? It's filthy! I can't be expected to live here!"

"Then clean it up! It's good enough for her daughter to live here. Apparently, whoever left your sister here didn't think it was too terrible for her, either." Oleg gave Ercan a glare, threatening to expose his shameful secret. "How quickly you have become so much better than the low people whom Jesus loves, Brother Ercan."

Ercan's mouth twisted and opened for a rebuttal, but he was cornered and remained silent. Oleg gulped the contents of his cup again.

"Very well. Ercan agrees. Rikta, if you please? Then we will see to putting this brothel out of business."

Oleg bowed his head as Rikta stood and placed her hand on Oleg. She gestured to Ercan.

"Are you too proud to kneel?" she asked, challenging him. "I see you and I will be like two goats pounding our heads together until you accept your lot, my big friend."

Ercan didn't respond as he knelt, his back to the beaded doorway. Rikta placed her other hand on his head and prayed for her street and God's will to be done in the brothel.

Oleg put his arm around Ercan. If Titus had been there, Oleg guessed the Serval would've done no differently with the bodyguard from Iran. But the dread of what they'd find in the brothel seemed to overshadow his joyful anticipation.

CHAPTER ELEVEN

Haung River – One Year Ago

Lisa woke up in a white, tented clinic. She wasn't immediately sure how she'd gotten there. It was daytime according to the sunlight pouring through the tent flap. A prison guard was sleeping on a cot next to her. Five others lay on cots beyond hers—peasants she didn't recognize, so she guessed they were probably from a nearby town, or the Hudie Valley rice paddies.

Her fever was gone. She didn't know how long she'd been unconscious, but she wore new clothes and she wasn't in the prison. The air smelled so fresh—almost scented like her mother's flower shop.

In bare feet, she slipped out of her cot and approached the tent opening. A doctor and a nurse were lounging in camp chairs, their backs to her, and were drinking something hot from plastic cups. Lisa's stomach craved something, but this wasn't the time for food. This was a time for flight while her guard slept!

Carefully, she withdrew into the tent again. Passing her guard, she approached the back wall of the tent and peeked under the canvas. A river! It had to be the gentle Huang. She crawled under the canvas and ran. At the water's edge, she looked back. No one had seen her. She'd rather die than return to the cold, damp, depressing cell. How far away was Hudie Valley? It didn't matter. Freedom was before her. All she could think about was getting away, contacting COIL, and finding Steve. She prayed he was still alive.

She plunged into the water, which was warmer than she expected. Smoothly, she stroked into the lazy current of the swollen river. Downriver, where civilization hugged the banks, the water would be polluted, but here, it was clear and peaceful, the grassy banks empty except for a few farm animals grazing and peasants washing clothes, but no one was paying attention to her in the middle of the river.

Treading water, she floated with the current, letting it take her away from the clinic on the hill, away from any notion of the prison. If she could, she wanted to float all the way to the ocean, but she knew there were dams miles ahead, as well as boat traffic.

Swimming reminded her of Steve. Though he was the competitor, she'd often swam with him, diving into the water after his training exercises. Now, the water both washed away her past and connected her to her future: Steve.

An hour later, she stroked toward the southern shore. Miles of winding river lay behind her. She climbed through reeds and mud to lay in tall grass. On her back, all she could see was blue sky above. This was a gift from God, she imagined—this moment, this peace, this freedom. Whatever trials arose on her trek east, this would be the moment she'd remember most—the warmth of the sun, the beauty of the sky, the thought of Steve's arms around her and—

The sound of a motor interrupted her moment of paradise. She sat up and studied the river for a boat. But the sound wasn't from a boat; it was a motorcycle on land! The rider was nearly on top of her when she leapt to her feet and scrambled toward the water.

The rider's foot, like a knight's lance, struck her from behind and sent her sprawling into the mud on the bank. Disoriented and bleeding from the mouth, she clawed at the reeds to get away. She couldn't feel her leg on the side where he'd struck her. Her mind screamed for help, to flee, but her body wouldn't respond.

She recognized the prison guard as he rolled her over. He punched her twice in the belly, then once in the face. Limply, she felt him cuff her hands and shackle her feet. A truck arrived, and she was manually thrown into the back.

"We just watched her float down," the guard told someone outside the truck. "She had to get out of the water sooner or later."

"That answers our question if she's well enough to be taken back to Hudie. The warden will be pleased."

Lisa opened her swollen eyes. She'd been beaten, but she was alive. Being alive wasn't necessarily great news, she realized, if she were back in the prison. They'd shoved her into a cell so small, she could touch all four walls by sitting in the middle of the floor.

She'd found what accounted for a source of water, which oozed from a crack in the wall. To drink, she had to press her lips against the crack and suck. It made her gag to think how many mouths had done just that in years past. Without a constant flow, her toilet was clogged, or barely draining, from the previous occupants in the cell.

"What are You doing?" she prayed, and rolled onto her other side. The walls were so close, she couldn't stretch her legs. "Why won't You help me?"

She thought of Bible stories she knew. Even terrible circumstances had been turned into startling blessings for God's faithful people. But those were Bible stories. And this was a pitch black cell in the heart of China. Was God even listening? How could this end with a startling blessing?

$\int$

Hudie Valley – Six Months Ago

Steve started teaching the Bible to the farmers of Hudie Valley by introducing story night outside his cottage. Sharing chicken eggs and becoming the farmers' hope for change in the valley had opened a door to the hearts of his fellow laborers, and he started with the children.

Only the very young came to his cottage for the first month of story night, but word spread to the older children, and then to various adults. Wu-Li never missed a night, seated in front, hugging Wong-wei through the suspense of certain stories. Steve narrated the Bible with dramatic intrigue, teaching as he stood upright, acting out various scenes and tragic dramas.

Because the youngest children started attending first, Steve instilled a praying tradition from the very beginning. He opened in prayer by kneeling in front of them all, folding his hands, and bowing his head.

"Dear Father in heaven," he prayed, "we are Your servants. You made us and You love us. We are Your faithful children, no matter what circumstances befall us. Teach us to be kind and to love one another, and to trust in You to turn us from evil, in thought and deed. Please bless Warden Fongdu Jen and his two children. And please watch over our families inside the prison. Comfort them through another night. Please urge Warden Fongdu Jen to be merciful as You are merciful. We pray to You because of what Jesus Your Son did for us. Amen."

By the time the adults began to attend story night, the order of each service was strictly enforced by the children. They knelt and bowed their heads in honor of the God whose might was apparent in the stories of seas parting and walls falling, of children striking down giants, and brave men willing to forgive their enemies as they died.

The warden's son, Zou, began to attend, which everyone believed was an answer to Steve's very prayers, that God would bless the warden and his family. Instead of distancing themselves from Zou, several boys his age befriended him. Their friendships manifested themselves throughout the daytime as well, at the swimming hole, and while running wild in the trees that bordered the valley. Steve's prayers to his powerful God cast no doubt in the minds of the farmers now. One by one, they submitted to the gospel of Jesus Christ.

Steve started writing another rice paper book, recording more events from the Bible, using it to try to teach some of the children to read and write. But the adults seemed more interested than the children in learning the discipline of writing. The children were more interested in running free and playing, not studying, so Steve began to tutor three adults to read and write.

One day, Shek-jai, one of his students, approached Steve as he carried twice the amount of soil across the paddy than anyone else could carry in the valley. His sturdy leg had made him a mule amongst his new friends and Christian family.

"My . . . husband." Shek-jai wouldn't meet Steve's eyes. Her Mandarin was improving slowly from his lessons, and Steve was patient. He set down his load with a small splash.

"Yes, Shek-jai? Your husband?" He pointed at the prison. Her son, Wu-Li, called for him to continue working so they would have time to play later. "He's in the prison, your husband?"

"Yes, Yes. You help? I need."

"Yes." Steve was overwhelmed with emotion, unable to deny her his help or withhold his tears that rolled down his cheeks. He didn't know how to help her husband—or any of the prisoners—but he would continue to pray about God's impact. "Yes, I will help, and God will help."

"Thank you." She bowed, and returned to her work.

That day, Steve doubled his time spent alone in prayer for Warden Fongdu Jen. He hadn't heard from or seen the man in months, not since the chicken gesture, but Zou was often in the valley with his new friends when he wasn't doing school work each morning in the fortress.

The terrors of hopelessness in the valley faded, and Steve became the champion of the farmers' optimism. Their gloom departed and smiles peeked through their downcast eyes. Steve continued to pray, almost frightened at how God would move next.

Hong Kong – Present Day

Titus glanced at his wrist out of habit, but realized he still didn't have his sat-watch, and no one in COIL knew where he was. If he got into trouble now, he'd be on his own with Song Sakana. At least he'd called Annette and told her he loved her. He'd given her an update and admitted he was working through a blunder. She'd prayed for him and his health, then they'd said goodbye. It felt as if gravity were pulling him back to her arms, but responsibilities demanded his attention.

He stood in an office building in downtown Hong Kong. The riots outside had reached their peak, drowning out most of the sound of a Japanese-style stringed instrument playing through a wall speaker. In the polished waiting room, Song Sakana sat across from him.

"This can't be comfortable for you," Titus said. "You used to run this city. Now your brother runs it alone."

"I don't envy him. I was thinking how uncomfortable this is for you." Song's face was calm, his voice soft. "Your face was recently in the newspapers."

"This social unrest will keep the authorities busy." Titus tapped his fingers on his knees, nervous regardless of his claim. "I'm more focused on finding Steve, and not making a bigger mess of things."

They listened to the chants of the rioters as they marched past on the street—a million strong now. More Hong Kong journalists had gone missing, and the government was being blamed. The semi-autonomous city was experiencing the end of its freedoms to criticize the government. Chinese law enforcers, without constitutional right to operate in the city, had been seen enforcing Beijing's protocols in secret. The result was more missing journalists. It was an ongoing cycle.

Titus glanced up when the office door opened and a heavy-set man in a suit waved them forward. Song followed Titus into the office.

"So! The coward returns like a kitten!" boomed Chin Sakana, a heavier version of his younger brother. He dismissed his bodyguard from the room with a wave. "Family business. Leave us!"

Chin spoke in a British accent instead of Japanese as Titus had expected. Song bowed before his brother, but Chin merely crossed his arms and laughed. Titus felt out of place, considering whether he should come back later after the two brothers worked through their feud.

When Chin refused to greet his brother, Song rose from his bow and signaled to Titus.

"This is the man I wrote to you about, the Serval."

"The Serval of Egypt? Bah!" Chin shrugged his shoulders. "This is Hong Kong. I've permitted this meeting only to—"

Faster than the fat mobster could ward off the attack, Song smoothly jabbed his brother in the side. Shocked, Titus blinked as a flurry of motion ended with Song standing over his older brother, Chin's arm pinned to the desk with little effort by Song.

"Do not mistake my recent absence as weakness, Brother," Song said in almost a whisper, which made his power more terrifying. Chin's reddened face twisted in discomfort, especially when he tried to move against Song's submission hold. "Your disrespect of others kept your inheritance in my hands for years. I may be your lesser, but honor dictates you show grace in your position of power. Is this understood?"

"Yes, Song. Let me go! I'm sorry! Okay?" Song released his brother and patted Chin on his shoulder as the heavy man rotated his wrist to check for injury. "I thought you were a Christian, a pacifist."

"Don't confuse a Christian for a Buddhist monk, Brother." Song led his brother to a chair meant for guests, and seated him in it, as if Chin were about to be interrogated. "And don't confuse love for evil. It's my love for you that corrects you, and doesn't kill you."

"Okay." Chin eyed Titus, then looked away shamefully. "Don't talk like this in front of him."

"I'd speak to you in Japanese, but you never learned, remember?" Song sat behind the grand desk made from imported oak. "You preferred father and me to feed you and spoil you with *geishas* and *sake*. The Sakana name has never been weaker in Hong Kong, but you still have a little strength, and that's why I'm here. You have what I asked for?"

"I do, but moving around inland is risky for you. I've made inquiries. May I?" Chin asked permission to rise from his chair, then he approached his desk. From a file, he drew a chart and offered it with two hands to Song. "I pressured a Xi'an official, and another in Chongqing. I've used them to transport product on the trains. They each compiled lists of re-education centers where they've heard that foreign criminals may be housed."

Titus licked his lips, anxious to get his hands on the list Song reviewed. There was a chance again that Steve and Lisa could be recovered. It was time to call COIL. It was time to partner with Oleg again.

"You've done well, Brother. You've possibly saved lives today." Song closed the file. Chin humbly returned to his lowly chair. "I thank you for helping us. But now we must talk about Father."

"I swear, Song, I didn't do anything to him. I don't want to run Hong Kong alone!"

"I know, Brother. Father's past caught up to him. He volunteered to retire, and in pursuit of a clear conscience before the Creator, he has also become a Christian."

"What? Both of you?"

"The ugliness of our sins and the compassionate healing offered by Jesus—these two forces must be considered, Brother. In the world, we have been gluttons. But there is more to life than food and money and women."

"But what would I do? I've always lived in your shadow, following Father." Chin looked broken, disappointed. "I don't know how to be a Christian."

"It may be time to live in the shadow of Jesus now, and not in the shadow of other men." Song rose from the chair behind the desk. "You have a home in Akita, Brother."

"And leave all this?" Chin's face showed his shock.

"We can gain the whole world, Brother." Song moved to the door, and Titus opened it for him, viewing the humble man's strength differently having seen his grace in action. "But it can cost us our soul. I love you, Chin. Don't make the same mistakes Father and I made in our earlier lives."

Nepal – Present Day

Oleg's mood was dark, and he was nervous that his flesh would rise above the Holy Spirit's influence as he dealt with the brothel situation in Kathmandu. Since his weakness was so evident in his eyes— yearning to take vengeance into his own hands for Ercan Sanli's sister—he prayed in the bathroom of their hotel room for thirty minutes before departing.

Ercan stood from his seat on the bed when Oleg emerged from the bathroom.

"I heard you praying," Ercan said quietly. "Following Jesus is very confusing. I've never felt so vulnerable, and yet so confident."

Oleg smiled and clapped his large friend on his massive shoulder.

"When our flesh is weakest, and we see ourselves in a truly needy state, then we are strongest in the power of Christ." Oleg removed his silenced COIL sidearm from under his mattress and inserted it into the shoulder holster he hadn't unstrapped since returning from the red light district. "We need the fullest measure of God's grace tonight. Titus—the Serval—taught me to withdraw to empty myself for God to fill me up as often as possible, not just before operations. But some- times I don't remember to do so until I face a weight beyond my strength."

"While you were in there, I prayed, too. God has given me peace about staying in Kathmandu." Ercan pointed at Oleg's sidearm. "But I'll need a tranq-gun of my own, you understand. Carrying that shotgun for so many years—killing is the way of the *Soldiers of Mahdi*. But it's no longer my way."

The two left the hotel and took a taxi to the avenue where Rikta's beauty salon was open late into the evening, serving the women of the night as they made themselves presentable to nationals and foreigners alike. Since both Oleg and Ercan were obviously foreigners, they received subtle offers as they walked down the street.

"I can imagine cleaning up this street," Ercan said with a nervous chuckle. "And that Rikta woman is the right kind of ally to have beside me."

"God will guide you as you seek to further His Kingdom."

Oleg nodded at Ercan as if to say they'd continue their conversation later, then he left Ercan on the street outside the brothel that was owned by the father and son pair. Inside, Oleg was reminded of a cathouse he'd once seen in an old American Western movie. There was a counter where tea was served instead of beer, and empty tables where clients could sit and wait. A rickety stairway clung to a wall that led to a balcony level of closed doors.

Three women sat on worn sofas against the wall opposite the stairway, but no clients were in sight. An older man stood up behind the counter, setting aside his cell phone.

"Do you speak English?" Oleg asked. He'd already decided to handle the situation as Titus had taught him—with complete transparency and boldness. And wit, if it came to him.

"Yes. English." He set a cup on a coaster and filled it with herbal tea. "Welcome to Kathmandu."

"Thank you." Oleg picked up the cup and pretended to take a sip. He wouldn't drink from the cup of a man who kept women locked in servitude. Considering the three prostitutes, he noticed they tried to present themselves in Westernized fashion, but seduction was the same everywhere, and Oleg felt a frown forming on his face. "Are you the owner?"

"Yes. My son and me." The man glanced at a closed door behind the counter, which perhaps led to their residence. "Is there something I may offer you? Or . . . someone I may introduce to you?"

"All three girls—how much for all three for one hour?" Oleg produced a wad of American bills. "I hear it's about ten dollars for one. How about I give you one hundred?"

"*One hundred?*" The man fidgeted and picked at a mole on his jaw. "Why would you do that?"

"I'd like the girls to make themselves scarce while you, me, and your son talk." Oleg set the bill on the counter and slid it toward the man. Usually, he enjoyed watching Titus flash his riches around to accomplish his goals for God. Now, he understood why Titus gave so much so often; the riches of the world moved the hearts of the world. "I insist."

The man swiped the money into a pocket and signaled the girls to approach.

"Room number one at the top of the stairs."

"No, I said I want your workers to leave." Oleg smiled like Titus would've smiled, even though he knew he wasn't as charming as Titus. "You and I are going to talk. They can go spend time with my friend outside. He's actually an old acquaintance of yours."

The girls, apparently understanding English, hesitated, and looked nervously at their owner.

"They're not allowed to leave." The man's hand drifted out of sight behind the counter. Oleg wondered if he had a weapon. Probably. The girls were certainly kept under control somehow. "They belong here."

Rather than invite any violence, Oleg smoothly withdrew his firearm and set it on the counter. His intentions seemed obvious.

"They don't belong to you right now." Oleg nodded his head. "I just paid for them, right? Go outside, girls. My friend is waiting for you."

The gun seemed to remove any immediate threat the owner held over the girls. They stumbled in high heels out the front door to where Ercan had agreed to escort them down to the salon for Rikta to explain everything.

Focusing again on the owner, Oleg noticed the man's hand was once again in sight.

"I'm putting you out of the brothel business in Kathmandu." Smiling again, Oleg felt the presence of God wash over him, the peace and confidence that empowered him to shine brightly in the darkness. "If you don't leave peacefully, you'll be brought up on charges of kidnapping and torture."

"What? I've never done any of those things!" He pointed after his absent prostitutes. "They all came to me. I gave them a home! A job!"

"What would the authorities say about Irem Sanli you're holding upstairs?" Oleg bluffed, praying she was still there. "Is she here willingly? I don't think so."

The owner's eyes gazed up at the ceiling as if he could see into the room where Irem was locked away.

"Why do you care about her? She's just a dirty Kurd. Her family didn't even want her!"

"Her family wants her back. They were wrong to sell her. And you were wrong to buy her. Look at me. I'm a foreigner. So is Irem. I could raise such a ruckus that you would become the most wanted man in Nepal."

"This is my home!"

The door behind the counter opened, and a young man walked out. His face was greasy, and he held a chicken bone in his hand. He stopped at the sight of Oleg and the gun.

Oleg saw the opportunity to punctuate his seriousness to the owner. He picked up his sidearm and shot a silenced round into the son's chest. The young man dropped his chicken bone and collapsed, but his father fell against the back shelves as if he were the one struck. His mouth gaped as he stared down at his son.

"You have twenty minutes to collect your things and leave." Oleg holstered his gun. "And you'll never return. Understand?"

"I understand!"

Oleg escorted the man through the back apartment to collect a bundle of possessions. Then Oleg explained that his son wasn't dead, only tranquilized, so he collected belongings for his son as well.

By the time Ercan returned from Rikta's salon and walked into the brothel, the son was groggily regaining consciousness.

"I remember you," the owner said to Ercan as he helped his son toward the front door, their possessions tied to their backs. "You have betrayed us!"

"No, I betrayed my sister." Ercan gazed up at the closed doors on the second story. "Oleg, get him out of my sight before I forget to love my enemies as Jesus would."

Following the two previous owners outside, Oleg watched them walk solemnly down the smelly street. As triumphant as he felt, his joy wasn't the same as it would've been had Titus been there, confronting evil with him. He missed his brother, the man who'd led him to Christ.

Back inside the brothel, he was struck by a wail from the second story. The door was ajar to one of the rooms, and he could hear Ercan cry from within. His words were indiscernible as he wept before his sister. Oleg hopped onto the counter to sit. He closed his eyes and felt bittersweet tears well up. Sin had caused the Sanli family such anguish, and the sounds he heard from upstairs—it was too painful to bear, but he listened, anyway—to Ercan's brokenness, and a woman's gentle voice, her weeping, and her forgiveness. It was tender music to God's heart, Oleg knew—the reconciliation of a brother and sister under the worst strain imaginable. It was too terrible and too beautiful all at once.

Shanghai – Present Day

Commander Tond-zu felt invincible. Shanghai's princes wanted to be his friend, and the princesses of Beijing invited him to dinner. No one commented about his yawning or his missing teeth any longer. He wore the best suits and enjoyed the fiercest loyalty from police agents around the city.

In his office in Shanghai Tower, he picked up his phone and tapped his finger on the CALL icon over Warden Fongdu Jen's name. He hadn't seen his old military friend in twenty years, but they'd grown up on the streets together, committed atrocities together. Tond-zu didn't need to see his old friend to know he could trust him implicitly. Several times a year, he sent the warden prisoners, oftentimes Christians, to warehouse until death at Hudie Valley Prison. The place stunk of death, Tond-zu felt, but he paid Fongdu Jen well from an automated account each month.

The warden never complained, and only wrote Tond-zu occasional official briefings about the prison's status: occupancy, deaths, and arrivals. Tond-zu barely glanced at the briefs, usually. But the deaths always intrigued him. There were a lot of deaths in Hudie, whether from illness or mistreatment, Tond-zu didn't care. The deaths were important only for the sake of knowing how many more inmates he could send to Fongdu. Hudie's dungeons were really only equipped to house about forty prisoners comfortably. How Fongdu housed over three hundred, Tond-zu didn't know. But the overflowing capacity limited Tond-zu from sending more prisoners there. So, he usually sent only those criminals who had offended him personally, which meant Christians.

Touching his bruised knuckles, he relished the memory of the torture from the day before. A young Christian evangelist had been his subject. Tond-zu had felt certain the weak pacifist would talk and finally disclose the secrets of Steve Brookshire's sub-net that secured the Christian network across China. But no. The man had died and Tond-zu was left with his bruised knuckles. Later, he would write up the man's death as a suicide. No one in China asked questions about suicides.

Leaving Steve Brookshire alive didn't feel like the victory Tond-zu was hoping for. Besides, Steve was one of Peng's pets. It was time for Steve to die, and die badly.

Warden Fongdu Jen picked up after the third ring.

"How are you, old friend?" the warden asked. "Sorry, I'm winded. I was down in the courtyard, overseeing a . . . procedure."

"Ah, then I'm the one who is sorry for interrupting." Tond-zu chuckled, imagining the enjoyment the warden could relish as sovereign over his valley. "Listen, things haven't gone well hunting down some government conspirators. I'd like Steve Brookshire's other leg, and then I want him dead."

"His . . . leg?"

"Yes. The Sakana family took his first leg, trying to make him talk. I'd come do it myself, but I drove out there almost two years ago. Just send me his other leg, and don't use anesthetic, like the first time."

"And then you want him killed?"

"As slowly as you want." Tond-zu chuckled. "Put the leg on dry ice, too. I don't want it to stink up my office. It'll be my trophy, among others."

"That sounds like something my men would enjoy doing. I'll fit it into our schedule."

"I thought you'd like that." Tond-zu yawned. "I'll include a little something extra in next month's deposit. Get to it when you can. I've been meaning to ask, do you still have a prisoner name Cao Yutong?"

"Uh, I haven't seen the name among the deceased recently," Fongdu said. "You want him dead, too?"

"No, no." Tond-zu considered what he'd like his old predecessor, Peng Zemin, to endure, who he'd had put away under the new name. "Put him in a leper cell. I like the thought of him having leprosy."

"I'll have him moved."

"Excellent. I look forward to receiving Brookshire's leg—when you get to it."

He hung up. His office door opened and Tond-zu drew his sidearm and aimed it at the intruder. His secretary froze, her mouth gaping in fear.

"Get out! Get out! I told you never to enter without knocking!"

"But I did knock, sir."

"Get out! Get out!"

She fled without closing the door. Tond-zu took a couple deep breaths, calming his heart. He was still edgy about his past interactions with Rashid al-Sabur. The mastermind had made him put Peng away, then Tond-zu hadn't received his cut of their deal over the coal-bearing land. Tond-zu had the distinct impression that he'd been used by Rashid for something sinister, but he didn't know what. Twice in the past week, he thought he'd seen Rashid from a distance, stalking him, maybe planning to kill him, to shut him up about what he'd done. Search as he might, Tond-zu couldn't find the land Rashid had said he meant to steal. It all seemed like a farce now, and what Tond-zu didn't understand made him very paranoid.

He holstered his weapon. What he needed was a victory for himself, a true triumph. The leg of Steve Brookshire would suffice, for now. Finally, the Christian behind the sub-net would be no more!

CHAPTER TWELVE

Hudie Valley – Present Day

Steve tried to smooth the wrinkles from his peasant clothing as he stood nervously outside the Hudie Prison gate. The night before, Zou had visited his cottage to tell him his father wanted to see him the following day—inside the prison walls. Though Steve had never been invited inside before, he expected no less from God to move this way—after Steve had prayed so fervently the past months.

No longer was Steve drawn to plans of escape from the valley. He viewed this change of heart as nothing less than a miracle by God inside him. It seemed insane to remain in captivity when he could easily escape on foot now. His body was lean and strong, maybe stronger than before he'd lost his leg. His walking ability had been fully restored by the iron leg held fast by the woven cups, and attached to his stump. And yet, through much prayer in seeking God's desire for his life, his own desire had conformed to God's, regardless of his comfort level or the threat of Tond-zu attempting to kill him.

His relationship with Warden Fongdu Jen's children had developed, though his daughter Lijia was often attending a school in Bayan Nur. But younger Zou was too unruly—as he himself had confessed to Steve. Therefore, his father chose to continue to educate him inside the prison. Zou was more than happy with the arrangement since he'd learned to swim, and he'd made many friends with the farmer children. And, of course, there was story night!

The gate squeaked open. The guard who'd treated Steve harshly months earlier now bowed his head in greeting. Steve made a point to bow lower, however, to show his willingness to submit.

"The warden will see you now."

Steve walked through the gate and gazed up at the massive walls that now encompassed him. The rock was clean of mold, unlike the outside, and the central lawn was trimmed almost perfectly, making it seem artificial.

"*Bao'r!*" Zou called from the balcony two stories up. "Come up! I showed Father the story book you gave us!"

"Wonderful!" Steve said, though immediately broke into a cold sweat.

He'd inquired carefully about the Bible story book he'd given the children months earlier, and Zou admitted he'd been reading it. Steve's impression had been that the child had cherished it as a fairy tale book, and as such, Steve's concern that it would fall into the wrong hands had faded away. But Steve's careful and direct challenges to Zou, backed by the Holy Spirit, were working on the boy's eternal soul. It was only natural that Zou should eventually speak to his authoritarian father about his ideas. The whole valley seemed to be talking about story night and the hope they now held in God.

As Steve climbed a stairway of stone, he looked down at the courtyard. Several guards stood, gazing up at him. They were hard-faced men with bamboo batons in their belts. If the conversation with Fongdu Jen went badly, Steve had no doubt he would get to know those guards and their batons much more intimately.

Behind the guards, an archway led into a dark-throated chasm to forty subterranean cells, as Steve had discovered through Zou. Steve wished he could enter the dreadful pits. He felt like weeping at the very thought of humans stored so near, and wanted to love them, encourage them. Perhaps, he thought, the way God would use him to show love would be for Steve to join them.

When Steve reached the balcony, Zou took his hand and led him through a white-curtained doorway into a luxurious office of rugs and lamps. Steve stopped and wondered if he'd entered another world— from misery to lavish comfort.

Warden Fongdu Jen rose from behind a desk Steve would've expected to find in a professor's private study. Framed paintings from China's culture and others, hung on the walls between military banners and large mirrors, giving the crowded room a strange dimension. On the desk sat the Bible story book, open about midway.

"Zou, go to your room to study."

The boy didn't hesitate, and Steve was reminded of the first day he'd met the strict man with one sagging eyelid. That day, Steve had almost been shot for saving Zou's life. What would happen once his father found out he'd made sure Zou was saved from eternal death?

Fongdu gestured to a polished wooden chair, and Steve sat down.

The warden sat on the edge of his desk.

"Thank you for coming."

"Thank you for receiving me." Steve's nerves were twitching, but he tried to relax since Fongdu's voice wasn't overly severe. Besides, how much and how often had Steve prayed about the warden? This was the moment in which God could move! "The farmers had the construction of a new containment wall in mind for me today. I enjoy the work, but this impressive collection of art is worth the visit."

"You've been teaching my son about *Li-mien tang-cia tih*."

Steve blinked. It was a phrase he'd used in the Bible story book, which many Chinese Christians throughout history had called the Holy Spirit, meaning *Resident Boss*, who guided His people from the inside. Denying the accusation was pointless. No one else would've taught the boy or written the book. He also couldn't deny that the story book was more than a collection of myths. He'd prayed too long for this moment!

"I'm in this valley for far greater things than building rice paddy containment walls, Warden."

The warden turned and spun a world globe on its axis, causing it to wobble as it rotated. As the man seemed distracted by the globe, Steve glanced at the curtained doorway. The summer air was warm. He imagined himself outside those terrible walls, among the farmers, wading through the flooded paddies, transplanting seeds from seed-beds to the rice terraces so they could mature. But if the warden chose, Steve might never leave those walls.

"Your answer tells me that you know what you've been teaching my son is wrong." His hand stopped the spinning globe. "Wrong, according to my government."

"Please understand, Warden, that I would rather break a government's ruling than deny the truth about the Creator. That's how much I care for your son and the others in this valley."

"Even if it means death?"

"Even if it means death, yes."

Fongdu stood and walked around his office. Steve waited for panic to overwhelm him, but God had brought him through too much to doubt His presence now. Silently, he thanked God for designing this visit, even if it did lead to his death!

"My son is under the impression that Resident Boss now lives inside him. When I asked what he meant, he showed me the book you compiled."

"I see." Steve fought a smile. "There's an ancient saying: sometimes the purest truths of all come through the mouths of children."

"Zou doesn't know any better. I'm just glad he told me first, rather than one of my men. They are loyal to me, but they are devoted first to the Communist Party. I trained them to be this way."

"It was not my intention to offend or—"

"I'm not offended." Fongdu turned sharply toward Steve. "I already witnessed your care for my children when you saved Zou from drowning, then taught them both to swim. You're not a wicked man, Steve Brookshire, regardless of Tond-zu's accusations against you. This leaves me in a very . . . sensitive situation."

Steve nodded, but without understanding. His every breath was a prayer for wisdom, clarity, and guidance.

"Please, help me understand."

"I read your book." Fongdu picked up an ornamental sword, and Steve felt his heart flutter. "I started it last night, and couldn't stop reading. I still haven't slept. I have many questions. There are things I don't understand."

"I see." Steve bit his lip. He felt like a triathlon finish line was in sight, and his race was almost complete. "The truths about God often have that effect on people."

Fongdu swished the sword in the air, testing the weapon's balance.

"I am exhausted from . . . facing many things you wrote about. If I believe that this One died for me, then you understand I am thrust into a situation of conflict." He set the sword down, and Steve sighed with relief. "The Communist Party is my god. If I take another—I cannot have two. I must leave one to take the other."

The joy welling in Steve's heart was almost too much to quench. He wanted to leap up and shake Fongdu's hand. Hug him, cry with him . . .

"I see. As a Party official, you're caught between two mountains."

"No, I'm not caught." Fongdu sat on his desk once again. "I'm fully convinced your words are true. There is power in them. I stand firmly, as of this morning on one mountain. I share my son's fascination with Resident Boss now inside me. That's why I cannot continue the life I have known. But I still have many more questions that your book didn't elaborate on. For instance, what should I do now?"

"Help me understand." Steve leaned forward.

"Half the prisoners below were sent to me by Tond-zu. I know they're Christians. As you can see, Tond-zu has paid me well for years." Fongdu held out his hands. "Now, I'm one of them; one of you. I can't be loyal to my new God if I kill my own people—His people."

Steve didn't want to awaken from this wonderful dream!

"All of this happened through the night?"

"Perhaps my pride and greed wouldn't let me see the truth earlier. Of course, I've never heard the words before, either. Now I understand. You've been a Christian for many years? Your file doesn't say."

"Almost twenty."

"Twenty! Well, then you must know. What should I do?"

"Regarding?"

"My loyalties to my new God. Aren't you listening? I can't release all of you. Tond-zu will catch you all immediately, and I would be executed. My children would be re-educated by force. But I think even force wouldn't work here. God is more powerful, isn't He? That's why losing even your leg didn't persuade you?"

"Yes, that's correct."

"My men will report me as soon as they notice something is amiss."

"I'm startled, Warden, that your first desire as a Christian is to release the Christians, but your discernment is wise for their safety and your own. This isn't a matter to rush into, but I'm certain God has the answer for you. This is where we can depend on Him to excel."

"Well, I refuse to be like Herod in your story. He took John's head for a hasty promise made to a dancer. The Party was my mistress. There will be no more victims as long as I am warden here." He indicated a pile of papers on the floor. "But who is a Christian and who is a legitimate criminal? This is hard to investigate from Tond-zu's confusing files. There are many false charges, I know, and some prisoners have no file at all."

"You'll need to interview each prisoner." Steve relished the idea of meeting fellow Christians in such a place! "I'll help you. But your guards need to be dismissed first, or they'll grow suspicious."

"How will this place operate without guards?"

"Perhaps you could institute new guards." Steve smiled. "Maybe from the prisoners, or from the farmers in the valley. Some of the young men are nearly of age. And I will volunteer, of course."

Fongdu brushed at a spot on his uniform

"I could transfer my men to other facilities. No, this won't work. We can't make a single prisoner into a guard as long as any of my men are still here."

"There's a solution." Steve eased himself from the chair to the floor. "We may not know what it is yet, but God will show us. Come down here. We need to pray like we've never prayed."

"You want me to get on the floor?"

"We're Christian brothers, now. There's no shame in bowing together to the Master over our lives and eternal futures."

Fongdu considered that for a moment, then sat down facing Steve. "What do we do?"

"Well, God is right here." Steve smiled. "We're going to talk to Him."

New York City – Present Day

When Corban Dowler was first abducted—crutches and all—off a street in New York City, he thought he was surely being transported to his death. There were a vast number of enemies who wanted him dead. But those who could smoothly kidnap him from downtown Manhattan, right off the sidewalk, were few.

His wrists were duct taped behind him, and the black hood over his head remained in place for over an hour. When his captors stopped the van in which they drove, they carried his crippled body across a windy expanse and up stairs. In minutes, he heard the hum of a small engine, and then he felt vibrations of the fuselage as the plane took off.

Once airborne, his hood was removed and his wrist tape was cut. Three tough-looking Korean youths sat across from him, almost daring him to say or do something contrary. They each had a firearm tucked into their waistbands.

Corban looked out the window. They were flying west. It didn't mean much to him, yet, but he hadn't waited to understand his situation before he'd started praying. He'd sponsored COIL operations into North Korea for years. If they'd finally tracked him down as the instigator of thousands coming to Christ, then the abduction and his pending death were worth it.

The plane descended to another remote airfield in what Corban guessed was Western Pennsylvania. He was duct taped and carried into a larger aircraft, then his wrists were loosed again. The jet flew west still, and Corban realized they'd upgraded planes to cross not only states, but seas. He was being transported to the Orient—in style.

One of the Korean thugs handed him an orange juice and napkin. Corban received it with two hands, as was polite in Korean culture, and sipped from the cup. He frowned at the interior of the jet. Some of the seats were missing in the rear of the cabin, as if removed for transporting bulk items. They hadn't hooded his head during the change of planes, so he'd glimpsed the jet's make and model. It was a Pilatus PC-24 twinjet, a recent favorite of smugglers, its reinforced landing gear and low drag making it an ideal short-field asset.

He chuckled to himself.

"Smugglers," he mumbled, and drank the rest of his juice. "For a minute there, I thought I was in trouble."

The nearest Korean refilled his juice without communicating. Corban didn't expect them to speak, which was certainly what they'd been ordered. By Titus.

Corban closed his eyes, crossed his arms, and settled in for a long flight overseas. He'd scheduled a couple meetings at COIL head-quarters for that day, but meeting with Titus was more important. And knowing the ex-smuggler's history as the Serval, he expected a meeting invitation in no other way. But he would have some choice words for Titus when they did finally meet.

As Corban felt the jet climb in elevation, he prayed for the right heart to deal with Titus at this stage in his Christian growth. The Serval was an influence in the world, having made whole countries shudder with annoyance, but he was a young Christian, still learning how God teaches His people, breaking the outer man at just the right moment to teach them to conform more fully to His will—for their own good.

Underneath it all, Corban knew the meeting would be tempered with disappointment. The meeting itself meant that Titus wasn't isolating himself any longer, but his recent failure had hurt them all. Finding Steve Brookshire and Lisa Kennedy alive now seemed to be an impossibility. That was a burden Titus would need help carrying.

The Steve Brookshire file was all but closed.

ʂ

South Korea – Present Day

Titus scooped the last of the chicken and rice stew from a shared bowl and slurped it down. Closing his eyes, he savored the rich flavors of Korea's Bukchon Hanok Village in Seoul. Not far away, the Han River split the sprawling city in two: the south with its modernism, and the north with its traditionalism.

Across the round table, Jeong Byeong-Cheol, also known as White Eye, touched his earpiece to turn off his phone.

"Your friend, Corban Dowler, is almost here." White Eye smiled mournfully. "I may regret not owing you a debt, Titus, because we won't have a reason to share a meal after this."

"Friends don't need a reason to share a meal." Titus rubbed his belly and studied White Eye's fellow gangsters, most of them professional thieves, all carrying weapons. "And I haven't decided if your debt is cleared yet."

"If you weren't so likeable, I would've killed you rather than pay the debt." White Eye rose from the table as a white car rolled up the street and stopped two feet away. "I never met a smuggler who convinced me that Jesus was worth knowing."

"So, you're convinced?" Titus remained seated.

"Perhaps at our next meal together, I will have an answer for you."

White Eye buttoned his jacket and waited as his men opened the back door of the white car. Corban Dowler struggled with his leg braces and crutches to stand. Titus hopped up and pulled his boss by his shoulder from the car and steadied him on his feet, then White Eye climbed in and sped away.

"That man looked familiar." Corban looked after the white car. "A friend of ours?"

"His uncle was Choi Jin-Seon. Our table's right here." Titus pulled out a chair for him. "He was one of the Christians Oleg and I pulled out of North Korea a few months ago. I didn't know his nephew was White Eye Jeong, a local criminal, until recently. I convinced him he owed me for getting his mother's brother out of a death camp."

"And he paid you?" Corban unlocked his braces and sat down.

"He paid me by listening to the gospel." Titus grinned. "And bringing you to me."

"And delivering your plane, apparently."

"You can't expect me to leave Asia. We're possibly days from cracking the Steve Brookshire mystery—me and Song Sakana." Titus signaled a waiter with two fingers. "*Ganjan-gejang.*"

"My Korean is a little rusty." Corban took a sip of water. "What did you order? I'm famished."

"Raw crab, soaked in fruit vinegar, sugar, and red chilies for four days. It's a little rich, but they serve it with rice for our sensitive pallets."

"Oleg should be here for this." Corban folded his hands on the table cloth and Titus met his eyes. "He's missed you, and he's not nearly as adept as you with the sat-watch."

"I really blew it in Shanghai, Corban." Titus' right hand touched his wrist where it was white from the missing Gabriel device. "I let everyone down."

"Except the refugees you saved. You didn't let them down. They're alive because of you." Corban frowned. "You had a decision to make. I may have tried to juggle with the same things, Titus. We can't withdraw from saving lives just because there's a risk it may mess up another operation. You and I are the type of men who believe God expects us to trust Him through everything He sets before us. Wes Trimble and Rashid, and even Oleg, may not understand that yet, because it's a special calling. A special burden. A *blessed* burden. That's why some are leaders, some are followers, and some are loners."

"Wow. This is unexpected. You're not mad?"

"Oh, I'm mad." Corban chuckled. The raw crab for two was placed in the center of the table, along with a huge bowl of rice. "Didn't you just eat with White Eye?"

"Song Sakana has had me fasting off and on for a week." Titus prayed for them both over the food, then gestured with a wooden serving spoon. "Go on, tell me how mad you are."

"I'm mad that you vanished."

"Well, I messed up."

"We're not your accusers, Titus. We're your family. God's our Judge, and His love is always offered graciously. Your family may correct you, but that's because we're your support system. If we all ran away every time a mission went sideways, we'd never rescue anyone from anywhere. And if you're back on the trail of Steve Brookshire, obviously, a vacation of self-pity was pointless."

"It connected me with Song Sakana."

"Don't take credit for God turning your insecurities into diamonds. You left us questioning our confidence in you. And Oleg relies on you more than you think. You led him to Christ. When we have a lapse in faith, it affects others."

"It ain't easy being perfect," Titus said with a full mouth. "Is that what you expect?"

"It's not about perfection, Titus. It's about communication. When something goes dark, we communicate. Communication sheds light on the darkness. We communicate with God. We communicate with one another. Only fools separate themselves. Proverbs 18:1."

"That verse has been coming up a lot lately." They ate in silence for a moment. Titus felt an inch tall. He hadn't even thought about Oleg and the others still needing him—only about his own embarrassment. "I was wrong to run away. I see that. But that's something I can correct."

"Then I forgive you for kidnapping me." He smiled. "You know, Luigi tries to surprise me with his antics, too. It's possible you're not invincible in this game, if it's a game you're starting."

"It ain't easy reaping what I sow!" Titus grinned and slapped the table. "Challenge accepted. Now, tell me where I can find Oleg."

"I'll tell you, but him—you better not kidnap. He's liable to hurt someone."

"Like a bull in a playpen."

"Just get your watch back on and get to work." Corban locked his braces and stood upright. "Write me a report when you can. You've probably been calling your wife all along, haven't you? That's why she hasn't been calling COIL nonstop."

"She helped me through this, too. Where are you going?"

"COIL has contacts in the city I haven't seen in a couple years. I'll get home on my own." Corban held out his hand, and they shook firmly. "Bring Steve and Lisa home, Titus. We'll be praying."

"I'm all over it."

Titus watched his boss hobble away. He pondered running after Corban to tell him about the cancer, and that he hadn't felt better in months. As soon as he could, he would get home and see his oncologist. God's healing hand couldn't have come at a better moment!

He'd known his time on earth was limited, but now? If he'd truly been healed, then he would celebrate by offering his life more fully back to his Healer. Anything less, he'd seem ungrateful!

Hudie Valley – Present Day

Steve realized he'd entered a new phase of his work for Christ in China, and he knew his effectiveness would be directly connected to his closeness to the Lord. He continued to devote himself to prayer and seeking God's face as he trembled at the possibilities ahead.

Two days after Warden Fongdu Jen had first invited him to the prison, their plan was roughly in place—to correct injustices under Fongdu's reign in the valley, and to protect those who were vulnerable. Everything had moved rapidly, and though rushing things made Steve nervous, he understood the urgency in Fongdu's heart to set right the many wrongs he'd presided over for years. His first desire was to set free his Christian brothers and sisters who were housed in the dungeons below, but this was no easy task, especially with Communist Party guards as prison personnel.

There was too much for only two men to accomplish, especially with the five seasoned prison guards who'd been trained by the Communist Party to suspect any notion of disloyalty in their comrades, even in their superiors. Hudie Valley was isolated from the politics of the east, but the communist hammer had been so restrictive for generations that Fongdu simply couldn't trust his own men to defy the government with him. Even in a secret defiance.

After an especially late story night at Steve's cottage, which had been purposely planned with the lengthy story of Joseph, the farmers returned to their own cottages. Steve remained outside, gazing up at the sky and sensing the actual presence of the God of Joseph, who made lives profitable even in captivity.

One by one, the adults arrived back at his cottage, their children now sleeping on their mats in their own cottages. Steve had tried to remain casual about his visits with the warden the last two days, but he couldn't proceed without his fellow farmers being aware of what was happening. And they were only too willing to meet secretly in the night, by his invitation, to discover what the warden was up to.

It was well after midnight when everyone was finally gathered inside Steve's small dwelling. He stood against the wall to make room. The four elderly basket-weavers sat on his mat, and he held a single candle close to his face. A hush went through the room.

"The only true God has touched Warden Fongdu Jen's heart toward our favor," Steve said.

A gasp and hushed cheer erupted inside the cottage. It was a full minute before Steve was able to continue, his own suppressed excitement matching theirs.

"There's great danger for Fongdu Jen if we betray him, so for his sake, for our sakes, for God's sake—let's not think lightly of this new brother who has joined us in compassion."

"Who would we tell, *Bao'r*?" a young mother asked. Her brother was reportedly housed inside the prison. "We never leave the valley. We're here for our families."

"Fongdu will make it possible for you to leave the valley. If you want to. With your relatives freed from prison."

Steve expected a cheer so loud that they'd hear it inside the prison walls. Instead, no one made a sound. Finally, little Shek-jai raised her hand.

"*Bao'r*, where we go?" she asked in broken Mandarin. "Arrest again at home."

"Maybe." Steve nodded, feeling the weight of their fears, their trust. "Maybe Hudie Valley becomes our new home, permanently. Fongdu has designed a way for us to remain safe. This valley provides everything we need. We can live here, and learn more about the Creator who has blessed us so richly."

"How will the warden release our families?" an elderly woman asked. She wasn't one of the weavers, but many of the others looked up to her since she'd worked in the valley for over thirty years, hoping her husband was still alive. "Fongdu doesn't have that authority to do what you say."

"He has God's authority, and if we agree, he'll have our help." Steve tried to smile, but the whole plan in his mind seemed more questionable now that he had to explain it to others. "We need to find guards for him from nearby towns. The warden will transfer the old guards out when their replacements arrive. That means some of you need to go into Bayan Nur to find guards to hire. We need five in exchange for the old guards. Then, Fongdu can begin to release our families."

A young man Steve knew as Vu Qing stood up in the back of the room. Almost twenty years old, he'd remained in the valley when all the other men had left. As an orphan, he'd worked in the fields for years with his mother in the prison.

"Make me a guard, *Bao'r*," he said, "and I'll hire four more."

No one seemed to oppose the idea. Vu Qing was young, but the work in the field had given him the shoulders of a man.

"Very well. I'll have the warden drop a uniform over the wall tomorrow. You can wear it into town."

"How will we remain safe if we have to live here, *Bao'r*?" a woman asked. Steve had taught her son how to swim. "Won't Shanghai suspect the warden?"

"The warden will maintain appearances, and the government will send supplies monthly as it always has. Once the new guards are in place, the warden and I will begin the long process of interviewing the prisoners and releasing them with warnings. Warden Fongdu Jen has said that Shanghai never visits to inspect their disorganized records. They only communicate through the computer. The facade could work for years, but some of you may want to relocate to feel safer."

Steve bit his lip. The people were uncertain. For years, even decades, the valley had been their home. Their misery and despair had become familiar to them. Now that he was upsetting their lives with the very liberty they wanted, they were afraid.

"I'll be staying in the valley," he assured them, "until all of your families are complete again. But this process will take months. There are almost three hundred prisoners inside. Some are actual criminals, and some are political prisoners. This is a very sensitive situation, so I'm willing to answer your questions and concerns as they arise. But for now, Vu Qing and I need to coordinate the hiring of four more guards, and we all need to continue to work as usual."

"We should pray again," Vu Qing suggested. "Pray for us, *Bao'r*. This plan of yours is very strange."

Without hesitation, the entire room moved to their knees. Even the four weavers knelt on Steve's mat, bowed their heads, and folded their hands.

Steve watched them for a moment, as they waited for him to pray. They'd never seen a Bible. They'd never heard a proper hymn sung or been inside a chapel. But they'd learned to believe, simply because they'd heard the truth about Almighty God. They believed, and that was enough to change everything.

Kneeling, Steve prayed with tears.

CHAPTER THIRTEEN

China – Present Day

Titus tightened his sat-watch around his wrist and checked its functions before he nodded at Oleg. Behind them, two jets were parked on a dusty airstrip in central China.

"Really, I don't mind you wearing it. You sure you want to give it back?"

"I never even figured out how to use all the functions." Oleg scratched his head. "Besides, it's your watch. It was enough trouble doing your job while you were on vacation, let alone figuring out how to operate COIL tech."

"Sorry about that, Oleg." Titus shook his head at himself. "I was wrong to leave. The Lord helped me see some things. Did you have any troubles?"

"You mean while I was pretending to be you, running your operation?" Oleg slugged Titus on the shoulder, sending him sideways as they approached Titus' smuggler jet. "I had a break from your holey socks. How could I be missing that? What's the point of wearing socks at all if they're hardly there? I hope you got some new ones."

"How do you think my old socks would feel if I just one day replaced them with new ones?" Titus climbed into the cockpit of his jet. Outside, the plane that had brought Oleg to their secret rendezvous taxied north, and took off. "It ain't easy being loyal to a pair of old socks, Oleg, but once disloyalty sets in, it trickles down to other areas of your life."

"Hey, you're the one who went on vacation, abandoning me." Oleg fastened his shoulder straps. "Talk about sock loyalty! How do you think I feel?"

Titus bowed his head, then slowly turned to Oleg.

"Oleg, brother?"

"Yeah?" Oleg raised his eyebrows. "What is it?"

"I wasn't being sensitive. I see that now. You could've just told me. Deep down, you really want my socks, don't you?"

Titus reached to unlace his boots.

"Would you just fly the plane?" Oleg crossed his arms. "Now I see why Annette doesn't mind you going on missions so often. She can't stand your mouth—or your socks!"

Titus laughed and flew the jet west. They talked and prayed together, and Titus finally shared his news with Oleg about the cancer. He told him he needed more testing, but he was feeling no more symptoms. Oleg wept openly and praised God that his closest friend wasn't leaving permanently quite yet.

Two hours later, Titus set the plane down on a straight stretch of dirt road outside Golmud in the Kunlun Mountains. The wilderness of Western China sprawled in every direction, but the search for Steve and Lisa had to begin somewhere.

Donning pointy grass hats that shielded their faces, and traditional tunics that covered their sidearms, they left the plane in an open field and walked toward a village not yet in sight, though visible on Titus' watch. He prayed aloud as they hiked closer to the village, the darkening sky threatening the jagged mountains. The rugged scenery and foreboding weather seemed almost spiritual—a showdown between two forces as the two men applied themselves to the mission.

The closer they walked to the village, the more Titus kept his head bowed to hide his white face, and he kept his hands under the sleeves of his tunic. Since Oleg was shorter, he was less conspicuous than Titus, who was over six feet. The private citizens of the secluded village hurried past them with suspicious glances.

"There it is." Oleg gestured with his elbow, drawing Titus' attention to a complex on the edge of the village. Cement and barbed wire rose grotesquely from the landscape. "It's hard to believe we've got Christian brothers and sisters in that place."

"Just keep walking." Titus splashed through a puddle and angled down a street toward the tallest building in the village. "Song Sakana said he'd meet us up here."

"You have a plan to bust Steve out of that place?" Oleg sighed. "Never mind. You never have a plan. Our TNT and rifles in the plane will be enough, right?"

"There's a long list of prisons where Steve could be. This might not be our last stop in China. He may not even be here."

They reached the building, which had a cement foundation, then stepped behind it under an awning as it began to rain.

"We're wanted foreigners," Oleg mumbled, "but we're hiding from the rain behind a Chinese Communist Party administration building. How long do you want to wait for this guy?"

"All night, if we have to."

"What if he gets caught? Plan B?"

"Now, you know I don't even have a Plan A." Titus stepped into the rain. "There he is. Let's see if we're gonna be up all night or if we're flying to the next village."

Oleg hung back to cover Titus as he moved forward to intercept Song Sakana on the muddy street. Taking Song's arm, Titus led him toward the intimidating cement structure in the distance, doing their best to avoid mud puddles and the attention of onlookers.

"Seems they could use some of that prison cement to pave these muddy streets," Titus said.

"They're too busy inside the prison to tend to the needs of the village." Song glanced over his shoulder. "The prison was built around a coal mine—four shafts, straight into the mountainside. I paid a guard for information, but my questions made him nervous. He gave the money back."

"Then he's a liability." Titus looked around, then put a spy glass to his eye to study the prison walls. "You can't let Party officials know we're in town, Song, especially if they're nervous."

"Don't worry. I tranquilized him." Song smiled. "You're not the only Christian with a past, remember? You gave me that tranq-pen for a reason."

"Where is he?"

"Tied up in his home. He lives alone."

"So, give it to me straight, brother. Is our guy or Lisa here?"

"There are Westerners inside, but not Steve or Lisa."

"I guess that's both good and bad." Titus pocketed his spy glass. "It's bad he's not here, since that means we haven't found them, yet. But it's good we don't have to figure out how to infiltrate that place. It looks impregnable."

"But the guard said there are other Christians in there." Song's face appeared pained. "I thought that's what you COIL people do—rescue the persecuted. They'll die in there. They're being worked to death."

"How many guards are inside?"

"Thirty, and about twenty civilian miners who oversee the prisoners' work. But there are five hundred prisoners."

"Whoa." Titus paused in thought. "It ain't easy leaving people behind, but we're not equipped for that kind of prison break. We'd need a month to prep and twenty operatives to bust in there. We're after one man and one woman. There are a lot of wrongs I wish we could set right, but a true Christian knows the score. We should all expect persecution, but Steve and Lisa—they have secrets that could possibly affect millions. We have to keep our eye on the—"

A sharp whistle drew Titus' attention up the street. Oleg had whistled the warning. Four Party officials were walking toward them.

"How far away is your plane?" Song asked.

"Too far for us to run to." Titus turned his back to the officers and reached inside his cloak to unclip his holster.

"Good thing we don't have to run." Song set his hand on Titus' arm. "You can keep that gun hidden. I have a truck two buildings away."

"I'm beginning to like working with you!" Titus clapped Song on the back as Oleg reached their position.

"But it's still two buildings away." Song's eyes grew larger. "How do we get out of town alive if they're onto us?"

"It's no problem." Titus winked. "Oleg, we have a Joshua 8:15 situation."

The officers were hastening their pace, marching straight through puddles to reach them. Civilians hustled indoors, sensing a conflict.

"Where's my retreat?" Oleg asked.

Titus glanced back at the officers.

"Two blocks east. Song has a truck. Careful, they're armed."

"Aren't they always?" Oleg chuckled and shoved Titus away.

Titus guided Song down the street, away from the soldiers. Song looked back as they left Oleg behind.

"He's sacrificing himself?" Song asked.

"No, nothing that drastic, or permanent." Titus moved around the corner of a building. His last glimpse of Oleg was of the big Russian flopping on the muddy ground and convulsing at the officials' feet. "We made an agreement a long time ago that he'll keep me from being captured, and I'll fetch him back if he gets caught."

"You're very casual about this. You're not concerned?"

"He's Oleg Saratov, and there are only four guys. He probably already tranquilized them."

The two reached the truck and Song climbed behind the wheel. Titus held up his hand.

"Start the engine, but don't drive away." He touched the screen of his watch and zoomed in on the overhead drone image of the village. "Okay, back up along this street about fifty yards."

Song reversed the truck fifty yards. Oleg stumbled out of an alley. He was covered in mud and gasping for air. Titus threw the door open and moved over so Oleg could leap in.

"Punch it, Song!" Titus held mud-caked Oleg as Song swerved the truck and almost lost Oleg out the door before he could close it. With the door closed, Titus used a finger to touch Oleg's muddy cheek. "You are Oleg, aren't you?"

"I tranquilized those four, but ten more were already on their way!" Oleg tucked a tranq-pen into a pocket and drew his sidearm. "Our take-off is going to be tight."

Song drove madly out of the village onto the rutted road leading into the countryside. The plane came into view, but Titus continued to study his watch.

"They're coming after us in their own vehicles. Song, block the road with the truck. I don't want them driving up on us as we take off."

"We didn't even break anyone out!" Oleg rested his hand on the door handle, ready to lunge out. "Why all the fuss?"

"We're foreigners poking around a secret labor prison camp. And Steve and Lisa aren't inside." Titus covered his watch with his sleeve and prepared for his own exit. "China doesn't like people to know where they keep the critics of the communist government. We may have discovered nothing, but they'll still keep us as guests until we confess something. If they catch us."

"Make sure they don't catch us!" Song hit the brakes, causing the tires to slide in the mud. The truck came to rest across the road between steep ditches on each side of the road.

Titus piled out of the truck with Oleg and leaped a ditch. Twenty yards later, he crawled under the belly of the jet to pull down the steps. But he suddenly stopped and pointed at Oleg who was panting not far behind.

"Hey! You ain't climbing into my spotless plane like that!"

Titus laughed as Oleg made a face and pulled off his muddy cloak while he ran.

In the cockpit, Titus flipped switches, ignoring Song's yells from outside the plane. The engines roared to life. Stripped to his shorts, Oleg scrambled aboard, holding his bundle of mud-caked clothes. Song slipped into the copilot seat as the jet began to roll down the field.

"The ground is soft." Titus winced, applying more power. "The fuselage may be coated with Teflon, but prayer at this point is probably in order."

Song instantly clasped his hands and mumbled in his native Japanese. From the cabin, Oleg shouted incoherently in Russian, probably peering out the port windows at the Chinese vehicles roaring up the road behind them. They could hear gunshots popping outside over the whine of the two engines.

Titus clenched his teeth as the jet gained speed and lifted off. They climbed quickly, then he corrected his altitude to fly low, in case a radar station was near.

"The cargo bay took a couple rounds," Oleg reported. "Is that bad?"

"Not nearly as bad as our fuel tank being hit." Titus tapped a gauge on the control panel. "We're too deep in China to fly out. I've got to set her down."

"None of us can be taken." Song's face was pale. "They'll execute us after what we just did back there, even if we didn't do much but tranquilize a few people."

Titus considered their options for a moment. He'd been fortunate to spend little time locked in a cell, but this deep in China as a tall, white man—it wouldn't be easy to get to the coast without being arrested. Now, they were wanted in the west, and because of Shanghai, his face was still on wanted bulletins in the east. Deep down, he wondered if God were telling him to abandon the search for Steve altogether, and focus on saving themselves. They'd barely started to search for the missing COIL personnel, and already it was over.

"I can patch the bullet holes," Titus finally said, "but it'll take time on the ground—dangerous time."

"I'm not willing to abandon our search for Steve." Song looked to Oleg. "Are you?"

"I didn't come to China to depend on a plane." Oleg's voice was low and serious. "This plane is just a convenience. We can move on foot and on train across the country, even if it takes us ten times longer to check all the prison sites."

"This is a ten-million-dollar loss I'm not willing to write off quite yet." Titus checked his instruments. "You two go to the next prison site and check it out. If we find Steve, we'll need the plane to make our exit fast to Japan. So, I'll stay back and repair her."

Flying out of Qinghai, Titus entered into his logbook that they'd crossed into Ningxia, a northern Chinese province. He set the plane down in a field of waist-high grass, far from the nearest city of Yinchuan on the other side of the Yellow River.

"We're here." Titus pointed to a spot on a map, and logged the coordinates from his watch into Oleg's sat-phone. "There are three other prisons for you guys to check in this neighborhood called Gansu. I'll leave you text updates, and you do the same for me. If you find Steve, I'll look for another landing strip farther upriver to arrange an extraction."

"The train can take Oleg and me through Gansu, and we'll find rides along the way. I just want to say . . ." Song covered his mouth for a moment. "Thank you for this. Thank you for helping me right this wrong. You're risking everything!"

"Song, if we weren't looking for Steve," Oleg said, "Titus would just find some other risk to dive into without a plan, or whole socks."

"It ain't easy being jealous of my socks." Titus raised his chin in mock pride. "Don't you two have some miles to cover before dark?" He touched his watch. "I'll have Marc put a Gabriel on you to track your phone, Oleg. Don't drop it in the river, or I'll be looking for four people instead of just two!"

Hudie Valley – Present Day

Steve couldn't remember being this nervous, even before a triathlon. The day had finally arrived, and Warden Fongdu Jen was about to receive the four newly-hired guards from the next town. And the five guards from the prison were gathered in the courtyard with their belongings. The warden was there with them, thanking them for their years of loyalty and expressing his regret that with their transfers to new posts, their families at the river town would also have to relocate.

From the balcony of Fongdu's quarters, Steve gazed beyond the wall at the ridge where five men approached the valley on the descending trail. One of the five was young Vu Qing, who put on a good show, his uniform freshly pressed like the others. Of course, the other four believed they were being hired for an actual job.

To the west, through the rice paddy expanse where the farmers had work to do, no one was working. Perhaps they were going through the motions of looking busy, but Steve knew enough about the flooded terraces now to see there was nothing actually being accomplished that day. There was too much anticipation for the success of Steve and the warden's plan for all their lives. They weren't about to miss the event by rebuilding containment walls and transplanting seeds for the second rice crop later that year.

Steve stepped away from the balcony and sat down on a sofa with hand-stitched seams. He bowed his head in prayer, thanking God for the drastic change in Fongdu's life. The man had even volunteered his expensive furnishings and paintings to finance released prisoners' newfound freedom, if they wanted to leave the valley.

Lifting his head, Steve acknowledged Fongdu's closed laptop on his expansive desk. In all the excitement of the warden's conversion and the strategizing for the farmers, contacting someone on the outside hadn't occurred to Steve. Until now. Now, he wondered if he had the perseverance to continue where God had planted him—when his ticket out of China was literally an email away. But a COIL rescue team, or any commotion at all, could disturb the fragile secret he and Fongdu had arranged. What was there to return so quickly to? Lisa was gone. After nearly two years missing, he doubted COIL was actively looking for him any longer. A few more months of silence wouldn't hurt anything, and a few months was just what he would need to screen all the prisoners for release.

"What's happening?" Zou emerged from the back bedroom rubbing his face from a night of sleep. "*Bao'r!* You look funny!"

Steve grinned and touched his shaved cheeks and trimmed goatee. His full beard was gone, and a PRC officer's uniform was draped over the chair in front of him. One of the weavers had tailored it for his tall frame.

"Your father is dismissing his old men." Together, they went to the balcony. For now, Steve still wore his peasant pajamas, which he wasn't especially quick to discard since he feared it would frighten his valley friends. But to operate inside the prison, he would need the sense of authority the uniform would project. "Your father's the bravest man I know, to risk all this for prisoners he doesn't even know."

"He won't even let me see them." Zou frowned. "Of course, he used to not let me play with the rice kids, either. Now, we're like family, right?"

"In the family of Christ, little brother."

Vu Qing and the new guards entered the prison gate. They looked very dapper in their crisp uniforms provided by Fongdu, and they stood for an instant, facing the men they were replacing, before they saluted. Fongdu saluted next, and the formalities were complete. The old guards filed out the gate and started up the ridge trail. From the balcony, Steve could barely see the roof of a bus in the parking lot waiting to take the men south to the river where they were meeting their families, unless their families were already on the bus. Prisons upriver had been found who needed more guards. Steve and Fongdu both hoped that Shanghai didn't notice the minor discrepancy: other prisons were receiving new guards transferred from Hudie Valley Prison, but Hudie wasn't receiving any transfers itself—on the books, anyway.

Below, the prison gate crashed closed. The five new guards continued to stand at attention as Fongdu addressed them as new employees. They weren't trained for such a job, but Fongdu would whip them into sharpness in their temporary roles. At least, they weren't wise to Communist Party regulations.

As Steve disrobed and drew on his own uniform, he listened to the warden's speech.

"You will not treat the prisoners badly. You will treat them as your own families. The slightest breach of this first rule will result in the gravest discipline!" Fongdu slapped his leg with a bamboo baton—an item none of these new guards had been given. "You have been hired for a short time only to keep the order as we release or transfer prisoners. You will feed the prisoners twice per day without speaking to them. The female prisoners are not to be touched. A female officer will be here momentarily to oversee the female prisoners. The slightest breach of this final rule will result in the harshest discipline!"

Steve cleared his throat as he descended the apartment rock steps to the courtyard. The new arrivals gawked at the tall, white man, and Steve affixed his most grim scowl on his face.

"This is Party Official Nee," Fongdu introduced. "Do not let his Western appearance confuse you. He is your superior in every way that I am. If he gives you a command, you obey as if it came from my very mouth!"

The guards cowered under Steve's angry stare as he paced in front of them. Only Vu Qing beamed with pride, his smile creeping onto his young face.

The men flinched at the pounding on the outside of the prison gate. Steve crossed the courtyard and wrenched down on a counter-weight that released the locking mechanism. He opened the gate, and Shek-jai walked stoutly through. In a PRC uniform, tailored into a skirt, blouse, and cap, the young mother from the field appeared quite attractive. Her hair had been brushed and pinned up under her cap. She'd been the only woman from the valley to volunteer for guard duty, leaving her son in the care of Wong-wei and the weavers.

Shek-jai fell in line beside Vu Qing and stood at attention.

"We have prisoners to process." Steve spoke in formal Mandarin as he walked in front of them. "Warden Fongdu Jen and I will be busy processing prisoners, but we won't be too busy to discipline any of you for an infraction. Sergeant Vu Qing and Sergeant Shek-jai, you have both been briefed on your duties. You will report to Warden Fongdu Jen the instant someone disobeys. You were each promised respectable wages, so do not ruin for yourselves this fruitful blessing!"

Steve nodded at Fongdu.

"You are dismissed!" the warden growled.

Though Vu Qing and Shek-jai had never been inside the prison before, they immediately instructed the other four as to where the kitchen, store room, and cells were located. Fongdu had gone to the valley cottages himself in the night to explain the routine to them, so his guards wouldn't know. Shek-jai's Mandarin was halting, but her aggressiveness didn't offer a hint of weakness in her authority. Steve knew her voluntary service was completely influenced by the possibility that she would find her husband still alive inside one of the subterranean cells. In Steve's breast pocket was a list of names from the farmers of their family members he would look for and release as fast as he could process initial prisoners.

The guards walked out of the courtyard and entered the dark archway that led to the cells. Steve watched them go, knowing that soon, he would venture below as well. But for now, as an officer, he was expected to leave interaction with the prisoners to the enlisted men.

"Officer Nee?" Fongdu waited on the stairs. "Are you ready?"

Steve smiled. The disorderly files on the three hundred prisoners awaited. The warden was wasting no time!

"Yes, I'm ready."

China – Present Day

Oleg held his rifle steady as he peered through the scope at Song Sakana a half-mile away. It'd been two days since he and Song had left Titus with the plane, and Oleg had felt uneasy ever since. In Song, he'd found a man of prayer, but Oleg was still concerned about their lack of support in the vast country. He just hoped Titus would abandon his plane if it were discovered on the grassy plain.

Far below the knoll on which Oleg lay camouflaged, Song stood with two PRC officers. He'd already discreetly handed them each an envelope of cash to pay for information, and according to what Oleg witnessed through the scope, the two officers were sharing plenty of intel. Even if they found out nothing about Steve and Lisa, they could pass on to COIL contacts what they learned from each secret prison and labor camp.

Swinging his scope up and away from the banks of the Yellow River, Oleg surveyed the prison they'd come to infiltrate, if Steve were found to be inside. This prison was nothing like the cement fortress up in the mountains. Here, the long prisoner shacks were made of corrugated metal, and there was no perimeter wall, only a fence with rusty wire strung carelessly from pole to pole. Oleg could see gaps in the wire he guessed he could squeeze through if he needed to sneak inside the prison during a night raid, but he wouldn't do so without proper coverage from Titus. He'd learned from experience that Titus would do just about anything for him, which gave Oleg a boldness to do just about anything to complete a mission. Song was an experienced Japanese mobster from Hong Kong with a special set of skills all his own, but Oleg preferred to place his confidence in Titus' sniper coverage more than Song's fluent knowledge of Chinese culture.

Thinking of Song, Oleg swept the banks of the river for his partner. Had he finished talking to the officers already? He realized he should've never taken his scope off the man! Frantically, he searched the edges of the river, two hundred yards upriver from where a dozen women toiled over laundry. The floating bridge near them was unoccupied. No Song.

Suddenly, Oleg spotted him. The Japanese man was being forcibly escorted toward the prison! Oleg exhaled smoothly as he used his scope to follow the two officers, with Song between them. Apparently, Song had approached the wrong two officers for information.

Oleg adjusted for the wind and settled his cheek against the stubby stock of the bullpup. Range five hundred yards and climbing, as Song was taken away at a brisk walk. He fired first at the man on the right. The .308 cartridge exploded from the barrel causing waterfowl on the river to take flight. As the officer collapsed, Oleg fired another round at the second officer.

An instant later, Song was running, his thick arms pumping, his small body surging down toward the river. The village and bridge seemed clear, but two dozen guards on the prison grounds were suddenly alert. Though their reaction to the gunshots was delayed, they certainly had an armory with more guns in it than Oleg had bullets.

Patiently, Oleg monitored Song's flight across the village and into the grass to the south. Song was a quarter-mile into the rolling plain before anyone in the prison spotted him. Three guards were crouched over the two unconscious officers, but there seemed only confusion as to how to respond.

Finally, an all-terrain vehicle laden with five guards roared out of the prison gate. They careened through the village, sending chickens squawking and civilians sprawling. When the ATV reached the bridge, Oleg fired two rounds into its windshield. They skidded to a halt, then reversed back into the village for cover.

By now, Song was over a distant hill, heading toward a rendezvous point. Not willing to make himself obvious, Oleg rose from his belly to his hands and knees, and crawled at a snail's pace over the knoll that had been his height advantage. Five minutes later, he brushed off the grass camouflage and stood upright. Prayerfully, he started walking northeast toward their rendezvous, hoping they didn't have to infiltrate the very prison they'd just stirred up!

Thirty minutes later, he came upon Song as he rose from hiding along the river grass.

"No one-legged foreigners here," Song reported as he recovered his pack from the reeds. "The guards took the bribe and they were still arresting me!"

"It's two days' hike to the next prison site." Oleg touched the screen of his sat-phone. "Unless we can catch a ride, it'll be a long two days, but word will be out now to watch for suspicious travelers."

"Then we walk. And pray"

Song started walking, but Oleg hung back. They couldn't expect to escape unscathed from too many more close calls. Oleg didn't like the thought of Chinese torture, even though he'd patiently endured his Iranian captors weeks earlier.

He used the sat-phone to text Titus a message: *"Still no S."* And the message from Titus was no more encouraging: *"Patched holes. Now must enter Wuzhong for fuel."*

Oleg let out a growl at the delay, not liking the idea of Titus walking alone into a small city so near where news of their shenanigans would have every government official on high alert.

CHAPTER FOURTEEN

Hudie Valley – Present Day

Steve and Fongdu Jen had agreed to process the female prisoners first. Vu Qing, in his crisp guard uniform, was all too pleased to fetch the first prisoner Steve asked for: Ghuning, his mother.

In the courtyard grass, a table had been set up where the warden was to sit, but Steve preferred to stand. That day's prisoner files lay fanned out before Fongdu. Steve occasionally glanced over to check details, though what few specifics the files held, he knew by heart from studying them diligently as he'd prepared to process the first few days of prisoners.

Ghuning was a defiant woman in her fifties. She held her head erect, her eyes daring the warden. Occasionally, she peered at Steve's face, who was certainly an odd presence in a PRC uniform. But nothing about the "hearing" was normal. Vu Qing held his mother by her arm, but neither mother nor son openly reacted, though Steve noticed Vu Qing's jaw trembling when his teeth weren't clamped shut. It was possible Ghuning didn't recognize her own son! The four hired guards, two on each side of the table, stood at attention, and for their sakes, even Shek-jai appeared vigilant and glaring to maintain the façade.

"You are Vu Ghuning?" Fongdu asked.

"You know I am. You were here when I came fourteen years ago."

Steve did his best not to show his shock. *Fourteen years!* Vu Qing had been only six when his mother had been taken from him.

"Your file says here that you are to be released upon conditions." Fongdu tapped his finger on the release orders, which had been written recently in his own official scroll. "Will you comply?"

Ghuning seemed to sway on her feet. She'd received an indeterminate sentence originally, meaning the government intended her to die for her journalistic criticisms against the Communist Party.

"What are the conditions?"

"You may not return to your province of origin, or you will be immediately arrested again. And your release must be transitioned by a residence with the valley rice growers. Do you agree to these terms?"

"You're releasing me—when?"

"My file says today."

"How long will I be required to remain a resident of the valley?"

"Vu Ghuning," Steve said, "the conditions of your release are not open for discussion. Your son still resides in the cottages nearby. I would think to be reunited with him would be worth any required term beyond these walls."

A moment passed. Steve realized as a political prisoner, Ghuning was a woman of principle and pride. The release certainly made no sense to her, yet. Vu Qing glanced nervously at Steve. No one had planned on the possibility of a prisoner denying her release!

"I accept." She suddenly didn't seem as defiant. "May I ask why I'm being released?"

"When you speak to your son," Steve said, "all will be apparent. Sergeant Shek-jai? Please escort the prisoner to collect her belongings."

Shek-jai disappeared through the archway with Ghuning, and Steve led Vu Qing by the arm out of hearing range of the others.

"Your mother is the first to be released. Take her to Shek-jai's cottage and spend as much time as you have to with her. Tell her everything. She'll be instrumental in the safe release of others to the valley. For all of our sakes, no one can break from this plan until the warden can dismiss the hired guards. Otherwise, we'll risk someone making a report to Shanghai, and we'll all be imprisoned!"

Fongdu joined them, holding his house phone.

"We have a change of plans." The warden looked nervous. "An unscheduled prisoner transfer will be on the ridge in minutes. They just called from the river."

"Nothing changes," Steve said. "Receive the new arrivals as normal. Do the transfer guards ever come to the prison?"

"No, never. But they'll expect an officer to receive custody up there." He nodded at Vu Qing. "You'll need to go to keep up appearances, young man."

"But, my mother—"

"She'll be fine," Fongdu said. "As soon as we confirm all visitors on the ridge are gone, we'll still release her. Go on. Take the men with you. That's protocol."

The warden returned to his table, obviously upset about the arrival of new prisoners the very first day that he intended to release prisoners from the horrible conditions below.

"*Bao'r?*" Vu Qing asked. "Will you tell my mother it's me?" The boy who'd been raised in the valley smiled, then corrected himself to look stern. "I don't know how to tell her. I just want her to know before I take her to the farmers."

"I'd be honored to tell her."

Vu Qing and two guards exited the gate. A moment later, Shek-jai returned to the courtyard with Ghuning, and brought her before Steve. Ghuning held only a blanket, a cup, and a few scraps of paper.

"We cannot release you for a few minutes, Vu Ghuning." Steve set his hand on the gate. "We're expecting new prisoner arrivals shortly."

"More people to treat like animals in cages?"

"No, all that's changing here, beginning with you." Steve glanced at the two remaining hired guards, well out of earshot. "You should know that you have your son to thank for your release today. He's risking his life for you and the others."

"What do you mean, the others?"

"You're not the only prisoner about to be released." Steve smiled. "Your son—he about fainted when you hesitated to accept the conditions of your release."

"My son?" She gasped. "I don't understand."

"Can you keep a secret?" Steve leaned close. "The tall, young sergeant? That's Vu Qing, your son."

"No! My son would never become a PRC officer!"

"He'll explain everything to you. Come, stand here and act like a prisoner."

He took her by the shoulders and positioned her back against the rock wall beside the gate. Tears rolled down her stoic face as she struggled to accept Steve's words.

When Vu Qing arrived with three new prisoners, Ghuning reached for her son, but Steve gently pushed her back.

"Not yet," he said. But a moment later, Vu Qing had handed over the prisoners to the warden's harsh welcoming speech, and Steve gestured to him. "Sergeant, take prisoner Vu Ghuning into the valley and get her situated."

Vu Qing saluted, and gripped his mother's arm to lead her through the gate. Steve watched them go, then closed the gate himself.

"Thank You, Lord," he mumbled, his heart light, praying each prisoner release was this satisfying. "One down, three hundred to go!"

This was better than being released himself!

China – Present Day

The city airport of Wuzhong had recently paved two new runways long enough from which small jets could land and take off. But instead of landing on either airstrip, Titus was hiding in the bushes at the end of the longest runway. As darkness fell across China, he received a text update from Marc Densort in New York, COIL's Gabriel technician. The tech was monitoring regional communications in China, and gave Titus the bad news:

"*The military has deployed a state of the art radar system across Gansu and Shanxi provinces to find you. If you take off, they'll get you for sure, Serval.*"

Titus texted back: "*In every direction, we're at least five hundred miles to the nearest border. If we don't fly out, we'll die here. We cannot burden anyone in China with helping us. It could mean their death.*"

He contemplated the stealth cargo DRIL he'd used in Iran to smuggle Bibles. The machine could avoid radar and come rescue them, but it only had a range of three hundred nautical miles, and they'd still be left with the issue of fuel. The mission to rescue Steve and Lisa was now a mission to escape China alive. Titus didn't mind dying for Steve, a Christian brother he'd never met, but if he died now, it wouldn't be for Steve at all; it would be just a useless death, he felt.

Near midnight, Titus stalked onto the runway and prowled toward one of the two open hangars. Two smaller planes taxied in the distance on the shorter runway, and took off. Behind the first hangar, he used his watch to search for warm bodies inside, but the angle of the Gabriels above didn't allow him a good view, or the roof was shielding their heat signatures. He drew his sidearm and sneaked through the open hangar door.

The fuel truck was hard to miss. It was parked in a service bay next to a private jet. However, there were four mechanics in overalls seated nearby, playing *mahjong*. They laughed and talked as they lay their triangle tiles down, so Titus guessed he could climb into the fuel truck without them hearing, but starting the engine was another story. He needed a head start!

Titus crouched behind a barrel. If he didn't know better, he'd think God was arranging circumstances against him to test his mettle. First, the bullet holes in the fuel tank, and now, more opposition to get fuel. Once he got the fuel, he intended on wiring payment to the city rather than be the thief he once was. So, why did God seem to be against him?

He saw no way to proceed but to tranquilize the *mahjong* players. If no one found them for an hour, he'd have an hour head start to reach his plane, refuel, and relocate to a field closer to Oleg and Song. If a fighter jet didn't shoot him out of the sky first.

Moving from behind the barrel, he drew his sidearm. One man facing him stood up, but there was nowhere to flee.

"*Bao qian*," Titus said in Mandarin. "*I'm sorry.*"

Their faces portrayed fear, but the men didn't even try to run as he tranqed them. Surely they thought they were dying and Titus felt guilty to be the cause of their terror. Searching one man's pockets, he found an identification card and pocketed it—not to steal his identity but to compensate him later. He'd have one of the COIL agents who knew fluent Mandarin to write the man a letter to explain what had happened to him this night. His sensitivity to the feelings of inconsequential strangers convinced him that God wasn't absent from these events. But he still wasn't certain what else God intended him to do.

Rather than hop into the fuel truck, he climbed instead into the private jet and used a pocket all-purpose tool to access the plane's transponder. He didn't know how else to reach Mongolian airspace to the north except by impersonating another jet.

The fuel truck was half full, which was more than enough for his Pilatus PC-24. The truck engine rumbled to life. With the headlights off, he drove it out of the hangar and turned left, away from the tower and central buildings. At the end of the dark runway, he rolled into the grass he'd already scouted, and pushed through a simple fence. He reached the highway two hundred yards later.

With the airport behind him, he switched on the headlights and floored the peddle. He had lives to save. No more messing around!

Hudie Valley – Present Day

Steve used scissors to cut up a British woman's file. Her real name was Vicky Jones, but her file had erroneously labeled her Vi Jong. After interviewing her, he and Fongdu had found her to be a kidnapped journalist from Hong Kong from eight years earlier. Destroying her file erased her identity, he hoped, along with her charges in China.

"Solitary prisoners don't mingle with other prisoners." Fongdu frowned. "I kept her isolated as Tond-zu told me to do. It's a miracle she's still alive. We didn't even let her outside with the others once a week."

"For eight years?" Steve looked away from Fongdu. He couldn't fathom such brutality, but then again, before Steve had come to Christ, he'd been in bondage to countless offenses against God and others as well. "It's in the past now. Ghuning will care for her in the valley. How many other foreigners do you have below?"

"About a dozen among the men. A virus killed some Westerners three years ago. And this one." He opened a file. "Li Ken. The last woman. She tried to escape a few months ago. My men caught her down by the river. She's been in solitary ever since. She's white, but I don't know if she's a Westerner or Russian."

"With a name like Li Ken?" Steve read the file. "Drug possession and trafficking. From Tond-zu, you wrote here."

"I don't recall ever hearing her speak. Maybe she doesn't know Mandarin. Being sent from Tond-zu, she could be here for anything."

"She could be a Christian?"

"Here she comes now." Fongdu gestured to a raggedy skeleton of a woman, her frame bent, her stringy hair hanging partly across her face, making her look like a wild woman.

Steve turned away with her file to pray. She wasn't the first female prisoner who'd aged twenty years in the dungeon, and that he'd had trouble looking at. Their conditions sometimes were too sickly. Two leprous women held in one cell together had been sent directly to the river clinic, regardless of the security risk to expose the prisoner release program.

With Steve's back to Li Ken, Fongdu started the interview.

"Do you speak Chinese?"

"If you speak slowly." Her voice was weak, like a sixty-year-old woman.

"Your file says you were a drug dealer. Is this true?"

"Does this really matter?" the prisoner asked.

"It does matter. Officer Nee? Her file please." Fongdu accepted the paperwork from Steve as he turned to face the proceedings, praying for mercy from God upon one more soul—and so many more in the dungeons below. "This hearing is to determine your suitability for your release."

The woman's legs seemed to weaken. Shek-jai caught her and helped her into a chair in front of the table.

"My release?" the woman's voice squeaked, her head lifting slightly. "Is this your way of teasing me?"

Steve titled his head. This woman's voice . . .

"It's not a joke," Fongdu said. "You're not a drug dealer? Your file says heroin."

"Lies." She shook her head. "They forced me to take it."

"Hmph." The warden grunted. "Sounds like Tond-zu. Officer Nee?"

But Steve wasn't listening too closely. He moved around the corner of the table toward her, then remembered the hired guards, two of whom stood near the archway to the cells.

"You two!" Steve shouted. "Quit standing around. Get below and feed the prisoners!"

"We fed them already this morning, the extra portion as you said," one man stated humbly.

"Then feed them again. Go on!"

They scampered below, and Steve instantly knelt beside the prisoner. His hand trembled as he reached for her hair, to pull back the stringy strands from her face. But the woman shrank away from his hand, turning in her chair and hiding her face behind her shoulder.

Steve stared in shock. *It wasn't possible!* But it was her. It was Lisa! What was left of her. This . . . crippled skeleton was his fiancée!

He was tempted to wrap his arms around her tiny frame and hold her, but he'd already witnessed the fragile psyche in the other prisoners. Ghuning had been a defiant exception to those who followed. They'd been scarred, diseased, and as crippled as this from malnourishment, mistreatment, and filth in the dark cells.

Standing upright, Steve walked to Fongdu's side and spoke in soft gasps.

"I . . . know this woman. I was told that she was dead. We don't need to question her anymore. She's a Christian."

"I'm sorry. I—" Fongdu closed her file. His jaw trembled. "How can I ever be forgiven?"

"You've already been forgiven, Warden." Steve set his hand on the warden's shoulder—to steady them both. "She's been here the whole time I've been in the valley?"

"Yes, almost two years."

"She tried to escape?" Steve closed his eyes. "She's the one your men caught by the river?"

"That's what her file says. You want Vu Qing to take her to the clinic with the other two?"

"No. She's a foreigner." Steve looked back at Lisa, her posture bowed and defensive. "We have to keep her in the valley, like Vicky Jones, until we can smuggle them out somehow."

"This is so dangerous!" Fongdu put his visibly shaking hand to his forehead. "Anyone who leaves could talk, then we're all dead!"

"Fongdu—"

"I'm not saying we should stop, but Steve, I have my children." He looked up at the balcony at his quarters where Zou was supposed to be completing his morning studies, but he ducked out of sight at their gaze. "We have weeks left of this. How can I risk so much?"

"I don't know, but I do know this: I'm taking her to Ghuning and the others. Continue without me."

"But we start on the men next. I need you for that."

"Then wait until I get back." He returned to Lisa and gently touched her shoulder. "I'm going to take you to the farmers outside the wall. They're good women, Lisa. They'll take care of you. It's okay now. I'm going to pick you up. It's too far for you to walk right now. Easy, I'm not going to hurt you."

He slid his arm under her bony knees and one arm around her back. She tensed for an instant, then stopped resisting as he pulled her against his chest. Standing tall on his iron prosthetic, he guessed it would hold since he'd carried workloads in the valley heavier than Lisa's seventy or so pounds.

Shek-jai wiped at tears on her face and opened the gate for them to exit. Immediately outside the gate, Wu-Li and Wong-wei leaped from the tall grass.

"*Bao'r!*" the child called.

"Run ahead, Wu-Li. Tell them I'm coming with another one. Run!"

Steve couldn't hold back the sobs as he walked up the path, past the rice paddies toward the cottages. He didn't know whether to hate or to rejoice. Even the leprous women had been able to walk and stand more ably than Lisa. Tond-zu was responsible, but his boss, the commander, Peng Zemin, was to blame! First his leg, and now Lisa!

His tears of rage ran down his face and dropped onto the folded frame in his arms. She was unresponsive now, and Steve didn't trust her fragile state to tell her it was him, yet. It would break her completely, he was afraid—just the shock alone.

At the cottages, he was met by the weavers and five other women. Ghuning, released four days earlier, stood in the doorway of one cottage.

"Bring her here!" she said and waved him over. "I didn't know she was still alive."

"You know her?" Steve asked.

"She was housed with us before she got sick." Ghuning cradled her head as Steve laid her on a grass sleeping mat. "How is she still alive? That was so long ago! Lisa? Can you hear me? I was teaching her Mandarin."

"Take care of her." Steve backed away. "I'll be back tonight, as soon as we process some of the first men. We're moving as fast as we dare."

"Sergeant Shek-jai's husband?" she asked, having been briefed by the other farmers.

"Yes, he'll be the first." Steve smiled and wiped his face with his sleeve. "She found him in a cell with six other men. She almost told him who she was. But that'll come now."

"Then, go. And take care of my son, *Bao'r*. That's what they call their hero? *Handbasket?* You're a *handbasket?*"

"It's a long story." He laughed. "And yes, I'll watch out for Qing. We couldn't have gotten this far without him!"

New York – Present Day

Corban Dowler received a China update text from Titus directly. The ex-CIA field operative was in his COIL office alone, and had been reviewing resources needed in Syria for Christians who'd stayed in harm's way after many others had fled. With COIL and other Christian agencies' support, those Christians had made an impact in the most dangerous fighting arena in the world. Some had even led ISIS militants to Christ—militants who'd murdered other Christians.

The situation in China, however, was bleak on a very personal level. Corban felt confident that Titus and Oleg could exit China eventually, even if it were on foot across several hundred miles of wasteland. But the search for Steve Brookshire and Lisa Kennedy was impossible when the searchers were running for their own lives. If China had been less restrictive and not so corrupt, the search could've progressed diplomatically.

Corruption. Corban circled two names on his tablet as he prepared to take all these matters to God in prayer. The two names were Peng Zemin and Tond-zu. Rashid al-Sabur had convinced Tond-zu to remove Peng, but now Tond-zu was in charge and Peng was missing, possibly even dead. If he was alive, Corban felt COIL needed to correct that injustice as well. And Rashid hadn't reported in since Titus and Oleg had left Shanghai. Luigi Putelli was also in the wind, possibly reverting back to his standard COIL over-watch stance, since he couldn't easily trail Titus and Oleg in China. At least Luigi had Heather Oakes—his girlfriend who now worked for COIL—to draw him home periodically. Annette had been calling him several times a day for news, but the situation in China was moving so slowly!

Considering himself prepared to pray, Corban locked his braces and stood upright, leaning heavily on his forearm crutches. At his office door, he opened it to see his wife, Janice, at her medical aid desk, and Chloe Azmaveth nearby, talking on the phone. She waved at him and he nodded back, guessing she was talking with an operator in the field, or a diplomat overseas, or a pastor wondering how to get involved in COIL's activities.

Corban closed his office door and locked it. Alone and hidden, he leaned against his desk and set his crutches aside. One hand at a time, he reached down and unlocked his braces by the lever behind his knees. Instead of collapsing, he supported his own weight. Carefully, he stood on one leg and lifted the other, bent at the knee. Then he exercised the other. Gradually, since his accident in Gaza, which had left him paralyzed from the waist down, he'd been regaining both feeling and muscle control. Annette had confided in him about Titus' recent bout with cancer and possible healing, but Corban hadn't said anything to Annette about his own health status.

Normally, Corban confided in his wife, or Chloe, or the others closest to him. But this secret of his functioning legs—that his spinal severance wasn't as complete as the neurologists had first said—it was his knowledge alone. Every morning, he strapped on his leg braces and hobbled around with no one the wiser. But in reality, he was exercising to strengthen his legs to one day walk free of any aids, even a cane.

He wasn't keeping his recovery secret for deceitful intentions, but as a spy, he certainly could think of ways he could use some craftiness with the ultimate results! As a paraplegic, Corban had been under-estimated by some COIL critics, and that kept COIL out of the line of fire. If opponents of his Christian efforts overseas knew he was able-bodied again, they might guess he would regain political and intelli-gence status that seemed to have waned the last couple years. And then, they would attack him again, in the press, or by harassing him with surveillance. If he kept a low profile, enemies might overlook COIL altogether.

There were dark foes who seemed supernaturally inspired to afflict Christians, and they simply didn't need to know he was back on his feet again. Almost. If he kept up his secret therapy, he guessed he might be walking unimpeded again in about three months. Running would come after that.

But for now, with his legs sufficiently exercised for the morning, he eased himself to the floor in a kneeling position. For almost two years, he'd missed praying on his knees, humbling himself before God—to implore and petition and listen.

He'd learned years ago to lay his problems before God. Sometimes he didn't, and in those moments of lacking faith, the burdens of responsibility stunted his growth as a son and diminished his discern-ment as a leader. But now, he prayed, stating plainly his thoughts and worries before God. After a few minutes, his eyes moist with concern for the China situation, he stopped talking and merely listened for something from God. He didn't expect an audible voice, but he did expect an impression or fresh ideas to touch his heart and mind, a motivation that corresponded to the Word of God in him, to guide him.

God seemed to direct his thoughts to Steve rather than to Titus.

Those thoughts were suddenly overwhelmed with comfort and even joy. And why not, he reasoned. Steve had been a devoted man of God for many years, serving on the front lines in the battle over souls. Why wouldn't the man be at peace wherever the Lord had planted him now?

Rising from the floor, Corban wiped his eyes and locked his braces. He took up his crutches and unlocked his office door to receive case workers if they needed his counsel. Finally, he sat down at his desk again and composed a brief message to Titus: "I'm praying. Stay safe. Steve is in God's arms."

CHAPTER FIFTEEN

China – Present Day

Titus drove the fuel truck through the night, aware that he had less than an hour head start. The tranquilizer would wear off the four men in an hour, but how soon would the missing fuel truck be noticed?

When he reached the programmed coordinates, Titus' watch beeped and he eased off the highway into an uncultivated field. Weeds smacked against the front bumper as he turned off the headlights in case any other vehicles came up the highway. Trusting the Gabriels' view ahead, he rolled through a grove and into another field where his jet rested.

He reached the plane and backed up to refuel. Hopping out of the truck, he laughed his praise skyward as he reflected on how smoothly getting the fuel had been. In the middle of China, he was about to secretly refuel his jet!

Reaching the back of the truck, he froze. Kneeling, he glanced under the tank, then hastily crawled on top of the tank to confirm his mistake. Standing on top of the truck, he sighed in defeat.

"So, the joke's on me," he said aloud. "It ain't easy refueling without a refueling hose!"

He wondered if the mechanics back at the hangar were laughing at him right then. A thief had stolen their fuel truck, but hadn't checked to make sure the hose was attached. It may have been removed for patching or replacement, but it definitely wasn't there.

Still standing on top of the truck, he looked down at the front of his jet. It was sloped at an awkward angle. Now, he laughed and threw his hands into the air. The entire wheel of the front landing gear had sunk into thick mud, all the way up to the fuselage belly! Since the nose-wheel was naturally short, he hadn't noticed it earlier in the darkness. There would be no moving the jet now, even if he were somehow able to transfer fuel into the plane.

Titus knew God was communicating something to him, but he

couldn't put his finger on what. Did He not want Steve Brookshire rescued? That hardly seemed likely! He left a text for Oleg: "*Pilatus out of commish. Need to focus on leaving, coming back later. Give me ur coords to meet.*"

Inside the jet, Titus turned on a small light and added to an already-stuffed go-bag. The armaments and explosives from the cargo hold were important, but he knew he couldn't take it all. He concentrated on removing only weapons that identified the plane as a COIL asset. With a change of clothes, a few identifications, food, and water, he set a timed explosive and drove the fuel truck a distance away.

Having determined to destroy the expensive plane, he smiled at the thought of the entertainment it would provide the Chinese government. Here he was leaving their fuel truck behind, undamaged. They would laugh at him, realizing something had gone wrong because his plane had burnt up, even after he'd commandeered their truck. Then, they would realize he was on foot, and begin a manhunt—more feverishly than the one already occurring.

Dawn was an hour away, so there was no hope he could burn the jet without drawing attention to the black smoke before the sun rose. He set the detonator for three hours and shouldered his eighty-pound pack. Until Oleg and Song responded with a rendezvous point, he didn't know exactly where to meet them. But Marc Densort was tracking Oleg to the southwest, using one Gabriel drone seventy thousand feet overhead. By heading toward the Himalayan Mountains, he knew he would eventually find them, even if it took him a week. As an Arkansas boy taught to live off the land, he guessed God would show him how to survive. But he knew Annette wouldn't be happy about his delay to meet her parents. Like so many other operations, this one had over-extended its welcome.

China – Present Day

Oleg and Song trudged through the grasslands of China, their hearts heavy. After surveying three different labor camps, they'd still not found Steve Brookshire.

Leading the way, Oleg occasionally checked his heading on a compass to save power on his sat-phone. At their pace, even with Titus marching toward them, they were three days from meeting up.

"Truck," Song mumbled behind him.

Shifting his pack, Oleg wondered if they could stretch their two days of food to last three. Water was just as scarce—drinking water, anyway. The Yellow River was nearby to the northwest, but it was too filthy to drink, and they had no purification tablets.

"Truck," Song said a little louder.

Oleg stopped, realizing his Japanese partner had repeated himself. Ahead of them, the green grassy steppes stretched into low hills and a few lonely trees. It was hard to imagine that a land so green could be so barren. If they didn't find more food before it ran out, he'd have to call Corban Dowler and—

"Truck!" Song shoved Oleg out of his stupor. "Run!"

With Song's hand drawing him forward, Oleg pumped his legs for two hundred yards before he stopped to catch his breath and looked back. Song continued straight ahead, toward Mongolia hundreds of miles away.

Gazing westward, Oleg saw the truck Song had spotted. It wasn't so much the presence of the truck that bothered Oleg, or the road they'd apparently been so near. It was the eight or nine uniformed soldiers climbing out of the back of the truck that made Oleg wince. Evidently, their tactless intrusion into China to search for Steve and Lisa at various prisons had finally caught up to them.

Even though Oleg had a gun that could out-distance the soldiers' weapons, he didn't fire on them. They certainly had a radio, and if he tranquilized a few of them, someone would simply call in heavier fire-power, maybe even a gunship. There was nowhere to run and nowhere to hide on the grassy landscape. When outnumbered and outmanned, a man had to prepare for the worst.

Oleg let Song run, and he was surprisingly fast for as weary as they both were. Since Song had a sordid past, they'd certainly not favor the Japanese visitor deep inside their country. Song wasn't going to make his capture easy, and Oleg wondered if the ex-Hong Kong mobster might actually get away.

Instead of following his partner, Oleg turned and found the road. The truck roared up the gravel behind him, the troops tromping in their boots alongside, jostling for what looked like a clear shot. Bounding off the other side of the road, Oleg passed several short trees, then leaped down the bank of the Yellow River. Though the sand was soft, he landed wrong and felt his knee snap. He fell into the shallow water, then crawled away, hidden from the soldiers by the high bank.

Instead of continuing northeast, he reversed to the southwest, limping and splashing, certain his gasps were heard by the enemy since he could hear their shouts. He guessed they were torn between capturing him and chasing after Song.

In a cleft of the river bank, Oleg climbed into the damp soil and hanging roots. The river was low that summer, but the spring run-off had carved deeply into the hillside.

Finally resting, Oleg shrugged off his pack and dialed his sat-phone. With his free hand, he clutched his knee. It wasn't broken, he figured, just over-extended.

Marc Densort answered. As COIL's Gabriel tech, he was always monitoring the feed from the three high-flying stealth UAVs.

"I'm minutes from capture," Oleg panted. "Busted my knee. Song and I split up."

"Okay, I'll direct one of the Gabriels off of Titus and lock onto Song's heat signature."

"I'm burying my phone and rifle and pack at these coordinates, against the river bank."

"I see you."

"Things didn't go well on this trip. Tell Corban I'm sorry."

"I'll tell him."

"And tell Titus I won't be too happy if he gets caught, too, since I'll have to depend on someone else to rescue me."

"He's ninety miles northeast of you. I've got all three of you on screen."

"Pray for us, Marc."

"Lean on God, brother."

Oleg turned off the phone and shoved it deep into the soil. He tugged at the roots and bank overhang to cascade the earth onto his rifle and pack. If he hadn't witnessed God's provision at other moments of capture, he would've been more concerned than he was. Instead, he was preparing himself for the discomfort of capture and subsequent waiting that he hoped would quickly proceed to a rescue— presumably by Titus. Already, he was anticipating Titus' gloating when he would be rescuing him from prison. Again.

Limping away, he fell into the river, then crawled on one knee, dragging his injured leg behind. A gunshot made him fall flat in the shallow water. He rolled onto the dry bank and lay prone, his arms outstretched, as a half-dozen soldiers surrounded him. Two more stood on the bank above and yelled orders.

With satisfaction, Oleg realized he'd drawn at least that company of soldiers away from Song. The man could still get away, but he was a long way from linking up with Titus. And Oleg had just buried the bulk of their provisions. If Song wasn't captured, he was in for a hard few days.

⚡

Hudie Valley – Present Day

Steve leaned on a shovel next to Warden Fongdu Jen as they stood over a mound of dirt. East of the prison wall, at the side of the smelly refuse pond, were dozens of other gravesites, most of them unmarked.

"I wonder who he was," Fongdu said. They'd discovered a dead prisoner while processing one cell's occupants for release. "So many of the files are fictionalized, it's hard to tell who is really who. If we would've processed him a week sooner, we could've sent him to the clinic. If only I had—"

"No, brother. We can't move any faster than we are." Steve swung the shovel over his shoulder. "We've released twenty prisoners this week already. Whoever he was, we've got what we need to continue our work. Here, why don't you take the shovel, and I'll carry that."

Fongdu gladly received the shovel as Steve stooped to pick up the dead prisoner's left leg, which Steve had crudely hacked off with the shovel. It was sobering for Steve to realize Tond-zu had indeed ordered his gruesome death—and a leg to memorialize his execution.

"Once you ship this thing to Tond-zu," Steve said, holding the leg in a soiled shirt, "I'll be dead to him. There's a little bit of liberty with that thought. It's like the Bible says, life comes from death, freedom from darkness."

They started around the edge of the pond toward the prison gate.

"Maybe now you should know my thoughts about that." The warden stopped and turned to Steve, but his eyes didn't meet Steve's face. "We're still weeks away from emptying the last cell. For me and my family, that may not be soon enough."

"I don't understand." Steve adjusted the heavy thing in his hand. "I thought processing all the people was a matter of conscience for you."

"It is. But I don't need to be here for you to do it." Fongdu lifted his head. "Besides, with your fiancée recovering, you'll be here. You've spent time with Tond-zu. You know personally the brutality he's capable of. I'd stay with you, but I have two children to think about. The weight of this risk has . . . made me a coward."

"No, you're not a coward, Warden." Steve wasn't about to argue with a good man, to convince him to stay in harm's way when he had a mind to leave. "You have somewhere to go?"

"West. I could disappear with Zou. Change our names. Lijia will be close to leaving home in a few years. She wants to go to the cities, where she'll be safer and able to disappear. I'll find a new school for Zou or teach him myself, far beyond Tond-zu's reach or influence."

Steve gazed up at the prison walls, considering the logistics of processing the remaining prisoners alone. They weren't even halfway through yet!

"My hesitation to see you go is selfish," Steve said. "We've enjoyed a rich time together, doing good for God that very few would believe possible."

"And you've taught me all about Jesus." Fongdu's eyes were moist. "I'll never forget our evening talks. You have saved my family from eternal damnation, but now we must think about safety. With Shek-jai and Vu Qing as your officers, you have a good team. I'll teach you how to use the computer as long as you want to stay in Hudie Valley. Your Mandarin is nearly as good as mine ever was. Most of the paperwork is digital over the Internet. Shanghai will not know otherwise. I'll leave the antiques to help finance your work and release of prisoners, and Shanghai will continue to supply you monthly."

"It's risky." Steve chuckled. "But I like it. It's God's work. You're a fine man, Warden."

"No, you're a fine man, Steve Brookshire, and you're the new warden now. Warden Nee."

Hudie Valley – Present Day

Vu Ghuning was hesitant to believe everything her grown son had told her, but the evidence was hard to dispute. She was free from the prison cell, Qing wore a PRC uniform as a fictitious sergeant, and the one-legged "round-eyed" officer had come to visit her each evening to check on Lisa Kennedy. The God who Qing continued to boast about was confusing to Ghuning, but the circumstances seemed to provide proof. The whole valley was talking about this good God. Was a deity really responsible for all of this?

She moved to the door of the cottage she shared with Shek-jai, her recovering husband, and Lisa—who'd been sleeping or delirious since her release almost a week earlier. Up the valley, several released men worked in the rice paddies beside their families. A few had left the valley, taking their families and leaving cottage space for those willing to stay or unable to travel.

Qing had carefully explained the situation to her, so Ghuning wasn't as apprehensive about staying in the valley, but hearing that the warden was leaving added some consternation. The others had asked for her advice, but she didn't know enough to give any. She hoped that could change this evening.

A few minutes later, the tall figure of Steve Brookshire—the man she'd first known as Officer Nee—walked up the pathway toward the cottages. The farmers who weren't in the fields poured out of their homes to welcome and honor him, as well as receive what gifts he brought them from the prison. Usually, he gave food generously, but that night it appeared to be cookware, which they desperately needed. Even those whose family members had died in the prison treated the tall American like a hero—one of their own. Some seemed more concerned about that week's story night than the possibility of a visitation of officials from Shanghai.

With his arms finally empty, Steve reached her cottage.

"Good evening, Ghuning." He bowed low like a peasant, though he wore his officer's uniform. It all seemed so strange to her! "Has there been any change with Lisa?"

"No change." She glanced over at the mat where Lisa slept. "Sometimes she talks, but it's all in English, so I don't understand much."

"Okay." He sighed heavily and started to turn away.

"Wait, uh, Steve. Please don't leave so quickly tonight. I have questions." She noticed his countenance lift, as if he were as interested in conversing with her as she was with him. "My son, your sergeant, told us the warden's leaving soon."

"It's time. I understand why he must."

"But you're staying? Isn't it dangerous?"

"I'm learning how to protect us. I've been involved in security strategies in China for many years. Hudie Valley is so remote, the only visitors we get are the deliveries of food and supplies from town, and the occasional prisoner transfers. No one wants to come near the prison since it has such a bad reputation for leprosy. Besides all this, God has shown Himself strong on our behalf, and our work isn't done yet. I think we're safe."

"I would feel better if I were involved." Ghuning gestured to Lisa. "She should be moved into a dwelling that at least has a door, and you should make me a PRC administrator to ensure all the paperwork is properly addressed. I was a journalist in Hong Kong before my arrest. I know better than you what we're facing by staying here."

Steve was silent for a moment as he looked out across the valley.

"Has anyone moved into my old cottage yet?"

"No." She smiled. "They don't want to dishonor you. It's your cottage. It's where you tell the stories. Everyone is waiting for story night to start again. I have to admit, I'm curious myself."

"This week." He nodded. "Story night will resume this week, and to address your offer—yes, I could use you as an administrator. It would be arrogant of me to think I can do everything Warden Fongdu Jen was doing. Now, I'll need to do it all under disguise."

"What about the guards you have on staff? They'll recognize me as a past prisoner."

"But they know you were released, so they won't question when I tell them I'm hiring you to help with paperwork. We could even tell them it's forced labor."

Together, they watched the valley darken. Lisa whimpered, and Steve knelt over her. Ghuning listened to him speak in English to her. No, she decided. He wasn't speaking to her; he was speaking to his God. She looked at the dark sky. Was God really up there? Everyone around her was honoring Him. Though a skeptic at heart, she smiled at the sky, imagining a benevolent Being looking down on her.

"Thank You for returning me to my son," she said, and immediately burst into tears of joy. She hadn't cried in all the years of her captivity. Now free, she wept openly. There had to be a God!

ς

China – Present Day

Titus knelt and used his magnified rifle scope to view the grassland to the southwest. He'd been in constant contact with COIL tech Marc Densort to locate Song Sakana, who was on foot and alone in China. It had been three days since Titus had left the jet behind, and two and a half days since he'd gotten word that Oleg had been captured. As often as he and Oleg had been in the clutches of the enemy, nothing had gone well, especially recently. Since Oleg was a foreigner, Titus figured the authorities wouldn't execute him outright, but they'd link him to the recent disturbances around several western prisons that were supposed to be secret facilities.

Using his watch, Titus confirmed there were no soldiers around the sleeping Song Sakana, who lay under a dark green tree, which was one of a whole grove of trees. Swinging his pack off his back, Titus walked up to the Japanese man and touched his shoulder. Song startled awake and opened bloodshot eyes. The haggard traveler's clothes were muddy and torn.

"I knew you'd find me," Song said, and accepted Titus' canteen to his lips. "I didn't hear the jet land."

"Yeah, I texted Oleg about that, but you guys were in the process of getting hassled by troops. I lost the jet. We're on foot."

"I fear that I am more adept in the city, my brother."

"There's certainly a difference between growing up in Hong Kong, and growing up in an Arkansas wilderness." Titus indicated the tree above him. "Of course, it ain't easy starving to death under a mango tree, huh?"

"This is a mango tree?" Song sat up with Titus' help. "All these trees look alike to me."

"Well, they should." Titus chuckled. "We're in a cultivated mango grove. There's a farm about two miles south. Might even find a vehicle there."

"I confess, my weariness had led to some despair." Song frowned. "Shall we look into this transportation? My feet are unfamiliar with so much walking."

"My energy level isn't much higher." Titus reached around Song's shoulders to support him. "However we feel, we have to keep moving, or we'll be joining Oleg in prison instead of rescuing him."

"Do I look like I can rescue anyone?" Song pulled at his tattered clothes. "I think we're in need of rescue ourselves."

"Obviously, Oleg never told you about the week we spent in Azerbaijan, running from apocalyptic Muslims!" Titus helped Song through a hedge as they started south. "The hardships of the past—God uses them to prepare us for the hardships of the future. You know the guy who taught me that? A Japanese sage named Song Sakana. I've grown rather fond of the guy, so he'd better not give up and die on me!"

"I'm from Akita of the Tohoku." Song's posture stiffened as he walked. "Samurai blood runs through these veins."

"Well, the Samurai warrior almost starved to death under a mango tree."

"Maybe I was fasting?" They paused and Titus handed Song an energy bar from his pack. "And now my fast is over."

Titus laughed.

"It ain't easy winning arguments with a Christian Samurai!"

China – Present Day

Oleg was transferred to three different local jails before he arrived in Wuhai at an administrative office that wasn't a jail at all. The city sprawled on both sides of the Yellow River, expanding recently from displaced farmers caught in flood zones.

His captors were three young PRC soldiers who hadn't let him sleep in almost three days. They worked together around the clock to jab or smack him awake when he began to doze. Oleg had begun to try to sleep standing upright, with his eyes partially open, just so they thought he was awake. But it wasn't working. His mind was foggy and he was afraid they were trying to break him, to get him to talk and spill all his secrets.

"This is your hearing," an official at a polished wooden desk explained in perfect Russian. Now, Oleg couldn't get away with saying in Russian that he didn't understand. "You are being charged with subversion and espionage. Would you like to respond to the charges?"

"Yes." Oleg looked down at the floor. They'd given him a strong cane to stand with, but his knee was still in no condition to run on. The waist chain shackles extended to his wrists, so he couldn't raise his arms to use the cane as a weapon. "I'm not a spy. I'm a traveler, a servant of my Master."

"What's your Master's name?"

"Jesus, the Son of God."

"Ah. You're a Christian?"

"Yes."

The administrator made several notes in a file, then referred to an outdated computer. The phone rang, to which the administrator answered in Chinese. Oleg waivered on his feet. He thought foggily about Titus trying to rescue him. He smiled to himself. Hopefully, Titus wouldn't rescue him before he caught a little sleep!

His contemplations were interrupted by a sharp baton strike to his right kidney. Catching his breath from the pain, he realized the administrator had been speaking to him.

"That was an official in Shanghai. I asked him what we should do with you." The man shook his head and made more notes in his file. "You're to be charged now as an anti-government conspirator and sentenced as a political prisoner at the worst prison I've ever heard of: Hudie Valley."

"What about my hearing?" Oleg tried to think past his weariness.

"This was your hearing. You'll now be transferred to where Christian foreigners are often housed. You'll wish you never came to China to do whatever it is you're here for. A sentence to Hudie Valley is a sentence of death."

"Hudie Valley?" Oleg was yanked aside and marched outside to a minivan. He repeated the name of the prison several times, but he was certain that name hadn't been on the original list of prisons in which Steve Brookshire may have been held.

On the way to the van, Oleg was struck repeatedly until he complied with climbing into the van. When he fell on his side onto the floor of the back seat, his escorts laughed, but didn't harass him again. They left him cramped in the small space between the middle and back seats. Then, the soldiers climbed into the front and pulled away.

After Oleg's initial feeling of claustrophobia diminished, he realized with some clarity that the cramped quarters might be his coffin. He couldn't move! He began praying for God's protection, but before sixty seconds had passed, he fell fast asleep.

CHAPTER SIXTEEN

Hudie Valley – Present Day

Steve turned his face left and right, studying his skin and goatee in the mirror. Fongdu Jen was gone, with Zou and Lijia. Now, Steve was warden, and appearing to be Chinese was even more important since the prisoners he released mustn't see him as an imposter, or as a mere Westerner, but as a fearsome PRC official—at least, initially. And though the chances were slight, if anyone from the east visited without warning, he needed to appear native as much as possible.

With a snip of scissors, he sculpted the last few hairs of his droopy mustache. His tan and thick eyebrows really did make him look Oriental, he thought, or Mongolian, at least. Well, almost. His eyes were light brown and he was taller than anyone for miles around, so he stood out, regardless.

"You received a text from Wuhai, Warden Nee," Ghuning announced from the living room that doubled as their office. "It's a prisoner transfer!"

"Is it Tond-zu?" Steve dropped the scissors and used a towel on his face as he left the back room. "We have to get used to this."

She studied the computer screen.

"Tond-zu did order it." She'd been told about Steve's past and the history of the prison, which seemed to be Tond-zu's private death camp for select prisoners. "A Russian man. Tond-zu wants him questioned. But he's a Christian! What are we going to do? A report is expected after we interrogate him!"

"It's okay." Standing beside her, Steve prayed under his breath. "We stick to the plan. As long as Tond-zu continues to communicate only through the computer, we'll be safe."

Lisa now slept in Fongdu Jen's old bedroom where Ghuning was boarding as well, since she took care of her. Vu Qing and Steve had moved into Zou and Lijia's old bedrooms.

The hired guards worked in pairs rotating through the night shift by sleeping in a small barracks room above the dungeons. The off-shift guards returned to their homes along the river.

Steve walked onto the balcony and looked down into the courtyard where the table awaited the day's proceedings. They had prisoners to process and release. Several more Christians had been found in the lowest levels, some too ill to travel. They'd been relocated to his old cottage in the valley where the farmers were caring for them.

"Sergeant Vu Qing!" Steve called to the young man in the courtyard. He was organizing the day's responsibilities for the four hired guards. "Postpone prisoner processing for now. Take two men and go to the ridge. A new prisoner is being transferred into our custody."

"Yes, Warden!" Qing snapped a salute and immediately selected two guards and left through the gate.

Sergeant Shek-jai continued, in broken Mandarin, to instruct the two remaining guards, all four of whom had been young farmers, Steve had discovered. He didn't suspect them to have actual Communist Party ties, and their job at the prison had been helpful for their growing families. He didn't believe they would report them to Shanghai, even if they did notice what was going on, though Steve didn't want to expose the prison's secret to anyone who had nothing to lose by reporting them. The entire plan was fragile, and he remained in prayer, that God would protect them and keep mouths shut where their safety was concerned.

Ghuning joined him on the balcony.

"When you relieve the four guards from duty," Ghuning said, "if they say anything to anyone in the town about a Caucasian warden, an official may come out to investigate."

Steve turned from the balcony.

"Who's the next prisoner for processing from below?" he asked, not willing to explain to Ghuning yet how he believed God would protect them. He wouldn't kill or imprison the four guards just to keep his secrets safe. "What's his name?"

"Cao Yutong. Fongdu Jen made a notation that he was sent from Tond-zu in Shanghai."

"I know our files are full of blanks," Steve sat in one of the soft chairs, "but I'd like to process all prisoners sent from Tond-zu first. Can you put them at the top?"

"I can. What're you thinking?" Ghuning thumbed through the pile of files.

"Tond-zu's prisoners are almost certainly Christians," Steve said, "since we know from Internet news reports that he's the magistrate now in Shanghai over subversive anti-government tactics. From the last prisoners, we should be able to find men willing to act as servants so we can relieve our four hired guards sooner. That way, we'll have complete control of the prison, without anyone inside that we need to carry on this facade for. We could move faster."

"But the facade does need to be continued to some degree." Ghuning handed him a dozen files. "My son can be on hand, with others he'll need to train, so they can accept the monthly supplies, as well as prisoner transfers up on the ridge."

Regardless of his faith, Steve was feeling anxious. What he was attempting was unprecedented, but he now realized how his whole life had been ordered for this precise situation. His security experience with the sub-net, his knowledge of Mandarin, and his disciplined boldness to share Christ to win the farmers and eventually the warden—all of it was specifically designed by his God. And yet, a single visit from Tond-zu could bring the wrath of a military division down upon Hudie Valley.

Beyond the wall, Vu Qing led a prisoner and two guards down the trail from the ridge. The prisoner limped severely and leaned on a cane. As they neared, Steve noticed the prisoner's Russian features— his broad face, thick neck, and shoulders the size of an ox.

Ghuning stood next to him.

"The digital file they sent says he speaks only Russian. Do you know any?"

"None. And I don't think anyone in the valley does, either. How does Tond-zu expect us to interrogate a Christian who speaks only Russian?"

"He was in China to share about your God. He must know some Chinese, unless he was using a translator."

"I think every prisoner transfer will be like this." Steve chuckled. "It'll be a challenge with each individual."

"Just be aware that the Party could send someone to test us at any time. Some facade will always be necessary."

"I understand." He nodded to his administrator and donned a small green cap, its bill covering some of his Western features.

Vu Qing seated the Russian in the chair in front of the processing table as Steve descended the rock stairs and assumed his place as warden, standing behind the table. The Russian seemed as curious about Steve as Steve was of him, each studying the other's appearance. Steve recognized the bruises on the Russian's face from the hospitality of PRC interrogators.

"Do you speak Mandarin?" Steve asked, then he tried Cantonese. Nothing. He studied the file. The Russian had had accomplices, yet they weren't caught. Maybe one of his partners had translated for him. Was he a Russian missionary to China?

Steve prayed for guidance. The Russian was bold enough to meet his gaze, and his muscled frame seemed to point more toward a soldier or laborer than a lay worker for Christ in a foreign field. Maybe he was the bodyguard of a missionary. His hands bore the calluses of a hard worker.

"See to your other duties!" Steve barked at the hired guards. "Sergeant Shek-jai and Sergeant Qing, you're the only ones I need here."

The other four left. Steve closed the man's file and drew a cross on the blank cover. He turned it toward the man, but the Russian didn't react when he saw the drawing.

"I'll get him some rice and water," Qing offered, and dashed away. Returning a minute later, he set the food and cup on the table.

The Russian tentatively reached for the water. Steve could see the distrust in the man's face. Even though he was famished, he'd been mistreated during his capture and transfer to the point of fear of . . . what? Poisoning? Finally, the man took a sip, then a gulp. The cup was empty in three swallows. Qing ran for a refill. The Russian gobbled at the rice as Steve watched him, remembering his own starvation and abuse two years earlier.

"English?" Steve tried on a whim. "Do you speak English?"

The Russian stopped eating. He'd understood. Steve smiled. No one else in the courtyard knew English, but here was a Russian who at least understood some of it.

"Can you tell me your name?" Steve asked.

"We're a little too deep in China for a Chinaman to speak good English," the Russian said, and leaned forward. "Take your hat off."

Steve frowned, and looked at Shek-jai, but she didn't understand.

"He told me to take my hat off," he said to her.

"Maybe he recognizes you." She shrugged.

"How could he? I've never seen him in my life."

"Maybe he's a Party spy."

"Are you a Christian?" Steve asked the Russian in English. "You were arrested and sent here to be tortured and probably executed."

"Who are you?" The Russian cocked his head, a grin spreading across his scarred cheek. "If I said James and John, what would you say?"

Steve bit his lip. *James and John*. It was an early COIL prompt for security purposes among underground Christians. Only a COIL operative would use it at such a moment as this. Unless the call and response had been beaten out of another Christian. If the Russian was really a Christian, then he would know a more difficult call and response from consistent Bible reading.

"Who did the son of Jesse fight?"

The Russian smiled broadly now.

"Answer mine first, then I'll answer yours."

"Who are you?" It was Steve's turn to allow a smile to creep onto his face. "I say Zebedee."

"And I say Goliath." The Russian looked around and suddenly removed his smile and whispered. "Steve? Is that you?"

Steve took a step backwards, a chill running up his spine. *COIL was here! They could ruin everything!*

"How many other COIL operatives are here?" Steve glanced at Qing, whose face showed his nervousness. "I'm barely in control of this place. If COIL does anything, word will get to Shanghai, and we're all dead! I have a whole valley to think about!"

"Whoa, whoa, slow down, Captain." The Russian surveyed the courtyard. "I'm the last one trying to mess up your play here. Just tell me how many of these officers are yours."

"These two sergeants and the administrator on the balcony are mine. The four other guards are temporary hires. They're not even PRC. We hired them from the next town."

"How is this even possible?" The Russian shook his head. "Did you have me transferred here?"

"Absolutely not. I'm trying to release prisoners, not take more in.

Having COIL in the area threatens my whole plan. You were caught?"

"Steve, we're here to find you and get you out. Obviously, the tables have turned. Yeah, I was arrested a few days ago. I want to know about you!"

"There's a story behind all this, I assure you. Who else is with you?"

"Two others. Titus Caspertein, a hotshot of Corban Dowler's, and Song Sakana, a guy from—"

"*Song Sakana!*" Steve felt his face go pale as he looked up at Ghuning on the balcony. "We have to get out of here now! Song Sakana was the man who—"

"Easy, Steve. He's a Christian now." The Russian's voice and face softened. "Because of you, he's a Christian. We've been looking for you for two years. Well, Corban Dowler has been. Song Sakana came to Christ and contacted an American embassy. We've been on the hunt personally only a few weeks. By the way, Song said he chopped off your leg?"

Steve pulled up his pant leg to show his homemade iron prosthetic.

"That's all part of the reason I'm warden here." Steve took a deep breath. "Maybe if God's been in control this far, I can trust Him through this, too."

"Hey, you'll hear no complaints from me. I just spent two days sleeping on the floor of a van, and like you said, I've been scheduled for torture. But your whole setup here—you need to call Corban immediately so Titus and Song don't blow your cover. Calling him earlier could've avoided this mishap in the first place."

"I didn't need a rescue." Steve felt his countenance fall. "I did at the beginning, but the last year has been, well, I've learned that none of this is about me."

"I believe you. I really do."

"Okay, well, I have to put you in a cell until I replace the hired guards with my own personnel. Shouldn't be more than a couple days. Just play the part, will you?"

"No problem, Steve, but you'd better call Corban, or Titus will bust me out and make a big scene."

"I'll call him. Right now." Steve explained briefly to Vu Qing his plan, then turned toward the stairs.

"Hey, Steve?" the Russian asked. "Any word about Lisa Kennedy? She hasn't been on our radar for almost two years, either."

"That's another act of God." Steve pointed to the sky. "She's up-stairs."

"Oh, I'm sorry, Steve. We're too late for her."

"No, I mean, she's literally upstairs in the warden's suite!"

New York – Present Day

Corban turned off his office phone, buried his face in his hands, and wept. He didn't yet know the full story, but receiving a call from Steve Brookshire himself, via a secure router in India, was almost too much relief to bear. It was because of victories like these that he wanted to shout of God's might from the rooftops. But he couldn't. Steve was impersonating a warden. The situation was sensitive, and in the heart of communist China, that meant the situation was deadly. Christians were still being hunted, and somehow Steve had a whole valley of Christians under his care!

"Father," he cried, "how do You turn prisoners into princes?"

The situation in China was far from being sorted out. Titus and Song were on foot a hundred miles southwest of the Hudie Valley coordinates Steve had just given him. And Oleg was wounded, but recovering. And Lisa was alive! Prayer was absolutely still necessary, regardless of God's obvious working already.

It was time to exercise his leg muscles, but Corban flipped up his laptop screen instead. Using Marc Densort, Corban had an open line to Titus through his sat-watch. But before he typed Titus a message to report Oleg's safe status in Steve's providential hands, Corban considered his last contact with Titus. The operative had literally kidnapped him and showed off his prowess by transporting him in a jet to South Korea! It was time to give the prankster a taste of his own medicine. After all, Titus had accepted the challenge to compete in covert tactics.

"*Your best route out of China is to get captured,*" Corban said to Titus in a text. "*Surrender to Hudie Valley Prison. Nothing else will prevail.*"

Then, Corban left coordinates, and called Marc Densort, instructing him not to assist Titus with more information. Radio silence, for now.

Satisfied with his scheme against the wily Serval, Corban unlocked his braces and knelt on the floor. Before exercising, his soul yearned to worship God for His generosity. The situation in China for all COIL personnel was even better than he'd imagined!

𝄢

Shanghai – Present Day

Tond-zu held the oblong postal package under his arm as he rode the elevator up Shanghai Tower. He knew what the package contained. It was from Warden Fongdu Jen. Finally, Steve Brookshire was out of his life. The unbreakable Christian's last leg was in the package!

Once in his office, Tond-zu locked the door and set the box on his desk. Using a letter opener, the handle of which was a human bone, he cut the tape and plucked off the top of the box. He yawned at the black skin of Steve's leg wrapped in double-walled plastic and encased in dry ice. He waited for the dark thrill to make his heart quiver, but there was nothing. He'd imagined an overwhelming sense of triumph at the sight of the leg, but he felt nothing, *nothing*—for the dead man who had eluded Peng first, and then him.

With a swing of fury, he knocked the open package off his desk. It landed on the floor and scattered dry ice against the wall. The frozen leg slid into the corner. From that angle, the leg appeared far too small to have belonged to a man as tall as Steve Brookshire, but the cold must've shrunken and deformed the limb.

As soon as Tond-zu imagined how Fongdu had removed the leg, the sense of satisfaction he wanted finally coursed through his veins. Yes, the man had suffered horribly. That evidence lay on the floor in front of him. Steve's imaginary God hadn't protected him.

Tond-zu returned to his desk and ran his finger down a list of prisoners arrested in the city in the past month. Fongdu never asked for money or recognition—beyond the funds and supplies he was allotted monthly already. But Tond-zu felt he understood what the sadistic warden would like: more victims.

From the list, Tond-zu identified four more Christians he'd decided to have murdered rather than sent for re-education for a third or fourth offense for their subversive activities against the Party. As he climbed in power, Tond-zu had to be careful that he didn't show himself as a sadist, cruel and merciless against the people. But Fongdu Jen was under no such scrutiny. The warden who shared Tond-zu's same sick heart—together, they could exterminate a generation of mind manipulators who relied on an invisible God!

Typing frantically, Tond-zu sent a transfer order to the local jails. More prisoners would be sent to Hudie Valley. More Christians!

China – Present Day

"He's got to be messing with us."

Titus showed his watch face to Song as they stopped walking through a field south of the Yellow River.

"Surrender?" Song scratched his head. "Is surrendering standard protocol for COIL operatives behind enemy lines?"

"Never!" Titus punched a response for clarification, misspelling several words in his haste and frustration. "Corban won't respond, either. These coordinates are two days' hike away still, unless we can beg another truck ride from someone, which isn't likely."

"If Corban means for us to turn ourselves in, then why not to the nearest police station? Why to these coordinates specifically?" Song sat down in the field and used a boot lace to tie on the sole of his boot. All their gear was falling apart. "I don't think I can walk two more days."

"There must be something about Hudie Valley . . ." Titus shook his head. "Yep, I'm certain of it. Corban's showing off. He's testing me. He doesn't think I'll do it."

"Surrender? You can't!" Song rose to his feet. "There's no reason to turn ourselves in. You said yourself that's never protocol. We still have supplies left. Perhaps, we could turn toward Mongolia. I cannot be taken prisoner, Titus. And you—how's Oleg ever supposed to be rescued if we're sitting in prison, waiting for COIL to diplomatically extradite us? We'll never get back to China."

"There are ways, still . . ." Titus clenched his teeth. "Song, I value your input more than I would anyone else I recently met, but out here in the field, there's a unique rationale that is, well, irrational."

"Well, it'll be rational of them to interrogate us. That's what Chinese interrogators do. I've had experience doing it. They'll try everything. And Hudie Valley Prison could be a labor camp. You want to risk a mine shaft collapse as they force you to dig deep underground? There are no human rights in China, Titus, not for prisoners."

"But Corban said to do this." Titus growled. "Man, I should've never kidnapped him two weeks ago. He's getting even now."

"Please, let's pray together, brother. You know I'm willing to risk my life for our Lord, and even for others, but not for foolishness."

"Jeremiah's message was the same for the people of Jerusalem, remember? Surrender to live. We're going to Hudie Valley."

Hudie Valley – Present Day

Lisa opened her eyes and stared at the ceiling. The bed under her, the blankets covering her, and the sweet smell of cinnamon made no sense. Had God transported her out of prison to some castle with stone walls and expensive tapestries? Was this heaven?

She sat up and touched her head. There were memories, but maybe they were dreams—of being carried, of living in the cottages of Hudie Valley. And the presence of Steve. The wishful thought nearly made her cry, but she set the thought aside to climb out of bed. With hesitation, she approached an open doorway. Someone was in the next room.

Peering through the door, she saw a familiar face—though cleaner now.

"Ghuning?"

The woman at the desk stood up and smiled.

"You're awake. There were days I had my doubts if you would ever wake up."

"Where . . . are we?"

"In the warden's suite." She moved to Lisa's side and guided her to a sofa. "You're safe now. It's okay."

"Safe? The warden took me to bed? I don't—"

"No, no. We have a new warden." Ghuning pulled away from Lisa's hold, even as Lisa clung to her as a child clings to her mother. At the entrance of a doorway to outside, Ghuning paused to yell. "Warden Nee! She's awake!"

Lisa touched her hair. This was worse than waking up in an underground cell. Was she the object of a new warden?

Ghuning moved back inside and stood expectantly. A uniformed figure filled the doorway. Lisa blinked rapidly through the tears that flooded her eyes. This giant man was Warden Nee? She was his property now, she understood. Still, she glanced around the furnished apartment for a weapon, or a hiding place, or for anything familiar that could fill in the blanks.

The warden knelt in front of her.

"Don't cry, sweetie," he said in English, then reached for her face.

His voice was familiar, but his appearance was so strange. She cringed at his touch, and he withdrew quickly.

"She doesn't recognize you," Ghuning said. "Lisa, it's Steve."

"It's me." He laughed softly. Yes, she knew that voice. Steve. Again, he reached for her. "We're here. We're really together again."

"Steve?" She frowned, peering through his disguise, the goatee and uniform. "You don't look like . . . you."

"I thought I'd lost you." He squeezed her hand, then kissed her fingers. "We made it. God did this. Even through the worst of it, He knew this would be the end. Or the beginning. This moment."

"Steve!" She fell into his arms and he held her. This dream was too perfect. She closed her eyes tightly and refused to let go. "This is real?"

"Yes, it's real." He stroked her hair. "You're speaking Mandarin!"

"You're alive."

"I'm alive. I'm not the man you remember, not completely, but—"

"You're a better man," Ghuning said. "And she's a better woman. Both of you—this is your God's design. It couldn't have happened any other way."

"God's design." Lisa pulled away to look at the strange goatee covering her fiancé's face. "How did this happen? Where are we?"

"We're still in Hudie Valley. But God has shown us His favor. I'm, well, the warden now."

"Ghuning?"

"Yes, Lisa, it's true. We're releasing the prisoners one at a time. All the women, our friends, are already free."

"How?" Lisa sobbed. "The last I saw you, you were swimming in the ocean."

"Actually, connecting some pieces with Ghuning here, the last you saw me would've been a few months ago, when you looked up the valley. You all saw me, she said. I was the crippled man up the valley. For a while I used crutches."

"You're . . . crippled?"

"All by God's design." Steve pulled up his pant leg and rapped his knuckles on the iron shin. "As you know, sometimes God's plans take some twists and turns. We just have to hold on through the suffering, but it's all for our good."

"This is— You're the warden?"

Together, the three laughed and wept.

CHAPTER SEVENTEEN

Hudie Valley – Present Day

For months, Peng Zemin had been starved nearly to death. And sleeping on the floor of a damp rock cell was much different than sleeping in his silk sheets as Shanghai's commander of the secret police. Now, he spent his days tormented by the memories of his past evils, and the fear of the painful death that awaited him.

The atmosphere in the prison dungeon was changing. Peng heard the conversations between prisoners in other cells as they whispered under their doors to one another. The guards were new, and they came daily to pull one prisoner at a time from the cells. For processing, they said. But Peng and the others suspected a worse fate. Processing could mean interrogation, torture, or execution. He knew about those.

Peng pinched the skin that hung loosely over his ribs. He'd lost weight faster than his skin could shrink around his skeleton. The rice diet was probably healthier than what he used to eat, but the portions were so small! Well, until recently. Until the "processing" started. Now, the rice was flavored with grease, and he'd even found a piece of chicken a few times, and vegetables at other times.

Whatever was happening in the prison, Peng knew there was no hope for him. Tond-zu would never let him go free. Of course, Peng couldn't combat the charges against him, so Tond-zu had nothing to fear. But Peng knew the dark heart of the yawning man. The man would torture him for a few years, then kill him in some gruesome way, maybe even asking the warden to keep a piece of his body as a trophy. It wouldn't be the first time, Peng thought, remembering Tond-zu's habit of taking souvenirs since he was a young PRC soldier.

"Feet!" called a prisoner a few cells away. That was the whispered warning when guards were descending to their level of the prison.

Peng used the wall to stand upright. His head bumped the ceiling, and he cursed the architect of such a cramped cell. Then he remembered he'd sent dozens of prisoners to Tond-zu's secret inland prison for this exact kind of torment.

The key turned in the lock in his door! A flashlight in his eyes made him flinch away.

"Cao Yutong?"

Peng despised the name. It was so . . . peasant-like! But that was part of Tond-zu's torture. After all, telling anyone who he'd really been could get him killed by other prisoners, if they found out.

"Yes, that's me."

"Come with me." It was the new sergeant he'd heard the others talk about. One other guard was with him.

"For what?"

"Processing. The warden is waiting. Warden Nee."

Peng crouched to exit through the opening. The guard took him by the arm and led him up the tunnel. So, this was it, he thought. He'd be processed to death. The world would never know what happened to him. The world wouldn't even care. The hundreds he'd sent to their own deaths, or manipulated evidence to send them to labor camps—it was his just reward now, he knew.

When he emerged through the archway, he saw the sun for the first time in weeks. It almost brought him to his knees, except for the firm hand on his arm.

"Sit in the chair," the sergeant said.

With his hands shielding his face from the brightness, he shuffled barefoot onto the courtyard grass and sat down in front of the table. The grass felt so wonderful against his filthy toes. He expected to see blood all over the ground from other "processed" prisoners, but instead, he found a tall PRC officer seated opposite him. The officer had Caucasian eyes, which meant he probably had foreign blood from his mother or father.

He felt the scrutiny of the officer's strange eyes, but Peng wasn't about to waste his time in the open air. He'd been in darkness too long. He turned his head this way and that, gazing up at the fortress ramparts. So, this was Tond-zu's infamous death prison. It really was magnificent, with a balcony and towers and—

"You're not Cao Yutong," the officer suddenly stated.

Peng straightened in his chair like he'd been slapped.

"Yes. That's my, uh, name."

"You're from Shanghai?"

Peng tried to gauge the officer's tone as to his level of aggressiveness since his eyes were strange, not disclosing anything. His true identity could only hurt him, he guessed.

"Yes, I'm from Shanghai."

"What did you do there?"

"You mean, what was my crime?" Peng glanced at the nearest guard. They already had his file. This was a test. He expected they would strike him if he answered wrong. "I was a Christian."

"What kind of Christian?"

Peng frowned and looked down at the grass. How he longed to lay on the soft grass instead of on hard rock!

"The normal kind, I guess."

"The normal kind?" The officer chuckled. "If you're a Christian, you must have read the Bible, right?"

"The Christian religious book? Yes, of course."

"What is your understanding of the love of Jesus Christ?"

Peng shook his head, searching for an answer. He had interrogated plenty of Christians in his earlier years. What kind of questions were these? It had to be some form of manipulation. How hard could it be to pretend to be a Christian?

"Love. It's amazing. I can't imagine my life without it."

"Really? Which book of the Bible is your favorite?"

"I don't remember. Zechariah?"

"I see." The officer folded his hands. "Why are you pretending to be a Christian?" Again, the officer chuckled. "Your charges are clearly not true. Who did you cross, Peng? Your file says Tond-zu sent you here. I would've processed you sooner if I had known Cao Yutong was Peng Zemin."

Peng took a deep breath.

"So, you know who I am. Fine, I'm no Christian. Where do you process prisoners?" He turned and looked back at a gate in the wall. "Out there?"

"Out where?" The officer frowned. The more Peng's eyes adjusted to the brightness of the courtyard, the more he believed the officer wasn't Chinese at all, though his Mandarin was perfect. "Oh, no. I have orders here from a friend of yours that says, despite your many evils, you're to be freed instead of executed."

"What?"

"Yes, a man came forward and has pleaded for your life. I've chosen to let you go, but I'd like you to remain in the valley as a rice farmer. If Tond-zu finds out you're alive, he'll definitely have you murdered. You understand?"

Peng glanced at the young sergeant nearby, but the man was stone-faced.

"This isn't a joke? You know Tond-zu?"

"Oh, yes. I know him very well. Better than most."

"And you dare to cross him?"

"He's in Shanghai. We're hundreds of miles away. Besides, Tond-zu never convinced me that he has the keys to life and death."

"And you do?"

"Well, like I said, a man who knows you has asked that I spare your life. He says you may want a chance to live differently in the valley—a change from your life and thinking in Shanghai."

"A man spoke on my behalf?" Peng shook his head. He had no friends. He had destroyed everyone close to himself in his rise to power. Not even his most distant acquaintances would risk their lives or livelihoods for him if it meant defying Tond-zu. "No one would do that for me. I don't believe you."

"Do you accept the gift of life, or shall we place you back in the cell for the rest of your life?"

"I choose life!" Peng struggled to control his breathing, as if he were still obese and had just climbed two flights of stairs. "But who is this man?"

"A Christian. A real one."

"A Christian?" Peng felt his face redden. "No Christian would ever vouch for my life, not after what I've done to them. You already know who I am."

"Christians are not ignorant of the evils done against them, but they are not controlled by the evil. They submit to God, whose kindness promotes change especially in the most evil of hearts. But not everyone wants God's kindness. Do you receive it?"

Peng wiped at his eyes. This cursed brightness was making his eyes water!

"Of course! I accept this kindness. But who is the man? Tell me who would show me this kindness."

"Steve. Steve Brookshire."

Peng stared at the government official as the name cut deeply. He'd kidnapped Steve and his girlfriend, then tortured Steve and drugged his girlfriend to be condemned under Tond-zu's craftiness.

"It can't be. The man you speak of—his leg was cut off. Because of me. He couldn't possibly do this thing for me. It wouldn't be . . . normal."

"I know all about it. But it's all true. What you meant for evil against him, the only God of heaven and earth—the Christian God—He has meant it for good to bring about this kindness on you."

"I can't believe it!" Peng's fist went to his chest. "No! This cannot be!"

"Steve Brookshire is interceding on your behalf. This is the attitude of the God of the Christians."

"God?" Peng turned his face to the blue sky. He couldn't look into the brightness without squinting. And there were more tears distorting his vision. "He knows me?"

"Of course. He's been trying to get your attention for a very long time."

"I don't deserve this." Peng gasped. "I deserve this least of anyone. I swear it! This isn't . . . justice!"

"Then you'll spend your life as a testimony to God's grace. Do you still accept this kindness?"

Peng bowed his head. None of this was right. How could he receive grace from anyone?

"I accept." He lifted his head, abandoning the effort to hide his tears. "Is Steve Brookshire still alive?"

"Yes, he's in the valley somewhere."

"And he and I . . . will live in the same valley now?"

"Is that a problem?"

"No. No, it's not a problem. I've never actually met him. But after this, I'll owe him everything."

"Well, that's something you two can talk about. You're free to go."
Peng didn't rise.

"I'm to go live in the valley? Now?"

"Yes. The valley is full of Christians. They'll take care of you."

"More Christians? Then others know me as well? You know I sent many of them here through Tond-zu. To die."

"Steve will keep you safe. The farmers are loyal to Steve, and to Steve's God."

Peng used the table to steady himself as he stood.

"I don't know what to say to Steve Brookshire when I see him. Someone who has done this for me, after I have done . . . what I did to him . . ."

"You can start with an embrace when you see him," the official said, "and move on from there. God will guide you."

Peng nodded and walked to the gate. A guard unlocked and opened it. Pausing, Peng looked back at the official, aware suddenly that he hadn't asked if the official himself were a Christian. But now it was too late. He had so many questions!

Outside, the gate closed behind him and Peng was alone. He looked up the ridge trail that he knew led to a road and the river. But his safety from Tond-zu depended on never returning to his old life. Rather, he needed to remain in the good graces of the warden, who obviously favored Steve Brookshire.

So, Peng Zemin faced the rice paddies. Farmers were scattered here and there. He wondered which one was Steve until he remembered Steve had only one leg. Surely, the Christian was confined to a bed.

Steeling himself, he walked slowly onto the worn path that led to the group of cottages. It was time to meet Steve Brookshire. He owed the man his life. The thought brought a fresh burst of sobs to his frail, shuffling frame. He was free!

✣

Hudie Valley – Present Day

Titus watched from the ridge above Hudie Prison as a slender man in drab clothing walked slowly up the path to the cottages on the northern side of the valley.

"I don't like it," Titus said.

"I can smell it from here," Song said at his side. "It stinks like death."

They both wore camouflage as they hid in the foliage, totally still for fear of being spotted.

"That's a serious prison." Titus measured its perimeter through his rifle scope. "It's built into the hillside. It looks like the cells must be underground. There's no escaping a place like that once I go in."

"Maybe now is a good time to listen to reason." Song set a gentle hand on Titus' shoulder. "Something is wrong. Your friend, Corban, would never intend you to be trapped beyond rescue."

Titus scrolled backwards on his watch to read the text from Corban for the hundredth time: *Your best route out of China is to get captured. Surrender to Hudie Valley Prison.*

"No, I've got to surrender here. We're out of options. Soldiers are searching everywhere for us. We have one canteen, and the terrain north of us is even drier." Titus closed his eyes. "I think—I'm assuming Corban is proving something to me."

"Would he send you to your death?"

"No. Never. Not Corban."

"You're sure?"

"I'm sure."

"Let me." Song started to rise, but Titus pulled him flat onto the hillside. "What? If it's a trap, you'll have a better chance to escape than me. If it's safe, I'll signal you. Look at me, Titus. I won't make it another mile."

"It might take me a month or two to get you out of that place." Titus glared at the prison, then locked eyes with Song. "You sure about this?"

"It would be my honor."

"We should plan more, signals and whatnot."

"If you trust Corban, I'll trust you." Song smiled. "You're too stubborn to walk away, and I'm too tired to argue with you. So, one of us has to go in."

"Not without prayer." Titus set down his rifle. "Oh, Lord, we're an unlikely pair, me and Song . . ."

Hudie Valley – Present Day

Steve stood beside Lisa on the balcony as they watched Peng Zemin approach the rice farmers.

"That was the most supernatural conversation I've ever heard." Lisa wrapped her arms around Steve. "He took so much from us, and yet I felt so much sorrow for him. I'm ashamed of how desperate I've been living while you've been leading people to Christ this entire time!"

"We were in it together." Steve held her. "We just didn't know it at the time."

There was a clang on the outside of the gate. Steve checked his watch, one of the many gifts inherited as warden, and saw it wasn't shift change yet. With the hired guards excused a few days earlier, several released men from the valley had begun to act as guards—not to guard but to keep order in the prison and to serve the handful of true prisoners.

Sergeant Vu Qing opened the gate after a signal from Steve to go ahead. In walked a slender Japanese man, his clothes stained and torn. One of his boot soles looked to be tied onto his foot.

Qing looked from the Japanese man to Steve for direction. Since Oleg had told him a man named Titus Caspertein and Song Sakana were in the area, Steve knew this had to be his old torturer, though the thick-armed man had changed much in two years. He had softened.

"Lisa, come with me." Steve led the way down the stairs, and took Lisa's hand at the bottom. Song was watching them closely, and Steve prayed for Lisa as much as for himself—for the right words for this reunion.

They stopped in front of one another.

"Warden Nee?" Vu Qing asked. "The gate?"

"You can close it, Sergeant." Steve said. "Mr. Sakana is a guest here."

Song stared for a moment, then bowed low. When he straightened upright, Steve noticed the older man's lower lip trembling in a vigilant effort to contain his emotions. He looked down at Steve's leg, then up at Lisa.

"I've heard you've been looking for us." Steve held Lisa's hand. "We've been waiting for you. Shouldn't there be another—"

Lisa left Steve's side and put her arms around the neck of Song. Steve watched Song remain rigid for a few seconds, then he crumbled into a sob that drew Steve to support them both.

After several seconds, they moved to the courtyard grass and sat down where Song could rest. Qing brought water as Ghuning watched from the balcony.

"Your leg?"

"An iron prosthetic."

"I see." Song nodded, wiping at his tears. "I'm in your debt—both of you."

"We've had two days to talk about your arrival." Steve took Lisa's hand again. He never wanted to let her go! "We're not angry with you. It's important you know that. We've forgiven you. As impossible as that should be, well, our God does miracles."

"This meeting is no small miracle!" Song gestured to Qing. "Did he call you warden?"

"We'll tell you everything, but this isn't the only reunion today. Commander Peng Zemin was a prisoner here, too. Tond-zu had him sent here under a different name. I barely recognized him from newspapers when I worked in Shanghai and all the time I spent avoiding him as I networked there."

"Peng is here?" Song sat in thought for a moment. "Was he the man who just left?"

"That was him. He understands he can't leave or Tond-zu will kill him."

"Of course, but did you lead him to Christ?"

"He's planted the seed." Lisa ruffled Steve's hair. "Give him a couple days. Steve'll have Peng reading Bible stories to the kids."

"I have no doubt." Song sighed. "After all, you taught me the love of Christ, Steve, two years ago. I took so much from both of you, but all you did was give."

"This is the kind of God we serve," Steve said, "and we'll continue to see His truth touch lives—with us at the heart of all the suffering."

"You're staying here?" Song suddenly held up his hand. "Wait, don't say another word. Can you open your gate? COIL Operative Titus Caspertein needs to hear the whole story, too. Just wave up at the ridge. He'll come down."

Steve exited the gate and waved at the hillside. A moment later, a tall man with blond hair marched down the trail. He carried a rifle, but Steve knew it was surely loaded with non-lethal rounds.

"Titus Caspertein, I presume?" Steve said in English. They shook hands as Titus frowned at Steve's appearance. "You probably have a lot of questions."

"Steve Brookshire?" Titus threw his head back in laughter. "It ain't easy being rescued by the man I was sent to liberate! I've been fretting for our lives for weeks, and you're sitting pretty in here?"

"I called Corban as soon as Oleg showed up." Steve smiled, immediately liking the casual American and his Southern accent.

"Oleg's here?" Titus held up his rifle. "Say, you don't mind if I tranquilize him for making me worry, do you?"

"Can you shoot in the dark? He's camped out in a lower cell."

"In a cell?"

"We had to put him there until I laid off some guards, but now that his cell door is open, he's just hanging out, talking to prisoners. He says it's cooler down there, anyway."

"Well, I'm not used to being the last one to join a party, but if you have an extra cell, I could get out of this heat, too."

"How do you all plan to get out of China now?"

They walked back into the courtyard to join Song and Lisa.

"We're not far from the Mongolian border now." Titus winked at Song. "I suspect Corban's already making arrangements, especially since it looks like you're in charge around here. But the way you're talking makes it sound like you're comfortable here."

"Comfortable? No." Steve sat down on the grass. "But God couldn't be more clear about wanting me here than if He used a bullhorn. And I'd rather be uncomfortable in God's will than comfortable out of His will. We'll call it contentment."

"Well said." Song passed water to Titus. "With your permission, I'd like to be the first among us to pray."

"You never have to ask permission to pray around me," Steve said, taking Lisa's hand again. "I've craved the company of more praying people for months."

"Just tell me this," Titus said after draining the cup of water, "how long would you wait to unlock Oleg if I locked him in a cell below?"

"What?" Lisa gasped.

"He's kidding, sweetie," Steve said.

"No, I'm serious. He keeps teasing me about the holes in my socks."

"Perhaps," Song interrupted, "I should just start praying . . ."

Hudie Valley – Present Day

Peng Zemin heard the commotion outside and set down a basket he'd been weaving. His mother had weaved baskets, he remembered, so the art was a nostalgic exercise under the watchful eye of four elderly weavers.

As he stepped outside the cottage, he took a deep breath. This was the moment, he told himself, that he was to meet his savior. The farmers, who'd given him a mat in one of the cottages, had already revealed to him that Warden Nee was Steve Brookshire.

The commotion was caused by dozens of farmers and released prisoners greeting Steve as the tall foreigner walked up to the cottages. The man had changed into peasant clothes, as Peng wore.

Finally, the crowd parted and hushed themselves as Steve reached Peng. The former Shanghai official stood up straight and almost saluted the tall American, but decided that was an inappropriate gesture. He resigned to bow low, lower than he'd ever bowed to anyone.

A hand touched his shoulder, bringing him to stand upright.

"Peng Zemin," Steve said, his eyes more gentle than Peng could imagine.

"I had some words . . ." Peng hung his head. "But I can't recall them now."

"It's okay. There'll be time to talk later. I have to get back to the prison."

"I understand." Peng found that he couldn't look Steve in the eyes. "Thank you for . . . this."

"I'm just a servant, Peng."

"Of course. Your God is to be honored. The people have told me."

"I'm sure they have."

"I've heard of this . . . story night." Peng motioned to the farmers, whose faces were so bright and smiling. "They make it sound better than the theater."

"Everything's better when done amongst friends. We'll talk soon. I'm glad you're doing better."

Peng couldn't hold himself back, and he couldn't allow Steve to return to the prison without expressing himself. He stepped forward and slowly wrapped his arms around the tall man, his teary eyes pressing into Steve's chest. Peng couldn't remember ever embracing another man, but it felt like the only natural response to all that he'd received.

"I hate the man I was!" he blurted. "I'm so sorry! I'm so sorry!"

Steve hugged him, and instead of the farmers standing around awkwardly, they laid their hands on the reconciled man. After all, until recently, every Christian in the valley had been sent there by Peng. It was a day of reconciliation for everyone.

New Jersey – One Month Later

Corban Dowler sat in a church pew next to his wife, Janice. On this Sunday morning, they were attending a small assembly in Franklinville, in Southern New Jersey. Jenna, their blind daughter, now in high school, sat next to her mother while Corban sat on the aisle, his crutches between his knees.

The pastor was speaking about the importance of missions—nationally and worldwide—but Corban was having trouble concentrating. He was thinking about the phone call from Titus he'd received right before the service. Titus, Annette, and Oleg were in Nepal for the grand opening of a woman's shelter that was run by Ercan Sanli, an ex-killer from the Soldiers of Mahdi militants. Corban wanted to be there in the field, witnessing the miracles in souls, seeing first-hand as God changed lives, even in the midst of strife and violence.

But his legs weren't ready yet, and he didn't have a good excuse to start disappearing for days at a time to run his own missions, either. He was able to walk short distances now, but with a cane. Soon, he would be able to run. Keeping his secret was paramount to COIL's security. Enemies were always lurking—physical and spiritual enemies.

Across the aisle, someone cleared his throat. It was Luigi Putelli, his shadow—not too invisible that day as he attended the church with his girlfriend, Heather Oakes. He'd walked into the church and pretended not to know the Dowler family, which delighted Jenna, since she could play along with his exaggerated need to remain a secret agent. At the back of the church, she'd drilled him for fun for several minutes, testing his legend: *What's your name? Where are you from? Why do you have an accent? What brings you and your girlfriend to Franklinville?*

With Heather shaking her head, Corban had let Luigi endure Jenna's test without rescue, and the Italian had passed every question—his careful identity foolproof under Jenna's scrutiny.

Luigi wasn't the only secret agent on Corban's mind. Rashid al-Sabur had reported in from China, finally. The COIL man was still keeping an eye on Commander Tond-zu's activities in Shanghai. When Corban briefed him on Steve's work in Hudie Valley, Rashid committed to remaining in China for Steve's security. Corban approved of the intelligence officer's intent to shadow Tond-zu and keep the Hudie Valley Christians safe. Steve and Lisa were not alone.

Corban's phone vibrated with a triple "ring" signal. Emergency. He shifted his crutches to his other hand, then slipped the phone from his pocket. Next to his leg, he checked the screen.

"Code red, Corban, Qatar. Christians abducted. Danger high. I'm on site. Send the best you've got.—Nicole."

He slid his phone into his pocket. Wynter Caspertein was on her first big assignment. She was seeing Christian persecution first-hand, and she wanted the best COIL team available. Available or not, the best COIL had now was her own brother, Titus, and of course, Oleg, whose knee injury was still recovering from their China escapade. Titus would have to send Annette home and fly himself and Oleg to Qatar. Wes Trimble might've already gotten there, since he and Wynter were a couple now, rumor had it. It was going to be a busy summer.

". . . So, it's my honor to welcome today," the chapel preacher said, "our brother, Corban Dowler. He has a little experience with Christian missions. Corban, the floor is yours."

Corban used the pew in front of him to lean on as he locked his braces and stood quickly—maybe too quickly since he sometimes cheated now by using his functioning legs. He used the crutches to walk to the podium, then turned and gazed for a moment across the forty people in the room. The fellowship already believed in the Great Commission, so he wouldn't preach to them. They'd already sent several men and women overseas or across the country to minister, so he wasn't there to recruit anyone, either. What could he say to such dedicated believers who'd already faithfully sent people into the harvest?

"Not long ago," he began, trying to put Wynter Caspertein's Qatar emergency out of his mind until later, "a Christian man was kidnapped in a foreign country. It wasn't in the news. No one even knew he was serving God while in that dangerous place. The people hired to kidnap him, tortured him for information about a Christian underground network. In the process, they cut off his leg and beat him nearly to death.

"Today, I want to tell you about Christ's work in an unnamed country, and this man with one leg. We'll say his name is . . . Joseph."

DISTANT HARM

BOOK THREE

The COIL legacy

D.I. TELBAT

Note from the author

Dear Reader,

First, it is worth noting that the five *Kindred of Nails* (KONs) characters in *Distant Harm* are based on real people, though of course, I have changed their names. They are sacrificial and courageous servants of Jesus Christ on the front lines in their ministries, so I wanted to memorialize them in this fictional story.

Secondly, many facts in this book about North Korea's labor camps are accurate, from the voltage of the electric fence, to the amputations of prisoner body parts. It is not my intention to disgust readers, but to reveal what our brothers and sisters in Christ are enduring right now. This is real.

Next, it should be mentioned that I have fictionalized one building inside Pyongyang's city center. For reasons of safety for real believers inside the repressive capital, the People's Palace of Remembrance is a figment of my imagination, though the rules for worshipping and photographing the statues is very real inside the city's other museums.

As in my other COIL novels, the DRIL and Gabriel technology is all based on actual developed drones already used in the US military.

The *Juche* idea of the North Korean Communist Party really is developed like a cult, with dictator worship demanded in brainwashing classes where the populace is told to "think through the personality of the Great Leader" to maintain national supremacy and unity. Eating sawdust and grass roots is actual advice the "Great Leader" has given for his people to endure the current famine in the land. They are starving to death—even the elite members of society.

Though the oppression of the North Korean regime is highlighted much in this book, the regime is comprised of people who need Jesus. Satan and sin are our enemies, not North Koreans, and there are sometimes instances of high-ranking Communist Party members coming to Christ in the real world.

When we pray for our enemies, and wait on God to move, miracles happen, as is illustrated in this book. Although North Korea is not very racially diverse, foreigners who submit to the government's rule are allowed to become citizens, though under strict supervision. There are even defectors—Americans included—who have sought refuge in North Korea, and remain there to this day. This reality has been the basis of some of the plot in this novel.

The Hamgyong Prison in *Distant Harm* is fictional, but it is based on the actual Hoeryong Concentration Camp in North Korea. Its official name is Kwalliso Number 22. Prisoners and their families are worked to death day after day. They are the "politically unreliable," and include Christians, returnees from Japan, and descendants of prisoners of war from South Korea.

Some children are born in the labor colonies, since whole families are given housing inside the prisons. The children are raised to work beside their parents, where they will spend their whole lives. Hundreds die every year in these camps. Although executions do occur, the government prefers to kill its condemned prisoners by working them to death in the mines or at the factories.

Because of the oppression inside North Korea, the Christian Church is thriving in quiet, underground circles. They do not want American or South Korean pity. In smuggled communications, Korean Christian leaders have said they want only our prayers that Jesus Christ will be glorified through their sufferings, which is their cross to bear. Their faith in the midst of such misery challenges us, does it not?

I have tried to capture some of the bold selflessness of suffering Christians in this COIL novel. May we remember the prisoners, and may we have the same hope they have for heaven.

I look forward to your thoughts on this final Legacy novel. And remember—the COIL story continues in the *Last Dawn Trilogy*. May God be glorified.

David Telbat

Dedication

This book is dedicated to the real-life
Kindred of Nails (KONS),
who sacrifice for Christ daily
while being despised, poor, and miserable.
Their service is not seen by society,
but they are well-known
by God and their brethren.
May their love inspire us all.

Laos

Avery Hewitt splashed through the stream as gunfire ripped through the jungle. He had no time to think, only to run. Next to him, a teenage girl fell on the bank of the stream. Whether she'd been shot or she'd just slipped, Avery wasn't sure. All he knew was that he couldn't abandon anyone within arm's reach.

Other villagers fled into the jungle, some adults dragging their children or the wounded with them. A body floated face down in a widened stretch of the stream where the secret baptism had been taking place. More soldiers emerged from the trees farther upstream. Heading west was out of the question. Avery needed to leave Laos behind and get into Vietnam, even with its own potential dangers for Christians.

Though he was slender and only five-nine, Avery had known nothing but a hard life that had left him both weathered and strong. As the only white man at the jungle baptism that afternoon, he guessed the army would make an example of him if he were captured. The government would use him as a prisoner—or display his dead body—to frighten Westerners away from sympathizing and supporting the Hmong believers.

Regardless of the increasing risk in those few seconds, Avery dropped to one knee and took hold of the fallen teen's arm. She struggled and pulled back, but he had no time for her fear-stricken paralysis. It seemed she wasn't injured, just panicked. He drew her over his shoulder and darted stiffly into the bushes with his burden.

Almost instantly, the gunfire ceased, but the cries of the wounded continued. An officer blew a whistle, and orders were shouted. Avery continued through the chest-high tangle of vines, then emerged on a well-worn path, much like the one he'd hiked ten miles on to reach the secret baptism. Panting, he set the girl down. She immediately darted down the path toward the sounds of other escaping villagers.

Once again, Avery was alone. He crouched as the bushes near him rustled. Suddenly, two uniformed soldiers stepped onto the trail, one soldier on each side of him, twenty yards apart. They were young, maybe not yet twenty years old. Glancing from soldier to soldier, Avery tensed to dive back into the foliage. Reading their faces, he could see the young gunmen realized their opportunity to kill or capture a white man. They leveled their rifles simultaneously and fired.

Searing heat slashed across Avery's chest and knocked him backward. He knew he'd been shot. As he lay on his back, half on the trail, he felt the trickle of blood running down both sides of his torso. There was a burning sensation, but he distinctly acknowledged the pain was being compartmentalized by adrenalin.

Sitting up, he looked to his left and right. Both soldiers were down. In that instant, Avery gasped with the realization that the soldiers had each shot one another, though one bullet had grazed his own chest, bloodying and tearing his shirt across his front.

Ignoring his wound, he crawled to his left and touched the first young man's neck. He was dead, shot in the chest. Next, he checked the other, and found the soldier gazing up at the sky, panting with shallow breaths. The man had a debilitating injury to his shoulder, but not life-threatening, unless he was left to bleed.

Avery gently helped the man out of his backpack straps and dug through the pack for a first aid kit. The soldier carried no kit, but he had an extra shirt, which Avery tore into strips.

The soldier whispered foreign words and stared at Avery's face while he tied the shirt around the man's shoulder and under his armpit.

Before other soldiers doubled back and found them, Avery lifted and dragged the wounded man off the trail, where he propped him against a stump that was consumed by mushrooms and moss. Having helped the soldier, Avery now needed to consider his own survival.

There was no returning to the airport in Laos. For all he knew, the soldiers were in the jungle that day hunting for him after he'd entered the country with three suitcases of Bibles. Airport security may have reviewed their camera footage of him offering a customs officer a gift for his family to let him pass. The customs officer had accepted the gift—an electronic Bible and digital stories for his children. Avery had left the airport, but that didn't mean the officer hadn't reported him thirty seconds later.

Or maybe the twenty Christians in the jungle that day had been tracked, and Avery had simply been at the wrong place at the wrong time. Whatever the case, he needed to leave Laos behind immediately.

From the wounded soldier, Avery took the man's canteen, lighter, and rifle. He patted his patient's good shoulder, then leaped into the forest to the east. A four-hour visit to Laos had become a trek across the country. If necessary, he'd hike all the way to Vietnam's east coast, but he guessed he'd come across a highway and transportation in a day or two.

Avery slipped under tree branches and leaped fallen logs like he'd been born in the jungle. He gloried in the fact that God had taught him to let go of the world, carrying nothing, owning no possessions. At a moment's notice, God could direct him somewhere, and he wanted to be free to go without looking back. Back home, he'd heard puzzled Christians in churches discuss his awkward way of living—the fact that he carried only a Bible, a toothbrush, and a compass.

In America, Avery had visited various churches, preached in parks, and slept wherever he happened to lay his head. Sometimes believers who received his words of revival and self-sacrifice gave him a bed for the night, but most often, Avery was too radical for most American professing Christians. He'd given up all to follow Christ and preach the gospel while so many chased the American dream.

No one lived like Avery. Many had sneered, and judged him insane. Thus, he knew the discomforts of scorn and sleeping on the streets with the destitute, but that merely gave him a chance to speak to the homeless about Jesus Christ. Only recently had a church leadership allowed him to sleep in their basement, and they had financed a short-term mission effort to equip Christians in Laos with Bibles. Avery hoped the courage of this first church to associate with him was a sign of open doors to come.

Prior to this invitation to smuggle Bibles, Avery had never left the States, but he now trekked through the vines and trees without worry. In his mind, he scoffed at fear and steadied his nerves by reminding himself that he served the God who had made this jungle. What did he have to fear?

At sundown, he shot a small deer and built a fire. He sensed the Laotian soldiers were far behind him. The fates of the other Christians and the Bibles he'd risked his life to give them were out of his control. God would see to them all, Avery pondered as he watched the stars blink through the jungle canopy above.

He fought away feelings of loneliness and drew out his pocket Bible to read by the light of the fire. From Psalm 34, his soul was refreshed, and he dried his eyes before lying down. His visit to Laos had been spontaneous, like much of his life had been since leaving prison. Establishing a routine hardly seemed like a call placed upon him by God, especially when his heart was so burdened with standing boldly for Christ wherever he went.

As Avery settled into a restful sleep on the twigs and grass of Vietnam, he wondered for what great thing God was preparing him.

CHAPTER ONE

Russia

Corban Dowler stood motionless in the freezing rain outside Vladivostok in Eastern Russia. Long past were the days when, in his prime, he'd hunted Cold War spies for the CIA. Now, he would be the one hunted, if anyone figured out who he was.

A medium-sized fishing vessel flying a Japanese flag approached the pier below. The town was hunkered down as dusk closed and the Siberian chill choked the landscape in a late fall storm.

Under his overcoat, Corban felt the hard steel of a revolver loaded with COIL's non-lethal gel-tranquilizer cartridges. Except for the gun, he had no backup if this meeting went badly. No one within a thousand miles knew who he was. Even his family and closest friends thought he was visiting missionaries in Singapore.

The fishing vessel bumped against the pier, and sailors tied off the sixty-foot vessel, but Corban remained where he stood. Behind him, the engine of his Volvo purred, ready to race him to safety if danger arose.

In 1945, Vladivostok had been the launching pad for North Korea's Communist Party leadership. Now, Corban hoped the Russian port city would host the arrival of news from North Korea that would contribute to the Party's demise.

Corban drew his collar tighter around his neck, trying to keep out the chilling moisture. He was approaching his mid-sixties now, and though he was confident in his skills to impact the international theatre for Christ's sake, his body had been prone to injury and illness the last few years. He now stood on his own two legs, free of braces and crutches, but he had no confidence in his flesh to ward off ailments or enemies, as he had in his youth.

Below, three sailors carried a limp body off the boat and laid it on the cement pier. Corban glanced around the harbor. No one obvious was watching the shoreline or paying attention on the freezing fall day.

"There's no waste with You, Father," Corban mumbled in prayer as he started down the steps to the wharf. He needed the affirmation of God's might in that moment as he realized the limp body below was the courier he'd needed to speak to about a critical situation in North Korea. But Corban knew the man's death wouldn't be wasted by God.

The three Japanese sailors stepped back as Corban drew close and knelt at the side of the Korean man lying on the pier. The man was dead, as suspected. There was a tear in his thin jacket stained with blood. A bullet had wounded the courier, Corban guessed, but he'd managed to still get aboard the fishing boat to come see him. Corban had never met the man personally, but through the underground Christian network, they'd made contact. The situation was worse in Pyongyang than Corban suspected if God's hidden ambassadors were being shot mid-mission.

"Money," one of the Japanese men said.

Corban didn't rise from his knees. He unbuttoned his coat and reached past his revolver to an envelope of cash. The Japanese fishermen weren't really fishermen, but criminals he'd hired through Song Sakana in Akita. They were crooked men, but the only men daring enough to have approached North Korea to fetch the courier.

"There may be more work for you in the next few weeks." Corban handed the nearest man the envelope, but he didn't move to button his coat again. If necessary, he could draw his revolver in an instant. It was possible the criminals were waiting to receive payment before they killed him, if they'd received a counter-offer from North Korean agents. "May we call upon you again?"

The men looked down at the dead body.

"No. It is too dangerous. Our job is done."

Backing away, the men hopped onto their boat deck and cast off the lines. Corban waited until their bow was pointed southeast and their stern was fading behind the sheets of rain before he searched the body before him. He couldn't be certain this man had been the courier he'd been expecting to receive unless he found something to identify him.

The dead man's clothing was of poor quality and worn thin. Opening the man's shirt, Corban studied the fatal wound closer. It wasn't a bullet wound after all, but some sort of puncture, as if from something blunt. Maybe even a hammer. Someone had killed him up close, face to face—someone deadly, merciless, and cold-hearted.

Though Corban wanted to discover more, he couldn't do so on the open pier. He could speak fluent Russian, and his identification was flawless, but there was too much happening within COIL for him to be delayed by police, if he were discovered examining a dead body.

He drew the Korean's light frame over his shoulder and stood upright, though shakily. His legs weren't the powerful limbs they'd once been, but he'd been exercising them during his recovery from a paralysis suffered in Gaza years earlier.

Mounting the stairs from the pier, he gasped at each step. The cold air burned his lungs. He contemplated stopping to rest, but pushed himself forward. When he reached the top, he froze. A thin, gaunt-faced man stood at the rear of Corban's Volvo. The trunk was open. There was twenty feet between them, an easy shot to make if Corban pulled his revolver now. But there was no need.

"You're not supposed to know I'm in Russia, Luigi," Corban said.

"And you're not supposed to be able to walk." Luigi Putelli didn't move to help, but he was clearly gloating as he chewed on a wad of bubble gum. He was never a man to miss an opportunity to use his tracking skills to impress Corban. "I suspected you weren't as disabled as others believed."

"What gave me away?" Corban continued with his burden to the car. "Not the trunk. He deserves better."

Luigi closed the trunk and opened the back door to help Corban load the body into the back seat.

"I found your leg braces in your car parked at JFK airport," Luigi said. "That's a little suspicious, don't you think?"

Corban steadied his breathing from the exertion, but Luigi seemed to be in peak condition, though he'd suffered debilitating injuries over the years as well.

"No one can know I'm physically able to infiltrate anywhere I please," Corban said, "or COIL will return to the radar of those who once thought we were a threat."

"My lips are sealed, as always." Luigi blew a bubble with his gum and gestured at the dead man. "Where are we going with him?"

"We?"

"A dead Asian in Russia?" Luigi hooked his thumbs in his belt, which Corban knew doubled as a non-lethal weapon, its buckle tipped with tranquilizer toxin. "I may keep your walking a secret for you, but not even you can make me step away when there's danger nearby."

"For Christians, there's always danger nearby." Corban moved to the driver's door and climbed in. "Come on."

Though Luigi's own rental car was parked nearby, the slim Italian agent climbed into the passenger seat.

"Normally, I can figure out what you're doing." Luigi adjusted the rearview mirror and checked out the windows for anyone approaching their position. "You've left North Korea's underground work to other agents for years. Why the interest now?"

"A contact disappeared, including his pregnant wife."

"There was nothing in the news feeds."

"I know." Corban took a deep breath, thankful to include someone else in the operation. "This is personal to North Korea's regime, but there's an international threat as well."

"Is he one of ours?" Luigi turned in his seat. "He's young. His hair is styled, so he wasn't in the wilderness or a village. He was probably from the city, maybe Pyongyang or Hamhung. His fingers aren't calloused, so he wasn't a laborer. His shoes are better quality than North Korea's normal working class, I'm guessing, since they're Swiss imports. North Korea's dictator has ties in Switzerland where he went to university. Might this be someone who was near to the regime's leader?"

"Let's search him."

Luigi jumped out and climbed into the back seat as Corban turned in his seat to pick through the dead man's pockets, even checking his skin for identifying marks. Luigi slipped off the man's shoes, pulled up his pant legs, then tugged off his socks. A folded-up piece of paper tumbled from one sock. Delicately, Luigi picked up the soaked paper and placed it in Corban's palm.

"Any idea what this might say?"

"I have an idea lives will be affected by what it says." Corban set the note on the dashboard near the heater. "We need to dry it out before trying to unfold it. I have a feeling we'll be calling Titus Caspertein. Unless I'm mistaken, North Korea is about to get the full attention of COIL."

"It'll be a pleasure to see COIL back in top form, Corban, especially with you at the front."

"The world has changed a lot since you and I wrote the rules of espionage, Luigi." Corban couldn't hold back a smile. "But yes, it seems God is calling out the best of COIL for an op that will test us all."

"What do we do with our brother here?" Luigi frowned. "Do you even know his name?"

"No, and I doubt we'll ever know it." Corban gripped the steering wheel. "God knows best the sacrifice he made for others, but now we need to bury him where he'll never be found. North Korea can't know we're coming!"

𝆕

Utah

Thirty-six miles outside Salt Lake City's International Airport, Titus Caspertein wore a utility belt as he sauntered down the hallway inside Deer Valley's lush Montage Resort. That night, if he cared to peek out the windows at the mountain, he'd find the ski runs lit up, and the fresh powder seemingly aglow after the first early blizzard in the Rockies.

But Titus wasn't there to ski or to enjoy the spa. His tool belt held all the traditional hardware for any fix-it man to repair any number of breakdowns in the resort, except one pocket held a non-traditional tool. His hand brushed the handle of a small caliber pistol. Like all COIL weaponry, it was loaded with gel-tranqs, and he'd already screwed a silencer onto the muzzle.

Before he rounded a corner and walked up a short flight of stairs to a second floor landing, Titus palmed his phone and held it to his ear.

"Yes, yes, the heater's working now. I opened it up myself and checked the temperature in every room of that residence." He approached a hotel doorway where two Sudanese men in suits were standing. "I don't know why they're still complaining. It's the beginning of the season. What do they expect? A few appliances need a little understanding."

Titus stopped in front of the doorway guarded by the two bodyguards. Though he was taller than both men, they each outweighed him by thirty pounds. A physical tussle didn't appeal to the Arkansas native, so he hoped his wit would prevail.

"I'm here about the leaky pipe." Titus held up a wrench. "The water pipe? Water? Drip, drip? You don't speak English?"

Both bodyguards glanced at one another. It was obvious they were professionals. They wouldn't be on guard duty for a wealthy African warlord unless they were the deadliest their boss could afford.

"Well, where should I put this?" Titus held up the wrench and seemed to search his utility belt for a loop to hold it, but then changed his mind. "Here, you hold it."

He tossed it lightly to the larger of the two Sudanese men. The tool was heavy enough to injure a foot, so the bodyguard fumbled to catch the steel object. With his right hand, Titus drew his silenced pistol and shot the second guard in the upper chest, then turned to the other, who now held the tool with a shocked look on his face. Both men collapsed to the floor, the tranquilizer coursing through their bloodstreams. They'd wake without serious injury, though the bruises would remind them that their lives had been spared.

Titus touched the communications button on his neck hidden under his flannel collar.

"The two in the front are down. How's the view outside?"

"Forget the view!" Oleg Saratov growled through the comm. "I'm freezing out here. We rented a lodge with a hot tub. After this, you're not going to stop me from climbing in and warming up!"

"I've never met a Russian who was so afraid of the cold."

"That's true." Oleg's voice calmed. "It would seem your spoiled American whining is rubbing off on me."

Titus chuckled.

"Let's crash this party and get you into that hot tub. I'm making an entrance in five, four, three, two . . ."

Titus backed away from the door, then heel-kicked it where the deadbolt was secured. The alpine ornamental frame burst inward. With his handgun leveled, Titus entered the residence as he heard a crash of glass from across the room. Oleg had made his entrance through the tall living room window.

Skirting the kitchen, Titus passed into the living room. Two men stood holding firearms—a sidearm and a carbine—and seemed torn between firing at the window where Oleg's short but powerful form advanced from the wintery weather, or at Titus as he moved deftly behind a large sectional sofa.

Oleg fired first, and Titus pulled the trigger an instant later. Both men dropped unconscious onto the carpeted floor as Titus reloaded and nodded at Oleg. The broad-chested Russian threw open a bedroom door, then leapt aside, expecting gunfire. Titus dove into the bedroom, rolled over his shoulder, and came up on one knee. His weapon was aimed at a bare-chested, middle-aged African man. A woman in a bathrobe screamed from the open door of the bathroom.

"Get back in there!" Titus yelled at her, then at Oleg, "The room's clear!"

Oleg stalked into the bedroom as the woman slammed the bathroom door. Her whimpering was muffled from inside.

"Is this him?" Oleg asked. "The Butcher of Rumbek?"

The Sudanese man held his empty hands up and glared at Titus.

"The Serval! What are you doing here? I have no business with you! We have had no deals in over a decade!"

"So, you *do* remember me." Titus plucked flex-cuffs from his tool belt and tossed them on the bed. "Put those on, but I suggest you get dressed first. It's cold outside, and it's a long ride back to the city."

"What about the hot tub?" Oleg asked. "I thought we had a deal. I need to recover from this mountain weather."

"You want to sit in the hot tub while I take him alone to the federal office?"

"I have diplomatic immunity!" The Sudanese man drew on pants and shook a finger at Titus. "You cannot prosecute me! I am immune to your government's prosecution!"

"You *had* immunity," Titus said, "but once we saw you coming into the United States to play, we informed your government of the atrocities you committed in Rumbek. The International Criminal Court wants you for genocide, so your government revoked your diplomatic status earlier today. You killed a lot of Christians in Rumbek, old friend, and now you're going to The Hague to stand trial."

"Christians!" The man spit on the carpet. "I spit on their unmarked graves! I curse the bones we burned to ashes! If I could, I would return to that valley and—"

Titus tranqed the mass murderer with a shot to his bare sternum. The man fell face-first onto the bed.

"I'd heard enough." Titus holstered his weapon.

"You could've waited until he finished getting dressed." Oleg held up a shirt. "Now I have to wrestle this shirt onto him on my own."

"It ain't easy doing all the hard work in this partnership, Oleg."

Titus laughed, then reached for his phone as it vibrated. "Looks like we got a text from Corban. It says, 'Code: *Philemon.*'"

"Philemon? I can't remember all the code words you two come up with." Oleg grunted over his efforts to put the shirt on the sleeping Sudanese man, then he stood upright. "Which op is Philemon?"

"Corban's recalling all the top tier field agents. Something big is coming up." Titus shook his head at the unconscious man. "Look at him, Oleg. You put his shirt on backwards! Now, you have to start over. Go on. I'll pull the car around."

"I'll fix his shirt if I get thirty minutes in the hot tub in our room."

"I'll tell you what. If you fix his shirt, cuff him, and put his shoes on him, we can take ten minutes in the hot tub."

"Oh, now you want to join me?" Oleg shook his finger at Titus. "I knew you wanted a good soak as much as me."

"Come on, Oleg. Corban's waiting!"

California

After delivering the Bibles to Christians in Laos, Avery Hewitt had nearly died while attending the secret baptism of underground believers. His chest was still scabbed from the bullet wound. Escaping from Laos, he'd then spent three desperate days and nights in the humid jungles of Vietnam, avoiding poisonous snakes, scrapping for food, and praying that he'd find favor when he reached a coastal airport.

Providing his US passport, he was given passage on a Canadian Aid C-130 transport plane to North America. He was finally safe. But when Avery returned to California from his short-term mission, he didn't receive the homecoming he'd anticipated from God's faithful people. Instead, he came back to discord and animosity.

"There's been a lot of talk while you were gone, Avery," said Pastor Scott, a white-bearded tall man with kind eyes. Two other church elders and two deacons sat in the circle in the otherwise empty Sunday school room. "It concerns your past. There've been complaints."

"I see." Avery's eyes settled on the carpet. He realized he'd gotten his hopes up a little too high regarding the people who'd taken him in. "I was honest and open with you all when I came here. I didn't hide the time I'd spent in prison. I didn't lie about my criminal past, or the life I took over two decades ago. I'm assuming that's what the complaints are about?"

"We took you in," Pastor Scott continued. "We let you live in the basement. As we got to know you, we found you worthy of sponsorship for the Bible delivery to Southeast Asia. But it seems not everyone approved of our decision to send you. While you were gone, there was a vote."

Avery felt like weeping, but he was too tired. After three days on the run and sleeping in the jungle, he was exhausted.

"What was the decision?"

"We believe that you're not the influence we want here, nor do we want you to be the face of this church's mission activity."

"You have others who would like to go to Laos and other places from this congregation?"

"Well, no." Pastor Scott smiled. "But the money we spent sending you to Laos could've been spent on a new sound system. And as for the basement—we'd like you to find another place to sleep. We're not a hotel for unemployed vagrants, as some have said. I'm sorry, Avery. Please don't make this more difficult than it already is."

"Okay." Avery rose to his feet, realizing that there were those in the room who probably disliked him enough to call the police and make a false report if he said too much more. As an ex-con, his word would mean little to the authorities. "I really don't have much, so I can leave now."

He started for the door. The men behind him mumbled, and Pastor Scott cleared his throat.

"Um, Avery, where will you go?"

Avery stopped and turned to study the men who'd welcomed him off the streets where he'd been living since his release from prison. They'd even contacted the State Department to clear him for an overseas passport.

"I'm not sure." He tried to smile, to show his confidence in God, but he was too disheartened and tired. "The Lord will provide. He always does."

The men of the church remained silent and looked away.

With his toothbrush, pocket Bible, and compass, Avery walked out of the church. Nothing else was his. Even the air mattress and blankets in the basement had been gifts. But he left it all. It hurt to leave, and he felt like weeping, but even crying would require too much energy.

Outside, his gaze fell on the interstate in the distance. There were other churches in Fresno, Avery knew, and in time, he guessed God would guide him to those who might be willing to work with him. Though he needed the help of the body of Christ, he decided what was more urgent was to simply be a presence of Christ in the City of Fresno. It didn't matter where he laid his head.

He started walking toward the interstate, his feet dragging. Internally, he lay his petitions before God. After twenty years in prison, he'd known life on the streets would be difficult, yet he hadn't expected to feel such discouragement. But he refused to give up. God had been preparing him, he believed, to think less of himself and more on the needs of others. After all, prison had taught him to live selflessly for God, day after day, to care for inmates who had yet to find the Hope of eternity.

"Hey, pal, you got a couple bucks you can spare?"

Avery stopped on the side of the street where an empty lot was overgrown by weeds. A cardboard shelter had been erected in the center of several piles of topsoil, as if an old excavation had halted in the midst of a project.

The man who'd asked for money was panting, as if he'd recently run a great distance. He sat on a soiled cushion next to a stack of old newspapers. His skin was covered with sores, he was missing several front teeth, and his hair was gray and greasy.

"No, friend, I have no money, but I have time for you."

"Time?" The old fellow, struggling to breathe, shrunk away from Avery as he stepped through the weeds and plucked a few newspapers off the stack. He spread them on the ground and sat down.

Beside the homeless man, Avery gazed over the bushes at the street and admired the concrete view beyond.

"I was in Asia just a few days ago," Avery said.

"Asia? What was you doing there?"

"It was a calling, so I responded. You ever had a calling?" Avery touched his chest. "It's something in here. Something you know you've got to do."

"No, I never had no calling." The old man didn't take his eyes off Avery. "You really don't have any money? Two bucks. I just want a burger."

"I don't even have a penny." Avery shook his head. "You and I need food, my friend, but we have a bigger need to get right with our Creator."

"Our Creator? I don't believe in God. He never did nothing for me."

"You know, we're going to be dead pretty soon, you and I. Maybe we didn't live the life we wanted to, but we'll definitely have to face God about the way we behaved for Him. You have any regrets?"

The homeless man lowered his head.

"I have lots of regrets. I wouldn't be out here if things were wonderful."

"Ever been to prison? I did a lot of years in prison."

"Nah. Just jail. Lots of jail. Many times. You don't seem like someone who spent any time in prison."

"Yep, spent many years there. And you say you were arrested lots of times, huh?" Avery sighed loudly. "I thought you said God never did anything for you. Man, all those times you were arrested, God was knocking on your skull to wake you up. How could you say you don't believe in God? Your life is full of moments, I bet, where God was calling you into line."

"I walk my own line."

"Not anymore, you don't. Come on." Avery rose to his feet and offered his hand to the grimy old timer. "You want to go get some food? You show me to the nearest homeless camp."

"There ain't no food at those homeless camps. There's just death and more arrests. Why do you think I hide in these bushes?"

"It's time for you to start trusting God. Come on. Give me your hand, or do you want me to carry you? I will if I need to."

"What kind of crazy are you?"

The man took Avery's hand, and Avery lifted him up and steadied him on his own feet.

"You good? Here, put your hand on my shoulder. Lean on me as we walk."

"I can't walk far." The man was already panting. "Emphysema."

"We'll rest whenever you need to. Now, which way to the nearest homeless camp?"

CHAPTER TWO

New York City

Corban watched the COIL agents arrive one or two at a time. He sat in a soft chair by the fireplace in a hotel suite on Manhattan's Upper East Side two blocks from Central Park. His crutches were leaning against the chair, and his pants bulged awkwardly from the leg braces underneath. Across the room, Luigi stood against the drawn drapes. The Italian agent appeared cagey, but Corban was glad his old gum-chewing friend had agreed to attend the meeting that demanded attention from the best agents the organization could gather.

Chloe Azmaveth, the Jewish ex-Mossad woman and COIL's PR attorney, arrived first. After nodding at Luigi, whom she knew from past operations, she seated herself on a divan to Corban's left. She set up a laptop on a chair in front of her, but remained quiet as the others filed in.

Bruno and Scooter, from COIL's first Special Forces team, arrived next. The two were shoving and horseplaying even as they entered the suite, but upon seeing Corban, they immediately straightened up and took seats on a sectional sofa in the center of the room. The two men couldn't have been more dissimilar, Corban mused with appreciation. Yet God had made the giant, bald, black man and the short Mexican close brothers in arms for years. Corban could see a few wrinkles appearing around Bruno's neck. And Scooter still wore his tall crewcut left over from his Marine days, but now a little gray salted his temples.

Next, Fred "Memphis" Nelson arrived behind Johnny "Mapper" Wycke, two of COIL's most dependable pilots, often inserting equipment into dangerous countries days in advance of COIL operations. Memphis had married June, who now worked closely with Chloe at COIL's New York offices. Johnny Wycke, Corban reflected, hadn't changed much since he'd joined COIL at the beginning. The sizeable pilot and geologist rarely took time off and never complained about the dangerous regions Corban asked him to fly into—always to smuggle something in or someone out of a country.

Nathan "Eagle Eyes" Isaacson arrived alone and with a limp—the product of an old bullet injury. His handlebar mustache and iconic angled eyebrows hadn't changed much in the last ten years, except when he needed to briefly alter his appearance for an undercover operation. Though he and Scooter had been best friends in the marines, Corban observed a distance between them now, as they nodded solemnly at one another across the room. Nathan chose to stand against the wall beside Luigi. Corban had sometimes wondered if he'd chosen wisely—making Nathan a solo agent, isolating him from his old team. But the results spoke for themselves. Not only had he met his wife, Chen Li, the broad-shouldered agent had saved hundreds of Christian lives and impacted countless international criminals with the grace and mercy of Jesus Christ.

Wes Trimble walked into the room next, his confidence almost visible, though Corban guessed the extra bounce in his step might've been from being in love. He'd been courting Wynter Caspertein for more than two years, and a wedding date had been set recently. The CIA's PRS Director was wearing a dark blue eye-patch that day, and his blazer was open to reveal his Desert Eagle sidearm, which Corban knew was loaded with COIL's non-lethal gel-tranqs.

Titus Caspertein and Oleg Saratov arrived fashionably late, though there was nothing fashionable about Oleg's appearance. The Russian's shirt was wrinkled, his hair was askew, and it looked like he hadn't shaved in a week. Titus, on the other hand, seemed that he'd just walked out of high school, in blue jeans and a faded jean jacket. His blond hair had a natural wave, and his blue eyes reflected the flickering fire. The two unlikely partners took seats in the middle of the living room, facing Corban.

"Good evening, everyone." Corban paused and browsed his personnel—many of them single-handedly having toppled regimes and interrupted empires. Now, they were together. "I'm aware that some of you haven't seen each other for a long time. Before we have a little reunion, we need to cover the business at hand. Bruno, open this meeting with prayer, would you?"

Often the preacher of whatever team he was in, Bruno's deep baritone voice dedicated their time together for God's purposes, and he asked for wisdom and attention that only the Lord could provide.

"We've all been through a lot." Corban paused and tried not to react as Luigi popped a bubble that brought a snicker from Scooter. "Friends have even been lost over the years. Now, I'm asking you to come together for not one but two operations inside the most oppressive and secretive country in the world: North Korea."

Wes Trimble's face turned a shade of pale, but otherwise, no one moved or responded. Perhaps they were in shock, Corban thought, but he knew they would accept any challenge that they were given for the sake of the persecuted.

"It cost a life to get me the intel I'm about to share, so you understand why I requested a meeting farther uptown from the COIL offices. No one can know we're coming. Each of you will play a role, and the past is evidence of the danger we're all in by confronting North Korea's government. Guard your communications. Watch your backs for tails. Double your security considerations. We have one shot at rescuing two lives in the coming winter months, and no one but us even knows these two people are still alive, except for the North Korean government that holds them. And don't be too distracted by recent overtures by the regime to make peace. What's still happening inside that country and what's happening for the camera are two different things."

Corban glanced at the fireplace. Somewhere up the chimney, the smoke was being filtered and the ashes were washed down a drain. The hotel was one of the few buildings in Manhattan that still offered a wood-burning fireplace.

"For years, North Korea's missile program has been driven forward by a home-grown engineer name Jeong Byeang-Rea. At some point, he became a Christian, and fled to South Korea, thinking that without him, the Christian underground would be safer. During his two years in South Korea, I met him through a professor at the capital. He was distraught about leaving the Christians in the north, and not long after we talked, he snuck back into North Korea, where he remained in hiding while teaching and discipling other believers.

"Not long after, he married another Christian at a secret wedding in the mountains. Her name is Han Ji-Jin. Jin is now about six months pregnant, and she's been arrested for crimes against the Great Leader. In other words, she was arrested for being an active Christian. But there's more.

"Her husband—our rocket scientist, Rea—was also arrested. He was the North Korean dictator's leading engineer, and as a Christian, Rea is being put on display, and his wife and child will be used as examples. As soon as the child is born, he or she will be executed in front of Rea and Jin, and then they are to be publicly executed. Sentences like this are handed down by North Korea's regime to torment their prisoners until the day of execution arrives. COIL's job will be to make sure that day never arrives."

Corban opened a briefcase and drew out two files.

"Rea is held in a maximum security men's prison in the northern mountains of North Korea. This is the worst prison you've ever imagined. Nathan, you're team leader of that rescue. There are hundreds of guards you'll be facing, so the operation will require precision that I know you can handle.

"Jin, on the other hand, is pregnant, and she's being held inside the City of Pyongyang under guard by a torturer hand-picked by the dictator to keep Jin uncomfortable. With some planning, we believe we can get in to Jin. We might even be able to get her out of the build-ing she's being held in, but it's looking like a one-way trip for the team who goes into Pyongyang to get her. It's a death trip."

"Boss," Nathan said, "we've faced tough prisons before. We can get her and get out. Put me on her detail instead, and I'll find a way. All of us together can come up with something."

"It's not just the building she's in that's the problem." Corban spoke quietly and slowly in the silence of the room. "North Korea *is* the prison. The streets are broad, the courtyards are wide and empty. Every citizen for two generations has been trained to report on strangers or strange events. There's no possibility of a bunch of Westerners sneaking into or smashing out of that city. And the Palace where she's being held is right in the center of it all. I've been in the city before, so I know it well enough.

"The dictator has an unnatural fascination with control—to a sadistic level. It's nothing like his paranoid father was. I knew how to use him, but not the son. He's more obsessed with war, security, and self-exaltation. The sentence he's personally passed on to the unborn child of two Christians is an alert to us all of how ruthless this man is. Thousands of other Christians have already been imprisoned and tortured to death in the terrible work camps by his orders."

"If she's six months pregnant," Chloe said, "we've only got three months to figure out how to get to her and get her out."

"I wish it were that simple." Corban swallowed and paused. "According to the intel I received, there's talk of inducing labor early on a specific date that I don't have. That means we have only weeks, not months, to get Jin out."

"There's got to be a way, Corban," Titus said. "If we had all the facts, we can put something together."

"I think I know how to get Jin out before the baby's born." Corban frowned. "I just don't know how to get the team out safely, once they get to her. I'm aware that you're all willing to give it a shot, but Nathan needs to lead all of you in the north to recover Rea. Though Rea was debriefed in South Korea, I understand he may have information that could help us with new problems regarding the regime."

"The US has always wanted Jeong Byeang-Rea," Wes Trimble said. "He defected to South Korea, though, so the Agency could only collect data that was second hand. We've believed Rea knows secrets he hasn't shared yet simply because he hasn't been asked the right questions. But the president will back COIL for something like this, if we can manage to pull Rea out of the prison. His wife could shed some light and confirm her husband's testimony as well. Getting the husband and wife out together is of international interest, not just a Christian operation. We need better intel on the status of the North Korean missile program to date."

"Corban?" Titus held up his hand. "Who's going in to get Jin? Oleg and I can get into that country using old contacts."

"A lot of us can get in, Titus." Corban handed one of the files to Chloe. "Remember, it's getting out that's not realistic. Nevertheless, I'm sending in a different team. It's a team of men none of you knows yet. The leader has already volunteered to go. Well, he's volunteered to some degree. That team, except by some miracle, won't be returning. Titus and Oleg, you two will be training them to get in and rescue Jin. If you can figure out a way to bring them home alive, even better. But our priorities are Jin with her baby in the city, and Rea up in the north at the prison."

"Training? Oh, come on, Corban." Titus scoffed. "Oleg and I are used to a little more action than what training has to offer. Turn us loose. We'll go into Korea and get this lady, Jin, out."

"Speak for yourself." Oleg frowned. "They burn people to death in that country. And if they don't kill you, they torture you until you lose your mind. I'd prefer to keep what little mind I have left!"

"No one's courage is being doubted here," Corban said. "This is about putting us all where we each excel. Now, Nathan, Chloe has the file for *Operation: Harm's Way*. That's what we're calling this double-mission op. Take your team into the other room and start planning. I need to discuss the Pyongyang rescue with Titus and Oleg."

"Uh, who's exactly on my team?" Nathan rose to his feet. "You didn't say, Boss."

"Who's on Nathan's team?" Corban asked the room of agents.

Bruno and Scooter stood, then Johnny and Mapper. With Chloe and Nathan, the operation to rescue Rea comprised of six agents who had worked together before. As they left the room, Corban focused on who remained—Titus and Oleg, with Wes Trimble and Luigi Putelli listening in. Corban had trusted Wes with sensitive COIL intel for years, and he hadn't been disappointed with the one-eyed agent's subtle way of keeping COIL in the president's favor.

Luigi hadn't been a negative presence in years. Briefly reminiscing, Corban recalled the grace he'd shown to the Italian assassin that had won him over as a close ally. Corban's own family had been kept alive by Luigi's sacrificial commitment to him as a friend. And since coming to the Lord, Luigi's value had doubled in Corban's eyes, since the man now shared the mind of Christ.

"Titus, you'll be acting as support on *Operation: Harm's Way*." Corban handed the Arkansas man the file for the Pyongyang rescue of Jin and her unborn child. "God has provided us with a unique group of men, selfless men, who seem like good fits for getting Jin. But they need you and Oleg to turn them into a COIL team."

"These men are volunteering to die to rescue Jin?" Titus flipped through several profiles, then handed them to Oleg to browse. "What are they, diagnosed with terminal illnesses or something?"

"No, they seem healthy enough. Read their profiles, and it'll make sense. Then teach them everything we know now about where Jin is held in Pyongyang. Extensive moves have already been made to prepare the way. As soon as I became aware of Jin's abduction, and her husband's arrest, I put several pieces into play. You and Oleg can present the plan to the five men, once you round them up. If they're the kind of Christians I think they are, they'll want to help, even though it's a lot to ask of them."

"But Oleg and I aren't really into training agents, Corban." Titus closed the file dismissively and handed the whole packet to Oleg. "You have two whole branches of COIL for this type of preparation—the compound in Mexico with Brody Sladrick, and the advanced teams training with Eero Haug in Idaho."

"Yes, but you'll be in the States for a little while, Titus. While you're here, I'm asking you to train these men. They need to be trained by the best for what they have to do. Nathan's the best team leader for storming a prison, but you and Oleg are the best at subversive and tactical infiltration. That's what these men need to learn. They'll be under a lot of mental pressure and spiritual opposition."

"Okay, Corban, I'll train the men." Titus folded his hands and leaned forward. "But you're not making sense. It ain't easy following your statements. What do you mean I'll be in the States for a while? Oleg and I have a list of overseas missions that need our attention right now."

"Unfortunately, those missions will have to be put on hold. Or if we can, we'll send other teams—maybe Brad Alden and Heather Kooper's team will be available." Corban paused and looked at the fire. "I know you want details, Titus, but I'll need to speak with you in private."

"That would be nice." Titus threw up his hands. Wes and Luigi understood they were being dismissed and headed toward the door. Oleg rose to his feet, taking the file with him into the next room where they could hear the team discussing their part of the North Korea operation. "Okay, Corban. We're alone. Why are you treating me like COIL's whipping dog?"

"Titus, I trust your skills, and I trust you to train others to use the same skills and resources, but doubt has been cast on your methods to implement COIL standards, particularly those that represent Christ's compassion for our enemies."

"I haven't killed anyone since I joined COIL!" Titus clenched his jaw muscles, then softened them. "Oh, I get it. You know, don't you? The phosphorus ammunition I've been stockpiling. I was going to tell you."

"Phosphorus is poisonous, Titus. And you *didn't* tell me. I had to find out on my own, and that means you were keeping something dangerous a secret from me. Phosphorus is highly reactive. Once it starts burning, the compounds you're mixing will melt metal like wax. And it'll kill anyone who gets it on their skin. It'll eat them like an acid. The government would come after COIL in an instant if they found out you've weaponized this stuff for a .308 cartridge. Since you hid it from me, I know you know what you're doing is wrong. You've jeopardized everything I've built, and all the lives COIL is responsible for. So? Why have you done this?"

Rising silently to his feet, Titus went to the fireplace. He set his clenched fists on the mantle and stared up at a painting of several Mallard ducks in flight.

"Incendiary shells will keep us ahead of our enemies. The gel-tranqs we introduced for any .22, .5-millimeter, or .308 are more versatile and carry more stopping power than your old water-soluble NL pellets." Titus turned and faced Corban. "Imagine the ability to melt the trusses of a bridge from a mile away, or burn through a prison's concrete wall from a safe distance. It'll work, Corban!"

"And what happens when it doesn't work?" Corban raised his eyebrows. "COIL's priority isn't placed first upon ourselves or even on winning, but upon our enemies and those we are tasked to help. The phosphorus rounds could kill someone."

"They're not for shooting at people, just machinery we want to disable, or structures we want to destabilize."

"But that kind of ammunition could be misused. It could be deadly. That's my point. And that goes against COIL's ethics and our Christian morals."

"I disagree." Titus held up his wrist and pointed at his oversized watch. "You equipped me with this sat-watch. It could be used to hurt others, too, but we use it for good. I'll use the phosphorus rounds the same way."

"We can control the Gabriel technology if you lose your watch," Corban said. "We can't control the way phosphorus will burn if it gets on someone, or if the ammunition falls into the hands of an enemy. Would you agree with that?"

Titus thrust one hand into his pocket, stalling.

"Yes, I agree with that. But I can't dismiss the usefulness of phosphorus ammo. You might as well know—I've test-fired quite a bit of it. I haven't just been stockpiling it."

"Is it in circulation yet?"

"No, and I don't intend to let it out of our grasp. I was waiting for the right time to show you what it can do. I'd like to keep it warehoused in San Diego until you can see how useful it is."

"I know you didn't mean any harm, Titus, but you've got to destroy that ammunition before it's discovered. It's too deadly." Corban gestured at the sofa. "Come sit down. There's something else we need to talk about."

Titus seated himself and rubbed his face with his hands.

"Okay, what else?"

"Annette called while you and Oleg were in Utah. Someone from your past has shown up on her doorstep. A fourteen-year-old named Levi."

"What? I don't know any kid named Levi." Titus reached for his phone in his pocket. "I knew I should've called Annette before coming here."

"This is Levi." Corban held his own phone up for Titus to view. "Levi Novarro."

"Levi Novarro?" Titus took the phone, his hand trembling. "What'd someone do, clone me? This is me as a teenager! Is this a joke?"

"His mother was Gloria Novarro, a light-skinned, red-headed Mexican woman from Jalesco. The best I could piece together from your past is that you spent some time in a village outside Chamela, laying low, after you pulled an arms heist in Argentina. Apparently, you met a woman named Gloria."

"Gloria Novarro . . . Oh, yeah." Titus returned the phone, his face suddenly drawn. "Wow. That was a wild time in my life."

"Now you understand why I said I think you'll be spending some time in the States for a little while."

"I need to talk to Annette." Titus rose to his feet and dialed his phone for his wife. "She must be going crazy."

"She's not too happy." Corban locked his leg braces and fit his forearms into his crutches. "Titus, can you handle all this? The men who need to be trained need your attention, even if you do suddenly have a son."

"Yeah, um. Yeah, I'll do it, Corban. I'm just— You know, it ain't easy getting ambushed by all this stuff on one day. Wow."

"That's one way to put fatherhood. But the Titus I know—the Titus who Christ has been renewing—will be just the father this young man needs right now."

"Sure, I can be a father in a pinch, but what about Annette? I'm wondering if she's ready for motherhood!"

Pyongyang, North Korea

Han Ji-Jin opened her eyes to screams. She was relieved to discover they weren't her own. Darkness surrounded her, except for a little light that shined through the cracks around her steel cell door. The corridor light outside her cell wasn't very bright, but it gave her something to focus on besides the darkness.

"My perfect God is perfect Light," she whispered. Tears immediately poured from her eyes. They were tears of joy and supernatural comfort. "In You, there is no darkness at all. Hold me, Father. Love me in my fear. Protect Rea. Do not let him worry too much about us."

Her hand went to her belly. The child was awake and restless. Thinking of him or her, she stilled her dread as a shudder rose up within her. Every day, the People's Palace of Remembrance guards escorted her to a cold and gloomy office room where she was seated in a chair in front of a Caucasian official who wore a tight North Korean military uniform. His name was Yuriy Usik, he'd said, and his purpose was to inform her daily that he would execute her baby the day it was born.

Four weeks earlier, Jin had been arrested. She'd met Yuriy Usik the following day, and that very afternoon, she'd begun to pray for the man whose cruel words and gruesome threats revealed his own tormented soul. Jin understood that all things were spiritual, and if Yuriy Usik was so wicked, it was because he was horribly enslaved by sin. He needed God's love more than anyone, so she prayed desperately for him as often as she thought of him.

Slowly, she rolled off her hard cement bunk and walked across the cold floor to the largest crack next to the door. She didn't want to look into the corridor. She only wanted to gaze at the light. Imagining heaven, in her Lord's presence, gave her comfort. Every moment she was awake, she fought the despair that Yuriy Usik tried to inflict.

"They may take you from me," she whispered, thinking of her baby, "but I won't change. There will be a resurrection. I will not be afraid. My Savior is kind, gentle, and compassionate. I may suffer, but only because I am not in glory yet. Soon, Father, I will stand in Your gaze and feel Your warmth. Rea will be there, too, and I will serve You for eternity."

Peering through the crack soon caused Jin's neck to ache. She went back to her bunk and lay down, praying constantly, drifting in and out of memories, feelings of terror, and then immense comfort from God. It was an exhausting cycle as she waited for her baby to be born and killed, and to suffer her own death.

She didn't know where the regime had taken Rea, but she understood he was still alive, even kept alive to witness his child's death, then her own. Afterwards, he would die from some painful invention under the dictator's hand. Rea had once been a prominent scientist for the dictator's ambitious missile program. Even after he'd become a Christian, Rea hadn't known how to leave the dictator's team, so he had remained, contributing to harmless though successful missile tests that had defied Japan's sovereign airspace and unsettled American interests.

But Rea had suddenly vanished, and Jin had thought the man she'd met in a secret Bible study had been found out as a Christian. For two years, she'd prayed for him, and wondered if perhaps he were still alive and being held in some brutal *kwanliso*.

However, two years after he'd disappeared, Rea had approached her on a rainy day. He was alive! Rather than wait in North Korea to be arrested, he had explained, he'd fled to South Korea, but admitted that he'd not been able to stay away—from the work for Jesus, or from her, the woman he loved.

As a fugitive, he'd lived in the hills near her government assigned housing district in Haeju, on North Korea's southwest coast. She had smuggled fish to him from her job as a fish processor, carrying fish out in her boots to avoid detection from the strict supervisors. In a cave in the hills, Rea had taught other Christians in hiding, until they were all arrested. Someone had been caught earlier, and that person had helplessly divulged information as they were interrogated.

Jin didn't care now who had informed the authorities. She didn't hate them. Perhaps the informant had received a little extra rice, or a residence in Pyongyang, which was reserved for the country's loyalists. But larger rations and a nice house wouldn't take away the offense against the holy and just God of the universe. Someday that informant would stand before the eternal Judge. No, Jin didn't hate the informant, but she prayed for him or her.

The screams from down the hallway finally stopped, and Jin thanked God for the quiet, even if it lasted only long enough for Yuriy Usik to bring a new victim to his office down the corridor. For now, Yuriy said he wouldn't harm her since he didn't want to induce premature labor. He'd said it like he was showing her favor, but quickly followed with, "But there will be a time when we will induce labor. Think about that, and think about your crimes against the Party."

Jin had been to Pyongyang for two parades as a teenager. She still remembered the magnificent buildings—square, rigid, and monstrous! The museums had fascinated her, their walls displaying holy relics of the dictator, who was to be revered by silence and meditation when gazing upon his family's artifacts.

One of those buildings she'd seen as a youth had been the People's Palace of Remembrance, its columns holding up an impossibly high ceiling, with engravings that would take a year to study fully. The People's Palace of Remembrance had been erected to honor those who'd fought the American capitalists in the war. In glass cases, their life stories could be read beside their pictures in black and white photos. They were true heroes of the People's Republic.

But in the bowels of the Palace, a secret hell had been constructed. The marble floors of the Palace above her head that day were thick enough to muffle the screams of the persecuted below, under Yuriy's torture. Though she hadn't spoken to any other prisoners in those basement sub-levels, she guessed the Palace dungeons were reserved for the country's "heaven people," as Christians were scornfully called by the government's media.

As alone as she sensed they all felt, Jin closed her eyes and prayed to the God who was very present and with each one. And she fought the dread of the sentence her family had been given.

New York

Sitting at the dining table, Titus stared out the window at his back-yard in upstate New York. The boy named Levi, who claimed to be his son, was wrestling with Kobuk, a giant St. Bernard. As if Titus didn't have enough going on, his brother Rudy had dropped by with his Search and Rescue dog. The two adventurers had recently returned from a seismology expedition across Greenland, but Titus wasn't too excited to sit and listen to his older brother's tales that morning.

"Do I need to tell you how upsetting this is for me?" Annette said from behind him at the kitchen counter. "You've been a *father* all these years? Are there any more Caspertein kids out there that I should know about? Or ex-wives?"

Titus turned from the window. He could think of no right words to comfort his wife of only a few years. Her eyes were red from crying. After arriving late the night before, Titus had slept on the couch.

"He just knocked on our door and told you he's my son?"

"Look at him, Titus!"

"I have been looking at him."

"He looks exactly like your old pictures that Wynter gave us. No doubt. He's your son."

"I'm not denying that." He folded his hands. "I'm just surprised. I haven't kept in touch with any, uh, old . . ."

"Girlfriends?"

"Yeah. I didn't know I had any kids, Annette. I would've told you. I wouldn't wish this on you."

"What? Motherhood? Now I'm supposed to be a mother, Titus? Just like that?"

"No, I'm sure he's just . . ."

"What? Just visiting? He's fourteen." She scowled at him. "You're his father. Where are you going to send him? He's still a child!"

"Right. I'm trying to think."

"He came here because he has no one else now. His mother just died—your *girlfriend!*"

"Just an old friend. I was with her for only a few weeks."

"Oh, that's comforting."

"Annette, please." Titus pointed to the nearest chair. "Would you please come sit down?"

Reluctantly, she seated herself at the table, but in the farthest chair from him.

"Well?"

"I'm not excusing my lifestyle before coming to Christ, and before meeting you." He looked up at the ceiling, seeking help from God. "I was a selfish jerk, running all over the place. I didn't circle back to see old friends, and I never cared to find out how they were doing. Or if I had a kid or not. Would you have preferred that we both rehearsed details of our old lives and partners?"

"Of course not."

"I'm just saying, when you and I got married, we agreed to leave our pasts behind. I regret my lifestyle from back then. This is one of the consequences of the way I once lived. I've hurt you, and that's not something I've ever wished to do. I lived loose and I didn't think about who it could hurt in the future. Now, I'm in the middle of my life, enjoying our marriage based on Christ's love. And suddenly, this comes up.

"Corban has even sidelined me since I need to have things under my own roof in order before I can take care of others. This is all because of bad choices I made in the past. Please believe me when I say that I now need the love of my life to help me make choices for the future. I'm . . . at a loss."

Annette sighed and brushed at a strand of brown hair that had stuck to her wet cheek. Her silence was hard to read, but Titus was truly out of ideas. On top of everything, the sofa hadn't been comfortable, and his mind was foggy from lack of sleep.

"I guess . . . it's a small miracle I don't have any children of my own from my past." She frowned. "I'm not saying that to hurt you for your ways. I'm just stating a fact."

"I understand," Titus said softly.

"He's fourteen, Titus. He's your son. We're parents now."

"It looks like it."

"We need to get him back into school. It's amazing he didn't get arrested while driving all the way out here from California. It was his mother's car, he said."

"We Casperteins always looked older in our teen years, and he's already the size of a man."

"What are your feelings about moving closer to my parents?"

"California?" Titus leaned back.

"That's where Levi has been going to high school. It'll be easier on him if he doesn't have to change schools in the middle of the year. And he's on the football team."

"Well, it would be handy to be on the West Coast for this operation Corban has for me."

"What operation? I thought you were sidelined."

"It's a new team for something in Asia—I'm supposed to train them. The West Coast would be more convenient if we were living there, even temporarily. I have some other COIL things progressing in California, too."

"When are you supposed to start training this new team?"

"Right away. Oleg's already gone ahead to round up the personnel. He was going to bring them to New York, but it won't take much to redirect to Southern California. Corban has a couple facilities there."

"So, what do we do with Levi?"

Titus turned in his chair as the back door opened. The tall, gangly youth strolled in. His clothes had grass stains from wrestling with Kobuk, who was panting at his side.

"Hello, Levi." Titus rose from his chair and held out his hand. "I'm Titus."

The youth shook Titus' hand. Levi's hand was slender but his grip was firm.

"Mom showed me a picture of you." Levi blushed. "She said you were a spy or something. Like you were always on the run, too busy to come home. I guess she was just trying to protect me since you had another life or something."

"No." Annette stood and walked around the table. "She was telling you the truth. Your father is a world-famous traveler and hero. And he and I are here for you. We want to be your family now. If you'll have us."

"Well, I don't have anyone else." Levi smiled sheepishly.

"It won't be easy," Titus said, "jumping into all this right in the middle of everyone's lives. But with God's help, I think we'll make a good team."

"You're religious?" Levi raised one eyebrow. "Mom used to take me to Sunday school, but I never really listened."

"It'll take us time to get to know one another." Annette held out her arms. "Come here."

Titus felt his heart stir with hope as his wife and son embraced. For now, Annette's arms could envelope the youth's frame, but by the look of the fourteen-year-old, in a few years, he'd be as wide and tall as his father. *Titus Caspertein had a son!*

"What's going on?" The bear-like bulk of Rudy Caspertein lumbered from the back bedroom. The six-six giant scratched at his full beard and Kobuk greeted her master by nuzzling his leg. "Whoa. So, I wasn't dreaming this. Titus' younger self has come from the past!"

Levi laughed nervously from all the attention and Kobuk barked.

"Levi, meet your Uncle Rudy," Titus said. "Rudy, meet my son, Levi."

California

Oleg Saratov climbed out of his rental car and pocketed his phone after reading the message from Titus. They would be training the Pyongyang team for *Operation: Harm's Way* in Southern California instead of staging in New York. That pleased Oleg, since he preferred the moderate winters of the West Coast. It seemed, though, that the change in venue wasn't the only change in the wind. Many things inside COIL felt to be on the verge of modification. The early generation of operatives was getting older, and the new generation seemed reluctant to commit as fully, or if they did, they were fewer in number.

The whole world was changing, Oleg reflected. Mass shootings and suicidal drivers were inflicting as much damage as possible at every conceivable social event. Politicians struggled to keep up the appearance of government as corruption and scandal tore the ranks of authority to pieces, even as civil and racial unrest ripped through every city. Oleg didn't see how he and Titus would be able to justify overseas operations in another year or two—as the need for their attention on the US mainland seemed to be taking precedence.

And now Titus had a son? Oleg didn't like to think of his new life without his friend and partner, if Titus was thinking about leaving COIL to be a father. In the back of his mind, Oleg had always guessed he and Titus would die together on some foreign field, holding off terrorists, saving the lives of God's precious saints. But now, fatherhood was facing the great arms smuggler, who many criminal networks still called the Serval. And COIL itself had never seemed so miniscule on the world stage, without its old influence, as its agents aged and support for Christian missions waned.

Compartmentalizing his sadness, Oleg lifted his eyes to take in one of Fresno's largest homeless camps. The homeless camps across America always startled Oleg when he came across them, since America seemed so wealthy and prosperous. Million-dollar homes literally stood a mile away from this camp. But the focus of self among those who had much had only pushed those who had nothing further down the social ladder.

Though the criminal element was obvious as Oleg walked through the camp, most of the people were victims of wild fires, earthquakes, or financial ruin. Whole families sat around smoking grills, too depressed to even lift their faces as he passed their shelters. America was falling apart from the inside, burdened with poverty, mental illness, and disregard for their spiritual state. It wouldn't take much of a national catastrophe to push the country over the edge. Collapse was around the corner, he felt, and everyone seemed to sense it, but no one seemed to know what to do except to keep playing at pleasure and self-gratification.

As Oleg neared the center of the mile-wide camp, he heard the loud, clear voice of an evangelist.

"You may have fallen on uncomfortable times, but God has not looked away!" the preacher shouted over a crowd of one thousand men, women, and children. "He hasn't looked away, but we have! Yes, we have few possessions, yet our souls aren't measured by what we have, but to whom we have surrendered. The terror of our poverty and hunger is nothing in comparison to the terrors of our sins, and in eternity, hell is what waits for all those who don't repent and turn toward the cross of Jesus Christ. Our sins are an ugliness that we cannot cleanse ourselves from, but by the sacrifice of Jesus for you and me, we can receive by faith a peace that secures our futures with Him. Look above, my friends! Let the Creator of the heavens and earth renew your lives. Let Him give you a new life on the inside! Who will come forward today? Who will take this invitation seriously? Will you be ready for the return of Jesus Christ? Don't allow another day of guilt and shame hold you back and smother your soul!"

Oleg expected the whole crowd to surge forward at such a fiery closing to the gospel message, but instead, the people shrugged and drifted away, trickling back to their tents and fires and sleeping bags. In a matter of minutes, Oleg was left standing alone, facing three men. He recognized the man in the middle from a photo on his phone.

"Have you sensed the call of God, my friend?" the middle man asked. The men at his sides seemed older, one black and one Mexican. Though their appearances were haggard, their faces were friendly, almost lit with a light that Oleg knew was the love of Christ. "Do you know that God wants you to come to the cross of Jesus Christ today?"

"I do know," Oleg said with a smile. "I've been with Him for a few years now. I'm not here to be served but to serve. You must be Avery Hewitt?"

Avery stepped toward Oleg, away from his two friends whose Bibles identified them as fellow evangelists.

"This is a little embarrassing." Avery grinned and held out his hand. "I thought someone was finally responding to our preaching. I've been here a month and have led only these two men to Christ so far."

"No need to be embarrassed, Avery." Oleg shook the slim man's hand. His gaze held a fierceness. His hair was salt and peppered, giving him an older look, but the evangelist was several years younger than Oleg. "Maybe God is telling you to change directions."

"Interesting you say that, since I was praying about that very possibility this morning." With his Bible in one hand, Avery rested his hands on his hips. When he did so, the top of his shirt opened enough for Oleg to see one of the man's many prison tattoos on his chest. "What brings you to Fresno's Tent Garden? You have an accent . . ."

"My name is Oleg Saratov. I'm originally from Russia, though I've lived all over while working for the government. Now, I work for the Commission of International Laborers, known as COIL. It's my understanding that you wrote a letter to a church or church organization in the past, volunteering to go where no one else wanted to go for the Lord, no matter the cost."

"I wrote a few of those letters when I was still in prison." Avery nodded. "I just wanted to serve. No one responded, though. Maybe they didn't take me seriously since it seemed I was just looking for a handout. There was a church that took me in for a little while. I ran a mission into Laos for them, but I've been living on the streets since then. What church did you say you were with?"

"I'm not with any specific church. I'm just a member of the body of Christ, Avery, and COIL wants to take you in and train you for something. But I must warn you: it's for a mission not many would be willing to accept."

"It's dangerous?"

"Extremely."

"Is it for God's people and His purposes?"

"It's a rescue mission of the condemned overseas."

"There are no jobs around Fresno for someone like me, and I don't even have enough money to get a bus ticket to leave. These two men can continue to share the gospel in this camp without me. I'm willing to see what's around the next corner."

"Okay." Oleg nodded. "You have any belongings? My car's parked a short walk away. I can help you carry whatever you have."

"A toothbrush, a compass, and a Bible." Avery held up his worn pocket Bible. "It's all I own. Lead the way, Brother Oleg Saratov!"

Pyongyang, North Korea

Chinese Christian Lu Yi paddled her canoe up the Taedong River on an overcast autumn night. Though the whole quarter-mile-wide river was available to her, the city lights were bright enough to reveal her vessel if she didn't remain in the shadows of the north bank. Trimmed bushes scraped her shoulder, but the bushes created a boundary for the shoreline park in Central Phongyang.

The river was empty of boats, and the street on the other side of the park was still. All of Pyongyang was quiet, but Lu Yi wasn't fooled. One loud splash from her paddle, or one accidental loud bump of her hull against the riverbank's concrete containment wall could alert someone. She'd be interrogated, tortured, and either imprisoned to work to death, or executed outright. But the danger didn't cause her to hesitate. Maybe she'd been afraid as a teenager, when her mother and father had first started helping North Koreans flee across the Yalu River. But she hadn't been a teenager for several decades. Besides, the reward for helping troubled people far outweighed any risk. Even if she were caught, her only fear was of accidentally betraying her network of underground believers across the harsh country.

Lu Yi squinted her eyes to gaze ahead. Was that the rendezvous place? A number of boats were tied off along the bank. Her instructions had been vague, but the urgency had been clear on the Italian man's face. Her English was rather good, and he'd spoken slowly. Using a map, he had instructed her to deliver two heavy parcels up the river to the middle of the city.

She wasn't surprised that a Christian organization had asked for her help. Thousands had been aided by her parents, and they knew she could be trusted with the most sensitive information. Her contacts were many up and down North Korea's rural west coast, but inside Pyongyang, where the fierce regime ruled among the elite socialists, Lu Yi knew of few believers. The city was barred from all but the most loyal subjects, and bands of teenagers regularly patrolled the streets, searching for violators of the *Juche* idea, which was North Korea's religious ideology that directed citizens to worship and present themselves like their Great Leader. Violators were beaten, imprisoned, or lost their residence inside the city.

From her safe house in China across the river from Sinuiju, she had accepted the two packages, then made plans to take her boat out into the Yellow Sea. It was an old tug boat, best equipped for harbor navigation, but Lu Yi had been taught by her father to navigate on the open sea, then arrive by GPS at the exact location on the North Korean coastline where a meeting was to occur. Sometimes she picked up fugitives who needed to flee the peninsula. Other times, she dropped off South Korean missionaries to labor for Christ in the windswept valleys of North Korea's Rangrim Mountains. Most often, though, she left the tug boat in the hands of a brave Chinese couple as she used the canoe to paddle ashore. Deliveries of coats, blankets, and food were the norm.

But that night, the packages that the Italian man had given her—she knew they contained nothing she'd ever smuggled before. She knew because she'd made him open the packages first. Without touching anything, she'd briefly studied some sort of machine, communications gear, food, and several weapons. Lu Yi had raised alarm about the weapons, but the Italian man had picked up one gun and fired it at the wall. A small, harmless slime appeared on the wall, then slowly evaporated. A non-lethal weapon, Lu Yi had understood. At least one Christian organization she knew of used non-lethal weaponry to incapacitate the enemy. Thus, she had agreed to use her expertise to transport the packages into the middle of the country's most dangerous city for an unknown purpose.

The boats against the river bank had no visible lights outside or inside. Lu Yi set down her paddle and took hold of the first boat, guiding her canoe alongside, careful not to bump it. In the dimness, she studied the hull of the boat for the sign she'd been told to look for: a flame with tongues of fire in the shape of the cross of Christ.

The river current wasn't strong, so she had no trouble moving her canoe up the side of the boat using her arms and torso. Now in her sixties, she wasn't the strong young woman who could carry heavy packs for miles, or canoe for twenty hours straight. But what she lacked in physical strength, she realized, her Lord had compensated with His wisdom and protection. She preferred the latter!

The first boat bore no such symbol on its hull, and after hearing quiet voices inside, Lu Yi pushed off and glided to the next boat tied a couple meters upriver. This was a tourist boat, with an open top but, by the shape of her, it had a cabin below deck. As she worked her way up the side of the tourist boat, she found no fiery symbol—until she reached the bow, which was aimed upriver. There, she squinted at what could've been mistaken for the North Korean enduring flame of *Juche* self-reliance. But no, the flame was subtly crossed with flames on each side. This was the cross of Christ, not the flame of dictator worship.

Lu Yi steadied her canoe, then stood and stepped onto the strange boat. She kept one foot in her canoe to keep it from drifting away. There were rows of white, empty seats from which tourists could sit and admire the city from the river. A helm sat at the back of the vessel in a small square house. But no one appeared or approached her. Doubt and fear crept up into her throat. Perhaps she had misunderstood the night she was to come? Perhaps the contacts in North Korea had been arrested, the secret plot tortured out of them? Perhaps an ambush was about to spring, and she was minutes away from a beating and a torturer's blade?

"The Lord is my Shepherd . . ." she recited, and her fears abated.

Whatever happened, she realized, wouldn't be a surprise to her Lord, even if she weren't aware of what others intended for her. No one in her line of ministry was ignorant of the dangers involved. Over the last forty years of interaction with North Korean Christians, she knew of dozens who'd been arrested or murdered by state officials. Sometimes, the bodies were found and buried. But often, no evidence was left behind of the regime's crimes. But still, God's people persisted in faith. Why? Because they couldn't deny their Creator and Savior.

The sound of a motor reached Lu Yi's ears. She glanced toward land for a vehicle, then a light far upriver caught her eye. She rarely traveled up the Taedong River because of the threat of patrol boats. After paddling in from the ocean and seeing no patrols, she'd hoped that she'd avoided them completely. Now, she was trapped, unable to paddle away faster than the motorized vessel coming toward her!

The patrol boat crept along her side of the river. It had a spotlight that cast a blinding light toward the shore. Lu Yi guessed she had two minutes before the patrol reached her location on the tourist boat. She gazed down at her canoe. Being trapped inside North Korea wasn't as horrible a thought as being caught and forced to expose an operation that Christians were planning. Informants were rampant through the underground. If she could help it, she wouldn't even risk being caught nor placed in a position where the regime's doctor could inject her with truth serum and question her.

The flame-cross symbol on the bow of the tourist boat was the only indication that she would find safety there, but even a little hope was hope enough. From her canoe, she hefted the first of two packages onto its side, then tilted it onto the edge of the canoe. Rolling it up to the deck of the tourist boat strained her back, but she couldn't think of her own health now. Others were certainly dependent upon the contents of what she'd been tasked to deliver.

The second package was lighter, but since her back was strained, and she awkwardly straddled both vessels, it wasn't any easier to transfer onto the deck of the other boat.

Finally, she reached back into the canoe and gripped her own small backpack, which contained a radio, water, and food for her journey. For now, her journey was over. After decades of helping Christians in North Korea, she would rely on those same Christians to help her.

Kneeling on the tourist boat, she leaned far overboard and turned her canoe until its bow aimed across the river. With a grunt, she shoved the canoe away. It glided into the great expanse of the river, then the current carried it gently away.

There was no time to gaze sadly after her canoe as it disappeared down the dark river. She hopped to her feet and dragged the packages across the floor and left them between rows of the white tourist seats. It was all the time she had left. Scrambling on all fours, she reached the pilot house, found the door unlocked, and slipped inside. Her heart pounded as the spotlight on the patrol vessel swept over her tourist boat, the blinding light lingering for a few moments on the pilot house windows. Lu Yi prayed that the two packages weren't noticed. If they were, her journey inland would be wasted, she would be caught, and the people of God who had trusted her would be sorely disappointed.

After what seemed like an eternity, she heard the motor rev up and the patrol boat slowly move on. But Lu Yi didn't move for several minutes, until the sound of the motor was completely out of earshot.

With a wince from the pain in her back, she climbed to her feet and checked out the windows. Pyongyang had a population of over three million, but the people lived under such harsh control that upon watching the city for several minutes, Lu Yi wondered if the city had been all but abandoned.

Quietly, she opened the pilot house door and crept out to the two packages. She dragged them one at a time into the interior, then closed the door. For the moment, she was safe. Her contact in the tugboat couldn't be left waiting off the coast once dawn broke, so she would have to tell him what happened. With a click, she turned on the radio from her backpack.

"Yellow Fish, Yellow Fish, this is Yellow Bird. Come in."

"Yellow Bird, this is Yellow Fish. I am here."

Lu Yi squeezed her eyes closed. His voice from miles away could be the last friendly voice she ever heard. God had blessed her with selfless coworkers for many years, but she couldn't put a single one of them in unnecessary danger for her own sake.

"Yellow Fish, I have reached my destination, but I can't return tonight. Please return in forty-eight hours for another communication. I'm sorry."

"Do not be sorry. Be safe, Yellow Bird. I will return in forty-eight hours. We will be praying. Goodbye."

Hoping to save her battery life, Lu Yi turned off the radio and bowed her head. She'd been on countless risky missions to coastal villages and rendezvous, but this was the most frightening, and the first one in which she'd been trapped inside North Korea. So much was at risk, she sensed, that she had to plan and act with great care.

Lu Yi acknowledged the door that led to the cabin below deck. It was time to investigate what awaited her. If she found no friends, it wouldn't be the first time a Christian's property had been confiscated and given to regime loyalists. After all, this was Pyongyang, where only the dictator's most ardent supporters were allowed to live inside the city limits.

Daringly, she opened the door.

New York

Chloe Azmaveth drove her Range Rover onto the lot of an abandoned roller skating rink. It had been neglected for so long outside Albany, New York, that trees had actually grown up through the pavement of the parking lot. She parked amongst several cars and trucks belonging to Nathan's team who was there to prepare and stage for the coming rescue of Rea in the northern prison. A semi-trailer of equipment was parked next to the building, and a long COIL RV sat beside the trailer.

Bruno and Scooter's wives were there as well, and they waved at Chloe as she stepped from her vehicle. The women had committed to at least a week at the rink as support staff while the men planned the mission. Such selfless servants were necessary for operatives to focus completely on the mission at hand.

After fetching a duffel bag and a laptop from her vehicle, Chloe walked into the skating rink building. It was cool inside, but warmer than the weather outside that was blowing into the area. She set her gear on a booth where she imagined teens had once loitered, and walked to the edge of the rink floor. Nathan, Bruno, Scooter, and Memphis were out on the floor, constructing some sort of miniature model of the prison complex where Rea was being held in the northern part of North Korea. A wood saw buzzed, and a two-by-four clanked loudly onto the floor. Someone cracked a joke, and laughter echoed across the rink. It caused Chloe to smile. This was the original COIL Flash and Bang Team, back together again for the largest operation COIL had ever staged. There'd been more operatives at the beginning, but Milk had become ill from a sadist's poisoning, and Toad had died during an operation in Malaysia years earlier.

"This will be a difficult one." The voice came from behind Chloe. Luigi Putelli stepped from the shadows of what was once the restaurant area. "They'll need this time to train carefully, or they won't return home."

"I figured you'd be with Corban, wherever he is." Chloe didn't move away as the Italian spook came up to stand next to her to watch the construction out on the floor. As always, he was chewing on a wad of gum that made his cheek bulge. Once, she'd felt edgy around Luigi, like when he'd first appeared with Corban in Malaysia, but now she knew he was a Christian, and a man who had risked his life beside them all, and for them all. "Where is the boss, anyway?"

"He's in California, helping Titus' team. He believes there's much more at risk here than a man, woman, and unborn child. There's also a missile program that shouldn't escape our notice."

"What do you think?" Chloe asked. "I mean, this is a lot of resources and lives we're putting on the line."

"I learned long ago in a Lebanese desert not to underestimate Corban Dowler." Luigi turned his head, and his gaunt face had never appeared so hollow to Chloe, as if the years were catching up to the man. "I've also never seen him layer so many contingencies for a single task, even though this is a double operation."

"Well, Wes Trimble was at the briefing last week. That means even the president knows what we're doing."

"I'll tell you something that not even Wes Trimble knows." Luigi's voice was low. "We have experienced our first challenge for *Operation: Harm's Way*."

"What happened? Did they move one of the prisoners?"

"Not as far as we know." Luigi looked behind them, as if checking for eavesdroppers. "We've begun sending equipment into Pyongyang for Titus' team. We've used multiple contacts in the Christian underground from China to South Korea. One contact made it in with our gear, a trustworthy woman, but she didn't make it out."

"She was caught?"

"No, but she's in hiding. If we're not careful, we'll be rescuing more than just Rea's family on this operation."

"When I was in the Mossad, I used to read briefings about North

Korea's zeal to build nuclear weapons. For years, people have called them a communist or socialist country, but only now we're realizing we're dealing with a state-wide religion of dictator worship. The missiles are its symbol of success, it seems."

"*Juche.* I know of the idea. They teach the people that they must think through their Great Leader."

"It's a nation of brainwashed civilians. They need to be set free."

"Not all of them are in captivity to the cult." Luigi lifted his head. "The elite in Pyongyang are often the ones we hear about, but they are only one-percent of the country's population. Outside the cities are whole villages who don't wear the pin of the leader's family. Thousands of Christians won't bow to his image or his shrines. There's danger where we're going, but there are also many of our brothers and sisters in Christ. The Christian church is thriving in North Korea, and in their persecuted isolation, their zeal for God might embarrass even this country's interest in Christ."

"Persecution has refined the church before, so I'm not surprised. Wait a minute." Chloe looked at Luigi sideways. "A minute ago, you said there's danger where *we're* going. What's really your place in all this, Luigi?"

"Just coordinating." He looked away. "For Corban. Wherever he needs me. I'm not picky."

"Uh-huh." Chloe chuckled and crossed her arms. "You and Corban never just *coordinate.*"

She watched Luigi's face, but he betrayed nothing, making her wonder even more what sort of schemes Corban was planning on the side. They were only two months from infiltrating North Korea with two teams. Those would be a long two months of prayer and planning—in that order. And she didn't want to be anywhere else in the world than there!

CHAPTER THREE

Idaho

Fifty-eight-year-old Job Buck turned the wrench until he was afraid he'd strip the bolt. His burly forearms barely fit through the apparatus that housed the outdated boiler in the church basement. Grunting with effort, he hefted his sizeable bulk away from the boiler and wiped his hands on his pants.

"That should hold it," he stated. "At least until we get new parts."

"The money we had for new parts went to you, to pay for your new life." The man who spoke was named Buddy Diamond and he'd hardly been a buddy to Job since Job had arrived at the Boise church. "Keep the boiler running, or I'll make sure you go back to prison for extorting us."

Job felt the weight of the wrench in his hand and set it quickly in the toolbox before he was further tempted to do something he would regret.

"I understand you don't appreciate me helping out around here, Buddy, but the elders of the church approved me to work here part-time while I look for another job. Would you seriously send a brother in Christ back to prison on trumped-up accusations?"

"I know your kind!" Buddy jabbed his finger at Job. "Try me. Just try me! You're on parole. I know what kind of damage I can do to users like you!"

Before he said anything reckless, Job stepped around Buddy Diamond, the church's custodian who seemed threatened by the ex-con's presence, and climbed the stairs to the church's first floor. He couldn't imagine working beside Buddy and listening to his threats for another day, let alone the whole winter. Fresh out of prison, no one would hire Job, especially at his age with his past.

Plucking a rag from his back pocket, Job wiped his hands clean of grime before he picked up his worn Bible he'd left on the rear pew of the sanctuary. It wasn't a large Bible, but its pages were wrinkled and worn from many years of study and tearful prayer. A few years into his twenty-five-year sentence for murder, he'd submitted to God's call on his life. After several years of learning beside another Christian inmate, Job had stepped out and begun to shepherd other prisoners. For years, he'd discipled inmates, raising them up to be mighty men of God even inside prison, and some of them had left prison to continue their walks with Christ.

But now, Job felt cheated. After all his years of faithfulness, God had placed him beside Buddy Diamond to be abused and threatened? Job opened his Bible as he sat on the back pew, frustrated about what to read for God's counsel in such a situation.

"Give me patience, Lord," he whispered. "You're humbling and breaking me a little more right now, and I sure don't like it, but if it's coming from You, I'm sure I need it."

Lifting his head, Job imagined the sanctuary filled with people on Sunday. His flock in prison rarely numbered more than a faithful dozen on a prison yard of one thousand, but that dozen had lived Christ-like and impacted those thousand men with kindness and counsel no one else would offer the condemned. Maybe someday, Job thought, he could preach to a crowd this size. First, however, it seemed that God wanted him to serve a bunch of strangers, including Buddy Diamond, who despised him without knowing him.

"What are you doing?" Buddy loomed over Job. "You're filthy! Why are you sitting on the pew! It cost us thousands to have them cleaned. Get up! Get up!"

Job leapt upright, and Buddy pushed him aside to examine the pew for stains.

"You need to watch your attitude, Mr. Diamond." Job felt his neck burning. "People in prison spoke nicer to me than you do, and that wasn't just because they knew of my past. You may not know me, yet, but I bet we could get along fine if we—"

"Get along?" Buddy stepped into Job's personal space. "You don't get it, do you? People like you are a ticking time bomb. I know it. We all know it. The elders are fools to trust you, giving you a room in the traveler's apartment. That place is for servants of God, not killers! You're as good as prison-bound already. You're just too stupid to know it!"

"I'd rather be back in prison!" Job roared, and thrust his rock-hard belly at Buddy, forcing the custodian backward. "Prison would be better than tolerating a false brother who is supposed to represent Christ!"

Job used his belly once more to shove Buddy backwards. Buddy lost his footing and was in the process of falling when he was caught in the arms of a dark-haired man with shoulders like an ox. Another man, a tall blond, stood next to the first. Buddy recovered and shook his fist at Job.

"You are finished!" Buddy screamed at Job. Spittle flew from the custodian's snarling mouth. "I even have witnesses now of your assault. Start packing, Job Buck! I'm calling the police!"

The heat around Job's neck diminished as he stared at Buddy and the two strangers. Job's gaze lowered. This was happening as he'd feared it would. The pressures of the world were dictating his life when he needed to simply take the abuse. Buddy had pushed him, but he'd pushed back, and the police would never heed the word of an ex-con over a long-time church-goer like Buddy Diamond.

"You're Job Buck?" the tall blond stranger asked, and extended his hand, smiling with perfect teeth. "We've been looking for you. The name's Titus Caspertein. This is Oleg Saratov."

"I'm Buddy Diamond," the custodian said, offering his hand.

Much to Job's surprise, the blond named Titus frowned at Buddy and didn't shake his hand.

"Are you worthy of the hand of fellowship, Buddy Diamond?" Titus asked. "We arrived several minutes ago and witnessed your display of so-called hospitality toward Job Buck. Tell me, Buddy Diamond, do you have any idea how many men Job has led to Christ and discipled in the last fifteen years?"

"Him? I don't think—"

"Tell me, Buddy Diamond, are only clean people allowed to sit on your pews? What if they are dirty with sin and need help? What if they are God's servants from prison, still wearing stained jeans? How clean do people need to be to attend Buddy Diamond's church?"

"I—" Buddy blinked. "You don't understand. This is Job Buck. He's an ex-con!"

Titus looked away from Buddy and back at Job. Job lifted his head, the intensity of the blond man's confidence giving him confidence.

"We just came from your parole officer, Mr. Buck." Titus unfolded a paper and handed it to Job. "That's a release from all state obligations, signed by the US District Attorney, backed by the President of the United States. Oleg and I work for a Christian relief organization. We need men who are sold out and sacrificial like Jesus. You want in, or . . . do you want to stay here?"

With a look of pity on his face, Titus glanced at Buddy, who appeared both confused and on the verge of tears.

"I'm in," Job said, clutching his Bible in both hands, "if I'm welcome even though I have a really messy past."

"COIL doesn't welcome folks based on their clean or messy pasts," Titus said. "We welcome them based on their reception of a Savior who cleans up messy hearts."

"Amen," Oleg said with a chuckle, then nodded at Buddy. "How about you? Is it time to get cleaned up and get to work?"

"I am clean!" Buddy ran a hand down to his stain-free slacks. "I'm calling the police!"

Job watched the custodian stomp away.

"You ready?" Titus asked Job. "We have a long flight ahead of us."

"What about him?" Job gestured after Buddy. "I think he's really going to call the police."

"Like I said, the president is backing you now." Titus threw his arm around Job's shoulders. "And Oleg and I will vouch for your character. You don't need to worry about anything else."

"As far as I'm concerned," Oleg said as the three walked to the front door, "that used Bible in your hands tells me all I need to know about how seriously you take your faith."

New Mexico

Francisco "Shorty" Hernandez wiped his brow and stretched his back in the middle of the hay field that extended beyond the horizon. Hay bales nearly as heavy as himself lay scattered across the field, the season's last hay harvest. A flatbed truck sat parked a few yards away, half-loaded with bales Francisco had hefted up and stacked himself.

He looked up at the sky and sighed, knowing God was pleased with him. Though many convicts released from prison had returned to their old lives of crime, Francisco had sought out the hardest labor he could find, knowing that he'd find work doing only what no one else wanted to do. It was a long ways from teaching Spanish-speaking prisoners the Bible in prison, but Francisco believed that God would eventually guide him toward a ministry outside of prison. For now, his main objective was to remain employed and out of prison, and to be a good example for Christ to his coworkers. Not even the gang life appealed to him any longer, since he'd become a new person.

With gritted teeth, he tugged his leather gloves on tighter, then picked up another hay bale, New Mexico's chief crop, and carried it to the flatbed. The bed was higher than Francisco's chest, but he propped the bale on its edge first, then shoved it up. After several more bales were on the bed, he climbed up to stack them more orderly. It was at least a two-man job, but he was alone, so he worked the best he could at his own pace.

As he walked over to another bale, he noticed two four-wheelers appear over a small rise, from the direction of the main barn. Probably the foreman and his son again. They'd been decent enough a week earlier when they'd hired him, but there was no telling when his criminal history would rub someone wrong, and he'd be asked to leave. He'd been honest about his parole status, but sometimes people demanded more—an impossible standard of more.

The four-wheelers drew closer, and Francisco acknowledged that the drivers weren't men he knew. One wore a jean jacket, and the other one with large shoulders wore a heavy sweater to ward off the chill of the season.

"You must be Francisco Hernandez," the one with the jean jacket said. The wind ruffled his hair, but it was the man's eyes that Francisco noticed. His eyes seemed to smile, like he'd just witnessed something funny.

"Yeah, I'm Francisco Hernandez." Francisco's Spanish accent was barely discernible, he'd been told, when he worked at it. His English vocabulary was extensive, mostly from years of studying the Bible with English-speaking Bible students in prison. "How can I help you? Sell you some hay?"

The man in the sweater laughed at the joke.

"I like this guy already," the big man said to the blond guy.

"It ain't easy lifting these bales all alone, is it?" The blond turned off his four-wheeler and hopped onto the flatbed truck. Without gloves, he easily lifted the bales Francisco had barely shoved onto the bed.

"Don't just sit there, Oleg. The guy at the barn said he already paid Hernandez to get this hay in, and these bales won't lift themselves."

"Can you drive?" the man called Oleg asked as he abandoned his four-wheeler as well. "Go ahead. You drive real slow. Titus and I will take a turn back here."

Francisco climbed into the truck cab and put it in its lowest gear. Through the side mirrors, he saw the men with their stronger physiques bend to the work. The truck crept forward, but the two strangers came and went again and again with bales lined on the left and right of the truck. They talked and laughed between themselves, but Francisco couldn't quite hear what they were saying. All he knew was that two strangers were doing his job three times faster than he could do it alone.

Finally, Francisco could stand it no longer. He leaned out of the open window of the driver's door.

"Hey, who are you guys?"

"A letter you wrote from prison finally reached us," Titus said. "God's people need you for something risky, if you're still up for doing what no one else wants to do. Or maybe bucking bales is your idea of a good time."

Francisco laughed.

"Is it dangerous, this risky thing you're talking about?"

"It's dangerous," Oleg said. "Seriously, pal, you may not live through it. Of course, you may not live if a pile of bales fall off that truck, the way Titus is stacking them."

"But you said it's for God's people." Francisco turned the steering wheel into another row of baled hay. "So, what is there to fear?"

Oklahoma

Donny Walters sat on a lawn chair to mix paint and paint thinner as he studied the next interior wall he was to paint. He sat because standing for too long caused his old hip and spine injuries to flare up. Chases from police had ended in car crashes, motor bike accidents had ended in broken bones, and brawls in prison had ended with more joint aches and pains than he could count. But even through his youthful years of wild living, he'd learned to paint. Now, a friend of a friend at a church in Lawton had employed him upon his prison release. His employer at the moment was a real estate developer named Peter Mitchell, who had seemed almost put out that the friend had asked him to give Donny a job. But Donny had taken the job, because he was desperate, even if his employer was still warming to the idea of hiring him.

Wetting his roller, Donny stood and reached with ease the corner at the top of the wall. His legs and arms were long and slender, and until he'd stopped working out to devote his time to ministry in prison, his shoulders had been broad and muscled. Now, he heard most people refer to him as slim or lanky, but he could still reach higher standing flat-footed than most people could jump and reach.

"Can I talk to you?"

Donny turned to find nineteen-year-old Clive Mitchell, his boss's son. They'd met the day before when Peter had shown Donny how he wanted the interior of each house painted.

"Sure, Clive." Donny set the roller on the tray and looked at his paint-spattered hands before offering Clive his hand. "I didn't hear your car."

"I rode my bike." Clive's hand was limp in Donny's grip. "There's a trail through the trees to the subdivision."

"Oh, you'll have to show me sometime. My bike is my only form of transportation right now, too." Donny smiled warmly, but sensed discomfort from the youth. After over a decade of using the Bible to counsel other inmates, Donny could read the signs of a hurting soul. "Listen, Clive, you can't say anything I haven't heard before, and you haven't done anything that I haven't tried, so you just rest assured, whatever it is that you want to say, it's a personal matter between the two of us, and we'll handle it together. Okay?"

"Okay." Clive sniffed and his eyes focused on everything but Donny.

"Here, let's take a seat." Donny motioned to the floor. His lawn chair would've been more comfortable, but there was only one, so they sat on the plastic-covered floor. Once seated, as Donny picked at paint around his fingernails, he prayed for openness and wisdom with the young man.

"I just feel so empty inside," Clive mumbled. "And lonely. I don't get the point of living anymore."

Donny nodded slowly, accepting the situation with which he was being entrusted, to respond as Christ would respond. He'd been involved with many suicide interventions in prison, so he knew the common nature of Satan's lies bombarding his victims.

"Well, you're talking to me, so something inside you knows that killing yourself requires some serious attention, right?" Donny studied the youth closer, and noticed something around one of his wrists that may have been due to him trying to hide cutting marks. "You can lie to your dad and to others, but you can't lie to me. If we're going to have a serious conversation, you need to get real with me. Pull up your sleeves."

Clive's frame slumped a little, but he pulled up his sleeves, revealing crude, homemade bandages that were stained through with blood.

"I didn't cut very deep."

"That's good, because nothing in that direction is the answer. Satan's twisting your mind to thinking that off-ing yourself is the answer to loneliness. And believe me, if you aren't trusting in Jesus Christ as your Savior, death will only bring you pain and loneliness that'll last an eternity. Satan wants that for you, but you have to want what Christ offers instead. It's time to trust what God has to say about you, Clive, and not listen to what others say about you. Sometimes, we even need to shut out what we think of ourselves and just place our faith in the real Friend we have in Jesus."

"I hear it all the time at church. I'm done with all that."

"Well, God's not done with you, or He wouldn't have brought you to me. Now, let's figure this out spiritually, and you need to listen to me, because I've been where you are. It's time to realize the hope you have right in front of you."

"Hope?"

Donny spent the next two hours explaining how God's gospel truth rescues the lost and hurting from bondage. The two prayed together, wept together, and laughed together. Clive faced his thinking errors by the insistence of Donny's abrupt style of confronting problems. Then Donny explained the danger of future emotional struggles, and how to deal with such spiritual attacks through the Word of God and prayer.

Before Clive left, he agreed to get involved in the young adult group at church, and he and Donny would talk more often about their mutual struggles.

After Clive was gone, Donny remixed the dried paint and committed to work until dark to make up for the time he'd lost. Nevertheless, he didn't see the last two hours as a loss. As near as he could tell, Clive had grown up in his father's church, but no one had explained to him how personal the gospel was or how real God could be in his life.

For an hour, Donny worked until he heard an engine outside. Peter Mitchell, the boss, walked into the house and surveyed the walls.

"What have you been doing all day?" Peter had a chiseled jaw and a mug that belonged on a magazine cover. The neighborhood subdivision was just one of his many investments around Oklahoma. "This should've all been painted by now. Why isn't it finished? I thought I was hiring a painter!"

"I won't leave here tonight until these last three walls are finished. I'll get it done, Mr. Mitchell."

Donny cared too much for Clive to use him as an excuse as his father demanded better work results.

"This isn't working out, Don." Peter shook his head. "I know your body has its limitations and you're getting up there in age. I feel for you about all the time you spent in prison, but seriously, if you can't finish a simple paint job in the time I ask, what good are you to me?"

"Well, I don't know, Mr. Mitchell." Donny set the roller back on the tray. It was strange for him to call a younger man "mister," anyway. "Maybe I'm no good to you at all."

Donny collected his jacket and thermos, and hobbled outside. The sun had gone down, and the late afternoon was cool. He peered up at the sky and smiled, imagining God was smiling, too. Though he'd lost his job, he'd saved a soul. Not a bad day, he decided.

A silver sports car raced into the housing complex lane. Dust rolled past Donny as the car turned tightly and came to a stop directly in front of him. The driver's door opened and a blond man in a jean jacket stepped out and stretched.

"You Donny Walters?"

"Yeah. Can I help you?"

"What're you doing?"

"Nothing now. I'm pretty sure I just got fired."

"Then why do you look pleased?"

"Because I got fired for doing the right thing."

"That's the best reason for getting fired, I suppose."

"Who are you?"

"Someone hiring people who will do the right thing, even if their lives are on the line."

Donny frowned. There was a dark-haired man in the car who looked about his own age.

"I don't drink or do drugs or steal, and my faith in Jesus Christ takes precedence above all."

"Sounds like we have the same heart." The blond man smiled and held out his hand. "I'm only here because your faith in Jesus Christ takes precedence above all."

Texas

Ernesto Colosio, nicknamed "Spider," donned a hazmat mask and crawled into the closet to capture a possum that had kept a young family awake for days, causing them to think their house was haunted. Starting his own pest control business upon his release from prison had been a complete accident for Ernesto. Initially, he'd been homeless, but after rescuing a woman and her cat from a family of raccoons in her attic, Ernesto had slowly accumulated the equipment necessary to handle rodent control complaints, as well as deal with insect infestations.

In a matter of six months, Ernesto had gone from being a homeless man, to a man with a mobile home to live in, a truck to use for work, and a business card that drew more business than he could respond to in a day.

Regardless of his work, he kept Saturdays and Sundays free for ministry. Down at the bus station in Austin, he'd gathered a number of vagrants, introduced himself, and handed out Bibles. Now, on Saturdays, he preached in Spanish to a small group of men, women, and children, and on Sundays, he preached in English to a different crowd in the same community. Many of those he'd led to Christ were illegal immigrants who spoke only Spanish, and many he discipled in English were ex-cons like himself, who sought true deliverance from the power of sin in their lives.

The police often cruised through the bus station area and gave Ernesto warnings. They threatened to write him a citation for having religious gatherings in a public area, but Ernesto was only going to the needy, where they were already gathered. He remained in prayer about the authorities, and continued to preach and teach.

It wasn't by choice that Ernesto ministered and worked alone. Upon leaving prison, he'd experienced much animosity and distrust since he was an ex-con, but he didn't want to be around homeless shelters that seemed overrun by drugs and abuse. Circumstances had thrust Ernesto into lay ministry, in which he worked alone, though it was the same work he'd committed his life to in prison after coming to Christ twelve years earlier. His work was to save souls from condemnation and to disciple believers to become courageous men and women for God. As long as he was able to do that, he wasn't about to fuss about the circumstances.

Inside the upstairs bedroom closet, Ernesto pushed a box trap ahead of him and listened for the cornered possum somewhere in the dark space. The whimpers of two young children downstairs in the care of their mother, gave him a sense of heroism. He was the mighty hunter of terrible creatures that no city-dweller would dare to tackle! But really, he knew the critters he caught were scared, hungry, and uncomfortable. For months, he'd been repopulating a small forest halfway to San Antonio where he loosed his captives.

The possum in the closet panicked, and instead of darting into the cage, it scrambled over the trap and came face-to-face with Ernesto. By instinct, Ernesto reached out and grabbed the possum by the neck and upper body, but the critter twisted around and bit hard onto his thumb. Ernesto felt the teeth grip, but his gloves, as tough as armor plating, protected his skin. Though the possum only weighed ten pounds, he still wrestled awkwardly with it until he was able to force it into the box.

Before he left the closet, he searched for any babies or a nest that needed to be cleaned out as well. The only casualty was what appeared to be someone's old Christmas sweater, which went into a sack on Ernesto's belt for disposal.

Downstairs, he was loading the trap into the back of his truck when he noticed a silver sports car idling at the street curb. Two occupants in the car were obviously watching him, and Ernesto immediately began to pray for God's watchcare. Any number of misunderstandings could arise from someone like him who visited a number of residences where oftentimes single or married women were home alone. The sports car could belong to a jealous boyfriend or an angry ex-husband.

From his truck, Ernesto returned to the house where the woman paid him electronically, and Ernesto left her with another pest-themed business card, on the back of which contained the gospel message.

"I may be a stranger to you, ma'am," Ernesto said, "but I'd be irresponsible if I didn't keep my clients safe from all kinds of dangers. Do you happen to recognize that silver car on the corner?"

"No." The woman withdrew from the porch and gathered her children to her at the door. "I've never seen that car around here. Should I call the police? They're just parked there. What should I do?"

"Let's find out before we cause a scene." Ernesto licked his lips, feeling anticipation. He was familiar with keeping people calm about their fears concerning the smallest of God's creatures, but here were some people who might be dangerous. "I'll go speak to them, and if they don't belong here, I'll send them away."

Ernesto walked to his truck and drew out a single-shot air rifle from behind his seat. Under extreme cases, he'd had to use a tranquilizer dart to capture raccoons or rabbits that didn't cooperate with his traps. With the rifle in one hand, he approached the sports car. The rifle was loaded with an animal tranquilizer, which wouldn't hurt a human, other than make them groggy for a few minutes. But Ernesto's intention was to provoke the flight of evildoers who might think the rifle was something more aggressive than it truly was.

When Ernesto was a few steps from the car, both the driver and the passenger emerged abruptly, their hands raised.

"Whoa, whoa, whoa, pal!" The blond driver gasped. "No need for that!"

The other man was wider, huskier, and shorter with wrinkled clothes. Ernesto kept his rifle aimed at the ground, but didn't back away.

"There's no need to sit suspiciously in a car and watch this nice lady's home, either. She'll call the police if she sees you around here again."

The blond man smiled, and Ernesto realized neither man showed actual fear, but they still didn't make a move to depart.

"You're just the kind of guy we're looking for, Ernesto Colosio." The blond thumped his hands on top of his car. "It ain't easy trying to talk to you with that dart gun in your hands. Besides, Oleg's likely to wrestle it from you before you can even cock it."

Noticing the man with wrinkled clothes was indeed poised to spring forward, Ernesto frowned and glanced down at his rifle. As the blond had apparently noticed, Ernesto hadn't cocked the rifle, and it really was only a dart gun.

"You know my name." Ernesto lifted his rifle to rest it over his shoulder. "What're you here for? You know me from my past? Or did we meet at the bus stop?"

"No, we've never met. My name's Titus Caspertein. This is Oleg Saratov. Before you got out of prison, you offered to help in some extreme operations for Jesus Christ. You still interested?"

"You're Christians?" Ernesto frowned. "I wrote that letter like two years ago."

"We only recently found a mission for you, something most people wouldn't want."

"Why wouldn't they want it?"

"It'll probably cost you your life," Titus said, "but there are lives you'll be saving."

"Would those lives be other Christians?" Ernesto asked.

"Yes."

Ernesto felt like his heart constricted. The snakes and raccoons of Austin could wait. Even his work at the bus stop could wait. Somewhere, Christians needed his help.

"I'll go tell the lady it's safe and get my truck."

CHAPTER FOUR

Pyongyang, North Korea

Yuriy Usik had defected from the Ukraine to Russia ten years earlier, but not even the Russians had been comfortable with his methods. As a large, fit man now in his forties, he'd never coped well under those in power over him until he found work that appealed to him in North Korea. In Pyongyang, his distaste for authority figures was appeased by the opportunity to exercise his appetite for brutality against enemies of the regime.

Intrigued with suffering, Yuriy Usik had excelled under his North Korean commanders to force confessions out of disloyal civilians, called untouchables, many of whom were Christians. The Great Leader of the country had a particular distaste for the traitors who worshipped an invisible God instead of himself, and Yuriy's techniques and results had excited the dictator for years. As such, Yuriy had been welcomed into Pyongyang's elite, or core, citizenship—one of the one-percent who occasionally met with the dictator, though never alone, and worked with government officials.

Deep inside the People's Palace of Remembrance, in a sub-level below ground, Yuriy Usik performed the most vicious examinations of state criminals. If they survived his interrogations, they were sent to one of the many *kwanlisos* around the country, the infamous "special control institutions," where life expectancy was only five years.

Yuriy Usik, in his cement office in the basement, straightened his uniform and adjusted the carpenter's hammer on his belt. The hammer wasn't a normal tool found on a pressed and pristine North Korean uniform, but Yuriy, as a foreigner and an extreme loyalist, was given certain privileges. As he awaited the expected prisoner, he removed the red pin on his breast, polished it, and fastened it more precisely over his heart. The perfect order demanded of North Korean officials would've driven him nuts in his youth, but he'd grown to appreciate the rigidity that now directed his entire life. He'd even learned to bow with practiced flawless posture to the state monuments that stood between his high-rise apartment and the Palace.

There was a light knock on his cast iron office door.

"Enter!" he called in Korean, and stood at attention like the perfect North Korean he'd become. His fists were lightly clenched at his sides, as he'd been taught years earlier, with the backs of his hands facing forward. His elbows were tucked tightly against his sides and his shoulders were squared and slightly shrugged.

One of his guards directed Han Ji-Jin into the office for her daily indoctrination, as ordered by a regime tribunal. The small woman stopped in the middle of the room, her pregnant belly at six and a half months clearly making her arch her back lest she double over forward. Her feet were bare, and Yuriy knew the floor was cold. He'd intentionally removed the rug his predecessor had placed on the floor, just to witness his subjects squirm from the chill. Watching people suffer excited Yuriy.

But as triumphant as Yuriy wanted to feel, Jin's face was calmly defiant. Her chin was raised just slightly, but her eyes weren't focused on him. He wanted to slap her, to put her in his torture chair as he had before, but her sentence and prescribed treatment had been carefully dictated to him, especially now that she was so advanced with child. The full term of her pregnancy was to be encouraged, and then the execution of child and mother could commence. Until then, his daily chiding would have to suffice his hunger to torture her.

"You have shown yourself to be a traitor to your people," Yuriy stated, walking around the prisoner. He shoved the guard out of the way to stand against the wall where the torture chair was placed. "You have distributed texts that have turned the country's people against the Eternal Leaders. By doing so, you have harmed many, and for this you will be punished.

"Today, I have brought in something new to show you." Yuriy noticed Jin's eyes twitch, maybe surprised that he had broken from his normal recitation of charges against her. "Look here. This camera was brought in special from China to record the event as you give birth in this very room. And it will record your baby's execution, and then your own death.

"The country will celebrate as someone so evil is destroyed so completely. The footage will be shown publicly inside Rungrado First of May Stadium. The whole country will celebrate your death and laugh at your shame. Children will mock you and rejoice for the Great Leader's wisdom to rid this country of you and your kind.

"The video will be sent up to Hamgyong Prison where your husband is paying for his many crimes. He will be forced to watch the recording every day until he dies. Turn and sit in the chair where you will soon die."

Yuriy stepped to the stainless steel chair, and the guard helped him fasten the straps around Jin's neck, arms, and ankles. He stood back to gloat at his prisoner, but Jin's face was blank. If he wasn't mistaken, she appeared peaceful! She stared straight ahead at the wall, as if she weren't afraid at all to die. Her lips were moving a little, but he could hear no audible words.

Everyone was afraid to die, Yuriy told himself, and the rest of his speech that morning left his mind. He turned from Jin and the chair, and sat on the edge of his desk. Many Christians had died under his hammer, and they had all seemed to be just like Jin, when he thought about it. Now, the most brutal execution the regime had ever imagined was coming to the woman in his office, and she was unresponsive?

Pulling his hammer from his belt, he examined the steel head on the end of the rubber-gripped steel handle. He'd kept the tool clean over the years, but upon closer examination, it still had tiny spots of rust on it. Weeks earlier, he'd used it on a disloyal official in Chongjin who had protested the regime's handling of Jin and her well-known husband, Rea. That official had been struck in the chest and left on the beach for the tide to carry away. But thinking back, Yuriy hadn't seen any real fear in that man's face, either. Had that official also been a Christian? A traitor to the people of Korea?

He thought back briefly to all the Christians he'd tortured. Many of them had been forced to react physically to their treatments, but he realized now that they hadn't actually been afraid. Nor did they come to a place where they regretted their crimes against the Great Leader. For the first time in his blood-thirsty career, Yuriy was shocked to realize that his methods of torture were ineffective to bring true change in the hearts of the people! Was Christian defiance actually stronger than the suffering he so carefully designed?

Looking up sharply, he caught Jin watching him. She turned her eyes away, again focusing on the blank wall. For weeks, he'd been threatening her. If anything, she appeared more peaceful in her discomfort. It wasn't possible! *Juche* couldn't possibly be weaker than this Jesus these traitors worshipped! How were Christians any different from other state criminals? How could they suffer silently while others pleaded and begged for his mercy?

"Take her back." Yuriy slid his hammer back into his belt and waved his hand. "Go. I'm done with her today."

Once he was alone again in his office, he unbuttoned his collar and sat carefully in the torture chair. It was made of several steel plates with edges jutting out awkwardly, pressing painfully into his skin, but he forced himself to remain reclined for a few seconds. When he got up, he rubbed the skin where the metal left small impressions. How was pain not making Christians react any longer? Or, had it ever?

To ask such questions aloud was dangerous, Yuriy considered, since the regime taught that the Korean people were the greatest, richest people in the world, reliant on and united around and thinking through the Great Leader. That was the *Juche* idea, the word that literally meant "subject," but had been translated by other nations as "self-reliance." What suddenly concerned Yuriy at that instant wasn't whether he asked others about Christian endurance through suffering, but if that endurance was somehow really greater than North Korean *Juche!* It was unthinkable that the machine of domination that so organized a whole nation could be thwarted by a silent, weak, pregnant woman!

Yuriy hated himself for pondering such thoughts, but he had to know why his threats against Jin had no effect. His life devotion to inflicting pain and projecting his power over others was being threatened. He had to know what force was causing this!

California

Titus Caspertein knew that *Operation: Harm's Way* was like no other operation he and Oleg had planned. For one, he'd never staged a mission where the operators were knowingly expected to die. In other missions, there were always risks, but nothing like what they faced inside North Korea.

And second, he and Oleg had an audience on the first day of training. That was far from standard protocol, especially with such sensitive intelligence involved. However, he, Corban, and Oleg had agreed that the subjects of the mission wouldn't be discussed until the whole team arrived in Akita, Japan, for their final preparation. But leaving for Japan was still several weeks away.

"Each of you has volunteered to be here," Titus began, standing like a drill sergeant in front of the five men he and Oleg had gathered. They stood on a stretch of pavement in front of a dormitory of an Olympic training center, now owned by COIL. The walled center covered one hundred acres, and, with the help of Wes Trimble, had been bought by COIL a year earlier for the training of COIL agents, as well as for a retreat for missionaries on furlough. "In less than sixty days, I will tell you who you are going to help, but until then, it's my job to prepare you to complete your job.

"For now, I'll tell you this: you will face cold, you will face hatred, you will face discouragement, you will face violence, and you will face death. For this operation to be successful, you must be despised by the modern world. That's part of your cover. You must become enemies of the state. You must abandon all attachments to your past. And you must, without exception, cling with unwavering faith to the invincible God who raised Christ from the dead. Why is that so important? Because if you don't identify fully with Christ's death, burial, and resurrection, you'll have no strength to face the horrible pressures before you. And without your mind on the resurrection Christ promises to His faithful, you'll have no courage to face death selflessly. Most, if not all five of you, will be dead in a couple months. You'll train for sixty days for what may be only sixty minutes of madness. The people you are being asked to save are God's people. They also have information that will save lives, but you will receive no credit. Your names will be slandered and scorned and forgotten by the world, but you'll grow spiritually through all this to appreciate Jesus Christ like few others have, if you surrender all."

Titus paused to let his words sink in. Avery Hewitt, on one end of the line of five operatives, seemed cool-tempered. Oleg had found the slender man in Fresno, preaching and starving nearly to death in a homeless camp. His gray eyes seemed to sparkle, as if willing to face the trial of death then and there, that very day. In fact, Avery was the only one of the five who had overseas experience. But Titus was aware that each of the five had already been screened by Corban as having made remarkable impacts in various ways.

Job Buck stood next to Avery, his feet wide, with thick forearms betraying years of hard work as a carpenter and handyman before he went to prison, as well as while he was there. The man was in his fifties, and his belly extended just barely over his belt, but Titus saw the man's solid frame behind his overweight appearance. And there was no fear in Job's face, either.

Next, Francisco "Shorty" Hernandez stood with a grin on his face. He was the shortest of all the operators, and the youngest, but he had the brightest face, and was seemingly amused by Titus' words. No doubt, Titus thought, the young man was just happy he wasn't still wrestling hay bales onto a truck.

Ernesto "Spider" Colosio stood next to Francisco. His black hair was tied back into a ponytail, and if Titus wasn't mistaken, he saw eagerness on the man's face. Every few seconds, the pest controller shifted his hands from having them folded in front of him, to tucking them into his pockets, to ringing them at his sides. It seemed he could barely contain his excitement.

Donny Walters, with paint still spattered on his jeans, was the most relaxed, at least in appearance. The tall Oklahoman was in his fifties. Titus had read his medical file after Janice Dowler had completed a brief physical on all the men. Donny's back and joints were plagued with arthritis from past injuries, and some days, moving around was a struggle, he'd admitted.

But Corban's plan to get the men into Pyongyang was flexible, and in time, each of the five would adjust to the role that fit them best.

Off to the side, Corban Dowler sat in a golf cart with his wife, Janice, a short-haired woman in her early sixties. Titus had learned that she was one of Corban's secrets to him living with stability and consistency for Christ. Before Corban had founded COIL years before, she'd led her husband to Christ, and the woman remained a stoic helpmate to that very day.

Standing next to the golf cart was Jenna Dowler, the adopted daughter of the older couple, and blind since childhood. She was now in high school, and Corban had boasted in her ability to read Braille in languages she didn't know, to digitally record the Bible and other study materials. So far, she'd learned to read words in the Urdu, Sindhi, and Pashto languages. Her ability to pronounce and enunciate clearly what she read had made her an effective COIL operator in her own right.

Titus' wife and son were sitting in a second golf cart. Annette had begun house hunting in San Diego, and Levi had returned to school the day before. Corban was never one to exclude people from an influential moment, so he'd suggested that Titus wait until that afternoon to give the operatives his opening speech when Levi was out of school and could join them. Though Titus hoped his fourteen-year-old son was witnessing the unflinching faith of the five believers, one look at Levi told him that the boy was more interested in the pretty blind girl a few yards away.

After clearing his throat, and noting to himself that he had some serious fathering to do with the boy, he continued.

"We need each of you in your best physical condition, so you'll be on strict diet and exercise routines. Your ages and health differ from one another, so we'll be pushing you according to your abilities, not by a universal standard. As your roles in the operation become clearer, we'll fine-tune your training to fit your responsibilities. You were briefed yesterday when you arrived about COIL's overall work worldwide, so you know non-lethal weapons training is on the itinerary.

"Spiritually, Oleg, Corban, and myself will provide what we have to offer, but you've all been Christians longer than we've been, and we're aware that you've all lived for Christ under pressure for years. You've led hundreds to Christ and discipled countless believers, so you five will probably be your own best fellowship and support in the dorms.

"I don't mean to be morbid, but preparing to meet Christ face-to-face should be first on your minds. That should be a priority for all Christians, but all the more so when we knowingly go into a life-threatening situation. I suspect this will be the best training for eternity anyone can undergo. It ain't easy, men, preparing to die so others can live. It's important that you count the cost in following Christ in this way."

Titus glanced at Corban, who gave a single nod. Though Titus didn't feel like he and Corban had finished their last conversation about improving COIL's weaponry, they were like-minded in their efforts and goals to stand boldly for God and His people around the world.

Oleg stepped up next to Titus.

"Rest and pray," the Russian commanded. "Tonight, we begin training. Tomorrow, you find out where you're going."

Hamgyong Province, North Korea

Johnny "Mapper" Wycke had never been a prominent COIL leader, planning and rescuing endangered Christians, but he'd remained on call for Corban Dowler since the beginning of COIL. With *Operation: Harm's Way* quickly approaching, Mapper's skills as a forerunner to any COIL team were in full demand.

On a frozen, isolated road in northeastern North Korea, Mapper drove a four-wheel-drive truck slowly up the sparsely forested mountain. The landscape was gray, and an early winter had cursed the land in Hamgyong Province. If something went wrong while in the oppressive country, he couldn't possibly escape on foot into the wilderness. Even though he was healthy and strong, the brutal cold and hunger would break him. Now eighty miles south of the Russian border, he was on his own in enemy territory.

But Mapper wasn't entirely alone. North Korean government jeeps, before and after his truck, escorted him as they drove to Hamgyong Prison.

Mapper's truck had been lightly searched before he'd been allowed entry across the Tumen River. His cover as a junior Russian diplomat had bought him access into the country, but his false identity wouldn't secure his departure if something went wrong. He was aware that others were being trained to risk their lives during *Operation: Harm's Way*, and Mapper had somberly agreed to Corban's recent plans to recon the prison where Nathan's team would soon extract Jeong Byeang-Rea.

Regardless of the search of his vehicle, Mapper had still brought gear secretly into the country. Though the temperature was bitter cold, he rolled down his window and kept an eye on his rearview mirror. Two men were in each jeep. That was eight eyes that could spot what he was about to do, unless he timed it perfectly.

As they approached a sharp bend along a mountainside, Mapper pulled up his right coat sleeve. A device, the size of a small salt shaker, was attached to a spring-fired wrist rocket. The slope out his window angled gradually down to a dry riverbed laden with boulders. As the jeep in the front reached the bend, Mapper propped his elbow on the windowsill. Then, it was his turn to drive around the bend. He supported the steering wheel with his knee as he used his left hand to press the trigger on his right elbow. The wrist rocket fired with a puff of air, as quietly as a slingshot.

An instant later, he'd pushed his sleeve back down, and taken hold of the steering wheel. He did all this without turning his head. He hoped if anyone had seen the flashing device fly through the air, it would be mistaken for a bird, or even a sun flash off the windshield.

The jeep in front didn't tap its brakes, and the jeep behind made no indication of alarm. A moment later, as Kwanmo Peak loomed in the distance, Mapper rolled up his window and sighed with relief. In such a large operation as this, COIL operators needed up-to-the-minute weather reports from the vicinity of the prison. The device, which had landed somewhere in the dry riverbed, would broadcast an intermittent weather report to COIL satellites. Knowing the exact weather patterns over the next two months could make the difference between a successful extraction and a failed mission. By knowing the weather, Nathan's team would know what clothes and food to bring, and what gear to leave behind.

A mile farther, Mapper braked as the three-vehicle convoy approached a double-gated perimeter fence. They had reached Hamgyong Prison.

Mapper gripped the steering wheel with his melon-sized fists and prayed internally for success. It wasn't safety he prayed for, only the success of the mission. Nathan's operation to fetch Rea from that prison was contingent upon fresh and accurate intel from inside.

Uniformed soldiers with rifles, grenades on their belts, and dogs on leashes walked casually along the fence that stretched north to south as far as Mapper could see. From satellite photos, he knew the prison spanned over one hundred and fifty square miles to accommodate everything from the barracks for guards and their families, a school for the guards' children, leather and rubber workshops, a farm, and limestone and coal mines.

A guard in a tower leaned out of his perch as Mapper's escorts spoke to the man in Korean, which Mapper didn't know. That was the moment Mapper chose to turn on the radio to a predetermined frequency, which played light static—an indicator that the camera mounted in the headlight was recording. After several shouts and commands, the double-gated entrance was opened for his truck and the two jeeps. He hadn't doubted he'd get this far, since his escorts were ranking officials from Pyongyang, overseeing his visit, but Mapper was more concerned about getting out, not getting in.

He let his eyes drift across the prison interior, taking mental note of prisoner dorms in view. A path led down a rocky embankment, perhaps to the limestone mine, he guessed, though everything on the ground seemed different than the satellite angles he'd seen.

For a minute, he drove along the eastern perimeter fence behind the lead jeep. Out of the corner of his eye, he measured the double fence height, an inner electric fence, and an outer barbed one. The ground immediately in front, between, and behind both fences was bare, as if sown with salt. The barren ground made for an easy killing zone with an unobstructed view for the guards, whether in the towers or on the ground, if a prisoner dared to attempt to scale the fences.

They drove past a massive square building, which Mapper had deduced was the shoe factory. Intel reports had described the four sides of the building. It had a courtyard in the middle, and housed different factory operations—cutting, designing, assembly, and repair.

Near a long, narrow warehouse, which was the leather and rubber workshop according to some reports, Mapper studied a single-file column of prisoners marching slowly in unison. Though he didn't want to draw attention to himself, he slowed his truck slightly to examine the prisoners closer. Knowing the condition of the prisoners could prepare Nathan's team for any number of scenarios. If the prisoners were healthy, then Nathan might possibly expect Rea to be able to walk or run alongside the operatives once they broke him out of his housing or cell. But if the prisoners were unhealthy, then that intel might be interpreted by Nathan that he'd need to be ready to carry Rea out of the prison.

It took Mapper only a few seconds to determine the prisoners' condition. Children as young as six carried bundles in their arms, the same as the adults. This was a column of workers coming or going from their work shift, and their bundles were probably their dormitory bedding to keep them warm while seated at their work stations. They wore drab-colored coats, layered, it seemed, one inside another, though the material looked like North Korea's vinylon fiber, literally made from coal and limestone.

Risking a glance backward, Mapper saw their faces. His glance lingered and took in the image of walking skeletons, some with scars on their faces. Many had missing eyes or ears, and several were even missing hands or arms.

He looked away and focused on the jeep in front of him. Mapper had been in some dreadful places around the world, doing recon and prep for COIL teams, but what he'd just seen would stay with him forever. The size of the camp, and from what he'd seen down several avenues where other prisoners were marching, the prison may have housed as many as one hundred thousand men, women, and children.

His convoy pulled up to an administrative building, clearly built differently than the prisoners' dorms not far away. He guessed the dorms were made of mud. The administration and guards' buildings were made of unpainted wood, which was weathered and cracked.

Mapper remained in his cab until one of his escorts signaled to him and moved to his door. From beside him on the seat of the truck, Mapper took two large suitcases, each weighing as much as fifty pounds. He was briskly escorted toward the building entrance. His guards were adult men in their prime, but malnutrition had stunted their growth. The tops of their heads reached almost to Mapper's shoulder. In the background and from the direction of the prisoner dorms, he heard a loud speaker droning with propaganda. Posters on the outside of the administration building, in writing that he couldn't read, had images of missiles blasting and fields with abundant food that seemed to project a message of supremacy and prosperity. It was all brainwashing, he knew. He'd heard that most North Koreans had never even seen anything that resembled a hamburger patty, yet they claimed to be wealthier than America and the rest of the world.

He was shown into a room where more national banners hung on the walls. Two men in uniforms that differed from the guards' attire rose to their feet from soft chairs. A small deer the size of a dog was stuffed and mounted in a corner where a coal stove warmed the room.

"We and our Great Leader welcome you to Hamgyong Prison," the eldest of the officials said in perfect Russian, then bowed stiffly.

"You are very gracious to host me, thank you," Mapper responded in Russian, and bowed in return. "I am told this may be the first of many transactions between our two countries, regardless of the capitalist sanctions."

The two officials seemed pleased with Mapper's greeting, and they indicated that he take a chair. His four guards remained posted intentionally across the room, as if barring Mapper from leaving without them. He fought an instant of panic, then focused on his objective. Corban and an old Russian agent named Fost Ivanovich had arranged this meeting, with him impersonating a Russian diplomat. But the smallest detail could derail everything, and Mapper could spend the rest of his life inside the labor camp—a life which would certainly be reduced in years.

"What is your interest in Sergei Tarmak?" the elder official asked.

To Mapper, the two North Korean officers looked like factory-produced twins. Their faces and ages were different, but their physique was the same and their haircuts resembled the dictator's haircut, which was enforced country-wide, intelligence said, and absolutely mandatory among the social elite.

The question the official asked was a test, Mapper understood. Corban had warned him something like this might happen. All the details of this visit had been communicated already, but information was power, so the North Koreans were seeking more information.

"I am just an errand boy," Mapper stated. "But I can tell you that my superiors want Sergei Tarmak because in Moscow, he has offended powerful families. He will suffer for his crimes, and your country's generosity will not be ignored. Because of the sanctions, we will not boast too loudly about this growing relationship, but I have heard there are already letters of appreciation drafted on your behalf, meant for Pyongyang, if patience and secrecy is exercised."

The officers couldn't quite hide their satisfied smiles and greed. They were certainly thinking a promotion was in order. No one wanted to live out in the barren, cold mountains when they could be eating imported cheese with the dictator in Pyongyang. Of course, there were no letters, and no such officials, and no such offended families in Moscow, but Mapper and the prisoner he wanted would be long gone by the time that was discovered, if it ever was.

"He has not cooperated as a laborer." The official's face seemed ashen and serious. "He has been punished."

Mapper restrained his real reaction and smiled instead.

"The disobedient must be disciplined." Having seen the other prisoners' scars and missing body parts, he understood that the discipline Sergei Tarmak had endured had probably mutilated him. "Is he still alive?"

"Yes, but he is no longer mobile." The officer waved with two fingers at a guard against the wall. "He ran into the woods in the northern quadrant of the complex and hid for two days. He was near death when we recovered him, but workers who refuse to work must be punished."

"Of course." Mapper turned his head to see an interior door open, and a thin white man in his early fifties was guided into the room. Sergei Tarmak was on crutches. His left foot had been amputated at the ankle, but the man's face matched the photos Mapper had seen, so he was sure this was Sergei. "Taking him back to Russia will not be as difficult now."

"Agreed, agreed!" the official cheered, apparently relieved that their harsh treatment wasn't being criticized. "The funds are all here?"

"Fifty thousand euros." Mapper pointed to one suitcase, then the other. "And as many chocolate bars as I could carry."

The chocolate bars were Chinese sub-par knock-offs of Hershey products, but in North Korea, no one would know or care.

"Will you be spending the night with us?" The official bowed slightly. "We have a room available."

"It is generous of you to offer." Mapper could hear the propaganda bullhorn blaring in the distance, and guessed no room in the whole prison could block out that noise. Spending a single night in the wretched place of suffering was unimaginable. "But I cannot be late for a jet to return the prisoner to Moscow. I'm sure you understand."

Sergei Tarmak's face showed both confusion and relief. His relief was certainly from the prospect of leaving the camp of horrors, and his confusion was probably because he was a petty Russian con man who'd been caught exporting stolen Swiss watches inside North Korea. As far as Corban had known, the Russian thief was a legitimate criminal, but he fit COIL's needs precisely, and buying his release would send no flags about Rea, whose freedom could never be purchased since the regime had a personal vendetta against him. The same went for any other natural-born Christian.

Sergei was led into the passenger seat of Mapper's truck, and gagged and tied for transport. The thin man didn't protest. Mapper still read relief on the crippled man's face. Once back in Russia, Mapper was scheduled to hand off the prisoner to Russian Christians for the thief's reintegration back into society, and hopefully to see the man come to Christ and change his ways.

As Mapper drove out of the camp of death, he wondered in which building Rea was housed. The criminal hobbled next to him probably wouldn't know about a single man in a camp the size of a city, but he would certainly know intel COIL didn't already have, so Sergei would be extensively questioned within forty-eight hours. Regardless of what Sergei revealed, Mapper had now been inside the prison. He'd seen the razor wire and the suffering, the weapons the guards carried, and the attack dogs on leashes.

Nathan's team of infiltrators would have their work cut out for them!

California

At the old Olympic training center east of San Diego, Avery Hewitt walked slowly around a model of the city of Pyongyang rather than joining the others for lunch. The rest of the gym floor beyond the expansive, three-dimensional model was where Titus Caspertein and Oleg Saratov had been training them all morning in hand-to-hand combat and submission hold techniques.

A sign on the outside of the building door read "gym," but most of the exercise equipment had been removed or pushed against the mirror-lined walls. Now, the building was kept locked at night, even to the casual Christian vacationers of the one-hundred-acre retreat facility.

"You're not hungry?" Titus wandered over to the model. "You need to keep up your calorie intake for this kind of training."

"Our survival in a few weeks depends on me knowing this city." Avery crouched down, visualizing the capital's broad streets and imposing monuments. "I feel it, you know."

"Feel what?" Titus stood beside him, hands in his pockets.

"God has shown me this has been my calling all along. Like you said at our orientation, I've counted the cost."

"That ain't easy for a lot of people to accept," Titus said softly, "that God has called His people to suffer. Some people love their lives too much."

"My choices and crimes have brought me to a place where society has rejected me." Avery walked over and knelt on another side of the model to view it from a different angle. "After everything I've done wrong, and after everything God has opened my eyes to—my whole life has been lived in preparation to die in this city if I need to—to die for Jesus by dying for His people's safety, to live more meaningfully."

A silent moment passed between them as Avery envisioned himself darting down shadowy Korean streets, burdened with gear, escorting the subject or subjects to an evacuation zone. Through prayer and the unfolding task before them, Avery had begun to embrace his role in the operation, though he hadn't been told the exact strategy of rescuing someone in Pyongyang. His physical fitness alone assured him a central part that would test his body to its limits, as well as his faith. Panic under such pressure could get himself and others killed before the mission was completed.

"Come on." Titus started toward the door. "Let's join the others."

Outside, Avery walked next to the tall blond agent as they descended a steep hill to the facility's cafeteria.

"In the third century," Titus said as they neared the building, "there was a group of Christians in North Africa who survived persecution in prison. Some of them were criminals who had come to Christ through other Christians imprisoned with them. They were released after years of suffering when a new emperor rose to power in Rome. But those released Christians were too radical for most of society, even for the Christians in the empire who hadn't suffered. Their passion for Christ was greater because they had fellowshipped with Christ through tremendous strain. They were misunderstood and labeled as crazies by some, but the fruit they bore later speaks for itself. They went to the leper colonies where others wouldn't go. They became missionaries and martyrs when others chose to remain in the cities. They lived poorly, ate poorly, and eventually they died in poverty. But I think Christ would call those ex-prisoners His family. Do you know what they called themselves?"

"What?"

They reached the cafeteria and stopped outside.

"They called themselves a Latin term that translates as the *Kindred of Nails*. They were kindred of Christ's suffering for them, and they weren't ashamed to suffer for Him. Ironically, in English, we would call them the KONs. Now, with you, Job, Francisco, Ernesto, and Donny, I think we're witnessing a new generation of KONs willing to do what no one else can or will do, because you've lived through what no one else has."

"We were all criminals," Avery reminded him. "None of us were in prison for missing choir practice."

"But like some of the third century KONs, you came to Christ while in prison. Tell me the truth: was living as a faithful Christian easy in prison?"

"No. Every day was hard. The others will tell you the same. There was pressure every single day."

"Why was it so hard on you five?"

"Maybe because each of us stood and spoke up. We didn't remain in hiding. Everyone on the yard knew we were Christians. We taught, counseled, and discipled. We were vocal."

"And everyone treated you well?"

"No. We've talked about that in the dorm. We were threatened, slandered, and sometimes mistreated."

"You suffered for Christ, but you endured." Titus placed a hand on Avery's shoulder. "You five are today's *Kindred of Nails.*"

Avery stared at the pavement for a moment, then raised his eyes to meet Titus' eyes.

"Thank you for telling me this. I'll share it with the others. It will mean something to them, too."

Inside the cafeteria, Avery and Titus were greeted by a chorus of cheers and laughter for arriving so late. As had become tradition for the five new operatives, Avery joined the other four at their own table. COIL support staff and vacationing missionaries were seated at other tables.

"We were just discussing our prison nickname," Donny said to Avery, "and the guys don't believe me that I didn't have a handle."

"Everyone's got a handle," Avery said. "Mine was *Chevy.*"

He unbuttoned his shirt enough to show a giant Chevrolet emblem tattooed on his chest. The men roared in laughter, drawing attention from the nearby tables where Titus and Annette ate with Corban and his family. Avery discreetly buttoned up his shirt under the critical eye of Janice Dowler, but Avery knew the older woman wasn't as tough as she seemed. She'd been teaching the team basic first aid, and her laughter at Francisco's failed attempts to give a dummy CPR proved the woman had a joyful heart and a sense of humor.

"My handle was *Hammer* before I came to Christ," Job said, raising a fist that made Avery think of Thor's mythical hammer. "Nobody messed with the Hammer in my youth!"

"Or they'd get nailed?" Francisco asked straight-faced.

"Exactly."

"Then why didn't they call you the *Nailer?*" Donny laughed.

Job slammed his fist down on the table in mock rage. The noise drew more attention from the other tables, and Ernesto shushed the rowdy men.

"I was *Shorty*," Francisco said, "but I don't know why."

The men chuckled.

"Let me give you a hint," Donny said, leaning forward to whisper. "It's not because you're too tall."

"I was *Spider*," Ernesto said, "but I'd rather not tell you why."

"Aw, come on!" the men cried in unison.

"All right, all right, but you have to promise me you won't call me *Spider*."

"Yeah, well . . ." Donny shook his head, "I don't see us making any such promise. Come on. Out with it."

"Okay, um, I was a new Christian, and I was having a hard time settling in to the discipline of studying the Bible. I liked to work out on the yard and socialize. One day, I woke up with my armpit swelled up like a grapefruit."

"A spider bite?" Avery asked.

"That's what they said, but who knows? I was on different antibiotics for months. Nothing worked. Every day, I was in the yard clinic getting my armpit abscess drained. Word got around I was bitten by a spider, so it stuck."

"So it's not because you have spider skills, like climbing tall buildings and solving crime?" Donny teased.

"I'm afraid not." Ernesto grinned. "But that's not the end. I hated spiders after that. I mean, I still have a scar in my armpit! But I learned through all that how to sit still and study the Bible. When you're sick and you can't move your arm, what does a Christian do? You get to know God a little better. And then, when I got out of prison last year, I started my own pest control business."

"Oh, I get it!" Donny howled. "You took revenge against all the spiders. Beware, the *Spider* who kills spiders!"

"Okay, okay," Ernesto waved his hand. "But let's not forget two things: you can't call me *Spider*—we all agreed—and we're here to find out Donny's nickname."

"Oh, yeah!" Avery rubbed his hands together. "If you don't have a handle, Donny, your caring brothers in Christ will do the honor of choosing something classy for you."

"Just make it something that highlights my finest qualities," Donny said. "Something like *Handsome Don*, or *Delightful Donny*."

"I was thinking more like *Okie*," Avery said. "You're straight out of Oklahoma, brother."

"Okay, okay, I'll accept my new handle," Donny said, "but only if it comes with extra late-night cookie privileges from the cafeteria."

The men laughed.

"Hey, on the serious side, guys," Avery said. He lowered his voice and the others leaned closer to him. "I think I've got a name for us. Titus was telling me about some prisoners back in Roman times. They came to Christ in prison, and when they got out, they served God in ways no one else could or would. They were probably marked as outcasts, like us, but they served God without flinching."

"Well?" Ernesto asked. "What were they called?"

"They were called the *Kindred of Nails*."

"The *Kindred of Nails*," Francisco repeated with a broad smile. "I like it. *The KONs*. That's us!"

"Yeah, that's us." Job nodded. "It fits."

Donny and Ernesto nodded, and their name was settled.

The cafeteria door opened and Oleg Saratov walked in and scanned the dining area. The COIL personnel occupied two tables near the salad bar. Oleg marched straight over to Titus and Corban. Avery hushed his table so they could all hear what was said. Oleg was clearly disturbed, indicated by his deep frown.

"News from Mapper," he told Corban. "It's worse than we realized."

Avery watched Titus' face for a reaction, to read the situation. So far, the KONs hadn't been told who Mapper was, but Avery knew it had to do with North Korea.

"Let's get back to the gym." Titus rose from his chair and touched Annette on the shoulder. "It's time everyone knew more details about Nathan's operation. Come on."

Looking down at his half-eaten plate of food, Avery prayed for courage. He picked up several cold-cuts, slapped them onto dry wheat bread, and followed his friends out of the cafeteria.

CHAPTER FIVE

New York

Nathan Isaacson lifted his head from praying in a carpeted corner of the roller skating rink as the front door opened. A familiar form entered to stand in the booth area of the closed establishment. The others who'd been in prayer remained where they sat, some of them in small groups, but Nathan jumped to his feet and ran across the hard floor to his wife, Chen Li. Like Mapper, she'd been overseas gathering intel for the coming operation.

For a few moments, the two held each other tightly. They'd fallen in love several years earlier when Nathan had been sent into the South Pacific to rescue Chen Li from underwater demise. Since then, the two COIL agents had operated together on missions as often as possible.

"How was China?" Being several inches taller than she, he held her at arm's length and looked down into her brown eyes. "Every time we're apart . . ."

"I know." She took a deep breath, seeming to hold back a sob. "The believers who hosted me were amazing, but there are things you need to know. The barriers to get Rea out of that prison are mounting."

"Come on. Let's lay it out for the others." Nathan held her hand as they walked back to the carpeted section of the rink. The carpet had been laid to ward off some of the chill when the team gathered for briefings or fellowship. He whistled to draw everyone from their scheduled prayer time. "Let's huddle up."

From all over the building, his team and the support staff drifted toward him. Bruno and his wife, Scooter and his wife, Fred and June, and Luigi and Heather took seats on various chairs or benches brought in to accommodate the team. For the moment, the enormous model of Hamgyong Prison in the middle of the floor was ignored.

As the couples settled in, and Chloe set up her laptop on a card table, Nathan prayed in his heart over the people God had given him to lead yet again. Their faces seemed to shine, even though great danger was before them. He attributed that shine to the time they'd all spent in morning prayer for the last hour. They'd been with the Lord. Standing next to Chloe's table, Nathan raised his hand to silence those gathered.

"We've made good progress getting to know a few details about Hamgyong Prison, but now we're going to fill in some blanks that still exist. We've heard from two more sources in the field. First, Chloe?"

Chloe remained seated in front of her laptop as she spoke loudly and confidently, as if she were still the Mossad veteran directing an operation.

"Mapper just arrived back in Russia with a prisoner he paid to get out of Hamgyong Prison. Since Mapper was inside the prison himself, he has fresh intel for us." Chloe paused as the team exclaimed with excitement at the brazen courage of their teammate. Luigi even stopped chewing his gum for a moment as he seemed to consider how dangerous it must have been for Mapper to go inside the razor wire. "Every detail we can get will make the team's job safer. The California team has been briefed that our data collecting is now complete. Everything we need to get Rea out of this prison is in our hands. We just need to finalize our entry and exit strategy."

She tapped a couple keys, and everyone swiveled to acknowledge a projection of points on the wall.

"The prison's inner perimeter fence is fifteen feet high and electrified with 3300 volts. The outer fence is the same height, with barbed wire and razor coils on top. There's about fifteen feet between the two fences, and this space appears to be planted with traps and maybe nails under the soft dirt.

"Instead of having unmarked structures to study in our model, we can now finish assigning labels to the rest of the buildings in the prison's southern section, where we believe Rea is being held in detention. We'll be facing about one thousand armed guards, and about five hundred administrative soldiers, which we can expect to be armed to some degree as well."

Scooter whistled and whispered something to Bruno, who nodded with concern.

"And we're seriously doing this with only a handful of us?" Scooter gestured at Bruno. "I nominate Bruno to distract all those guards while the rest of us rescue Rea."

"What am I, a rodeo clown?" Bruno smiled. "You're my distraction while I pole-vault over the fences and hang glide out to safety with Rea."

"You two haven't changed." Nathan chuckled with the rest. "Now that we know where we need to go inside the prison to free Rea, which is pretty deep inside farthest from the front entrance, we'll be discussing additional personnel to help us when it comes to the towers."

"Who'll that be?" Memphis looked around. "Whoever's going to back up the incursion team should be here training with us."

"We are." Chloe rose to her feet and stepped in front of the card table. "Bruno, Nathan, Memphis, and Scooter are the front-runners on this team. They're responsible for the part of this mission that involves going inside the prison. But that's not enough, as Nathan has pointed out. You four need extra coverage. June, Chen Li, Heather, and myself aren't here only for logistical and moral support. We each have NL-X2 battle rifle training. In pairs, we can hold a couple of the corner towers as long as we need to, providing the insertion team coverage as you go inside. June?"

Everyone looked to the investigative reporter who was often Chloe's right hand in Manhattan's COIL office. Since coming to Christ and marrying Memphis, she'd also become a mother of two.

"I figured there was more to you having us ladies here than just cooking meals," June said. "I haven't been in the field for a while, but I can still shoot. I'll need to ask my relatives to watch the kids a little longer."

"Bring them here," Scooter's wife said. "We'll be holding down this fort until you all get back."

Bruno's wife nodded at her friend, and Chloe seemed satisfied.

"Okay, then. Luigi, do you have something to say?"

Always aloof, Luigi stood slowly from a worn-out sofa he and Heather were sitting on. The tall, gaunt Italian was silent for a moment, then he spoke purposefully.

"The two DRIL combat drones are on a freighter, heading for Japan. They can each carry a payload of thirty-five-hundred pounds. That's enough for twelve people plus gear in each drone. Please explain to everyone why we're extracting only one person from the prison. That's all."

He sat down, and Nathan gave the floor to Chloe to respond.

"Only one DRIL is for our team in the north," she said softly. "The other will carry its own fuel for a refueling to fly south, to support the team that Titus is training, if they can use it. That means we'll have ten of us crammed into the belly of one combat drone. Under tight conditions, with one or two of us possibly wounded and needing to lie down, the DRIL space will be at capacity. I wish we could take out more people, or even free all the prisoners, but Rea's value isn't just as a Christian, but also as a missile engineer. He's a special priority. Corban says the Pentagon has questions to ask him immediately about the North Korean regime's missile program that could affect the entire world. Of course, rescuing someone who was so close to the dictator, who is now the dictator's obsession, will be a statement made on behalf of persecuted Christians everywhere. God hasn't abandoned His people. Even if we can't rescue everyone, Christians everywhere will celebrate Rea's rescue, and hopefully his wife's extraction as well."

"Okay." Nathan said. "Now for Chen Li."

The Hong Kong native took a step forward.

"I was recently in Fushun, China, and spoke to an ex-guard from Hamgyong Prison." Her voice was quiet, so everyone listened closely to hear her, but Nathan knew Chen Li's resolve was anything but soft. Her deep care for God's children had made her a determined operator, sacrificial and zealous. "He left North Korea four years ago, but I think I was still able to get valuable information from him that'll help us. Like the train schedule that runs on a track east of the prison. It might aid in our escape from the area if we are pursued after we rescue Rea. We can also better understand the mining practices on the north end of the prison and how prisoners are marched to work every morning and at what time. Even if we don't use all this information, the intel will be passed on to other organizations who may be able to capitalize on little weaknesses to assist believers inside the camp. Between what Mapper received from the recovered prisoner, and what I have to label on the model, we're ready to get to the specifics of the operation."

"Our training has expanded," Nathan said as Chen Li sat down behind him. "The four ladies who will provide cover fire, you'll each be paired depending on your marksmanship. You need to be on the range out back for a couple hours each day, firing the .308, until your accuracy rivals Scooter's. And men, it's time to define our roles before, during, and after the op. We now have one month until we fly to California, pick up Titus' team, then continue on to Japan. That's only thirty days to determine every single minute we spend inside that prison.

"We may have performed rescues before, but never with over one thousand armed guards inside a country that lives and breathes death for Americans and most other foreigners. And keep the California team in prayer. Our part is dangerous, but those boys out west signed on for what's probably a one-way trip to rescue Jin. She's no less important to the government, since she may corroborate what her husband knows about the missile program, but we want her out as a sister in Christ as well."

Nathan took a deep breath as everyone slowly dispersed. Chen Li and Chloe compared notes to update the floor model of the prison. Luigi signaled to Nathan, and the two met privately on the edge of the carpet.

"This is the moment I must leave." Luigi appeared almost melancholy, and in his obvious discomfort, he offered Nathan a piece of gum from an open pack. "Corban has another part for me to play in all of this, and I must prepare for it."

"Contingencies, huh?" Nathan accepted the piece of gum. Though normally he wasn't a gum chewer, he'd never seen Luigi share his gum before, so he thought maybe the spook was making an attempt to bond in a new way. "I guess something this big needs a few surprise back-ups to everything we're planning, just in case we don't all make it out."

"We're all in God's hands." Luigi shook Nathan's hand. "Watch over Heather. She's still new to this level of evil, even if she was a police officer."

"We'll keep her close, brother. Go with God."

Luigi turned, embraced his wife, and walked out. Nathan watched him leave, imagining what Corban could be sending the Italian super-agent to do. The terrain around Hamgyong Prison was so rugged and isolated, he wondered if Corban was sending Luigi to further recon the prison, or maybe make preparations for situations that could go awry.

But the more Nathan considered Luigi's skills, he guessed Corban was utilizing Luigi in Pyongyang, where the less-experienced KONs were being trained for the rescue of Jin.

Bummer, Nathan thought. It would've been nice to know that

someone unflinchingly dependable was there in the wilderness around the prison to back them up. But if Luigi was needed elsewhere, then the team in the north would just have to depend that much more on God's watchcare.

San Diego

Levi Caspertein set two boxes marked "clothes" in the living room of the small house that was his new home with Annette and Titus. He gazed at the mountain of boxes his stepmother had hauled from New York. Of course, she'd been a model of some sort in her youth, but this much clothing seemed impossible for one person!

"Levi," Annette called from the kitchen, "you want a sandwich?"

"Just one?" Levi frowned at his manners an instant later. "I mean, yes, please."

"Sorry, I forgot you're a growing Caspertein," she said, poking her head out. "Two sandwiches? Three?"

"Two." Levi felt himself blush, then indicated the boxes. "The house isn't big enough. This is only half of what's in the truck."

"You bring it in, and I'll find a place to put it. Most of it's going to the shelter, anyway." She laughed, a pleasant sound that reminded Levi of his own mom. "We'll worry about how we'll live with all this later."

Levi was about to return to the truck outside when he noticed a box marked "Titus" on the bottom of one stack. He moved two clothes boxes to get to the one that belonged to his father. It was the only box he'd seen labeled with his father's name. With an excited flutter in his stomach, he opened the box that could hold the secrets to the man who hadn't known he existed until a few weeks ago.

On top of a collection of junk was a photo album. Levi opened the cover. One faded photo was of two skinny juveniles next to a large boy with curly hair. All three were in their swim clothes at a swimming hole in the middle of the woods. With a grin, Levi recognized Titus at about nine years old as one of the skinny kids, standing next to Wynter, his sister. Levi had never met his Aunt Wynter, but he recognized Rudy, the hefty boy with curly hair.

The next photo framed teenage Titus between Rudy and Wynter, each holding up their catch of fish. Titus' catch was more than Rudy and Wynter's combined. Levi inhaled with pride that his father bested his competition, even if the competition were just with his siblings.

Next, was a photo of Titus, now a little older, leaning against a dark blue Mustang car. Titus wore a jean jacket, like he still wore, and his blond hair was the same color as it was almost twenty years later.

Levi turned the album page, but found no more photos. With disappointment, he closed the album. *Only three photos?* Even if Titus had grown up before the age of smart phones, Levi had expected more pictures.

"You found his box." Annette handed Levi a paper plate with two-and-a-half sandwiches as she ate a half herself. "We wouldn't have anything at all from his years growing up if Wynter hadn't given me those things."

"What's this?" Levi picked out a wood-carved giraffe from the box. The wood had aged and blackened, but blotchy paint was still obvious on the exterior. "Dad was in Africa?"

"He was in Africa more than America for many years, running guns, smuggling archaeological treasure, starting wars. We'd have to ask him what all this stuff means to him."

Suddenly, Levi tugged on the head of the giraffe and it slid off, exposing a short dagger on the end of the neck.

"Whoa!" Levi tested the tip of the blade on a fingernail. "I don't think this is a kids' toy."

"What else is in here?" Annette stepped closer. "Put that thing away. It could be tipped with poison or something."

Levi carefully replaced the giraffe head and held up a tribal mask. The front was ordained with gems and rocks in swirls and globs of paint. When Levi held it up to his face to peer through the eye holes, he noticed turquoise paint on the mask interior.

"Look at this." He held it up for Annette. "If I hold it flat, it looks like dripping paint. But when I tilt it sideways . . ."

"It looks like a map!" Annette snatched it from his hand and tilted it left and right. "Wynter's probably had this hanging on her wall for years and didn't even realize what was on the inside. I wonder if Titus knows what the map is for."

Though Levi was listening, he'd already turned his attention to the next item in the box. Clearly, what he'd first thought was junk were items of intrigue, each holding a mystery that could take a lifetime to discover.

In the bottom of the box were a couple of ornamental daggers, journals in strange languages, and a blown glass rattle full of sand and rocks. The outside of the glass was smoky-red and scratched.

"This is Portuguese, I think." Annette frowned at a leather-bound journal. "Maybe from some explorer. Titus was probably trying to find more treasure by it."

"I think he found it." Levi tapped his finger on the rattle's glass. "Well, it's some sort of treasure."

"A baby's rattle?" Annette studied the glass, then her eyes widened. "Oh. Those are diamonds! And the little rocks look like other uncut gems."

"Did you know he had stuff like this? Did Wynter?"

"I don't think anyone knows half the secrets from your father's past." She set the rattle carefully back in the box. "At least we know where he keeps some of his emergency funds, huh? Maybe we should keep unpacking and ask him about this stuff in person."

Levi didn't object as she closed the box. He remembered his lunch and took a bite of a ham and pickle sandwich as Annette returned to the kitchen. But as Levi chewed, he continued to ponder about the items in the box. They spoke volumes about the man who was his father. Though Annette had told him in days past that Titus was a better man now than he once was, Levi wanted to know the man his father had been, the man who had known his mother.

That evening, when Titus came back from the COIL training center to eat dinner at their cluttered home, Levi asked Titus about the items in the box.

"I don't remember half that stuff." Titus shrugged. "I was on the road a lot. During those first years traveling away from home, I wouldn't even write my family. I'd just send some artifact to Mom and Dad. When they died, I guess Wynter kept a few things she could fit in a box. Hey, don't teenage boys have better things to do than to poke through boxes of the past? We moved to the West Coast for you to finish high school with your friends."

"I don't know." Levi set down his dinner fork and rested his elbows on the table. "Ever since Mom died, I feel like the world has changed. I go to football practice, but it doesn't mean too much to me anymore—you know, the cheerleaders and getting invited to parties. Now that

I'm a sophomore, maybe I'm not such a kid anymore."

The family of three was silent for a few moments. Levi wondered if he'd laid too much on the young married couple. What did Titus and Annette know about raising someone like him who didn't know anything about life?

"It ain't easy going through what you've been through, Levi," Titus said. "I know God well enough to tell you that you need to pay close attention to what He's doing to mold you. If you sense change, now's the time to trust Him to guide you through that change. The people at the training center might be just the type of people you need to be around right now."

"Those Christians? The ex-cons?"

"They have their priorities in life sorted out. God may be trying to get your attention about that right now. It doesn't matter that you're fourteen. What matters is that you get ready for what God wants to use you for in the years to come."

"Use me?" Levi sat back from the table. Though he had many questions, his father's words were making some sense. "Maybe God has been trying to talk to me, but I don't know anything about Him."

"It might be time to get to know Him," Annette said. "Come on. Eat your vegetables. They're fresh."

Levi studied his father as he ate. *Get to know God?* Titus had been a powerful man, even feared, his mother had said. Those few relics from his past showed that he'd been a treasure hunter, wealthy and well-traveled. But now those relics were in a box, and Titus was talking about God and Christians and life priorities. And Annette had been a clothing model and spokesperson. She'd given it all up to live like this, in a middle-class house, taking care of her adopted son and a husband who talked about Jesus and rescuing Christians.

"How can I get to know God?" Levi asked.

"We have a couple Bibles around here." Titus pointed his fork at Levi. "That's where Corban started me. I've done just about everything there is to do in this world, so I can tell you from experience that there's nothing like living for God. The Bible is definitely from the God who created everything. It's worth reading daily and getting to know Him."

"And after football practices are over," Annette said, "we can start eating dinners as a family up at the training center. You'll have a better chance of talking to men like Oleg, Corban, and the others with questions you may have."

"It's okay to hang out with all those guys?" Levi asked Titus. "I won't be in the way?"

"Well, there's no sense in just hanging out. I don't see why you can't participate in some of the training, too. You ever shoot a .308 battle rifle?"

"Titus!" Annette frowned.

"It fires a standard sniper rifle cartridge." Titus shrugged at his wife. "He's a Caspertein. He needs to know how to shoot a rifle. It's practically in his genes."

"I've never shot a rifle." Levi felt breathless. "Can I, uh, Mom?"

"Oh, all right. Who am I to stand in the way?" Annette chuckled. "Yes, Levi, it's fine. It can't hurt for you to be trained by responsible men."

"And Jenna will be there." Titus nudged Levi's shoulder. "Corban and his family will be living at the training center until the operation in a few weeks. You know, just because Jenna is blind doesn't mean she doesn't know when you're watching her."

"Dad!"

"Titus!" Annette dropped her fork. "Stop teasing him!"

"Oh, was it a secret?" Titus laughed and winked at Annette. "It ain't easy being in love."

"Titus!" Annette scowled through her own amusement. "Levi, you ignore your father's joking. Jenna's a nice girl, and she's your age. There's no reason you two shouldn't hit it off."

Levi stared at his half-eaten plate, embarrassed but excited.

"What's my life becoming?" he asked, barely realizing he'd spoken aloud.

"It's just beginning." Titus saluted with his glass of milk. "Don't worry. We'll be right beside you until God wants you to move for Him on your own."

Levi took a deep breath. Yes, he felt it in his heart. God, whoever He was, was trying to speak through all these events. Among other things, God seemed to be trying to turn him into a man before he had expected to become one. And Levi wasn't backing down, not if it turned him into half the man his father was!

❦

Hamgyong Prison – North Korea

Jeong Byeang-Rea lay on his side in his detention cell in the infamous Hamgyong Prison. The soiled sawdust that covered the floor no longer repulsed him, though he knew it contained bits of dried refuse, and even bones and flesh of dead prisoners. Insects never died in such an abundance of food, even though the winter weather pierced the building's thin plywood and particle board walls. His body was covered with sores from bug bites and his thin clothing seemed designed to keep him perpetually cold.

The four other prisoners in the cell with Rea were dead, and they'd been dead for days. Soon, the guards would take them away, only to bring other dead prisoners into his cell to decompose for a while. It was their way, he realized, of torturing him psychologically as well as physically. The labor camp's conditions took many lives, and the deceased seemed to find their way into his cell before they were taken out to be buried.

Though the dead weren't company, Rea hadn't been entirely isolated from human contact, and he praised God for this small joy. At dawn and dusk each day, a guard opened his cell door and tossed in two corncobs. There was no corn on the cobs, since someone else had eaten the corn off already, but he'd learned to suck and gnaw on the cob for a little flavor. However, it was these brief interactions with the guards that lightened his heart.

Every time the door opened, Rea greeted the guards with kindness, even if he managed only a few words. He prayed for them as often as he prayed for his wife who was with child. The guards had ordered him not to speak to them, but he was under no such restriction by God to wish them glad tidings, so he didn't stop, even when they beat him.

A little sunlight seeped through the wall cracks in the mornings, so Rea had come to understand he was housed on the eastern wall of the detention center. He'd learned that his building was reserved for prisoners scheduled for execution or for urgent interrogations. The little bit of sunlight each morning was his call to prayer, and though his legs were bruised from beatings every day, he managed to kneel through most of his morning prayer time.

In his prayers, he discovered many ideas he believed were small blessings for which to be thankful. For one, he'd found peace in his limited time in the detention center. Soon, he would be executed, probably by strangulation, he guessed. Some of the dead in his cell had neck markings that indicated how they'd died, which he'd discovered when moving them against the wall. And with his life on earth near its end, he didn't worry about such things as germs, or the discomfort of the many torments the guards had been tasked to place upon him. Soon, he would go to his Savior, who would embrace him in everlasting and perfect joy.

Though Rea wasn't troubled about the illnesses he now endured, he was aware that his body was indeed failing more and more each day. Every time a corpse was brought to his cell to rot, he moved it against the wall, dragging and rolling it. As his strength waned from malnutrition, the activity took much longer than when he'd first arrived weeks earlier.

Over two years ago, before he'd married Jin, he'd defected to South Korea. While the South Korean agents had debriefed him for intel from when he'd worked on the missile program in North Korea, he'd undergone treatment for parasites. He'd been a leading engineer, close to the North Korean regime's powerful figures, and he'd enjoyed what he'd thought was favored status, but he'd still had horrible, large parasites living inside him like leeches. And that was under the best conditions North Korea had to offer him. He guessed he now hosted a much more thriving variety of parasites, since his water and food were as filthy as his detention cell. But all of this was to strengthen his faith, so he didn't hate the suffering for his Lord Jesus. This was his cross to bear, and he knew glory would be that much sweeter because of it.

Peace from God enveloped Rea as he spent the days in prayer and Scripture recitation, but he still wept, for his sorrows for Jin were great. Somewhere, she was suffering through her pregnancy. Rea did not—he could not—allow his thoughts to dwell on her treatment. He missed her, and he prayed for her endurance through unthinkable torment. And he thanked God for their time together as husband and wife, however brief it had been.

In the best moments, Rea laughed aloud at good memories. Before Jin had given herself to be his wife, she'd worked at the fish processing factory in Haeju. It had been cold, back-breaking work, day after day for many years. But at the gutting bins, Jin had led many women to

Christ by sharing Scripture in secret, and the Christian underground had been fed by her smuggling efforts. Every day, she'd placed fish in her boots, and walked out of the fishery. The extra protein had kept many alive as Rea and other fugitives hid in the mountain refuges, teaching the Bible to all who fled the cities and villages.

Rea didn't know who exactly had betrayed them by informing on them, but he had his suspicions. Someone had been caught with a Bible, and that person had been enticed, probably under torture, to betray the believers in hiding around Haeju. Some family members had been publicly executed immediately, including Jin's mother. Others who had more political symbolism, like himself, had been set aside for a more prolonged and torturous demise, but it would be no less public, he was told. He'd been harassed by his torturers with the idea that soon his child would be born, and the whole country would witness the execution of his family before he himself was killed. This was the sentence for being caught as a Bible teacher in the wilderness of Eastern Hwanghae.

Stretching out an arm, Rea swept sawdust across the floor toward him, piling it against his ribs. He did the same behind him, doing his best to conserve his body heat against the chilled air. Months earlier, the dictator himself had announced to the country that eating finely-ground sawdust mixed with grass roots was an acceptable food source, during the nation's famine, but Rea hadn't entertained the idea of eating the sawdust around him. It was too filthy to eat, but it wasn't too uncomfortable to lay on as he recited Scripture and awaited his next torture session, mixed with indoctrination lessons.

As he drifted to sleep, he prayed for the Westerner who'd been in the cell next to his and had been recently removed. The man had been Russian, but Rea had known only a few words in his language. Rea had heard from the guards that the Russian's foot had been cut off for trying to escape. He prayed the man was finding peace in his Creator and Father, if he was still alive.

California

Titus stood next to Oleg as they each held stopwatches beside an oval track once used to train Olympians. Now, it was the site for ex-convicts training for a deadly mission.

"They're already improving," Oleg commented as Avery "Chevy"

Hewitt crossed the finish line after a one-mile run. Behind him, Francisco "Shorty" Hernandez plodded steadily beside Ernesto "Spider" Colosio. In the rear, having slowed to a walk two laps earlier, were Job Buck and Donny Walters. "They're starting to act like a team, sticking together."

"Yep." Titus pressed his stopwatch as Shorty and Spider passed him. "Forty seconds off last week's time for those two."

"Job and Donny are the same." Oleg held up his watch. "Everyone's falling into place."

"The real question is . . ." Titus glanced over his shoulder at the bleachers where Corban sat in his wheelchair. Luigi Putelli stood next to him as they spoke quietly with one another. "What are those two up to?"

"There are a hundred other international COIL concerns right now." Oleg pocketed his watch. "They're probably just coordinating other operations."

"I don't like not knowing what people around me are planning. Come on." Titus walked with Oleg toward the five KONs who were resting on the grass of the infield. "They're planning something about our operation, Oleg, except they're leaving us out."

"If it concerns us," Oleg said, "they'll tell us. We have enough to focus on, don't we?"

Titus didn't answer. The approaching operation had him on edge, besides the other issues looming in his life. He still hadn't destroyed the stockpile of phosphorus ammunition cached in a bunker near San Diego's waterfront. Corban hadn't mentioned it again, but Titus knew he needed to either deal with the cache right away, or convince Corban to keep the incendiary ammo.

And with all of his time devoted to the KONs, teaching them about self-defense, security, and North Korea, he hadn't had much time to get to know his son, though Annette had begun to bring Levi to the training center after school. The teen participated in various exercises with the KONs, but the boy remained distant—observant, but distant, nonetheless. Titus had noticed the boy watching him when he didn't know Titus was aware, but Titus was still waiting for a moment alone with him to find out what the young man had discovered about God since their last talk at the dinner table.

"All right, let's take a knee." Titus was the first to kneel on the grass amongst the KONs. The men circled around and gave him their attention. "We've now analyzed your strengths and weaknesses enough to know where to place each of you for the mission. You've all received the same training so far, but all that changes today. Oleg and I have outlines for each of you to work through, and your personal instructions to follow for the mission's success."

"When do we find out who exactly we're helping in Pyongyang?" Donny asked. "If I'm risking my life, I'd like to put a face to all our praying."

"It's too dangerous for that person or persons involved for us to openly talk about their names right now. That will all be disclosed when we reach Japan. What I can tell you now is that you're being split up into two groups from now on. Group One will consist of Chevy and Job. Group Two will include Shorty, Spider, and Donny. This hasn't been easy for Oleg, Corban, and me to decide, but each of your physical traits, skills, and faith have all been considered. This is where your training takes a more serious turn."

"More serious than training to die?" Donny joked, but no one laughed this time.

"No, not more serious than dying, but I will need to speak plainly about dying well, if it comes to that. Our objective is for the persons you're rescuing, to be rescued. After that is accomplished, we want you to evade capture if possible, and make it back here. We're putting things into place to bring you home, but there are many unknowns. Things could go a variety of ways."

"Nothing is predictable, exactly," Oleg added.

"We're already here," Chevy said. "We've counted the cost. Give it to us straight, Titus."

Titus smiled sadly. The KONs had all been believers longer than he. Though he had more experience at running international operations, these were veterans of the faith.

"Okay, Group One—that's Chevy and Job—you two will be inserted covertly to rescue the subjects. Your job will be the most secretive work. Group Two will be inserted overtly, meaning under the watchful eye of the government. We've been setting up your identities as if you're defectors from the United States. North Korea will allow you into their country, but they'll be watching you very closely. It won't be easy to gain their trust enough to slip away to help with the rescue, but you've got to do it somehow. Both groups—the covert group or the overt group—will be close to danger and death the entire time. One slip and you're done.

"Now, part of your gear is in the country already. Once all of you get into the country, Group One will set out to rescue the subjects. At that time, Group Two will do their best to join you, but they've got to get away from their government escorts to support Group One. If anyone falls or is compromised, the others need to push on and get the job done. This strategy of inserting two teams from two different directions doubles our chances at getting to the subjects."

"We know where the subjects are held?" Chevy asked.

"We do." Titus took a deep breath. "We even have safe sites inside Pyongyang for you to flee to, but nothing is guaranteed. We call this a fluid operation. There are many variables. Things could change throughout the mission that you've not been trained for. You'll have to improvise."

"We need to pray," Job said, "then you can begin teaching us our individual duties. We'll be ready for them."

Titus watched the men throw their arms around each other in a huddle, and then Job prayed for them all. The gentle sincerity that came out of the large and gruff KON's mouth showed his big heart for God's purposes. These men may have lived most of their lives inside a prison around criminals, but they themselves were criminals no longer. They were lambs, he realized. They were lambs willing to sacrifice themselves for others.

With an hour until the next bout of training, the men dispersed to their dorm to shower and rest up. Oleg went over to Corban and Luigi, but Titus joined Levi and Annette as they arrived. Titus shook his son's hand, still fascinated to find his own face on the growing youth. He was almost as tall as Titus, and Titus wondered if Levi would take after his Uncle Rudy and be even taller than his own father.

"You two hang out," Annette said, turning away. "I need to help Janice and Jenna inventory some gear before it's shipped off to Singapore."

For the first time, Titus was completely alone with his son. The two stood shoulder to shoulder on the edge of the oval track and stared off to the west where a manmade lake catered to a number of wildlife, though it had once hosted the Olympic rowing teams as they had trained.

"It ain't easy being a father to a son I didn't know I had," Titus said, "but I'm glad you're my son. And I'm glad you're here with us. From what I can tell, your mother raised you well."

"It ain't easy being the son of a man I only heard stories of." There was sadness in Levi's cracking voice. "You're nothing like what Mom said you'd be."

"When I knew your mother, I was a different person—violent, selfish, maybe a little angry about life. Your mother deserved better."

"She said you were a hero, but I didn't understand." Levi threw his hands in the air, then let them fall to his sides. "I don't get it. I thought Christians were just a bunch of do-gooders who drove expensive cars and played dress-up for church on Sundays."

"That's what I thought, too. Come on. Let's go up to the training gym." Titus walked beside his son, measuring the boy's stride as they moved past the cafeteria to the gym. Levi's gait was nearly the same as his own. "A person can call himself a polar bear, but does that mean he is one?"

"No."

"Many people call themselves Christians, but it doesn't necessarily mean they're really Christians. Jesus defined who His followers are— those who follow in His character and service for others. As you read the Bible, you'll see that there's a clear definition of what a Christian is. There are still many who believe and follow Jesus Christ, even though they are becoming fewer all the time."

"People like COIL?"

"Yes, COIL is an organization that tries to gather a few of the faithful to help support those who serve Christ."

"And the guns I've been learning to shoot—you don't kill people any longer, not ever?" Levi sounded almost disappointed. "Mom said you killed a lot of bad guys to get rich and you had to stay on the run. That stuff in the box at home—I'm still trying to make sense of it all."

They reached the gym and walked inside. No one else had arrived yet.

"I hurt a lot of people, Levi. There was nothing glorious about my life back then. I chose a path that separated me from my own family.

Rudy and Wynter became adults thinking I didn't want to be around them, and I was such a fool that I even had a son I didn't know I had. A real man would've been responsible for his girlfriend, and loyal to his family. I was neither to you or your mother. There was no honor in my life, even if I was good at what I did. Corban taught me a few years ago that true honor comes from being sacrificial and courageous, and doing the right thing against all odds, even when others won't. Those are things you can't learn from anyone but Jesus."

"But He died on the cross." Levi sat on a chest press exercise machine and set the weight high. "Why would anyone want to follow Someone who gets killed in the end? I've been reading a little of the Bible you gave me."

Levi strained through ten reps, then stood up, flexing his chest and shoulders. Titus sat down, then put one hundred more pounds on the cable.

"If you only look at Jesus' death, you miss out on two life-changing things."

Titus pressed out ten reps at the much heavier weight, straining a little but hiding it. He knew there was more that God intended to teach through their time alone than merely talking.

"What's bigger than death?" Levi asked, then looked closer at all the weight his father had lifted. "I thought you'd moved the pin to less weight. That's almost twice what I lifted!"

"Go ahead." Titus offered him the bench and Levi sat down again. "Give it a shot. Arch your back. Bring in your elbows a little. There you go. Now, breathe out as you press. Push it! Push it! There!"

Levi let the weight drop from the top, having barely lifted it once.

"I did it!"

"You did!" Titus clasped his son's hand and pulled him to his feet. In a brief half-hug, he clapped his son on the back. "That was some good form, too."

"No one on the football team lifts that much. Wow." Together, father and son looked down at the conquered weight machine. "So, Jesus' death wasn't that big of a deal?"

"Oh, it was a big deal, but it's not the end of the story. First, Jesus was God in human form, and that leads to the second point. He couldn't stay dead. He died a public death, sure, but He rose to live publicly, too. There were witnesses to His resurrection. The Bible records eye-witness statements that were written while many of those people could refute what was said. But no one did. Jesus had walked around after they'd killed Him. It really happened.

"So, yes, I follow Jesus who died for my sins, but I also follow Jesus who rose again, and showed Himself to be more powerful than death. Now, think of the big picture. We all die, Levi. Do you want to follow Someone who gives you the gift of life because He's conquered death, or do you want to enter eternity with a question mark over your eternal soul?"

Levi was silent for a few moments, then frowned.

"You really believe that? That Jesus was God?"

"I believe it and I know it." Titus touched his chest. "If He isn't God, He wouldn't be alive and inside me. He changed my life and gave me peace. He's alive, and that gives me the courage to face death for others."

Oleg walked into the gym and shook their hands, then glanced at the weight machine.

"Is the pin stuck?" Oleg asked. "Won't it go any higher?"

"Higher?" Levi gasped.

Titus chuckled as Oleg sat on the bunch.

"Go ahead, Levi. Put all the weight on."

Levi placed the pin on the bottom weight, and Oleg's thick chest trembled under the strain.

"One to get the blood flowing . . ." Oleg pressed out one rep. A vein bulged on his forehead. "And two to feel the burn . . ."

"That's not a burn," Titus said. "That's a muscle tearing in half."

Nevertheless, Oleg controlled the weight all the way up, then eased it down.

"You try it, Dad!" Levi waved at his father.

"Oh, no. Not me." Titus laughed. "For one, I don't want to go to the hospital after I show up Oleg. And two, it'll be some time before Oleg is able to get off that bench."

"Are you hurt?" Levi asked the Russian.

"Just . . . give me a minute . . ."

Titus folded his arms.

"Seriously? I think you're just finding an excuse to soak in the therapeutic hot tub again."

"These old bones need it." Oleg frowned. "Go ahead. I'll catch up in a little while."

Titus put his hand on his son's shoulder as they walked over to the arriving KONs.

"There's a difference, Levi, between making a point and crippling yourself."

"I made my point!" Oleg yelled after them, still on the machine, panting. "I just won't be able to move for a few days."

CHAPTER SIX

Pyongyang, North Korea

Lu Yi had been trapped inside Pyongyang for over four weeks. She was certain she was starving to death as she could feel her ribs through the clothing she still wore after canoeing up the Taedong River. Even after decades of ministering to the North Korean people, she'd never actually eaten what they ate until now, and her body wasn't adjusting well.

"We have to go to the parade assembly," her male host explained, and without further words, the thirty-year-old man ushered his young wife off the boat. All their conversations were like that—a single statement, with nothing ever personal.

Being alone on the tourist boat during the days was nothing new, but the impersonal hospitality Lu Yi received from her host couple had been almost depressing. She understood the people of Pyongyang lived under a canopy of fear, but the man and wife hadn't even shared their names for fear of her informing on them, if she were caught.

Nevertheless, the couple had conceded to allow their house guest to remain on the boat, and to stay below deck except at night, when she could emerge for fresh air. On the port side of the living quarters, the woman cooked the daily *onban*, Pyongyang's warm rice. Only once in two weeks, Lu Yi had seen a single mushroom slice given to the husband, and twice, Lu Yi had thought she'd tasted chicken grease in her rice, but otherwise, the rice was plain.

Three times, they had shared a *bindaetteok* for an evening meal. The pancake, made from ground mung beans and vegetables, was bland, but with tea and thanksgiving in a whispered prayer, Lu Yi had eaten and not complained. After all, her hosts weren't just allowing her to live in their home; they were splitting all their food with her! Her male host had fishing line, but he was afraid to fish even in secret to feed his wife or their guest. Thus, Lu Yi was starving.

Carefully, Lu Yi drew aside a curtain that covered a window below the deck of the boat. It was an overcast day and snow was in the air, but the whole city had been summoned out to the parade ground across the river from Juche Tower. The muffled loudspeaker and occasional barrage of celebratory artillery reached Lu Yi's ears, and it weighed on her soul immediately. The country, and especially the city, was so bound by fear and propaganda, the gospel message couldn't be spoken in anything but whispered tones. Even then, her hosts had hushed her completely during the daytimes, if she started to speak words from the Bible. But on the parade grounds, the guns of communism barked loudly.

From under the narrow bench that had been her bed for the past month, Lu Yi dragged both packages she'd smuggled for the Italian Christian. Every day, she had resisted the urge to draw them out, and her male host had insisted the bundles remain hidden under the bench, covered with a tattered blanket.

Lu Yi gave her attention first to the smaller of the two packages. The zipper slid down freely, with only a hint of rust setting in, and she opened the top. Nothing had been disturbed since she'd received the items in China, but her circumstances had changed. Trapped inside North Korea, she had to utilize what she'd smuggled in. Besides, she was fairly certain the food in zipped plastic were emergency rations for an operator, or maybe food to share or to be used as a bribe.

She found two pouches of powdered milk, and four pouches of beef and gravy. Setting one of each aside, she dug deeper and found water purification tablets, ten chocolate bars, and a squishy unlabeled plastic pouch that felt like chunky peanut butter. All of the items confirmed her assumptions. Only a special operations team or person from the West would be able to afford such high protein, nutritious food to aid in their calorie-burning operation, whatever it was.

Ignoring the food for the moment, Lu Yi opened the second bundle of gear and studied the equipment before her. Part of it was a bulky motor the size of her head. A turning shaft extended from the motor, which seemed to need some assembly with ten three-foot lengths of metal. The ten lengths of metal had links on them, obviously meant to be connected to make five six-foot lengths. It was like a drone she'd seen in Beijing a few years earlier, except this one, once assembled, would have propeller blades longer than the height of a person.

Next, her fingers tore open a Velcro pouch that contained a satellite phone. She touched the power button and found it fully charged. It was an expensive phone, so it would have its own scrambler, she realized, and unique frequency for security.

She glanced at the food she'd already chosen to share with her hosts, and touched the dial button. Though her weekly communication with her tugboat operator had been consistent, she desperately yearned for outside contact. The river had become heavily patrolled, so an escape at the moment was impossible.

The phone rang three times before it was answered by an English speaking man. It didn't sound like the brisk Italian Christian who'd given her the packages to deliver. She'd expected someone to answer in Chinese, or maybe Korean, since Chinese and South Koreans were most often available for Christian underground work in North Korea.

"Yes?" the person answered. "Is someone there?"

Lu Yi gathered her thoughts, aware that their conversation needed to be brief.

"This is Yellow Bird," she said in carefully enunciated English. "I delivered two packages, but I am trapped. Do you know who I am or where I am?"

"Just a moment." There was a pause. "I don't know who you are, but I have your frequency, so I know the equipment you are using and where it supposedly is. Who was King David's father, please?"

Lu Yi smiled. Of course, caution needed to be used. After all, anyone could use the phone, but only a Bible reader would know the answer to such a question.

"His father was Jesse, and Jesse's grandfather was Boaz, the husband of Ruth."

"Very good. How can I help you?"

"I may have to remain where I am in hiding for many days still to come. There is food in these two packages. I have to share it with those who are starving to feed me."

"That is understandable. It is my understanding that the food you have was packed excessively for a contingency plan. I will communicate your use of it to the principals involved."

"So, I am allowed to share it?"

"Yes, you are allowed to share it. It might be wise to reserve enough for one small meal for two men, if that is possible.

"I will leave at least that much. There is quite an abundance here, possibly as much as some might eat for three months."

"Very well, sister, it is yours."

"Thank you." Lu Yi bowed her head as she sobbed quietly. "That is all I wanted to ask."

"Are you safe, Yellow Bird?"

"I am. My Savior's grace is sufficient, even if I am in a bad place."

"I will pass on your words to our appropriate friends."

"Wait! May I call you again?"

"The phone you have should have a charger with it. I will be monitoring this frequency regularly, so you may call as often as you would like, until you are home safe."

"Thank you. Thank you."

Lu Yi turned off the phone and wept in her hands. After a few minutes, she repacked all the gear, except for the food she wanted to share, and hid the packages under the bench. She wrapped the food items in a blanket, then returned to the window to watch for her hosts to arrive home. She couldn't wait to share the food with them!

California

Titus leaned against the golf cart where Corban and his daughter, Jenna, sat in the front seat on the comfortable fall day. They wore ear protectors as the KONs fired their battle rifles at targets downrange. This was Levi's third time shooting with the operatives, and Titus was thrilled to see that his son was quickly getting the feel of the bullpup against his shoulder.

After several volleys, the operatives paused to reload.

"What are the results?" Jenna asked her father as she leaned forward, wearing her dark glasses. "Did Levi improve?"

Corban steadied a spotting scope against his brow, though Titus didn't need to see the targets to guess who was most accurate. He'd read each shooter's form when they'd fired, to determine who was shooting most accurately. The .308 caliber carried a healthy punch, and not everyone was comfortable shooting it from any position.

"Job has the best grouping on the bullseye," Corban said, "then Chevy. But Levi is probably the next best. Shorty, Spider, and Donny are improving, though."

"In a couple weeks," Jenna said triumphantly, sitting back in the seat, "Levi will improve to be more accurate than everyone. He's young, and he's already as good as or better than them all."

"Yes." Corban cast Titus a knowing look. "It seems he may have inherited something from the Caspertein bloodline in that regard."

"It ain't easy being a natural." Titus chuckled. "The hard part isn't teaching him to shoot straight. It's keeping his ego down to earth so God can do something meaningful with his God-given abilities. I was only a couple years older than Levi when I got too big for my britches, and left home."

"You were a good rifle shot when you were a teenager?" Jenna asked.

"Rudy and I were carrying pellet guns in the forest before we were ten years old. Even then, though, Wynter was a better shot than both of us boys."

"Wynter was a better markswoman?" Jenna grinned. "Fascinating!"

"Yep, she had a steadier hand when it came to target shooting, but Rudy and I bagged more game than anybody in our county."

"What do you suppose this is about?" Corban gestured at the operatives and Levi.

Titus walked a few feet away from the golf cart to watch the shooters approach Oleg and huddle in a tight group, clearly discussing something serious. Levi was shoulder to shoulder between Chevy and Spider, and the others seemed to be directing their concerns or grievances toward Oleg.

"What's happening?" Jenna asked.

"The KONs are appealing to Oleg about something," Corban said. "It's a good sign, seeing them like this. They're consistently showing that they're working together like a solid team of operators should."

As they waited to hear what the issue was, Titus returned to the golf cart. Corban hadn't been present at all of the training sessions lately, but he and Luigi hadn't left the center for days. They were staying in one of the many apartments up on the hill. Titus and Oleg hadn't asked what the two were planning, but Titus sensed it had something to do with *Operation: Harm's Way*. There was simply too much volatility inside North Korea for Corban not to be focusing on additional schemes while the KONs invaded the country. The question was, what schemes were he and Luigi up to?

It was also hard for Titus to see Corban so disabled. He remembered how he'd first met the older man in Gaza, where Corban had made it difficult to keep up with him in the war zone. Now, the man was reduced to observing from a golf cart with his blind daughter.

"Something on your mind, Titus?" Corban asked, apparently noticing that Titus had been staring at his legs.

"I was just thinking how you probably have some tricks up your sleeve still, even though you seem to be put out to pasture." Titus smiled. "Knowing you, I wouldn't be surprised if your legs, those braces, and your crutches are just—"

"Hold it," Corban interrupted. "Here comes Oleg. Let's hear what this is about."

Oleg arrived and plucked a sports drink from a cooler on the back of the cart. He guzzled it, making the three wait.

"They want to get shot," Oleg finally stated.

"What shot?" Corban turned in his seat. "Janice already gave them all their shots."

"No, I mean, they want to *be* shot." Oleg gestured at the operatives who waited at the firing line, along with Levi. "They don't like the idea of shooting people with tranquilizers, without knowing how bad it feels."

"That's an interesting request," Corban said. "Who proposed it first?"

"Donny seemed behind it, but they're all in agreement."

"It's out of the question," Titus said. "This close to the mission, we can't have our guys going into North Korea all bruised up."

"Use a smaller caliber," Jenna said. "And I want to be shot, too."

"Jenna, your mother would *not* approve." Corban raised his eyebrows at Titus. "You're team leader. Is this something your team needs to do together?"

"It seems so." Titus sighed and unclipped his shoulder holster. "I do have the .22 loaded with gel-tranqs."

Titus left the golf cart and marched out to the operatives. He and Oleg stood looking them over for a moment as they stood idly waiting for a decision.

"Well, lean your rifles against the hut," Titus said. "Now, everyone line up, facing away from me. Levi, help Jenna. She wants to be part of this, too."

Jenna stumbled over uneven ground as she joined the operatives. Levi took her by the arm and turned her with the rest to face the targets, their backs to Titus and Oleg.

Titus glanced at Corban, mostly for approval to shoot his daughter with the others. Jenna clung shakily to Levi's arm, and Levi, perhaps because of her, stood more squarely and confidently than Titus had ever seen him stand. Corban responded with a shrug.

"I don't know about this, Titus," Oleg said softly. "Those things really hurt."

"That's what they want to know." Titus drew his sidearm. "At least the grass is soft. And they get to take a little nap for an hour."

"Oh, I don't want to be here when Janice finds out you shot Jenna." Oleg backed away. "If I didn't already know how much those things hurt, I'd have you tranq me just so I could claim I had nothing to do with this."

"Just make sure they're all resting comfortably, would you?" Titus said. "Or I'll tranq you for my own amusement."

Titus aimed and fired at Chevy's left shoulder blade, where the impact of the round would bruise, but it had no chance of injuring the operative for the coming mission. He went down the line, firing rapidly, hitting them all in the same place. The tranquilizer had a half-second delay after impact, so each recipient flinched from the round, then crumbled in slow motion onto the grass. As he shot Jenna, Oleg was already arranging the limbs of the first unconscious operatives.

"No one can ever say COIL training is conventional," Corban said once he drove the cart closer.

"Let's just hope they gain consciousness before Annette and Janice get back," Oleg said. "I don't want to explain to them why seven of our trainees are laid out."

"Yeah, it might be a good idea for me to reload my pistol," Titus said with a straight face. The three burst into laughter an instant later.

New York

Chloe Azmaveth read the Yellow Bird report from Marc Densort, where he was stationed in a mine shaft in the Catskills. Marc had been one of COIL's leading global technicians for years, supporting primarily Titus and Oleg's missions that required constant attention for the Gabriel spy drones at seventy thousand feet. He also controlled the

DRIL combat drones, when they were deployed.

The Yellow Bird report, Chloe realized, didn't regard Nathan's operation into Hamgyong Prison, but it could affect the KONs' mission into Pyongyang, so she sent the briefing about the woman named Yellow Bird to Titus in San Diego.

With the morning's messages read, Chloe stepped out of the RV into the parking lot of the roller rink. The trees had already dropped their autumn leaves, but the forest around them was still beautiful and peaceful. The quiet town nearby couldn't be seen through the forest. Peering up at the blue sky, Chloe basked in the wonder of the life God had given her. She was married to Zvi, a Christian businessman who supported her efforts for the persecuted, and she was surrounded by caring, courageous believers. For a moment, there weren't hundreds of thousands of Christians needing aid or rescue. There weren't two tormented people in North Korea who needed COIL's help. There weren't overwhelming worries that remained out of her control. No, there was just her and her God. And peace.

She wanted to stand there forever in His presence, fellowshipping quietly with her Creator. However, her Creator hadn't made her only to acknowledge Him, but He had placed His life in her to also act on His behalf.

Chloe walked into the rink and approached the team gathered around the sprawling model of Hamgyong Prison. The night before, they'd spent an evening of laughter and feasting on *naengmyeon*, a cold buckwheat noodle soup, originating in Pyongyang. But now, an attempt at North Korean cuisine was farthest from their minds as they returned to the challenge of rescuing Rea. Heather, Luigi's wife, June, and Chen Li stood with Nathan, Bruno, Scooter, and Memphis.

"I don't like our exit plan," Nathan stated. "It was my idea, but I still don't like it. It leaves too much to chance."

"What're you working on exactly?" Chloe asked.

"We have five steps figured out," June said. "Step one, take over the west tower to command the gate and this side of the compound. Step two, take over the southeast tower to command the eastern perimeter and railroad. Step three, the insertion team crosses the fence up by the mines and hikes down to the prison dorms. Step four, get Rea out of the detention building. But step five, to leave the prison covertly and quickly—we don't quite know how, yet. Not safely, anyway."

"Go back the way they come in," Chen Li suggested. "They'll have to carry Rea, but it's safer to exit the prison up by the mines in the mountains. Trade speed for safety."

"All this assumes everything goes perfectly." Bruno used a laser pointer to highlight a building inside the prison's southwest perimeter. "If an alert is sounded, can we sufficiently hold off the hornets' nest that will spill from here?"

"The towers' line of fire is limited." Scooter stepped into the model itself and used a straight edge to measure angles. "Look, the interior buildings are too high for us to see into the avenues from the towers. We'll have no cover from our tower shooters if we have to weave through the dorms and other buildings to exit to the north."

"Maybe the nearby ridge is high enough to place a shooter," Memphis said. "A shooter a little higher could watch over everyone."

"If we exit too loudly, like by blowing up the fence to get away," Bruno said, "our rendezvous back to the DRIL will be a mess. We'll all arrive at separate times. That won't work if we have soldiers on our heels."

"Agreed." Nathan nodded. "No loud exit, unless it's absolutely necessary. Of course, if the alarm sounds, or a shot is fired, it'll be a mess anyway. Everyone will have to scramble out the best way they can, which is out the front gate, or back across the fence up by the mines. We have a week, everyone, before we go to Japan. Let's keep praying about this, and come back after lunch."

Chloe waited until the others dispersed, then she approached Nathan who was standing with Chen Li. The two had been married for a few years, but they still looked at one another like newlyweds.

"The Pyongyang side of things with Titus is on track," Chloe said. "Word came in from one of the inside agents. Equipment is in place. It'll be up to the KONs' training now to get that pregnant girl out."

"We're supposed to have the more straightforward mission," Nathan said, "but we can't figure out how to get out of this prison safely. We have no edge out in the Korean wilderness. We're totally isolated. Striking at night isn't even really an edge since the whole place may or may not be lit up by electricity."

"Right—depending on whether they divert power to the electric fence or the perimeter lights," Chen Li said. "I didn't want to say anything earlier, but what about sabotage or a diversion?"

"Yeah." Chloe smiled. "Something remote-controlled. Throw every-one off. I like it."

"I'd like to think making noise would be a last resort," Nathan said, "but you both might be on to something, especially if the prison lights come on in the middle of all this."

Chloe watched Nathan's face. She remembered a time when the two of them had planned another prison rescue together. Nathan had been young and over-confident, and a little mouthy. But operating alone for a few years and being married had calmed him, made him wiser. His intensity was still there, but gone were his immaturity and recklessness. Viewing him in this new light strengthened Chloe's own confidence in his leadership, which was important since he had the final word on mission decisions.

They were all about to risk their lives for a single prisoner held inside a potentially deadly country. Chloe couldn't wait to pull Rea to safety and reunite him with his pregnant wife—assuming the KONs succeeded in rescuing Jin from her dungeon. In the end, the two would finally reveal what they knew about North Korea's missile program. She prayed they could help protect the US from a potentially disas-trous series of agreements with the dictator.

Pyongyang, North Korea

Han Ji-Jin was strapped to the torture chair inside Yuriy Usik's office. The air was cool, but not as cold as her cell down the corridor. However, she preferred the isolation of her cell over the company of leering guards and Yuriy Usik's smirking face. And he smelled like fish.

Once she was secured to the chair, Jin noticed an older woman in a business suit wheel an electronic device over to her side. Though Jin had mentally resigned herself to endure any number of horrors before she and her baby were murdered, she had to force her mind to reach out for the hand of Jesus in those terrifying and uncertain seconds.

"You may call to Jesus now," Yuriy said in her ear, "but I will see to it that you cry out to the Great Leader for salvation before you die."

Jin didn't realize she'd called aloud for the whole room to hear, but she guessed there was no harm in it. After all, they already knew she was a follower of Jesus.

"Hold still, *Dongmu*," the woman in the suit instructed, and folded up Jin's top to expose her belly. "I don't want to do this more than once, so don't move."

Cold jelly was applied to Jin's belly. At first, she thought this was some sort of torture. After all, she was sitting in the torture chair! Instead, she identified on a monitor what she'd heard was called an ultrasound image. They were looking at her baby!

Yuriy leaned over her to squint at the granulated, pulsing image.

"Is it healthy?" he asked. "Will it live if we induce labor now? Here?"

Jin stopped breathing. *They wanted her to have the child now so they could carry out the executions!* They were tired of waiting.

"She is around thirty weeks, *Dongji*," the lab woman said. "If something were to go wrong during the delivery, I cannot guarantee survival. All of my maternity equipment is at the hospital, and half of it is outdated or broken. I advise that you do not induce labor, or if you do, wait at least three more weeks. This is her first baby. Let it come to term."

"Is it a male or female?" Yuriy asked.

Jin looked up, the question making her feel more violated than she already was. Everything was out of her control. Tears ran from the corners of her eyes, but she didn't sob for Yuriy's delight. She felt helpless, but God was her comfort, and even her baby was in His hands.

"It is a male." The woman wiped off the lubricant and turned off the monitor. "I will write my report and return next week to check again."

"Yes, yes." Yuriy dismissed her with a wave, and the woman left the office. He glowered over Jin, his hot breath on her face. "It won't be long now. The whole nation is waiting for your family's extermination. You are not worthy of *Choson*. We will be a better nation once your disloyalty is purged, while on display for everyone to witness."

Jin was unstrapped, and without further abuse from Yuriy, she was escorted back to her cell. Once there, she reclined slowly, her hand on her belly. She closed her eyes and prayed for strength to remain faithful to the end, like Rea certainly was.

She was having a baby boy!

ʄ

California

Avery "Chevy" Hewitt held a small motor with both hands as Job Buck attached a small propeller to a horizontal shaft on the back of it. Next, a gallon of fuel was set on top of the motor then locked into place with a sharp twist. The fuel tank was filled with water, since this was just an assembly exercise.

Together, Chevy and Job fit the motor, the small prop, and the fuel tank onto the back of a narrow chair that consisted of a rigid backrest, a seat, and harness straps. Chevy held the contraption in place as Job lifted the final piece—a large propeller assembly, with five six-foot propellers—and locked it onto the shaft that extended vertically from the motor.

"Time!" Chevy called.

"Got it." Titus hit his stopwatch. "Four minutes and nine seconds. That was your fastest time. The props took the longest, but now you know how much time you'll need to put it together on that night."

"Then we hit the starter?" Job reached around to the front of the motor and pressed a black button. Nothing happened. "And it'll do the rest?"

"The motor is wired to an altimeter and GPS. Yes, it'll do the rest."

"On one gallon for the whole flight?" Chevy frowned. "It depends how heavy this person is, but this thing can't go that far. Pyongyang is thirty miles from the coast. I'd be surprised if this thing could fly even five miles with even a small man sitting on it."

"The replica you'll be using is already in Pyongyang." Titus pocketed his watch. "It ain't easy lacking all the details, but that's the way these operations need to be."

"Because we could get caught, I know." Chevy began to take apart the contraption while Job held it. "I just want to make sure we're not wasting our time. Job and I know motors, and this isn't like any motor we've ever seen. What'll the fuel be? Can you tell us that much?"

"Hydrogen peroxide." Titus looked around the training gym. The three men were alone in the middle of the night. "The other three KONs can't know anything, since they'll most likely be drugged and questioned."

"Hydrogen peroxide isn't a fuel," Job said, "is it?"

"It's a propellant." Titus helped them lay the pieces of the machine on the floor. "Hydrogen peroxide reacts with stainless steel as a catalyst. And it'll be nearly silent once you push the button. It'll generate enough lift for one person for about twenty minutes of flight, and carry our subject far enough to connect with the next relay point of the extraction. This is the primary method for getting the subject out. After that, you'll both follow your own escape and evade routes to the DRIL and rendezvous with the other three KONs, if you haven't already done so."

"And if Job and I fail with this thing?" Chevy asked.

"The other KONs will extract the subject their way. A different way."

Chevy stepped away from Job and Titus. The plan was simple, but it was filled with danger. They would be running all over Pyongyang at night, where the streets were normally empty of civilians. Thousands of troops patrolled the region day and night, and the subject was under guard in a basement level prison. Now more than ever, Chevy understood why he'd been told at the very beginning that this was a mission from which he probably wouldn't return.

"Thank you for getting us ready," Job said, and offered his meaty hand to Titus. The blond man shook Job's hand. "We won't let you down."

"Just stick to the script." Titus turned and shook Chevy's hand as well. "Oleg and I will go with you as far as Japan where you'll receive your final instructions, then I'll be coming back here to wait for your return, Lord willing. Oleg will stay in Japan for a few days to respond to any urgent needs."

"Then what?" Job asked.

"Yeah." Chevy chuckled. "We've been talking in the dorm. Let's say we pull this off and make it back alive. What happens to the KONs then?"

"You're already part of the COIL family." Titus smiled warmly. "COIL doesn't turn its back on its people. When you return, we'll continue the work together. There's always more to do for Christ."

As he tried to fall asleep that night in his bunk, Chevy rehearsed in his mind how to assemble the flying machine. He guessed Job was doing the same. Since they'd been paired together for the mission, the two had begun to spend more time visiting and sitting together during breaks between training sessions. The three other KONs had begun to do the same. If they were to die well together, it seemed natural that they wanted to live well together, too.

Job wasn't the kind of man Chevy would've picked to be friends with, he admitted to himself. Their physiques were different, and their interests outside the Lord didn't align. They were also too much alike though a generation apart. Both preferred action rather than explanation, and neither had much tolerance for excuses. They expected much from themselves, and their personal comfort wasn't a high priority. Though they were different ages, their sense of humor was the same—dry, Chevy thought, which further distanced them from the others. And though Chevy preferred to do things his own way, with Job, he was learning to submit to other options.

All in all, Chevy had come to appreciate Job's gruffness, as well as his sincerity, regardless of their differences or the things that normally would make them incompatible. Both men were at the top of the class as marksmen, which was one of the reasons they were paired together for their part of the mission, and both were mechanically inclined. Through exercises with Titus and Oleg, they'd learned to trust each other, and they'd need to—whether during a gunfight or while trying to enter North Korea in an unsuspecting way.

Suddenly, Chevy opened his eyes wide. The clock showed it was after midnight. He'd heard crying! Someone in the dorm was crying, though muffled and quietly. This wasn't someone looking for attention, Chevy knew, but someone struggling with the reality of the danger and a lonely death they'd be facing in a few days' time.

Rising from his bed, Chevy touched Job's forearm in the bed next to him. He felt Job tense the instant he woke. Neither spoke in the darkness. Knowing Job, Chevy figured the man was listening to the night as Chevy's hand remained on his arm.

When Job sat up, the crying nearly went silent.

"We're under spiritual attack," Job whispered. "Let's all pray."

Chevy moved across the room and roused the other three. No lights were turned on, and Chevy didn't explain why he was waking them. It didn't matter which of the KONs was hurting, only that one of them was hurting.

"Let's all pray," he invited, and they all knelt around Spider's bed.

"The bad we're about to face in North Korea can be fought only by all the good that God is. He is love, and nothing can separate us from His love. We can't rise from here tonight until we're all reestablished in this truth."

"I'll start," Job said.

In just a couple sentences of Job praying, they were all stirred in their hearts, and they wept for a time, then recovered and called upon God with fresh devotion. Toward dawn, Chevy rejoiced as he showered before one of the last days of training. Their night of prayer together seemed like the most important training they could receive, since death was so near. They were giving their lives so others could live. It was a bond Chevy knew that no one outside of their COIL group would understand.

At breakfast, Chevy noticed how everyone seemed more pleasant and bright.

"You see it, too?" Job asked.

"I see it," Chevy said. "We're ready for North Korea."

Hawaii

By the time Nathan awoke inside the C-130 cargo plane, they were landing in Honolulu for refueling on their way to Japan. Around him, his *Operation: Harm's Way* teammates had also slept through the night, since most of them were familiar with overnight transports in loud, shaky planes. Only Heather hadn't been on many missions, but she'd settled into a seat between Chloe and June, and gone to sleep as well.

No one left the plane as it refueled, and Nathan stood up to walk around the hold. The brace on his leg supported his knee, but the joint was still prone to aching unless he exercised it often.

Away from his team, Nathan observed the *Kindred of Nails* men— five misplaced operators lounging around Titus and Oleg toward the rear of the plane. Nathan thought of them as misplaced because, like many COIL personnel, they didn't seem to have the ideal field agent qualifications, but since they were willing and dependent upon God, they were exactly what Christ and COIL preferred to use.

On their own headset channel, the KONs joked and visited. None of them seemed the least bit concerned that they were flying into a country that would kill them without hesitation at the slightest infraction. When Nathan moved closer, Titus glanced up and smiled.

Nathan had been skeptical of Titus joining COIL a few years earlier, precisely because Corban had recruited the ex-arms smuggler known as the Serval straight out of a foiled arms deal in Israel. But since then, Nathan had used Chloe to keep an eye on the casual Arkansas man. His exploits in China to rescue Steve Brookshire were still a matter of hushed admiration, so Nathan knew Corban's choice of Titus was a good one, even if they'd never run a full mission together.

Titus rose to his feet and changed headset channels to speak to Nathan over the noise of the airplane and the US Pacific Command airfield outside.

"Your team looks relaxed," Nathan said. There was no need to apologize for sleeping through the night when the KONs boarded, since they all knew how much rest they'd need for the coming days. "I expected to see Corban with you guys when you got on in San Diego."

"Corban and Luigi left us a week ago," Titus said. "You know those two—secretive. I got the impression Corban was more concerned about what North Korea is up to than he admitted. Something to do with their missile program. I bet Wes Trimble is in on it, too, but no one is talking. It's got me drawing some conclusions of my own about North Korea and the bigger picture. I think we're risking so much for Jin and Rea because they know a lot more about the dictator's intentions, even though peace is on everyone's minds."

"It's like it always is, huh?" Nathan chuckled. "Us grunts kept in the dark and expected to do the dirty work."

"Except it's not just us grunts this time." Titus motioned with his hand toward Chloe, June, Heather, and Chen Li. "How far are they going?"

"Getting Rea out of prison is proving more difficult than first suspected. We needed four more shooters, and still, our plan isn't perfect, I feel. Maybe it's my old age, but I don't like winging it anymore."

Nathan watched Titus frown and look away, seeming to be in deep thought. Then, the Arkansas man pulled up his sleeve and unstrapped his bulky sat-watch.

"You won't be blind with this." Titus offered him the watch. "You know what this is, right?"

"I've heard of it." Nathan accepted the device. "Can it see what I've heard it can see?"

"The Gabriels are flying at seventy thousand feet over that watch on a perpetual basis. You'll have thermal imaging and telescopic enhanced vision over any battlefield. It's guided me through some pretty harsh environments."

"What about you?" Nathan strapped it to his wrist.

"I have some domestic business to deal with, some of it COIL-related, and some of it personal."

"The son?"

"You heard, huh?" Titus sighed. "It ain't easy learning to be a father after I never stopped being a kid myself."

"What's Annette think of it all?"

"She and Levi took to one another. I have some work to do as a father and a husband, but the Lord is helping me. After our final briefing in Akita, I'll be going back to San Diego to keep them both company. Maybe Corban wants me on standby for the mission—just in case, you know? I'm telling you, there's more going on right now than we're aware of."

"Believe me, I know." Nathan touched the top of his leg brace. "This thing never lets me forget how quickly circumstances can change. But I've got your watch now. Seeing what's happening all around us will solve our blindness. How're the KONs, though? You'd not rather give them the watch?"

"They'll be in the midst of Pyongyang from day one. We can't take the chance of the watch falling into enemy hands and being reverse engineered. It's a tough mission for those five. They'll be walking a razor's edge. Not much margin for error. They definitely don't need a piece of equipment like that watch throwing off what they've learned to do by instinct."

"Well, thank you, Titus." Nathan shook the Serval's hand. "I think you gave us the edge we needed. I look forward to telling you how the watch helped us."

The two men parted, and the two North Korea teams remained in their individual groups. Nathan sat next to Chen Li and looked back at Titus. The man wasn't used to being left behind, and Nathan almost wished he could trade places with him, to stay home and raise a son.

"What're you thinking?" Chen Li asked. Her small feet were resting on top of her heavy pack, which contained everything she'd need for a week on foot in the Hamgyong Mountains. Her NL-X2 battle rifle, no longer than her arm, rested on her lap. It was partially disassembled as she cleaned it. "He's not going in?"

"No." Nathan drew his own bullpup across his lap. "You know how Corban covers all the angles. I think he's using Titus' son as a reason to keep Titus out of harm's way, just in case the rest of COIL's primary agents fall. COIL can still continue to operate with Titus' help."

"It could happen, I guess." Chen Li frowned. "We've been close to death before, you and I. We'll all go sometime."

"To live is Christ," Nathan quoted, "and to die is gain. Maybe this is it, Mrs. Isaacson. I'll see you in heaven. It's been a pleasure knowing you."

She elbowed him hard in the side.

"Don't take it that far! I'd prefer we enjoyed each other in this life a little while longer."

"In that case, I'll do my best to bring us all home together. Alive."

Nathan noticed the others chattering lightly and joking together as they cleaned their rifles. The whole rifle was only eight pounds, and though the stock was short, with the action behind the trigger mechanism, the barrel was a lengthy eighteen inches. It was as dependable as any other bullpup some Special Forces used—effective up to six hundred yards, especially with a strong scope attachment.

COIL had mass-produced the weapon for its own missions after Titus had raised concerns about the deficient old NL series, and Nathan was happy about the upgrade. The NL-X2, with the NL-X1 sniper rifle accurate up to one thousand yards, put COIL on equal if not elevated ground against any fighting force in the world.

Looking up from his rifle, Nathan locked eyes with Titus once more. There was worry in the tall blond man's face, but he gave Nathan a sharp nod just the same. Nathan nodded back, realizing now more than ever that if he or any of his team were captured, Titus would be the only one capable of rescuing them all. With Oleg at Titus' side, the Serval was a force to be reckoned with.

CHAPTER SEVEN

Pyongyang, North Korea

Yuriy Usik left the People's Palace of Remembrance in Pyong-yang's Central District and crossed Sungri Street. The early morning haze suited his mood as the sun hadn't yet risen. He didn't favor being summoned to the Mansudae Assembly Hall, but his responsibilities as an authority figure in his adopted country came with its share of politics and oversight as well.

With Kim Il Sung Square on his left, he moved through the sparse trees of the park that hugged the riverbank. When he reached the water, he stretched in the cool air, taking in the wide river before him. This was his favorite spot in the whole city, if he had to leave the sub-basement of the Palace. One hundred yards to his right was the Taedong Bridge, and far to his left was the Okryu Bridge. Both bridges were testaments of North Korean engineering, conquering a mighty river that was frequented by freighters.

Across the river was the Juche Tower, the one-hundred-and-seventy-meter-high monument built out of granite. It was built with over twenty-five-thousand blocks, each representing a day in the life of the Eternal Leader. The monument symbolized his vision for the country to follow his every immortal thought.

Normally, Yuriy embraced the structure and mindset of the Korean people, but lately, he'd been more reflective of his status. The cult that *Juche* had introduced to the peninsula was also responsible for giving him a home and a place to exercise his intrigue into the suffering of humanity. Until recently, the exacting, strict rule of the regime over the people seemed to portray the ideal government. Everything from population control to the extermination of disabled people kept the city striving toward its highest potential. Even Yuriy had yearned to do his part to purify the people for a stronger union and a more powerful military. Of course, that yearning had come with his own sense of personal ambition, but no one seemed to interrupt his work, even though they monitored him constantly.

He checked the mandatory pin of the Great Leader worn over his heart on his uniform, and adjusted the hammer on his belt. Most officers carried sidearms, but Yuriy liked the intimidation factor that the hammer presented when he walked among his peers or those whom he considered below him. None of the officers had ever used their sidearm as it was mostly ornamental in the city. But they'd all heard stories, Yuriy knew, that he regularly used his hammer on subjects of the state. Often, men and women had been mangled physically before he sent them to labor camps to work and to die. Going that morning to the Assembly Hall was simply another opportunity to remind everyone who they would face if they projected their individuality over the unity of the *Juche* idea.

Frowning suddenly as the sun rose, Yuriy gazed down at the tourist boat that always floated snuggly against the river bank. It tugged and creaked against its mooring lines, and a woman emerged meekly from below deck. Yuriy noticed her Chinese features, and wondered how she, a foreigner like himself, had come to live on one of the city's tourist boats. The boat, as he recalled, hadn't been out on the water for months, since there'd been no tourists due to friction with the West. Many other nations had prohibited its citizens from even coming to Pyongyang, since the regime had mistreated so many foreigners. The downside of such rigid internal discipline was that it affected tourism. Perhaps all that was about to change, he thought, since there was now talk of sanctions being lifted, and even transportation being resumed with South Korea.

For a moment, Yuriy contemplated walking down to the boat and arranging a ride with the woman. Maybe he owed her that much—a little business. He was, after all, one of the elite and privileged in the city who had extra *wons* to spend each month. Sometimes, he even went to a store for a soda or a candy bar. The stores were always empty of customers, and the shelves were nearly empty of exotic Chinese imports. But Yuriy liked such privilege, which he doubted this Chinese woman had ever known. She and her husband had probably been assigned to live in a mere boat that saw no tourists. What a sad existence.

Perhaps another day, Yuriy decided. When he had no meeting to attend, he would arrange a boat ride, maybe to motor around Rungna

Islet and to see the monstrous May Day Stadium. It had been a long time since he'd taken a day to relax and see the latest architecture the regime had raised, even if most of it was an uninhabitable facade. The appearance of greatness was as wonderful and as powerful as actual greatness.

When Yuriy moved away from the bank, the Chinese woman glanced up sharply and shrunk away on the deck of the boat. Yuriy recognized the fear in her that all North Korean civilians had when they were observed by a powerful officer. But this woman hesitated, seemingly caught between two actions—to leave the deck of the boat or to continue what she was doing on deck.

Instead of departing for his meeting, Yuriy decided to investigate. The woman saw him coming, and she bowed herself low, like some peasants did when regime officials went into the countryside.

"What do you have there?" he called to the boat. Though Korean wasn't his first language, he'd been told his Ukrainian accent wasn't too distinguishable. "What are you doing?"

Rather than answer, the Chinese woman moved her hand, and a fish flipped and flopped on the deck until she captured it again. She remained bowed, frozen in fear, Yuriy realized.

"Do you not trust in the Great Leader's provision enough," he asked, "that you must steal his fish? You could be punished for this. You and your husband could lose your boat. Do you wish to be sent to Pujon? Or to Taechon?"

"I am sorry, *Dongji*." Her Korean was rough and halting. "It will not happen again."

"I doubt that." He pointed at the side of the boat. "You have more fishing lines in the water, and they are wiggling with fish!"

"Yes, *Dongji*. I will set them loose and never commit this crime again. Please forgive me, *Dongji*."

Yuriy remembered his initial desire to honor the boat owners with a little business, then he recalled his youth, fishing in Cherkasy on the Dnieper in his homeland. Fresh fish had been rare in Pyongyang lately. The best they received even in a restaurant was frozen and thawed from the fisheries in Haeju.

"How do you prepare the fish?" he asked, then looked around the shore. No one was near. "Trout soup?"

"Yes, *Dongji*, but I have no black peppercorns or salt, just trout."

"I want trout soup, and you will make it for me." Yuriy rested his hand on his hammer. "Look at me. Do you know who I am?"

The woman lifted her head hesitantly. She was in her sixties, healthy-looking with red cheeks from the cool air.

"I am sorry, *Dongji*. I am not well-acquainted with the respectable personalities in our fine country."

"I am Yuriy Usik, the highest ranking non-*Choson* official in all of Pyongyang. I work for the Ministry of People's Security. Once a week, on this day, I want trout soup. Tonight, I will send a runner with a pail of peppercorn and salt, enough for two people. You will make me one serving once a week, and you may keep the second serving. If you do this, I will overlook this crime."

"Yes, *Dongji*. Thank you, *Dongji*. I will do as you request."

"Good." He nodded his approval at her subservience, guessing she wouldn't report him since she was in danger of punishment herself. "I will see you in one week. Do not get caught fishing anymore."

"Yes, *Dongji*."

He walked away briskly, feeling strangely empowered by the mercy he'd expressed. Mercy wasn't something he ever expressed to anyone. Was he growing soft, he wondered? First, he was questioning the effectiveness of his torture methods, and now he was conspiring with a starving boat operator. For a moment, he wondered if he should return and check her identification to get her name, but there would be time another day to do that. Trout soup was harmless enough.

As he approached the magnificent twenty-columned entrance, he found himself winded from walking all the way to Mansudae Assembly Hall. The expansive lawn out front was brown from the constant frost that time of year.

Inside the hall, he marched unchallenged past lesser guards and higher officials who seemed to identify him on sight. They feared him, he decided, which was good, unless they intended to remove him, at which point their fear would bring upon him their brutality without warning. For now, he guessed, they still needed him, since he performed the regime's most gruesome and politically-delicate work.

In the office of the People's Security, he was offered a chair in which to wait until the interior door opened a moment later. Much to his surprise, an assistant showed him into a room already full of officials, and they all turned their heads to look at him. One of the adjustments Yuriy had had to make years earlier was the acceptance of the clone-like appearance of the people of North Korea. It was part of the *Juche* idea to model one's self after the Great Leader. From clothing to body posture, their appearance was exactly the same.

But Yuriy had also learned the hierarchy within the various ministries that supported the regime. He quickly picked out Minister Jo Jong-Oh of the Ministry of People's Security, and saluted to the superior and the most influential man in the room of twelve men, each heads of their bureaus. Due to Yuriy's own rank and position, he had files on several of the heads of state in the room, and if any one of them continued on his own current personal agenda, independent lifestyle, or unique form of ambition, the man would suddenly become a guest of his at the Palace. However, Yuriy could play along as well as the rest of them. Respectfully, he greeted each of the men in turn, then seated himself in the only empty seat remaining—directly in front of Jo Jong-Oh's desk.

If Yuriy wasn't so confident in his undying loyalty to the regime's way, he would've thought the meeting was a tribunal against him, for the position of his chair was clearly a matter of focus. But internally, he knew no one had seen him make a deal that morning with the Chinese woman, and no one knew he was questioning the effectiveness of his skills at making people suffer.

"What we are about to discuss, *Dongji* Usik," Jo Jong-Oh said softly, his voice monotone, "is strictly confidential. Only the Supreme Commander and we in this room know what I am about to explain to you."

"I understand, *Dongji*." Yuriy nodded succinctly. "My life and mind are the Great Leader's."

"Very well." Jo Jong-Oh folded his hands. Except for a little gray around the temples, the minister could've been the dictator's older brother. He had the same plump figure and jowls, signifying his wealth and liberal diet, and the same half-closed eyelids while looking down his small nose at others. The only difference between all of the uniformed men were their medals on their breasts. "There will be a missile launch in thirteen days from today. The codename for the event is *Gimbap*. You have been briefed before. Further communication about that day will remain under the codename *Gimbap*. The Supreme Commander has ordered Han Ji-Jin's child to be executed in the May Day Stadium earlier on the same day as the *Gimbap* event. Is that clear?"

"In thirteen days?" Yuriy resisted the urge to glance at the other faces in the room, lest his gesture be mistaken for questioning the Great Leader's sovereign and perfect wishes. The *Gimbap* missile plan was suicide for North Korea! Wasn't the country having meetings to bring hostilities to a close? "Shall I have the doctor induce labor before that day? Thirteen days would still be a premature birth."

"The Supreme Commander has spoken." Jo Jong-Oh's face was without emotion. "Do what you must to fulfill his desires for the people. Each of us has our own duties to coordinate for the unprecedented launch. Yours is the most symbolic. You must not fail."

"Yes, *Dongji*. I will see that all is ready. Originally, I was to film the execution of the child and mother inside the Palace, for national viewing. Shall I prepare the mother for public execution at the stadium as well, or is the child the only one to be executed publicly?"

"Prepare them both for public execution in thirteen days at the stadium. There will be a pageant, and the Supreme Commander will attend. Everything must be precise."

Yuriy fought a little panic. He controlled how people died, but the regime was requiring him to control how a child was born, and born alive and healthy, as a proper offering for the Supreme Commander. He felt the blood drain from his face. This wasn't an execution. The deaths of Jin, Rea, and the child were a public sacrifice. A blood sacrifice on the day of a missile launch? An unprecedented missile launch!

"I will do as you have commanded." Yuriy did his best to keep his jaw from quivering, but he dared not clench it for fear that he be mistaken for being unsettled about the order. "Is that all, *Dongji*?"

"That is all. You may go."

Yuriy rose, saluted the room, and walked out of the office. He moved quickly through the Assembly Hall corridors and out to the front porch where he stopped next to the nearest column. Though he hoped he was thought by bystanders to be taking in the glorious view of the park and city below Moran Hill, he instead steadied himself against the column lest he collapse.

"What is happening to me?" he whispered to himself and blinked away moisture from his eyes. "I am Comrade Yuriy Usik!"

But no amount of self-proclamation settled his soul. For years, he'd known he was a sadist. Too gruesome for Russia's methodology, he'd come to North Korea to exercise his intrigue over the suffering, starving, political prisoners. Hundreds had died at his hand, hundreds by the hammer. None had been shown mercy. The machinery of the great nation had required the terrible awe that he had provided to a people susceptible of drifting apart if fear and control were not constantly enforced by all of its officials.

So why was he upset over the life of a child not yet born? This was about more than the sacrifice in the stadium in less than two weeks. No one ever knew when a missile launch was to occur, even when the missile program was fully functional. That's what this was really about. Knowledge of a launch was too dangerous. But now, there was immense coordinating of the heads of state, and he had been told. *Gimbap* was actually going to happen. This wasn't a missile launch, but an attack, and a sacrificial child was commemorating for the world the true insanity of the dictator. The *Gimbap* launch, Yuriy realized, would be the end of North Korea. They would never be able to withstand a counterattack.

But who would the regime attack? Yuriy continued to walk away from the Assembly Hall. Surely, an attack would be against South Korea and America. Japan might even join in, if provoked, and the Supreme Commander had already been provoking them for years. Attacking one superior nation was stupid. Attacking three at once was insanity. The people were starving, even though there were rumors of food trucks sitting at the border, waiting for the sanctions to lift. The nation's infrastructure was a façade. War with anyone couldn't possibly result in any kind of a win for North Korea! Negotiations with the West must've fallen apart, or old offenses could not be ignored. The Korean people were a proud people.

The Palace down the street came into view, and Yuriy imagined it being bombed to rubble, like he'd seen buildings in the Ukraine. Russia had a mighty military, but nothing like what America could hurl with non-stop accuracy at North Korea. Pyongyang would be obliterated, if not nuked outright.

For the first time in his life, Yuriy Usik was truly afraid.

Akita, Japan

Avery "Chevy" Hewitt stood against the living room wall of the small middle-class residence of a stout man he'd been told was named Song Sakana. The rest of the KONs and the COIL agents crowded into the room as well, sitting on the floor or a few padded chairs. The true heart of Song Sakana, Chevy noticed, was best displayed in that moment as the host helped his ailing mother-in-law out of the room so the COIL gathering could speak privately. The woman seemed to have dementia, and a stroke had disabled her to the point that Song needed to carry most of her weight as she moved.

Titus and Oleg stood in the doorway of the kitchen and commanded the room's attention without saying a word. Chevy observed how even the COIL operatives, whom he'd recently met, respected the tall blond and the Russian at his side. Wherever COIL personnel weren't standing, gear for the mission was piled in duffel bags against the walls and between chairs.

"In a few days," Titus began after praying, "the first of you will leave for North Korea. You've all been trained and equipped. Now, it's time to implement what we're here for. Since we haven't heard any new intel in weeks, we're going on faith that God has prepared the way for us."

Chevy watched Song Sakana reenter the room and crouch discreetly next to the sofa. In prison, Chevy had known two Asian men who were doing life terms for trafficking for the Sakana Crime Syndicate in Hong Kong. However, this Sakana was clearly not part of the family business, but rather a trusted confidant, maybe even a COIL agent and peer to Titus, judging by the reverence Titus and Oleg had paid the man upon arriving.

"Those of you with folders," Titus continued, "please open them now."

The KONs opened their folders. Chevy's file contained one grainy photo of a plain-looking Korean woman, and one page of text, which consisted of the woman's profile. Her height, weight, and age were included.

Glancing over Job's shoulder, Chevy observed that Job had the same information as he did. Immediately, Chevy took note of the woman's approximate weight. She was under the weight limit of the P-Rox vehicle he and Job had practiced assembling.

"This is Han Ji-Jin. We'll call her Jin. In Korean, personal names are ordered last. She is the pregnant subject, the one you're being sent to save before she is murdered, along with her child. The other operatives in this room will be going far north to rescue her husband from a maximum security prison. This is a joint mission—*Operation: Harm's Way.* Both extractions must be executed on exactly the same night. If one is rescued first, then security will increase for the other or the other may be moved.

"Having said that, you'll need to be able to adjust for changes. Jin is held inside the People's Palace of Remembrance. But what if she's moved to somewhere else in the city? Each of you knows the city intimately now as well as any citizen of Pyongyang. You know the safe houses, and you know the holding facilities. You'll have one night to locate her, and get her out in your respective ways. Jin and Rea, her husband, aren't only our brother and sister in Christ, but they also may hold intel pertinent to America's national security. We're unofficially acting on behalf of the president's need for knowledge to prevent an attack from North Korea, and to determine if the US should indeed enter any agreements with the country."

Titus continued to review the risks and demands on their lives, but Chevy was distracted by his own personal mission, since his rescue subject now had a face. It seemed a lifetime ago when he'd been homeless in Fresno. Now, he would rescue Jin, a stranger—even die for her if necessary. It was a sobering thought, but he would see and know her one day in heaven. That made it a wonderful thought as well.

"There's only one thing left to do," Titus said, raising his chin. "We all know what Jesus said about counting the cost. It's time to say it aloud. Have you counted the cost? Satan and his cohorts are going to be fighting something fierce against all of you, so before anyone gets on a plane or climbs into a boat to go to North Korea, we need to hear that you've counted the cost. No one can head out on this mission and draw back at the last second. We need to know if you have any apprehension about following through. If you do, no one will look down on you. You'll just fly back with me to the States. Each of you needs to say something, not for legal purposes, but for the purpose of confessing aloud, for everyone here and for the angels who witness your confidence, that you've counted the cost, because make no mistake, this will cost you something."

Chevy hadn't been expecting to be put on the spot like this in front of so many he was still getting to know. All he knew was that he was a simple believer who'd volunteered for an operation to care for God's people in a dangerous land. But Titus was right, he decided. This wasn't a time for timidity or false humility. This was a time for courage and unwavering faith.

"I'll say it." Chevy raised his hand. "I've counted the cost. I'll be true to the testimony of Jesus Christ and rescue Jin, even at the cost of my life. That would be an okay way to exit this world, though I'm also content to stay alive through the mission to be a part of what COIL will be doing next. Thanks."

Titus and Oleg exchanged glances, nodding to each other. Chevy took that as a sign of their approval, though he knew his own heart without their approval. He knew he would die for this stranger, or even his fellow KONs, if necessary. Her life was valuable to him, regardless of the information she carried. If it came to it, he would even die for the North Korean oppressors, to see them rescued from their twisted thinking and turn to their Savior.

"I've counted the cost," Nathan said. "I'm ready, if it comes to that, for the sake of Christ."

"He speaks for both of us," Chen Li said, taking her husband's hand. "I've counted the cost."

"I'm ready, too," Scooter said. "I've counted the cost."

"Amen to that," Bruno stated. "I've counted the cost."

"I've counted the cost," Heather said. "I'd be honored to die for Jesus."

"We've counted the cost," Memphis said as he held June's hand. "We talked about this on the plane, June and I."

"I've counted the cost," June confirmed.

"If there were ever a mission on which the cost needed to be counted," Chloe said, "this is the mission. I've counted the cost. Zvi and I talked on the phone this morning, and we've both known it could come to something like this. He's counted the cost with me."

The four remaining KONs were the only men who had said nothing so far, and though no one else looked their way, Chevy's gaze fell on the men he'd trained with. They'd spoken of this very subject, and each of them had expressed their cost-counting faith many times, so he didn't understand their hesitation. A few quiet moments passed. There was no rescue without these men, so Chevy felt a mixture of emotions when they delayed their responses.

"I was in prison a long time," Job said suddenly. His head was lowered. "We had some tough years—me and the other Christians in the joint. We encouraged each other to stand strong in the face of persecution, or ridicule from other faith groups. Some men couldn't handle the mockery. I wanted to go last right now because I wanted to hear what kind of people I was with. I'm only here because I've counted the cost, and I'm proud to be among others who've done the same."

"I've counted the cost." Shorty smiled. "I didn't want to seem too eager to go first. I'm ready to go, if the Lord calls me home along the way."

"I've counted the cost as well," Donny said, "though the life I'm offering isn't too costly. My body's falling apart and I don't have anything to show for my years, but it's all God's, completely and fully."

"I'm happy to count the cost," Spider said. "The days ahead will be tough on us, I know. Before I go to be with the Lord, I'm okay with suffering for Him a little more."

"That's everyone." Oleg studied their faces for a moment. "We didn't really think anyone would turn back, but these things must be said. Don't take what's been said for granted by the person next to you, and don't hesitate to repeat it when the risks are highest. Let each other know in an affirming way that you indeed have counted the cost. It'll help all of you to work together when you know that you'll do what must be done, even if it costs you your lives."

When the briefing was finished, they all prayed, one at a time, and several were moved to tears. Yet, there wasn't much sadness through it all. The tears, Chevy felt, were from the greatness of the sacrifice that was about to be given for people they didn't know. It was so beautiful to have the honor to die for someone they didn't even know. None of them could hold back at least some emotion. Their own sacrifice reminded them of their Savior's sacrifice for each of them.

While they prayed, the hearts of the COIL operators he'd not known were revealed to Chevy. He was used to the vulnerability that

Titus and Oleg showed, though they were still in the early years of their faith. Nathan was soft-spoken to his God, and Bruno's great size was matched by a great heart and plain words. Scooter was casual but frank, and Memphis' prayer was simple and short. No one competed for attention and there was no time restriction. Their prayer time lasted over an hour, and they only rose when their souls sensed that God had indeed heard their praise and petitions.

After the prayer, Chevy walked onto the back porch of the home where a large wall tent had been erected to house the men, while Chloe, June, Heather, and Chen Li would occupy the house overnight.

"They're tight quarters," Titus said as he joined him on the porch, "but North Korea has spies even in Japan. A gathering of Christian operatives like us would stand out at a hotel."

"The quarters aren't too tight for us," Chevy said, referring to the KONs' former residence. "Remember?"

"Right." Titus chuckled. "Well, all we'll need to do is put up with Oleg's snoring."

"My snoring will be a favor," Oleg said, and Chevy understood Titus' jest had been made because he knew Oleg was within earshot, entering the porch. "My snoring will cover up the weeping of Titus, because he can't go on this mission."

"I could go," Titus argued, "but my responsibilities are elsewhere right now, and I'll be in San Diego when you guys return."

"So, there won't be any weeping?" Oleg continued to tease. "Maybe the real weeping will be when you take your boots off in the tent, and everyone smells your feet."

"I washed them especially for this occasion," Titus said. "Perhaps I will weep a little that I can't go on the mission. But the laughter will be louder tomorrow."

"What laughter?" Oleg asked.

"The laughter from the others. They'll learn it ain't easy trying to sleep with your snoring!"

That night, regardless of the concern and excitement about the coming mission, when Chevy thought he was the last one still awake in his sleeping bag, he heard Oleg snoring. Then, from across the tent, someone snickered. Moments later, the whole tent erupted in laughter.

But Oleg never woke up.

Pyongyang, North Korea

In the monotony of living aboard the tourist boat on the Taedong River, Lu Yi had fallen into a routine that made her a valuable guest rather than only a dangerous burden. Sharing the food from the smuggled packages with her two hosts had opened up further communication with the couple, and she found that they were fearful but true believers in Jesus, starving for the Word of God.

Though Lu Yi had arrived in Pyongyang with no Scriptures on her person, her decades of reading and studying the Bible had left her with numerous memorized Bible passages she was now able to write down in Korean Hangul characters to be read by other believers. The threat of death seemed less as her hosts drank in the precious Word of God which Lu Yi wrote onto scraps of wrinkled wrapping paper. Each day, the couple returned from indoctrination rallies or marches to find Lu Yi had prepared not only physical food for them, but spiritual nourishment as well.

Having been in Pyongyang for some weeks now, Lu Yi wasn't merely submitting to her confinement on the boat; she had fully embraced God's purpose to build up the couple in charge of river tourism in Pyongyang!

The morning came, one week after meeting Yuriy Usik, that Lu Yi was to give the official his trout soup. It was a cold winter morning, and a thin layer of ice had formed on the surface of the water along the shoreline. Though Lu Yi's hosts had been terribly concerned that the renowned Ukrainian torturer had accidentally made contact with Lu Yi, she'd settled their hearts by explaining there were no accidents with God. Somehow, she'd assured them, He would use this interaction for His good purposes.

"Our Lord will not waste this opportunity," Lu Yi had said, "to reach the iron heart of an evil man. Let us pray for truth to be revealed to him that he cannot deny—about himself and about his Savior."

And so, Lu Yi stepped onto the deck of the tourist boat that morning with the confidence that their God had indeed been moving in some way in the life of Yuriy Usik.

She gazed through the trees between the river and the cold, plain buildings of the city. The pail of trout soup was wrapped in scratchy vinylon, keeping it warm as she waited. Prayerfully, she sought the

Lord's courage and wisdom for the coming interaction. There were brave underground Christians throughout North Korea, and she knew some of them. But few of them would meet like this with the People's Security officer whose headquarters was rumored to reside inside the People's Palace of Remembrance. She didn't want to waste this moment!

Then, she saw Yuriy Usik walking quickly through the trees, emerging a short distance downriver at the water's edge. He motioned subtly with his hand, and Lu Yi understood that she was to go to him.

Carefully, because of the ice, she stepped off the deck and onto the shore. As she approached him, she prayed for God's will. Her eyes fell on the hammer on his belt, the hammer that her hosts had said was responsible for the public executions of whole families in Hakdangol Fountain Park, only a kilometer away. They'd seen those executions. If she had any brains, Lu Yi told herself, she would've found a new hiding place and never agreed to fish and cook for the murderer. After all, what if he asked for her identification? She wasn't even a Korean citizen! But sometimes, stepping through God's open doors made no safe sense. The step simply had to be taken, for God's sake.

"You received the salt and peppercorns from my runner?" he asked without greeting.

"Yes, *Dongji*." Lu Yi gave him the pail still wrapped in the blanket. She hadn't planned on giving him the whole blanket, but he clearly had nothing with him in which to wrap the soup to ward off the cold. "And the extra fishing line as well. Your generosity has brought you to my thoughts often this week."

"Oh?" He glanced at her, but otherwise his eyes remained on the water, or across the river on East Pyongyang. "What are your thoughts? You have told no one of this arrangement, I trust."

"Our secret is safe," she said. "There is an old story of a man who lost his inheritance when he traded it for a bowl of soup. But I think you, *Dongji*, are on the path to learning of your inheritance because of this bowl of soup."

"Last week, I caught an old woman catching fish illegally." He frowned at her. "Now, you share foolish wisdom and ancient stories?"

"It is not foolish wisdom. Are you to tell me that your soul hasn't been stirred with thoughts of kindness since we met?"

Yuriy Usik took a full step backwards. His mouth opened and his eyes glared, then blinked rapidly. Finally, he shook off his reaction.

"You are a witch! I knew there was something about you." He shifted the bundled soup into his left arm and placed his right hand on his hammer head. "I should kill you now. I have that power. Or I will drag you before the court and let them hear your words. My soul stirs for *Choson* alone, and the *Juche* idea!"

"Do not be troubled, Yuriy Usik." Lu Yi folded her hands and smiled. "There is no need to pretend in my presence. I know you are a great man and I am just a small woman. I have lived a long time, and I know the seasons of the heart may change like the weather. Tell me, are you in the season of spring, summer, autumn, or winter?"

Yuriy's hand remained on his hammer, but his countenance softened. Lu Yi kept her gaze squarely on his white face.

"I am not in a season. I am in a desert. Alone." He swallowed, his emotions on the surface for her to read. "My world is crumbling, and I cannot leave it. I have not prepared for what is to come."

"Eternity?"

"Eternity? No. I mean, I have not prepared for the end of *Choson*. But it is run by fools, so I should have known it would end like this. *Juche* was first beautiful to me. A machine of war and unity. But its leaders are corrupt and too proud to move *Choson* into the next era of prosperity."

"What do you mean, the end of *Choson*?" Lu Yi suppressed a shiver from the cold, or maybe it was from the despair in his voice. "Tell me, my friend. Share the burden that weighs on your soul."

"Friend? We are friends? How do I know you are not a spy for—?"

"For whom? You are a People's Security Officer. You came to me. Yes, we are friends. You may call me Yellow Bird. We have shared food and we have shared our true thoughts. Look at us now. I am of Chinese origin, and you, it is said, are from the Ukraine. Our uniqueness demands that we stand beside one another."

"You speak like no other *dongmu* I've ever known."

"Tell me about your fear of the end of *Choson*. Share your heart with an old woman, Yuriy Usik."

"It is a secret."

"I have many secrets, one of which is my trout caught for my friend's trout soup."

"I don't doubt you have many secrets." He glowered at her. "You don't speak like a *dongmu*, so your secrets plunge as deep as your heart is old."

"It is a tragedy to wander through life as dark as your mood seems to be, Yuriy. My people have a saying, 'Keep yourself in the light, and the darkness cannot harm you.' Let the light be cast upon the darkness you hold onto, my friend."

"You have boldness, old woman, but also a sincerity I cannot withstand." He paused, carefully eyeing the area around them. "There will be a missile launch, and I was warned ahead of time. It isn't customary to tell anyone at my level, so I know the truth of it. An old protocol is being followed for the launch, called *Gimbap*. It is insanity to launch a missile at a time like this, with peace so close with the West. Do you understand?"

Lu Yi looked away. Missile launches were old news, but an *announced* missile launch that officials were meant to keep secret—it made little sense at such a moment of peace talks.

"Then, an attack is imminent," she said. "*Choson* cannot win. I know this, even if others don't know it. But apparently, you know this."

"I do know it. My life is over. There will be war and I will die. We will all die."

"*Choson* is not your life. Your life is more than *Choson*."

"That is blasphemy, old woman! How can you say this?" He sighed and gritted his teeth for a moment. "If I had prepared, I would have somewhere to go. But six days is not enough time. Now, I wait with the rest of *Choson*. For death. I fear America will not spare Pyongyang. Japan will target Chongjin and Hamhung. And South Korea will invade *Choson*. It is over."

"It is not over, Yuriy Usik. Six days is enough time to prepare your heart for eternity. It is enough time to turn from your harmful wickedness and surrender to Someone greater than yourself or *Choson* or the Great Leader."

"Surrender? You mean defect? No, I cannot defect. I am a wanted man. You call me wicked, so you know I have committed many crimes. I cannot surrender to anyone."

"You surrender from in here." She stepped closer and laid her palm flat on his chest, upon the pin that represented his allegiance to the

Supreme Commander. "*Choson* is a country of broken people. We have no way to fix ourselves, Yuriy Usik. We must surrender from our hearts to the Creator who made our eternal souls. He is the One who has called on your heart this week to turn to Him. Call out to Him in your grief and desperation."

"*God?*" He swept her hand away and checked the shoreline for any onlookers. "You speak of God. Now, I know you are a fool! Do you know how many heaven people I have executed? *Choson's* stability relies on the unity of its laboring people, not upon imaginary gods!"

"There is one God, Yuriy Usik, and He loves you sincerely. Besides, you know *Choson* will be no more, and *Juche*, as beautiful as it may have seemed, relies on a perfect people, yet we are not perfect people. We have a need in our hearts to be forgiven for our many harmful deeds. Deep down, we are not good, but bad, and this must be corrected not by human unity, but by divine unity. God came as a Man, and the death we deserve as bad people—He died for us. Now, we must rely on this truth to experience unity with Him. Then, you will have peace, Yuriy Usik."

"You *are* a heaven person!" He looked down at the soup. "Have you poisoned my soup as well as my mind with your blasphemy against the Great Leader?"

"Friends do not poison their friends. The heaven people, Christians, have never hurt you, and I am not hurting you now. The truth I tell you is spoken at great risk, but the truth is too valuable not to share it. You have told me the truth about the *Gimbap* missile launch in six days. You care deeply about this. And so I have told you the truth about the need of our eternal souls. The stirring in your soul has been real, has it not?"

"No, it is not real." He backed away. "I do not believe what you say. Never speak to me again. Tell no one we spoke, or I will kill you in the most dreadful way. You keep silent, old woman!"

"I will pray for you, Yuriy Usik," she said louder as he walked away. "And in seven days, if we are still here, I will have more trout soup for you!"

Lu Yi watched him stomp through the park trees and back into the city streets, which were beginning to stream with morning commuters.

"God, please help us," she whispered, then turned and went back to the boat.

Below deck, her hosts wanted to know the details of her conversation, which they had witnessed covertly through a port window, but she couldn't tell them just yet. Instead, she unwrapped the sat-phone and dialed the number before she'd completely formulated her words. The same man's voice answered in English on the other end.

"This is Yellow Bird. I have news."

"I am recording, Yellow Bird, and our signal is encrypted."

"In six days, there will be a missile launch. An official is troubled by it so much because he believes it will be an attack, which will provoke a military strike on Pyongyang by America, Japan, and South Korea."

"Oh. Six days?"

"That is what he said. He called it *Gimbap*, but I do not understand what that means. *Gimbap* is a food sold on the street in Korea. It must be a code word."

"Are you still in the same location?"

"Yes. Patrols have been frequent on the river. Now, perhaps, we know why."

"Yellow Bird, you're caught in much more than either of us understands. I must communicate what you've said to my friends, and they'll need to arrive at your location before the launch occurs. Expect two messengers in a matter of days. Everything will happen quickly now."

"I will expect your two messengers."

"They are men of the heaven people, and they'll perhaps show you a way of escape out of the city."

"I will be waiting."

When she turned off the phone, Lu Yi looked into the concerned faces of her Korean hosts. They'd listened to her English conversation, but they clearly hadn't understood much, though most Koreans in the big cities usually took English courses in school as children.

"Pray with me first," Lu Yi said, "and then I will tell you what I can. We are in terrible danger, but God's hand is not small. Even if we die soon, we are safe forever because we know who our Savior is. Kneel with me. Let us not be afraid."

CHAPTER EIGHT

Pyongyang, North Korea

Donny Walters was calmer than he thought he'd be on the jostling flight from Beijing, China, into Pyongyang. By faith, he believed God was closely involved in this operation, and he was seeing the impact of His Lord everywhere. Just a couple months earlier, he'd been painting houses, then Peter Mitchell had fired him. Getting fired would've seemed like a desperate time for an ex-con like himself, but he'd come to know, while in prison, that God really did provide for His children.

Titus and Oleg's invitation to join the *Kindred of Nails* hadn't been merely an opportunity to avoid homelessness, but a way to use his life to honor God and those who were in great need. Though he'd been with the other KONs for only a few weeks, he couldn't imagine having lived his life without them. They were imperfect, uneducated, and poor, but they'd been with Jesus Christ for years, and their heart was his heart.

It was nighttime when the plane landed and taxied on the runway. Donny nodded at Francisco "Shorty" Hernandez and Ernesto "Spider" Colosio. The rest of the plane was empty. There were no stewardesses, and the Chinese pilots, who spoke good English, had said if they weren't being paid for a full flight, the Air China flight would've been canceled due to lack of passengers. That's when it hit Donny: *this is real!* North Korea wanted the three of them bad enough that they'd bought up empty seats on the plane just to get them into Pyongyang that night. So far, the plan was working beautifully. They were the first team of COIL agents to enter North Korea for *Operation: Harm's Way.*

"We're finally where we belong," Spider said from another row as the plane came to a stop.

"Yep," Donny said. "We're home."

Nothing was further from the truth, Donny thought, but Spider was already acting the part of a United States defector, using a cover Corban Dowler had begun to foster the minute he knew operatives would need to enter North Korea to rescue Jin. Titus had shown them some of the fake press releases COIL's misinformation specialists had posted on US government bulletin board systems. All three KONs had been painted as North Korean sympathizers and anti-American antagonists who were wanted by the FBI for the bombing of a church in Wisconsin. Of course, there'd been no bomb and no church, but the news releases and warrants for their arrests had made them popular fugitives overnight.

As soon as the jet's cabin door opened, a rosy-cheeked Korean woman in her thirties entered and walked down the aisle. She wore slacks and a plain blouse, but the two men on her heels wore military uniforms with caps pushed so far forward, Donny couldn't see their eyes.

"Hello!" The woman smiled brightly, showing bleached white teeth and freckles on her little nose. "I am An Sum-Mi, your companion in Pyongyang. My English is excellent, with first-rate grammar. I have practiced my whole life for this moment to meet and welcome you to our wonderful country. From your communications, I know you already."

She pointed to Shorty and called out the fake name COIL had given him. Then she did the same for Spider and Donny.

"I am very impressed!" Donny clasped his hands loudly. As the eldest of the three, he was expected to speak first. "We are honored to finally be somewhere safe. America has continued to promote its agenda of capitalism, and we are three men who spoke up. For our stand, we were called criminals. We thank you ahead of time for your hospitality, and we look forward to serving this fine country and its people. After all, it is our country now as well."

"Yes, we are pleased as well with our superiority over America in every way. Phones, please? And your luggage? All luggage. You have no need for anything that is not provided already from the Great Leader."

"Of course." Donny drew his phone from his pocket. He, along with Shorty and Spider, gave up all their possessions, which contained the most subtle hints that they were the anti-capitalists they claimed to be. "We will cooperate in all things. We are your guests."

Their phones and bags were passed to the two soldiers who carried them off the plane. So far, everything was going exactly as Titus, Oleg, and Corban had said it would. But beyond this point, they had only speculation as to what would occur to three supposed American defectors to North Korea.

As Donny followed their government escort off the plane, he considered the other COIL operatives and their roles. In the far north, Nathan was about to lead his team into Hamgyang Prison for Rea. They could already be approaching the North Korean coastline right then, since their timelines had been moved up. And Chevy and Job were about to be inserted covertly into the country to also go after Jin at the Palace.

That left Donny and his two companions to convince their North Korean hosts that they were real defectors, so that security around them would decrease enough for them to slip into the city undetected. Five days wasn't much time to do all that, but their stories had been carefully constructed and their mission was well-defined.

If they couldn't slip away to join Chevy and Job in five days, they would be left behind.

In the airport terminal, there were no civilians, only a rigid line of twenty soldiers standing at attention with their sidearms. An Sum-Mi snapped an order at the soldiers, and the twenty split into three groups, one group per defector.

"Go with them, please," An Sum-Mi instructed Donny and his friends. "They must search you. It is okay, my comrades. You are in Korea now."

Donny was forcefully guided to the nearest wall, and the soldiers began to strip him of his clothes. Since he was well over six feet tall, he could see over the heads of the small Koreans, most of them in their twenties. Shorty and Spider were already naked as their clothes and bodies were inspected. There was a man with a notepad in each group who took notes. Every mole, scar, tattoo, and skin blemish was noted in the file while An Sum-Mi supervised from a short distance away.

Seeing as she'd given orders to the soldiers, Donny understood she wasn't merely a government escort, as most tourists would've been assigned. No, she was an administrator with some authority. She was cute in a simple way, but Donny had no illusions. If she suspected they were infiltrators, she would send them to prison in an instant.

Once Donny was allowed to dress again, he was given new stiff and scratchy clothing, but he didn't complain. He'd worn worse while incarcerated. Even the strip search didn't bother him much since, depending on which work detail he was assigned in prison, he'd usually been strip-searched twice a day for years.

Next, Donny was walked outside into the blowing winter wind and loaded into the back of a four-door car. One soldier sat on either side of him. Shorty and Spider were each loaded into other cars, and Donny quickly lost track of them.

They cut through dark sections of the capital city, which was clearly experiencing power outages, and Donny didn't notice any other headlights in front or behind them. Shorty and Spider had been taken elsewhere, it seemed. They were being split up to be interrogated, Donny figured, but he wasn't troubled. Death held no sting for him, so if he faced it, he would die without fear. He'd counted the cost. His only regret if he had to die early was that he wouldn't be able to help Jin reach safety. For now, however, he had a facade to maintain, so he faced straight ahead and asked no questions.

Japan

Nathan stared at the blackness that surrounded the rising and falling freighter ship. Icy rain slashed at his face, but his goggles protected his eyes. He also wore a waterproof parka, but the rest of his gear for the North Korea operation was already sitting in one of the two DRILs, which were each secured to the foredeck. The Drone Resupply Insertion Landers would be pushed to their max on this mission, and Nathan prayed the machines and their giant propellers were up to the freezing weather.

Wearing his combat boots and full gear, Scooter slid across the deck to the railing next to Nathan.

"Are we having fun yet?" the rowdy Mexican-American joked. "Hey, this is perfect weather for us, right?"

"Perfect?" Nathan chuckled. "Yes, it's perfect. And deadly. No one else is foolish enough to be out in this weather."

He glanced over his shoulder. Half the team, including his wife, was already lounging inside the shelter of the DRIL. The bay door was open and ready for the rest of them. Everyone wore their gear for immediate deployment.

"How's that thing working?" Scooter gestured to the bulky sat-watch on Nathan's wrist.

"It feels like cheating—being able to see everything from the sky." Nathan touched the watch screen and swiveled the three-dimensional view to another angle. "We're farther out to sea than I wished we were, but there's a North Korean battleship patrolling in this direction. We need to deploy and send the freighter back to Japan."

"Roger that." Scooter trotted across the sloping deck to share the news with the others.

Nathan mounted the stairs to the bridge and stepped inside the small pilot house. Song Sakana stood at the controls.

"We're leaving," Nathan said. "Point the bow into the wind, and get out of here the minute we leave. It's not on your radar yet, but in a few minutes, there'll be a North Korean navy ship off your port side."

"I understand." Song turned the ship to a northwest heading, then offered his hand. "Go with God, Eagle Eyes."

They shook hands, then Nathan left the bridge. This was his first time working with Song Sakana, but he hadn't been disappointed in the ex-Hong Kong gangster. Titus had assured him that Song was a dependable and sincere brother, especially when others were in a tight spot. Though Nathan was used to relying on Corban for COIL dependencies, he was learning that Titus had been thoroughly inserted by Corban into every area of COIL. Though Titus and Corban weren't on the mission with them, Nathan felt the confidence of the two capable leaders backing his team's moves. After all, he wore Titus' sat-watch now.

Down on the deck, Nathan opened the cargo door of the second DRIL for a final check. No one was riding in this machine. It was loaded to its capacity weight with fuel, and programmed to fly deep into North Korea's southern territory to potentially aid the KONs in their extraction. Everyone with Nathan understood that the DRIL couldn't refuel itself, so it was rendezvousing with someone else who was inside the country. Since Nathan hadn't seen Luigi for a few weeks, he wondered if the gum-chewing spook was already in the country, pulling the strings from the shadows for Corban.

Thinking of Corban, Nathan wondered where he was, too. Paralyzed from the waist down, the man could've retired by now. But Corban and Luigi had left San Diego together. Corban's family, Janice and Jenna, had returned to New York, and Luigi's wife, Heather, was there in the DRIL with the others. But Nathan doubted even Heather knew any more than he did about where her husband was lurking.

Nathan closed the cargo door, then punched a code into the keypad under the port side wing. He stepped back to steady himself next to the first DRIL as the drone loaded with fuel containers thundered to life. Its nine-foot-wide fans on each side of the fuselage were powered by two nine-hundred-horsepower helicopter engines, so the noise was louder than anything on board the freighter and the rainstorm combined. His parka flapped harshly as the machine rose and wobbled above the deck. Thousands of miles away, Marc Densort was coordinating such tech, so Nathan tried not to worry too much, but there was nothing simple about launching two giant drones from the moving deck of a freighter in the midst of an ice storm.

The DRIL seemed to collect its wits, then lifted straight up into the windy darkness. In seconds, its engine noise drifted and faded away to the west.

"Piece of cake," Nathan said to everyone as he smiled and counted heads packed into the DRIL bay. "Hold onto your hats."

"Is now a good time to tell you," Bruno said, "that I don't do well inside vibrating, enclosed spaces?"

"I agree," June called from the rear corner. "I could use a couple windows punched in the wall back here."

Nathan tapped in the code, then hopped into the DRIL bay as the door ramp raised and closed. For a moment, as the noise and vibration rose in complete darkness, Nathan wondered if this was the dumbest idea they'd ever had. The DRILs were equipped with stealth capabilities, not to deploy troops, but to deliver Bibles and supplies across closed borders.

Memphis cracked a glow stick, and Chen Li found Nathan's arm. In the tight space, Nathan stood prayerfully with the other seven operatives, wondering if the whole contraption would keel overboard and splash into the water right then and there.

They felt the DRIL jolt and rise into the air and hover. No one breathed, moved, or spoke. Then, the machine tilted forward, and its momentum seemed consistent with normal flight through turbulent air.

"If you have to move," Nathan yelled, "move slowly. I don't want anything to upset the balance of this bird."

"I'm afraid to move at all," Scooter said. "How was it that we trained for everything on this mission, except for this?"

"Probably because," Heather said, "if we knew we were about to be flown in a shuddering metal coffin, none of us would've come!"

There was light laughter, but Nathan's stomach was greatly unsettled. He took several deep breaths, then crouched down to sit on his pack next to Chen Li. The space was so tight, his knees brushed the back of Chloe, but she remained silent.

For a while, no one spoke. They just stared at each other's faces in the green light of the glow sticks. The coast was two hundred miles away, and flying at two hundred miles per hour, they had an hour to wait to land. Once on land, they were to use the fuel canisters in the bulkhead to refuel the DRIL for a hasty take-off. Since the drone had a range of only three hundred miles, they couldn't fly it all the way to the doorstep of Hamgyong Prison, but they were four days ahead of schedule. There was plenty of time to hike thirty miles through the mountains to reach the prison.

Much to Nathan's delight, his sat-watch worked without a glitch from inside the bay. He watched the shoreline of North Korea draw nearer. The North Korean destroyer had changed course for its own waters when Song Sakana's freighter turned back to the east.

Suddenly, Bruno's deep voice started a chorus, and over the otherwise deafening noise of the turbines, together they sang *It is Well with My Soul*. On the second verse, Nathan wept tears of joy. To serve with such faithful people was overwhelming. He wondered if Rea had any idea of the kind of men and women that were coming to rescue him from death. But of course, he didn't know.

North Korea

Chevy stood next to Job in the basket of a hot air balloon with its black canvas above them. The altimeter and GPS around Job's neck, like a coach's stopwatch, was their only source of information a quarter-mile up in the air. If all went right, they were on track to drift inland over the Taedong River and into the heart of North Korea.

The two operatives had been the last to leave Akita, Japan, traveling first to South Korea, then taking a chopper out to a fishing trawler in the Korean Bay west of North Korea. Due to an ice storm, they'd nearly missed their window to launch the giant balloon. But thanks to the help of a sizeable COIL man who had introduced himself as Mapper, they'd made it.

At dusk, the two had risen silently into the sky and floated over the ocean on invisible air currents. For the last three weeks in San Diego, the two men had been training with a hot air balloon pilot, amongst their other training at the COIL center, but neither man had experienced flying at night.

"We just passed over the coastline," Job announced quietly. "We're twenty-five miles north of the river's mouth, and about forty miles from the city."

"Altitude?" Chevy asked, whose job was to manage the elevation.

"Thirteen hundred feet."

"We'll stay here for another ten miles." Chevy gave the balloon thirty seconds of burn to maintain elevation. "It's so dark, you'd never know a whole country was down there."

"No electricity." Job leaned his thick forearms on the basket edge. His bulk shifted the whole basket. "Makes you think about life in America as not being so bad, huh? All the misery we've seen and been through is nothing compared to what those people down there have lived for three generations. It's all they know—fear, starvation, and spiritual darkness."

"A year ago, we were both still in prison. Can you believe this? I would've never thought we'd be in North Korea within a year of getting out. And in a matter of hours, we could be standing before the throne of heaven."

"Could be," Job agreed. "But before we run off and get ourselves killed, let's try to send Jin and her baby off to safety, huh?"

An hour passed during which the two rehearsed their landing and checked their gear for the tenth time. Unlike Donny, Shorty, and Spider, who'd entered the country with no gear, Chevy and Job had gear to spare—enough for all five, if they met up as planned some-where in the city.

Two more hours passed, and Chevy felt a twinge of anxiety in his belly. If they had launched the balloon too late from sea, then they'd be floating over Pyongyang in the sunshine, for the whole nation to see! As it was, they'd moved up their schedule by two days due to a communique Nathan said they'd received from inside North Korea. In three more days, a war could possibly start. If they waited any longer to get Jin out, they'd all be stuck inside North Korea, and maybe killed by the air strikes.

With three hours of darkness remaining, both men finally spotted the city lights of Pyongyang far to the east.

"It's too far," Chevy said. "We're moving too slowly. The air is so still."

"Can you make us go faster?" Job asked.

"You mean like flap my arms or something?" Chevy laughed. "I don't think that'll work, but I'm as new at this as you are."

"If we can't go faster, then we're going the right speed."

Tensely, they edged closer to the lights. With one hour before daybreak, they passed over the first lights on the outskirts of the city. The Taedong River was a black avenue splitting the city in two.

"Can you hit that?" Job pointed at the river. "We're at six hundred feet."

"Yeah, I can hit it. Hold on. I'm not going to burn again until we're over the river bank."

The balloon began to drop more swiftly the longer Chevy withheld adding more hot air. From so high up, both men pointed out landmarks they recognized from maps and satellite shots.

"There's the Revolutionary Site!" Chevy announced. "We're still too far downriver."

"Central District is coming up. Look, to the north. Moran Hill is all lit up with the Arch of Triumph and the stadium. I think our angle is okay."

"Job, look!" Chevy pointed straight down. "The Palace!"

Both men leaned over the basket as the roof of the Palace of Remembrance passed mere feet beneath them. The wind was moving them east-by-northeast, so they didn't have time to gaze long. Chevy gave a three second burn to lift over what looked like park trees at the river's edge, then Job knelt on the basket floor to fit a CO_2 canister to the valve of a raft.

"We're over the river!" Chevy whispered harshly. "Hang on!"

But there was no hanging on for Job. He was gathering gear to throw it overboard with the raft at the last second.

"We're feet away!" Chevy said. "Oh, this is gonna be cold!"

As planned, seconds before the balloon skidded across the surface of the water, Chevy pulled on the gas and hooked a loop in the line around a knob on the basket wall. The balloon reacted slowly to its burn as Job tumbled overboard with a splash, and Chevy dove out of the basket an instant later.

The chill of the water took Chevy's breath away, even though he was wearing a dry suit. He surfaced, gasping and splashing, trying to orient himself. Job caught his arm and drew him to the raft. But for a moment, Chevy didn't climb into the raft. He searched the sky, then found it. The balloon was nearly invisible as it lifted quickly, stuck on burn until it would run out of fuel. It passed over the light on top of the Tower of Juche, then continued to rise out of sight.

"We're drifting downriver!" Job warned, and helped Chevy into the raft.

Two short paddles gave them propulsion toward the west shore, but Chevy could feel the current pulling them south. He recited the names of the four bridges that spanned between the Central District and East Pyongyang. Chongryu Bridge in the north, then Rungra, Okryu, and finally, Taedong. Each bridge was designed differently, and he'd memorized their appearances for the landmarks they were.

"We're between the Okryu and the Taedong," he said.

"That's good, right?" Job was winded, but he didn't stop paddling.

Dawn painted the horizon.

"Yes, that's good. Except we're still outside, and we're two white boys in the middle of North Korea. That's bad. It'll be full-on daylight in ten minutes!"

They paddled across the current toward three thirty-foot boats tied to the bank, facing upriver. Chevy aimed at the middle boat and dug deep with the paddle. Pictures hadn't done justice to how wide the river was. Frantically, he studied the boat hulls for a fiery cross emblem. It was the middle boat, he realized, which was a type of platform-keel hybrid for tourists on top, with living quarters below. On its bow, there was a fiery cross painted in gold and black.

Chevy dropped his paddle in the raft and hopped onto the deck of the boat. Though he and Job had rehearsed every move they made, nothing could have prepared Chevy for the cold, the fear, and the exhilaration of the actual mission being played out. But there was no time to think!

From the raft, Job shoved two bags of gear up to Chevy, and Chevy slid each onto the deck. Finally, Chevy caught Job's hand and helped the older, heavier man onto the boat. They both reached back and released two air valves on the raft, rather than deflate it with knives, in case they needed it again. Once deflated, Job hastily rolled the raft into a bundle the size of a pillow.

The sky was blue. They were out of time. Chevy grabbed one bag of gear and dragged it after Job, who was dragging the other. Together, they entered the pilot house and closed the door after them. Panting, they leaned against one another, chuckling a little to release tension from the danger they'd averted.

A wooden door opened from a narrow companionway that led below deck. An elderly Asian woman's face appeared. Chevy and Job froze.

"Maybe we got the wrong boat?" Job said.

"No," the woman said in fair English. "You are welcome here. I am Yellow Bird. I have been waiting for you for weeks."

Leaving their bags in the pilot house for the moment, Chevy and Job squeezed and ducked low to descend the stairs to the low-roofed cabin.

"I've been in cells bigger than this," Chevy whispered to Job.

Besides the first woman, two middle-aged Koreans stared at them from the other end of the room. Chevy wondered if he and Job were the first Americans the man and wife had seen. Casting aside all social protocol he'd been taught in San Diego, Job lumbered forward and embraced the man who stood in what seemed like terror and shock. Then, Job turned and embraced the wife.

"Please excuse us," Chevy said to the first woman, who looked more Chinese than Korean. "We've worked hard to get here this morning."

The woman held out her arms and Chevy gave her a tight hug. Job seemed to have started a new greeting in Korea.

San Diego

Titus sat on a soft chair in the living room of their house at the edge of downtown San Diego. He needed to take a break from assembling bed frames and moving boxes into the attic. Since he had very few possessions of his own, he puzzled over Annette's need to have shipped dozens of boxes of belongings from New York, only to put them into storage. She'd given several boxes to the nearest shelter, but by Titus' estimation, it wasn't nearly enough. Perhaps it had something to do with her feeling at home, he thought, which he hadn't appreciated since he'd been a teen, so he simply did what Annette wanted him to do. Besides, all of this should've been done weeks before, but he'd been consumed with work at the COIL training center.

He'd arrived from Japan the day before, but Oleg had remained on call in Akita for a few more days. In months past, Titus had tasked a COIL tech with the job of duplicating the first COIL sat-watch. The differences between the original watch that Nathan had, and the duplicate on Titus' wrist, was that this one was silver instead of black, and it only received a signal. It didn't send data or coordinate the Gabriel drones in any way. From his living room, Titus studied his watch to see what image it mirrored from Nathan's position in North Korea. He guessed Corban, Luigi, and Marc Densort were all following Nathan's progress, too, but on computer screens.

The team had made landfall a few miles inland from the coast. Now on foot, Nathan's team was making good time, with two days left to arrive at the prison. Meanwhile, there was no way to track Chevy and Job, unless they called in on the sat-phone at their first safe house on the river. But Titus was supposed to be domesticating, according to Corban's orders, so he wouldn't pry too much into the mission status by contacting Marc Densort.

"Levi's home, Titus," Annette called from their home office room, then she came into the living room. "He just pulled up on his bike. Reveal things to him gently, would you? What you've told me is hard enough for me to accept, and I'm a follower of Christ. It won't be easy for him to swallow what you're about to tell him, especially while he's still hesitating to surrender his life to God."

"We'll talk it out." Titus rose from the chair, not too disappointed to escape from box duty. "Be back around sundown."

He plucked his Mustang keys from her fingers, kissed her on the cheek, and opened the door as Levi was reaching for the handle. Titus took one look at the youth's red eye, fat lip, and torn shirt, and knew the youth had been in a fight. He closed the door before Annette had a chance to see the condition of her son.

"Let me see your hands," Titus said, not moving from the doorstep.

Levi held up his hands, which Titus turned over to examine his knuckles. The skin was broken and red over both fists. He dropped the boy's hands and looked into his eyes. There was shame and concern in his young, battered face.

"I see what happened to you," Titus said quietly, not wanting to bring Annette into the matter yet. That would come soon enough. "How about the other guy?"

"There were two of them." Levi's gaze fell. "Both seniors."

"This isn't cool, Levi. God made us Casperteins too strong to get into petty fights that can hurt people permanently. Come on. We're going for a drive."

Together, they climbed into the Mustang and drove away. Instead of turning right to race out of town to the training center, Titus turned left toward the waterfront.

"What was it over?" Titus asked.

"A girl. A sophomore."

"What a surprise."

"He made her cry, so I got involved. Then another guy jumped in."

"We can't solve problems with our fists, Levi."

"I didn't put my fists on them, not even once."

"Your knuckles say otherwise."

"That's from when they knocked me onto the pavement. They tried to stomp me out, Dad. But I grabbed onto them one at a time. I used the submission holds you and Oleg and the KONs taught me. I might look beat up, but I put them to sleep without hitting them once."

"You're serious?"

"And I asked the girl out."

Titus shook his head, trying his best not to laugh.

"Well, you're definitely a Caspertein." Titus sighed. "We have a tendency for trouble, and God makes sure we take our lumps to keep us humble, but if you do the right thing by Him, you'll come out all right."

"And I got the girl." Levi sat proudly in the passenger seat.

"You may have gotten the girl, but you'll have a lot of explaining to do to another girl when we get home."

"Annette? I mean, Mom?"

"Exactly. And somehow I think she'll blame me for this."

They drove down to Seaport Village on Harbor Drive and stopped in front of the Convention Center, which was in the process of renovation. Scaffolding littered the outer wall, and plastic tarps flapped in the breeze from the roof. Titus shut off the Mustang engine, but he didn't open the door.

"I have to tell you something." Titus gripped the steering wheel tightly. "If what I tell you doesn't happen, then we can forget this conversation. But I know something of villains, and evil, and the prophesies of the Bible. We may be days or weeks away, Levi, from some sort of world-wide calamity, and COIL operatives who you know are in the middle of it all inside North Korea."

"What's happening?" Levi turned in his seat. "Is that why you didn't go on the mission with the others? You're too valuable because you know too much?"

"No, I would've rather gone, and I'm not that valuable. Like you, I don't mind a little battering if it's for a good cause, especially for Jesus Christ and His people. It seems to be the Caspertein way, now."

"I don't understand. What else is happening in North Korea? There's nothing on the regular news about anything. And I listened to the briefings before you guys left for Japan. It's just a rescue, right?"

"While I was still in Japan, we heard word from a source inside the country that forced COIL to move up our rescue of Rea and Jin. We think North Korea will be attacking America in the next couple days. It'll change our world."

"But, we're the United States. I mean, we can use lasers or something to shoot down any missiles they fire."

"We're confident we can." Titus nodded. "I think that's part of the problem. We in America are too confident, and for a long time, we've boasted in everything we can do. But it may not be true. North Korea knows we can intercept a percentage of their missiles, and we'll try, if our defense system isn't all hype. But that's why I think North Korea is up to something. All this nuclear missile testing for years and now their sudden interest in peace—it seems to be a smoke screen for something else. North Koreans are out of touch, but they aren't stupid. The dictator has remained in power for years while others have wanted him gone. That means he's crafty, and we still know very little about him. I think he's using everything we don't know against us, even drawing us into peace talks like everything is okay. I'm just suspicious."

"Well, what could happen?" Levi looked down at his scabbed knuckles. "I'm just fourteen."

"I know, but you'll need to become a man, I think, sooner than expected. And I have no doubt you'll do well. We need to keep your mother safe, and we need to remain self-sufficient so we can help others who need help."

"Does Mom know about this?"

"I've explained everything to her so that she understands why we Casperteins have to get ready. That's why you and I are here tonight."

"At the Convention Center? This is where I learned to skateboard."

Titus climbed out of the car and used a key to enter a maintenance door to the Convention Center. There was more scaffolding inside, and Titus stepped past equipment to an empty space on the floor.

"You can never bring anyone here, but if something happens to me, you need to know about this." Titus pointed at the floor. "This. It's a trapdoor. While this place was being remodeled, I decided to hide my own little stash in plain sight."

Titus used the keys to pry up part of the dusty panel to expose a vaulted door beneath.

"I have safes, accounts, armories, and weapon caches all over the world. This is my latest one in San Diego."

"Mom always said you were a famous smuggler."

"Before I came to Christ, I used all these sites for my own purposes." He punched a code into the vault door. "Now, I use them for God's purposes. I'm hoping you'll do the same."

"Can you tell me the code?"

"Of course. It's your name, numerically. L-E-V-I. Each letter is assigned a number sequence, so you'll never forget. A is one, B is two. So the code is twelve, five, twenty-two, and nine. Help me. This is heavy. Oleg was here with me last time, and we both know he's strong enough to do this on his own, but your old man is, well, getting older."

Together, they swung open the vaulted door, which exposed a set of stairs into darkness. Titus led the way down, and picked up a flashlight from a shelf. When he turned it on, he revealed a corridor along the Convention Center's outer wall. The corridor was lined with shelves and racks of army surplus, survival supplies, and short, bulky rifles—the NL-X2.

"You're already familiar with the battle rifle. I've stockpiled all these just in case we need them during whatever scenario plays out around here. They're a tough rifle, compact, and have superior range to anything on the market."

"It's enough for an army!"

"Well, they were meant for COIL operatives going on missions, and for training, but now I'm putting them in storage down here. I've also shipped two more crates—one to Colorado to your Uncle Rudy, and one to Corban's place in New York. Look here. These rifles take three types of ammunition—regular metal jacket .308 cartridges for deer hunting, and these over here are the gel-tranqs that you've been shooting at the COIL training range. I have them in several calibers."

"I know the .22 caliber!" Levi felt his shoulder and grimaced. "I'll never forget that feeling. I talked to Jenna on the phone. She's still bruised! What are these over here?"

He touched a shelf that held dozens of slick black containers.

"This is another type of ammunition, called phosphorus. Basically, it burns through anything, like acid does. It's deadly stuff, Levi. Pray we never need to use it. Corban wants me to destroy all of it, but I think he'll come around."

Titus watched Levi wander down the corridor as long as a basketball court, using another flashlight to examine all the different types of gear.

"So, you think we'll need all this stuff?" Levi walked back to his father. "I thought you believed in God and stuff. You said prophecy, so, like, the apocalypse is coming, and all that, right?"

"I trust God with my eternal soul and I want Him to live through me daily." Titus picked a battle rifle off the rack. "This rifle has already saved lives internationally. It was designed as a non-lethal alternative to keep bad guys alive while we rescue the persecuted. What I'm telling you is this: we're ready if we become the persecuted right here at home in America. If that happens, yes, it'll seem like some sort of apocalypse."

"But I'm not a Christian. I'm reading the Bible you gave me, and it's interesting, but I'm still not sure about all of it."

"That's something we can keep talking about." Titus smiled and replaced the rifle on the shelf. "For now, you simply need to know where this place is. Come on."

They climbed out of the storage bunker.

"Where are we going now?"

"To the training gym at the COIL facility. We were going to lift weights, but seeing that you're into saving the honor of weepy sophomores, I should probably teach you some more submission holds."

"I thought the world was ending."

They reached the car. Titus checked his watch and noted that Nathan and the team were making good time through the mountains of North Korea.

"The world is ending, Levi. Every passing minute, we're getting closer to the day Jesus Christ returns for His people. That doesn't mean we stop preparing in case we're around for a little longer than we expected. We need to be good stewards of our time and resources, and all the things God gives us to use to honor Him and to care for others."

"How real is this, Dad? Some of it sounds, I don't know, made up."

Father and son's eyes locked over the roof of the car.

"It's real, son. I just don't know in what form it'll come. Believe me, I wish I were wrong. I wish I could travel the world with you and take you to places your mom and I have visited. I wish I could take you to meet amazing men and women of God in distant lands. I wish you could see the look on a Christian's face when you save him from a Saudi Arabian sword, or from a prison cell where he's been condemned to rot. I wish we could go to Israel together and stand with the Israelites against enemies who've sworn to wipe them out."

"Israel? Mom told me that's where you two met."

"It is where we met, but I don't think you'll see any of those things, because we'll be busy surviving right here in this very city."

"Why doesn't anyone else know all this? How come no one else is getting ready?"

"They don't want to know what's happening. They're enjoying their lives too much, Levi. Oh, I wish I were wrong, but it's my business to gauge these kinds of threats. When things fall apart, this city will need us. It'll need you. Sometimes, it ain't easy being a Caspertein."

CHAPTER NINE

Pyongyang, North Korea

Yuriy Usik wondered what it was like to die. He'd seen many people die, and he'd killed many. It shocked him now to think that in all the years of his fascination with suffering and torture, he'd never wondered what death held for him, or what followed death.

Sitting in his dungeon office, he found himself grumbling aloud about the aging Chinese woman at the river. He liked her immensely, her sincerity and boldness, her direct words spoken without a hint of malice toward him. But she was a Christian, one of the heaven people! She wasn't loyal to the *Juche* idea. Her heart and life weren't dedicated to the people's revolution in *Choson* and abroad.

For days, Yuriy hadn't interrogated anyone. He saw no point in it now, not if they were all about to die in an air strike from American missiles. Though he was expected to deliver Jin and her baby by the following day, he hadn't made a single arrangement.

The Palace guards had been whispering about him. He'd heard them. News about his procrastination and withdrawal may have already reached the regime's eager ears. The ruthless work he'd been doing for so many years, without question or flinching—he'd stopped. There were officials who feared him, since he was a brutal, ambitious man, so they would be eager to see him removed and executed. After all, he was a foreigner.

Underneath it all, there were the words of the woman at the river. Her words haunted his soul and troubled his spirit. She knew him completely, he felt, and for that he was ashamed. He was an intimidating official, and she was a poor citizen who lived on a weathered, tiny boat. What did she have to offer him or anyone else?

He opened the file on his desk. It was Han Ji-Jin's file. There was no fire inside him any longer to see her suffer, nor any of the other nine hundred prisoners in the Palace dungeon. His heart sank at the hopelessness they must have felt. If they didn't die by his hammer in his office, then they would be maimed for life and shipped off to work to death at one of the labor camps spread across the country in the north.

They would all die. He would die. Everyone would die. His eyes widened. There were no exceptions! Death was guaranteed. But the woman at the river had implied an answer to death, or after death, or a payment for death that might rescue him from death's grip or the fear of death. In his sleep-deprived, anxious mind, he couldn't remember what the answer was. God had something to do with it. That was all he knew. For years, his god had been the dictator, even if he was just playing a role to live his life his way. He wondered if maybe he'd made a god of himself, placing his satisfaction and pleasures before all others. None of this could be too pleasing to the real God, he guessed.

Death had to be appeased in some way, he decided, and he rose to his feet. Sacrificing Jin's baby wouldn't appease death. No, there was some other metaphysical way to placate death's hungry demands, and he needed to hear it explained by the woman at the river, lest he make an irreversible mistake in his zeal to preserve himself.

He opened his office door and found four guards standing idly in the corridor. They straightened up and saluted.

"Keep the prisoners fed," he ordered, "and wait for my orders. The Supreme Commander is about to make an important pronouncement against the enemy."

That would pacify them for another day, he decided, and marched past them to the elevator that led up to the Palace main floor. As controlled as North Korea was, it hungered for gossip, Yuriy realized, like any other people. The country was already awash with rumors of three American defectors, men who had embarrassed the United States severely, then had fled to North Korea where they would be safe from American prosecution. Yuriy understood that the regime was spinning everything in its favor for the baby's public execution and missile strike the following day.

Outside, Yuriy marched quickly toward the river under the afternoon's overcast sky. Military vehicles were about, even more than normal, and Yuriy knew what that suggested, even if the people thought it was business as usual. Following years of vocal taunts at America, and on the eve of its attack, North Korea was moving with secret precision. After all, the whole world believed the country had conceded to international sanctions.

Yuriy was nearly to the trees by the river when two vehicles raced toward him on Sungri Street. He glanced left and saw four soldiers walking briskly toward him—and four more on his right.

It seemed so absurd that they would come for him like this that he stopped in the middle of the street and waited for them all to pass him by. Instead, one soldier drew a baton and swung it at his mid-section. Yuriy backed away and drew his hammer. Two vehicles parked in the street, and suddenly the whole unit of soldiers was upon him, grabbing his arms, pinning him down on the pavement.

He didn't cry out as his arms were bound and his head was hooded. This was how traitors were arrested. Though he'd not yet acted against the regime directly, he'd most certainly been monitored by his own guards for the security of party officials. His quota of interrogations had vanished in number since hearing about the missile launch, and he'd made no move to induce labor for Jin's baby for the following day. His lack of cooperation made him a liability, he knew. And now, he would be replaced. It had happened hundreds of times before— maybe thousands of times.

As he was stuffed into one of the vehicles, he thought of the Chinese woman at the river, Yellow Bird. He'd nearly reached her, but now he would never know the answer to his question about death— how was death appeased? His depression weighed even more, and the brutal Yuriy Usik wept quietly for himself. The heaven people had known something all this time, and he'd tortured them instead of listening to them.

Donny Walters didn't know what day it was. Maybe it had been three days since coming to North Korea. Maybe it had been ten. The questioning, the sleeplessness, and the drugs they'd given him had completely thrown off his grasp for how much time had lapsed.

But as he woke in a plain bedroom with only a bed in it, he remained perfectly still while he gathered his wits. He didn't know what he may have confessed under drug-induced interrogation, but he wasn't yet in a labor camp, so that was a good sign. And the drugs seemed to be out of his system now.

He was fairly certain he was still in or around Pyongyang, since he couldn't recall traveling far from the airport. There'd been no sign of Shorty or Spider since they'd been strip-searched on arrival. During the marathon questioning, he hadn't been able to focus on much except what questions he was being asked. By the grace of God, he seemed to have retained his cover.

"My life is in Your hands, Lord," he whispered under the covers. "No one and nothing can remove me from Your hand. I am loved by You forever. For ages upon ages for all eternity, I am Your child. Your grace is sufficient even in my loneliness and despair. I will not be ashamed. You will never leave me nor forsake me. Give me courage to live well and to die well, and to bring You glory."

His bedroom door opened, and An Sum-Mi stood in her slacks and plain blouse—either the same ones she'd worn on another day, or she had many exactly like them. The daylight that shined through the bedroom windows illumined her blemish-free skin, and the woman seemed quite pretty, but Donny was aware that everything around him could be a test and a trap. Anything that seemed nice or strong about North Korea, he'd learned, was just a facade.

Fully clothed in the scratchy material, he sat up in bed.

"Good morning, Comrade," she said with a bright smile. "You have the honor of waking in the illustrious Ryugyong Hotel. Come. Look! The whole city is before you. It is a great day. Tomorrow, I am told there will be a national celebration, and you will be an honored guest. See, it is already evening. There is much to do to prepare."

Donny walked weakly to the floor-to-ceiling windows and looked out upon the City of Pyongyang. His body needed much recovery from the last few days, but they had at least not physically tortured him. They'd wanted to be certain he was not an infiltrator, and though he had a good cover and had claimed to be loyal to the Juche idea, they would certainly still be suspicious of him for months.

"It's beautiful," he said, but not from the heart.

Instead, he used the view to orient himself. He was indeed in Pyongyang. There was the Taedong River winding around the Central District. Though he couldn't see the boat or boats on the river, he could see the Taedong and Okryu Bridges, and he imagined Chevy and Job hiding near there, preparing.

Then his eyes drifted west from the river to the grand People's Palace of Remembrance. Its roof was unmistakable. Jin was there, yet he was far from her.

"What day is it?" He tried to disguise his anxiety.

She told him, and he quickly did the math, accounting for the lost time while drugged and delirious. He'd been in the country for four days. That meant he'd come to his wits in time, barely. *A national celebration tomorrow?* Then, Jin must have had her baby already. They were about to execute it. And the news of a missile launch, having reached them before leaving Japan, was somehow connected to the celebration.

That night, he would need to apply all the training he'd received, but he'd never felt less capable.

"May I eat something?" He turned from the window.

"Of course." An Sum-Mi smiled and stepped closer to him. "But first, here is your pledge of loyalty to the Supreme Commander of the *Juche* idea. You are now a member of the Party. Congratulations, Comrade!"

She carefully attached a pin to his shirt over his heart. It was red, white, and black, with the images of the dictator's father and grandfather.

Donny admired it briefly, trying to act proud that he'd been given the token, but he was thinking about the way many Christians in North Korea viewed the pin. New followers of Christ often refused to wear the pin any longer, since it represented loyalty to a false god. But those who refused to wear the pin, even to follow the God of the Bible, were instead sent to the labor camps, along with their children and their parents, where they were worked to death.

Though Donny hated the pin on his chest, for him, it was a means to an end, and he hoped that after sundown, he no longer had to impersonate a loyal Party member.

"Are my companions well?" He smiled as pleasantly as he could. After all, he'd been given asylum in North Korea. "The journey here hasn't been pleasant, but we all wish to celebrate together."

"Of course." She gestured to the hallway. "Come with me. I will be your guide both today and through tomorrow, during the celebration."

"Wonderful."

Donny followed her out of the room, interpreting her words for himself. After the celebration, there would be no need to keep a government escort on him and his friends, because North Korea would be a battlefield. That was, if the United States indeed retaliated with a missile strike once North Korea launched its own missiles.

Two guards awaited him in the hallway and accompanied him to a freight elevator. The dirty cement floor of the "hotel" confirmed everything Donny had learned about the city's most iconic landmark. It had been built to be the tallest hotel in the world, with three revolving restaurants at its triangular peak. But economic crisis had halted its construction midway. The building had been left exposed to the elements, weakening its infrastructure to the point that a highly qualified European Union inspector had deemed the structure irreparable. The official noted that certain crooked elevator shafts was an example of the terribly-constructed embarrassment.

As the freight elevator descended with jerky movements, Donny acknowledged the empty building where even some of the walls were incomplete. It was a condemned building now, apparently used only as an isolated location to interrogate foreign defectors.

The elevator stopped, and the cage door opened to Shorty and Spider, accompanied by two guards each. His two friends smiled broadly.

"Hello, sleepyhead!" Spider greeted as they walked into the elevator. "We were wondering when you would wake up."

They shook hands briefly, and Donny intentionally withheld his inner delight at the fact that they all wore the political party pins, meaning they'd passed at least the initial screening of acceptance into the country. Since he was the last to come to his senses, Donny wondered if his interrogators had given him more serum than they'd given their other two guests, and if he'd gone through more in depth questioning.

The elevator continued to descend.

"We're going to eat," Shorty informed. "Can you believe we're finally here?"

"It's spectacular," Donny said. "It's like living a dream."

But he understood that every word they spoke was measured and not merely conversation. Their words were laced with information for one another. What was spectacular was that they were all still together to perform the operation. On the surface, they meant to show a loyal front for the six guards and their pretty government escort. But below the surface, they needed to carefully coordinate their escape and evasion into the city. All their training had been for this one purpose.

Besides the boat at the river, there were two more Christian safe houses on the west side of the river. Chevy and Job would be making their move toward the Palace before midnight. If Donny and his companions made their move any later, the three of them would miss the rescue op altogether, and they'd need to focus on escaping the city to the evacuation point.

"We are going to Songyo Restaurant," An Sum-Mi said as the elevator reached the bottom of over one hundred floors. "At the restaurant, you will each review your speeches for the celebration tomorrow."

"We're giving speeches already?" Spider asked. "I'm not really ready for that kind of thing."

"Oh, the Pyongyang Party Committee already wrote your speeches. You have only to read them aloud. It will be wonderful."

"Just read them, huh? That makes things simple." Donny clapped Spider on the back, as if to say, *Just go with it. We'll either be gone or dead by tomorrow, anyway.*

Songyo Restaurant was across the river, and Donny looked casually off the Taedong Bridge as they crossed it in two vehicles. A number of boats were tied to the west bank far below. At a passing glance, it was impossible to see which one Chevy and Job might be hiding in, if they had survived their insertion at all.

Sundown was approaching, and Donny prayed for calm. Shorty and Spider were being model guests, asking An Sum-Mi questions that urged her to boast about the country's greatness, which was actually sub-par to most third world countries, but the North Koreans were brainwashed to think otherwise.

At the restaurant, which was empty of patrons except for themselves, they were served two dishes, *Pyongyang onban*, which was cooked rice topped with mushrooms and chicken, and *bindaetteok*, which were pancakes made from ground mung beans and vegetables. It was just what Donny needed to recover his energy for the eventful night ahead, but his nerves were so jumpy, he had no appetite as An Sum-Mi presented their speeches on paper. Donny nodded and agreed with her points, while he force-fed his mouth. He wondered if Shorty and Spider were feeling the same nervous anticipation for the night as well.

It was now dark outside, and though they were on the wrong side of the river, the Taedong Bridge and the boats would be within view if they stepped outside to the street. The time to make their move was already upon them.

Their speeches were attempts at boasting in the might of North Korea, and they were to deliver them to over one hundred thousand people at the May Day Stadium on Rungna Island north of the city, at noon tomorrow. One at a time, the men rehearsed their speeches aloud.

Spider's speech emphasized America's corrupt and weak military, and how the North Korean soldiers were far superior. Shorty's speech spewed hatred about American intellectuals and self-centered farmers, but North Korea's scholars were smarter, and its farmers were generous, because plentiful food overflowed miraculously for the citizens who were most loyal to the Supreme Commander.

Finally, Donny's speech was to focus on American capitalism, its greed, and inferiority to North Korea's unity and wealth. He was disgusted by the lies and manipulation in each speech. Yes, America had its share of immoral rot that seemed to be growing, but America had also been the vehicle by which God had reached nations with His Word and brought many children to Himself. America's laws, though sometimes twisted for harm, were designed for the sake of liberty and justice for all. Not like the totalitarian oppression and state-regulated existence in North Korea, built around a single dynasty of absolutism.

The speeches were to be read as declarations, the woman said to them all, and Donny understood that the power of the words would be that much more poignant against America since the three of them had once been Americans.

From everything Donny had learned about North Korea, the quantity of food they were fed at the restaurant was rare—enough for a large family to eat for a week. The man-made famine in the country was widespread, and even Pyongyang's elite were being forced to resort to smaller portions. As such, only Donny, Shorty, and Spider ate as the guards and An Sum-Mi looked on, sometimes with wistful glances. But when the monitors noticed they were being watched, they gave stoic smiles. At the moment, it was in the Party's interest that the three ex-Americans gave an impression of strength, and that required that some starved that day.

To reject the food would've been disrespectful, so all three ate, mostly to maintain the facade, but also for the nourishment after the days of questioning with little food.

As their meal concluded, Shorty sighed loudly and sat back, rubbing his belly.

"Yes, it will be nice," he said, "to get a good night of sleep and have the celebration tomorrow."

"Here, here." Donny raised his glass. There was no ice in his water, but the water wasn't bad tasting, just tepid. "To tomorrow!"

Spider raised his glass as well.

So, everyone was agreed, Donny thought. Their toast was a sort of rally. They needed to make their move soon. Jin was waiting.

Hamgyong Province, North Korea

Nathan Isaacson lay on his belly next to Scooter as they gazed through their night vision rifle scopes at the prison below. They were a quarter-mile away from the prison, on the mountain ridge that ran adjacent to the prison.

"It's dark enough." Scooter swung his scope across the fenced area. "I've never seen a prison this size. You?"

"This whole country's a prison." Nathan focused on the nearest perimeter tower. "We have a good plan, but now that we're about to do this, I don't like the idea of leaving Chen Li and the girls in the towers. They look flimsy."

"The women?" Scooter asked, obviously joking, even at a time like that.

"No, the towers." Nathan turned up his scope magnification, trying to get a closer look. "We couldn't have known from satellite photos that the siding on those towers would be nothing more than some flimsy plywood. If there's gunfire, bullets will just pass clean through them."

"Don't tell Chloe you're second-guessing her ability to withstand a little gunfire." Scooter chuckled. "You seem to forget she was Mossad for over a decade. She's been trained to attack people in more ways than either of us. When they get into the towers, they'll know to reinforce the two sides that might take gunfire. Are we moving out or what?"

Nathan didn't answer for a moment. The last few days since leaving the DRIL, had been brutal on all of them. Cold days and freezing nights. And marching up and down endless mountainsides.

"We're moving. If we sit and wait any longer, we'll freeze to death." Nathan turned his head to look at Scooter's smaller frame in the starlight. "Let's pray the KONs are moving right now, too, because this country is about to explode—and I'm not just talking about whatever missiles are supposedly being launched tomorrow."

"Okay. I'll round them up."

Scooter backed away on his hands and knees, but Nathan remained on his belly on the frozen ground, studying the prison. It was a city enclosed by an electric fence, self-contained and self-sufficient, with farm fields, mines, sawmill, leather shops, and other unidentifiable buildings.

In the southeast corner, he located the detention building, where Rea was supposed to be held. The building appeared small, but Corban's intel said that, between the two floors, it was a two-thousand-square-foot building. It had no windows and appeared to be made of wood. Almost all the buildings were wood, except for the prisoner dorms in the northern half of the prison, which were made of mud.

The administration building was next to the detention building. It was five times larger, and looked like a log hunting lodge, complete with upper-level bay windows and two balconies.

Someone bumped Nathan's elbow. It was Chloe, belly-crawling up for a view. She held her battle rifle, but on her back was a .22 rifle with a silencer attached to its barrel.

"No lights on the fence line," she said. "That's good for us, but who doesn't keep their perimeter lit up?"

"They don't expect anything like us to approach them, and all their power is probably diverted to that electric fence."

"I'm just saying." She shrugged. "They're making our job easier."

"Easier?" Nathan growled. "Remind me of that if we have to get into a gun battle with over a thousand guards. Besides, you're not one of the ones who has to climb across a line hanging over that buzzing fence."

"Even if they do catch on to us, they won't know what hit them." She patted him on the shoulder. "Don't you have somewhere to be?"

"I'm going." But he didn't move. He checked his sat-watch for a three-dimensional view of their location. There were no vehicles approaching the prison. Nothing but an occasional lonely animal, or heat signatures like deer, seemed to be bedded down around them in the mountains. Not even the train from up north was on its approach quite yet. "Nothing's moving around us. Just some deer."

"Of course there's nothing around us. It's twenty degrees out here." Chloe laughed quietly, exasperated. "Are you stalling, or what?"

"Of course I'm stalling! I want this to be perfect."

"You haven't changed." She shook her head. "All these years, you're still just a big kid."

"Not true. I have changed." He covered his scope with lens protectors as he prepared to leave. "Chen Li says I got fat."

"Yeah, right!" She laughed almost too loud. "Just go, would you? We're in God's hands here."

"See you in a couple hours."

He patted her arm, then crawled back to the others, who were crouching on the snowy mountain slope. June blew on her mitten-covered hands and Heather rubbed warmth into her arms, but the rest of the operatives were motionless warriors, hungry for action.

"It's time," he said to Bruno and Memphis. "Let's roll out. Scooter, don't miss the train."

"You got it, Eagle Eyes." Scooter saluted and shouldered an NL-X1 sniper rifle. He was staying on the ridge to cover everyone with his rifle, accurate up to a thousand yards. "'To live is Christ, to die is gain.'"

Nathan kissed his wife on the cheek. They'd said their verbal good-byes earlier that evening as they'd waited for the cover of darkness. He shouldered his gear and, at a brisk walk, led the way north. Memphis followed close behind him, and Bruno brought up the rear. As large as Bruno was, his footfalls were as quiet as a man who wore moccasins.

Happy to finally be moving, Nathan picked up the pace to warm his limbs. He'd seen battle as a Marine, fighting desert enemies he couldn't always identify. But this night, his enemy was well-known, well-studied, identifiable, and about to be caught sleeping. Good odds!

When the unit of three came out of the mountains, they were a mile north of the others, but they were still alongside the prison's perimeter fence. They could see the sooty mountainside deeper inside where, even from space, the coal mine was visible. It had claimed thousands of prisoner lives, yet still remained in operation sixteen hours a day, all week long.

Memphis climbed a rocky outcropping above the road outside the fence, where the road carved away part of the mountainside. He aimed a crossbow with a grappling hook, angled it toward the sky, then fired it over both fences at a tall, gnarled pine tree fifty feet away, inside the perimeter fence.

Below, Nathan and Bruno covered the fence line, aiming their rifles north and south, ready to engage any enemy who wandered past.

"Line feels secure," Memphis said on his comm. "Driving it home."

A moment later, Nathan glanced up at Memphis as he used a rubber mallet to pound two mountain climbing stakes into the rock above.

"We're crossing the fence now," Nathan announced over his comm to the two teams of women and Scooter a mile to the south. "Anything moving?"

"Nothing new," Scooter reported. "Chloe and Heather are taking Tower One."

Nathan watched as Memphis slid hand over hand up the cable. The cable bowed dangerously toward the top wire of the electrified fence, but Memphis, being the lightest of the three of them, cleared the razor wire coils by six inches.

Once Memphis was over the two fences and inside the perimeter, he continued up the cable to the heights of the pine tree, where he tightened and better secured the cable around the tree.

"Go," Bruno said, tapping Nathan on the shoulder.

While scampering up the rock, Nathan was still waiting for a report from Scooter. Had Chloe taken the tower assigned to her and Heather? If they failed to silently tranquilize the two guards there, the rest of the rescue was jeopardized.

He took off his pack and fastened one strap onto the cable, then another to his ankle. Since his hands were gloved, the almost invisible cable didn't cut into his palms as he took hold and threw his feet over the line. Hand over hand, faster than Memphis had gone, Nathan moved above the road, crossed the fences with feet to spare, and reached the tree. All the while, his pack was towed behind, attached to his ankle. At the tree, Memphis took hold of Nathan, unfastened the pack, and handed it to Nathan.

"Go," Memphis said. "I've got Bruno."

Nathan climbed down the tree carefully, from a height of around fifty feet, and leaned against the base of the pine, his rifle leveled.

"Tower One secure," Scooter finally reported. "Chloe took out both guards with one shot each. Moving on Tower Two."

Managing his breathing, Nathan thanked the Lord for safety so far. Taking the towers to control the prison perimeter was paramount to covering their infiltration. Using the silenced .22 loaded with gel-tranqs had been Chloe's idea, once she drew the two guards out of the tower and into her sights. Now, it was up to Chen Li and June to take Tower Two.

Bruno dropped down beside Nathan five minutes later, and Memphis joined them both in seconds. Together, they studied the sky above the road and fence. The cable was hard to see. A car or truck could even drive under it without ever noticing it was there.

"We're on the ground moving south," Nathan reported.

"Tower Two secured," Scooter responded. "We're ready for you, Eagle Eyes."

Nathan checked his watch for hot spots. No one was north of the prisoner dorms a mile to the south.

"We're clear," he said. "Bruno, take point. Memphis, take our six."

Though they'd rehearsed this arrangement many times, Nathan had found that in the midst of an exhilarating mission, a team leader still needed to keep them alert. With Bruno in the front and Memphis in the back, Nathan could keep tabs on the sat-watch for movement.

The op had gone remarkably well so far, he realized, but he'd never been on a mission where everything had gone as planned. They were about to enter the rows of buildings of the prison proper, and there was no way to plan for what over one thousand guards might do in the middle of the night. Nathan hoped they were all fast asleep, but that was a lot to hope for.

Pyongyang, North Korea

Chevy zipped up his dark coat in the tight living quarters below deck on the tourist boat. In the low candlelight of the cabin, the older woman he knew as Yellow Bird and the two boat owners watched him and Job suit up for their excursion across several blocks of the city to the People's Palace of Remembrance.

Before Chevy and Job's arrival, the three boat inhabitants had dipped into the food rations, so with all five together the last three days, their meals had been light. Chevy and Job had agreed that the couple who lived on the boat had sacrificed enough, and they were taking Yellow Bird with them, rather than leave her behind to wait for another way out of the city. With so many patrols on the river, and with war potentially devastating the region, Yellow Bird had to leave now, or maybe never.

After one final sat-phone call to Marc Densort, Job shoved the phone into a Velcro pocket on Chevy's backpack and chambered a non-lethal round into his battle rifle.

"Ready?" Chevy checked the time. It was after ten o'clock at night. "If we wait any longer, the other three will beat us to the subject."

Yellow Bird embraced the boat hosts, then placed her hand on Chevy's arm. Chevy nodded, understanding the Chinese woman was indicating her readiness and trust. Her clothing seemed in no way able to ward off the bitter winter air outside, but she was a hearty woman who had shared enough stories of daring ministry for Chevy to know she wouldn't be a burden to them. In fact, he hoped she could help them with Jin when the time came.

"Let's go." Chevy climbed the steps to the pilot house. Through the windows, he checked the river, the bridges, and what he could see of the city streets through the park trees. The Taedong Bridge and the Okryu Bridge were experiencing light military traffic, all heading out of the city, east and south.

"They're on the move," Chevy said. "Traffic toward the DMZ. A few foot patrols on the streets. Let's keep it casual. No panic. We're just out for a stroll. Hopefully, we can blend in."

He walked onto the platform of the vessel as Yellow Bird and Job came up behind him. The couple in the cabin below had been told to erase all sign of their presence. Chevy and Job, and even Yellow Bird, had never known their host's names, since it was too dangerous to share them. God knew them and they would be reunited in heaven.

"Okay." Chevy allowed his rifle to hang on its sling until he would need to use it. "Nice and steady."

His pack contained no survival gear, only his half of the contraption meant to fly Jin to safety. Job carried the other half in his pack. They stepped off the boat onto land. Immediately, Chevy resisted the urge to dash for cover when he saw a vehicle drive along the street on the other side of the trees. But running would draw attention, so he spoke quietly to his companions, urging them to remember that from a distance, the three walkers would seem normal. He hoped.

Chevy directed the three of them into the trees as they walked abreast.

Donny sat between Shorty and Spider in the second of two vehicles driving across the Taedong Bridge into the Central District. Though it was after ten o'clock at night, military traffic flowed against them out of the city.

"Everyone is getting ready," An Sum-Mi said from the front passenger seat, "for tomorrow's celebration."

"We are honored to be included." In the cover of darkness, Spider elbowed Donny lightly in the ribs.

The vehicle was nearly to the other side of the bridge. The lead vehicle driving in front of them was filled with their accompanying soldiers.

"Would you like to drive?" Donny softly asked Shorty, since he was behind the driver's seat. "This seems like a manageable time."

"I would be delighted," Shorty answered calmly.

An Sum-Mi turned in her seat and smiled, but Donny guessed she hadn't caught the entirety of their few words. Even if she had, only she and the soldier driver were in the car.

"Sungri Street," Donny said as they drove off the bridge. "Green light."

"Okay." Shorty understood he was to initiate their mission's next phase.

Twenty seconds passed as the vehicle approached the second street from the waterfront. As they reached the intersection, Shorty drew up his short legs on the seat under him, and launched himself over the driver's seat onto the head and shoulders of the driver, entangling the soldier completely.

Simultaneously, Donny and Spider reached for An Sum-Mi. Spider circled an arm around her neck and Donny grappled with her left arm as he fell between the two front seats. The vehicle swerved and a gunshot blasted in Donny's face, causing his ears to ring, but he hadn't been shot—or his adrenalin was so high, he hadn't felt the wound.

Reaching farther across her, he grabbed the woman's other arm and wrenched a small firearm from her hand, which she'd drawn in the scuffle. Spider's chokehold incapacitated her an instant later. Then Donny pressed the gun threateningly against the ribs of the driver, who was losing the wrestling match with Shorty over the steering wheel. The driver surrendered, and Donny and Spider pulled him from the front seat into the back as Shorty took full control of the car.

"Where are we going?" Spider climbed into the front passenger seat as Donny situated both unconscious North Koreans in the back with him. "To the boat or to the art theater? Nothing else is close."

"The art theater." Shorty drove steadily and calmly behind the lead vehicle. If the soldiers in the lead vehicle suspected anything was amiss, they hadn't indicated by their driving. "Get ready. I'm going to swerve off."

At the next intersection, near Pyongyang University of Medicine, Shorty turned the wheel to the right onto Chollima Street, and hit the gas. Spider looked out the back window.

"They'll be coming for us now!" Excitement made Spider's voice tremble. "There's no turning back!"

"We need to dump the car." Donny took off the jacket of the unconscious soldier and handed it to Spider. "Let's get our gear then move on foot to the Palace."

"I'll dump the car," Shorty said. "You guys go ahead."

"No." Spider tugged on the jacket. It was too tight around his chest, but it was more than what he had on to fight off the cold. "We need to stick together until there's a very good reason to split up."

"This is a good reason," Shorty said. "Trust me. We don't have time. I'll lead them on a good chase, maybe even out of the city."

"It seems unnecessary to split up this early," Donny agreed with Spider. "We're barely on our own. Shorty, we need you at the Palace."

The car flew down the street, and at the next available right, Shorty drove east. The Mansudae Art Theater was an L-shaped building several stories tall that loomed on their left.

"Get ready to jump out!" Shorty hit the brakes. "Go!"

Spider didn't argue. The enemy could spot them at any minute. Donny climbed into the front seat to exit through the passenger door. He paused and, with the door light on, looked back at Shorty. Blood soaked his side, from his shoulder down to his hip—a lot of blood.

"I'd wondered where that bullet went," Donny said.

"We underestimated her." Shorty gasped in pain, but kept both hands on the wheel. "Get going. You don't have time for this. I'll draw them west. So far, they don't know what we're up to."

"If they catch you—"

"When they catch me, I'll be dead." He glanced down at the blood that pooled between the seats. "I have ten minutes, no longer. Go, Donny. Get Jin to safety. Don't worry about me. I've counted the cost, remember?"

"See you in heaven, brother."

Donny slammed the door and ran. Behind him, the car zoomed away.

On Spider's heels, Donny darted around to the north side of the building. Spider was more athletic, so he arrived at the storm drain much faster.

"It's here!" He yanked off the drain cover and drew on a nylon rope to raise a weatherproof bag of gear. "You ready?"

"Ready." Donny was still panting from the run as he drew on a winter parka. Next, Spider shoved a small pack into his hands, and a battle rifle. "It's nice to have friends in hidden places."

"Roger that." Spider donned his own coat and pack, and shouldered his rifle. "To the Palace."

"Yeah, but slowly now. Until we need to run."

Their packs were light, with more winter clothing and food for themselves and Jin, if they had to march her out of the city on foot.

Though their instinct was to run, their training directed them to walk now. Shoulder to shoulder, so they didn't appear to be anything but citizen soldiers of the city, they walked southward on the shoulder of the road.

In front of them, near the Grand People's Study House, a military vehicle crossed the street.

"Steady now," Spider said. "Keep moving."

A tall, slender man walked out between two buildings, then paused in the shadows.

"That guy's watching us." Donny crossed his arm, ready to raise his rifle. "I'm going to take him out."

"Pull your hood on your head," Spider said. "Of course he's watching us. You're the tallest white man in the country."

"Wait." Donny stopped, still on the side of the street, and gazed toward the man in the shadows. The man withdrew into deeper darkness, then was gone. "*No way!* I think that was Luigi, Corban's guy from the training center!"

"Keep moving," Spider urged. "How else do you think our gear made it into the country? Titus and Corban have been planning this for weeks."

Donny continued, his head hidden by his parka hood, which hindered his view from side to side, but at least he wasn't so conspicuous.

"Shorty was shot in the side, maybe the lung," Donny said. "He's probably dead by now. Our mission's barely started, and he's already gone."

"He played his part. We'll share in the reward together. Look. We cross Kim Il Sung Square, and we're at the Palace. You ready for this?"

"I'm ready."

Donny flipped the safety off his rifle. Ahead of them, somewhere far away, muffled gunfire thundered. A gun battle was raging without them. *They were too late!*

CHAPTER TEN

Pyongyang, North Korea

Chevy's heart pounded from the tension as he walked beside Job and Yellow Bird toward the People's Palace of Remembrance. The city seemed so quiet, so deserted, and he knew it wasn't the cold weather that caused people to stay indoors. Over four million people lived in Pyongyang, but the regime kept them held in torment and need so they could be controlled. It was the *Juche* way.

"Here we go," Chevy said as he drew a silenced handgun and held it against his hip. "Yellow Bird, stay behind us."

"Just get us through the door, Chevy," Job said. "I've got your back."

As they climbed the granite steps to the porch of the Palace, two guards stepped into sight. They'd been standing between two columns that seemed like massive guardians on either side of the glass entrance.

The gun was cold in Chevy's hand. He'd shot at targets in San Diego while being trained, but he'd never shot at a person. It was a frightening prospect, even if he knew he was only firing gel-tranqs. The people he intended to shoot could shoot back!

To steel his nerve, he remembered what they were in the country for, and for whom they were risking their lives. Jin was inside. She was alone, cold, and frightened, maybe even feeling hopeless. Whether she'd given birth to the child yet or not, he was there to bring her and the baby out to safety.

He raised the handgun and steadied it with both hands as Titus had drilled into him. Before either guard could respond, Chevy fired twice into the left guard's chest, then twice at the right guard. The impact of the rounds forced the men backward, and by the time they would have realized they hadn't actually been fatally shot, the tranquilizer had pulsed through their systems within two heartbeats, and incapacitated them as completely as an anesthetic.

Job, using his greater bulk and strength, dragged both guards farther out of sight from the street below. Chevy lowered his handgun and surveyed the block. He could barely see the outgoing light traffic on the Taedong Bridge in the distance. Otherwise, nothing else moved.

"Let's go," Job called as his work was finished, and he opened the glass door for Chevy to enter first, followed by Yellow Bird. "It doesn't look like Donny and the boys will be joining us."

Chevy didn't respond as he swept into a marble foyer with high walls and dim lighting. Since he and Job had trained to complete the mission alone, he set aside his hope to see the other three. Something had gone wrong if Donny and the others weren't there, but they had each known the risk. Now, it was up to him and Job, Chevy realized.

Against the right-hand wall, Chevy walked straight forward, the silenced sidearm leveled. Over his left shoulder, he glimpsed Job's battle rifle muzzle covering their flank, like they were a two-man SWAT team.

They came to a corner and paused. Before them, a thirty-foot-tall bronze statue of the dictator stood in a lobby the size of a basketball court. A velvet rope cordoned off the statue, and a plaque in ten languages instructed tourists and citizens alike how to approach, bow, and correctly frame the statue in their camera if photos were taken. Another sign warned that it was illegal to take a photograph of the Supreme Commander that didn't encompass the statue fully so as to capture his complete grandeur.

"Elevator," Chevy said. "Two o'clock. Clear?"

Moments passed. Yellow Bird said nothing behind them. The lobby was indeed so expansive that it took both men a few breaths to confirm that no one else was in there with them.

"Clear. Go."

Calmly and directly, they approached the elevator and Chevy pressed the button. The car arrived without a chime, and the doors opened with a clunking sound.

There were three buttons inside the elevator, but none were labeled.

"Now," Job said, "we find out if Titus' intel from Corban was accurate."

Chevy touched the bottom button, then holstered his sidearm. He raised his battle rifle and pulled it snuggly against his shoulder. Along with Job, he aimed at the door.

The elevator stopped and the door opened. Chevy flinched as they suddenly stood face-to-face with five armed guards. The guards' mouths fell open in startled shock, which bought the team a little time.

Job moved up next to Chevy and fired a deafening burst of automatic gunfire into the five guards. The men wore only sidearms and batons, and at such close range, the gel-tranqs hammered them each like mule kicks.

Chevy fired an instant later, and moved into the corridor to secure the rest of the basement.

"Help us with Jin," Job said to Yellow Bird. "Stay behind us!"

Without looking back, Chevy charged up the long corridor. Another guard stepped out of a cell, his sidearm drawn. He fired at Chevy, but the bullet zipped past him. Chevy tranqed him and continued advancing toward an iron door at the end of the corridor.

The iron door opened, and three uniformed men emerged, firing handguns. Chevy dove to his belly, bruising his elbows, and fired from the floor, barely aiming. When his eyes focused again, the three men were down.

Lunging to his feet, Chevy charged the steel door and entered a cement office complete with desk and wall posters boasting the Supreme Commander's wisdom and strength. There was a chair behind the door that reminded him of a dentist chair. In it sat a bloodied Caucasian man wearing a North Korean official's uniform.

Job entered the office and touched the tortured man's neck.

"He's alive, but not for long. They worked him over pretty good."

The victim in the chair opened his eyes. When he spoke in a whisper, it was in a language Chevy didn't know.

"We can't help him." Chevy unstrapped the man from the chair, and Job carried the victim to a desk chair. "He's lost too much blood. I'll go search for Jin."

As Chevy left the office, he glanced back to find Job on his heels. Yellow Bird fell into step behind them. Chevy wished they could save everyone in the dungeon, but they couldn't. Jin was their mission focus. Countless lives depended on her and her husband's knowledge!

"Han Ji-Jin!" Chevy called, pounding on cell doors as he marched down the corridor. He realized their time was limited since there was at least one other sub-basement, and more guards were certainly on the way. It would be ignorant of him to think that some sort of alarm hadn't been sounded.

"Just start opening doors!" Job tossed Chevy a set of keys from one of the guards' belts. "Here! You open. I'll cover."

Chevy caught the keys and let his rifle hang on its sling. He was almost afraid of what he'd find behind the doors. Yellow Bird set a calming hand on his shoulder. She would help with whatever they found.

Jin couldn't sleep that night. Not only had she been assured that she would be forced to have her child early the following morning, there were new officials in the dungeon enforcing the dictator's ruthless will.

As wicked as Yuriy Usik had been by taunting her for weeks, she wept on her hard bunk for his soul as his screams echoed down the corridor. He was in the torture chair, she imagined—his own torture chair. The regime had found some fault in him, and now he was being tortured. She wondered if his torture had anything to do with her prayers for him. Regardless, his screams held no hope for herself or her baby. His screams meant evil people—more evil than even Yuriy Usik—were now in charge.

For the last week, Yuriy hadn't called her into his office. She hadn't known what it meant exactly, but apparently, he'd been found wanting in his duties for the regime. As a foreigner, Yuriy had surely been disliked by some officials. As an interrogator, he'd probably been shunned by all.

"Save him, Lord." Jin wept into her hands. "Let him see You. Rescue Yuriy Usik somehow."

Thunder suddenly filled the basement. Jin sat up and listened, pulling a thin blanket to her chin. Gunfire deafened her, and she dropped the blanket to cover her ears with her hands. It lasted thirty seconds. Slowly, she took her hands from her ears. Yuriy Usik's screams had stopped. Had they executed him in the dungeon? It seemed strange, since the regime would've wanted to make someone like Yuriy suffer longer, maybe by dying in a labor camp, not by shooting him in secret. Unless he'd attacked them.

A strange voice and language was yelled outside her cell door. *English!* She remembered her English lessons as a child in Haeju, before she'd gone to work at the fishery with her mother. She hadn't spoken it since, but she could understand it if she listened closely.

She heard her name! Oh, no, she thought. They had killed Yuriy, and now they were about to induce her labor. For weeks, she'd refused to think about the coming pain. There seemed no joy in the birth of this child. If only she could hold the baby boy while she died, and spare him the anguish of living a short life and dying miserably in the hands of cruel strangers!

Again and again, a man yelled her name, then two men, then their voices were joined by a woman's voice. Jin stood and approached her cell door. These weren't North Koreans. They were foreigners searching for her! The thought of freedom brought a weakness to her legs more than the thought of execution. Holding her belly with one hand, she approached the door and slapped it with her other hand.

"Here! I am Jin!"

Through so much noise outside, she wasn't sure how she could be heard, but keys rattled, then her door swung open wide. She took a step backward. A white man with a big belly faced her. He wore all black clothing, a bulky backpack, and carried a rifle.

"Jin?" he asked.

"Yes," she answered in English. "I am Jin."

He held out his gloved hand to her. It was a simple gesture, but Jin saw it as a hand of love. This was no enemy. He had come as an avenging angel!

Suddenly, another white man ran up the corridor. He was slender and wild-eyed in the hazy basement lighting. An older Chinese woman followed him closely.

"We need to go," the second man said. "There are more guards coming. Yellow Bird, help her to the elevator."

Gunfire thundered from down the corridor. The big-bellied white man shoved them all into her cell, but not before he was struck by a bullet. The slender man returned fire, replaced a magazine, and fired some more. Jin knelt with Yellow Bird to see to the husky man who'd been shot. His wound was high on the chest, close to his neck, and he was bleeding profusely.

The gunfire lasted another thirty seconds, then ceased.

"Job, can you walk?" the slender man asked.

Jin held the wound with her hands, his blood covering her fingers.

"No. I'm done." He panted, and moved weakly to unbuckle the pack strap across his chest. "Take the P-Rox."

The man offered his pack. Yellow Bird took it and the other man helped the Chinese woman into the straps. Still kneeling, Jin laid a hand on the wounded man's forehead. She understood that they were leaving him behind. He was too wounded to continue.

"You are blessed," she said in Korean, her eyes welling with tears. "I will not forget you."

He closed his eyes.

There was more gunfire, and the slender man fired back. Jin rose to her feet and huddled close to Yellow Bird, but they were still in her cell. With so much gunfire, leaving seemed impossible. They were pinned down, trapped by the arrival of more guards.

Suddenly, more automatic gunfire roared, and Jin heard yelling by others who spoke English. The pitch of the battle changed. In seconds, there was silence, then two more Westerners jogged up the corridor. One was tall and white, the other was a broad-shouldered Hispanic.

"You're clear all the way to the elevator," the Hispanic man said. He acknowledged Jin by nodding to her, then noticed the wounded man. "How's Job?"

"He's done," the slender one stated. "It's good to see you guys, but we need to get Jin out of here before we're hosting the whole army!"

The tall white man led the way and the Hispanic man brought up the rear. In the midst of them, next to the Chinese woman, Jin glanced back. The heavy-set man opened his eyes again, and Jin prayed he would be comforted in his final moments.

Job's shirt front was soaked with his blood, but he was still conscious and he still had a little strength left. He rolled to his side and looked both ways up and down the corridor. Unconscious North Korean guards lay heaped along the wall. With his left arm disabled from his chest wound, he used his right arm to cling to the door as he climbed to his feet.

He couldn't run after the other KONs, but he felt drawn to stagger down the corridor to the office. Gritting his teeth against the pain, he focused on entering eternity in mere minutes. His life had been first spent on pleasure and drugs. But prison had opened his eyes to his great need for a Savior. Now, he would die in a North Korean secret prison, and he wasn't ashamed of it. The mission he'd been sent for was completed. Jin had been rescued. The other *Kindred of Nails* would see that she was flown to safety. Now, he could focus on dying well, as he'd been trained.

In the dungeon office, he sat on the edge of the desk and looked down at the tortured Caucasian man in the Korean uniform. He was still alert, though disabled from the recent abuse.

"English?" the stranger asked through broken lips.

"Yes." Job leaned heavily on his right arm. His strength was fading, but he intended to move no farther. "Together, we will die. You aren't alone, my friend."

"I am always alone." The man coughed blood from internal injuries. "Now, I am alone and afraid."

"Afraid to die?" Job closed his eyes for a few breaths, then opened them again.

"I have not known the answer."

"What is the question?" Job prayed for focus for the man's sake. He couldn't imagine dying with fear about what lay beyond death. "What would you like to know?"

"What is the answer for death? Has God condemned us all?"

Job smiled. It was just like his sovereign God to somehow prepare a man's heart for the end like this. Now he knew why he'd felt the need to come down the corridor to die rather than die in Jin's cell.

"The payment for death was paid for by Jesus, the Son of God. He died for your sins. You and I, my friend, were born bad. We need God to save us from our bad nature."

"I have done too much bad." The man spit blood onto the floor. "Death is my finish. I deserve it a thousand times. There can be no payment."

"No, God in the flesh died for you. His life is enough. He sent me to you right now to tell you this. With your last breath, believe this truth. He died for you, so that you may live in the resurrection."

"I have hated too many people." The man wept. "I made them suffer. Now, I am afraid."

"Forsake your evil. Admit you need God. He is your only option. Let Him be merciful to you."

"I do need mercy. So much mercy."

"There is no fear in love. Surrender to Him, my friend, and He will welcome you. Do you believe? This is the answer. Just believe."

"I believe, Yellow Bird." The man's body convulsed, then he was still.

Job smiled. *Yellow Bird?* Though he knew not how, this man had known Yellow Bird! And Yellow Bird had told him enough of the gospel to make him question death. It was too much to fathom how God had arranged their lives to save this stranger, but Job was content in being part of His plan.

Peace washed over Job, and he lay down on his side on top of the desk. On the desk was a bloody hammer, but it didn't bother Job. Nothing bothered him. His pain from the bullet wound left him.

"Thank You, Lord," he mumbled, then fell asleep.

Outside the Palace, Chevy followed Donny to the north. Directly behind him, Jin and Yellow Bird walked together, and Spider trailed behind, his rifle shouldered.

When they reached the edge of the open space of Kim Il Sung Square, Chevy stopped and unbuckled his pack.

"This is good, Donny."

He helped Yellow Bird take off Job's heavy pack. Without his partner, Chevy began to assemble the P-Rox. As he worked, Donny and Spider helped Jin into a bulky parka and heavy winter pants with a waistband that covered her pregnant belly. When she was ready, Spider and Donny took up positions around Chevy, their rifles leveled.

By the few lights in the city, Chevy assembled the propellers of the P-Rox, attached them to the motor and guidance system, then mounted it all onto the foldout chair set on the pavement.

Yellow Bird waited for Chevy's instructions, then helped Jin into the chair and buckled the harness over her shoulders. She spoke Korean to the shivering, pregnant woman, but Chevy didn't take time to find out what she said. Words of comfort, he guessed.

"Vehicle!" Donny called. "Car from the south! Hurry, Chevy! I'll draw their fire away if they start anything."

Chevy didn't look up. He turned on the P-Rox guidance system and pressed the motor starter. The props immediately started to spin, so he stepped back. A hissing sound fizzled from the ends of the props as hydrogen peroxide reacted with the stainless steel. It expelled as pure water from the hollow props.

The chair lifted slightly, and Jin fearfully grasped her harness straps. Then, the machine rose straight up, following its programmed route. On the edge of the square, the transport lifted her high into the night even though there were no tall buildings to avoid.

The car Donny had spotted stopped one hundred feet away, and four soldiers quickly climbed out. Apparently, they could see something of Jin for they angled their rifles and fired into the sky. Donny fired at them, then Spider and Chevy joined in, though they had no safe cover from which to take a stand.

Spider knelt in front of Yellow Bird to protect her as the four soldiers gave up on shooting at Jin and began firing at the KONs. One soldier fell, then Spider was struck by a bullet in the neck. Chevy shifted his gaze to Spider for an instant and noticed the man stared sightlessly toward the heavens. He was gone, but he had shielded Yellow Bird.

"Jin is out of range!" Chevy yelled. He scooped up Spider's rifle and pushed it into Yellow Bird's hands. "Let's move!"

Donny didn't need any more coaxing. He sprinted directly away from the gunmen, who were down to two now. Chevy started to call out to the tall man, to yell at him to get out of the square, but Donny's body jerked twice, and he went down. Without Donny, Chevy considered, he and Jin would still be pinned down inside her cell. God had used the painter from Oklahoma to save the lives of His people, then the Lord had taken Donny home with the others. Donny's physical ailments were no longer bothering him.

Chevy hustled Yellow Bird to the west, not tempting further reliance on the tourist boat owners by traveling to the east. In the shadows of the buildings near the Grand People's Study House, Chevy and Yellow Bird skidded to a stop. They were the only two left.

"Where do we go?" Yellow Bird gripped Chevy's arm. "This is not a safe place. Nowhere is safe!"

"The Arch of Triumph," Chevy said. "If we can get there without being noticed, we'll be safe!"

"I do not know the way," she said. "I am not from here."

"It's okay." Chevy touched his thigh, realizing he'd been wounded by a bullet that had grazed his leg through his pants. "I know where it is, but it will take us till dawn to get there."

"But tomorrow, North Korea will be attacking America. There will be war. We are not safe anywhere in the city."

"We'll have to take our chances in God's hands in hiding rather than in the North Korean's hands in the daylight. Let's go."

Chevy's watch said they had six hours of darkness left, and they would need every minute to avoid the hornet's nest that was sure to be humming as soon as the regime learned about Jin's rescue and escape.

Looking northward, Chevy prayed Nathan and his team were similarly rescuing Rea.

With a heavy heart, he walked away with his Chinese companion. Four of his brothers had been killed. They'd died for Jin and for each other. Chevy was the only *Kindred of Nails* left alive. So far.

Hamgyong Prison, North Korea

Nathan, Memphis, and Bruno emerged from the trees on the northern segment of Hamgyong Prison, and together they took a knee in the thin layer of snow. Seven rows of prisoner dorms sat one hundred feet away.

"Now, for the tricky part," Nathan said to his two companions as he studied his watch face. "Tower One, report."

"No alarms," Chloe said, "but I see guards on patrol all over the place."

"Tower Two, report."

"My corner is quieter than what Chloe sees," Chen Li said. "Maybe the administrators don't have a night shift."

"Scooter, report."

"I see standard foot patrols in pairs between all buildings, and more around the central leather shop where there's more lighting. A few guards have dogs."

"Okay." Nathan took a deep breath. "Let's see if we can do this without waking anyone up."

Nathan led the three at a jog, crossing the space between the trees and the dorms in fifteen seconds. Two guards were walking the perimeter fence on the east side of the dorms, so Nathan cut through the maze of buildings. From one to the next, they darted across avenues. Since the dorms were made of mud, Nathan figured the cracks in the walls allowed the freezing temperatures outside to torment the residents inside.

Suddenly, Nathan stopped and crouched.

"Back up!" he whispered to Memphis and Bruno. "Dog!"

Even as Nathan spoke his warning, a dog around the next corner started barking. Bruno scrambled backwards, but it wasn't fast enough for Memphis. Memphis darted down another avenue, and Nathan took a right-hand turn at an intersection. For the moment, he figured avoiding detection was more important than staying together, but now Bruno and Memphis were blind, each scattered in different directions.

The dog kept coming, but the two men with the dog spoke Korean casually, as if the dog on their leash had often led them on fruitless chases. Nevertheless, Nathan couldn't retreat any farther without being discovered by the dog patrol or the perimeter fence patrol.

The door on the nearest dorm had no handle or lock. It was only ill-fitted plywood on leather hinges. He drew it open, slipped inside, and closed it gently with one hand. In the darkness, his nose adjusted before his eyes did. Disease still stinks even in freezing weather, Nathan thought, but he didn't react. These weren't animals—only men, women, and children treated like animals.

As his eyes adjusted by the small light coming in through wall cracks, he got the impression of stacks of bunks, three or four high, with narrow walkways between the many rows. The disease he sensed had a smell like gangrene. If their intel was accurate, prisoners died daily in Hamgyong Prison from gangrene, starvation, beatings, and work injuries gone untreated. Of the hundreds who died every year, many of them were Christians—their brothers and sisters.

Listening to the darkness, he heard the breathing and quiet mumblings of several hundred sleeping people. He knew families were housed in partitioned dorms on the east side of the leather shop. This dorm held single men and boys, or perhaps women and girls.

But over the gentle sounds of sleeping, he could hear the growls and sniffing of the security dog outside. His sizeable boot tracks were probably visible in the snow outside if anyone used a flashlight to look. In his mind, he imagined the door opening, and then him trying to flee across the crowded bunk room. If that happened, there would be no escape in such tumult, and he'd probably get some prisoners shot if the guards started shooting. The rescue of Rea would be over before it began!

After an agonizing, breathless few moments, the guards outside seemed to move on. Nathan pulled up his sleeve and adjusted his watch view several times, trying to differentiate between Memphis and Bruno's heat signatures from those of the guards. It was impossible. Only the heat signatures of the dogs were different and slightly smaller. There were bright spots all over the compound, several of them single and several in pairs—any of which could be Memphis and Bruno.

"Memphis, report."

He didn't respond. Either he was hiding in the vicinity of a guard, so he couldn't talk, or his comm wasn't working.

"Bruno, report."

"Bruno here. I'm over by the north side of the leather shop. I just ran for it. Memphis is not with me."

"Roger that." Nathan could at least zoom in on his own location and see that the guards and dog had indeed moved down the row of dormitories. "Bruno, I'm coming to you. I'm four dorms away from you. Memphis, if you can hear us, we're rallying at the north side of the leather shop, then continuing to the subject. Over."

Nathan opened the door of the dorm and paused, allowing more light into the overcrowded building. He wanted to remember this moment—the sight, the smells, the sadness. Turning this many people loose in that kind of weather and terrain would only kill them all, so Nathan couldn't rescue them. Brokenhearted, he stepped outside and closed the door. The prisoners were safer to remain where they slept, rather than come with him. But he would write a report about every detail he'd witnessed, so everyone who cared could be informed, pray, and respond in their own way.

The suffering wasn't all gloom, however. Nathan knew many of the people in that prison were Christians, and their confessions of faith, even in the face of torture, wasn't an ugly thing, but a thing to be celebrated. Some guards, he'd heard, had even been saved from sin by the testimony of condemned prisoners.

Outside, Nathan walked quickly up the rows of dorms, weaving twice to avoid patrols, to reach the leather shop. The lights on the outside corners of the leather shop were a dull yellow, as if the glass fixtures hadn't been cleaned in years, emitting only faded light.

For an instant, Nathan aimed his rifle at a form across the avenue whose back was against the leather shop wall. Then the form raised his hand, and Nathan knew it was Bruno. The avenue was clear, so Nathan ran and threw himself against the wall next to the big man.

"No sign of Memphis?" Nathan asked.

"No sign." Bruno aimed his rifle in one direction, and Nathan covered the other.

"Scooter, Chloe, either of you see Memphis?"

"Negative," Chloe said.

"Nothing, Eagle Eyes," Scooter reported. "I think he went into one of the dorms to hide."

"Roger. Bruno and I are continuing."

It bothered Nathan immensely that Memphis was missing, but he couldn't search for someone without any leads. Patrols walked everywhere, many with canines. The only consolation was that no alarm had sounded. If a well-armed Westerner like Memphis were captured, the whole prison would already be buzzing.

"Hey," Bruno said. "Let's go through the shop. It seems quiet."

"Okay." Nathan nodded once. "Let's try it."

He walked to his right and opened the corner door to the leather shop. The Gabriel was having trouble identifying any heat signatures through the roof. But upon peeking inside, Nathan saw a dark interior. It smelled like leather and boot polish, but no one was there.

Bruno closed the door softly behind them, and they crept into the building along an aisle on the east side of the building. Nathan flipped his night vision scope on and observed the long wooden tables and benches where countless prisoners surely worked during the long days, cutting leather and assembling shoes. The building was massive, as large as a football field. A courtyard was in the center where a few windows allowed some light to shine inside.

As interested as Nathan was at seeing where some of North Korea's political prisoners were worked to their deaths, he brushed aside his fact-finding, and continued to the opposite wall where they found another door in the corner.

"We can leave by this route, too," Bruno whispered. "This opens near the detention building."

"I agree." Nathan touched the door and paused. "Memphis, if you can hear me and if you can move, get inside the leather shop and wait for our exit through the east side. We're heading for the subject."

He was thankful they'd been able to cover so much ground under concealment of the shop interior, but the administration building was flanked by a large open lot, presumably for parking, though there were few vehicles on the prison grounds.

"Let's stay to the left," Nathan said to Bruno. "From this approach, let's come at the detention building clockwise and make our entrance by the fence."

"Roger that," Bruno said. "Let's go get Rea."

Nathan took a calming breath, saw on his watch that the avenue and parking lot were clear, and moved silently into the cold night.

Jeong Byeang-Rea wished he had the energy to remain awake during his last night alive, but he didn't even have the strength to stand upright any longer. So, he had to be content with praying when he occasionally woke from bouts of shivering.

He lay in the soiled sawdust in the same cell where he'd been left for weeks. The only difference from day to day was when he was dragged by two guards into the back of the administration building and given an update about his demise, and then he was beaten with batons. Just that evening, he had been informed by several crude officers how his wife would be forced into labor that night. Then she would be transported to the May First Stadium and executed with their newborn son for the whole nation to see what happens to heaven people. Rejecting the Supreme Commander's infinite compassion, they had said, was met with merciless slaughter. By the blood of his family, the regime intended to spark a new revolution around the world.

They had taunted him about the work he'd once done to advance the regime's missile testing agenda. Now, the work he'd completed was contributing to the nation's superiority over America. Rea understood that half of what was said was repeated brainwashing propaganda from news releases. He'd become numb to their threats long ago. Their harassment didn't make him afraid, for his life, death, and eternal soul had been in the hands of his Savior from the beginning.

Weakly, Rea moved only his left arm to sweep more sawdust against his back. Yes, he decided, he was ready for death. This endless cold, the sleepless nights, and the starvation was torture in its own way. It would've been kinder to amputate one of his limbs, as the guards had done to other prisoners who refused to cooperate.

"Into Your hands, I commit my spirit," Rea mumbled over and over. That he was dying for Christ gave him an immense sense of closeness to Christ, and he felt that Jesus' own words of trust on the cross were the right words for him in his final hour of need. He had no more worry, no more concerns. Even Jin, and whatever horror she experienced, was in God's hands as He completed in them all He desired for their refinement to enter eternity. They were His inheritance, and Christ was theirs.

"Rea, are you there?"

Rea breathed in through his nose, immune to the odors around him, and exhaled through his mouth.

"Yes, I am here." His body was still, not shivering as much, perhaps because he was hypothermic. He imagined the warmth of paradise with Jesus in the next breath. "I am here."

Suddenly, he opened his eyes. *English?*

"Rea, are you there?" someone asked, this time louder. In English! "Rea!"

Moving only his head, and in the dim lighting, Rea eyed the dead bodies the guards continued to lay in his cell. Was someone still alive among the dead? Perhaps he should've checked more thoroughly before assuming all were dead and rolling them against the wall.

"Rea, are you there?" This time, the voice was even louder, and it sounded like it came from outside his door!

"Yes!" he responded hoarsely. "I am here."

He sat up, hating the thought that he might be hearing voices, and spoiling the warmth he'd secured in the sawdust he'd piled around him. But a delusion in English seemed unlikely.

The sound of cracking particle board destroyed any further idea that he was imagining someone outside his cell. Someone who knew his name, who spoke English, was breaking into his cell! He tried desperately to greet the intruder by standing, but his legs wouldn't hold him. But by the time the door was torn away by a man in black, Rea was sitting at attention, gazing up from his place on the sawdust-covered floor.

"Are you Rea?" The man pocketed what looked like a small crowbar as he climbed through the hole he'd made in the door. "Don't be afraid.

Is your name Rea? What is your wife's name?"

"Han Ji-Jin." He trembled and felt like an infant in this large Westerner's presence. "I am ready to go."

Rea could think of nothing else to say to express his sound-mindedness and willingness to cooperate and escape with this man who was clearly there to save him.

"I'm Eagle Eyes." The man knelt and took off his pack. "I'm here to take you out of the country. Quickly, undress. Are you injured?"

Rea didn't slap away the man's gloved hands as he helped him discard his tattered shirt and soiled pants. He shook with nervous anticipation in the cold air as he was just as quickly forced into a wool shirt, fleece trousers, and a hooded parka.

"No, I am not injured." He found himself crying. "But I am too weak to run."

"Don't worry about a thing. I'll carry you all the way. Bruno, report."

Rea didn't know who Bruno was, until he heard another man's indiscernible voice in the hallway outside his cell.

"My wife isn't here," Rea said. "Please, you have to help her in Pyongyang. Leave me if you have to. She's in the capital city!"

"We know, sir." Eagle Eyes loosened the straps on his pack. "If everything goes according to plan, your wife is already safe and in the hands of God's people. You'll meet her in Japan when you get there."

Rea's body felt like fluid. At the promise of safety, his limbs seemed to give up, and he fell into the arms of the man who was thrusting his feet into wool socks.

"Don't worry about a thing," Eagle Eyes repeated. "God has taken care of the details. Even if we are shot on our way out of here, we won't stop relying on our Lord, right?"

"At least you are honest." Rea tried to chuckle, but it came out as a sob. He suddenly felt talkative. "If you would have told me we had nothing to worry about, I would think you were insane."

"No, we're far from safe." Eagle Eyes fit Rea's legs and arms into his backpack's netting. "I'm just saying you have men and women on your side who've done this a hundred times and will take care of you as much as anyone can. Okay, now, I need you to try to stand."

Before Rea could remind the operative that he had no strength, the man used one arm to effortlessly lift him to his feet. Rea put his hands on the man's shoulders as his knees wobbled. Eagle Eyes stooped down and took the pack straps over his shoulders. When the Westerner straightened up, Rea was lifted a foot off the ground. His feet dangled until his ankles were pulled around front and held by a sling.

"You good?" Eagle Eyes asked.

"I am a human backpack!" Rea laughed. "Even if I die now, I will die with a smile."

"Well, focus on smiling, not dying."

Eagle Eyes picked up a short rifle against the wall and climbed carefully through the ruined door where a light bulb hung from the ceiling. The largest black man Rea had ever seen stood against the wall of the hallway. This was Bruno, he understood. Bruno took off the stocking cap from his own head and fit it over Rea's head, covering his ears with a quick tuck. Rea opened his mouth to ask how such fierce warriors could show such gentle kindness, but then he knew. These were Christians. They were with the covert units he'd heard about while in South Korea, teams of believers who carried non-lethal weapons and cared for their enemies and friends unconditionally.

"Back the way we came," Eagle Eyes said to Bruno. "Let's hope to pick up Memphis along the way."

Suddenly, Rea felt Eagle Eyes flinch as two gunshots sounded somewhere outside.

"Who fired?" Eagle Eyes asked through a radio mic. "Who fired?"

"Oh, we're in for it now!" Bruno said and aimed his rifle at the end of the hallway.

Rea's hands rested on top of Eagle Eyes' shoulders. By peeking around the soldier's neck, he could see what Eagle Eyes saw. More lights came on inside the detention building, and through a window in the outside wall, he noticed the lights outside came on as well.

"Chen Li!" Eagle Eyes roared. "Kill the generator!"

CHAPTER ELEVEN

Hamgyong Prison, North Korea

Scooter heard the two gunshots as well, while stationed on the mountain ridge overlooking the prison. He heard Nathan's question and he saw the prison light up like an airport.

"Who fired?" Nathan asked again. "Us or them?"

"I heard one of each," Chloe said on her comm. "It was somewhere by the north dorms. I heard a bang and a clack."

Scooter used his NL-X1 scope to study for movement in the avenues between the dorms. He'd heard that Memphis was lost somewhere, and off-comm. From Chloe's description, he understood she meant a battle rifle had been fired, followed by a Chinese AK-47, which made a distinct sound as well.

"Eagle Eyes, it's starting to come alive out here." Scooter pivoted to scope the officer quarters. Uniformed men were pulling on coats as they emerged from their homes. "You've got about two minutes before we're facing an army. Over."

"Chen Li," Nathan called again. "Hon, we can't step outside until the lights are out."

"Okay." Her voice chimed back. Scooter imagined the sweet Chinese woman in Tower Two with the powerful rifle who was about to wake up anyone who wasn't already on high alert. "Here I go."

Gunfire exploded in short bursts from Tower Two. Scooter noticed sparks flying around the fencing near the officers' quarters where the generator and transformer were housed. Chen Li was the only one who had a full clip of armor-piercing .308 cartridges, since she and June had a clear view of the generator from their position. Two bursts later, the lights flickered and went out.

There was complete silence for a moment. Scooter applied his night vision scope to view the prison in the dark.

"Anyone see Memphis?" Nathan asked. "Chloe? Scooter?"

"Negative!" Chloe's frustration was obvious. They'd come to rescue Rea, not lose one of their own in unnecessary confusion!

"Negative." Scooter, as much of a veteran as Nathan, calmly studied the northern dorm quarter. "There's a lot of movement down there, but no one seems to have captured him. He's hiding somewhere, Eagle Eyes."

"We have to get Rea out," Nathan said. "We're going through the east fence. Lay down cover fire. Tower One, pull out after we get through the fence. Tower Two, cover us until Tower One reaches you. Scooter, hunker down."

"Roger that." Scooter swallowed then clenched his teeth. He knew how Nathan thought. Everyone else was pulling out to exfiltrate across the railroad tracks, but he was to stay in place. As long as they were missing one of their own, they weren't pulling out completely. "I'm settling in. Handle it, Eagle Eyes."

"But what about Memphis?" June asked about her husband. "Eagle Eyes? Memphis!"

"Quiet, December!" Chloe snapped, using June's call-sign from her first operation with COIL in Germany. "Scooter's staying back. If we all stay, we all die. Memphis would want it this way. Eagle Eyes, go!"

Scooter frowned at Chloe's tone, but she was right. The subject was in their hands. They'd gotten what they'd come for.

"Cover fire now," Nathan ordered.

Both muzzles blasted from Tower One, and Tower Two opened up a breath later. Scooter nuzzled his cheek against the stock of his sniper rifle and focused on the milling soldiers around the administration building. None of the guards had trained for a full-on assault coming from two corners of the prison. In the darkness, no one knew who was shooting, or why.

Scooter picked out a knot of officers in the parking lot area, and fired. At eight hundred yards, his five-dart tranquilizer would have a spread of several feet. He chambered another round and focused in time to see three guards drop from his first projectiles. Guards scattered for cover.

Bruno suddenly entered Scooter's scope view, firing as he ran toward one of the vehicles.

"So, that's how you're getting through the fence," Scooter mumbled to himself.

He shot twice more, covering Bruno. The two towers weren't

covering so much as they were drawing fire. Two mobs of about one hundred guards each with rifles were massing to assault the towers.

"Tower One," Scooter called, "you have to cover Tower Two now. Tower Two, you have to cover Tower One. You're both about to be overrun."

There was a brief pause as the towers shifted their firing from shooting at nearby targets to shooting over the buildings to protect the other tower. As such, no guard had a safe place to hide unless they remained crouched behind the taller buildings.

Meanwhile, Bruno reached a stout transport truck behind the administration building, and climbed inside. Scooter had yet to see Nathan and Rea, but he guessed they were both somewhere in the shelter around the detention building. Whenever Nathan decided to emerge, he would face an ever-increasing number of guards filtering through the buildings and alleys from the guards' quarters, so Scooter continued to fire into small clusters of confused guards. Every shot he fired, he tranquilized at least two guards.

At one interval, as he reloaded his rifle with another ten-round magazine, he heard a squeaky footfall on the frozen snow behind him. From his chest holster, Scooter drew a tranq-pistol and rolled over. He was shocked that someone from the prison had gotten the drop on him from behind! Since he was a quarter-mile from the perimeter fence and hidden both in terrain and darkness, it was inconceivable that he'd been located in the ten minutes since the first shots had been fired.

However, he was too slow. His sidearm was knocked aside even as he fired, and the gel-tranq blasted unsilenced into the sky. The heavy frame of his attacker dropped upon him, carefully pinning his legs and arms in a cross-brace so that Scooter uselessly fought for control.

"Easy, Scooter. It's just me," a familiar voice said. "Shouldn't you be covering your team?"

"Corban? Boss? What're you doing here? *You're walking!*"

Corban eased off Scooter, then crouched at the top of the ridge.

"I was never here," the veteran spy stated. "You never saw me."

"If you say so." Shaken, Scooter holstered his sidearm and picked up the NL-X1 in time to watch through the scope as Bruno drove the transport vehicle recklessly up the avenue toward the detention building. "I think Bruno's making a back door."

"I saw where Memphis went down." Corban's voice was calm—

much calmer than Scooter felt about the mission that was boiling over. "I'm going in while the others are drawing fire."

"You'd better hurry, Boss. We're looking to pull out in a few minutes."

"As soon as Memphis and I are in the clear, get to your own L-Z. Don't wait for us."

"You got it, Boss."

Scooter fired again, and far below, two guards fell. Prison personnel scrambled to avoid getting hit by the transport Bruno was driving. He picked up speed and passed the detention building. The delayed sound of Bruno blaring the vehicle's horn reached Scooter's position, and he watched for a few seconds to make sure Bruno's plan worked.

The vehicle bounced over the inner perimeter road, then smashed into the inner electric fence without slowing. A few yards later, the second fence was torn from its foundations and the transport was forced sideways. He had damaged both fences, but the vehicle was now caught in the wire.

"Come on, Eagle Eyes!" Bruno called. "I made a hole, but you'll have to climb through it."

"Tower One," Scooter said, "prepare to evacuate in sixty seconds."

"Roger that," Chloe said. Her voice could hardly be heard over the gunfire around Tower One.

Scooter looked up from his scope to find he was alone again on the ridge. Corban had slipped away.

Staccato rifle fire blasted at the towers below, and Scooter guessed the COIL agents in the towers were getting off fewer effective shots. Hundreds of guards were now involved in a steady advance toward both towers. Scooter had fifty rounds left, which wasn't enough to tranquilize everyone. The towers had hundreds of rounds, but firing safely was impossible now. Their only security blanket, Scooter realized, was that the towers were outside both fences. The guards could only shoot at the towers, but under such an overwhelming barrage of bullets, the operatives in the towers were in grave danger.

Across the compound, a bulky, burdened figure picked his way through the mangled fences. It was Nathan, with the subject on his back. Scooter fired three hasty shots at guards who were running up the avenue next to the detention building. In their plan to attack

Nathan from behind, they'd neglected to consider that Nathan was covered from on high.

"Tower One, evacuate. Nathan and Bruno are through the fence. The subject is safe."

COIL gunfire ceased from Tower One, so Scooter fired the rest of his magazine into the advancing crowd of guards now near the fence line. With seven shots, he guessed twenty dropped, enough to halt the advance and scatter a few of their number. At such a distance, they would have difficulty even seeing his muzzle flash, but they would hear his gunfire if they stopped firing their own rifles.

Chloe and Heather emerged from the tower's outer door, which faced outward, and they sprinted across the cultivated grounds between the prison fence and the access road. Heather looked back and fell, but she recovered quickly. Either she'd been lightly wounded or she'd tripped. Whatever the case, Luigi's wife wasn't quitting.

With Chloe and Heather momentarily safe, Scooter focused several rounds on those moving on Tower Two. Chen Li and June were firing desperately from the crow's nest, sometimes not even looking as they fired blindly by holding their rifles outside and pulling the trigger.

"What about Memphis?" June shouted over her own gunfire.

Scooter scanned with his scope across the ground around the northern dorms. Corban was running full-charge toward the buildings. He'd abandoned both his pack and rifle to dash unhindered. Scoffing, Scooter wondered how the founder of COIL had kept his secret quiet. His legs certainly weren't crippled that night!

"I've got Memphis covered," Scooter said, though he couldn't see exactly where Corban was going. "Everyone keep moving. Memphis is extracting the way he came in. I won't move until he's safe."

He chuckled, already trying to think of how he was going to explain Memphis' rescue without revealing to others that it was Corban who'd saved the day. The man had clearly been watching and listening to the scene unfold for just this reason, but he apparently wanted his presence and abilities kept secret.

Nathan, with the subject, continued east beyond the railroad tracks toward the DRIL extraction point. Bruno cut to the south to help defend Tower Two. Scooter found Chloe and Heather in his scope as they rounded the southwest corner of the prison, jogging wearily toward the second tower.

Far to the north, a train was rolling toward the prison.

"Tower Two, go ahead and retreat." Scooter fired four times into the crowd below the tower. His shots seemed to make little impact among so many people. "Get out now. There's too many to hold off. Use the train as cover. It's coming quickly."

"Chen Li is wounded," June said. "It's not fatal. Just her leg."

"Get her to the ground," Bruno said. "I'll help her."

With Tower One and Two evacuated and on their way to rendez-vous in the darkness, Scooter exhaled and swung his scope back to Corban. It took a moment for him to find him creeping along a dorm in the third row. With the guards grouped on the south end of the prison, Corban had a quiet approach up to one door. He disappeared inside.

The gunfire on the south side dwindled and went silent. A dozen guards inspected the wrecked transport and demolished fence section. Others helped those who were unconscious, though Scooter figured everyone would think they'd been killed. Only later when they woke up, they'd realize their lives had been spared.

The train rolled slowly past the prison, just a few yards beyond the east fence. It cut off the prison from viewing the fleeing operatives. But in the darkness, no one inside the prison seemed anxious to leave the prison gate to pursue their attackers.

Scooter gave all his attention to the dorm Corban had entered. He had no rifle, but Scooter guessed the boss had a sidearm. Regardless, if Memphis was wounded, Corban would need everything Scooter could offer if someone were to patrol in their direction.

Pyongyang, North Korea

Jin stared into the dark void in front of her as the machine flew her through the sky. Her eyes teared from the force of cold wind in her face, and her ears were drawn to the hissing of fuel and throbbing of rotors directly over her head. It was impossible to know how far off the ground she was or where she was being carried. Her rescuers could be trusted, she decided, since they'd sacrificed themselves for her safety. It was an exercise of her faith to fight worry as the machine whisked her away from the city lights far behind.

The machine lurched, and one of her hands went to her belly, and the other went to the harness strap. The pitch of the rotors changed, and forward momentum was checked. With wide eyes, she stared across the landscape, unable to distinguish distance or depth, only the impression of the night sky and a dark land.

With shocking force, her feet hit the ground. She kicked them out in front of her as the seat settled roughly onto the ground. The sound of hissing fluid ceased, and the rotors slowed their spinning until they finally stopped completely.

The wind was blowing. Jin tucked her chin into the collar of her parka. This wasn't right. She was in the middle of nowhere. Central North Korea was a rugged and untamed land of mountains and forgotten ridges. The underground church had used its remoteness to hide in, but she couldn't survive out there. She had no food, no shelter. In the cold, she guessed she could last for maybe two days.

Something had gone wrong, she was sure. All of the effort and sacrifice of her rescuers had led to a deserted location? Anything was better than the torture chair, she thought, which had been intended to be used as a birthing chair that very morning!

She unclipped her harness and stood. Since the regime had wanted her to birth a healthy baby, she'd been fed well enough to have a little strength, unlike most prisoners. In the darkness, she felt the rotors and motor and fuel tank. Tapping on the tank, she guessed it was empty and needed more fuel. Was there more fuel attached? Feeling all over the basic contraption, she found no additional fuel, and she could recall no instructions from her rescuers to refuel the machine if it stopped.

"Father, what do I do?" Strangely, she wasn't panicked or saddened, not even for her child. She was more fascinated by God's timing than anything. Even if she were to die now on the barren slope of the open range, she would be no less thankful for the life she'd been given. However, she didn't want to waste the opportunity to stay alive, if there was something she could do to help herself.

Minutes passed. She stared in every direction away from the haze of city lights far behind. The wilderness gave no indication that a vehicle was approaching. No flashlights beamed in her view to indicate further angels of mercy were coming to guide her onward.

Then she heard it: an animal's breath. A creature panting in the night. It was coming for her. She'd heard stories of fantastic beasts around Mount Paektu, the legendary birthplace of the Korean people.

Her mind tried to reason against such nonsense, but so much had already happened that she couldn't explain.

The panting slowed as it grew nearer. She heard rocks rattle under its feet. Moving closer to the flying machine, Jin stood with the machine between herself and the beast.

"The heavenly Creator made all things great and small," she whispered from a Korean children's song. "I am safe in His arms, whether I am great or small."

The breathing quieted. The thing stood before her. It didn't attack, but it chewed loudly on something. The air carried a new scent of something sweet.

"Han Ji-Jin, I'm here to help you." The man's voice sounded gentle, perhaps even weary. "My name is Luigi. No harm will come to you now."

Jin didn't know this latest rescuer, but she moved around the machine's propellers and fell into this stranger's arms in relief. He felt slender and much taller than any man she'd ever known, and though she didn't know if he was young or old, she knew he was working with those who'd already died for her. She wasn't alone. God was sending His servants to care for her and her baby.

"My English not good," she said.

"That's okay. We won't be talking much."

He gently pushed her away to stand aside, then he began to work on the machine.

"More fuel?" she asked.

"I have more fuel, yes, but only one more container." He grunted, and Jin heard the clunk of a tool against metal. "We have to walk much closer to the demilitarized zone before you are flown farther south. If you fly again now, you'll crash still inside North Korea."

"I understand." Jin wiggled her toes in her boots. "We walk?"

"Yes, we walk. But I have to take this thing apart first, so I can carry it. Just stand there and watch for approaching lights."

Jin smiled and obeyed. As he worked beside her, she faced the north where Pyongyang's lights were still visible, and watched for a search party. While she surveyed the darkness, she thought of this man God had sent her. He wasn't a man who understood how to comfort a woman, but he provided security regardless. Perhaps he was a man accustomed to the military—a soldier, silent and direct, loyal and efficient. It was the kind of man this type of rescue required, and she thanked God through her tears as she relaxed.

"My husband safe?" she asked quietly.

"I haven't heard. I'll make a call soon, but we can't waste time. Your safety is my priority. If you can't walk fast, then we'll take our time, but we must get there. The way has been arranged."

"I believe," she said. "Thank you."

The man didn't respond, but she didn't expect him to. She prayed as he disassembled the machine for transport. She prayed for Rea, for their child, for herself, and for the man who'd been sent to care for her on this leg of her journey.

In the midst of laying her concerns before the throne of God, she realized that when she did once again climb into the seat of the machine, she would fly alone to South Korea. Alone, she would be leaving Luigi behind. Alone, he would remain in a dark and dangerous land. But even alone and threatened, he seemed like a man unafraid. God had made him special like that. Alone, he would be strong, for he was a man of God.

𝄢

Hamgyong Prison, North Korea

Corban stepped over two unconscious guards to enter the dorm where he'd seen Memphis crawl. Memphis had had a confrontation with the two guards soon after getting split up from Nathan and Bruno, and alone, he'd turned to the only refuge available: the prisoners of Hamgyong Prison.

For two nights, Corban had been scoping the prison from the mountain, high above even the COIL team led by Nathan and Chloe. In case anyone were caught and questioned, he'd kept his role in the op a secret, and Luigi's involvement had been an important detail added in the last weeks of preparation as well. While Corban was in the north, prepping for a fuel drop and contingency plan, Luigi had been planting gear in Pyongyang for the KONs.

Corban was exhausted, and he suspected Luigi was similarly running on empty, but contacts inside North Korea were few. And those Christians they did know about couldn't be asked to do what they hadn't volunteered to burden. If all had gone well, Corban pondered, Luigi had traveled the ten miles from Pyongyang to the point where the P-Rox would first run out of fuel. The mission had been a lot to ask of one man—caring for a pregnant woman and carrying the flying machine for many miles. But Luigi had never refused a request, and Corban knew COIL was a better organization because it had dedicated men and women with courage, like Luigi.

Inside the prison dorm, Corban left his night vision goggles on his face to see through the dark interior. Memphis had unsuspectedly crawled into one of the women's dorms! Hundreds of women, their faces bleak and empty, turned toward Corban, even though he knew they couldn't see him without light in the long, wide room. So many female prisoners here were forced to live two to a bunk in some cases. They were condemned by the regime, but Corban didn't think of them as criminals. They were sisters in Christ, most of them.

"Where is my friend?" he asked in the muffled silence. Women with matted hair, some with scarred faces, missing eyes or ears, didn't move or respond. "Please, I must take him and run away. I know you are friends. I'm a friend of Jesus the Christ. Who has my friend? Who is caring for him? Where is he?"

"Corban," a weak voice called from the depths of crowded bunks. It was Memphis.

Squeezing through the bunks, Corban reached the middle of the dorm where Memphis lay on a bunk. Two women hovered over him as his nurses.

"How are you?" Corban lightly touched Memphis' head, which had been bandaged. "At the moment we needed you, you thought you needed a little R and R?"

"He has a concussion," one of the North Korean women said in perfect English. She was older than most of the women in the dorm. Her scalp showed through her hair, and one of her hands had been amputated. "I hope you do not have to move him far. He should rest. A bullet grazed his skull."

"Unfortunately, we have far to go," Corban said, "and I can't carry him. Memphis, can you walk?"

"My head's pounding, but I can make it." With help, he sat up.

"Are you a doctor?" Corban asked the woman.

"In Chongjin Prison, I was a physician. The Christ followers in prison taught me the truth of Jesus, so I cast my pin aside. I follow Him now, and no more idols. Now, I am a leader of the women who are Christ followers in this prison." She swept her arm at the faces who crowded near to hear. "All these are Christ followers."

"You could be punished for helping us."

"We are already punished for loving Jesus." She reached out with her only hand, and found Corban's face. "So, we are not afraid to help His children. Go, my brother. Take your man. We will pray that you touch many more lives. But tell us this: for what have you come to Hamgyong Prison this night?"

"We came for a Christ follower." Corban didn't push her hand away from his cheek. "He's a special symbol of hope for the country, and what he knows may save many lives. His pregnant wife was to be executed as well."

"They are important Christ followers." The woman smiled sadly. "You defy the regime of Satan with us. Does the world know we suffer for Jesus here as well?"

"Everywhere I go, I tell people." Corban turned to look at all the women, young and old, little children and grandmothers. "And now, when I speak, I will tell them about the special women I spoke with tonight. Your faith is a light for the whole world. Jesus is coming soon."

"Here are his belongings." Two younger women carried Memphis' pack over and set it on the bunk. Corban saw no sign of Memphis' communications headset, and assumed it must've gotten knocked off during the confrontation. "We have taken nothing."

"He's in no condition to carry a pack, and I have my own outside the fence." Corban accepted Memphis' recovered battle rifle and flak jacket. "Can you dispose of the pack safely? You may keep what you want. There's food and clothing."

"We will share it with those who have little," the physician said. "You should leave. Incidents of gunfire require a special head-count."

"I understand." Corban drew the woman into a firm embrace. She was a national outcast, unbathed and visibly diseased, but he held her thin frame as tightly as he would have held Jenna, his own daughter. "I will see you in paradise, my sister. Every day, we will remember you."

The others were no less affectionate toward both him and Memphis as he readied himself to leave, though Memphis was unsteady on his feet. Corban had come without anything to carry, so he prepared to carry his man some if need be.

Exiting the dorm without a sound, Memphis leaned heavily on Corban. The two had spent a long time inside the dorm, and now they needed to hustle back to the pine tree. Corban glanced to the west where he knew Scooter was faithfully watching over them, along with the Lord above. They passed other unconscious guards laying on the ground, tranquilized during the battle. But now, there were no gunshots. Soon, Corban guessed, the perimeter lights would be turned back on. They had to hurry!

Corban reached the tree and Memphis leaned against the trunk.

"How're you doing, Memphis?"

"My head feels like it's going to explode, Boss. I can barely focus to see at all."

"Then keep your eyes closed and climb. Feel above you. Go ahead. We need to cross that rope before we're caught in daylight or head-lights. This whole prison will be swarming with officials as soon as they get organized."

"What about our evac?" Memphis started climbing. "How late are we? What if they don't wait for us?"

"I told Scooter not to wait. Everyone else has already gone. Plan B, son. We're on our own."

"How are you even here, Boss? I didn't know you were coming with us."

"I was never here, Memphis. You and Scooter keep it quiet until it has to be known. I'm just one man, but COIL enemies will continue to think we're not a threat if I'm crippled and useless in their eyes. Keep climbing, son. Just a little farther. Ten more feet, then reach to your left for the rope.

Nathan reached the repositioned DRIL transporter first, even though he was carrying Rea on his back. After punching in a code on the drone's keypad, the bay door opened. Carefully, he released Rea's ankles from his waist and shrugged out of his shoulder pack to lay Rea inside. The DRIL wasn't heated, but Rea could at least get out of the wind.

Leaving the man inside the DRIL, Nathan stepped outside and oriented himself with the view on his watch. In single-file, the rest of the team was marching toward him. One larger form appeared on his watch, which he recognized to be Bruno, now carrying or helping Chen Li across the two miles from the prison.

Hamgyong Prison was a blend of hot spots, but even after twenty minutes since the last shot was fired, he still saw no party in pursuit of them. The North Koreans simply didn't know who had attacked them, or where their attackers had fled. However, by dawn at the latest, Nathan guessed the guards would account for who was missing, and then all of North Korea would go on lockdown.

Far to the west, there were two hot spots about where the team had crossed the fence by rope. That had to be Memphis, but with whom? Whoever Memphis was with, they were too far away to catch up to the team by the time they needed to extract. But they couldn't leave anyone behind.

Chloe came into sight through his night vision. Her left arm was in a makeshift sling, and her shoulder was bleeding. Heather walked behind Chloe, her cheek bandaged, but she seemed to be in top form, carrying what gear Chloe couldn't carry.

June led Bruno as he carried Chen Li in his arms. As much as Nathan wanted to take Chen Li into his own arms, he patted Bruno on the shoulder as they reached him.

"Good work, everyone. Let's load up."

"We're not leaving without Memphis!" June stated. "We're *not!*"

"We'll figure it out, June."

He waved her on and steadied his gaze on the distant bluff. Scooter came into view, approaching at a jog like he was fresh from a long rest rather than from enduring days of restless cold in a threatening land.

Stepping farther from the DRIL out of earshot, Nathan met Scooter with a clap on the back.

"Who's with Memphis?"

"I can't say." Scooter shook his head. "It was a nobody, if you know what I mean."

"We can't wait another twenty minutes for anyone, not even Memphis. Rea is on board."

"They don't expect us to wait for them. They've got their own way home. Let's roll, Eagle Eyes, before they stick the hounds on our trail."

Scooter continued to the DRIL where he was welcomed with praise. Everyone there owed their lives to him, who had protected them all from his position on the ridge.

Nathan still stood at a distance, considering their options, and thinking of Scooter's words. Scooter had seen someone else go into the prison for Memphis. *A nobody*, he'd said, which was slang for a ghost agent that no one would expect to be there. It could be Luigi, Nathan guessed, but then dismissed that thought. There was no reason to keep Luigi's presence a mystery.

Chuckling, Nathan wondered what ghost Corban had kept hidden to rise up to help in the most dire of moments—maybe someone from his own past. Nathan had spent long enough as a solo field agent himself, while everyone thought he was dead, to know that Corban liked to keep a couple wild cards in his pocket to put into play when no one, especially an enemy, would expect it.

"December!" Nathan yelled.

June pushed her way past the others to emerge from the DRIL.

"Yeah? How're you going to get my husband?"

"Look." He held up his watch. "This is the prison here. And these two moving dots out there are your husband and someone else."

"They're moving away from us!" June put her hands on her head, clearly distressed. "How can we get to them?"

"We can't. We have enough fuel for one straight shot from here out to sea to Song Sakana's ship. Memphis is with someone, and they're on the move. At the moment, they're safe, and we have to call this mission complete."

"Who's he with?" Her hands went to her hips. "Is it that Luigi guy?"

"I don't know for sure. Seriously, Corban has had other people out here before us, prepping. It could be a guy named Brody Sladrick, or another COIL agent Corban brought in to watch over us. But Memphis is on the move. Whoever he's with most certainly has another way out of the country. If we try to reach them, or wait any longer, we put everyone at risk."

"Okay." She sounded resigned. "If you're sure he'll find a way back."

"He's in good hands, whoever those hands may belong to, besides God's." He set a hand on her shoulder. "It's time to go. It'll be a long flight out to sea. Make sure the wounded are comfortable."

"Okay." She lingered. "That was some firefight, huh? Reminded me a little of the Sudan a few years ago."

"Yeah, I remember hearing about that one. Come on."

Moments later, the bay door closed with them all inside. Bruno cracked a glow stick to light the interior as the drone hummed loudly to life. But no one spoke. Death by a thousand guards had been hurled at them, and they were leaving Memphis behind in enemy territory. The mission didn't feel like it was over, yet.

Pyongyang, North Korea

Chevy sprinted across Triumph Return Square and dove to his belly on the grassy island in front of the Arch of Triumph. A tank rumbled up the four-lane street, passed through the arch, and continued north-bound out of the city. A jeep with four men followed the tank. Until both vehicles were through the arch, Chevy kept his face down. Three hours earlier, he'd smeared street grime on his cheeks and forehead, but he was certain his camouflage had dried and crumbled off by now.

He signaled Yellow Bird. As soon as he saw her dart from the apartment buildings, he turned and watched for any enemy who might be moving into the square. The sky was growing lighter. Full dawn was twenty minutes away. All night, he and Yellow Bird had prowled through the city, even crossing two bridges to pass through Pothong-gang District since the Central District was overrun with soldiers radiating outward from the People's Palace of Remembrance. At one point, below Ryugyong Hotel, they'd hid behind the base of a rusty crane as soldiers had lounged on the street nearby. The delay had cost them precious time.

Yellow Bird hurdled dying decorative bushes, and slid headfirst into Chevy. For a woman in her sixties, she was doing amazingly well, but they were both feeling the fatigue of the night. Their hands, knees, and elbows were bruised and scraped from frequent dives to safety.

"Hurry," Yellow Bird said. "It is not safe here."

"Okay." Chevy drew a bolt cutter from his pack. "Bring my pack with you when I signal."

He dashed away, knowing Yellow Bird was dependable to trust with his pack. She'd carried it before when he'd needed to perform some limber activity without the burden.

Approaching the Arch of Triumph was no small step for the fleeing pair, for the sixty-meter-tall monument was lit by floodlights year-round. The massive arch even had its own single cylinder diesel generator in case the city power failed, which it had twice that very night.

After checking for more cars passing through the arch, Chevy walked through the light to the inside of the arch where he'd been told there was a door. He found it padlocked, as planned. Using the bolt cutters, he snapped the lock, stuffed it into his pocket, then waved at Yellow Bird.

Before she reached him, Chevy opened the door to a bare granite corridor and a forty-year-old elevator. He pulled Yellow Bird into the space and slammed the door as two more jeeps approached the monument.

The interior of the arch had been remodeled recently. The off-white paint over the granite stones gave off an odor that nauseated Chevy as he closed the elevator gate and pushed a button. Electricity hummed and counter-weights dropped. From schematics he'd memorized in San Diego, he counted two landings before he stopped the elevator midway before the third landing. There, in the wall, was a door the size of a cupboard. If he hadn't been looking for it, he could've easily ascended in the elevator without noticing it at all.

The little door swung inward to a small room. He climbed inside, with Yellow Bird close behind. They discovered it was about nine-by-six feet. Here, the wind whistled, since one wall was missing, fashioned into an observation platform. An enormous shelf of granite extended outward and over Chevy's head so that he couldn't see the brightening sky. But looking down, he could see most of Triumph Return Square.

There were two items in the little room—a fifty-foot rope that could reach the ground, and an off-white painted board meant to conceal the cupboard-size door in the wall.

"It's almost light outside. I see no anchor for our rope. Job was supposed to be here for this part, but now you'll have to tie this around your waist and drop the other end down to me."

"By God's providence," Yellow Bird mused, starting to tie the rope to her waist, "I've lost weight, but I think I still weigh more than you."

Chevy appreciated her humor at such a tense moment. Leaving Yellow Bird there, he exited back out through the small door, went down the two-and-a-half stories in the elevator, and emerged from the arch's underbelly. There, he placed a new padlock on the door that nearly matched the one he'd cut off.

He ran around the arch to the northeast corner and found the rope dangling from up high. After tugging firmly on the rope to let Yellow Bird know he was about to climb up, he applied his full weight and worked his way up.

At the observation platform he climbed around Yellow Bird's braced legs, and rolled onto his back to rest. After a few moments, he rose to his knees and took the off-white board in his hands and fit it diagonally outside the cupboard-sized doorway, then pulled it flush with the frame. It fit snugly, cut to be wedged into place. He guessed anyone from inside the elevator wouldn't even notice the board covering the small hole. Or if they did, they would need a crowbar to pry it out of the frame.

Sitting back, he exhaled. For the first time since leaving the tourist boat the previous evening, he could rest. With Yellow Bird, he moved to a back corner of the small room and sat side-by-side with her. He shared food from his pack and they sipped from his canteen.

"It's cold," he said, "but at least we're safe for the day. We'll leave at sundown."

"We are safe, yes—unless the Americans shoot back with their missiles."

"I wouldn't know about that." Chevy took out the sat-phone. With a heavy heart, he pushed the dial button, and it connected immediately with a COIL man Chevy knew to be named Marc, who was hiding in a mine shaft somewhere in New York. "This is Chevy. I have Yellow Bird with me."

"I have your signal and your location," Marc said. "Where are the others?"

"Job fell inside the Palace. Donny and Spider fell at the square where we got Jin airborne. Shorty was shot early on, and drove away to draw the enemy from Donny and Spider. They didn't tell me any other details."

"But Jin made it out of the city?"

"As far as I know, as long as the P-Rox did its job."

"Okay. It's a bittersweet day, then."

"Yeah." Chevy held the phone away from his head so Yellow Bird could hear. "Any word on the others up north?"

"Rea is in route with the others back to Japan. I'm a little unclear about the details, but they had to leave Memphis behind to get out another way. Something didn't go right."

Chevy recalled the man nicknamed Memphis who'd shared that he'd once been a gym teacher in Arizona. Now, he was married to June, and both worked full-time for COIL.

"But no other casualties?"

"A few bullet wounds, and Memphis is still in the wind, somewhere two hundred miles northeast of you. And there's no confirmation that Jin is safe yet. How soon can you get out of the city to your extraction point?"

"We'll try at sundown tonight. We'll rest until then. We need it."

"Good work, Chevy. I'm sorry about the other KONs. I'll tell Corban and the others, whenever they check in next."

Chevy turned off the phone and closed his eyes.

"It was a success?" Yellow Bird asked. "Your operation?"

"I think Jin and Rea are safe. But four men died. Good men. The closest friends I've ever had."

"Our brothers," Yellow Bird said, holding onto his arm. "We will see them again soon, but hopefully not too soon."

CHAPTER TWELVE

Hamgyong Province, North Korea

Leaving a wounded Memphis on a rocky ridge, Corban climbed to a high peak. From there, as the morning sun sparkled on the dew across the landscape, he used binoculars to gaze to the east. He shadowed the lenses with one hand so he wouldn't risk alerting pursuers by the reflection off the field glasses. The prison was down there about three miles back. It was out of sight from his point of view as he was too close to the mountain to see it. He was sure trackers were being organized, though. For five minutes, he watched for movement, but saw none.

Pocketing his binoculars, he descended to where Memphis sat leaning on Corban's pack.

"No one yet," Corban said, "but they have dogs trained to track humans. As soon as they figure out our trail, they'll come after us twice as fast as we can travel."

Memphis didn't respond. His head hung low, and his eyes were closed. Using a GPS, Corban checked their progress.

"We have about eighteen miles to go, Memphis. I'll carry you if I have to, but I'd rather you walked."

"I'm good." Memphis didn't lift his head, but he held out his hand in a weak attempt to show he had a little strength. "It's just my head. It was never of much use to me, anyway."

"Well, it'll be just our skin if they catch us." Corban glanced south, wishing he could see two hundred miles away at the progress of the KONs. "God help us if we miss our ride out of here. The Chinese border is too far away if we miss the DRIL refueling."

"Let me hang onto your pack," Memphis said, rising to his feet on his own. "You walk in front. My equilibrium is way off. And opening my eyes just makes the pain worse."

Corban pulled on his pack, and Memphis laid both hands on the back, leaning heavily. For now, Corban could cope with his own weariness, but he was worried about Memphis. The pilot was in top physical condition, but he'd been in the wilderness for over five days on minimal sleep. Now, he was experiencing some sort of head trauma, maybe even brain swelling.

They started walking off the west slope of the mountain, deeper into the Hamgyong Mountain Range. There were no towns for forty miles, all the way to the Tumen and Yalu Rivers that created the natural border with China. There might've been mountain villages hidden in the canyons, but Corban was determined not to upset their poor existence with a visit from two foreigners. The North Korean military had been known to enslave whole villages who had helped the Christian underground.

Around noon, Corban called for a break, and Memphis collapsed. He was almost immediately asleep. His fatigue and pain had wearied him beyond his own resolve. Corban used a tarp from his pack to cover Memphis from the mountain wind that bit the skin and burned the lungs.

He checked the GPS. Six miles since dawn. It was farther than he'd expected over such terrain, but they still had twelve more to go before they reached the next fuel depot Corban had staged a few days earlier. Now, he wished he would've found a closer location, foreseeing the possibility of trekking cross-country with a wounded COIL agent.

After pulling off one glove, he dialed his sat-phone. Instead of calling Marc Densort who was coordinating *Operation: Harm's Way* from America, he called the only other man he knew who could manage a dozen crises at once and objectively make the hard decisions. He called Titus Caspertein.

"I need your help," Corban stated first. "Can you talk?"

"Yeah." Titus' voice sounded strong, and Corban's confidence rose, simply by connecting with the Serval a world away. "I'm just with Levi at the training gym. We're going over some shooting techniques. What's up?"

"I'm on foot in North Korea with Memphis. He's experiencing a head injury from a bullet. I'd hoped to close off this mission myself, but you were always a safe second. I need two things from you since I'm not out of the country yet."

"Go for it. I'm listening."

Corban felt a peace wash over him that he knew was from God. The servants of the Lord who depended on other servants who had Christ within them—they would always experience immense comfort. Titus hadn't asked needless questions to waste time, nor would he compromise COIL by sharing intel with a third party. Yes, he was speaking to the right expert!

"First, I need you to get word to the KONs in Pyongyang to wait for two more passengers at the next fueling depot. The DRIL is already programmed. Marc will help you communicate that message. Hopefully, Memphis and I haven't already missed them."

"Two more passengers," Titus repeated. "Wait for them. Got it."

"Next, Nathan has Rea. They're probably back in Japan now, or nearly back. Nathan needs to ask Rea about this missile attack that's about to be launched from North Korea. It's supposed to be sometime today, maybe even this evening. What Rea tells us may determine what the US response might be to such an attack. Luigi should have Jin by now, and we need to question her as well—about what she knows of the coming missile launch or her husband's work. Whatever you learn about *Gimbap*, get it to Wes Trimble. It's a mission code or launch operation."

"Missile attack intel to Wes. *Gimbap*. Understood. I'll take care of it."

"That's it. I can focus on getting us out alive now."

"It seems rumors of your disability are greatly exaggerated." Titus chuckled. "It ain't easy saving the world while everyone thinks you're a cripple, Corban."

"Keeping that quiet may not matter after today," Corban said, "if North Korea launches what I think they're launching. You have old networks and contacts. Have you reached out? What's your read? Be candid."

"Uh, candidly?" Titus cleared his throat. "Nuclear miniaturization is highly unlikely for an ICBM. They're still behind schedule for that, but this threat of a launch isn't a bluff. There are other things they could be launching besides a nuclear weapon. It's a first strike of some sort, something we're probably not prepared for. They've pretended to be reforming, but while we've been focused on nuclear issues, we forgot they still think we're at war."

"Tell Wes everything you just told me. We need to avoid war with this country, if possible, but I also understand America needs to protect herself. If we can, we need to save lives, Titus."

"I'll tell him. Just get yourself home. Let me worry about missiles and war."

"Thanks. Tell my girls I love them. Oh, and Titus? I was never in North Korea."

"Of course. As far as I know, you're still in the apartment next door here at the training center. After all, you're paralyzed, right?"

Corban turned the phone off. It would've been nice to hear an update on Luigi from Marc, but there was no time to explain everything to the tech a second time. The op was now in the able hands of Titus.

"Memphis." Corban nudged the sleeping man. "We need to get moving."

Without grumbling, Memphis sat up and reached out his gloved hands, instantly ready to be led onward.

"Remember how we first met?" Corban asked, leading him uphill. "Russia."

"I still have the scar," Memphis said softly. "It's my favorite scar. I met June not long after."

"It's providential, you and I being together at the end like this. We met when COIL was really taking off, and now we're together at its conclusion."

"What conclusion?"

"The world won't be the same after today. COIL's mission will change from now on."

"I don't understand."

"Evil minds are hatching something we can't figure out. We saved Rea and Jin, but it seems God is allowing the wind to change, and we can't control the wind. We just remain obedient to the ministry of reconciliation, and surrender to all that remains in God's hands. Even if it's disaster."

"What's my job with COIL now?"

"I think it'll soon become a matter of survival on a local level. Those of us who know how to thrive under such a collapse need to help those around us who won't know how to survive. It's time to shift our focus from international aid and persecution, to steadfast, local ministry. We're in the last days, Memphis. We need to get back to

America to watch and be ready for Christ's appearing."

"No argument here." Memphis struggled over a rocky ledge, pulling hard against Corban. "If He came now, He could spare us this whole march. I wouldn't be sore at Him about that."

Japan

Nathan stood in the doorway of a back bedroom in Song Sakana's house. Rea was horribly emaciated from starvation and disease, but he was alive against all odds. He would pull through, Nathan thought, but it would take months for him to recover.

Returning to the living room, Nathan contemplated what there was for him to do next. He felt helpless, knowing COIL personnel were still in danger. After all, as far as he knew, the KONs were still in North Korea.

With his back against the wall, Nathan observed the room full of COIL operatives. The wounded had been cared for on the long boat ride back to Japan, but now the exhausted team was being fully pampered by the best Song could rally from around Akita and nearby cities. Unfortunately, those with actual bullet wounds—his wife especially, but also Chloe—couldn't be taken to the hospital. Two Christian doctors, who understood the sensitive nature of the situation, turned two of Song's bedrooms into treatment rooms where small medical procedures had been performed on the slightly wounded.

Of course, Rea's condition was the most serious, and Nathan awaited instructions from Corban regarding the survivor, who was attached to an IV. Normally, upon completing a mission, Corban or Chloe arranged for his team to return quietly to the States. But Corban hadn't called, and Chloe admitted that she didn't know Corban's intel regarding the best location in which to place Rea. He needed security in place, Nathan considered, since North Korean agents had been known to arrange murders outside their own country. If anyone would be targeted, Rea would be. So, speaking quietly with Chloe, Nathan had decided to stabilize Rea and the wounded, and await instructions for a complete departure for further treatment. Song's residence was no place to house all the COIL personnel post-mission. Even if the KONs hadn't returned, Nathan wanted to get his people home.

On one sofa, June sat with Heather, who had a nasty bullet graze on her cheek that Nathan was sure would be a scar for life. June glanced often at Nathan, and he could read in her eyes that she wanted to know the status of Memphis. Knowing June, Nathan guessed she was willing to participate in a second rescue mission if necessary to recover her husband.

Heather was remarkably poised and hadn't even taken pain relievers for her bandaged cheek. She seemed to share Luigi's calm demeanor under pressure. Luigi had won her heart a few years earlier by using both trade craft and compassion. And she was also aware of her husband's uncompromising loyalty to Corban.

Of all the operatives who'd entered Hamgyong Prison, Nathan was the least injured. Since he'd carried Rea out, everyone else had endangered their lives more than he, for Rea to escape safely.

"Nathan," Chloe called from the kitchen. Her arm was in a sling, so she was making sandwiches one-handed. Everyone in the living room looked up, anxious for something to happen or for some word to confirm that the KONs and Memphis were safe. "A moment?"

Nathan stepped over the gear that lay packed on the floor. Though he'd asked Chloe to keep the sat-phone on vibrate so no one was alerted by potential bad news, everyone seemed to understand Nathan's summons to the kitchen. Though the two leaders had no intention to hide news from the rest of the team, there were facets of the operation that needed to be compartmentalized for security reasons. Assets needed to be protected. It was always that way with sensitive operations, even if Nathan didn't know which compartment he was in.

"Corban?" he asked Chloe as she handed him the phone.

"No, Titus." She opened the back door to the patio, then closed it after they stepped out together into the winter air. "I tried to get something out of him, but he said he's to speak to you directly, but I need to listen."

"Okay." Nathan leaned over so Chloe could hear with him. "Yeah, Titus? This is Nathan. Chloe's here, too, but we're alone. What's happened to Corban? I don't understand what's going on."

"It ain't easy operating without the boss," Titus said, "but he asked me to handle a few things. You have Rea?"

"Yeah, we're waiting to find out what to do with him."

"Okay, first of all, we're on a peace-keeping mission now. We know that North Korea is supposed to fire off some sort of missile today— not a test. The thing is, we need to know from Rea immediately if he knows what the *Gimbap* Program is. Wes Trimble is waiting for this intel to counsel the president in how to respond to a pending attack. It's already the afternoon over there, so this is an emergency."

"Understood. Chloe and I will go in to him right now." Leading the way back into the house, Nathan went through the kitchen, and into the back room where Rea was being treated. Nathan moved to the side of the bed across from the doctor. "I need to ask you to please leave the room for a few minutes, sir."

The doctor understood enough English to comply, and Chloe closed the door behind him.

"Rea? Can you hear me?" Nathan shook the man's shoulder, and Rea opened his bloodshot eyes. "I need to ask you some questions."

"He's medicated," Chloe said.

"It is okay. I understand." Rea lifted his bone-thin hand. "Ask. I owe you everything."

"You owe us nothing. We honor you for your faithfulness." Nathan squeezed the man's hand and gave Chloe the phone to hold so Titus could hear everything. "I need to ask you this: back when you were coordinating the North Korean missile program, did you hear of anything called the *Gimbap* Program? Or the *Gimbap* Protocol maybe? *Gimbap* something?"

"*Gimbap?*" Rea's eyes drifted, then suddenly widened. "*Gimbap!* They are doing it?"

"What is it?" Chloe pressed him. "Can you explain what *Gimbap* is?"

"It was a biological weapon. Very unlikely. It was meant to contaminate the food supply, maybe the water."

"What kind of weapon?" Nathan asked. "Can you tell us? Was it developed enough when you were involved?"

"The regime wanted multiple delivery systems. When nuclear capabilities were behind, I was to develop other weapons, but in secret. *Gimbap* was one. We wanted everyone to think nuclear was our only priority, but no. *Damage* was priority. What has happened?"

"Nothing yet." Nathan took the phone to speak to Titus. "You hear that? A chemical weapon of some sort."

"No," Rea objected. "Not chemical. *Biological.* Infect, contaminate, spread. It would be a virus. Biological."

"Correction," Nathan said on the phone. "It's a biological weapon."

"I heard." Titus was silent for a moment. "Biological weapons launched against North Korean enemies would be a complete surprise. The whole world is focused on a nuclear weapon coming from them. North Korea has been throwing us all off their real advancements. No wonder they've been so quick to agree to give up their nuclear program. They have ulterior motives."

"The missile tests for years were a cover," Chloe said. "Even the underground nuclear tests have been secret and unverified. A nuclear launch is expected at this point. Anything else could possibly be dismissed by other nations."

"They're about to do the unexpected for that reason," Titus said. "I need to get this to Wes Trimble. It's as bad as I feared."

"Wait!" Chloe leaned closer to the phone. "Where's Corban?"

"He's engaged in what he does best," Titus said. "We all know Corban. He's probably juggling danger and a thousand complications that reflect this spiritual battle we're involved in."

"Yeah, that's not a vague answer." Nathan scoffed. "How about Memphis? Anything? No one is telling us, Titus."

"You guys just snatched a guy out of prison. He holds the key to avert a war where millions could die. I can't blame Corban if he wants certain operatives isolated and protected."

"Titus, June is worried sick," Chloe said. "We know Memphis was wounded in the prison. Nathan thinks he saw him get out with some-one. Are we going back to rescue them or what?"

"Negative. Bring Rea back to San Diego. The jet is being refueled and the paperwork is being completed by Janice. As for Memphis, his head got rattled by a bullet, but he's hiking to an L-Z right now. He's in good hands. I need to go. You guys did your part. Now, I need to do mine. See you all back home soon."

Nathan handed the phone to Chloe.

"Let's get everyone together," he said. "We'll crowd into Chen Li's room. We need to pray this thing out. Apparently, *Operation: Harm's Way* isn't over for COIL yet."

San Diego

When Titus got off the phone with Wes Trimble, he had an uneasy feeling in his stomach. Levi was gone to school, so Titus was at the training center, mingling with some COIL trainees. Oleg had recently returned to the States and he was teaching new operatives about international crime in relation to Christian persecution.

On the balcony overlooking the lecture hall, Titus felt tears roll down his cheeks. *Millions were about to die and no one was prepared.* They didn't know how to prepare. Even a recent false nuclear missile alarm in Hawaii hadn't been enough to spur people into readiness. Pleasure and comfort were more important than life itself. Everyone was being fooled by media reports about political overtures where true repentance was completely missing.

A biological attack. He shook his head. In speaking to Wes Trimble, the White House was only concerned about a nuclear attack, and they highly doubted a biological one. They felt there was no intel that suggested the hermit kingdom even had a developed biological delivery system. And if a missile were fired toward the United States, the president was certain he could have it shot down before it reached American airspace.

Besides, Wes had said, intelligence sources elsewhere were reporting nothing spectacular happening in North Korea, except preparation for a celebration of some sort, which always involved mobilizing their various military units.

Someone codenamed Yellow Bird wasn't a familiar CIA intelligence source, and it seemed a tortured, drugged, and half-dead engineer in Japan, who hadn't been part of the missile program for over two years, could not possibly be reliable.

But Titus believed the threat was real. North Korea had even been staging Jin's execution for that day in Pyongyang, along with the death of her child, to celebrate the missile launch. Titus believed Yellow Bird and Rea. They were two different sources, even if he didn't know who Yellow Bird was.

He palmed his cell phone again and dialed Annette.

"How are things going downtown?" he asked.

"The trucks are beginning to roll in."

He imagined her at the San Diego parking garage he'd bought with old gun-smuggling funds. Two levels of the garage had been closed and devoted to warehousing food and supplies. He had other stashes around the city as well, and Annette was quietly acting as the front-person for it all, so there wouldn't be any visible cause for panic.

"I'll be there this afternoon after I pick up Levi from school."

"This is scary, Titus. It's one thing to talk about threats. It's another thing to know something is about to happen. America's not ready for this kind of an event. Nine-eleven was horrible, but what you're talking about is beyond anything we've imagined."

"I hope it doesn't happen, believe me." He left the balcony. "I'm gathering all the COIL personnel we can to brief them. I'll tell you the details then, too. By tonight, secrets won't matter anymore. I don't know what Corban can rally, but we need to diversify funds to people's accounts before the economy collapses and banks close. Everyone needs to stock up in their own way."

"How long can we last with what you've allocated here and the other places?"

"Alone, if it's just the three of us, we could last decades. But we're warehousing for others who will need help, too. This isn't about our survival, Annette. We can survive easily enough, I think. We need to keep reminding each other about the fact that we're here to serve others. Even our own survival doesn't come before that. It's how Christ lived. And we follow Him."

"I'll remember. I love you, Titus. God has prepared you your whole life to be here for so many now. I see it all happening, and I'm so thankful to be by your side."

"We're a team, Annette. Team Caspertein. Speaking of which, I need to call Rudy and bring him up to speed. And Wynter, though she'll probably want to be wherever Wes Trimble wants to hole up. Air travel will cease gradually over the next few weeks or months, so we need to get where we're going to be."

"Call your family. Let's tell who will listen. Whoever won't listen, you've prepared for them as well, if they can get to San Diego in time."

Titus dialed Rudy next, and as the phone rang, he thought of Levi. God had brought his son into his life by no accident. He understood that very clearly now. Whatever was about to befall America, he needed to raise Levi well, to be able to embrace God's call for the years ahead, if the Lord tarried His appearing.

Rudy had moved to Colorado recently, having married a woman Titus had met only a couple times. Although Rudy wasn't a man who needed to be told how to survive under extreme conditions, he was a man who needed to know how they seemed to be approaching the last days of the America they'd all known and loved.

Pyongyang, North Korea

In the short time they'd been together, Chevy had begun to relate to Yellow Bird as his aging mother. Without revealing her own Chinese network, she shared ways God had used her the past forty years. Whole villages in northwestern North Korea had been impacted by the Bibles and food supplies Yellow Bird and other courageous believers had smuggled into China for concentrated discipleship classes. Then she'd smuggled the believers back into North Korea where they knew they were serving Christ only until they were arrested and sent to a prison labor camp.

There was no sense or hint of fear for her own life in what Yellow Bird shared with him. The gospel and the souls were too important to be fearful, or to allow fear to direct her actions. It reminded Chevy of the four men who'd just given their lives for Jin. They had scoffed at death and chosen to live by love instead. They had died physically, but they had followed Christ, so they still lived, never to die again.

"Look." Yellow Bird lay on her belly close to the edge of the balcony, watching the city fade into darkness. "Everyone is returning from the stadium. Street lights are not coming on, but this is not a power failure. Something is about to happen."

Chevy wiggled on his belly up to her side. All afternoon, buses had transported the city's citizens to the northeastern stadium on Rungna Island. The celebration had lasted into the evening. Cannons had fired, making Chevy wonder if the war had begun, but Yellow Bird had explained that they were just celebrating *Juche*—national submission to their god and his thoughts, which revolved around their supposed immortal dictator.

But now, sure enough, as the sky darkened, the only lights on were from the bus headlights as they drove a hundred thousand people back to their homes.

"Human shield." Yellow Bird pointed to five tanks parked on the edge of Triumph Return Square. A bus full of passengers parked directly behind the tanks. "Loyal citizens will die for their leader."

"I highly doubt America will shoot at five miserable tanks. This will be a war over missile silos and launch pads."

"*Choson* has mobile launchers," Yellow Bird reminded him. "Loyal citizens will die to add to the body count. America will look shameful if they shoot back and kill *Choson* citizens."

"We've got to get out of here before that starts." Chevy backed away from the edge and gathered the clothes they'd laid across the granite floor to offer warmth and padding. "We should be safe if we can get to the drone. Now, we need to worry about getting shot down by America as we're leaving. Supposedly, the drone has stealth technology, but I think every satellite over Asia is looking at this little country right now."

They departed from the Arch of Triumph the way they'd arrived. Chevy left the board leaning against the wall and the rope coiled neatly as he'd found them, in case the arch survived the bombing that was about to commence. And it was possible the Christian underground would need to use the room again.

In the eerie darkness, they jogged away from the arch, heading north on Karsun Street. Within two hours, with no delays, Chevy guessed they would reach the DRIL, where it was hidden in a canyon off the highway. As long as it remained undiscovered, they could be on their way to a fuel depot deep in the mountains before midnight.

Chevy paused and looked back at the city. The arch remained lit up with its own generator while everywhere else was hidden in darkness. The scene made him smile. It was just like God to hide him and Yellow Bird in plain sight for twelve hours while the whole country searched for them and prepared for war. Without the safety of the arch, they would've been caught. The arch was the pride of the city, standing thirty feet taller than Paris' own Arc de Triomphe, but God had used for preservation that which others looked to in national pride.

Suddenly, a bright light, like a light bulb, gleamed in the east. Seconds later, the rumble of the rocket reached Chevy's ears as it lifted with strange resistance into the sky. Yellow Bird came to stand beside him. Chevy had never seen a rocket launch into the sky before. It was huge, even from a distance. As tall as a building and as thick as the thickest cedars he'd seen in photos.

Soon, the glow of the rocket was all that was seen, burning so far into the sky that it seemed that a star was on fire. Then Chevy blinked and couldn't differentiate the rocket's burn from the rest of the stars.

Yellow Bird took his sleeve and drew him with her. He joined her, but his mind was numb. *It had begun.* The world would never be the same. Would there even be an America to return to?

DMZ, North Korea

Luigi looked back at Jin, whose pace had slowed to a crawl as night fell across the landscape of southern North Korea. Not once had he urged her to move faster, though their food and water was running low. Their energy was depleted. He couldn't imagine any other pregnant woman in her eighth month able to cover so many miles.

Just then, Luigi saw a missile reaching for the sky. He was fifty miles southeast of the city, but the air was clear and the rocket was monstrous. It lifted far above the landscape, and Luigi prayed that God Himself would strike it down, or that the United States would shoot it down, but there was no explosion, yet. The farther it rose, the more certain Luigi was that death flew with it. This wasn't a missile test. This was the beginning of the attack.

"What?" Jin asked as she arched her back, standing with him.

"I think there are many other missiles," Luigi said, "and they are launching from all over North Korea. We need to hurry, before the fighting starts, or you may never get over the border to safety."

"How far?"

He gave her the canteen for a drink. It had only a few swallows left, which he refused to finish when she handed it back. She would need it all. That's why he'd come—for God, for her, and for Corban. If he died now, it would all be worth the cost. The years serving beside Corban had been blessed years, even though he'd been wounded on more than one occasion. In Corban, he'd found a friend. By Corban, he'd come to know the God of the Bible. And because of Corban, he'd met Heather, the only woman he'd loved.

"One hour," he said, and in the darkness, he offered his arm to the small woman. "Someday, I will introduce you to my friends."

"What about men who save me?"

"Yes." Luigi smiled. "I didn't know them long, but they were my friends as well."

"Tell me."

And so, to pass their final hour together, Luigi told her about the five men who he believed had died for her to live—Avery "Chevy" Hewitt, Job Buck, Francisco "Shorty" Hernandez, Ernesto "Spider" Colosio, and Donny Walters. They weren't just his friends. They were his brothers.

Hamgyong Mountains

Corban limped the last few hundred yards up the rocky mountainside, pulling Memphis along. It was like carrying another heavy backpack. At an unstable moment, Corban had fallen and bruised his knee badly, but at least they were almost to the fuel depot—whether to die or to be flown to China. He couldn't go much farther unless Memphis was able to support more of his own weight.

"We're there." He turned to Memphis to help him sit down on a rocky mountain plateau. The plateau was an open area where the drone could land. But there was no drone. There were only three fuel containers that he and Luigi had packed up the mountain before Luigi had ridden the DRIL down to Pyongyang for the KONs' extraction.

"How much time do we have, Boss?" Memphis asked.

Corban sat next to Memphis and used his binoculars to search the dark mountain passes below.

"There they come. About three miles back. Three or four flashlights. Must have dogs to track us so well over all this rock and snow."

"Three miles?"

"Forty-five minutes, give or take." Corban sighed and wondered what to say on his last sat-phone call. He took off his pack and readied his battle rifle for conflict. The DRIL didn't seem to be coming, which meant none of the KONs had survived in Pyongyang. The mountain plateau would have to be the place for their final stand. "How do you feel?"

"Misery," Memphis said.

Corban laid down his pack as a pillow for Memphis, and helped him onto his side to rest with his back to the wind. Memphis would be of no use in a firefight. Besides, Corban had hurled the extra battle rifle into a ravine earlier since he didn't want to carry the extra weight. In a shoulder holster, Corban had a nine-millimeter loaded with gel-tranqs, but it wouldn't be much against the carbines the guards were surely carrying.

Memphis was safe from below as he lay concealed over the lip of the plateau, so Corban set about building up fortifications from which he could defend their position. However, as only one man, he knew he would be overrun in an extended battle. Anyone could flank him by approaching up either side, or up the back of the mountain, or from all sides at once.

He tried not to think about treatment inside a North Korean facility. It had taken four months to set up *Operation: Harm's Way*. No one would be able to come in and get him right away. The team was licking its wounds and Corban had used all the Christian underground contacts he dared to risk inside the country. The only man who might manage a rescue would be Titus, and of course, Oleg. Luigi would help, and Nathan and Chloe, if they weren't injured. But a rescue would take time, and time was what torturers enjoyed.

Shifting his thoughts, Corban considered his wife, Janice. Though she would be saddened by his passing, she was a strong, independent woman. During much of their marriage, he'd been on the road, even after he'd come to Christ. Someone had always needed his help. Their adopted blind daughter, Jenna, was now in high school, but she was already innovative like a Christian missionary, devising audio programs for people groups who needed Bible access. She could see people in need, Corban thought, better than many seeing people.

Sitting cross-legged, Corban used the night-vision scope adapter to gaze down the mountain. His pursuers were coming with two tracking dogs in the lead. They were German Shepherds, large enough to be a real nuisance if they were released to attack. He'd definitely have to tranq them as well, while they were still on the leash and relatively under control. But it was the seven men behind the dogs that he studied.

Three had flashlights. Except for the dog handler, every man carried a rifle, and they were moving quickly up the snow-covered rocks, which told Corban they were experienced, hardened men used to the most bitter of elements. He guessed they were probably guards from the prison with their lives on the line to catch the prisoner who they figured had gotten away.

Corban left his fortification and roused Memphis, who groaned at being disturbed.

"Take my sidearm." Corban thrust it into his gloved hand. "Listen,

Memphis, I know you're in pain, but you have to stay alert for a few more minutes, or we're finished. Can you hear me?"

"Tranq me, Corban. I'm dying here."

"Your brain got bounced around a bit. You need to stay awake through the pain, Memphis. Listen. In exactly fifteen minutes, I need you to shoot my pistol three times. Shoot it into the air. It'll confuse the enemy once I open up on them from the side. Got it? Look, I'm setting your watch. In fifteen minutes, you fire the gun. After that, if you must, you can tranq yourself."

"Fire three times? I'll . . . try."

"That's all I'm asking." Corban blew on his gloveless fingers after fixing Memphis' watch. The cold wind made any exposed flesh numb. He thrust his hands back into his gloves. "If this goes badly, it was a pleasure serving with you. COIL was better with you on our team. Stay awake, Memphis! I've got to go now, or we don't have a chance at all."

Corban had to leave him and get into position. This could work without Memphis firing a shot, but Corban preferred an edge against so many trackers. He already intended to use the superior ballistics of the .308 against their AKs, but he was only one man against seven and two attack dogs. Survival was unlikely, he knew. But he was willing to try for Memphis' sake.

♨

DMZ, North Korea

Luigi listened to the night a long time. The wind was blowing in from China, but he still expected to hear sounds of missile bombardments or gunfire from the DMZ, about eight miles away. The Imjin River was twenty miles east, and a highway that spliced Hwanghae Province hooked within sight from the north to the east.

The traffic on the highway was heavy, all going to the border. He guessed it was the most militarized any demilitarized zone had ever been. Luigi had guessed war was inevitable once the missile was launched, but nothing seemed to be happening, yet. Maybe the missile had been another test after all, and all the tension was for nothing.

"I think it'll be safe." He approached Jin and the assembled P-Rox. It had taken him an hour to assemble it, since the machine was strange to him, but after carrying it for nearly thirty miles, he was determined to figure it out. Otherwise, sneaking across the border on foot was on the agenda, and that was madness with a pregnant woman—walking through mine fields and sniper fire. "Are you ready?"

"What you do?" she asked as he harnessed her into the seat.

"It's fifty miles to the west coast. I can phone a friend who is waiting. It's nothing."

"What I do?"

"In South Korea? There are people waiting for you. The machine will fly you to them. After that, you go to your husband. You have your baby. Along the way, you will be with many Christian friends. God has provided everything. He always does, even if the path is sometimes difficult."

"Thank you." She laid her hand on his. "I have no words."

"You don't need any words." Luigi drew his hand away. "Someday in heaven, we will rejoice. We will know all the right words then."

"And meet your friends?"

"Yes, and meet the *Kindred of Nails*." He moved his hand to the starter on the motor. "God is with you, Han Ji-Jin."

"God with you. What your name?"

"Luigi."

"Luigi." She settled on the seat, her gloved hands gripping the harness straps. "Luigi."

He started the motor and backed away. In the darkness, Luigi couldn't see the propellers, but he felt wetness on his face from the expelled water as they spun, urging him to back away farther. Next, he heard the hissing sound elevate, then fade to the south. Jin was gone.

Never one to be too sentimental, Luigi started walking west that very minute. He needed to cross the highway before dawn, and get to the coast.

A few minutes after he identified his precise heading on his GPS, he used his sat-phone to call Marc. Instead, Titus answered.

"I rerouted all Korea calls through me," Titus explained. "Corban's orders. Are you okay?"

"I'm sending you my location now. Jin is flying over the DMZ as we speak."

"Good work. I'll contact our people in Seoul to make sure she made it safely."

"Where is Corban?"

"You're one of the few I can tell. He's over two hundred miles northeast of you. I asked Marc to use one Gabriel to monitor him. It's not good, Luigi. A unit from the prison is closing in on him, and I see no indication that the DRIL he and Memphis are waiting for is on the way."

"Is he armed? He had only a rifle when we parted ways."

"I think that's still all he has."

Titus was silent for a moment, and Luigi hoped he wasn't expected to offer false hope. If Corban's situation was grave, then he might die. For years, Luigi had shown Corban his true heart, and he believed in the moment of death, the old spy would know Luigi thought fondly of him, even though he wasn't at his side like he wanted to be.

"Mapper is in a boat off the coast, waiting for you," Titus finally said. "Make it back to San Diego when you can. There are some urgent developments."

"How is Heather?" Luigi asked, though he noted the concern in Titus' voice, which probably had something to do with the North Korean missile he'd seen fired. But for the moment, a global crisis wasn't his heart's priority. "Is she okay?"

"She's okay, but she'll have a memorable scar on her cheek. Everyone performed remarkably well. Now we're just praying for Corban and Memphis. It'll take a miracle, Luigi."

"I've seen God do miracles before." Luigi turned off his phone.

Thinking of Heather, he picked up his pace. He would miss Corban, but the agent was leaving behind many whom he had touched immensely for God. The legacy of Corban Dowler would go on through the lives of those who lived for Jesus Christ.

CHAPTER THIRTEEN

Hamgyong Mountains, North Korea

Corban was still picking through the mountain rocks in the darkness when he heard Memphis fire his gun early. Whether Memphis was delirious from pain or the watch had been set wrong, the early gunshots foiled Corban's plans. The seven guards weren't far enough up the slope, yet now they were alerted to Memphis' position on the plateau. However, Corban had two things going for him still— he was the only one who had night vision, and the battle rifle had a longer range than their smaller caliber rifles.

Climbing an adjacent ridge, Corban didn't waste time checking on what the seven men below were doing now. He needed to get farther away, and higher, where the .308 could command the scene and better cover Memphis. Besides, he didn't need to see the soldiers to know what they would probably do.

In his haste, Corban slipped on an ice-covered rock and fell hard, cutting his left hand through his glove. He recovered silently but remained seated. If he hadn't already spent days and nights hiding in those same mountains, he could've been fresher and more alert than he was, but he didn't have the option to recuperate and ambush the soldiers under perfect conditions.

He planted his feet where he sat, ignored his blood-drenched glove, and steadied his breathing. Calmly, he braced his elbows on his knees and peered through the night-vision scope.

The seven guards had turned off their three flashlights, but they were as clear in his scope as if it were daylight. They had split up into three parties. Three were moving north, three were moving south, and the two dogs with their handler stayed on the trail up to the plateau.

"One, two, three." Corban counted off, rehearsing his shots. "Four, five, six."

Due to his elevation over the enemy, far and up to their right, they were a whole sixty seconds away from reaching any sort of cover on their current headings. However, Corban recognized he had no cover himself where he sat on the south slope.

His bloody glove had cooled. Weariness strained his eyes. Fatigue made the battle rifle feel heavy. But his experienced years as a field agent were required now, if he were to save Memphis.

He tranquilized the dogs first, since if loosed, they had the potential to reach and attack Memphis first. Their handler was next, in rapid succession, since he was on a direct path up to the plateau.

By this time, those to the north and south were hustling for cover, and simultaneously trying to find the shooter. Corban aimed at those far to the south first, at three hundred yards. He hit one before those closest to him started firing back. He knew they couldn't see him, but looking for him, they would be able to see his muzzle flashes.

He rose from his seat to relocate as their wild and inaccurate rounds peppered the mountainside. Instead of moving toward them, he moved away and higher, banking on his superior firepower. While planting his boots hastily, he slipped again, and rolled into the fall to protect his rifle and his hands. His shoulder was bruised as he landed, and he slid a couple feet downhill, but he came up shooting. One of the closest guards fell. Four left.

Since he could relocate faster by moving downhill, Corban fired twice at the two in the south, then they disappeared behind the plateau before he could confirm a hit. A bullet whined next to his hip, reminding him even if the enemy's rifles were inaccurate at that distance, he could still die from a surprise round.

After reloading, he tried again for some elevation, hoping to get an angle on the two who were behind the plateau. Rocks underfoot, which he expected to be frozen in place, shifted loose, and he went down hard on his belly, landing with all his weight on the rifle. Though the bullpup was as sturdy as a rifle comes, he didn't realize he'd damaged it until he fired at the northern guards once, then the chamber jammed. He pulled the slide three times, as roughly as he could to unjam or force twisted steel back into alignment, but it was useless.

The only other weapon available was in Memphis' hands, up on the plateau, which wouldn't be too effective against the guards. The guards who had already fallen by his tranqs had dropped their rifles, but Corban wouldn't entertain the idea for a moment to use lethal rounds against even an enemy. His death was imminent, and he couldn't in good conscience pass into eternity with the blood of enemies on his hands, no matter his own danger. His Christ-like compassion even for these soldiers was unconditional. They were in need of their Savior as much as anyone. As he had with countless other foes, if he could reason with them and show them his care, he knew that love wouldn't fail to meet God's purposes even here. But these weren't men intent on talking, it seemed, even if they did happen to speak English.

Corban's options were limited to one. He had to get to Memphis before they did, and they had a huge head start. And even at Memphis' side, with the sidearm in his hand, it wasn't much against the four remaining rifles of the enemy.

Using the night vision at intervals, he picked his way down the slope to the tranquilized dogs. He heard no more gunfire now. It seemed everyone was focused on advancing and prowling. Corban wondered if they really knew to advance on the plateau as he feared they did. They couldn't know Memphis was as debilitated as he was.

The dog handler had no rifle, but he did have a handgun. Corban picked it up, chambered a round, and fired five rapid shots at the sky. The gunfire was meant to keep the enemy cautious and slow down their advance. He tossed the gun aside and charged straight up the slope to the plateau. No one fired at him, and no one seemed to be on the top yet, but he knew they were on their way, scouting around.

The last few yards to Memphis, Corban crawled through the darkness. Memphis was motionless, and Corban had to check the agent's neck to confirm he was still alive. The sidearm had fallen from Memphis' grip, so he took it up and unclipped his breast ammo pouch for one more magazine for the weapon.

It was awkward, but Corban used the night vision from the disabled rifle to scope the plateau, as he held the pistol ready to fire.

Men were whispering Korean off to his right. They were organizing about fifty feet away. Maybe they'd seen him moving below, his dark shape against the white and black winter landscape.

They would come all at once, he guessed. Maybe from two sides. It would be over in seconds, a brief gun battle in the rising wind that would end with his death. Memphis would be captured, and he would wake up in an interrogation room, knowing his boss had failed to protect him.

Grabbing onto Memphis' flak jacket, Corban dragged the unconscious man off the plateau. Now, behind the lip of the tabletop, they had a little more cover, but the fuel canisters for the DRIL were exposed in the open. In the dark, they appeared as an awkward collection of rocks. Snow had partly covered them. Maybe they would be ignored in the darkness, and after he was dead, Corban hoped the DRIL would still come and get refueled to fly on to China and out of immediate danger.

The wind howled louder, and that's when the enemy charged. They were fearless, Corban realized, approaching an enemy they knew was armed, but risking their own lives, anyway. It would've been senseless on their part, but Corban knew that their deaths out there would be more compassionate than the torturous deaths they'd receive under the regime if they failed their brutal government.

Corban let them come closer. They fired in his general direction, combing left and right with cover fire, trying to draw fire and locate him for a fatal shot. Patiently, Corban kept waiting, not wanting to reveal his exact location until they were upon him, then he would rise up and fire four rapid shots into them. Tranquilizing the guards was simply stalling the inevitable. After an hour, each man would wake up, and unless he somehow took seven men and two dogs captive, they would simply attack him all over again.

The howl in the wind turned into a roar an instant before Corban rose up to fire. The charge of the enemy was broken as a throbbing mass dropped from the dark sky, whipping snow and rocks into their faces at hurricane velocity. Even Corban was blinded, but unlike the guards, he knew what machine was landing on the plateau—*the DRIL!*

He squinted into the rotor wash as he rose to his full height. Three guards stood less than fifteen feet away, their backs to him since they were surely confused as they considered the metal wonder that had settled on the mountain. Not waiting for a better moment, Corban fired once at each guard. They fell an instant later.

Raising his hand, he shielded his eyes from the wind. The DRIL propellers were powering down. At least someone from the KONs had survived! But was there really no fourth guard left?

His question was answered a breath later as bullets ricocheted off rocks at his feet. He dove backwards, nearly landing on top of

Memphis. But the passengers in the DRIL needed cover! They'd never get off the hilltop if the last guard wasn't put down. In that instant, Corban wondered if God had kept him alive for this final purpose—to offer cover for a refueling, so the DRIL could safely take off again—even if it left him behind.

Corban couldn't think of only his and Memphis' safety now. He rose again and fired at the muzzle flash across the plateau until he clicked on empty. A bullet slammed into him and threw him backwards. When he landed, he hit the back of his head on frozen ground and settled on his back, trying desperately to breathe.

Snowflakes drifted from the sky and brushed his face. He wondered how long he would last with a lung shot, unable to inhale. Even in his final, frantic thoughts, he couldn't rationalize that he'd made any difference in North Korea. Memphis hadn't been saved and he'd not been able to clear the plateau for the DRIL's successful refueling.

Finally, he caught his breath again. But his first exhale was a bitter groan through agony. He hurt all over. Scoffing at himself, he vaguely recalled when he'd told wounded operatives that feeling pain was a good sign, because it meant they were still alive.

Moving his legs, he pushed off the mountainside to right himself, and sat up. Uncertain if he would find blood, he touched his chest to discover the gnarled remnants of the second sidearm magazine pressing through the fabric of his flak jacket. He pushed his fingers through where the bullet had torn his vest. With surprise, his hand came out dry, not caked with blood! The enemy's bullet had slammed into the very magazine for which he'd been in the process of reaching!

Only then did he realize there was tremendous gunfire blasting away on the plateau. He crawled up to Memphis, then beyond to the edge of the hilltop. Someone with a battle rifle stood in the open bay door of the DRIL and pounded the opposite side of the plateau with gel-tranqs.

Then, there was silence. Whoever was in the DRIL reloaded, but they didn't emerge. There were voices, one of which belonged to a woman! And they spoke English, so that was a good sign.

Corban lowered his head from sight, lest he be shot by accident.

"*Kindred of Nails*!" he called past the pain in his bruised chest. "The enemy is down. The hill is clear!"

"Who's there?" a voice challenged over the wind. "Come out! Keep your hands up! Get out here! Who are you?"

"It's me, Corban Dowler." He raised both hands and stood upright. "I have Memphis here, wounded. He's in bad shape."

"Corban?" the shape of the man approached. "What are you doing here? I thought you were paralyzed!"

"Chevy!" Corban fell into the younger man's arms for a brief embrace. "You made it! Come on. Help me with Memphis. We need to refuel and get out of here before more soldiers come."

"Where are we?" Chevy leaned over Memphis. "Is he alive?"

"For now." Corban flinched at the sudden presence of another figure. "Oh, hello."

"This is Yellow Bird." Chevy took Memphis by the shoulders, and Corban and Yellow Bird each took a leg. "Ready, set, lift!"

They hobble-walked across the space to the DRIL, wherein Corban sat down the instant Memphis was laid on the floor. Yellow Bird knelt on the other side of him.

"Where will we go now?" the Chinese woman asked. "We are still in North Korea?"

Corban knew who she was, so he didn't ask her unnecessary questions. He was just pleased that one of their contacts who'd been trapped in Pyongyang had gotten out!

"Yes, still in North Korea." Corban heard Chevy refueling the drone. "We'll fly to Fusong in China now."

"I know Fusong. I can get home from Fusong."

"Then we'll part ways there," he said. "We need to fly back to America with this wounded man as soon as possible. Thank you, Yellow Bird, for your help."

"They have been good weeks," she said, "but now it is time to return to my work."

"I hope we didn't interrupt your work too much."

"No. My time in *Choson* has been good. Chevy and I have become like family." She reached for Chevy as he entered the DRIL. The bay door closed and Chevy sat down with them, holding Yellow Bird's hand. "He is like a son now. My American son."

Corban closed his eyes, his emotions overwhelming him for the moment as the drone shook and lifted off. He was still surprised to be alive. God apparently had other plans for him on earth.

⚘

San Diego

"Levi, get up." The teen opened his eyes to his father's touch. "We've got to be somewhere. Come on. Your mother's waiting."

In his bedroom in the house he was still adjusting to, Levi pulled on jeans and a sweatshirt, then looked at the time. *Three o'clock in the morning?* What was happening now? He'd learned that living with a father like Titus, no day was ordinary. Something unexpected was always happening.

With his shoes still untied, he wandered out to the living room. Annette and Titus were waiting at the door, their faces weary but full of anticipation.

"What's going on?" Levi grabbed a baseball cap to cover his bed-head. "Is something wrong? Has the apocalypse started already?"

"Nothing quite that drastic, yet." Titus chuckled. "Come on. We're driving to the airport."

"Okay." Levi shrugged, and walked through the door as his dad opened it.

Oleg was sitting in an SUV on the street, and Janice Dowler sat in a back seat with a medical bag on her lap. When Annette, Levi, and Titus climbed into their Mustang, Oleg led the way out of the city to the airport. Levi yawned and stretched, wondering what his new parents were up to at this strange hour. His whole life had been flipped upside down since his mother had died, so he wasn't too surprised that there were still things happening he couldn't figure out. One thing he did know, however, was that God was definitely speaking to him through his circumstances. The more he read of the Bible that Titus had given him, the more he felt his heart tug toward wanting something he couldn't yet define. He had questions, but the people around him were slowly helping him find the answers.

At the airport, Oleg used a security pass to clear their two vehicles through the gate that separated the public from the tarmac, and both vehicles moved out onto the pavement where Levi was afraid a plane would land on top of them in the darkness. Levi liked that the people he was around had access to special areas and secret lives. Oleg, he'd heard, had once worked for Interpol, and now was partnered closely with his own father. *How cool was that?* He didn't even have the words to brag to his friends, nor did he know if they would care that he was part of something greater than social media, clothing brands, parties, and money.

They climbed out of their vehicles and the five of them gathered against the SUV, watching the jets arrive and depart out on the runways. So, Levi thought, we're here to pick someone up. Instantly, he knew who. *It was the KONs!* Their mission in North Korea was finished! He'd trained with them, and now Titus wanted him to be there for their grand homecoming. Oh, he couldn't wait to hear their stories—how they'd tranquilized the enemy, and rescued people condemned by evil dictators!

"Here they are." Titus gestured at a huge cargo plane, and another smaller jet, taxiing toward them. "Both of them, right on schedule."

Levi stepped forward with his father, not wanting to get in the way, but he felt like he was part of the COIL team now. After all, he knew some Caspertein secrets and Titus had gotten him up in the middle of the night to be here.

As the engines of the small aircraft were still winding down, the cabin doors opened and men and women started to emerge. The cargo door lowered and several people began to exit the back of the cargo plane. Titus walked over and embraced a huge black man Levi had never seen before. Annette ran to two women, one in a sling, and another lady with a leaking bandage on her cheek. Janice approached a man on a gurney who was being wheeled out by two men with battle rifles over their shoulders. So, Levi thought, these were COIL operatives, but where were the KONs?

The man on the gurney was North Korean, Levi noticed as he passed. So, at least part of the mission was a success, even though some had received wounds.

The last one out of the cargo plane was a Hispanic man with a tall crewcut who walked up to Levi to stand next to him as they watched the scene unfold. Janice seemed to be stabilizing the Korean man on the gurney.

"You're Titus' son, aren't you?" The operative offered his hand. "You can call me Scooter. All my friends call me Scooter."

"Yeah, I'm Levi." Levi firmly shook the soldier's hand. "Nice to meet you. Who are all you guys?"

"COIL personnel, like your dad." Scooter pointed with a gloved hand at the smaller jet. "See that pregnant woman? She and that guy on the gurney are why we risked our lives."

Levi frowned. The woman stepped carefully down the rolling stairway to the tarmac below. She appeared lost and bewildered until the woman with the wound on her cheek ran forward and took her by the arm and led her toward the gurney.

"Just two people?" Levi looked at Scooter. "That's all?"

"One would've been a lot." Scooter grunted. "North Korea's no joke, my friend. But this was special. They were supposed to be executed the morning after we rescued them. We got the guy there out of a prison that would embarrass a horror show, and the KONs rescued the lady there."

"Where are the KONs?" Levi studied the tarmac again, wondering if he'd missed someone in the crowd. Several people were loading into the SUV with Oleg's help.

The pregnant woman fell onto the man on the gurney, smothering him with sobs and speaking a foreign language.

"I don't think the KONs did too well." Scooter shook his head. "I heard it went bad for them, but at least they got their subject out. That's what they went in for. So, I guess they did pretty good after all."

"But . . ." Levi faced Scooter face on. "Donny and Spider? Shorty and Job? I mean, we were training together a week and a half ago."

"Sorry. I don't think they made it, Levi." Scooter patted Levi on the shoulder. "It's what we train for, my friend. To live well, and if we have to, to die well. This is my ride back to the training center. Catch you later."

Scooter jogged over to the SUV as Oleg climbed into the driver's seat.

Levi wiped at his eyes, angry at the tears he found wetting his cheeks. *God had taken his new friends?* This was horrible! This wasn't the homecoming he'd wanted. This wasn't worth getting up in the middle of the night for!

"You're Levi, aren't you?" The woman with her arm in the sling held out her hand. She was beautiful, for a woman around his mom's age. She had curly, brown hair flowing out from under a stocking cap. "My name's Chloe. I would recognize you anywhere. You're a younger version of your dad."

"That's what everyone always says." Levi smiled, still trying to wipe the moisture from his face. How embarrassing, he thought, to cry in front of a woman. "So, this mission was successful?"

"This is what we do it for." She gestured at the Korean couple. "They're a special pair, a symbol, really. In more ways than one, their rescues have changed lives."

"You know about the apocalypse?" Levi asked. "I mean, you know, the danger?"

"What danger?" Chloe's eyes suddenly seemed fierce, turning on him. "What happened while we were on our way home?"

"Uh, maybe I wasn't supposed to say anything." Levi took a step backward. "I don't know that anything has happened. Not exactly."

"What about the missile? The missile struck, didn't it?"

"You'll have to ask my dad. I shouldn't say any more. I thought you knew what I knew."

"Titus!" Chloe marched away.

Levi shook his head, wondering what kind of fire he'd started for his father. He realized he needed to be more cryptic with his words, especially around people who were apparently not supposed to know certain things.

"I see you met Chloe." A man as tall as Levi approached him. His eyebrows were angled deeply, almost to the bridge of his nose. "The name's Nathan. Don't let her upset you. Her job is to care for everyone. I heard a little of what was said. She just likes to know everything before other people do, to help COIL avoid any problems."

"I didn't mean to make her mad."

"Oh, she'll be fine. If anyone can handle her, Titus can. Here. Look at this." Nathan took off a bulky, familiar-looking watch and offered it to Levi. "This belongs to your dad."

"Yeah, I recognize it. The satellite watch. You had it?"

"He let me borrow it for the mission."

"Did it help?"

"I didn't lead my team into any ambushes, so I'd say it helped. Come on. It'll be a little while before Oleg returns for the rest of us. Let's have a talk. I hear you've got the makings of a good COIL operative."

"Aw, I'm just a kid, but I'm learning."

"It's easy to get trained to be a soldier." Nathan led him to a small pile of gear that remained on the tarmac. Together, they sat down. "It's not so easy to be ready for what the world may throw at you. You've got to be ready in your heart."

"Yeah, I've been reading about that." Levi sighed and looked up at his father and mother as they mingled with the remaining operatives. "Dad gave me a Bible. Every time I read it, I learn something new."

For the next thirty minutes, Levi listened as Nathan spoke quietly about the struggles of the Christian faith, but that there were nevertheless ultimate victories, and there was an unmistakable overcoming lifestyle as believers surrendered to the Spirit of Christ inside them. As Levi listened to the muscle-bound, broad-shouldered COIL agent, he thought his dad's friends must be the greatest people in the whole world—not only selfless heroes, but also people with a keen sense of spiritual matters. They seemed almost superhuman to him, and Levi was drawn closer to God, he felt, in those few minutes alone with Nathan.

When Oleg returned from the training center, the rest of the North Korea mission members and their gear were loaded into the SUV, including the two North Koreans. In a few minutes, the SUV drove away, and the jet and cargo plane taxied away toward a number of hangers off to the side. Titus and Levi stood in front of the Mustang alone, since even Annette had left with the operatives. Levi was so proud to stand next to his father, especially after hearing several of the operatives speak highly of his dad. He wondered how many teenagers his age had fathers who'd taken time to share with their sons the deep things of Christianity, and life, and even of the hardships of sacrificial living. It felt like Levi could have stood there and watched the airfield with his father forever, and everything would've been just right.

"Here they are," Titus said suddenly, and walked to the back of the car.

Levi looked around, not aware that they'd been waiting for anyone else to arrive. An ambulance with no flashing lights pulled up. Not wanting to miss a thing, Levi jogged to catch up to Titus as the ambulance driver opened his door.

"I need you to stand by, please," Titus said to a middle-aged driver and his younger partner in the passenger seat. "It'll be a few minutes, but they're on their way. Since this is a Homeland Security situation, you'll need to stick to the agreement we made on the phone. Keep this injury quiet and keep the hospital staff from asking too many questions. Here's my card."

"Yes, sir." The driver tucked the card into his breast pocket. "Our only concern is the patient. Whatever else is going on—that's your business."

"Thank you." Titus backed away with Levi to the car. "I'm glad they didn't ask any questions. We have enough going on without people blaming COIL for what North Korea has just done to America."

"You mean the missile?"

"Yeah. The missile."

A few minutes later, another small jet landed and taxied up to the Mustang. The paramedics understood that their patient had arrived, so they readied a stretcher, and Levi remained close to his father's side. He felt like everything he was witnessing was actually shaping him, maybe for something in the future.

The cabin door opened and Levi almost collapsed to see Chevy emerge at the top of the stairs.

"He's alive!" Levi gasped, and before he knew it, he was running toward the jet.

Chevy reached the bottom of the stairs and Levi stopped before him, fresh tears in his eyes. They paused, staring at each other, then Levi looked back at the plane door.

"I'm the only one, Levi," Chevy said. "The rest have fallen."

Levi couldn't stand the sadness in the man's voice. He wrapped his arms around Chevy, who was much shorter, and wept against the side of his head. Although he'd trained with the KONs for only a few weeks from the sidelines, he'd come to know they were special. And now, he realized how special they really were. They'd given their lives to get the pregnant woman and her husband out of North Korea. The sense of loss was enough to make him wonder how life could ever be free from sorrow again.

Next out of the plane was a man with his head bandaged. The paramedics insisted that he immediately lie down on the gurney they provided. At the bandaged man's side was a man Levi realized he knew—*but Corban Dowler was walking!*

"I'll be going with Memphis." Corban shook Titus' hand. "I'll make sure everything's in order with him, then I'll come to the training center. Send June over to the hospital when you get a chance. Everyone else made it okay?"

"Yep, just a few minutes ago." Titus took a deep breath. "We have a lot to discuss, Corban."

"The missile?" Corban glanced at Levi. "How bad is it?"

"No actual impact yet. That'll come later. But it's going to be bad."

The men stood in silence for a moment, and Levi wondered if they would've said more if he weren't there.

"It's out of our control," Chevy finally said. "Let's put our energy into doing what we can, and not think about what's out of our hands."

"I can't argue with that." Corban nodded, then acknowledged Levi. "You've grown some since I last saw you, Levi. I'll see you guys tomorrow. You can fill me in on the rest of what's happened."

Corban jogged to catch the ambulance before the paramedics drove off, and Chevy, Titus, and Levi walked to the Mustang.

"What'd he mean I've grown since the last time he saw me?" Levi asked. "I'm no taller than I was last week."

"Maybe he recognized another kind of growth," Titus said. "And I'm happy to say that I've noticed it as well."

The three climbed into the car. Even though the collapse of America seemed inevitable, Levi couldn't imagine a greater moment, sitting beside his heroic father, and the last living *Kindred of Nails*.

🐾

One Week Later – San Diego

Titus stood at the head of the lecture hall in the training center complex as COIL agents and their spouses filed in and took seats. One-eyed Wes Trimble was there with his fiancée, Wynter Caspertein. Chen Li had her leg in a brace, and Annette was doting over the Hong Kong operative since Nathan was on a mission with Chevy, and neither had returned yet.

Looking up from his phone where he was keeping an eye on the national news updates, Titus noticed Rea, in a wheelchair, with Jin in the back row. Both had spent several days at the hospital being checked out and starting medications meant to cleanse their bodies of parasites and diseases. Corban was sponsoring their immigration into the States, and to become part of the COIL family.

Luigi was standing off to one side, but only an arm's length away from Heather who sat in the outside row. Her cheek was still bandaged, but her eyes were bright. If Titus wasn't mistaken, she had a hunger in her to serve Christ even more because of the danger she'd seen and experienced for His sake.

Corban, Janice, and Jenna were in the second row, and surrounding them were dozens of agents who'd been gathered from all over the country, flown in on Titus and Corban's jets. In minutes, the room was filled and hushed. What once had been a hall used for teaching Olympic athletes about nutrition and training regimens, was now a room used for briefing COIL teams about America's last days.

From where he was seated at the side, Corban nodded at Titus. They'd prepared the briefing together, to best represent Christ's concerns within the COIL family. When the two had been alone, Titus confessed to his mentor that he'd not destroyed the new COIL phosphorus ammunition, and Corban had said, "Perhaps it's for the best. The world has changed since we last talked about it. I know you won't use it for harm."

"Can I have your attention, everyone?" Titus called. "Let's open in prayer. Bruno?"

Next to Levi, Bruno rose to his feet and dedicated their meeting to the Lord's will, placing their fears in His hands, and surrendering their circumstances to His sovereign direction.

When Bruno finished his short prayer, Titus glanced once more at his phone, then turned it off. He'd seen enough.

"We've asked you all to come today because of the missile that North Korea fired at the United States. It was all over the news for a few days, but now it's already fading from our focus. Nothing seems to have happened, even though the US military failed to shoot it down, and Americans are continuing to live as if nothing has changed. But let me be very clear. *Everything* has changed. We called you here to prepare you for those changes. Wes? This is the Pentagon's Wes Trimble, everyone."

The CIA's Pacific Rim Agent, liaison to the Pentagon, stood and took the front, as Titus stepped back and watched the room. Rudy, his brother, wasn't there, but he'd already been informed, and Titus had transferred funds to Rudy's personal account to prepare in Colorado as Titus was preparing in San Diego, and Corban would be preparing in New York.

"Good afternoon, everyone. I'm Wes Trimble. I'm the president's so-called inside-COIL man. I'm here to tell you what's really happened, so we're all accurately informed of the situation, since there seems to be an agenda to keep people acting and thinking like nothing has happened.

"The missile that North Korea fired at us didn't catch the US military off-guard, but we did respond late, much to our new president's embarrassment. It took twelve minutes for the ballistic missile to fly past Hawaii. Eleven minutes later, it crossed into US airspace. Nine seconds later, it dropped in altitude and detonated over the town of Meridia, Oregon. It detonated at ten-thousand feet, impacting nothing, it seemed. In the future, as everything begins to happen, few people will probably even link the disaster to the North Korean missile.

"Prior to that detonation, the military argued for and against shooting it down. Intel before and after the missile launch confirms what we still know, which is that all of North Korea's nuclear blustering the past few years was subterfuge to throw us off their true intentions. In the confusion of the missile launch, their intentions worked—the United States was confused. Our military's slow response to a non-nuclear attack allowed the missile to slip through our shield, though over thirty unsuccessful interceptors were fired at it. We suspect Russia's latest missile technology was leaked to North Korea to thwart our missile shield.

"The detonation seems to have been precisely planned. The missile payload was packed with live spores of a virus we don't yet understand. At ten thousand feet, it has now been carried across the continent. The government recovered the rocket fuselage to confirm the spore's presence. We're watching for symptoms to pop up, but we've seen nothing surface, yet. However, we expect to see cases of a mysterious virus within two weeks. North Korea planned this carefully. I don't expect to find that they sent us a fast killer, but something slow.

"The bottom line is this: it'll be a killer, and it's already all over America—maybe in our food, in our water, or in our lungs. The delay before we have any fatalities has given North Korea a way out of culpability. They can deny they've done anything but fire a test rocket, since related fatalities may not show up for days or even weeks. The president isn't willing to point the finger until we have harder evidence that we've actually been hit with a biological danger. He is still trying to encourage diplomatic agreements with North Korea, urged on by the United Nations.

"I presented the president with the evidence we have thus far, but his closer advisors have counseled him to keep the whole incident hidden from the media. It's an entire black-out, so they can avoid panic. When he said he wouldn't warn the public, I resigned. Wynter and I will be moving permanently out here to work with Titus. Thank you."

Wes sat back down with his fiancée, and Titus stepped forward again.

"So, let's talk projections. Some of you know I trafficked in arms before I came to Christ. I know weapons, and so does Corban. Together, we've come up with a rough timetable, based upon the worst-case scenario.

"Within the next few weeks, we expect some mysterious deaths in the Midwest, probably. Then, the sick will come in clusters, and the CDC will sound an alarm as rules for some sort of contagion are laid out. Infected neighborhoods will be placed on quarantine, then whole towns, then cities. But you can't contain an airborne agent with military force. This killer is complex, too complex for experts to devise an antidote or vaccine before it spreads wildly.

"This summer, fatalities will be in the hundreds, but it'll keep spreading. Businesses and banks will close. Transportation will be banned. Food and water will become scarce. Crime will spike, and there will be no law or order. The National Guard will hold for a few months, but even they will be overtaken by the virus, and their numbers will be decimated as they either die or they leave their posts to care for their families.

"So, you ask, what do we do? What I can tell you is what COIL will be doing. We're setting up resource zones here in San Diego, in Colorado with my brother Rudolph Caspertein, and Corban will organize a COIL center in New York. Our primary objective won't be to stay alive, but to offer stability and hope in a chaotic and dying land. This is what you've done with COIL in the past, and if you'd like to serve Christ in this way in America's future, we'll remain steadfast in these three zones as roads are closed and communication shuts down. I love my cell phone's many uses, but soon, it'll become a paperweight. Laptops, television screens, even cars will be useless. It's time to first brace ourselves in the faith, and then make ourselves available to the many lives who aren't yet caring to look into this situation further than what the media is inaccurately and falsely sharing."

The back door opened as Nathan and Chevy walked in. Both wore jeans and pull-over sweaters—like brothers. Chevy crossed his arms and took a position standing against the wall near Rea and Jin. Nathan nodded once at Titus, and Titus waved him to the front as everyone waited. With their heads together, Nathan spoke for only Titus to hear.

"Meridia is already on quarantine," Nathan whispered, "but it's all top secret. The spores that didn't get carried east on the wind, dropped down on the town in a measurable quantity. The government is testing to find infected blood, but it's still a mystery. No symptoms have emerged. Yet."

"Yeah, *yet*. Thanks, Nathan." Titus took a deep breath to address the group as Nathan took a seat. "Nathan and Chevy just arrived back from Oregon on a fact-finding mission. From the site of detonation, people are already being infected. It has begun. Now, we must be ready for what's to come. As long as the Lord tarries, we'll continue to live as His people.

"But this isn't a sad time. Rea and Jin, recent arrivals from North Korea, have been asking about the men who rescued them. Though four of them died during the mission, one of them is still with us, but they haven't yet met. Chevy? Rea and Jin? Can you three come up here? Nathan, could you come back up here, too?"

Jin stood shakily and pushed her husband's wheelchair forward. Titus moved away and sat between Corban and Annette. The old spy was back to wearing his leg braces and using his crutches, but Titus guessed the man's facade would soon be over. He would very quickly be relieved of COIL critics in the government with everyone's new pandemic concerns.

"You Chevy?" Jin asked Chevy, then wept as they embraced.

Titus had read Chevy's account of the rescue of the pregnant woman. It was a tale of legends, and Chevy alone had survived to share of his brothers' courageous and selfless deaths.

Next, Rea with tears shook Nathan's big hand. The muscled agent dwarfed the little Korean man as he gave him a hug. Titus had read the briefing on the prison rescue as well, how Nathan had carried Rea on his back to safety through gunfire and a wrecked perimeter fence.

"We needed this," Corban whispered to Titus. "With everything that's about to come, this is cleansing."

"Just tell me this," Titus said, "when are you going to lose the braces? Too many people know already. It's bound to slip out. When, Corban?"

"When being underestimated loses its usefulness. Get back up there and do the Q-and-A. Calm everyone's hearts. Remind them of their purpose on earth."

Titus took the front, as Rea, Jin, Nathan, and Chevy returned to the back of the room. No one's eyes were dry after the reunion.

For a moment, Titus surveyed the faces before him. He didn't know everyone, and even those he did know, he'd never met most of their spouses. Suddenly, his eyes settled on an unshaven face with a head of uncombed hair. This man had once been an enemy, but by God's grace, the two had served and bled together.

"Ladies and gentlemen, our next segment will be a question and answer time. I know you have some important concerns to ask about. I thought I'd be doing this alone, but I see Oleg has given the hot tub a break." Titus paused for a few chuckles. "Please welcome Agent Oleg Saratov to help me with your questions. Come on up here, Oleg!"

Oleg smiled shyly and lumbered to the front. He shook Titus' hand.

"You could've ironed your clothes," Titus whispered to his big-shouldered friend. "Come on, Oleg. The apocalypse hasn't started yet!"

Oleg ineffectively smoothed down his wrinkled shirt front and grinned at the crowd. Through his teeth, he spoke quietly to Titus, "Careful, Serval, or I'll return to the hot tub and let you answer questions you don't know about government quarantine protocols."

"I stand corrected, my Russian friend. The floor is yours." Titus set a hand on Oleg's shoulder. "Everyone, we'll begin with questions about quarantine procedures. Take it away, Oleg."

Standing to the side, Titus noticed Levi watching him. When their eyes met, the boy smiled. Titus smiled back, but his heart ached. Somehow, he needed to find time to raise his son to be a man of God. The world was becoming increasingly more sinful, and without a strong godly Caspertein presence, people would be left to wander like sheep without a shepherd. Titus wondered if Levi had it in him to become one of those shepherds as America entered her last days.

"It ain't gonna be easy!" he mumbled to himself.

Appendices

Character Sketch for *Distant Contact*, Book One

Arlin Skokes – Caspertein family attorney
Barry Baxter – US Secretary of State
Corban Dowler – Founder of COIL
Emily Gaultridge – Deputy Secretary of State
Luigi Putelli – COIL's shadow operative
Marc Densort – COIL's underground Gabriel technician
Nasser al-Hakim – Imam of the Soldiers of Mahdi in Iran
Oleg Saratov – Partner to Titus
Rashid al-Sabur – Treasure hunter from Cyprus
Rudy Caspertein – Seismologist in Alaska
Serik Tomir – Nasser al-Hakim's most trusted soldier
Titus Caspertein – Operative for COIL
Wynter Caspertein – Archaeologist from Arkansas

Map for *Distant Contact,* Book One

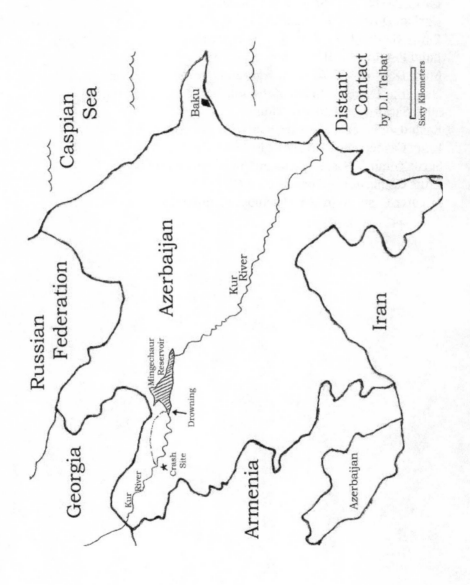

Caspian Sea

Baku

Distant Contact

by D.I. Telbat

Sixty Kilometers

Russian Federation

Azerbaijan

Kur River

Iran

Georgia

Mingechaur Reservoir

Drowning

Kur River

Crash Site

Armenia

Azerbaijan

706

Character Sketch for *Distant Front*, Book Two

<u>Ercan Sanli</u> – Imam Serik al-Hakim's bodyguard

<u>Fongdu Jen</u> – the most unmerciful prison warden China has ever seen. His prison in Hudie Valley is known for being a prison of death, its dungeons damp and cold, and its captives threatened by leprosy.

<u>Lisa Kennedy</u> – may have sordid past, but her commitment to Steve's work for Jesus Christ is unflinching. Now that they're engaged, this woman from California anticipates a life of service in China with Steve.

<u>Oleg Saratov</u> – may seem like Titus' shadow, but he's emerging as one of COIL's dependable agents, if only this ex-Interpol operative could put up with Titus' antics.

<u>Peng Zemin</u> – has his eyes set on rising the Chinese political ladder, and only the Christians stand in his way. As Shanghai's secret police commander, his methods to capture enemies of the Communist Party often delve into darkness.

<u>Serik al-Hakim</u> – Imam of *Soldiers of Mahdi* in Iran

<u>Song Sakana</u> – has led the Sakana Crime Family in Hong Kong for years, following his disgraced father. As <u>Japanese </u>mobsters in Chinese lands, they have proven their effectiveness through brutality and pro-fessionalism.

<u>Steve Brookshire</u> – has been organizing the Christian underground church in China for fifteen years. His language skills and his love for Jesus Christ has caused him to take dangerous risks to care for souls. His cover as a triathlete is thin, and he knows the Chinese secret police probably know all about him.

<u>Titus Caspertein</u> – has smuggled the black market's dangerous wares for most of his adult life, so it's no wonder that his transition to living fully for Jesus Christ isn't perfect. He wants to save everyone, and using his wit and smuggling skills, he just might!

<u>Tond-zu</u> – raised on the streets of Shanghai, found a career in the military, and now stands at Peng's side to destroy the Christian plague that saturates their largest city in the world. This deformed man isn't just thinking about arrests, but also about taking trophies from the bodies of his victims.

Map 1 for *Distant Front*, Book Two

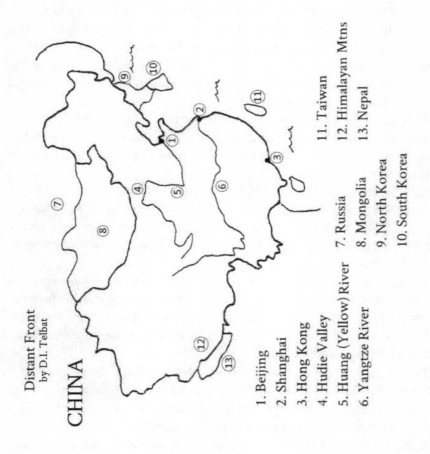

Distant Front
by D.I. Telbat

CHINA

1. Beijing
2. Shanghai
3. Hong Kong
4. Hudie Valley
5. Huang (Yellow) River
6. Yangtze River

7. Russia
8. Mongolia
9. North Korea
10. South Korea

11. Taiwan
12. Himalayan Mtns
13. Nepal

Map 2 for *Distant Front*, Book Two

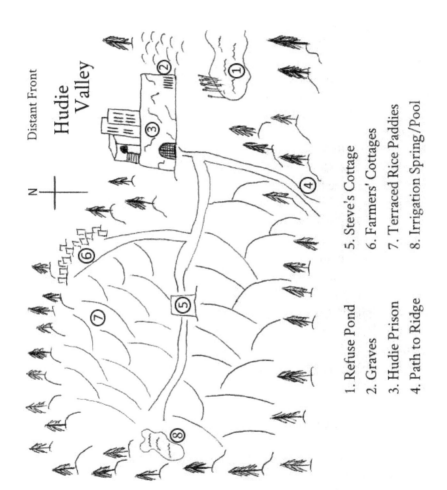

Distant Front

Hudie Valley

N

1. Refuse Pond
2. Graves
3. Hudie Prison
4. Path to Ridge

5. Steve's Cottage
6. Farmers' Cottages
7. Terraced Rice Paddies
8. Irrigation Spring/Pool

Character Sketch for *Distant Harm,* Book Three

Annette Caspertein – Once a clothing model, she now commits her-self to motherhood and standing beside Titus, her husband and COIL leader.

Avery "Chevy" Hewitt – This cool-tempered ex-con is in his element as an evangelist, but he's ready to move anywhere for God since he has only a Bible, a toothbrush, and a compass.

Bruno – This sizeable black man is part of COIL's old Flash and Bang Team. Besides offering comic relief with Scooter, he remains a gentle spiritual presence when the tension is highest.

Chen Li – a Chinese COIL operative from Hong Kong; now married to Nathan Isaacson.

Chloe Azmaveth – With a history in Israel's Mossad Agency, Chloe's reliability inside COIL is unmatched as she coordinates missions and even faces gunfire if she's called to help.

Corban Dowler – Now in his sixties, this ex-CIA agent continues to lead COIL, even through his own infirmities, to rescue the persecuted.

Donny Walters – After a life of upheaval, his ailing body is no match for his heart to counsel and care for the spiritual needy. From a painter in Oklahoma to a volunteer in COIL's ranks, this dry-humored ex-con lives to soldier up for God's people.

Ernesto "Spider" Colosio – From preaching in prison to killing bugs on the outside, this ex-con can barely contain his excitement at the prospect of risking his life for others.

Francisco "Shorty" Hernandez – Though this bilingual ex-con is more familiar with bucking hay bales in New Mexico, he's ready to sacrifice for God's purposes, wherever he's called. And he'll go with a smile!

Fred "Memphis" Nelson – Now married to June, Memphis remains a dependable operative, fitting in wherever Corban needs him to serve.

Heather – an ex-police officer from NJ, she is the newest COIL opera-tive; also wife of Luigi Putelli.

Jin – Han Ji-Jin married Rea then they were arrested for working in the underground Christian movement. She is very pregnant and is being used by the evil regime as an example.

Job Buck –While older and heavy-set, this ex-con from Idaho is willing to lay down his hammer to pick up his Bible and give his time to those who need the love spoken of in the gospel.

Cont—

Johnny "Mapper" Wycke – As part of the COIL support team, his skills are so broad, his expertise leaves a mark on every successful COIL mission.

June – an ex-investigative reporter, now a COIL operative married to Memphis.

Levi Caspertein – Titus' long-lost son whose blond-haired, blue-eyed looks offer a glimpse of Titus in his teenage years. This fourteen-year-old is thrust into the company of COIL operatives and international intrigue when he comes to live with Titus and Annette, but he must choose for himself whether or not he will follow Christ as his Savior.

Luigi Putelli – Even with Heather as his wife, this gum-chewing spook doesn't hesitate to risk his life for Christ and for Corban, to protect the people of God.

Lu Yi – A Chinese operative now in her sixties, with an extensive underground Christian network in rural North Korea.

Nathan "Eagle Eyes" Isaacson – Married to Chen Li, this aggressive operative emerges from the shadows to lead whenever and wherever Corban needs him.

Oleg Saratov – Having left Interpol, this light-hearted Russian with shoulders like an ox is Titus Caspertein's right hand, and is willing to sacrifice all for the cause of Christ.

Rea – Jeong Byeang-Rea was North Korea's leading engineer, working on the missile program, until he became a believer and fled to South Korea. He returned to find and marry his lost love, Han Ji-Jin, then to work with her in the Christian Underground Church until arrested to be used as examples for the evil regime.

Scooter – This Hispanic ex-Marine makes up for his small stature with a tall crewcut and a personality that lightens the most serious moments.

Titus Caspertein – This Arkansas native was once the world's most daring arms smuggler, but now he is mentored by Corban Dowler and has become a strong Christian leader inside COIL.

Wes Trimble – With an eye-patch for every day of the week, this one-eyed CIA man remains the president's liaison with COIL, as well as COIL's voice in the US government.

Yuriy Usik –This sadistic Ukranian is put to work as a torturer inside North Korea, where he thrives on the suffering of others.

Map 1 for *Distant Harm*, Book Three

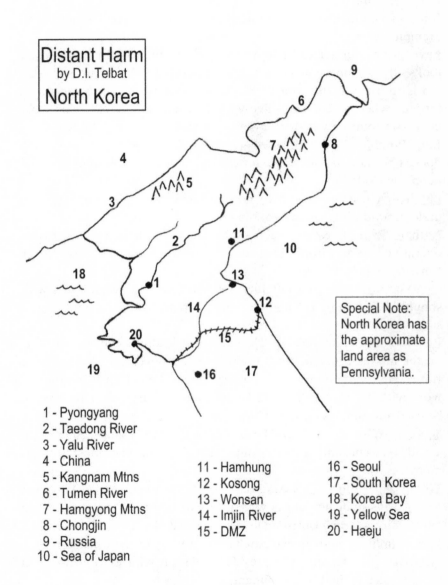

Distant Harm
by D.I. Telbat
North Korea

Special Note: North Korea has the approximate land area as Pennsylvania.

1 - Pyongyang
2 - Taedong River
3 - Yalu River
4 - China
5 - Kangnam Mtns
6 - Tumen River
7 - Hamgyong Mtns
8 - Chongjin
9 - Russia
10 - Sea of Japan

11 - Hamhung
12 - Kosong
13 - Wonsan
14 - Imjin River
15 - DMZ

16 - Seoul
17 - South Korea
18 - Korea Bay
19 - Yellow Sea
20 - Haeju

Map 2 for *Distant Harm,* Book Three

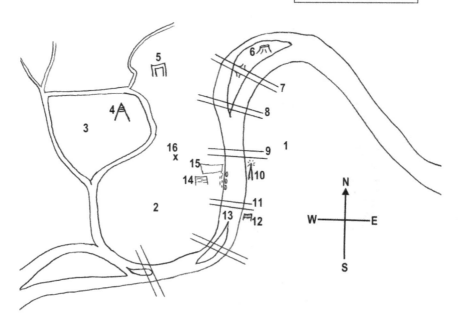

Pyongyang, North Korea

DISTANT HARM
by D.I. Telbat

N

W———E

S

1 - Tongdaewon District
2 - Central District
3 - Pothonggang District
4 - Ryugyong Hotel
5 - Arch of Triumph
6 - Rungrado First of May Stadium
7 - Chongryu Bridge
8 - Rungra Bridge

9 - Okryu Bridge
10 - Tower of the Juche Idea
11 - Taedong Bridge
12 - Songyo Restaurant
13 - Taedong River
14 - Palace of People's Remembrance
15 - Kim Il Sung Square
16 - Mansudae Assembly Hall

Other Books by D.I. Telbat

(in suggested reading order)

The COIL Series:
Dark Edge, Prequel
Dark Liaison, Book One
Dark Hearted, Book Two
Dark Rule, Book Three
Dark Vessel, Book Four
Dark Zeal, Book Five

The COIL Legacy:
Distant Boundary, Prequel
Distant Contact, Book One
Distant Front, Book Two
Distant Harm, Book Three

The RESOLUTION Series
Resolution Books One-Four

The STEADFAST Series
Steadfast Books One-Six

Last Dawn Trilogy
Dawn of Affliction, Book One
Dawn of Oppression, Book Two
Dawn of Subjection, Book Three

Standalone Books:
Arabian Variable
Called To Gobi
COIL Extractions
COIL Recruits for Christ
God's Colonel
Soldier of Hope
The Leeward Set, Bk1, *Fury in the Storm*
The Leeward Set, Bk2, *Tears in the Wind*

The COIL Series

International spies and Special Forces comman-dos are committed to saving at-risk Christians around the world. Join the Commission of International Laborers in covert ops and rescues—all with non-lethal weapons.

These novels of suspense, loss, love, and commitment to Christ will draw you, and you will see God is still in control even in the midst of chaos.

D.I. Telbat prays that your faith in Christ our Savior will be strengthened as you read *The COIL Series*. The adven-ture begins with the Prequel, *Dark Edge*, followed by Book One, *Dark Liaison*. Visit his author page: https://books2read.com/b/DarkLiaison.

~

Last Dawn Series

Twenty years have passed since Levi Caspertein found his father, and twenty years since the collapse of America due to the viral pandemic. Raised in San Diego, Levi has become a mighty man of God while in his father's shadow. Now, Levi must take his family and flee for their lives. They embark on a cross-country trek to discover what has become of the Dowler family in New York.

Levi has been trained in the disciplines of COIL's non-lethal tactics. As a Caspertein, he is strong-willed and determined to help everyone in need, even against great odds. With others at his side, Levi leads what is left of his family east-ward, fighting the entire way to stay alive.

Join Levi on this action-packed journey across America, with enemies on his trail, and desperate people to care for in every apoca-lyptic-ravaged community. *Dawn of Affliction*, Book One, will prepare you for steadfast courage in America's Last Days.

Visit author page: https://books2read.com/b/DawnofAffliction.

The STEADFAST Series

The STEADFAST Novella Series follows Christian survivalist Eric Radner through the heartache and heroism of living in the aftermath of America's collapse. The Meridia Virus has killed millions across N. America and brought out the worst in the US. Bandits roam, cities are left in charred ruins, fear cripples, and Christian persecution abounds.

But secluded deep in a Wyoming mountain range, Eric hides alone, finding refuge in a small cabin. He has committed his life to a desperate survival, yet with a determined, steadfast faith.

Emerging from the mountains to prove his faith in the face of a new breed of terror and persecution in America's Last Days, God guides him to reach out to others. https://books2read.com/b/SteadfastBk1.

~

Other End Times Novels by D.I. Telbat

Called To Gobi: A Christian End Times Chronicle begins on the brink of WW3. Andrew Foworthy finds Christ and his calling while in prison. Against odds and with little support, he leaves the US, but a plane crash hurls him into the Altai Mountains. Caught between Russia, China and End Times terror, he hopes to reach Mongolian nomads with the salvation message in time.

~

God's Colonel - As America collapses and Antichrist rises as supreme from the carnage, a broken family struggles to survive the devastation of the Final Tribulation. Caught in the crossfire of End Time plagues that strike the earth with fiery judgment, each family member faces hard decisions and trials as they witness noncompliant underground Christians dragged to the guillotine.

ABOUT THE AUTHOR

D.I. (David) Telbat is a Christian author best known for his clean Suspenseful Fiction with a Faith Focus. This includes his bestselling and award-winning *COIL Series, Steadfast Series, Last Dawn Trilogy*, and other Christian suspense and End Times novels.

David studied writing in school and worked for a time in the newspaper field. Getting into serious trouble with the law as a young man became a turning point in his life. The Lord used that experience to draw David into a personal relationship with Him. Re-focusing his life for Christ, he now seeks to honor God with his life and writing by doing what he loves most—writing and Christian ministry. At this time, D.I. Telbat lives on the West Coast, but keeps his home base in the Northwest US. You can find his complete list of books and his bio at https://books2read.com/ap/8NV7l8/DI-Telbat.

Through David's weekly blog posts, he offers free Christian short stories and related posts, to entertain, but also to bring attention to the Persecuted Church worldwide. Many D.I. Telbat stories and books are about persecuted Christians—their sacrifices and their rescues. His related posts include his novel news, author reflections, and challenges for today's Christian. To subscribe to his weekly posts, as well as receive several exclusive subscriber gifts, visit his author site under-lined above. Also, he'd love for you to visit right now and download some other items of reader interest from his Book Funnel page found at https://books.bookfunnel.com/for-all-readers.

Please leave your comments wherever you bought this book. Reviews greatly help authors, and David Telbat would love to hear your thoughts on his works. He takes reader reviews into consideration as he makes his future publishing plans. You can also reach him through email at ditelbat@gmail.com.

There is no redemption without sacrifice.

CPSIA information can be obtained
at www.ICGtesting.com
Printed in the USA
BVHW031923200122
626720BV00005B/40